101 MYSTERY STORIES

Edited by Bill Pronzini
and Martin H. Greenberg

AVENEL BOOKS
New York

Published 1986 by Avenel Books, distributed by
Crown Publishers, Inc., 225 Park Avenue South,
New York, New York 10003.

Printed and Bound in the United States of America

Library of Congress Cataloging-in-Publication Data
Main entry under title:

101 mystery stories.

   1. Detective and mystery stories. I. Pronzini,
Bill. II. Greenberg, Martin Harry. III. Title: One
hundred and one mystery stories.
PN6120.95.D45A112 1986   808.83′872   85-22428
ISBN 0-517-60361-6

h g f e d c b a

ACKNOWLEDGMENTS

MacDonald (THERE HANGS DEATH!)—Copyright 1949 by United News-paper Magazines Corporation; copyright renewed © 1977 by John D. MacDonald. Reprinted by permission of the author.

Brown—Copyright 1940 by Popular Publications, Inc.; copyright renewed © 1968 by Fredric Brown. Reprinted by permission of International Creative Management.

Westlake—Copyright © 1967 by Donald E. Westlake. First appeared in ELLERY QUEEN'S MYSTERY MAGAZINE. Reprinted by permission of the author.

Hoch (EVERY FIFTH MAN)—Copyright © 1968 by Edward D. Hoch. First published in ELLERY QUEEN'S MYSTERY MAGAZINE. Reprinted by permission of the author.

Sisk (THE LEAKAGE)—Copyright © 1970 by H.S.D. Publications. Reprinted by permission of the author.

Brewer—Copyright © 1956 by King-Size Publications, Inc. Reprinted by permission of the Scott Meredith Literary Agency, Inc., 845 Third Ave., New York, NY 10022.

Simenon (THE LITTLE HOUSE AT CROIX-ROUSSE)—Copyright 1933 by Georges Simenon. Reprinted by permission of the author.

Fish (PUNISHMENT TO FIT THE CRIME)—Copyright © 1980 by Robert L. Fish. First appeared in ELLERY QUEEN'S MYSTERY MAGAZINE. Reprinted by permission of Richard Curtis Associates, Inc.

Wellen—Copyright © 1979 by Davis Publications, Inc. First appeared in ELLERY QUEEN'S MYSTERY MAGAZINE. Reprinted by permission of the author.

Garfield—Copyright © 1978 by John Ives. First appeared in ELLERY QUEEN'S MYSTERY MAGAZINE. Reprinted by permission of the author.

Charteris—Copyright 1933 by Leslie Charteris; copyright renewed © 1961 by Leslie Charteris. Reprinted by permission of the author.

Pronzini and Malzberg—Copyright © 1976 by Bill Pronzini and Barry N. Malzberg. First published in ELLERY QUEEN'S MYSTERY MAGAZINE. Reprinted by permission of the authors.

Woolrich (THE RELEASE)—Copyright © 1968 by The Mystery Writers of America, Inc. Reprinted by permission of the agents for the author's Estate, the Scott Meredith Literary Agency, Inc., 845 Third Ave., New York, NY 10022.

CONTENTS

FOREWORD

Variety is the key word for this collection of mystery and suspense stories. The book you are holding is the largest ever compiled in terms of the number of stories included, and is also one of the largest in length. It includes outstanding stories by writers from several countries, as well as from various time periods, ranging from the nineteenth century to the 1980s.

You will find such classic early practitioners of the mystery-writer's art as Edgar Allan Poe, the father of the modern mystery; Guy de Maupassant; Charles Dickens; O. Henry (William Porter), of the twist ending; the multitalented Jack London; Stephen Crane; and a hard-to-find gem by Frank R. Stockton.

The authors of the "classic" period of the 1920s to the 1940s (some of whom are still active) are also well represented with stories by Georges Simenon of Belgium (now resident in Switzerland); Leslie Charteris; the immortal Ellery Queen (Fred Dannay and his cousin Manfred Lee); the undeservedly forgotten Fletcher Flora; the prolific but excellent Erle Stanley Gardner; and Melville Davisson Post, among many others.

Suspense in the "hard-boiled" tradition made famous by Dashiell Hammett and Raymond Chandler is particularly well represented here by such men as John D. MacDonald (with two of his least known stories); Fredric Brown; Gil Brewer; Cornell Woolrich, the "Poet of the Shadows," who set a pattern for suspense writing that has been widely imitated but never equaled; William Campbell Gault, still going strong after all these years; the late Jack Ritchie, one of the true masters of the short mystery story; Robert Bloch, famous for writing *Psycho*, an achievement that has unfortunately overshadowed his other excellent works; and John Jakes, a fine mystery/suspense writer who has moved on to bigger things with his Bicentennial series and such best sellers as *Love and War*.

We have not forgotten the contemporary scene, which is currently enjoying a burst of wonderful writing. Here you will find Donald E. Westlake; Edward D. Hoch, the most prolific of all mystery short story writers and one of the very best; Brian Garfield; Isaac Asimov, a fine mystery writer better known for his science fiction and science writing;

Robert Randisi, he of the fast and good typewriter; Evan Hunter, here found as himself and as "Ed McBain," the modern master of the police procedural; Lawrence Block; John Lutz; Harry Kemelman of Rabbi Small fame; Joyce Harrington and Marcia Muller, excellent representatives of a large group of outstanding women mystery writers; Michael Gilbert of Great Britain; and dozens of others.

We are also proud to offer fine examples of the work of writers we feel have been neglected and whose work deserves a wider audience, people like Edward Wellen, Arthur Porges, Talmage Powell, and Henry Slesar.

In the following pages you will read almost every type of mystery story ever written—the classic whodunit; the tricky whydunit; stories of police detectives, of private eyes, and of talented and sometimes lucky amateurs; armchair detectives; ethnic detectives; stories of suspense; and puzzle stories that will test your intellect as well as your instincts. We have also included a number of never-before-reprinted stories for your enjoyment.

The sources for these stories are as varied as their types—in addition to *Ellery Queen's Mystery Magazine, Alfred Hitchcock's Mystery Magazine*, and *Mike Shayne's Mystery Magazine*, thankfully all still going strong, we have chosen stories that first appeared in such publications as the terrific *Manhunt* (1953–1967), now legendary for its modern hard-boiled tales; and such rare pulps as the Munsey Company's *Double Detective* (1937–1943). The mystery field is somewhat unique for naming its magazines after its practitioners and their creations, and in addition to those already mentioned, we are proud to bring you stories from such magazines as *The Saint Mystery Magazine* (1953–1967); the very rare *Ed McBain's Mystery Book*, which existed during 1960–1961 for only three issues; and the equally difficult-to-locate *Charlie Chan Mystery Magazine*, which had a life of four issues in 1973 and 1974.

And now it's time for you to enter the world of thieves, spies, murderers, and their pursuers—read on, and enjoy!

BILL PRONZINI
MARTIN H. GREENBERG
1985

xiv

1

THE OVAL PORTRAIT

Edgar Allan Poe

THE CHÂTEAU INTO which my valet had ventured to make forcible entrance, rather than permit me, in my desperately wounded condition, to pass a night in the open air, was one of those piles of commingled gloom and grandeur which have so long frowned among the Apennines, not less in fact than in the fancy of Mrs. Radcliffe. To all appearance it had been temporarily and very lately abandoned. We established ourselves in one of the smallest and least sumptuously furnished apartments. It lay in a remote turret of the building. Its decorations were rich, yet tattered and antique. Its walls were hung with tapestry and bedecked with manifold and multiform armorial trophies, together with an unusually great number of very spirited modern paintings in frames of rich golden arabesque. In these paintings, which depended from the walls not only in their main surfaces, but in very many nooks which the bizarre architecture of the château rendered necessary—in these paintings my incipient delirium, perhaps, had caused me to take deep interest; so that I bade Pedro to close the heavy shutters of the room—since it was already night—to light the tongues of a tall candelabrum which stood by the head of my bed, and to throw open far and wide the fringed curtains of black velvet which enveloped the bed itself. I wished all this done that I might resign myself, if not to sleep, at least alternately to the contemplation of these pictures, and the perusal of a small volume which had been found upon the pillow, and which purported to criticize and describe them.

Long, long I read—and devoutly, devoutly I gazed. Rapidly and gloriously the hours flew by and the deep midnight came. The position of the candelabrum displeased me, and outreaching my hand with difficulty, rather than disturb my slumbering valet, I placed it so as to throw its rays more fully upon the book.

But the action produced an effect altogether unanticipated. The rays of the numerous candles (for there were many) now fell within a niche of the room which had hitherto been thrown into deep shade by one of the bedposts. I thus saw in vivid light a picture all unnoticed before. It was the portrait of a young girl just ripening into womanhood. I glanced at the painting hurriedly, and then closed my eyes. Why I did this was not at first apparent even to my own perception. But while my lids remained thus shut, I ran over in mind my reason for so shutting them. It was an impulsive movement to gain time for thought—to make sure that my vision had not deceived me—to calm and subdue my fancy for a more sober and more certain gaze. In a very few moments I again looked fixedly at the painting.

That I now saw aright I could not and would not doubt; for the first flashing of the candles upon that canvas had seemed to dissipate the dreamy stupor which was stealing over my senses, and to startle me at once into waking life.

The portrait, I have already said, was that of a young girl. It was a mere head and shoulders, done in what is technically termed a *vignette* manner; much in the style of the favorite heads of Sully. The arms, the bosom, and even the ends of the radiant hair melted imperceptibly into the vague yet deep shadow which formed the background of the whole. The frame was oval, richly gilded and filigreed in *Moresque*. As a thing of art nothing could be more admirable than the painting itself. But it could have been neither the execution of the work, nor the immortal beauty of the countenance, which had so suddenly and so vehemently moved me. Least of all, could it have been that my fancy, shaken from its half slumber, had mistaken the head for that of a living person. I saw at once that the peculiarities of the design, of the *vignetting,* and of the frame, must have instantly dispelled such idea—must have prevented even its momentary entertainment. Thinking earnestly upon these points, I remained, for an hour perhaps, half sitting, half reclining, with my vision riveted upon the portrait. At length, satisfied with the true secret of its effect, I fell back within the bed. I had found the spell of the picture in an absolute *life-likeliness* of expression, which, at first startling, finally confounded, subdued, and appalled me. With deep and reverent awe I replaced the candelabrum in its former position. The cause of my deep agitation being thus shut from view, I sought eagerly the volume which discussed the paintings and their histories. Turning to the number which designated the oval portrait, I there read the vague and quaint words which follow:

"She was a maiden of rarest beauty, and not more lovely than full of glee. And evil was the hour when she saw, and loved, and wedded the painter. He, passionate, studious, austere, and having already a bride in his Art: she a maiden of rarest beauty, and not more lovely than full of glee; all light and smiles, and frolicsome as the young fawn; loving and cherishing all things; hating only the Art which was her rival; dreading only the palette and brushes and other untoward instruments which deprived her of the countenance of her lover. It was thus a terrible thing for this lady to hear the painter speak of his desire to portray even his young bride. But she was humble and obedient, and sat meekly for many weeks in the dark high turret-chamber where the light dripped upon the pale canvas only from overhead. But he, the painter, took glory in his work, which went on from hour to hour, and from day to day. And he was a passionate, and wild, and moody man, who became lost in reveries; so that he *would* not see that the light which fell so ghastly in that lone turret withered the health and the spirits of his bride, who pined visibly to all but him. Yet she smiled on and still on, uncomplainingly, because she saw that the painter (who had high renown) took a fervid and burning pleasure in his task, and wrought day and night to depict her who so loved him, yet who grew daily more dispirited and weak. And in sooth some who beheld the portrait spoke of its resemblance in low words, as of a mighty marvel, and a proof not less of the power of the painter than of his deep love for her whom he depicted so surpassingly well. But at length, as the labor drew nearer to its conclusion, there were admitted none into the turret; for the painter had grown wild with the ardor of his work, and turned his eyes from the canvas rarely, even to regard the countenance of his wife. And he *would* not see that the tints which he spread upon the canvas were drawn from the cheeks of her who sat beside him. And when many weeks had passed, and but little remained to do, save one brush upon the mouth and one tint upon the eye, the spirit of the lady again flickered up as the flame within the socket of the lamp. And then the brush was given, and then the tint was placed; and, for one moment, the painter stood entranced before the work which he had wrought; but in the next, while he yet gazed, he grew tremulous and very pallid, and aghast, and crying with a loud voice, 'This is indeed *Life* itself!' turned suddenly to regard his beloved:—*She was dead!*''

2

THERE HANGS DEATH!

John D. MacDonald

THE DEAD MAN was face down on the dark hardwood floor. He was frail and old, and the house was sturdy and old, redolent of Victorian dignity. It was the house where he had been born.

The wide stairs climbed for two tall stories, with two landings for each floor. He lay in the center of the stairwell, twenty-five feet below a dusty skylight. The gray daylight came down through the skylight and glinted on the heavy ornate hilt and pommel of the broadsword that pinned the man to the dark floor.

The hilt was of gold and silver, and there was a large red stone set into the pommel. The gold—and the red of stone and red of blood on the white shirt—were the only touches of color.

Riggs saw that when they brought him in. They let him look for a few moments. He knew he would not forget it, ever. The bright momentary light of a police flash bulb filled the hallway, and they turned him away, a hand pushing his shoulder.

There were many people in the book-lined study. He saw Angela at once, her face too white, her eyes shocked and enormous, sitting on a straight chair. He started toward her but they caught his arm; and the wide, bald, tired-eyed sranger who sat behind the old desk said, "Take the girl across the hall and put Riggs in that chair."

Angela gave him a frail smile and he tried to respond. They took her out. He sat where she had been.

The bald man looked at him for a long moment. "You'll answer questions willingly?"

"Of course." A doughy young man in the opposite corner took notes with a fountain pen.

"Name and occupation?"

5

"Howard Riggs. Research assistant at the University, Department of Psychology."

"How long have you known the deceased?"

"I've known Dr. Hilber for three years. I met him through his niece, Angela Manley, when I was in the Graduate School. I believe he'd retired two or three years before I met him. He was head of the Archeology—"

"We know his history. How much have you been told about this?"

"Not very much. Just that he was dead and I was wanted here. I didn't know he'd been . . ."

"What is your relationship to his niece?"

"We're to be married in June when the spring semester ends."

"Were you in this house today?"

"Yes, sir. I went to church with Angela. I picked her up here and brought her back here. We walked. We had some coffee here and then I went back to the lab. I'm running an experiment using laboratory animals. I have to . . ."

"What time did you leave this house?"

"I'd say it was eleven-thirty this morning I've been in the lab ever since, until those men came and . . ."

"Were you alone at the lab?"

"Yes, sir."

"Did you see Dr. Hilber when you were here?"

"No, sir."

"Did Miss Manley inform you that she was going to stay here? Did she say anything about going out?"

"She wanted me to go for a walk. I couldn't. I had to get back. We sometimes walk up in the hills back of here."

"Did you know that Miss Manley is the sole heir?"

"I guess I did. I mean I remember him saying once that she was his only living relative. So I would assume . . ."

"Did you know he had substantial paid-up insurance policies?"

"No, sir."

"He opposed this marriage, did he not?"

"No, sir. He was in favor of it. He opposed it at first. He didn't want to be left alone. But after I agreed to move in here after we're married . . . you see, he wasn't well."

"You had many arguments with him, did you not?"

Riggs frowned. "Not like you mean. They were intellectual arguments. He thought my specialty is a sort of . . . pseudoscience. He was a stubborn man, sir."

6

"You became angry at him."

Riggs shrugged. "Many times. But not . . . importantly angry."

The study door opened and two men came in. The man in uniform who had come in said to the bald man, "Can't raise a print off that sword, Captain. It wouldn't have to be wiped. It's just a bad surface."

The bald captain nodded impatiently. He looked at the second man who had come in. "Doctor?" he said.

"Steve, it's pretty weird," the doctor said. He sat down and crossed long legs. "That sword is like a razor. It was sunk right into the wood."

"If it was shoved through him and he fell on his face, of course it would be stuck in the wood."

"Not like that, Steve. It's a two-edged sword. If he fell after it was through him it would be knocked back. Some of the shirt fibers were carried into the wound. No, Steve, the sword went into him after he was stretched out on his face."

"Knocked out?"

"No sign of it."

"Check stomach contents and so forth to see if he was doped."

"That'll be done. But does it make sense?"

"How do you mean?"

"If you're going to kill a man, do you dope him, stretch him out on the floor and chunk a knife down through him? Now here's something else. After we got him out of the way we found another hole in the floor. A fresh hole, about four inches from where the sword dug in. It's a deeper hole, but it looks to me as if it was made the same way, by the same sword. And there was only one hole in the professor."

The captain got up quickly and went out. Most of the men followed him. Howard Riggs got up and went out, too. He was not stopped. He saw Angela in the small room across the hall. He walked by the man outside her door and went to her. She stood up quickly as he approached. Her face was pale, her eyes enormous. He took her cold hands in his. "Darling," she said, "they act so . . ."

"I know. I know. Don't let it hurt. Please."

"But he's dead, and the way they look at me. As if . . ." She began to cry and he held the trembling slenderness of her in his arms, murmuring reassurances, trying to conceal from her how inept and confused he felt in the face of the obvious hostility of the police.

The hard voice behind him said, "You're not supposed to be in here." A hand rested heavily on his shoulder.

Riggs turned out from under the hand and released Angela. He looked back at her as he left the room. She stood and managed a smile. It was a frail, wan smile, but it was good to see. He hoped he had strengthened her.

Out in the hall the captain was on his knees examining the gouges in the dark wood. He craned his neck back and looked straight up. The men around him did the same. It was a curious tableau.

The captain gave an order and the sword was brought to him. The blade had been cleaned. He hefted it in his hand, took a half cut at the air.

"Heavy damn thing," he said. He glanced at Riggs. "Ever see it before?"

"It's from Dr. Hilber's collection of antique edged weapons. It dates from the twelfth century. He said he believed it was taken on one of the early crusades. The second, I think."

"You men move back down the hall," the captain said. He plodded up the stairs, the incongrous sword gleaming in his hairy fist. Soon he was out of sight, and they could hear him climbing the second flight. There was silence—and then a silvery shimmer in the gray light of the stairwell. The sword flashed down, chunked deeply into the floor and stood there, vibrationless.

The captain came back down. He grasped the hilt with both hands, planted his feet, grunted as he wrenched it out of the floor. He smiled at Riggs. "I look at her and I say she could just about lift a sword like this. She couldn't stick it through the old man, but she could drop it through him."

"You're out of your mind!"

"The other hole is where she made a test run when he was out, to see if it would fall right. She says she came back from her walk and found him. But I find clumsy attempts to make it look like a prowler did it. The jade collection in his bedroom is all messed up. We got to check it against his inventory. Dirt tracked into that room where the weapons are. Silver dumped on the floor in the dining room. If Doc wasn't on the ball, that stage setting might have sold me. *Might* have. But now we know it was dropped through him, and it was no theft murder, even if she tried to make it look that way."

They took Angela in on suspicion of murder. They did not let Riggs speak to her. They told him not to leave town. He did not understand why they didn't arrest him also. He sensed that he was being carefully watched.

Though he was emotionally exhausted that night, it took him a long time to get to sleep. A nightmare awakened him before dawn. In his dream a shining sword had been suspended high over him, in utter blackness. He did not know when it would drop. He recognized the similarity to the legend of Damocles. He lay sweating in the predawn silences until his frightened heart slowed its beat. It seemed then that it was the first time he had been able to think logically of the death of Hilber. He thought carefully and for a long time, and when he knew what he would do, he went quickly to sleep.

He walked into the captain's office at two o'clock on Monday. It was raining heavily outside. The captain was in shirt sleeves. "Sit down," the captain said. "You asked to see me, but I'll tell you some things first. The girl is sticking to her story. I half believe her. Besides, that corpse was in the center of the room with the sword sticking straight up. I can't see anybody throwing it and making it land that way, so we're trying to uncover other angles."

"Hilber had a good academic mind, but not what you'd call a practical mind."

"Keep talking."

"If he wanted to kill himself and make it look like murder, he would try to clear Angela by such clumsy business as the dirt tracked in, the silver on the foor, the disorder in the jade case. He'd never stop to think of the next logical step, that the police would accuse Angela of doing all that to mislead them."

"You try to read a dead man's mind and he can't tell you if you're wrong. You've got more than that, haven't you?"

"This morning I talked to his lawyer and his doctor, Captain, and I went to the house and they wouldn't let me in."

"I know that."

"He had very little money. His illness used up most of it. He had forty-five thousand in insurance, in two policies, one of ten and one for thirty-five thousand. There is a suicide clause in the larger policy."

"So he heaved a sword up in the air and it came down and hit him in the back."

"He was operated on two years ago. The operation was not completely successful. The malignancy returned and this time it was widespread. He had six months to two years, and in either case it would not have been pleasant."

"So?"

"Did you ever hear of the Sword of Damocles?"

The captain frowned. "They hung it on a thread over some joker's head when he wanted to be king, didn't they? It would take a special kind of nerve. Some timing device. Candle maybe. Let's go take a look, Riggs."

They looked. The captain brought the sword along. They experimented. It would have had to drop from the top floor. The railing encircled three sides of the stairwell. Nothing was tied to the railing. Nothing had been fastened to the skylight. They searched for a long time. The captain thought of the possible use of rubber bands, so they would snap back into one of the bedrooms. They could find nothing. The captain rubbed his bald head. "No good, Riggs. The sword had to be dead in the middle. Nothing could have held it. The girl didn't come upstairs. The house was searched after we got here. And who could have held the sword out that far—in the center of the room?"

"Let me look around some more, please."

"Go ahead."

Riggs finally wandered to the study. Dr. Hilber had spent most of his time there. He sat moodily in Hilber's chair and went back over every aspect of the previous day to see if he could remember anything that would help.

They had come back from church. Angela had opened the front door with her key, mildly surprised to find it locked. They had walked back through to the kitchen. He remembered that Angela had wondered if her uncle would put in his usual appearance for Sunday morning coffee, then thought that he was probably immersed in reading one of the many scholarly books that were so much a part of his life. She had decided not to disturb him.

The memory of the morning gave him no clue. The Sword of Damocles had hung over the stairwell. And it had fallen. And the means of suspension was utterly gone, as though it had never been. As though it had vanished. He sat very still for a long moment and then got up quickly.

Angela was released at six. Riggs was asked to perform the experiment again for the city District Attorney and two members of his staff. He and the captain had found the proper material after experimenting with various kinds of thread, and had purchased a sufficient supply of rayon tire cord yarn. Riggs took the sword to the top floor, knotted one end of the yarn around the metal railing and cut off a piece long enough to reach to the opposite railing. To the middle of that piece he tied a length sufficient to reach to the floor far below. He then tied the sword to the middle of the strand, took the free end around and tied it to the opposite railing. The sword danced and shimmered in the air and grew still.

They all went back down to the main floor. Riggs lighted a match and touched it to the strand of yarn hanging down. It caught at once and a knot of flame raced up the piece of yarn with stunning speed. Soon the heavy sword fell and imbedded its point deeply into the hardwood of the hallway.

By the time they reached the top railing, all traces of the suspension method had disappeared. The heat generated had not been sufficient to leave any mark on the metal railings.

The District Attorney sighed. "It's half crazy, but I guess I've got to buy it."

The captain shook his head and said, "It's the only thing possible. Nobody could have thrown that sword and made it land at that angle—or rather without an angle. And that stuff he used doesn't leave a trace. Without Riggs figuring it out, though, I don't know where we'd be."

The District Attorney stared curiously at Riggs. "How did you figure it out?"

"He was a classical scholar and with this setup—" Riggs indicated the open space above them and the railings. "It almost had to be based on the legend of the Sword of Damocles. That and the second hole in the floor. Those were the clues. He tested the method while we were out. That's why there were two holes in the floor. The Sword of Damocles gave him his idea. Modern technology gave him the method."

And then he was free to go to Angela.

3

TOWN WANTED

Fredric Brown

ON MY WAY in I looked into the back room. The boys were there. Alderman Higgings had a pile of blue chips in front of him and was trying to keep his greasy little mug from looking sap-happy.

Lieutenant Grange was there too. He was half tight. He had beer spots on the front of his blue uniform shirt. His hands shook when he picked up the stein.

The alderman looked up and said, "Hi, Jimmy. How's tricks?"

I gave him a grin and went on upstairs. I pushed into the boss's office without knocking.

He looked at me sort of queerly. "Everything go okay?"

"They'll find him when the lake dries up," I told him. "We won't be around then."

"You covered all the angles, Jimmy?"

"All what angles?" I asked him. "Nobody's going to investigate. A guy won't pay his protecton and Annie Doesn't Live Here Any More. Now the rest of them will lay it on the line."

The boss took out a handkerchief and wiped the sweat off his bald spot. You could see the guy was squeamish. That's no way to handle things. It would be different, I figured, when I took over.

I eased down and lit a cigarette. "Listen," I said. "This town is worth twice the take we're getting. Who do we move in on next?"

"We're letting it ride a while, Jimmy. Things are hot."

I got up and started for the door.

He said softly, "Sit down, Jimmy."

I didn't, but I went back and stood in front of him.

"Well?" I asked.

13

"About the boys you've lined up to buck me, Jimmy. When do you think you're going to take over?"

I guess I'd underestimated him. You can't run the rackets and not be hep.

I sat down. "I don't get you, boss," I stalled. "What's on your mind?"

"Let's settle this, Jimmy," he said. There were beads of sweat on his bald spot again and he wiped it off. I kept my yap shut and looked at him. It was his move.

" You're a good guy, Jimmy," he went on. "You've been a big help to me."

There wasn't any malarkey in that. But he was just winding up and I sat back and waited to see what he was going to pitch.

"But six months ago I saw it couldn't last, Jimmy. You got big ideas. This burg isn't big enough for you to stay in second spot. Right?"

I still waited for him to go on.

"You think you've bought four of the boys. You've only got two. The other two leveled with me. They're set to gum your works."

That was bad listening. He *did* know; four was right. And I didn't know which two ratted. All right, I thought, this is the showdown.

"Go on," I said. "I'm listening."

"You're too ambitious for me, Jimmy. I was satisfied to run the slot machines and the joints. Maybe just a little on the protection societies. You want to run the town. You want to collect the taxes. And your trigger finger's too jittery for me, Jimmy. I don't like killing, except when I have to."

"Lay off the character reading," I told him. "You've called the shots. Add it up."

"You could kill me now, maybe. But you wouldn't get away with it. And you're too smart, Jimmy, to stick you neck out unless it's going to get you something. I'm counting on that. I'm ready for you. You wouldn't get out of here alive. If you did, you'd have to blow. And if you blow, what's it get you?"

I walked over to the window and looked out. He wouldn't draw on me, I knew. Hell, why should he? He held the cards; I could see that now. He'd wised up a little too soon for me.

"You've been a big help, Jimmy," he went on. "I want to break fair with you. In the last year I've made more dough than I'd have made without you. I want you to leave. But I'll give you a stake. Pick a town of your own and work it. Leave me this one."

I kept looking out the window. I knew why he wouldn't bump me.

There'd been too many killings; the cops were beginning to take it on the chin. The boss wanted to pull in his horns.

And from his point of view I could see it all right. He could even drop the protectives. The slots, the joints, the semi-legit stuff paid enough to suit him. He'd rather play safe for a small take. I'm not that way.

I turned and faced him. After all, why not another town? I could do it, if I picked one that was ripe.

"How much?" I asked him.

"Ten grand," he said.

We settled for twenty.

You can see now why I'm in Miami. I figured I could use a vacation before I picked out a spot. A swell suite, overlooking the sea. Women, parties, roulette and all that. You can make a big splash here if you're willing to spend a few grand.

But I'm getting restless. I'd rather see it coming in.

I know how I'll start, when I've picked my town. I'll take a tavern for a front. Then I fnd out which politicians are on the auction block. I'll see that the others go—money can swing that. Then I bring in torpedoes and start work.

Coin machines are the quickest dough. You pyramid that into bookie joints, sporting houses, and the rest; and when you're strong enough, the protective societies—where the merchants pay you to let them alone. That's the big dough racket, if you're not squeamish. It's big dough because you don't have to put in anything for what you take out.

If you know the angles and work it so you don't have to start liquidating the opposition until you've got control, it's a cinch. And I know the angles.

Plenty of towns would do, but some are easier than others. If you pick one that's ripe it goes quicker, and if you can buy enough of the boys in office you won't have to force the others out.

I'm looking them over. I'm tired of loafing.

How's your town? I can tell if you answer me a question. Last time there was an election, did you really read up both sides of things, with the idea of keeping things on the up and up? Or did you go for the guy with the biggest posters?

Huh? You say you didn't even get to the polls at all?

Pal, that's just the town I'm looking for.

I'll be seeing you.

15

4

THE SWEETEST MAN IN THE WORLD

Donald E. Westlake

I ADJUSTED MY hair in the hall mirror before opening the door. My hair was gray, and piled neatly on top of my head. I smoothed my skirt, took a deep breath, and opened the door.

The man in the hallway was thirtyish, well-dressed, quietly handsome, and carrying a briefcase. He was also somewhat taken aback to see me. He glanced again at the apartment number on the door, looked back at me, and said, "Excuse, me, I'm looking for Miss Diane Wilson."

"Yes, of course," I said. "Do come in."

He gazed past me uncertainly, hesitating on the doorstep, saying, "Is she in?"

"I'm Diane Wilson," I said.

He blinked. "*You're* Diane Wilson?"

"Yes, I am."

"The Diane Wilson who worked for Mr. Edward Cunningham?"

"Yes, indeed." I made a sad face. "Such a tragic thing," I said. "He was the sweetest man in the world, Mr. Cunningham was."

He cleared his throat, and I could see him struggling to regain his composure. "I see," he said. "Well, uh—well, Miss Wilson, my name is Fraser, Kenneth Fraser. I represent Transcontinental Insurance Association."

"Oh, no," I said. "I have all the insurance I need, thank you."

"No, no," he said. "I beg your pardon, I'm not here to *sell* insurance. I'm an investigator for the company."

"Oh, they all say that," I said, "and then when they get inside they *do* want to sell something. I remember one young man from an encyclopedia company—he swore up and down he was just taking a survey, and he no sooner—"

17

"Miss Wilson," Fraser said determinedly, "I am *definitely* not a sales-man. I am not here to discuss your insurance with you, I am here to discuss Mr. Cunningham's insurance."

"Oh, I wouldn't know anything about that," I said. "I simply handled the paperwork in Mr. Cunningham's real estate office. His private business affairs he took care of himself."

"Miss Wilson, I—" He stopped, and looked up and down the hallway. "Do we have to speak out here?" he asked.

"Well, I don't know that there's anything for us to talk about." I said. I admit I was enjoying this.

"Miss Wilson, there *is* something for us to talk about." He put down the briefcase and took out his wallet. "Here," he said, "Here's my identifi-cation."

I looked at the laminated card. It was very official and very complex and included Fraser's photograph, looking open-mouthed and stupid.

Fraser said, "I will *not* try to sell you insurance, nor will I ask you any details about Mr. Cunningham's handling of his private business affairs. That's a promise. Now, *may* I come in?"

It seemed time to stop playing games with him; after all, I didn't want him getting mad at me. He might go poking around too far, just out of spite. So I stepped back and said, "Very well then, young man, you may come in. But I'll hold you to that promise."

We went into the living room and I motioned at the sofa, saying, "Do sit down."

"Thank you." But he didn't seem to like the sofa when he sat on it, possibly because of the clear plastic cover it had over it.

"My nieces come by from time to time," I said. "that's why I have those plastic covers on all the furniture. You know how children can be."

"Of course," he said. He looked around, and I think the entire living room depressed him, not just the plastic cover on the sofa.

Well, it was understandable. The living room was a natural consequence of Miss Diane Wilson's personality, with its plastic slipcovers, the doilies on all the tiny tables, the little plants in ceramic frogs, the windows with venetian blinds *and* curtains *and* drapes, the general air of overcrowded neatness. Something like the house Mrs. Muskrat has in all those children's stories.

I pretended not to notice his discomfort. I sat down on the chair that matched the sofa, adjusted my apron and skirt over my knees, and said, "Very well, Mr. Fraser. I'm ready to listen."

18

He opened his briefcase on his lap, looked at me over it, and said, "This may come as something of a shock to you, Miss Wilson. I don't know if you were aware of the extent of Mr. Cunningham's policy holdings with us."

"I already told you, Mr. Fraser, that I—"

"Yes, of course," he said hastily. "I wasn't asking, I was getting ready to tell you myself. Mr. Cunningham had three policies with us of various types, all of which automatically became due when he died."

"Bless his memory," I said.

"Yes. Naturally. At any rate, the total on these three policies comes to one hundred twenty-five thousand dollars."

"Gracious!"

"With double indemnity for accidental death, of course," he went on, "the total payable is two hundred fifty thousand dollars. That is, one quarter of a million dollars."

"Dear me!" I said. "I would never have guessed."

Fraser looked carefully at me. "And you are the sole beneficiary," he said.

I smiled blankly at him, as though waiting for him to go on, then permitted my expression to show that the import of his words was gradually coming home to me. Slowly I sank back into the chair. My hand went to my throat, to the bit of lace around the collar of my dress.

"Me?" I whispered. "Oh, Mr. Fraser, you must be joking!"

"Not a bit," he said. "Mr. Cunningham changed his beneficiary just one month ago, switching from his wife to you."

"I can't believe it," I whispered.

"Nevertheless, it is true. And since Mr. Cunningham did die an accidental death, burning up in his his real estate office, and since such a large amount of money was involved, the routine is to send an investigator around, just to be sure everything's all right."

"Oh," I said. I was allowing myself to recover. I said, "That's why you were so surprised when you saw me."

He smiled sheepishly. "Frankly," he said, "yes."

"You had expected to find some sexy young thing, didn't you? Someone Mr. Cunningham had been having an—a relationship with."

"The thought had crossed my mind," he said, and made a boyish smile. "I do apologize," he said.

"Accepted," I said, and smiled back at him.

It was beautiful. He had come here with a strong preconception, and a belief based on that preconception that something was wrong. Knock the preconception away and he would be left with an embarrassed feeling of having made a fool of himself. From now on he would want nothing more than to be rid of this case, since it would serve only to remind him of his wrong guess and the foolish way he'd acted when I'd first opened the door.

As I had supposed he would, he began at once to speed things up, taking a pad and pen from his briefcase and saying, "Mr. Cunningham never told you he'd made you his beneficiary?"

"Oh, dear me, no. I only worked for the man three months."

"Yes, I know," he said. "It did seem odd to us."

"Oh, his poor wife," I said, "She may have neglected him but—"

"Neglected?"

"Well." I allowed myself this time to show a pretty confusion. "I shouldn't say anything against the woman," I went on. "I've never so much as laid eyes on her. But I do know that not once in the three months I worked there did she ever come in to see Mr. Cunningham, or even call him on the phone. Also, from things he said—"

"What things, Miss Wilson?"

"I'd rather not say, Mr. Fraser. I don't know the woman, and Mr. Cunningham is dead. I don't believe we should sit here and talk about them behind their backs."

"Still, Miss Wilson, he did leave his insurance money to you."

"He was always the sweetest man," I said. "Just the sweetest man in the world. But why he would—" I spread my hands, to show bewilderment.

Fraser said, "Do you suppose he had a fight with his wife? Such a bad one that he decided to change his beneficiary, looked around for somebody else, saw you, and that was that."

"He was always very good to me," I said. "In the short time I knew him I always found Mr. Cunningham a perfect gentleman and the most considerate of men."

"I'm sure you did," he said. He looked at the notes he'd been taking, and muttered to himself. "Well, that might explain it. It's nutty, but—" He shrugged.

Yes, of course he shrugged. Kick away the preconception, leave him drifting and bewildered for just a second, and then quickly suggest another hypothesis to him. He clutched at it like a drowning man. Mr. Cunningham had had a big fight with Mrs. Cunningham. Mr. Cunningham had changed his beneficiary out of hate or revenge, and had chosen Miss Diane Wilson, the dear middle-aged lady he'd recently hired as his secretary. As Mr. Fraser had so succinctly phrased it, it was nutty, but—

I said, "Well, I really don't know what to say. To tell the truth, Mr. Fraser, I'm overcome."

"That's understandable," he said. "A quarter of a million dollars doesn't come along every day."

"It isn't the amount," I said. "It's how it came to me. I have never been rich, Mr. Fraser, and because I never married I have always had to support myself. But I am a good secretary, a willing worker, and I have always handled my finances, if I say so myself, with wisdom and economy. A quarter of a million dollars is, as you say, a great deal of money, but I do not *need* a great deal of money. I would much rather have that sweet man Mr. Cunningham alive again than have all the money in the world."

"Of course," he nodded, and I could see he believed every word I had said.

I went further. "And particularly," I said, "to be given money that should certainly have gone to his wife. I just wouldn't have believed Mr. Cunningham capable of such a hateful or vindictive action."

"He probably would have changed it back later on," Fraser said. "After he had cooled down. He only made the change three weeks before—before he passed on."

"Bless his soul," I said.

"There's one final matter, Miss Wilson," he said, "and then I'll leave you alone."

"Anything at all, Mr. Fraser," I said.

"About Mr. Roche," he said. "Mr. Cunningham's former partner. He seems to have moved from his old address, and we can't find him. Would you have his current address?"

"Oh, no," I said. "Mr. Roche left the concern before I was hired. In fact, Mr. Cunningham hired me because, after Mr. Roche left, it was necessary to have a secretary in order to be sure there was always someone in the office."

"I see," he said. "Well—" He put the pad and pen back into the briefcase and started to his feet, just as the doorbell rang.

"Excuse me," I said. I went out to the hallway and opened the door.

She came boiling in like a hurricane, pushing past me and shouting, "Where is she? Where is the hussy?"

I followed her into the living room, where Fraser was standing and gaping at her in some astonishment as she continued to shout and to demand to know where *she* was.

I said, "Madame, please. This happens to be my home."

"Oh, does it?" She stood in front of me, hands on hips. "Well then, you can tell me where I'll find the Wilson woman."

"Who?"

"Diane Wilson, the little tramp. I want to—"

I said, "I am Diane Wilson."

She stood there, open-mouthed, gaping at me.

Fraser came over then, smiling a bit, saying, "Escuse, me, Miss Wilson, I think I know what's happened." He turned to the new visitor and said, "You're Mrs. Cunningham, aren't you?"

Still open-mouthed, she managed to nod her head.

Fraser identified himself, and said, "I made the same mistake you did—I came here expecting to find some vamp. But as you can see—" And he gestured at me.

"Oh, I *am* sorry," Mrs. Cunningham said to me. She was a striking woman in her late thirties. "I called the insurance company, and when they told me Ed had changed all his policies over to you, I naturally thought—well—you know."

"Oh, dear," I said. "I certainly hope you don't think—"

"Oh, not at all," Mrs. Cunningham said, and smiled a bit, and patted my hand. "I wouldn't think that of *you*," she said.

Fraser said, "Mrs. Cunningham, didn't your husband tell you he was changing the beneficiary?"

"He certainly didn't," she said with sudden anger. "And neither did that company of yours. They should have told me the minute Ed made that change."

Fraser developed an icy chill. "Madame," he said, "a client has the right to make anyone he chooses his beneficiary, and the company is under no obligation to inform anyone that—"

"Oh, that's all right," I said. "I don't need the money. I'm perfectly willing to share it with Mrs. Cunningham."

Fraser snapped around to me, saying, "Miss Wilson, you aren't under any obligation at all to this woman. The money is legally and rightfully yours." As planned, he was now 100 percent on my side.

Now it was time to make him think more kindly of Mrs. Cunningham. I said, "But this poor woman has been treated shabbily. She was married to Mr. Cunningham for—how many years?"

"Twelve," she said, "twelve years," and abruptly sat down on the sofa and began to sob.

"There, there," I said, patting her shoulder.

"What am I going to *do*?" she wailed. "I have no money, nothing! he left me nothing but debts! I can't even afford a decent burial for him!"

"We'll work it out," I assured her. "Don't you worry, we'll work it out." I looked at Fraser and said, "How long will it take to get the money?"

He said, "Well, we didn't discuss whether you want it in installments or in a lump sum. Monthly payments are usually—"

"Oh, a lump sum," I said. "There's so much to do right away, and then my older brother is a banker in California. *He'll* know what to do."

"If you're sure—" He was looking at Mrs. Cunningham, and didn't yet entirely trust her.

I said, "Oh, I'm sure this poor woman won't try to cheat me, Mr. Fraser."

Mrs. Cunningham cried, "Oh God!" and wailed into her handkerchief.

"Besides," I said, "I'll phone my brother and have him fly east at once. He can handle everything for me."

"I suppose," he said, "if we expedite things, we could have your money for you in a few days."

"I'll have my brother call you," I said.

"Fine," he said. He hesitated, holding his briefcase. "Mrs. Cunningham, are you coming along? Is there anywhere I can drop you?"

"Let the woman rest here a while," I said. "I'll make her some tea."

"Very well."

He left reluctantly. I walked him to the front door, where he said to me, quietly, "Miss Wilson, do me a favor."

"Of course, Mr. Fraser."

"Promise me you won't sign anything until your brother gets here to advise you."

"I promise," I said, sighing.

"Well," he said, "one more item and I'm done."

"Mr. Roche, you mean?"

"Right. I'll talk to him, if I can find him. Not that it's necessary." He smiled and said goodbye and walked away down the hall.

I closed the door, feeling glad he didn't think it necessary to talk to Roche. He would have found it somewhat difficult to talk to Roche, since Roche was in the process of being buried under the name of Edward Cunningham, his charred remains in the burned-out real estate office having been identified under that name by Mrs. Edward Cunningham.

Would Roche have actually pushed that charge of embezzlement he'd been shouting about? Well, the question was academic now, though three months ago it had seemed real enough to cause me to set up this hasty and desperate—but, I think, rather ingenious—plan for getting myself out of the whole mess entirely. The only question had been whether or not our deep-freeze would preserve the body sufficiently over the three months of preparation, but the fire had settled that problem, too.

I went back into the living room. She got up from the sofa and said, "What's all this jazz about a brother in California?"

"Change of plans," I said, "I was too much the innocent, and you were too much the wronged woman. Without a brother, Fraser might have insisted on hanging around, helping me with the finances himself. And the *other* Miss Wilson is due back from Greece in two weeks."

"That's all well and good, Ed," my wife said. "But where is this brother going to come from? She doesn't have one, you know—the real Miss Wilson, I mean."

"I know." That had been one of the major reasons I'd hired Miss Wilson in the first place—aside from our general similarity of build—the fact that she *had* no relatives, making it absolutely safe to take over her apartment during my impersonation.

My wife said, "Well? What are you going to do for a brother?"

I took off the gray wig and scratched my head, feeling great relief. "I'll be the brother," I said. "A startling family resemblance between us."

She shook her head, grinning at me. "You are a one, Ed," she said. "You sure are a one."

"That's me," I said, "The sweetest man in the world."

5

EVERY FIFTH MAN

Edward D. Hoch

YOU PROBABLY WONDER why I'm still alive after all that has happened, and I suppose it *is* quite a story. I'd been living and training with the exiles for two years before the attempted coup, knowing—as we all knew—the penalty for failure. There were months of hand-to-hand combat and paratrooper training and even some explosives practice before we were ready for the big day, the day we returned to Costa-nera.

I'd lived the 25 years of my life in the cities and towns and jungle villages of Costanera. It was my country, worth fighting for, every inch of it. We left with the coming of General Diam, but now we were going back. We would drop from the skies by night, join the anti-Diam military, and enter the capital city in triumph.

That was the plan. Somehow it didn't work out that way. The military changed their minds about it, and we jumped from our planes into a withering crossfire from General Diam's forces. More than half of our liberation force of 65 were dead before we reached the ground, and the others were overrun quickly. By nightfall we found ourselves prisoners of the army in the great old fortress overlooking Azul Bay.

There were 23 of us taken prisoner that day, and of these one man—Tomas—had a bad wound in his side. We were crowded into a single large cell at the fortress and left to await our fate. It was hot in there, with the sweat of bodies and a mustiness of air that caught at my throat and threatened to choke me. I wanted to remove my black beret and shirt and stretch out on the hard stone floor, but I did not. Instead I bore it in silence and waited with the others.

A certain custom has existed in the country, a custom which has

25

been observed in revolutions for hundreds of years. Always faced with the problem of the defeated foe, governments had traditionally sent down the order: *Kill every fifth man and release the others*. It was a system of justice tempered with a large degree of mercy, and acted as a deterrent while still allowing something of an opposition party to exist within the country. Of course the eighty percent who were released often regrouped to revolt again, but the threat that hung over them was sometimes enough to pacify their activities.

This, then, was the fate that awaited us—23 prisoners in a gloomy fortress by the blue waters of a bay. We had reason to hope, because most of us had the odds on our side, but we had reckoned without the cold-blooded calculation of General Diam. The order came down early the following morning, and it was read to us through the bars of the cell. It was as we had expected: *Every fifth man will be executed immediately. The remaining prisoners will be released in twenty-four hours*.

But then came the jolting surprise. The oficer in charge kept reading, and read the same message four times more. General Diam had sent down five identical executive orders. No one was to survive the executions.

I knew something had to be done, and quickly. As the guards unlocked the cell door I went to the officer in charge. Using my deepest voice I tried to reason with him. "You cannot execute all twenty-three of us. It would be contrary to orders."

He looked down at me with something like scorn. "Be brave, little fellow. Die like a soldier!"

"But the first order says that every fifth man should be executed immediately. It means just that. They should be executed before you read the second order."

The officer sighed. "What difference does it make? The day will be hot. Who wants to die under the noonday sun? At least now there is a bit of breeze out there."

"You must obey the orders," I insisted. "Each order must be executed separately."

You can see, of course, the reason for my insistence. If the five executive orders were lumped together and carried out at once (as General Diam no doubt intended), all twenty-three of us would be shot. But if they were carried out separately, the orders would allow nine of us to live. I'd always been good at mathematics, and this was how I figured it—every fifth man would be taken from the original 23, a total of 4, leaving 19. The process would be repeated a second time, killing 3, leaving 16. On the third round another 3 would die, and 13 would be left. Then 2 shot, 11 left. A final 2 shot, and 9 of us would walk out of the fortress as free as the air.

You say the odds were still against me? Not at all—if the officer agreed to my argument, I was certain to survive. Because consider—how would the fifth man be picked each time? Not by drawing straws, for this was the military. We would line up in a single column and count off. And in what order would we line up—alphabetically? Hardly, when they did not even know our names. We would line up in the old military tradition—by height.

And I had already established during the night in the cell that I was the shortest of the 23 prisoners!

If they started the count-off at the short end of the line—which was unlikely—I would always be safe, for I would always be Number One. More likely, they would start at the tall end, and for the 5 count-offs I would always be last—numbers 23, 19, 16, 13, 11, and 9. Never a number divisible by 5—never one of the doomed prisoners!

The officer stared down at me for what seemed an eternity. Finally he glanced through the orders in his hand once more and reached a decision. "All right, we will carry out the first order."

We lined up in the courtyard—by height—with two men supporting the wounded Tomas, and started the count-off. Of the 23 of us, 4 were marched over to the sea wall and shot. The rest of us tried not to look.

Again—and 3 of our number died against the sea wall. One of the remaining 16 was starting to cry. He had figured out his position in the line.

The officer formally read the third executive order, and 3 more went to the wall. I was still last in the line.

After the fourth order 2 of the 13 were marched to their death. Even the firing squad was beginning to look hot and bored. The sun was almost above us. Well, only one more count-off and then 9 of us would be free.

"Wait!" the officer shouted, as the first man began to count off again. I turned my neck in horror. Tomas had fallen from the line and the blood was gushing from his side. He was dead, and the 11 was suddenly reduced to 10.

I was the tenth one as the last count began!

The fifth man stepped out of line—then *six, seven, eight, nine, ten*. I didn't move.

"Come, little fellow," the officer said. "It is your turn now."

You ask how I come to be sitting here, when I was so surely doomed, when my careful figuring had gone for nothing. I stood there in that moment, looking death in the face, and did what I had kept from doing all night and morning. I knew the officer would obey General Diam's order to the letter—to execute every fifth man—and that was what saved me.

I took the beret from my head, let my hair fall to my shoulders, and showed them I was a girl.

6

VENDETTA

Guy de Maupassant

THE WIDOW OF Paolo Saverini lived alone with her son in a poor little house on the outskirts of Bonifacio. The city, built on an outjutting part of the mountain, in places even overhanging the sea, looks across the foamy straits toward the southernmost coast of Sardinia. Around on the other side side of the city is a kind of *fjord* which serves as a port, and which, after a winding journey, brings—as far as the first houses—the little Italian and Sardinian fishing smacks and, every two weeks, the old wheezy steamer which makes the trip to Ajaccio.

On the white mountain the clump of houses makes an even whiter spot. They look like the nests of wild birds, clinging to this peak, overlooking this terrible passage where vessels rarely venture. The wind, which bows uninterruptedly has swept bare the forbidding coast; it engulfs itself in the narrow straits and lays waste both sides. The pale streaks of foam, clinging to the black rocks, whose countless peaks rise up out of the water, look like bits of rag floating and drifting on the surface of the sea.

The house of Widow Saverini, clinging to the very edge of the precipice, looked out, through its three windows, over this wild and desolate picture. She lived there alone, with her son Antoine and their dog Semillante, a big thin beast, with a long rough coat, one of the kind of animals that is used for guarding the herds. The young man took her with him when out hunting.

One night, after some kind of quarrel, Antoine Saverini was treacherously stabbed by Nicolas Ravolati, who escaped the same evening to Sardinia.

When the old mother received the body of her son, which the neighbors had brought back to her, she did not cry, but stayed for a long time motionless, watching him; then, stretching her wrinkled hand over the dead body, she promised her son a vendetta.

She did not wish anybody near her, so she shut herself up beside the body with the dog, which howled continuously, standing at the foot of the bed, her head stretched toward her master and her tail between her legs. The dog did not move any more than did the mother, who was now leaning over the body with a blank stare, weeping silently.

The young man, lying on his back, dressed in his jacket of coarse cloth torn at the chest, seemed to be asleep; but he had blood all over him—on his shirt, which had been torn off in order to administer the first aid, on his vest, on his trousers, on his face, on his hands. Clots of blood had hardened in his beard and in his hair.

His old mother began to talk to him. At the sound of this voice the dog quieted down.

"Never fear, my boy, my little baby, you shall be avenged. Sleep, sleep—you shall be avenged, do you hear? It's your mother's promise! And she always keeps her word, you know she does."

Slowly she leaned over him, pressing her cold lips to his dead ones.

Then Semillante began to howl again, with a long, monotonous, penetrating, horrible howl.

The two of them, the woman and the dog, remained there until morning.

Antoine Saverini was buried the next day, and so his name ceased to be mentioned in Bonifacio.

He had no brothers, no cousins—no man to carry on the vendetta. Only his mother thought of it, and she was an old woman.

On the other side of the straits she saw, from morning until night, a little white speck on the coast. It was the little Sardinian village, Longosardo, where Corsican criminals take refuge when they are too closely pursued. They comprise almost the entire population of this hamlet, opposite their native island, awaiting the time to return. She knew that Nicolas Ravolati had sought refuge in this village.

All alone, all day long, seated at her window, she looked over there and thought of revenge. How could she do anything without help—she, an invalid, and so near death? But she had promised, she had sworn on the body. She could not forget, she could not wait. What could she do?

She thought stubbornly. The dog, dozing at her feet, would sometimes lift her head and howl. Since her master's death she often howled thus, as though she were calling him, as though her beast's soul, inconsolable, too, had also kept something in memory which nothing could wipe out.

One night, as Semillante began to howl, the mother suddenly got hold of an idea—a savage, vindictive, fierce idea. She thought it over until morning; then, having arisen at daybreak, she went to church. She prayed,

30

prostrate on the floor, begging the Lord to help her, to support her, to give to her poor, broken-down body the strength she needed in order to avenge her son.

She returned home. In her yard she had an old barrel which served as a cistern. She turned it over, emptied it, made it fast to the ground with sticks and stones; then she chained Semillante to this improvised kennel.

All day and all night the dog howled. In the morning the old woman brought her some water in a bowl, but nothing more—no soup, no bread.

Another day went by, Semillante, weakened, was sleeping. The following day, eyes shining, hair on end, the dog was pulling wildly at her chain.

All this day the old woman gave her nothing to eat. The beast, furious, was barking hoarsely. Another day passed.

Then, at daybreak, Mother Saverini asked a neighbor for some straw. She took the old rags which had formerly been worn by her husband and stuffed them so as to make them look like a human body.

Having planted a stick in the ground in front of Semillante's kennel, she tied to it this dummy, which seemed to be standing up. Then she made a head out of some old rags.

The dog, surprised, was watching this straw man, and was quiet, although famished. Then the old woman went to the store and bought a piece of black sausage. When she got home she started a fire in the yard, near the kennel, and cooked the sausage. Semillante, wild, was jumping around frothing at the mouth, her eyes fixed on the food, whose smell went right to her stomach.

Then the mother made a necktie for the dummy with the smoking sausage. She tied it very tightly around the neck, and when she had finished she unleashed the dog.

With one leap the beast jumped at the dummy's throat, and with her paws on his shoulders she began to tear at it. She would fall back with a piece of food in her mouth, then she would jump again, sinking her fangs into the ropes, and snatching a piece of meat, would fall back again, and once more spring forward. She was tearing the face with her teeth, and the whole collar had disappeared.

The old woman, motionless and silent, was watching eagerly. Then she chained the beast up again, gave her no food for two more days, and began this strange exercise again.

For three months she trained the dog to this battle. She no longer chained her up, but just pointed to the dummy. She had taught Semillante to tear it up and to devour it without even hiding any food about the dummy's neck. Then, as a reward, she would give the dog a piece of sausage.

As soon as she would see the "man," Semillante would begin to tremble, then she would look up to her mistress, who, lifting her finger, would cry, "Go!"

When the widow thought that the proper time had come, she went to confession, and one Sunday morning she partook of communion with an ecstatic fervor; then, having put on men's clothes, looking like an old tramp, she struck a bargain with a Sardinian fisherman who carried her and her dog to the other side.

In a bag she had a large piece of sausage. Semillante had had nothing to eat for two days. The old woman kept letting the dog smell the food, and goading her.

They got to Longosardo. The Corsican woman walked with a limp. She went to a baker's shop and asked for Nicolas Ravolati. He had taken up his old trade, that of carpenter, and was working alone at the back of his store.

The old woman opened the door and called, "Nicolas!"

He turned around; then, releasing her dog, she cried, "Go!"

The maddened animal sprang for the murderer's throat. The man stretched out his arms, seized the dog, and rolled to the ground. For a few seconds he squirmed, beating the ground with his feet; then he stopped moving as Semillante dug her fangs into his throat and tore it to ribbons.

Two neighbors, seated before their door, remembered perfectly having seen an old beggar come out with a thin black dog which was eating something its master was giving her.

At nightfall the old woman was home again. She slept well that night.

7

THE LEAKAGE

Frank Sisk

WIGMORE, EXECUTIVE VICE-PRESIDENT of Great Greengrocers, Inc., addressed his secretary over the intercom. "Miss Dryson."

"Yes, A.C."

"Has that fathead of a detective appeared yet?"

"He's coming along the corridor now."

"Sober, I trust. At any rate, show him in immediately."

"Yes sir."

"And those figures that came in last night from Store Sixty-six, I want those, too."

"They're right here on my desk, A.C." The voice went a bit off focus. "Good morning, Mister Horner. We've been expecting you."

A moment later Miss Dryson, holding a manila folder to her meager chest, entered Wigmore's office in tandem with Lewis J. Horner, head of Confidential Research Associates.

Horner was hardly anyone's conception of a private detective. Short, portly, with a dozen strands of brownish-gray hair distributed sketchily across his round head, he had the blank look one sees in paintings of medieval monks given to cheerful sessions with the grape. The only emphatic feature of his face was the nose, shaped somewhat like a plum and of similar coloration.

Wigmore wasted no words. "We don't seem to be getting anywhere, Horner. It's seven damned weeks since you and your alleged staff started this investigation, and not a single result apparent to date."

"My dear man," Horner said in a surprisingly low, mellifluous voice, "what is not yet apparent to you may be quite apparent to us."

"Don't give me that line again, Horner. The president and the board of directors aren't buying it. All they see now—and I can't help but agree—is

33

that Store Sixty-six is being systematically robbed of thousands of dollars a week and you and your men are unable to find the leak.''

''We may give the impression of inactivity,'' Horner said, smacking his lips, ''but beneath this illusion we are extremely thorough. Our reputation is proof of this.''

''Your weekly statement for services rendered is thorough,'' Wigmore said. ''And mighty prompt too. As for the expense account that accompanies it, a few of its outlandish items are causing certain board members to wonder if your purpose here is to plug a leak or to create another.''

Horner chuckled quietly. ''To allay all such future speculation, Wigmore, I think I can now safely promise an imminent solution of your problem.''

''Good. Give me an inkling.''

''In short order. But first I suggest you send for a floor plan of the store under surveillance—an operational floor plan.''

''Miss Dryson.''

''Yes, A.C. I'll call Engineering immediately.'' Handing her boss the manila folder, Miss Dryson left.

A brief silence descended like a blanket woven from chain mail. Horner bettered the moment by finding and sitting in the second most comfortable chair in the room. Wigmore, appearing uncomfortable in the best chair, finally opened a copperish humidor on his desk, took out a long fat cigar and wordlessly offered another to Horner.

''I don't smoke,'' Horner said. ''But I'll accept a glass of cream sherry if you have it.''

''I don't drink during business hours,'' Wigmore said, biting the end off his cigar. Then he turned his full attention to the manila folder. ''These are the latest profit and loss figures from our newest and largest market—with a strong accent on loss—as you will see.''

Horner had closed his eyes and seemed to be dozing.

''Would you like to hear a few salient facts?'' Wigmore asked, vexed.

''I'm listening,'' Horner replied from behind shut lids.

''Well, this week our loss leader was a special on frozen turkeys. Twenty-nine cents a pound.''

''I bought one myself,'' Horner said with quiet satisfaction.

''Good for you. Anyway, we shipped fifteen hundred of these birds to Store Sixty-six. The retail value was estimated at six thousand five hundred and twenty-five dollars. As you know by now, all specials are assigned a code symbol which appears opposite the amount of the sale on the cash-register tapes. In the case of the turkeys the symbol was an asterisk.''

Horner dozed on.

''If we ever needed additional evidence of the ineptitude of your so-called investigation,'' Wigmore continued in a voice barely under control, ''we have it in hand now. The tapes from the twelve registers at the checkout counters show a sale of only one thousand three hundred and thirty-two birds. Are you able to draw a conclusion from this figure, *Mister* Horner?''

''The most obvious conclusion is that a hundred and sixty-eight birds are unaccounted for.''

''Precisely.''

''Of course they weren't in the remainder inventory?''

''There *was* no remainder inventory. The special was a sellout. Not a turkey was left. But one hundred and sixty-eight were not paid for, Horner. How do you account for that?''

''Quite easily, I believe.''

''Is that so? Well, edify me a bit. Explain to me, if you can, how anybody could walk out with more than a ton of turkeys and not be observed by one of your eagle-eyed operatives?''

''Also easily explained,'' Horner said, opening his eyes. ''As soon as Miss Dryson returns with the floor plan, I think I'll be able to verify my deductions.''

Wigmore peered narrowly at the detective. ''You mean you really think you know who's behind this systematic thievery?''

''We've known that almost from the beginning,'' Horner said.

''Then why in hell didn't you nail him?''

''We didn't know *how* he was doing it. After all, when a man is consistently stealing about three thousand dollars a week, and right under the noses of three of my best undercover men, we like to discover the trick he's been pulling.''

''Who is the magician? Can you tell me that?''

''The manager.''

''Jorgenson. I can't believe it. He's been with us for nearly twenty years.''

''Perhaps that explains something,'' Horner said.

''Meaning exactly what, Horner?''

''Twenty years is a long time to wait to become a store manager.''

''He wasn't really ready until now.''

''The personnel files contradict you there, I'm afraid. For a long time

Jorgenson's immediate superiors have been rating him as fully qualified for store management. In fact, he was first in line for the last several openings until you intervened in behalf of your deserving relatives.''

"You're a sassy cuss, Horner."

Mirth twinkled in the detective's eyes but he said nothing.

"Anyway, when I finally made Jorgenson manager I seem to have made a mistake. How did he think he could get away with it? Going into a new store and stealing at that rate right from the beginning? He must have known he'd be suspected and watched.''

"His method gave him confidence. He felt it would be foolproof for a certain period of time, I imagine, and he wanted only enough time to amass a little capital for a venture of his own. Within a few more weeks, I think, Jorgenson's resignation would have been forthcoming, based probably on the very fact that he was under suspicion and found the suspicion intolerable.''

At that moment Miss Dryson reappeared with a roll of blueprint.

Horner got to his feet, murmuring politely, and took the roll and unrolled it on Wigmore's desk. He studied it for half a minute, then grinned happily. "Ah, clever. Most simple and clever.''

"Out with it, man," Wigmore said impatiently.

Horner continued to grin. "One of the ironies here, Wigmore, is that you held the key to the riddle every time you told me about the symbol on the cash-register tapes.''

"How's that?''

"You always referred to *twelve* registers, *twelve* checkout counters.''

"What's wrong with that?''

"Nothing, if we go by this floor plan. For here, too, I see *twelve* registers and *twelve* checkout counters. But yesterday morning, as I stood in a line of housewives with my frozen turkey, I began an idle count of the checkout counters and they added up to *thirteen*. Immediately I realized where the leak was. Sometime and somehow, before the grand opening of Store Sixty-six, Jorgenson had set up his own register and checkout counter.''

"Well, I'll be a blue-eyed obscenity," Wigmore said.

"I dare say.''

8

THE GESTURE

Gil Brewer

NOLAN PLACED BOTH hands on the railing of the veranda, and unconsciously squeezed the wood until the muscles in his arms corded and ached. He looked down, across the immaculately trimmed green lawn, past the palms and the Australian pines, to the beach, gleaming whitely under the late morning sun.

The Gulf was crisply green today, and calm, broken only by the happy frolicking of the man and woman—laughing, swimming. His wife, Helen, and Latimer, the photographer from the magazine in New York, down to do a picture story of the island.

Nolan turned his gaze away, lifted his hands and stared at his palms. His hands were trembling and his thin cotton shirt was soaked with perspiration.

He couldn't stand it. He left the veranda, and walked swiftly into the sprawling living room of his home. He paced back and forth for a moment, his feet whispering on the grass rug. Then he stood quietly in the center of the room, trying to think. For two weeks it had been going on. At first he'd thought he would last. Now he knew it no longer mattered, about lasting.

He would have to do something. He strode rapidly across the room into his study, opened the top drawer of his desk, and looked down at the .45 automatic. He slammed the drawer shut, whirled and went back into the living room.

Why had he ever allowed the man entrance to the island?

Oh, he knew why, well enough. Because Helen had wanted it. And now he couldn't order Latimer away. It would be as good as telling Helen the reason. She knew how much he loved her; why did she act this way? Why did she torture him? She *must* realize, after all these years, that he couldn't stand another man even looking at her beauty.

Why did she think they lived here—severed from all mainland life?

37

He stiffened, making an effort to wipe away the frown on his face. He reached for his handkerchief, and swabbed at the perspiration on his arms and forehead. They were coming, laughing and talking, up across the lawn.

Quickly, he selected a magazine from the rack and settled into a wicker chair with his back to the front entrance. He flipped the periodical open and was engrossed in a month-old mystery story when they stomped loudly across the veranda.

Every step was a kind of unbearable thunder to Nolan. He was reaching such a pitch of helpless irritability that he nearly screamed.

"Darling!" Helen called. "Where are you—oh, there!"

She stepped toward him, her bare feet softly thumping the grass rug. He half-glanced up at her. She was coffee-brown, her eyes excited and happier than he'd seen them in a long time. She wore one of the violent-hued red, yellow and green cloth swimming suits that she'd designed for herself.

He abruptly realized how meager the suit was and his neck burned. He had contrived to have her make the suit with the least expenditure of material. It was his pleasure to look at her.

But not now—not with Latimer here!

"What *have* you been doing?" she asked.

He started to reply, looking across at Latimer standing at the entrance-way, but she rippled on. "You really should have come swimming with us, dear. It was wonderful this morning." She reached out and tousled his hair. "You haven't been near the water in days."

Nolan cleared his throat. "Well," he said. "Well, Mister Latimer. About caught up? About ready with your story?"

He wanted to shout: *When are you leaving!* He could not. He sat there, staring at Latimer. The sunny days here on the island had done the man good. He was bronzed and healthy and young and abrim wih a vitality that had not been present when he'd first come over from the mainland.

"A few more days, I guess," Latimer said. "I wish you'd call me Jack. And I sure wish you two would pose for a few pictures. It's nice enough, the way you've been about letting me photograph the island, your home, but—" Latimer left the protest unspoken, smiling halfheartedly.

Nolan glanced at his wife. She reached down and touched his arm, her fingers trembling. "After lunch Jack and I are going to take a walk, clear around the island," she said. "You know, we haven't done that in a terribly long while. Why don't you come along?"

"Sorry," Nolan said quickly. "I've some things I've got to attend to."

"Sure wish you'd come," Latimer said.

Nolan said nothing.

"Well," Latimer said. "I've got to write a letter. Guess I'll do it while you're fixing lunch, Helen."

"Right," Helen said. "I'd better get busy." She turned, and hurried off toward the kitchen, humming softly.

"By the way," Latimer said to Nolan. "Anything you'd like done in town? I'll be taking the boat across this evening, so I can mail some stuff off."

"Thank you," Nolan said. "There's nothing."

"Well," Latimer said. He sighed and started across the room toward the hallway leading to his bedroom. It had been a storage room, but Nolan had fixed it up with a bed and a table for Latimer's typewriter when Helen insisted the photographer stay on the island. Latimer paused by the hallway. "Sure you won't come with us this afternoon?"

Nolan didn't bother to answer. He couldn't answer. If he had tried, he knew he might have shouted, even cursed—maybe actually gone at the man with his bare hands.

He would not use his bare hands. He wouldn't soil them. He would use the gun. He listened as Latimer left the room, and sat there breathing stiffly, his fingers clenched into the magazine's crumpled pages.

Yes, that's what he would do. Latimer's saying he was going to remain on the island longer still clinched it. Nolan knew why Latimer had said that. He wasn't fooling anybody. Taking advantage of hospitality for his own sneaking reasons. Didn't Helen see what kind of a man Latimer was? Was she blind? Or did she want it this way?

The very thought of such a thing sent Nolan out of the chair, stalking back and forth across the room. He could hear Latimer's typewriter ticking away from the far side of the house.

Their paradise. Their home. Their love. Torn and twisted and broken by this insensitive person. He heard Helen call them to lunch then, and, moving toward the table in the dining room, he felt slightly relieved. He knew that while they were gone this afternoon, he would get everything ready.

With Latimer's unconscious aid, Nolan knew exactly how he was going to do it. He sat at the table, picking at his food, listening to them talk and laugh. He tried vainly to concentrate away from the sounds of their voices.

"This salad's terrific," Latimer said. "Helen, you're wonderful! You two've got it made, out here!"

Helen lowered her gaze to her plate. Nolan stared directly at Latimer and

Latimer reddened and looked away. Nolan grinned inside. He had caught the man. But the victory was empty. The long afternoon, thinking about her out there with Latimer would be painful.

They finished lunch in silence. Almost before Nolan realized it, the house was again empty. He could hear them laughing still, their voices growing faint as they moved down along the beach.

Helen had even insisted on taking several bottles of cold beer wrapped in insulated bags to keep cool, and carried in the old musette.

Nolan could not stand still. He paced back and forth across the extent of the house, thinking about tonight. If he didn't do it tonight, it might be too late. He did not want Helen too attached to Latimer and he felt sure it had gone very far already.

He knew Latimer intended to stay on and stay on—until he could take Helen away with him. But tonight would end it. He would go along with Latimer to the mainland. Only Latimer would never reach the mainland. The boat would swamp.

Nolan knew how to swamp a boat. He knew Latimer wasn't much of a swimmer, and anyhow, a man couldn't swim with a .45 slug in his heart. But Nolan could swim well. He would kill Latimer, take him out into the Gulf, weight him and sink him. Then he'd bring the boat in and swamp it and swim ashore. He would report it, and rent a boat and come home. He knew they were in for a bit of heavy weather tonight. It would be just perfect.

And Helen and he would be happy again. The way they had always been.

He looked back, thinking over the good times. The time before they'd come to the island, when he'd been hard-working at the glass-cutting business he'd inherited from his father. Then more and more he'd become conscious of Helen's beauty and the effect she had on men. And loving her as wildly as he did, he could no longer bear the endless suspense; the knowledge that sooner or later, she would leave him. So he sold the business, retired. His little lie. So far as she knew, he simply wanted island life—quite, unhurried, alone with her. It was true. But not a complete truth.

All this time they had been happy. Until now. Somebody'd got wind of the beauty of the island and Latimer had shown up, to do his story. Under conditions imposed by Nolan—no pictures of either himself or Helen. He had allowed one fuzzy negative of them standing against a blossoming hibiscus near the house, at twilight—that was all.

Wandering through the house, trying not to think of what they were doing now, he found himself in Latimer's room. The unmade bed, the photographic equipment, the typewriter set up on the table.

Beside the machine was a typewritten letter.

Nolan turned away. But something drew him over to the table. Pure curiosity in this man Latimer. He stood there, staring down at the obviously unfinished letter. An addressed envelope lay beside it. There was a half-completed sentence on the sheet in the typewriter, numbered *Page Two*.

The letter was addressed to the editor of the magazine where Latimer worked.

Nolan began reading, at first leisurely, then feverishly.

"Dear Bart:
   Really have this thing wrapped up, but I'm staying on a while longer, just to settle a few things in my own mind and maybe I'll come up with a bunch of pix and a yarn that'll knock your head off... sure beautiful scenery on the island... house is a regular bamboo and cypress mansion... unhealthy, Bart, really sick... he watches her like a hawk. He's ripped with jealousy and it would be laughable, except that they're both so very old. He must be in his eighties, but she's a bit harder to read. I did a lousy thing. I confronted her with it. You would have, too. She's so obviously just enduring everything for his sake. Humoring him. My God, think of it! All these years he's kept her out here, away from everybody, imprisoned. It's pure hell. She as much as admitted it. I'm staying on, just to see if I can't work it somehow. Get her back to civilization, if only for a vacation, Bart. She deserves it. You should hear her ask how things are out there—it would break your damned heart..."

There was more and Nolan read all of it through twice. For a moment longer, he stood there, seeing everything clearly for the first time in nearly a half century.

Then he walked through the house to his study, opened the desk drawer, took out the .45 automatic. He sat down in his chair by the desk, put the muzzle of the gun into his mouth and pulled the trigger.

9

THE LITTLE HOUSE AT CROIX-ROUSSE

Georges Simenon

I HAD NEVER see Joseph Leborgne at work before. I received something of a shock when I entered his room that day.

His blond hair, usually plastered down, was in complete disorder. The individual hairs, stiffened by brilliantine, stuck out all over his head. His face was pale and worn. Nervous twitches distorted his features.

He threw a grudging glare at me which almost drove me from the room. But since I would see that he was hunched over a diagram, my curiosity was stronger than my sensitivity. I advanced into the room and took off my hat and coat.

"A fine time you've picked!" he grumbled.

This was hardly encouraging. I stammered, "A tricky case?"

"That's putting it mildly. Look at that paper."

"It's the plan of a house? A small house?"

"The subtlety of your mind! A child of four could guess that. You know the Croix-Rousse district in Lyons?"

"I've passed through there."

"Good! This little house lies in one of the most deserted sections of the district—not a district, I might add, which is distinguished by its liveliness."

"What do these black crosses mean, in the garden and on the street?"

"Policemen."

"Good Lord! And the crosses mark where they've been killed?"

"Who said anything about dead policemen? The crosses indicate policemen who were on duty at these several spots on the night of the eighth-to-ninth. The cross that's heavier than the others is Corporal Manchard."

43

I dared not utter a word or move a muscle. I felt it wisest not to interrupt Leborgne, who was favoring the plan with the same furious glares which he had bestowed upon me.

"Well? Aren't you going to ask me *why* policemen were stationed there—six of them, no less—on the night of the eighth-to-ninth? Or maybe you're going to pretend, that you've figured it out?"

I said nothing.

"They were there because the Lyons police had received, the day before, the following letter:

"Dr. Luigi Ceccioni will be murdered, at his home, on the night of the eighth-to-ninth instant."

"And the doctor had been warned?" I asked at last.

"No! Since Ceccioni was an Italian exile and it seemed more than likely that the affair had political aspects, the police preferred to take their precautions without warning the party involved."

"And he was murdered anyway?"

"Patience! Dr. Ceccioni, fifty years of age, lived alone in this wretched little hovel. He kept house for himself and ate his evening meal every day in an Italian restaurant nearby. On the eighth he left home at seven o'clock, as usual, for the restaurant. And Corporal Manchard, one of the best police officers in France and a pupil, to boot, of the great Lyons criminologist Dr. Eugène Locard, searched the house from basement to attic. He proved to himself that no one was hidden there and that it was impossible to get in by any other means than the ordinary doors and windows visible from the outside. No subterranean passages nor any such hocus-pocus. Nothing out of a mystery novel . . . You understand?"

I was careful to say nothing, but Leborgne's vindictive tone seemed to accuse me of willfully interpolating hocus-pocus.

"No one in the house! Nothing to watch but two doors and three windows! A lesser man than Corporal Marchard would have been content to set up the watch with only himself and one policeman. But Manchard requisitioned five, one for each entrance, with himself to watch the watchers. At nine p.m. the shadow of the doctor appeared in the street. He re-entered his house, *absolutely alone*. His room was upstairs; a light went on in there promptly. And then the police vigil began. Not one of them dozed! Not one of them deserted his post! Not one of them lost sight of the precise point which he had been delegated to watch!

"Every fifteen minutes Manchard made the round of the group. Around three a.m. the petroleum lamp upstairs went out slowly, as though it had run out of fuel. The corporal hesitated. At last he decided to use his lock-picking gadget and go in. Upstairs, in the bedroom, seated—or rather half lying—on the edge of the bed was Dr. Luigi Ceccioni. His hands were clutched to his chest and he was dead. He was completely dressed, even to the cape which still hung over his shoulders. His hat had fallen to the floor. His underclothing and suit were saturated with blood and his hands were soaked in it. One bullet from a six-millimeter Browning had penetrated less than a centimeter above his heart.''

I gazed at Joseph Leborgne with awe. I saw his lip tremble.

"No one had entered the house! No one had left!" he groaned. "I'll swear to that as though I'd stood guard myself: I know my Corporal Manchard. And don't go thinking that they found the revolver in the house. *There wasn't any revolver!* Not in sight and not hidden. Not in the fireplace, or even in the roof gutter. Not in the garden—not anywhere at all! In other words, a bullet was fired in a place where there was no one save the victim himself and where there was no firearm!

"As for the windows, they were closed and undamaged; a bullet fired from outside would have shattered the panes. Besides, a revolver doesn't carry far enough to have been fired from outside the range covered by the cordon of policemen. Look at the plan! Eat it up with your eyes! And you may restore some hope of life to poor Corporal Manchard, who has given up sleeping and looks upon himself virtually as a murderer.''

I timidly ventured, "What do you know about Ceccioni?"

"That he used to be rich. That he's hardly practiced medicine at all, but rather devoted himself to politics—which made it healthier for him to leave Italy.''

"Married? Bachelor?"

"Widower. One child, a son, at present studying in Argentina.''

"What did he live on in Lyons?"

"A little of everything and nothing. Indefinite subsidies from his political colleagues. Occasional consultations, but those chiefly *gratis* among the poor of the Italian colony.''

"Was there anything stolen from the house?"

"Not a trace of any larcenous entry or of anything stolen.''

I don't know why, but at this moment I wanted to laugh. It suddenly seemed to me that some master of mystification had amused himself by presenting Joseph Leborgne with a totally impossible problem, simply to give him a needed lesson in modesty.

He noticed the broadening of my lips. Seizing the plan, he crossed the room to plunge himself angrily into his armchair.

"Let me know when you've solved it!" he snapped.

"I can certainly solve nothing before you," I said tactfully.

"Thanks," he observed.

I began to fill my pipe. I lit it, disregarding my companion's rage which was reaching the point of paroxysm.

"All I ask of you is that you sit quietly," he pronounced. "And don't breathe so loudly," he added.

Ten minutes passed as unpleasantly as possible. Despite myself, I called up the image of the plan, with the six black crosses marking the policemen.

And the impossibility of this story, which had at first so amused me, began to seem curiously disquieting.

After all, this was not a matter of psychology or of detective *flair,* but of pure geometry.

"This Manchard," I asked suddenly. "Has he ever served as a subject for hypnotism?"

Joseph Leborgne did not even deign to answer that one.

"Did Ceccioni have many political enemies in Lyons?"

Leborgne shrugged.

"And it's been proved that the son *is* in Argentina?"

This time he merely took the pipe out of my mouth and tossed it on the mantelpiece.

"You have the names of all the policemen?"

He handed me a sheet of paper:

Jérôme Pallois, 28, married

Jean-Joseph Stockman, 31, single

Armand Dubois, 26, married

Hubert Trajanu, 43, divorced

Germain Garros, 32, married

I reread these lines three times. The names were in the order in which the men had been stationed around the building, starting from the left.

I was ready to accept the craziest notions. Desperately I exclaimed at last "It *is* impossible!"

And I looked at Joseph Leborgne. A moment before his face had been pale, his eyes encircled, his lips bitter. Now, to my astonishment, I saw him smilingly head for a pot of jam.

As he passed a mirror he noticed himself and seemed scandalized by the incongruous contortions of his hair. He combed it meticulously. He adjusted the knot of his cravat.

Once again Joseph Leborgne was his habitual self. As he looked for a spoon with which to consume his horrible jam of leaves-of-God-knows-what, he favored me with a sarcastic smile.

"How simple it would always be to reach the truth if preconceived ideas did not falsify our judgment!" he sighed. "You have just said, 'It *is* impossible!' So therefore . . ."

I waited for him to contradict me. I'm used to that.

"So therefore," he went on, "it *is* impossible. Just so. And all that we needed to do from the beginning was simply to admit that fact. There was no revolver in the house, no murderer hidden there. Very well: then there was no shot fired there."

"But then. . . ?"

"Then, very simply, Luigi Ceccioni arrived *with the bullet already in his chest*. I've every reason to believe that he fired the bullet himself. He was a doctor; he knew just where to aim—'less than a centimeter above the heart,' you'll recall—so that the wound would not be *instantly* fatal, but would allow him to move about for a short time."

Joseph Leborgne closed his eyes.

"Imagine this poor hopeless man. He has only one son. The boy is studying abroad, but the father no longer has any money to send him. Ceccini insures his life with the boy as beneficiary. His next step is to die—but somehow to die with no suspicion of suicide, or the insurance company will refuse to pay.

"By means of an anonymous letter he summons the police themselves as witnesses. They see him enter his house where there is no weapon and they find him dead several hours later.

"It was enough, once he was seated on his bed, to massage his chest, forcing the bullet to penetrate more deeply, at last to touch the heart . . ."

I let out an involuntary cry of pain. But Leborgne did not stir. He was no longer concerned with me.

It was not until a week later that he showed me a telegram from Corporal Manchard:

AUTOPSY REVEALS ECCHYMOSIS AROUND WOUNDS AND TRACES FINGER PRESSURE STOP DOCTOR AND SELF PUZZLED POSSIBLE CAUSE STOP REQUEST YOUR ADVICE IMMEDIATELY

"You answered?"

He looked at me reproachfully. "It requires both great courage and great imagination to massage oneself to death. Why should the poor man have done that it vain? The insurance company has a capital of four hundred million . . ."

10

PUNISHMENT TO FIT THE CRIME

Robert L. Fish

HE WAS MY best friend—damn him! But I got even . . .

I'd better begin at the beginning. Jack Burnham had been my best friend since we were little kids, since the day, in fact, when I stopped a bigger kid from beating Jack up in the schoolyard. It was true that Jack had swiped this kid's pencil box, but that didn't seem to me to be reason enough for the bigger kid to try to take Jack's head off. But throughout our school careers that's what other kids tried to do, usually for similar reasons. Jack never learned to respect other people's property. It kept me busy keeping him from being murdered. But I suppose it wasn't his fault if he hated to buy something he could swipe, or if he wouldn's spend a dime if he could get someone else to spend it; it was just the way he was, the way he had been born. And people can't help that; I understood that.

In college I was lucky enough to get a job after classes, something Jack didn't happen to manage; so of course I had to cover most of the expenses when we ate away from the dormitory, or whenever we went out on a rare double-date. But I didn't mind. After all, that's what friends are for, aren't they? And I certainly didn't get angry with either Jack or Noreen when Noreen came to me after graduation and said she wanted to break our engagement, that she had decided Jack was a better bet than I was. Well, after all, you can't dictate love, or desire for security, or anything else; I understood that well enough.

After that we sort of went different ways, Jack to New York and a job in the brokerage firm that Noreen's father was president of, and me to the west coast and after a rather checkered career, into the TV writing business. We corresponded regularly, though, and we spoke on the phone whenever I felt flush enough to stand the phone charges—both Noreen and Jack loved to reminisce whenever I called. So, as I say, we kept in touch, and I still considered him my best friend—in fact, I considered the two of them my best friends.

And of course after I hit with the TV series, "Mugger's Lane," I was able to get to New York with greater frequency, and was able to take the two of them out to dinner, and to buy them a nice house-warming gift when they moved into the new big house on the sound in Mamaroneck next to the Yacht Club. I recall we would sit out on the wide porch and sip the Remy Martin I had brought as we remembered some of the scrapes we had got into as kids and remarked on how successful we had both become, but mainly Jack, who was now vice-president of the brokerage firm and slated soon to take over the top job on his father-in-law's retirement.

I never told Jack about the novel I was trying to write. I guess all TV writers, TV producers, even the office boys and stenographers in TV studios, hope some day to write the Great American Novel, to launch them into a more respectable area of the communications sphere. But chiefly TV writers, even—or possibly—mainly the successful ones. They dream of the day when the world will grant them the accolades accorded the Hemingways and the Faulkners, or even the Haleys and the Wallaces; the day when they can throw off the restrictive shackles and emerge into the light of freedom from the small dark cells where they pound out their lives on ancient Remingtons in some Ulcer Alley in one studio or another. They fantasize of the day when they can put their earnings into blue-chip stocks and gilt-edged bonds, rather than into providing those same earnings to some psychiatrist to help them maintain their sanity.

I didn't tell Jack because I wasn't sure the book would ever be published, assuming it was ever written. There is nothing quite as pitiful in this world as being asked what you do for a living and when you reply that you're a writer, being asked if you were ever published. No, better to say nothing. But I could not help but picture the day when, a copy of my novel in one hand and a rave review from John Leonard in the other—and my name being written across the heavens by skywriters—I would appear at Mamaroneck and receive praise from those from whom it would mean so much more than from anyone else—my best friends.

Someone once said that everyone wants to have written a novel, rather than to write one, but in time I actually managed to finish the book, and it was even published. The critics gave it fine reviews—and it sold about 400 copies, as best I could determine. But that all meant nothing; I hadn't written the book for money. The important thing was that I had written a book, that I held a copy in my hand, and that I was on my way to Mamaroneck with a copy for Jack and Noreen, expecting to be properly praised, if only for exhibiting the discipline necessary to complete writing a novel. And, if I must add my voice to those of the reviewers, it wasn't a bad book.

The reaction I received was all more than I expected—high praise, back-slapping, a kiss on the cheek from Noreen, a hearty two-handed handshake from Jack, with all the sincerity in the world in his eyes. Jack even broke out a bottle of fairly decent Scotch to celebrate. The two of them kept congratulating me on the imagination and talent necessary to have written a novel, a thing Jack confessed he could never do. They leaned over me affectionately as I carefully inscribed the flyleaf with: "To Jack and Noreen Burnham, my oldest and best friends, and the best friends a person could have," and signed it with a flourish. Noreen said the book would hold the place of honor on their book shelves; and I don't believe I ever felt as good about writing the book, or about anything else, as I did that moment. Until my next visit, when I noticed the book was missing, and Jack laughed as he put his arm around my shoulder.

"Leave that book out where one of our thieving friends might hook it?" he said, and shook his head. "No, that book is in my safety-deposit vault. It's too valuable to us to take any chances with." Then, I think, I felt even better.

I wrote a second novel, not a very good one I'm afraid, that was never published, and after that I started TV writing-producing, rather than just writing, and there just didn't seem to be time to do much of anything except my job. I slowly became reconciled to the fact that I was going to be a one-book author. But at least, I told myself, the one book had been a good one, even if it hadn't sold; how many people hadn't written any books at all in their lives? Many, many, many. The thought gave me a certain satisfaction, but not much; my major satisfaction remained in recalling the reception I had received when I gave Jack and Noreen their inscribed copy. Just remembering it always made me feel warm, made me grin.

I had to be in New York on a sudden call not long afterward, and after my business was completed I thought I'd drop in on Jack and Noreen. I started to phone them and then paused, thinking how much more fun it would be to drop in and surprise them; there had never been the slightest formality in our relationship. It was a lovely spring day, I had a rented car, and I figured the drive up to Mamaroneck would be pleasant, even if I found them out. So off I went.

To my disappointment they were out. Jack and Noreen, the housekeeper told me, were in Europe for a vacation and would not be back for about three weeks. So there I was in Mamaroneck with a full day ahead of me and with nothing to do. I drove back into the center of the small town, parked the car in front of a coffee shop, and got down to have a cup of coffee before starting back to New York. Then I paused, because next to the coffee shop there was a second-hand bookstore.

I must tell you why I paused. I'm not a collector of books, myself, but some of my friends are. In particular, I have a friend who lives in San Diego, a man named Ned Guymon who at one time had collected what was and is considered the finest and most valuable collection of rare first editions and original manuscripts relating to the mystery field that the world has ever seen, a collection that today is housed at the Occidental College in California. A book that Ned has often mentioned as being one he had never been able to even find, let alone own, is a book titled *Andrewlina,* by J. S. Fletcher, and I am sure that all of Ned's many friends, whenever they are near a second-hand bookstore, drop in for the one-in-a-billion chance that they might run across a copy of the rare book and give it to Ned, for we all know how pleased it would make him. And so, being near a second-hand bookstore in a town where the chances were few collectors would normally seek rarities, I stopped in.

The place was large and well-lit as most second-hand bookstores are, quite contrary to the impression most people have of such places as being gloomy warrens ankle-deep in dust. The proprietor at the moment was not present and I set about examining the stock. The books, as in a few such stores, were not arranged in alphabetical order, but were set in shelves that ran the length of the store and up to the ceiling, on both sides of narrow aisles. Fortunately, fiction was separated from nonfiction, and I patiently began my search at the fiction shelves, my head turned to read the titles, and beginning to get a stiff neck as I inched my way along the aisle.

And then I suddenly smiled. A copy of my own opus was here! With a grin I withdrew the book and opened it the the flyleaf to see what price the proprietor had placed on a used copy of my work. And got the shock of my life, my smile frozen on my face like an idiot rictus. There, before me in my own handwriting, were the words: "To Jack and Noreen Burnham—" and all the rest of the florid, insipid inscription. A bit of a shock, to say the least.

I carried the book to the front of the store and waited until the proprietor appeared from the basement, dusting his hands.

"This book," I said, and my voice sounded strange to my ears, as if I were listening to someone else speak. "Is there any way you can tell where you bought it, or from whom?"

"At times, but rarely," he said. "We buy from many sources, from bookstores with overstocks, from the libraries of estates, from garage sales, from church sales, or from people who just come in with a suitcase full of old books they're sure are worth a fortune. And rarely are. However, sometimes we mark them. Let me see."

He took the book from me and opened it to look at the inside of the back cover. A small mark there seemed to tell him something; he looked up, smiling.

"I remember this one, not because of the book itself, but because I bought quite a few at the same time at the same place, all of no particular value, although the way the man argued you'd have thought they were first editions of Poe. At a garage sale. One of those posh places down on the sound, next to the yacht club, as a matter of fact." He shook his head in nonunderstanding. "You wouldn't expect a garage sale at a place like that, would you?"

"No," I said, and then wondered what made me say it. I bought the book for $1.25, the price marked on the flyleaf above my inscription.

That was two weeks ago. I have spent the time between then and now trying to think up a proper punishment for Jack Burnham, and it only came to me this morning. A simple recrimination would never do; I wanted a chastening, a retribution that was fitting, something that would do to him what he had done to me by selling my book for a paltry sum, probably a half-dollar or so. It makes me smile when I think of my solution to the problem, but there is little humor in the smile, and a good deal of bitterness.

Jack and Noreen should be home from Europe in about a week. And when he gets back he'll find a letter from me. It will read:

"Dear Jack:

"Congratulate me! Bring out the beer and pretzels, strike up the band! This is going to make you happy. Happy? Overjoyed!

"Remember that one book I managed to squeeze out of my system? The one that got good reviews and then managed to disappear from the face of the earth? Well, believe it or not, one of the top film producers read it somewhere—he doesn't remember exactly where, but he thinks it might have been in Asia on a trip there to check locations, can you believe it?—he didn't bring the book back, and God knows where it is now. Anyway, he called me up and wants to buy it for the movies. And for a sum, my friend—for ig-bay ough-day—that would curl your hair. And on top of that, I'm going to do the script, the screenplay. For *more* dough. Can you imagine?

"There is one small problem, though; fortunately an easily surmountable one. I don't have a single copy of the blasted book, and the publisher went out of business not long after he published it—maybe that was the reason (don't *say* that!). I've checked libraries and written all around, and my magnum-opus is now a nonmagnum-opus, so to speak. But I remembered the copy I inscribed to you and Noreen, the one you keep in your safety-deposit box.

"Lucky you kept that copy, pal. Now it's worth its weight in gold. Gold, hell! Rubies, emeralds, diamonds, you name it. I know how much you value that copy, but a xerox will do fine. Be sure and include in the xerox the inscription on the flyleaf; I want to impress on the producer that I actually know Jack Burnham.

"And another thing—you and I and Noreen have been friends for a long, long time; you know I never married and I have no responsibilities. So my idea is we split everything the movie earns for me—which is going to be moola, pal—*moola!* Such as in the dreams of sultans and such-like folk. The producer is talking about a fifteen million dollar budget, and my—I mean *our*—share of that should be enough to keep the wolf a league or so away from the door for a long, long spell.

"So shoot the bookie to me, cookie, and we'll all be rich. That's about all the news, but what more could anyone want? Love to Noreen, and all the best."

And I signed with my fanciest flourish.

I wonder what he'll do? Suicide is possible but unfortunately, not very probable. A nervous breakdown is both possible and probable. An ulcer the very least.

Jack should never have said he put the book in a safety-deposit box; a fire would have handled the problem if it had been kept on his bookshelf. Or a theft by a visitor. Or many things. But a fire in his safety-deposit box? Or a theft there? Hardly. Poor Jack, he really has little imagination.

But I have plenty. I'm a writer, remember, Jack?

11

THE PLAN OF
THE SNAKE

Edward Wellen

FAR OUT ON the veldt one hundred years of weather have scoured and scattered the bones of the Bantu, the Boer, and the snake. If the bones have changed, the pebble half buried amid them has not. The wind and the sun have worked on the pebble, but it is the sun's beam that takes a polish and the wind's glassiness that gets scratched.

When the bones of the Bantu wore flesh, it was the Bantu who found the pebble. The earth in its long travail had worked the pebble to the surface. The pebble winked at the world in vain who knows how long till the Bantu happened by on his hunt for springbok.

The Bantu abandoned the springbok's spoor to answer the blinking call of the pebble. He stood staring down at it, then hunkered and picked it up. The hand holding his assegai went suddenly slick on the weapon's wooden shaft, and the hand cupping the pebble weighed it in wonder.

He had heard of these pebbles and even seen a few, but never in the wildest tales had there been talk of one this size. With it he might, if not cheated, buy a hundred head of breeding cattle, and much land for a kraal, and more than one woman to grow sorghum and children. He laughed at the play of light in his hand, picturing his woman carrying one child strapped to her back while carrying another within.

It was then that the Boer cast his shadow across the Bantu's present and future.

The Bantu closed his hand over the pebble, but it was too late. Turning his head, he knew the Boer had seen the pebble; the pebble's glitter was now in the Boer's eyes.

The Boer, also out hunting, had come upon him while he squatted dreaming. The Boer could stand beyond reach of the assegai's iron tip and speak death from the mouth of his gun.

The Bantu looked at the Boer, knowing the man without ever having seen him before. The elders had a saying: "If you refuse to be made straight when you are green, you will not be made straight when you are dry."

The Boer's mouth had the twist of old meanness. And now it spoke soft words that did not hide the crookedness behind them. "Good day, kaffir. Show me the *mooi klip*."

Unwillingly the Bantu's hand opened to show the Boer the pretty pebble.

The glitter grew in the Boer's eyes. The Bantu's hand closed on the pebble but the light did not go out. The Boer smiled.

"That pebble would make a nice plaything for my child. I will give you my hunting knife for the pebble." The Boer unsheathed his knife to show how it flashed.

The Bantu wrinkled his face in thought, pretending to weigh the offer, then slowly straightened. In pushing himself to his feet he palmed another pebble, a commonplace pebble, and held it in his fist along with the first.

The Boer extended the knife toward the Bantu. "So we see eye to eye. The pebble for the knife."

The Bantu shook his head. "It is a good knife, but I do not wish to trade the pebble."

The Boer slid the knife home in its sheath. "Then it is an even better bargain. I will have the pebble for nothing. Hand it over, kaffir." The Boer raised the gun so that the mouth looked at the Bantu.

The Bantu gestured around at the veldt with his closed fist. "The pebble belongs to the earth."

The Boer's mouth tightened and the gun's mouth grew perfectly round. "The pebble belongs to me."

The Bantu half opened his fist as though to give in. Then, while his two smallest fingers held the *mooi klip* fast, the other fingers flung the commonplace pebble spinning far. He made his voice shake with rage rather than fear. "If it is yours find it, as I found it."

The Boer's gaze followed the false flight and the gun's mouth dropped.

The Bantu whirled and ran. He remembered a dip in the earth along the back trail. But before the Bantu reached the dip and sank out of sight the Boer had seen through the trick.

The gun spoke.

So swift was the gun's word that it seemed to the Bantu his flesh heard the gun before his ears. A blow as from a flinty fist struck fire in his side.

Then he was slipping and sliding over the lip of the hollow. He lost his footing and rolled over roughness to the bottom, where dry grass grew and here and there a sizable boulder sunned itself.

He lay half stunned, half catching his breath. Plucking at his breath's raggedness only raveled it more. He did not want to look at the hole in his side but he looked. He was losing much blood.

To have any time at all, the Bantu knew he must haul himself behind a boulder before the Boer appeared at the rim of the Bantu's barren little world. He heard the Boer's shout of rage as he found strength to plug the hole with grass to leave no trail of blood and found will to make for the nearest boulder, the pebble digging into his palm as he thrust himself along.

Rounding the boulder, the Bantu began to stretch his own length and the assegai's in the boulder's grudging wedge of shadow, then saw he shared the shade with a snake.

The snake's tongue flickered.

The Bantu's mouth pulled against pain in a smile. "Snake, do not waste your poison. I am already dead."

But the snake did not listen. It coiled to strike.

The Bantu struck first. The assegai spitted the snake and the snake writhed and died.

The Boer's voice broke into the Bantu's world. "Kaffir, I know you are down there. You cannot hide from me or outrun my gun. Show yourself and give me the pebble and I will let you go."

The Bantu tightened his hold on the pebble and smiled at the hurt. The Boer did not have the pebble yet.

But neither was there anywhere to hide the pebble from the Boer. If the Bantu scrabbled a hole, the Boer would spot the digging. If the Bantu cast the pebble away, the Boer would never leave this cup of earth till he had found it.

The Bantu eyed the snake. "Where, oh, snake?"

And the dead snake answered silently.

The Bantu laughed. "Thank you, oh, snake."

He weighed the pebble on his palm. It looked too big to go down but the Bantu made one last scan of it, put it in his mouth, and swallowed.

The pebble started down, then stuck in his windpipe, blocking all air. The Bantu's eyes bulged and his throat convulsed. Then the pebble worked its way and went down.

Sooner or later the Boer would know the Bantu had swallowed the pebble and would slit his belly and writhe searching fingers through his slippery guts. The Bantu put his hands over the grass plug. For this plan of the snake's to work, the Bantu had to hold himself together and hang on to life till the Boer found him.

To hasten the Boer's coming, the Bantu twisted so that his feet left the boulder's shade. The Boer would see the movement.

Drumbeat of death, the Boer's boots trampled dry grass.

Carefully the Boer rounded the boulder. In a sweep the Boer's glance took in the Bantu and the spitted snake.

The Bantu looked up at the shimmer of heat that was the Boer. He let his hands fall from the wound.

The Boer looked down. The Bantu's hands lay open and empty. Fresh blood loosened the grass plug from blood that had crusted around the wound and the Boer saw the Bantu had not stuffed the pebble in the wound. The ground ringing the boulder showed no smoothing over. With his foot the Boer rolled the Bantu wound side down. The Bantu's body had not been hiding anything. The Boer rolled the Bantu back with his foot.

He prodded the Bantu with the mouth of the gun. "Where is the *mooi klip*? If you have swallowed it and cannot cough it up I will take my hunting knife and slit your belly."

The Bantu pointed to the snake. Trying to hide the rawness of his throat, he spoke. "What you seek is in the snake's mouth."

The Boer narrowed his eyes. "Kaffir, if you are lying, you are just putting off your belly-slitting a little and adding to my anger a lot."

The Bantu only steadied his pointing finger. "What you seek is in the snake's mouth."

The Boer hesitated but a moment. After all, the kaffir lay helpless, eyes glazing, and the snake lay dead. The Boer leaned his gun against the boulder and knelt to probe the snake's mouth.

Reptiles have lasting reflexes. Even dead, a freshly killed snake will sink its fangs into probing flesh.

The Boer cried out.

After a time all was stillness.

And all is stillness still, but for the wind through the bones.

12

TWO-WAY STREET

Brian Garfield

THE BODY WAS found along Route 783 just outside the town of Aravaipa. The woman who found it was a Navajo lady; I learned that she and her dogs had been herding a flock of sheep across the road at dawn to beat the morning traffic. She'd roused a dairy rancher and the phone call had been logged in at the Sheriff's office at 5:44 A.M. I was brought in around noon when one of the Undersheriffs picked me up in a county car; he filled me in on the way to Pete Kyber's office. "We've got a corpse and a witness. Or at least we think he's a witness."

"Who's the victim?"

"Name of Philip Keam. Thirty-something. Reporter for one of the Tucson newspapers."

"You notified next of kin?"

"Divorced, no children. The parents may be alive—we're trying to find out."

Officially the temperature went to 103° Fahrenheit that day, which meant that down along the surface of the plain it was near 140°. The asphalt of the Sheriff's parking lot was soft underfoot, sucking at my shoes, and I hurried into the air-conditioned saltbox before I might melt. Slipping off the sunglasses I made my way back to the Sheriff's private office.

Pete Kyber was long-jointed and Gary Cooperish: slow-moving and slow-talking but not particularly slow-thinking. His most noticeable feature was his Adam's apple. Pete was no relation to the redneck stereotype; he was by instinct a conservationist rather than a conservative. How he and I ever got elected to our offices in the rural county still mystified me.

He watched me sit down; he was gloomy. "We got a bloody one, Mike."

"I'll have a look on my way out. What's the story?"

"Bludgeoned to death. With a rock."

"No fingerprints?"

"On a rock?"

"Who's this witness you've got?"

"Larry Stowe. Just a kid."

"Would that be Edgar Stowe's son?"

"Yes."

Edgar Stowe ran the drugstore in Aravaipa. He didn't own it—it was a chain store—but he was the manager. His son Larry would be about 22, I calculated; one of my kids had been in the same high-school class. I remembered the Stowe boy coming around the house now and then, but that was five years ago. He'd struck me as an unremarkable kid, towhead and a bit vacuous.

"What's Larry got to say?"

"We're having a hard time getting a straight story out of him. You'd better talk to him yourself."

"All right. First tell me what you've got."

"Well, Keam was robbed. His wallet's gone. We called the paper in Tucson to find out what he was doing over here. The city desk man got lathered up and I had to calm him down. But I'm afraid we'll be knee-deep in newspapermen by this afternoon. Keam was up here investigating a story about land frauds. Digging into the Inca Land Company developments."

"Ron Owens."

"Yes." Pete Kyber made a face to indicate his opinion of Ron Owens— real-estate tycoon, despoiler of the wilderness. I knew Owens, not intimately, and disliked the man as much as Pete did. Usually Owens could be found sporting around in his Lear Jet, flying his pet congressman to Las Vegas, or partying with his Oklahoma oil chums and expatriate Detroit gangster buddies. The "desert estates" he sold were rickety instant-slum dwellings encrusted on drearily bulldozed scrub acres.

Dozens of lawsuits were outstanding against Owens, brought by home buyers who attested that the Inca Land Company had failed to make good on its advertising and had defrauded them in multifarious ways. Naturally Owens had a phalanx of lawyers, some of whom had practiced in Washington and all of whom were adept at delaying cases until hell froze over. Owens was as slippery as a watermelon seed.

Pete Kyber took me back to the interrogation room where Larry Stowe sat picking his fingernails. Pete said, "Larry, you know the prosecutor here, Mike Valdez."

"Yes, sir." Larry was still towhead, still vacuous—his mouth hung open most of the time—and, at the moment, uptight.

"Sure we know each other." I shook hands with Larry. "How are you, son?"

The kid's handshake was perfunctory, his palm damp; he had trouble meeting my eye. "How's Mike Junior doing, sir?"

"Fine, just fine. Finishing up at the University this year."

"That's, uh, that's great, sir."

"Pete, you want to leave us a while?"

"Sure thing." The Sheriff retreated and shut us in.

I sat down facing the youth across the chrome-and-vinyl table. "Okay, Larry, would you like to go through it with me?"

He was reluctant but I kept at him with gentle persuasion and finally it came out, sheepish: he'd spent the night with a girl at her parents' ranch a few miles up the highway and that was why he'd been walking back into town so early in the morning. He didn't want to involve the girl, didn't want her parents to know he'd spent the night—he admitted with a nervous laugh that he'd left by the bedroom window with his shoes in his hand.

Once we got past that obstacle he told a straightforward story. He'd been walking along the highway shoulder; it wasn't yet dawn but it was a clear night. Down along Mule Deer Creek he'd walked under the cottonwoods where the big corrugated culvert funneled the creek under the road and he'd heard voices raised in argument. Curious and cautious, Larry made his way past the trees into the brush beside the road. He saw a big car parked in the dust—a Cadillac. Larry didn't know much but he did know cars and he described that one in fabulous detail, right down to the license number, and I made notes as he talked.

Three men stood out on the slickrock and Larry recognized two of them—cowboys he'd seen around Tooner's Bar, drinking beer and pawing at the waitresses. The third man was a stranger to Larry; of course that was Philip Keam, the reporter from Tucson.

The cowboys were arguing about what to do with Keam. Larry said, "Bud Baker kept saying they ought to beat the guy up and dump him. The other guy, Sammy Calhoun, he was scared, I guess. He kept grabbing at Bud's arm and saying they better turn the guy loose or they'd get in trouble with the Sheriff. And then I heard Bud say that was what they were getting paid for, to put a good scare into this guy so's he'd quit nosing around. Then this guy between them, he interrupted the two of them and said, 'You two have only got two choices. You got to kill me or let me go, because if you start dumping on me I'll sign a complaint for forcible kidnaping and assault and battery.'"

Larry swallowed; I saw sweat on his forehead. "So old Bud Baker just says, real calm-like, he says, 'All right, if that's how you want it,' and I seen him reach down and pick something up and hit this guy over the head with it. He hit him three-four times while he was falling.

"Then Bud and Sammy, they went through the guy's pockets, and I guess they taken his wallet, and after that they run over to that Cadillac and I watched them drive away. It was starting to get light and this Indian woman come along with some sheep, and I stayed hid-up there in the brush till I seen her run for help, and then I run for home. I figured she'd give the alarm, you know, but then I kept, you know, thinking on it, and finally I come down here to see the Sheriff.''

I obtained warrants on Baker and Calhoun; Peter Kyber's men went out to arrest them. Pete and I picked at Larry Stowe in several sessions, trying to nail down evidential details; his testimony was direct, his memory clear, and I knew we had a first-class witness in him.

We tried to sweat Baker and Calhoun but they'd been coached. They stood mute, refused to answer any questions without their lawyer, admitting nothing. The lawyer was a skinny fellow from Phoenix who drove up in an air-conditioned Corvette. He wore a sharkskin suit and aviator sunglasses. His name was William Farquhart and he had a white toothy smile—''Just call me Bill''—and I loathed him on sight.

We were obliged by the rules of disclosure to give him the outlines of our case; we had to tell him we had an eyewitness and we had to tell him the substance of the witness' testimony. Before the trial we would also know we had a positive make on the car driven by the two killers: Ron Owens' Cadillac.

We forestalled the latter problem by impounding Owen's car on a bench warrant but this only alerted Owens & Company to their jeopardy and within 24 hours lawyer Farquhart had been reinforced by the importation of three powerhouse lawyers from Tucson and Phoenix.

And later that day Larry Stowe came into my office, scared white. "I got to talk to you. They want me to change my story."

He'd never seen the two men before. They'd hustled him into the backseat of their car. "It was a two-tone green '73 Chevy Suburban." They told him to shut up and just listen.

"This guy says in the first place they've got five respectable witnesses to testify Bud and Sammy was over to the Sonoita rodeo grounds that morning, so they couldn't possibly of been up here beatin' Keam to death with a rock. Then they told me they got a witness who'll swear he seen me throw something over the fence behind Tooner's Bar, and this witness went and picked it up and it turned out to be Keam's wallet.

"They told me I'd be accused of the murder myself unless I change my testimony and say it was too dark to see the two guys that killed Keam. They say if I don't identify Bud and Sammy in court they'll leave me alone."

"Thanks for coming forward, Larry. You've got guts."

I said to Pete Kyber, "It's dismally effective. At least we can see the defense tactics now. They intend to make it look as if Larry killed Keam himself—to rob him—and then tried to shift the blame onto the two cowboys."

"It's possible that's what actually happened, Mike."

"No. I know the kid. Larry's got a feeble imagination. He could never have dreamed up that story and kept to it so faithfully. He's not a killer—he never even goes hunting with the other kids—and I don't believe he's ever stolen anything in his life."

"Dumb but honest," the Sheriff said. "But we're still in a bind here. If they produce a gang of witnesses to impeach his testimony, we won't get a conviction. Reasonable doubt."

I said, "I'm disinclined to let them get away with murder, Pete."

"Sure, but I don't know what we can do about it."

I got up to leave. "Two can play at dirty pool, you know."

"Larry, if you took that wallet off the body after they killed him, you'd better tell me now."

"No, sir. I'd admit it if I'd done it. I didn't do that."

"All right."

Bill Farquhart, the oily lawyer, agreed happily to a private meeting with me. Of course he expected me to offer a deal and I didn't disabuse him of that misapprehension until we met over a lunch table in a poorly lit booth in Corddry's Steak House.

Farquhart's dark hair fluffed around his ears Hollywood style; in the sharkskin suit he was all points and sharp angles. But he was reputed to be a splendidly effective courtroom lawyer.

He ordered a dry martini and talked about the hot drought but I cut him off because I hadn't the patience for small talk. I said, "Ron Owens thinks he's got this thing framed up perfectly, doesn't he? Let's not waste each other's time—we both understand the situation."

"I guess we do, Mr. Valdez. Defense wins, prosecution loses. That's the score." He laughed gently at me, very sure of himself.

I said, "As far as I'm concerned you're an errand boy for Ron Owens. I've got a message for you to carry back to him. You just listen to it and carry it to him. Understood?"

He gave me a pitying look. "Valdez, I don't take that kind of talk from two-bit Mexican civil servants."

That elicited my hard smile. "I'm the elected prosecuting attorney of Ocotillo County, Mr. Farquhart. As for the other, I'm not Mexican, I'm American. It's my country here, not yours. My ancestors were right here in this county while yours were still burning witches in Scotland. But the key point on the table right now is this. I'm the County Attorney in a county where Ron Owens has eighty-three percent of his assets tied up. Does that suggest anything to you?"

He smiled slowly; he thought he understood. "Okay," he said, "what's the deal?"

"This time I'll settle for Baker and Calhoun. I want their heads in a basket. And I want Ron Owens out of this county, lock, stock, and barrel. Right out."

"I guess you know better, really."

"No. I'll tell you something, this isn't Phoenix where everybody's got his hand out for graft and things are big enough to provide anonymity for men like Ron Owens. You're in a small town now and we tend to be unimpressed by Sy Devore suits and Hollywood sunglasses and Corvettes and big-city methods of extortion and intimidation. You don't realize it but these are tough people out here. They have to be, to survive in this desert. They chew up clowns like Ron Owens and spit them out."

His eyes were hooded; he feigned boredom. "What's the message, Mr. Valdez? I'm getting tired of this small-town boosterism."

"You've listed six defense witnesses who may be called during the trial to impeach Larry Stowe's testimony and to alibi the defendants. Of course you won't bother to call those six witnesses if Larry fails to identify Baker and Calhoun, correct?"

"You're doing the talking."

"Here's the message, counselor. Commit it and pass it on. One. Larry Stowe is under police protection. You won't find him until he appears in court, so you may as well forget any further attempts to threaten him or assault him. Two—"

"Are you accusing me of—"

"Shut up. Two: Larry will testify to what he saw—the deliberate and unprovoked murder of Philip Keam.

"Three: you will fail to call the six perjurious witnesses. The trial will take its course on the basis of the truth, and we'll take our chances on getting an honest conviction.

"Four: should you or Ron Owens disregard my warning, and should you bring forward your six witnesses to give false testimony, then certain things will begin to happen in this county. Ron Owens will find himself up to here in property-tax auditors and land reappraisals. He will find every application for a building permit held up for months, perhaps years. He will find his heavy construction equipment impounded by the County for violations of safety and pollution regulations. He will find his car ticketed incessantly for violations of vehicular codes, and he'll find his home, his office and other real property cited for every conceivable violation of the building codes. He will find himself and his executives subjected to an endless barrage of bureaucratic foul-ups, lost applications, misplaced documents—a nightmare of red tape, a systematic campaign of official harassment that will bring all his businesses to a total standstill and result in the across-the-board bankruptcy of every enterprise controlled by Ronald Baylor Owens.

"And one more thing," I added in the same quiet voice. "It's conceivable that some fatal accident might just happen to befall me if I began to put such a campaign into action. You and Owens should be aware that this is a rural county and that my family is one of the oldest here. We've known one another for generations around here. Some of these old boys—friends of mine, I play poker and hunt deer with them—some of these gents can shoot the flea off a coon-dog's ear at six hundred yards. They're not above settling their grievances in the old-fashioned manner. I'd like you and Owens to understand that if anything happens to me, it happens to Owens. I doubt it's much fun spending the hours wondering when to expect the bullet out of the darkness."

I got up and left him then; I'd said all I had to say.

Part of it was a bluff. I don't number any killers among my friends. But Farquhart and Owens were city boys and they didn't know that for sure; we had a redneck reputation up our way.

The rest of it had been quite true. I was fully prepared to drown Owens' companies in bureaucratic obstructionism and it would have been perfectly legal to do so: if you can actually enforce every ludicrous regulation in the law you can cripple anyone. The reason it hadn't already been done in Owens' case was that he'd been pouring a great deal of money into the economy of the county. Folks are willing to put up with all sorts of shenanigans if prosperity comes with them. But people up in Ocotillo County are still a bit old-fashioned: they don't condone willful murder as an acceptable way of doing business. I'd have had no trouble getting the cooperation of the other county officials.

Coercion is a two-way street. Owens and Farquhart were dealers in fear; I'd given them their own medicine.

Farquhart and his supporting battery of big-town attorneys put up a good defense but they didn't produce the six lying witnesses; Baker and Calhoun were convicted on the steadfast testimony of Larry Stowe and the evidence of bootprints and a few other tangibles left at the scene. The killers were sentenced to twenty-year-to-life terms in the State Penitentiary at Florence. Rumor has it that Ron Owens had to pay both of them enormous sums to insure that they wouldn't implicate him in the murder. The presence of his Cadillac at the crime meant nothing; Owens simply gave out the story that he'd lent the car to the two cowboys but had no idea what they meant to do with it.

But Owens pulled out of the county with satisfying alacrity. It took him a while to liquidate his properties but by Christmas he was gone, his offices closed, his residence sold.

He wasn't really very tough. I'd been looking forward to squaring off against him but evidently he didn't enjoy playing a game against people who played harder than he did.

The law doesn't protect people unless people protect the law.

13

THE PAIR OF GLOVES

Charles Dickens

"IT'S A SINGLER story, sir," said Inspector Wield, of the Detective Police, who, in company with Sergeants Dornton and Mith, paid us another twilight visit, one July evening; "and I've been thinking you might like to know it.

"It's concerning the murder of the young woman, Eliza Grimwood, some years ago, over in the Waterloo Road. She was commonly called The Countess because of her handsome appearance and her proud way of carrying of herself; and when I saw the poor Countess (I had known her well to speak to), lying dead, with her throat cut, on the floor of her bedroom, you'll believe me that a variety of reflections calculated to make a man rather low in his spirits, came into my head.

"That's neither here nor there. I went to the house the morning after the murder, and examined the body, and made a general observation of the bedroom where it was. Turning down the pillow of the bed with my hand, I found, underneath it, a pair of gloves. A pair of gentleman's dress gloves, very dirty; and inside the lining, the letters TR, and a cross.

"Well, sir, I took them gloves away, and I showed 'em to the magistrate, over at Union Hall, before whom the case was. He says, 'Wield,' he says, 'there's no doubt this is a discovery that may lead to something very important; and what you have got to do, Wield, is to find out the owner of these gloves.'

"I was of the same opinion, of course, and I went at it immediately. I looked at the gloves pretty narrowly, and it was my opinion that they had been cleaned. There was a smell of sulphur and rosin about 'em, you know, which cleaned gloves usually have, more or less. I took 'em over to a friend of mine at Kensington, who was in that line, and I put it to him. 'What do you say now? Have these gloves been cleaned?' 'These gloves have been

67

cleaned,' says he. 'Have you any idea who cleaned them?' says I. 'Not at all,' says he; 'I've a very distinct idea who *didn't* clean 'em, and that's myself. But I'll tell you what, Wield, there ain't above eight or nine reg'lar glove-cleaners in London'—there were not, at that time, it seems—'and I think I can give you their addresses, and you may find out, by that means, who did clean 'em.'

"Accordingly, he gave me the directions, and I went here, and I went there, and I looked up this man, and I looked up that man; but, though they all agreed that the gloves had been cleaned, I couldn't find the man, woman, or child, that had cleaned that pair of gloves.

"What with this person not being at home, and that person being expected home in the afternoon, and so forth, the inquiry took me three days. On the evening of the third day, coming over Waterloo Bridge from the Surrey side of the river, quite beat, and very much vexed and disappointed, I thought I'd have a shilling's worth of entertainment at the Lyceum Theatre to freshen myself up. So I went into the Pit, at half-price, and I sat myself down next to a very quiet, modest sort of young man. Seeing I was a stranger, he told me the names of the actors on the stage, and we got into conversation.

"When the play was over, we came out together, and I said, 'We've been very companionable and agreeable, and perhaps you wouldn't object to a dram.' 'Well, you're very good,' says he; 'I *shouldn't* object to a dram.' Accordingly, we went to a public-house, near the Theatre, sat ourselves down in a quiet room upstairs on the first floor, and called for a pint of half-and-half apiece, and a pipe.

"Well, sir, we put our pipes aboard, and we drank our half-and-half, and sat a-talking, very sociably, when the young man says, 'You must excuse me stopping very long,' he says, 'because I'm forced to go home in good time. I must be at work all night.' 'At work all night?' says I. 'You ain't a baker?' 'No,' he says, laughing, 'I ain't a baker.' 'I thought not,' says I, 'you haven't the looks of a baker.' 'No,' says he, 'I'm a glove-cleaner.'

"I never was more astonished in my life, than when I heard them words come out of his lips. 'You're a glove-cleaner, are you?' says I. 'Yes,' he says, 'I am.' 'Then, perhaps,' says I, taking the gloves out of my pocket, 'you can tell me who cleaned this pair of gloves? It's a rum story,' I says to him, 'I was dining over at Lambeth when some gentleman, he left these gloves behind him! Another gentleman and me, you see, we laid a wager of a sovereign that I wouldn't find out who they belonged to. I've spent as much as seven shillings already trying to discover; but, if you could help me, I'd stand another seven and welcome. You see there's TR and a cross, inside.'

"'I see,' he says. 'Bless you, *I* know these gloves very well! I've seen dozens of pairs belonging to the same party,' 'No?' says I. 'Yes,' says he. 'Then you know who cleaned 'em?' says I. 'Rather so,' says he. 'My father cleaned 'em.'

"'Where does your father live?' says I. 'Just round the corner,' says the young man, 'near Exeter Street, here. He'll tell you who they belong to, directly.' Would you come round with me now?' says I. 'Certainly,' says he.

"We went round to the place, and there we found an old man in a white apron, with two or three daughters, all rubbing and cleaning away at lots of gloves, in a front parlor. 'Oh, Father!' says the young man, 'here's a person been and made a bet about the ownership of a pair of gloves and I've told him you can settle it.' 'Good evening, sir,' says I to the old gentleman. 'Here's the gloves your son speaks of. Letters TR, you see, and a cross.' 'Oh, yes,' he says, 'I know these gloves very well. They belong to Mr. Trinkle, the great upholsterer in Cheapside.'

"'Did you get 'em from Mr. Trinkle, direct,' says I, 'if you'll excuse my asking the question?' 'No,' says he; 'Mr. Trinkle always sends 'em to Mr. Phibbs's, the haberdasher's, opposite his shop, and the haberdasher sends 'em to me.' 'Perhaps *you* wouldn't object to a dram?' says I. 'Not in the least!' says he. So I took the old gentleman out, and had a little more talk with him and his son, over a glass, and we parted excellent friends.

"This was late on a Saturday night. First thing on the Monday morning, I went to the haberdasher's shop, opposite Mr. Trinkle's, the great upholsterer's in Cheapside. 'Mr. Phibbs in the way?' 'My name is Phibbs.' 'Oh! I believe you sent this pair of gloves to be cleaned?' 'Yes, I did, for young Mr. Trinkle over the way. There he is in the shop.' 'Oh! that's him in the shop, it is? Him in the green coat?' 'The same individual.' 'Well, Mr. Phibbs, this is an unpleasant affair; but the fact is, I am Inspector Wield of the Detective Police, and I found these gloves under the pillow of the young woman that was murdered the other day, over in the Waterloo Road.'

"'Good Heaven!' says he. 'He's a most respectable young man, and if his father was to hear of it, it would be the ruin of him!' 'I'm very sorry for it,' says I, 'but I must take him into custody.' 'Good Heaven!' says Mr. Phibbs again, 'can nothing be done?' 'Nothing,' says I. 'Will you allow me to call him over here,' says he, 'that his father may not see it done?' 'I don't object to that,' says I, 'but unfortunately, Mr. Phibbs, I can't allow of any communication between you. If any was attempted, I should have to interfere directly. Perhaps you'll beckon him over here?'

"Mr. Phibbs went to the door and beckoned, and the young fellow came across the street directly; a smart, brisk young fellow.

"'Good morning, sir,' says I. 'Good morning, sir,' says he. 'Would you allow me to inquire sir,' says I, 'if you ever had any acquaintance with a party of the name of Grimwood?' 'Grimwood! Grimwood!' says he. 'No!' 'You know the Waterloo Road?' 'Oh! of course I know the Waterloo Road!' 'Happen to have heard of a young woman being murdered there?' 'Yes, I read it in the paper, and very sorry I was to read it.' 'Here's a pair of gloves belonging to you, that I found under her pillow the morning afterward!'

"He was in a dreadful state, sir; a dreadful state! 'Mr. Wield,' he says, 'upon my solemn oath I never was there. I never so much as saw her, to my knowledge, in my life!' 'I am very sorry,' says I. 'To tell you the truth; I don't think you *are* the murderer, but I must take you to Union Hall in a cab. However, I think it's a case of the sort that, at present, at all events, the magistrate will hear it in private.'

"A private examination took place, and then it came out that this young man was acquainted with a cousin of the unfortunate Eliza Grimwood, and that, calling to see this cousin a day or two before the murder, he left these gloves upon the table. Who should come in, shortly afterward, but Eliza Grimwood. 'Whose gloves are these?' she says, taking 'em up. 'Those are Mr. Trinkle's gloves,' says her cousin. 'Oh!' says she, 'they are very dirty, and of no use to him, I am sure. I shall take 'em away for my girl to clean the stoves with.' And she put 'em in her pocket. The girl had used 'em to clean the stoves, and, I have no doubt, had left 'em lying on the bedroom mantelpiece, and her mistress, looking around to see that the room was tidy, had caught 'em up and put 'em under the pillow where I found 'em.

"That's the story, sir."

14

AFTER TWENTY YEARS

O. Henry

THE POLICEMAN ON the beat moved up the avenue impressively. The impressiveness was habitual and not for show, for spectators were few. The time was barely ten o'clock at night, but chilly gusts of wind with a taste of rain in them had well nigh depeopled the streets.

Trying doors as he went, twirling his club with many intricate and artful movements, turning now and then to cast his watchful eye down the pacific thoroughfare, the officer, with his stalwart form and slight swagger, made a fine picture of a guardian of the peace. The vicinity was one that kept early hours. Now and then you might see the lights of a cigar store or of an all-night lunch counter; but the majority of the doors belonged to business places that had long since been closed.

When about midway of a certain block the policeman suddenly slowed his walk. In the doorway of a darkened hardware store a man leaned, with an unlighted cigar in his mouth. As the policeman walked up to him the man spoke up quickly.

"It's all right, officer," he said reassuringly. "I'm just waiting for a friend. It's an appointment made twenty years ago. Sounds a little funny to you, doesn't it? Well, I'll explain if you'd like to make certain it's all straight. About that long ago there used to be a restaurant where this store stands—'Big Joe' Brady's restaurant."

"Until five years ago," said the policeman. "It was torn down then."

The man in the doorway struck a match and lit his cigar. The light showed a pale, square-jawed face with keen eyes, and a little white scar near his right eyebrow. His scarfpin was a large diamond, oddly set.

"Twenty years ago tonight," said the man, "I dined here at 'Big Joe' Brady's with Jimmy Wells, my best chum, and the finest chap in the world. He and I were raised here in New York, just like two brothers, together. I

71

was eighteen and Jimmy was twenty. The next morning I was to start for the West to make my fortune. You couldn't have dragged Jimmy out of New York; he thought it was the only place on earth. Well, we agreed that night that we would meet here again exactly twenty years from that date and time, no matter what our conditions might be or from what distance we might have to come. We figured that in twenty years each of us ought to have our destiny worked out and our fortunes made, whatever they were going to be.''

''It sounds pretty interesting,'' said the policeman. ''Rather a long time between meets, though, it seems to me. Haven't you heard from your friend since you left?''

''Well, yes, for a time we corresponded,'' said the other. ''But after a year or two we lost track of each other. You see, the West is a pretty big proposition, and I kept hustling around over it pretty lively. But I know Jimmy will meet me here if he's alive, for he always was the truest, staunchest old chap in the world. He'll never forget. I came two thousand miles to stand in this door tonight, and it's worth it if my old partner turns up.''

The waiting man pulled out a handsome watch, the lids of it set with small diamonds.

''Three minutes to ten,'' he announced, ''It was exactly ten o'clock when we parted here at the restaurant door.''

''Did pretty well out West, didn't you?'' asked the policeman.

''You bet! I hope Jimmy has done half as well. He was a kind of plodder, though, good fellow as he was. I've had to compete with some of the sharpest wits going to get my pile. A man gets in a groove in New York. It takes the West to put a razor edge on him.''

The policeman twirled his club and took a step or two.

''I'll be on my way. Hope your friend comes around all right. Going to call time on him sharp?''

''I should say not!'' said the other. ''I'll give him half an hour at least. If Jimmy is alive on earth he'll be here by that time. So long, officer.''

''Good night, sir,'' said the policeman, passing along on his beat, trying doors as he went.

There was now a fine, cold drizzle falling, and the wind had risen from its uncertain puffs into a steady blow. The few foot passengers astir in that quarter hurried dismally and silently along with coat collars turned high and pocketed hands. And in the door of the hardware store the man who had come two thousand miles to fill an appointment, uncertain almost to absurdity, with the friend of his youth, smoked his cigar and waited.

About twenty minutes he waited, and then a tall man in a long overcoat, with collar turned up to his ears, hurried across from the opposite side of the street. He went directly to the waiting man.

"Is that you, Bob?" he asked doubtfully.

"Is that you, Jimmy Wells?" cried the man in the door.

"Bless my heart!" exclaimed the new arrival, grasping both the other's hands with his own. "It's Bob, sure as fate. I was certain I'd find you here if you were still in existence. Well, well, well!—twenty years is a long time. The old restaurant's gone, Bob. I wish it had lasted, so we could have had another dinner there. How has the West treated you, old man?"

"Bully; it has given me everything I asked it for. You've changed lots, Jimmy. I never thought you were so tall by two or three inches."

"Oh, I grew a bit after I was twenty."

"Doing well in New York, Jimmy?"

"Moderately. I have a position in one of the city departments. Come on, Bob; we'll go around to a place I know of and have a good long talk about old times."

The two men started up the street, arm in arm. The man from the West, his egotism enlarged by success, was beginning to outline the history of his career. The other, submerged in his overcoat, listened with interest.

At the corner stood a drug store, brilliant with electric lights. When they came into this glare each of them turned simultaneously to gaze on the other's face.

The man from the West stopped suddenly and released his arm.

"You're not Jimmy Wells," he snapped. "Twenty years is a long time but not long enough to change a man's nose from a Roman to a pug."

"It sometimes changes a good man into a bad one," said the tall man. "You've been under arrest for ten minutes, 'Silky' Bob. Chicago thinks you may have dropped over our way and wired us she wants to have a chat with you. Going quietly, are you? That's sensible. Now, before we go to the station here's a note I was asked to hand you. You may read it here at the window. It's from Patrolman Wells."

The man from the West unfolded the little piece of paper handed him. His hand was steady when he began to read, but it trembled a little by the time he had finished. The note was rather short.

> Bob: I was at the appointed place on time. When you struck the match to light your cigar I saw it was the face of the man wanted in Chicago. Somehow I couldn't do it myself, so I went around and got a plainclothesman to do the job.
>
> Jimmy.

73

15

THE EXPORT TRADE

Leslie Charteris

IT IS A notable fact, which might be made the subject of a profound philosophical discourse by anyone with time to spare for these recreations, that the characteristics which go to make a successful buccaneer are almost the same as those required by the detective whose job it is to catch him.

That he must be a man of infinite wit goes without saying; but there are other and more uncommon essentials. He must have an unlimited memory not only for faces and names, but also for every odd and out-of-the-way fact that comes to his knowledge. Out of a molehill of coincidence he must be able to build up a mountain of inductive speculation that would make Sherlock Holmes feel dizzy. He must be a man of infinite human sympathy, with an unstinted gift for forming weird and wonderful friendships. He must, in fact, be equally like the talented historian whose job it is to chronicle his exploits—with the outstanding difference that instead of being free to ponder the problems which arise in the course of his vocation for sixty hours, his decisions will probably have to be formed in sixty seconds.

Simon Templar fulfilled at least one of these qualifications to the nth degree. He had queer friends dotted about in every outlandish corner of the globe, and if many of them lived in unromantic-sounding parts of London, it was not his fault. Strangely enough, there were not many of them who knew that the debonair young man with the lean tanned face and gay blue eyes who drifted in and out of their lives at irregular intervals was the notorious lawbreaker known to everyone as the Saint. Certainly old Charlie Milton did not know.

The Saint, being in the region of the Tottenham Court Road one afternoon with half an hour to dispose of, dropped into Charlie's attic workroom and listened to a new angle on the changing times.

"There's not much doing in my line these days," said Charlie, wiping his steel-rimmed spectacles. "When nobody's going in for real expensive jewelry, because the costume stuff is so good, it stands to reason they don't need any dummies. Look at this thing—the first big bit of work I've had for weeks."

He produced a glittering rope of diamonds, set in a cunning chain of antique silver and ending in a wonderfully elaborate heart-shaped pendant. The sight of it should have made honest buccaneer's mouth water, but it so happened that Simon Templar knew better. For that was the secret of Charlie Milton's employment.

Up there, in his dingy little shop, he labored with marvelously delicate craftsmanship over the imitations which had made his name known to every jeweler in London. Sometimes there were a hundred pounds' worth of precious stones littered over his bench, and he worked under the watchful eye of a detective detailed to guard them. Whenever a piece of jewelry was considered too valuable to be displayed by its owner on ordinary occasions, it was sent to Charlie Milton for him to make one of his amazingly exact facsimiles; and there was many a wealthy dowager who brazenly paraded Charlie's handiwork at minor social functions, while the priceless originals were safely stored in a safe deposit.

"The Kellman necklace," Charlie explained, tossing it carelessly back into a drawer. "Lord Palfrey ordered it from me a month ago, and I was just finishing it when he went bankrupt. I had twenty-five pounds advance when I took it on, and I expect that's all I shall see for my trouble. The necklace is being sold with the rest of his things, and how do I know whether the people who buy it will want my copy?"

It was not an unusual kind of conversation to find its place in the Saint's varied experience, and he never foresaw the path it was to play in his career. Some days later he happened to notice a newspaper paragraph referring to the sale of Lord Palfrey's house and effects; but he thought nothing more of the matter, for men like Lord Palfrey were not Simon Templar's game.

In the days when some fresh episode of Saintly audacity was one of the most dependable weekly stand-bys of the daily press, the victims of his lawlessness had always been men whose reputations would have emerged considerably dishevelled from such a searching inquiry as they were habitually at pains to avoid; and although the circumstances of Simon Templar's life had altered a great deal since then, his elastic principles of morality performed their acrobatic contortions within much the same limits.

That those circumstances should have altered at all was not his choice;

but there are boundaries which every buccaneer must eventually reach, and Simon Templar had reached them rather rapidly. The manner of his reaching them has been related elsewhere, and there were not a few people in England who remembered that story. For one week of blazing headlines the secret of the Saint's real identity had been published up and down the country for all to read; and although there were many to whom the memory had grown dim, and who could still describe him only by the nickname which he had made famous, there were many others who had not forgotten. The change had its disadvantages, for one of the organizations which would never forget had its headquarters at Scotland Yard; but there were occasional compensations in the strange commissions which sometimes came the Saint's way.

One of these arrived on a day in June, brought by a somberly-dressed man who called at the flat on Piccadilly where Simon Templar had taken up his temporary abode—the Saint was continually changing his address, and this palatial apartment, with tall windows overlooking the Green Park, was his latest fancy. The visitor was an elderly white-haired gentleman with the understanding eyes and air of tremendous discretion which one associates in imagination with the classical type of family solicitor that he immediately confessed himself to be.

"To put it as briefly as possible, Mr. Templar," he said, "I am authorized to ask if you would undertake to deliver a sealed package to an address in Paris which will be given you. All your expenses will be paid, or course; and you will be offered a fee of one hundred pounds."

Simon lighted a cigarette and blew a cloud of smoke at the ceiling.

"It sounds easy enough," he remarked. "Wouldn't it be cheaper to send it by mail?"

"That package, Mr. Templar—the contents of which I am not allowed to disclose—is insured for five thousand pounds," said the solicitor impressively. "But I fear that four times that sum would not compensate for the loss of an article which is the only thing of its kind in the world. The ordinary detective agencies have already been considered, but our client feels that they are scarcely competent to deal with such an important task. We have been warned that an attempt may be made to steal the package, and it is our client's wish that we should endeavor to secure the services of your own—ah—singular experience."

The Saint thought it over. He knew that the trade in illicit drugs does not go on to any appreciable extent from England to the continent, but rather in the reverse direction; and apart from such a possibility as that the commission seemed straightforward enough.

"Your faith in my reformed character is almost touching," said the Saint at length; and the solicitor smiled faintly.

"We are relying on the popular estimate of your sporting instincts."

"When do you want me to go?"

The solicitor placed the tips of his fingers together with a discreet modicum of satisfaction.

"I take it that you are prepared to accept our offer?"

"I don't see why I shouldn't. A pal of mine who came over the other day told me there was a darn good show at the *Folies Bergère,* and since you're only young once—"

"Doubtless you will be permitted to include the entertainment in your bill of expenses," said the solicitor dryly. "If the notice is not too short, we should be very pleased if you were free to visit the—ah—*Folies Bergère,* tomorrow night."

"Suits me," murmured the Saint laconically.

The solicitor rose.

"You will travel by air, of course," he said. "I shall return later this evening to deliver the package into your keeping, after which you will be solely responsible. If I might give you a hint, Mr. Templar," he added, as the Saint shepherded him to the door, "you will take particular pains to conceal it while you are traveling. It has been suggested to us that the French police are not incorruptible."

He repeated his warning when he came back at six o'clock and left Simon with a brown-paper packet about four inches square and two inches deep, in which the outlines of a stout cardboard box could be felt. Simon weighed the package several times in his hand—it was neither particularly light nor particularly heavy, and he puzzled over its possible contents for some time. The address to which it was to be delivered was typed on a plain sheet of paper; Simon committed it to memory, and burnt it.

Curiosity was the Saint's weakness. It was that same insatiable curiosity which had made his fortune, for he was incapable of looking for long at anything that struck him as being the least bit peculiar without succumbing to the temptation to probe deeper into its peculiarities. It never entered his head to betray the confidence that had been placed in him so far as the safety of the package was concerned; but the mystery of its contents was one which he considered had a definite bearing on whatever risks he had agreed to take. He fought off his curiosity until he got up the next morning, and then it got the better of him. He opened the packet after his early breakfast, carefully removing the seals intact with a hot palette-knife, and was very glad that he had done so.

When he drove down to Croydon aerodrome later the package had been just as carefully refastened, and no one would have known that it had been opened. He carried it inside a book, from which he had cut the printed part of the pages to leave a square cavity encircled by the margins; and he was prepared for trouble.

He checked in his suit-case and waited around patiently during the dilatory system of preparations which for some extraordinary reason is introduced to negative the theoretical speed of air transport. He was fishing out his cigarette-case for the second time when a dark and strikingly pretty girl, who had been waiting with equal patience, came over and asked him for a light.

Simon produced his lighter, and the girl took a pack of cigarettes from her bag and offered him one.

"Do they always take as long as this?" she said.

"Always when I'm traveling," said the Saint resignedly. "Another thing I should like to know is why they have to arrange their time-tables so that you never have the chance to get a decent lunch. Is it for the benefit of the French restaurants—at dinnertime?"

She laughed.

"Are we fellow passengers?"

"I do not know. I'm for Paris."

"I'm for Ostend."

The Saint sighed.

"Couldn't you change your mind and come to Paris?"

He had taken one puff from the cigarette. Now he took a second, while she eyed him impudently. The smoke had an unfamiliar, slightly bitter taste to it. Simon drew on the cigarette again thoughtfully, but this time he held the smoke in his mouth and let it trickle out again presently, as if he had inhaled. The expression on his face never altered, although the last thing he had expected had been trouble of that sort.

"Do you think we could take a walk outside?" said the girl. "I'm simply stifling."

"I think it might be a good idea," said the Saint.

He walked out with her into the clear morning sunshine, and they strolled idly along the gravel drive. The rate of exchange had done a great deal to discourage foreign travel that year, and the airport was unusually deserted. A couple of men were climbing out of a car that had drawn up beside the building; but apart from them there was only one other car turning in at the gates leading from the main road, and a couple of mechanics fussing round a gigantic Handley-Page that was ticking over on the tarmac.

"Why did you give me a doped cigarette?" asked the Saint with perfect casualness; but as the girl turned and stared at him his eyes leapt to hers with the cold suddenness of bared steel.

"I—I don't understand. Do you mind telling me what you mean?"

Simon dropped the cigarette and trod on it deliberately.

"Sister," he said, "if you're thinking of a Simon Templar who was born yesterday, let me tell you it was someone else of the same name. You know, I was playing that cigarette trick before you cut your teeth."

The girl's hand went to her mouth; then it went up in a kind of wave. For a moment the Saint was perplexed; and then he started to turn. She was looking at something over his shoulder, but his head had not revolved far enough to see what it was before the solid weight of a sandbag slugged viciously into the back of his neck. He had one instant of feeling his limbs sagging powerlessly under him, while the book he carried dropped from his hand and sprawled open to the ground; and then everything went dark.

He came back to earth in a small barely-furnished office overlooking the landing-field, and in the face that was bending over him he recognized the round pink countenance of Chief Inspector Teal, of Scotland Yard.

"Were you the author of that clout?" he demanded, rubbing the base of his skull tenderly. "I didn't think you could be so tough."

"I didn't do it," said the detective shortly. "But we've got the man who did—if you want to charge him. I thought you'd have known Kate Allfield, Saint."

Simon looked at him.

"What—not 'the Mug'? I have heard of her, but this is the first time we've met. And she nearly made me smoke a sleepy cigarette!" He grimaced. "What was the idea?"

"That's what we're waiting for you to tell us," said Teal grimly. "We drove in just as they knocked you out. We know what they were after all right—the Deacon's gang beat them to the necklace, but that wouldn't make the Green Cross bunch give up. What I want to know is when you started working with the Deacon."

"This is right over my head," said the Saint, just as bluntly. "Who is the Deacon, and who the hell are the Green Cross bunch?"

Teal faced him calmly.

"The Green Cross bunch are the ones that slugged you. The Deacon is the head of the gang that got away with the Palfrey jewels yesterday. He came to see you twice yesterday afternoon—we got the wire that he was planning a big job and we were keeping him under observation, but the jewels weren't missing till this morning. Now I'll hear what you've got to say; but before you begin I'd better warn you—''

''Wait a minute.'' Simon took out his cigarette-case and helped himself to a smoke. ''With an unfortunate reputation like mine, I expect it'll take me some time to drive it into your head that I don't know a thing about the Deacon. He came to me yesterday and said he was a solicitor—he wanted me to look after a valuable sealed packet that he was sending over to Paris, and I took on the job. That's all. He wouldn't even tell me what was in it.''

''Oh, yes?'' The detective was dangerously polite. ''Then I suppose it'd give you the surprise of your life if I told you that that package you were carrying contained a diamond necklace valued at about eight thousand pounds?''

''It would,'' said the Saint.

Teal turned.

There was a plain-clothes man standing guard by the door, and on the table in the middle of the room was a litter of brown paper and tissue in the midst of which gleamed a small heap of coruscating stones and shining metal. Teal put a hand to the heap of jewels and lifted it up into a streamer of iridescent fire.

''This is it,'' he said.

''May I have a look at it?'' said the Saint.

He took the necklace from Teal's hand and studied it closely under the light. Then he handed it back with a brief grin.

''If you could get eighty pounds for it, you'd be lucky,'' he said. ''It's a very good imitation, but I'm afraid the stones are only jargons.''

The detective's eyes went wide. Then he snatched the necklace and examined it himself.

He turned around again slowly.

''I'll begin to believe you were telling the truth for once, Templar,'' he said, and his manner had changed so much that the effect would have been comical without the back-handed apology. ''What do you make of it?''

''I think we've both been had,'' said the Saint. ''After what you've told me, I should think the Deacon knew you were watching him, and knew he'd have to get the jewels out of the country in a hurry. He could probably fence most of them quickly, but no one would touch that necklace—it's too well known. He had the rather artistic idea of trying to get me to do the job—''

''Then why should he give you a fake?''

Simon shrugged.

"Maybe that Deacon is smoother than any of us thought. My God, Teal—think of it! Suppose even all this was just a blind—for you to know he'd been to see me—for you to get after me as soon as the jewels were missed—hear I'd left for Paris—chase me to Croydon—and all the time the real necklace is slipping out by another route—"

"God damn!" said Chief Inspector Teal, and launched himself at the telephone with surprising speed for such a portly and lethargic man.

The plain-clothes man at the door stood aside almost respectfully for the Saint to pass.

Simon fitted his hat on rakishly and sauntered out with his old elegance. Out in the waiting room an attendant was shouting, "All Ostend and Brussels passengers, please!"—and outside on the tarmac a roaring airplane was warming up its engines. Simon Templar suddenly changed his mind about his destination.

"I will give you thirty thousand guilders for the necklace," said Van Roeper, the little trader of Amsterdam to whom the Saint went with this booty.

"I'll take fifty thousand," said the Saint; and he got it.

He fulfilled another of the qualifications of a successful buccaneer, for he never forgot a face. He had had a vague idea from the first that he had seen the Deacon somewhere before, but it had not been until that morning, when he woke up, that he had been able to place the amiable solicitor who had been so anxious to enlist his dubious services; and he felt that fortune was very kind to him.

Old Charlie Milton, who had been dragged away from his breakfast to sell him the facsimile for eighty pounds, felt much the same.

16

PROBLEMS SOLVED

Bill Pronzini and
Barry N. Malzberg

DEAR MR. GREY:

Thank you for consulting me, and for your expression of confidence that I will be able to solve your problem. I do take considerable pride in "Problems Solved," my consultation service. As you know from my magazine advertisements, this service by mail has been functioning successfully for seven years (with never a complaint, if I may add proudly).

Now then, to your problem. Mr. Grey, the question you pose in your last paragraph is obviously what has really been on your mind throughout your letter. Thus, in answer to this question, let me say that I do not believe your murderous fantasies are so unusual, nor do I think that you have any reason to feel as guilty about them as you say. *Most* people have murderous fantasies of one sort or the other, sometimes toward those who are closest to them and whom they love best. These fantasies function usually as a normal and healthy outlet, since the important thing is that they will never be acted upon. Seen in that context, then, they are definitely a healthy release.

Of course, guilt can be self-destructive. I am reminded of a case many years ago in the small upstate New York town in which my wife was born: a local man murdered several strangers for the confessed reason that he had "wanted to kill people all the time lately and I couldn't stand knowing I was as good as a murderer inside, so I just went out and did it." So, Mr. Grey, I urge you to work on these guilt feelings of yours more than on the fantasies themselves. It is *only* the guilt building up within you which could be dangerous.

Your accompanying check in the amount of $50.00 is exactly double my customary fee for a consultation of this nature. Therefore, I am entering a credit of $25.00 which you may use for another consultation. I *do* hope to hear from you again, since I believe your particular problem may involve at least one and possibly two or three additional consultations before we can safely mark it "solved."

Sincerely yours,
Dr. Harold Rawls
"Problems Solved"

DEAR MR. GREY:

I am in receipt of your second letter, and I must say first of all that I am sorry you were disappointed with my initial advice. I am also sorry that you feel continually disturbed, and although I agree that there is no accounting for "the range of human pain and the desire to inflict pain," as you put it, I must strongly repeat what I said previously.

Giving free rein to your murderous fantasies may actually be counter-productive, you know. The explicitness of detail in your letter would be shocking to a nonprofessional, and while I well understand the context in which this should be placed, I must tell you that I would not, if I were you, express these details to anyone but me.

Please Mr. Grey, you must understand that your fantasies are quite common and that you should not feel the kind of guilt which merely triggers further rage and pain. We live in difficult times, unhappy times: many of your best friends, perhaps, would secretly like to be murderers. It is the act of *commission* which makes all the difference.

This second consultation has been paid for, of course, by your $25.00 credit. When you write again, please enclose further remuneration. And please tell me something about yourself as well. You have been quite bare on personal details in your two letters to date. With more knowledge of who you are, what you do for a living, and so on, I can be much more specific in my advice.

Sincerely yours,
Dr. Harold Rawls
"Problems Solved"

DEAR MR. GREY:

I have received your latest letter and your $100.00 check for a total of four consultations. However, I am returning herewith my check in the amount of $75.00, which represents a total refund less $25.00 for this third, and unfortunately final, consultation.

84

You have given me no alternative, Mr. Grey. I cannot deal with you any longer. You have refused to confide any personal information beyond a name and a post office box address in upper Manhattan. You prefer to remain hidden in the shadows, as it were. As a result I have no idea of who you are or who you are talking about when you mention "this urge, this terrible, incessant urge to kill." Members of your family? Friends? Business associates? Strangers? I have no way of knowing.

You seem also and for no apparent reason to have taken a dangerously abusive attitude toward me, which I will not tolerate. Violent emotional outbursts and veiled threats such as those which marked your letter are pointless, childish, and misdirected.

It is my final opinion, Mr. Grey, that you are a seriously ill personality and that you should immediately seek a face-to-face consultation with a qualified psychotherapist. Do so, I urge you, before it is too late.

Sincerely,
Dr. Harold Rawls
"Problems Solved"

MR. GREY:

I suppose I should have foreseen the content of your most recent letter. That I did not is a comment only upon my heavy workload. I will say nothing about your vile and insane threat on my life. I will not attempt to reason with you, for it is obvious you have graduated beyond reason to psychosis.

I would like you to know, however, that I maintain careful files which include all letters sent to me and carbons of all my responses. These files are kept under lock and key, where no one but myself and my secretary have access to them, and in the event of harm to me they would immediately be turned over to the police.

Not, of course, that I anticipate any harm from you. Individuals such as yourself are very common in my profession. You obtain satisfaction from ventilating aggressions which you are unable to act out in reality. Thus, I am not at all frightened that you will carry out your threat. Threats such as yours do not disconcert me in the slightest, for I not only understand their origin, I have a great inner strength.

I suggest, once again, that you consult a qualified psychotherapist as soon as possible.

Sincerely,
Dr. Harold Rawls
"Problems Solved"

DEAR FRIENDS,

I'm sorry for this mimeographed note, but I don't have the time or the energy to personally thank all of you who sent flowers and other expressions of sympathy on the terrible death of my husband, Dr. Harold Rawls. I know you will understand. I also know you will understand why I must go away for a while. There are too many memories here, too much sorrow— and as long as the lunatic who murdered Harold is still at large, my own life may be in danger as well.

With gratitude,
Muriel Rawls

MR JOE VINSON CRISTOBAL HOTEL NASSAU GRAND BAHAMAS ARRIVING EIGHT FORTY TONIGHT FLIGHT 62 STOP PROBLEM SOLVED STOP LOVE YOU

MURIEL

17

THE RELEASE

Cornell Woolrich

I LEFT THE taxi with a splurge, like a man arching his legs to straddle a sidewalk puddle though no puddle was there. He called out something about my change; I showed him the back of my hand.

No elevator ever went so slowly as the one that took me up to Sutphen's office. There were never so many floors between; so many people never got off, never got on. So many latecomers never made it at the last minute and caused the doors that had already closed to a hair's width to reopen all the way again. The indicator sweep inside the cab never moved so reluctantly, never stayed on 3 so long, on 4 so long, on 5, on 6. Sweat never prickled so, along the pleats in somebody's forehead, in the crotches below his arms. A heart never beat so fast before, except in the hurtle finals of the Olympics, and everything else around it so slow, so slow before.

Then at last it was at 7, and I stepped on someone's toes, knocked someone else's hat askew, carried still someone else's handbag halfway out of the car with me, hooked onto the buttons of my coat sleeve.

Then I was out running, and no corridor was ever so long before or had so many people on it getting in your way before, playing that simultaneous impulse game, where they move to the left when you move to the left blocking, and to the right when you do, blocking you all over again.

He'd moved his office. The number on the door hadn't changed, but it was fifty doors farther down the line now and twenty-five more around the turn. I was on the other side of the door at last. There was a receptionist at the desk. She didn't try to stop me or ask me who I was. She saw my face, saw what was on it, had seen it before, but never with the shining light that showed all over me now. She just pointed. "In there, door on the left. He's by himself."

I pushed the door out of the way. Knocking was for other times; knocking was for times when there was time. And he was in there, walking back and forth.

I caught him doing that—no one with him—walking back and forth, one hand in his pocket like when you're broke, one hand hooked around the back of his neck like when you're at a loss. Sour in the face, disturbed, discouraged, disgusted—I couldn't tell what it was. Some other case, not mine. Mine was over; mine was squared. I didn't owe the law anything, anymore.

You know how lawyers are. They have dozens of cases. Some of them fizzle; some of them go wrong. You know how lawyers are—they have cases by the carload. He stopped his pacing and looked up to see who had come in. He said the funniest thing to himself. I heard him. He said, "Oh merciful God."

Then he asked me, after watching me, "What are you doing here? I thought they refused the parole."

"No parole." Triumph bubbling, escaping into the open. "A pardon."

He kept watching me. "How'd you come down here?"

"First by train and then by taxi." I wondered why he'd asked that. I was here—that was all that mattered—or should have mattered.

"Did it have a radio? Was it on?"

I frowned. "It had a two-way radio, steering it to pickups by its dispatcher. Why?"

"Oh, that kind." He seemed to lose interest—in the radio, not in me. "Did you tell her to expect you?"

"No, that was the whole idea." I whipped the thing D'Angelo had signed out of my inside pocket, pushed it at him. "Don't y'want to see what I've got here?" The jubilation was back. I was jabbering staccato. "Don't y'want to read it? I'm free, like I was born. Free, like I'll die. Free, like I was meant to be—" My voice slowed and started to dwindle. "Doesn't it matter?" was the last thing that came out. Then it faltered, and it died.

It didn't matter. He didn't say it didn't, but he showed it didn't.

He took the paper the statement was on, pleated one end of it like he was making a paper dart out of it, poised it over his desk wastebasket, and speared it in.

I was jolted. "What'd you do that for?"

He just looked at me. Everything that anyone was every sorry for was in that look. You could see it there.

"I can't tell you. I'll have to let the radio do it for me. They can do it better." He went over and thumbed the knob. "I'll see if I can get one of the all-news stations. It'll come around again. Sit down a minute."

He took a cigarette out of a gold-tooled desk box and put it in my mouth—even lit it for me. He put his hand on my shoulder and pressed down hard, as if to say, "Brace yourself."

In the background familiar names began to sound off dimly, names that were far away, that had nothing to do with me. Hanoi—Cape Kennedy—Lindsay—U Thant—Johnson—

He opened a drawer and took out a bottle of Hanky Bannister. I hadn't known he kept anything like that there. He didn't drink himself, not in the office, I mean. He kept it there for clients, I guess, and for sufferers who needed it for imminent shock, like he seemed to think I was going to. He passed me a good-sized drink.

I drank it down, still in happiness, although the happiness was now a little dazed—not dimmed, but dazed by his peculiarity. Even with the happiness I started to get scared by all this indirection—Like a guy waiting for surgery without knowing what form it was going to take.

It came. It hit. Before I knew it, it was already over. And the slow-spreading after-sting had only just started in.

He brought it up—the sound, I mean. Touched it with his finger. And I noticed as he did so he didn't look at me but looked the other way, as if he didn't like to look at me right then—couldn't face my face.

" . . . Mrs. Janet Evans took her own life early today in the apartment in which she had been living on East Seventy-eighth Street. Mrs. Evans, whose husband had been serving an indeterminate sentence in connection with the death of singer Dell Nelson, left a note which is in the hands of the police. The death occurred sometime between four and six A.M., when the body was discovered. . . . "

The cigarette fell out of my hand. Nothing much else happened. How much has to happen to show your life just ended, your heart just broken? Nothing shows it—nothing. Your cigarette falls on the carpet. After a while your head goes down lower, then lower, then lower. You stare, but you don't see. No words, no tears, no anything. It's a quiet thing. It's a your-own thing that no one else can share. You reach up behind you and turn your coat collar up and hold it close to your throat in front with your fingers, though you know the room is warm for anyone else.

You're cold, you're hungry, you're thirsty, you're scared, you're lonely, you're lost. And you're all those things together at one time.

"I saw her only two days ago," I heard him saying. "I spoke to her. I think she tried to tell me then what was going to happen, only I didn't catch on. 'It's too late now for both of us,' she said. 'We can't win anymore now; we've already lost. Get together again? Two strangers hardly knowing each other, grubbing around in the debris looking for something they once had? Two ghosts sitting in the twilight, with a bottle somewhere between them? After a while, if we didn't swallow the bottle, the bottle would swallow us. Both of those are worse than any prison is.' ''

I looked up at him and I complained. "I hurt all over."

But he couldn't help me. He wasn't a bandage.

I stood up finally and turned to the door, and he said, "Where are you going?" and he tried to hold me back.

"Home. I'm going home."

"You can't. You know that, Cleve. There isn't any home anymore for you. Stay here in the office awhile first. Lie down on the couch. I'll take you with me when I leave. I'll put you in a hotel for a week or two, pay all the expenses, see that you're taken care of until the worst is over."

"No. I'm going home. Home."

And when he tried to hold me, I shrugged him off. And when he tried to do it again, I swerved violently, flinging his hands off.

"I'm going home. Don't stop me."

"Or come up with me for a week to my place. We live in Bronxville. I have two kids, but we'll keep them away from you—you won't hear them. You don't even have to have your meals with us."

"No," I said doggedly. "I'm going home."

"But you haven't any anymore, Cleve."

"Everyone has—someplace."

The last thing he said to me was, "You'll die, left on your own. I hate to see you die, Cleve. It seems such a waste; you loved so well and so hard!"

"Don't worry," I assured him gravely. "Don't worry about me, Steve. I have to meet someone. I'm going out tonight. I'm late for it now."

And I closed the door behind me. And he didn't try to come after me, because he knew every man must find his own peace, his own answers. There is a point beyond which no man can accompany another, without intrustion. And no man must do that. It's not allowable. That's about all we're given, our privacy.

As I went hustling down the corridor (which had become very short again now), I heard a curious sound from inside where I'd left him. It sounded like a whack. I think he must have swung his fist around, punching into some leather chair with all his might. I wondered why he'd do a thing like that, what its meaning was. But I didn't have time to figure it out.

In the second taxi, the one that took me away from there, the driver did have his radio going this time. Unlike the one coming over, the one that Sutphen had asked me about, this one was only playing music—I guess to take the edge off the traffic sounds the cabby lived in all day long.

It was burbling away there. I didn't pay much attention until suddenly I seemed to hear the words.

> *Peace and rest at length have come*
> *All the day's long toil is past*
> *And each heart is whispering 'Home,*
> *Home at last.'*

"That's right," I thought. "that's where I'm going now." I spoke to the driver. "Stop at the next flower shop you come to," I told him. "I think there's one just up ahead."

I bought some yellow roses, barely opened, just past the bud stage, and those little things that look like yellow pom-poms. He wrapped them for me like I hope he would for festive giving—first in tissue, then in smooth lustrous green, then folded flat across the top and stapled into a cone. When I came back to the cab with them, I felt like her young lover all over again.

I rang. I wanted her to come to the door. I wanted to make a big splash with the flowers, shake them out, spread them in front of her face, and say, "A guy sent these to you, lady, with his love." But she didn't come, so I put my key in it instead and went in on my own.

I didn't see her, so I knew she must be in the bathroom, doing something to her hair or things like they do. I'd often found her in there when I came home nights like this.

I called her name. "Jannie, I'm back," like that. I didn't hear her answer, but that was all right. I guess she couldn't at the moment. Maybe shampoo was running down her forehead. I knew she'd heard me, because she had the door open in there.

("How'd it go?" she asked me. I could almost hear her.)

"Arrh," I said with habitual distraction. "Same old treadmill, same old grind. Want me to fix you a drink?"

(I could almost hear her. "Not too strong, though—")

I built us two Martinis from the serving pantry and the case I'd brought from the club; we hadn't run through it yet. One tiger's milk, the other weak as tears.

First I was going to take hers in to her, but I didn't. The bathroom is no place to drink a drink or toast a toast—all that soap around.

I called out, "Let's go out tonight. Let's go out like we used to at the start. Let's go somewhere and dance and eat where they have candles on the table. Let's forget the world and all its troubles."

("What's the big occasion?" I could hear her ask.)

"Who knows how long we have?"

("That's a cheerful thought." I could detect the little make-believe shudder that went with it.)

"Stella's, over on Second. Or the Living Room. Or Copain. Or that little Italian place on Forty-eighth where they have the bottles of wine in wicker baskets hanging round the walls and the man plays "Come Prima" for you on his guitar if you ask him. You name it."

(I could see her put the tip of her finger against her upper lip, like she always does when making a choice. "All right, the little Italian place on Forty-eighth, then.")

"What dress d'you want? I'll take it out for you, save time."

("Even if I told you, you wouldn't find it.")

"Try me."

("All right. That one you like the best. The one I got at Macy's Little Shop. You know, the one that's all gleamy and dreamy.")

I found it easy and right away and took it out and off its hanger. The scent of her faint but unforgettable and unforgotten perfume came up to me from it. More like the extract of her personality than any literal blending of alcohol and attar of roses. She had never used much of it, if any.

While I was waiting for her to come out, I put on that record we'd often danced to before, back in the first days. It was a favorite of ours. It *expressed* us. It said for us what we wanted to say for ourselves, thought of, and couldn't.

Then she came out, in all her sweetness and desirability, in all her tender understanding and compassion for a guy and his poor clumsy heart. All the things we live for and dream about and die without: a man's wife and his sweetheart, his mistress and his madonna. All things in one. Woman. *The* woman. The *one* woman.

Rose-petal pink from her showering in there. Sweet and soft and just a touch of moistness still lingering here and there. The two little strips crossing her in front, the bra and the waistband, both narrow as hair ribbons, separating revealed beauty from veiled. And the terry cloth robe slung carelessly over her back, as I'd seen her come out so many times.

She infiltrated into the dress I'd been holding ready for her, and I helped her close the back of it, as I had so many times. Once, in sliding the zipper,

I'd accidentally nipped her, and she'd turned partly around and pinched the tip of my nose and playfully shook it back and forth.

We started to dance, her dress floating in my arms, fluttering, rippling, as if it were empty. First in small pivots in the very center of the room. Then expanding into larger but still compact, still tight-knit circles. Then wider all the time, wider and wider still. Wider each moment and wider each move.

I put my hand down on one shoulder, then quickly brought it up again before it even had time to touch. "I just want your voice in my ear. Just want to hear your voice in my ear. Just say my name, just say Cleve, like you used to say Cleve. Just say it once, that'll be my forever, that'll be my all-time, my eternity. I don't want God. This isn't a triangle. There's no room for outsiders in my love for you. Just say it one time more. If you can't say it whole, then say it broken. If you can't say it full, then say it whispered. Cleve."

Then, because it warms you—dancing in a stuffy room—I broke off just long enough to throw both halves of the window apart as far as they would go. It was a picture window and nearly wall-wide. The city smiled in on us from out there, friendly, seeming to understand, sharing our joy and our rapture.

Back again to the spinning rounds of the dance, its tempo slowly mounting in a whirl. The lights, the sky, the monolith in the background swung now to this side, now to that, then all the way around and back again to where they were before, like a painted cyclorama around the outside of a merry-go-round.

Then at last, when we were as far as we could get from it, and it was as far as it could get from us, from all the way back at the back of the room, we turned as one and with one accord started to run, devotedly, determinedly, yet somehow without grimness, toward it, our arms tight around one another, cheek pressed to cheek. Then at the last moment, instead of turning aside, we crossed the low sill and the ledge beyond with a spread-legged leap, a buoyant arc, that never came down again—never ever came down again.

And as the suction funneled up around us and life rushed past our heads like the pull of a tornado gone into reverse, I heard someone cry out, "Wait! Let me catch up. Wait for the boy who loves you."

And the empty music played in an empty room, to a gone love, two gone lives.

18

WE SPY

Clark Howard

BENSON, THE SUBSTITUTE letter carrier, arrived at the main post office promptly at 7:00 A.M. He went into the sorting room and waited, along with three other substitutes, to be assigned a route. Presently the assistant postmaster came out of his office and passed out the route sheets. Benson got his last.

"You'll be out in the Glen Hill district," the assistant postmaster said. "It's a lot like the Park Forest route you had last week; takes a while to get out there but it's a nice, pleasant route once you get started. Nice upper-class neighborhoods, hardly any dogs at all."

"Thank you, sir," Benson said, taking the sheet. He was always careful to be polite with the assistant postmaster; it assured him a good route on the one day that he worked each week.

"How's your college coming along?" the assistant postmaster inquired.

"Very well, sir, thank you," Benson said. "This job helps a lot. I want to thank you again for putting me on."

"Glad to do it," the older man said. "Way I look at it, a fellow trying to get an education deserves all the breaks he can get." He patted Benson on the shoulder and sent him on his way.

The bus ride to the Glen Hill substation took twenty-five minutes. Benson checked in with the route foreman and helped the letter sorter finish collating his route. By eight-fifteen he had his mail in a delivery scooter and was driving into one of the Glen Hill residential sections.

It was, as the assistant postmaster had said, a nice, pleasant route. The houses, most of which were two stories, were set well back on large lots with curved driveways and manicured lawns. An occasional gardner could be seen working, and now and again Benson passed a parked delivery truck of some kind, but for the most part there was little or no activity on block

95

after winding block as he proceeded along his route. The mailboxes, without exception, were curbside; most of them were either wrought iron on black metal poles or tooled brass on wooden posts. They all had the house number on them and, more often than not, the last name of the occupant. One could not, Benson reflected several times that morning, have asked for an easier route.

It was getting on toward eleven when he happened to see the woman taking the mail out of the Manley mailbox. He was on Heather Street, in the eighteen-hundred block; he had just finished the east side of the street, which was still in the shade, and had turned around to go back up the west side. The Manley house was second from the corner, a Mediterranean affair with a balcony all the way across the front and lots of ivy climbing each side.

Benson had reached the fourth house in his return trip up the west side of Heather and had paused to sort through the next bundle of letters, when he happened to notice the woman in his rear-view mirror. She had crossed the lawn from the corner house, which was 1800, and taken mail from the Manley box, which was 1810. Of course, Benson thought, it could be Mrs. Manley; she could be visiting the neighbor next door and just have run out to get her mail. Then again . . .

Best to call Mr. Grey, he decided. Mr. Grey could check it out easily enough. It might be nothing at all, or it might be just what Mr. Grey was looking for. Best to call him.

Benson finished the block, then drove the scooter over to the Glen Hill Center. There was a drive-in restaurant there where he could eat lunch after he made his call. He wheeled onto the apron of a filling station, pulled up next to an outdoor phone booth and dropped his dime into the slot, then dialed the number Mr. Grey had given him, the number that was a private line to Mr. Grey's office. The phone at the other end rang only once before it was answered.

"Hello? Grey speaking."

"Benson, Mr. Grey."

"Benson, yes. How are, my boy? How's everything at school?"

"Just fine, sir."

"Splendid. Well, what can I do for you, Benson?"

"I—I'm not sure I should be bothering you, Mr. Grey, but you said to call if I even *suspected*—"

"Exactly what I said, Benson, exactly. What is it?"

Benson told him about the woman coming out of 1800 and taking mail from 1810.

"Hmmm," Mr. Grey said, and Benson could almost see him rubbing his chin thoughtfully. "You're positive she didn't come out of 1810, get the mail, and then walk over to 1800?"

"Yes, sir," Benson said. "There's a hedge between the two yards; I saw her come around it on her way to the box."

"Hmmm. All right, my boy, give me that name and the street again. I'll check it out."

Benson gave him the information."

It was just before noon when Fleck, the meter-reader supervisor at the electric company, answered his phone.

"Fleck, meter reading department."

"Fleck, Grey here. How are you?"

"Oh, hello, Mr. Grey. I'm fine, just fine. What do yo need?"

"A little favor, Flack. Will you look at your records and see how long before the meter is due to be read at the residence of an Edward Manley at 1810 Heather?"

"Sure thing, Mr. Grey. You want to hang on while I check on it?"

"Yes, I'll hold, thank you."

"Fleck put the receiver down and stepped outside his office to a large records room. He walked over to a clerk at one of the desks.

"Look up the file number for Heather Street, will you please?"

The clerk opened a large directory and turned several pages. "Bottom drawer of 33, top drawer of 34," she told him.

"Thanks." He walked along the wall of file cabinets, hoping that the eighteen-hundred block would be in the top of 34. His back had been acting up lately and he didn't want to do any more bending down than necessary.

He reached cabinets 33 and 34, looked at the index on the top, and smiled. He was in luck; the card he wanted was in the top drawer of 34. Pulling the drawer all the way out, he estimated with a practiced eye where the card for 1810 would be, and his fingers, with seventeen years of training in them, flipped the row of cards apart just three away from his objective. He backed up, took out the card, and returned to his office with it.

"Mr. Grey," he said, picking up the phone again, "that meter is due to be read next Tuesday."

"Hmmm," said Grey. "I wonder if you could move that up a bit, Fleck. Say this afternoon, perhaps, right after lunch? And do it yourself?"

"Well, yeah, I guess I could. Think you might be onto something?"

"Well, I'm not certain, of course, not yet; but there's a strong possibility. Can you call me as soon as you get back?"

"Will do," said Fleck, hanging up the phone and studying the meter card for a moment. Edward Manley; he idly wondered who Edward Manley was.

At quarter of three, the phone rang in the circulation department of the daily *Courier*. Percey, the circulation manager, answered it. "Yeah?"

"Percey?"

"Yeah. That you, Mr. Grey?"

"Yes. How's everything in the world of journalism, my friend?"

Percey grunted. "Don't ask me, Mr. Grey; I don't write the garbage, I just see it gets delivered."

"Yes, of course. Listen, Percey, I'm calling about a possible subscriber named Edward Manley. I've already checked with Tedland over at the *Journal* and McKee at the *Tribune*, so you're my last hope. The man must read *something*."

"Well, if he don't belong to the other two, he must be one of ours," Percey said. "Where's he live?"

"Eighteen-ten Heather Street."

"Glen Hill, huh? Okay, hold on." Percey flipped an intercom switch. "Bring me the collection stubs for district six," he said.

A moment later an office boy brought in a wide, rectangular tub containing probably a thousand collection stubs strung on two long metal rods, and put it on a table next to Percey's desk. Percey waited until the boy left, then walked his fingers along one of the rods until he found the stub for which he was looking.

"He's ours, all right," he said into the phone to Mr. Grey. He chuckled. "This makes three in a row for me, don't it? I'll bet Tedland and McKee are turning green."

"Sounds like you boys have a side bet on this thing," Mr. Grey said lightly. "But, to business. Can you have the collector cover that area this evening?"

"Well, let's see . . ." Percey counted the days on his fingers. "Yeah, I guess. It's a little early in the month, but I can cover for that. Want me to call you when the collector gets back?"

"Please. I'll wait for your call at my office."

"Right." Percey hung up. For a moment he drummed his fingers silently on the desk top, his lips pursed in thought. Then he flipped his intercom switch again. "Send the boy back in for this tub," he said. "And have the first eight routes in district six collect tonight and bring their tallies in when they're through. And don't tell me we'll be collecting early; I *know* we'll be collecting early—but I want to beef up this week's figures a little. I'll be back after supper to go over the tallies." He flipped off the intercom switch and went back to the work he had been doing when Mr. Grey's call interrupted him.

Percey got back to the office at eight o'clock and settled down, with a cigar and the late edition, to wait for his district route collectors to come in. They were not allowed to disturb subscribers after eight-thirty, and many of them—Percey knew because he used to be a collector—quit fifteen or twenty minutes earlier than that. He guessed that the first of them would probably arrive about quarter of nine, and that all of them, including the particular one in whom he was interested, would be in by nine.

He was halfway through the sports section when his intercom buzzed. He flipped the switch. "Yeah?"

"The collectors are in, boss," his assistant said. "They're tallying now."

"Okay."

Percey left his paper open on the desk, went out to the big circulation room and walked over to one corner where the collectors were working at a long counter. In front of each of them were two metal tubs such as the one the boy had brought to his office earlier. The collectors were sorting their collection stubs into two categories, collected and uncollected, and stringing the stubs into the tubs accordingly. On each uncollected account stub the routeman had penciled a notation, citing the reason for his failure to collect.

Percey walked slowly around the counter, stopping now and again to speak to one of the men or casually finger through the stubs in the uncollected tub. One of the stubs he looked at in this manner was the one for Edward Manley at 1810 Heather Street. After looking at it, he proceeded on until he was back where he started, then walked over to the cooler for a drink of water, and unobtrusively returned to his office.

Back at his desk, Percey dialed Mr. Grey's office. Mr. Grey, as usual, answered after only one ring.

"The collector couldn't collect from that guy Manley," he told Mr. Grey. "Nobody was home. He asked when he went to collect next door and the neighbor said that Manley and his wife were out of town to attend a wedding."

"A wedding, hmmm," said Mr. Grey. "Well, that's very interesting, Percey. Yes, indeed, very interesting. As a matter of fact, I think it's interesting enough to warrant immediate action."

"Is there anything else you want me to do?" Percey inquired.

"No, I think not," said Mr. Grey. "You've been a big help, as usual, Percey. Thank you very much."

"Don't mention it, Mr. Grey."

Percey hung up and resumed reading the sports page.

Exactly one week later, they all were invited to Mr. Grey's office—Benson, the substitute carrier, Fleck, the meter-reader supervisor, and Percey, the circulation manager. They sat in a row in front of their host's desk.

"Gentlemen," Mr. Grey said, "I'm delighted to be able to report that the information furnished by the three of you culminated in one of the most successful raids ever conducted by this office."

He sat back and smiled expansively at the trio. Momentarily his gaze rested on Fleck. "As usual, my friend, your evaluation of the doors and windows at the rear of the house was flawless."

Before Fleck could thank him Mr. Grey shifted his glance to Percey. "And you, upon whose information I have come to rely so completely, continue to maintain a spotless record as an informant. Needless to say, your determination of the whereabouts of the Manleys contributed substantially to our decision to act when we did."

Now Mr. Grey turned to Benson, the substitute carrier. His expression softened proudly. "We are all aware, of course, that without the initial information brought to our attention by this young man we would not even have been aware of the Manley house's existence. It was a result of his alertness in observing Manley's mail being taken by a neighbor, and his promptness in reporting that act, that initiated the action which ultimately led to our raid. For someone who is a newcomer to our ranks, I think that his performance was highly commendable."

Fleck and Percey both nodded their agreement, and Fleck reached over to hit Benson good-naturedly on the arm. "Nice going, kid," he said, and Benson blushed appropriately.

"Now," said Mr. Grey, "to business. As I said, it was a very successful raid; very successful, indeed." He opened a notebook and began to read aloud. "Aside from the jewelry and silverware, not to mention the cash in the wall safe, there were two portable color TV sets, three oil paintings of considerable value, about six thousand dollars in furs . . ."

The substitute carrier, the meter-reader supervisor, and the circulation manager all sat back and smiled as Mr. Grey's businesslike voice continued reciting the inventory before him.

19

THE LEOPARD MAN'S STORY

Jack London

HE HAD A dreamy, faraway look in his eyes, and his sad, insistent voice, gentle-spoken as a maid's, seemed the placid embodiment of some deep-seated melancholy. He was the Leopard Man, but he did not look it. His business in life, whereby he lived, was to appear in a cage of performing leopards before vast audiences, and to thrill those audiences by certain exhibitions of nerve for which his employers rewarded him on a scale commensurate with the thrills he produced.

As I say, he did not look it. He was narrow-hipped, narrow-shouldered, and anemic, while he seemed not so much oppressed by gloom as by a sweet and gentle sadness, the weight of which was as sweetly and gently borne. For an hour I had been trying to get a story out of him, but he appeared to lack imagination. To him there was no romance in his gorgeous career, no deeds of daring, no thrills—nothing but a gray sameness and infinite boredom.

Lions? Oh, yes! he had fought with them. It was nothing. All you had to do was to stay sober. Anybody could whip a lion to a standstill with an ordinary stick. He had fought one for half an hour once. Just hit him on the nose every time he rushed, and when he got artful and rushed with his head down, why, the thing to do was to stick out your leg. When he grabbed at the leg you drew it back and hit him on the nose again. That was all.

With the faraway look in his eyes and his soft flow of words he showed me his scars. There were many of them, and one recent one where a tigress had reached for his shoulder and gone down to the bone. I could see the neatly mended rents in the coat he had on. His right arm, from the elbow down, looked as though it had gone through a threshing machine, such was the ravage wrought by claws and fangs. But it was nothing, he said, only the old wounds bothered him somewhat when rainy weather came on.

Suddenly his face brightened with a recollection, for he was really as anxious to give me a story as I was to get it.

"I suppose you've heard of the lion tamer who was hated by another man?" he asked.

He paused and looked pensively at a sick lion in the cage opposite.

"Got the toothache," he explained. "Well, the lion tamer's big play to the audience was putting his head in a lion's mouth. The man who hated him attended every performance in the hope sometime of seeing that lion crunch down. He followed the circus about all over the country. The years went by and he grew old. And at last one day, sitting in a front seat, he saw what he had waited for. The lion crunched down, and there wasn't any need to call a doctor."

The Leopard Man glanced casually over his fingernails in a manner which would have been critical had it not been so sad.

"Now, that's what I call patience," he continued, "and it's my style. But it was not the style of a fellow I knew. He was a little, thin, sawed-off, sword-swallowing and juggling Frenchman. De Ville, he called himself, and he had a nice wife. She did trapeze work and used to dive from under the roof into a net, turning over once on the way as nice as you please.

"De Ville had a quick temper, as quick as his hand, and his hand was as quick as the paw of a tiger. One day, because the ringmaster called him a frog eater, or something like that and maybe a little worse, he shoved him against the soft pine background he used in his knife-throwing act, so quick the ringmaster didn't have time to think, and there, before the audience, de Ville kept the air on fire with his knives, sinking them into the wood all around the ringmaster so close that they passed through his clothes and most of them bit into his skin.

"The clowns had to pull the knives out to get him loose, for he was pinned fast. So the word went around to watch out for de Ville, and no one dared be more than barely civil to his wife. And she was a sly bit of baggage, too, only all hands were afraid of de Ville.

"But there was one man, Wallace, who was afraid of nothing. He was the lion tamer, and he had the selfsame trick of putting his head into the lion's mouth. He'd put it into the mouths of any of them, though he preferred Augustus, a big, good-natured beast who could always be depended upon.

"As I was saying, Wallace—'King' Wallace we called him—was afraid of nothing alive or dead. He was a king and no mistake. I've seen him drunk, and on a wager go into the cage of a lion that had turned nasty, and without a stick beat him to a finish. Just did it with his fist on the nose.

"Madame de Ville—"

At an uproar behind us the Leopard Man turned quietly around. It was a divided cage, and a monkey, poking through the bars and around the partition, had had its paw seized by a big gray wolf that was trying to pull off the paw by main strength. The arm seemed stretching out longer and longer like a thick elastic, and the unfortunate monkey's mates were raising a terrible din. No keeper was at hand, so the Leopard Man stepped over a couple of paces, dealt the wolf a sharp blow on the nose with the light cane he carried, and returned with a sadly apologetic smile to take up his unfinished sentence as though there had been no interruption.

"—looked at King Wallace and King Wallace looked at her, while de Ville looked black. We warned Wallace, but it was no use. He laughed at us, as he laughed at de Ville one day when he shoved de Ville's head into a bucket of paste because he wanted to fight.

"De Ville was in a pretty mess—I helped to scrape him off; but he was cool as a cucumber and made no threats at all. But I saw a glitter in his eyes which I had seen often in the eyes of wild beasts, and I went out of my way to give Wallace a final warning. He laughed, but he did not look so much in Madame de Ville's direction after that.

"Several months passed by. Nothing had happened and I was beginning to think it was a scare over nothing. We were West by that time, showing in 'Frisco. It was during the afternoon performance, and the big tent was filled with women and children, when I went looking for Red Denny, the head canvasman, who had walked off with my pocketknife.

"Passing by one of the dressing tents I glanced in through a hole in the canvas to see if I could locate him. He wasn't there, but directly in front of me was King Wallace, in tights, waiting for his turn to go on with his cage of performing lions. He was watching with much amusement a quarrel between a couple of trapeze artists. All the rest of the people in the dressing tent were watching the same thing, with the exception of de Ville, whom I noticed staring at Wallace with undisguised hatred. Wallace and the rest were all too busy following the quarrel to notice this or what followed.

"But I saw it through the hole in the canvas. De Ville drew his handkerchief from his pocket, made as though to mop the sweat from his face with it—it was a hot day—and at the same time walked past Wallace's back. He never stopped, but with a flirt of the handkerchief kept right on to the doorway, where he turned his head, while passing out, and shot a swift look back. The look troubled me at the time, for not only did I see hatred in it, but I saw triumph as well.

" 'De Ville will bear watching,' I said to myself, and I really breathed easier when I saw him go out the entrance to the circus grounds and board an electric car for downtown. A few minutes later I was in the big tent, where I had overhauled Red Denny. King Wallace was doing his turn and holding the audience spellbound. He was in a particularly vicious mood, and he kept the lions stirred up till they were all snarling—that is, all of them except old Augustus, and he was just too fat and lazy and old to get stirred up over anything.

"Finally Wallace cracked the old lion's knees with his whip and got him into position. Old Augustus, blinking good-naturedly, opened his mouth and in popped Wallace's head. Then the jaws came together, *crunch,* just like that."

The Leopard Man smiled in a sweetly wistful fashion, and the faraway look came into his eyes.

"And that was the end of King Wallace," he went on in his sad, low voice. "After the excitement cooled down I watched my chance and bent over and smelled Wallace's head. Then I sneezed."

"It . . . it was . . . ?" I queried with halting eagerness.

"Snuff—that de Ville dropped on his hair in the dressing tent. Old Augustus never meant to do it. He only sneezed."

20

THE LITTLE THINGS

Isaac Asimov

MRS. CLARA BERNSTEIN was somewhat past fifty and the temperature outside was somewhat past ninety. The air conditioning was working, but though it removed the fact of heat it didn't remove the *idea* of heat.

Mrs. Hester Gold, who was visiting the 21st floor from her own place in 4-G, said, "It's cooler down on my floor." She was over fifty, too, and had blond hair that didn't remove a single year from her age.

Clara said, "It's the little things, really. I can stand the head. It's the dripping I can't stand. Don't you hear it?"

"No," said Hester, "But I know what you mean. My boy, Joe, has a button off his blazer. Seventy-two dollars, and without the button it's nothing. A fancy brass button on the sleeve and he doesn't have it to sew back on."

"So what's the problem? Take one off the other sleeve also."

"Not the same. The blazer just won't look good. If a button is loose, don't wait, get it sewed. Twenty-two years old and he still doesn't understand. He goes off, he doesn't tell me when he'll be back—"

Clara said impatiently. "Listen. How can you say you don't hear the dripping? Come with me to the bathroom. If I tell you it's dripping, it's dripping."

Hester followed and assumed an attitude of listening. In the silence it could be heard—drip—drip—drip—

Clara said, "Like water torture. You hear it all night. Three nights now."

Hester adjusted her large faintly tinted glasses, as though that would make her hear better, and cocked her head. She said, "Probably the shower dripping upstairs, in 22-G. It's Mrs. Maclaren's place. I know her. Listen, she's a good-hearted person. Knock on her door and tell her. She won't bite your head off."

105

Clara said, "I'm not afraid of her. I banged on her door five times already. No one answers. I phoned her. No one answers."

"So she's away," said Hester. "It's summertime. People go away."

"And if she's away for the whole summer, do I have to listen to the dripping a whole summer?"

"Tell the super."

"That idiot. He doesn't have the key to her special lock and he won't break in for a drip. Besides, she's not away. I know her automobile and it's downstairs in the garage right now."

Hester said uneasily: "She could go away in someone else's car."

Clara sniffed. "That I'm sure of. *Mrs*. Maclaren."

Hester frowned. "So she's divorced. It's not so terrible. And she's still maybe thirty—thirty-five—and she dresses fancy. Also not so terrible."

"If you want my opinion, Hester," said Clara, "what she's doing up there I wouldn't like to say. I hear things."

"What do you hear?"

"Footsteps. Sounds. Listen, she's right above and I know where her bedroom is."

Hester said tartly, "Don't be so old-fashioned. What she does is her business."

"All right. But she uses the bathroom a lot, so why does she leave it dripping? I wish she *would* answer the door. I'll bet anything she's got a décor in her apartment like a French I-don't-know-what."

"You're wrong, if you want to know. You're plain wrong. She's got regular furniture and lots of houseplants."

"And how do you know that?"

Hester looked uncomfortable. "I water the plants when she's not home. She's a single woman. She goes on trips, so I help her out."

"Oh? Then you would *know* if she was out of town. Did she tell you she'd be out of town?"

"No, she didn't."

Clara leaned back and folded her arms. "And you have the keys to her place then?"

Hester said, "Yes, but I can't just go in."

"Why not? She could be away. So you have to water her plants."

"She didn't tell me to."

Clara said, "For all you know she's sick in bed and can't answer the door."

"She'd have to be pretty sick not to use the phone when it's right near the bed."

"Maybe she had a heart attack. Listen, maybe she's dead and that's why she doesn't shut off the drip."

"She's a young woman. She wouldn't have a heart attack."

"You can't be sure. With the life she lives—maybe a boyfriend killed her. We've *got* to go in."

"That's breaking and entering," said Hester.

"With a *key*? If she's away you can't leave the plants to die. You water them and I'll shut off the drip. What harm?—And if she's dead, do you want her to lay there till who knows when?"

"She's not dead," said Hester, but she went downstairs to the fourth floor for Mrs. Maclaren's keys.

"No one in the hall," whispered Clara. "Anyone could break in any-were anytime."

"Sh," whispered Hester. "What if she's inside and says 'Who's there'?"

"So say you came to water the plants and I'll ask her to shut off the drip."

The key to one lock and then the key to the other turned smoothly and with only the tiniest click at the end. Hester took a deep breath and opened the door a crack. She knocked.

"There's no answer," whispered Clara impatiently. She pushed the door wide open. "The air conditioner isn't even on. It's legitimate. You want to water the plants."

The door closed behind them. Clara said. "It smells stuffy, in here. Feels like a damp oven."

They walked softly down the corridor. Empty utility room on the right, empty bathroom—

Clara looked in. "No drip. It's in the master bedroom."

At the end of the corridor there was the living room on the left, with its plants.

"They need water," said Clara. "I'll go into the master bath—" She opened the bedroom door and stopped. No motion. No sound. Her mouth opened wide.

Hester was at her side. The smell was stifling. "What—"

"Oh, my God," said Clara, but without breath to scream.

The bed coverings were in total disarray. Mrs. Maclaren's head lolled off the bed, her long brown hair brushing the floor, her neck bruised, one arm dangling on the floor, hand open, palm up.

"The police," said Clara. "We've got to call the police."

Hester, gasping, moved forward.
"You mustn't touch anything," said Clara.
The glint of brass in the open hand—
Hester had found her son's missing button.

21

THE REINDEER CLUE

Ellery Queen

"ELLERY!" INSPECTOR QUEEN shouted over the heads of the waiting children. "Over here!"

Ellery managed to work his way through the crowd to the entrance of the Children's Zoo. The weather was unusually warm for two days before Christmas and the children didn't mind waiting.

If the presence of a half-dozen police cars stirred any curiosity, it was not enough for anyone to question Ellery as he edged his way forward.

"What is it, dad?" he asked, as the Inspector closed the wooden gate behind him.

"Murder, Ellery. And unless we can wind it up fast there are going to be a lot of disappointed kids out there."

"Are they waiting for Santa Claus?" Ellery asked with a grin.

"The next best thing—Santa's reindeer. It's a Christmas tradition here to deck the place with tinsel and toys and pass one of the reindeer off as Rudolph."

Ellery could see the police technicians working over the body of a man sprawled inside the fence of the reindeer pen. Off to one side a white-coated man kept a firm grip on the reindeer itself as the police flashbulbs popped. Another white-coated man and a woman were standing nearby.

"Who's the dead man?" Ellery asked. "Anyone I know?"

"Matter of fact, yes. It's Casey Sturgess, the ex-columnist."

"You've got to be kidding," Ellery exclaimed. "Sturgess murdered in a children's zoo?"

The old man shrugged. "Looks like he was up to his old tricks." Sturgess had been the gossip columnist on a now defunct New York tabloid.

When the paper folded he'd continued with his gossipy trade, selling information in a manner that often approached blackmail.

Ellery glanced toward the woman and two men. "Blackmailing one of these?"

"Why else would he come here at eight in the morning except to meet one of them? Come on—I'll introduce you."

The woman was Dr. Ella Manners, staff veterinarian. She wore straight blond hair and no makeup. "This is a terrible thing, simply terrible!" she cried out. "We've got a hundred children and their mothers out there waiting to see the reindeer. Can't you get this body out of here?"

"We're working as fast as we can," Inspector Queen assured her, motioning Ellery toward the two men.

One, who walked with a noticeable limp, was the zoo's director, Bernard White. The other man, younger than White and grossly overweight, was Mike Halley—"Captain Mike to the kids," he explained. "I'm the animal handler, except today it's more of a people handler.

"Our reindeer is tame, but it's still a big animal. We don't let the kids get too close to it."

The Inspector motioned toward the body. "Any of you know the dead man?"

"No, sir," Bernard White answered for the others. "We didn't know him and we have no idea how he got in here with the reindeer. We found him when we arrived just after eight o'clock."

"You all arrived at once?" Ellery asked him.

"I was just getting out of my car when Captain Mike drove up. Ella followed right behind him."

"Anyone else work here?"

"We have a night crew to clean up, but in the morning there's only the three of us."

Ellery nodded. "So one of you could have met Casey Sturgess here earlier, killed him, and then driven around the park till you saw the others coming."

"Why would one of us kill him?" Ella Manners asked. "We didn't even know him."

"Sturgess had sunk to some third-rate blackmailing lately. You all work for the city in a job that puts you in contact with children. The least hint of drugs or a morals charge would have been eough to lose you your jobs. Right, dad?"

Inspector Queen nodded. "Damn right! Sturgess was shot in the chest with a .22 automatic. We found the weapon over in the straw. One of you met him here to pay blackmail, but shot him instead. It has to be one of you—he wouldn't possibly have come into the reindeer pen before the place opened to meet anybody else."

Ellery motioned his father aside. "Any fingerprints on the gun, dad?"

"It was wiped clean, Ellery. But the victim did manage to leave us something—a dying message of sorts."

Ellery's face lit up. "What, dad?"

"Come over here by the body."

Ellery passed a bucket that held red-and-green giveaway buttons inscribed, "I saw Santa's Reindeer!" He ducked his head under a hanging fringe of holly and joined his father by the body. For the first time he noticed that the rear fence of the reindeer pen was decorated with seven weathered wooden placards, each carrying eight lines of Clement Clarke Moore's famous poem, "A Visit from St. Nicholas."

Casey Sturgess had died under the third placard, his arm outstretched toward it. He could only have lived a minute or so with that wound," the old man said. "But look at the blood on his right forefinger. He used it to mark the sign."

Ellery leaned closer, examining two lines of the Moore poem. *Now, Dasher! now, Dancer! now, Prancer and Vixen! | On, Comet! on, Cupid! on, Donder and Blitzen!*

"Dad—he smeared each of the eight reindeer's names with a dab of blood!"

"Right, Ellery. Now you tell me what it means."

Ellery remained stooped, studying the defaced poem for some minutes. All the smears were similar.

None seemed to have been given more emphasis than any other. Finally he straightened up and walked over to the reindeer that was drinking water from its trough, oblivious of the commotion.

"What's its name?" he asked the overweight Captain Mike.

"Sparky—but for Christmas we call him Rudolph. The kids like it."

Ellery put out a gentle hand and touched the ungainly animal's oversized antlers, wishing that it could speak and tell him what it had seen in the pen.

But it was as silent as the llama and donkey and cow that he could see standing in the adjoining pens.

"How much longer is this going on?" White was demanding from the Inspector.

"As long as it takes. We've got a murder on our hands, Mr. White."

He turned his back on the zoo director and looked at his son. "What do you make of it, Ellery?"

"Not much. Found anyone who heard the shot?"

Ellery went back for one more look at the bloody marks on the Moore poem.

Then he asked Ella Manners. "Would you by any chance be a particularly good dancer, Doctor?"

"Hardly! Veterinary medicine and dancing don't mix."

"I thought not," Ellery said, suddenly pleased.

"You got something?" his father asked.

"Yes, dad. I know who murdered Casey Sturgess."

Sparky the reindeer looked up from its trough, as if listening to Ellery's words. "You see, dad, there's always a danger with dying messages—a danger that the killer will see his victim leave the message, or return and find it later. Premeditated murderers like to make certain they've finished the job without leaving a clue. You told me Sturgess could only have lived a minute or so with that wound."

"That's right, Ellery."

"Then the killer was probably still here to see him jab that sign with his blood finger. And are we to believe that in a minute's time the dying Sturgess managed to smear all eight names with his blood, and each in the same way? No, dad—Sturgess only marked *one* name! The killer, unable to wipe the blood off without leaving a mark, smeared the other seven names himself in the same manner. He obliterated the dying man's message by adding to it!"

"But, Ellery—which reindeer's name did Sturgess mark?"

"Dad, it had to be one that would connect instantly with his killer. Now look at those eight names. Could it have been Donder or Blitzen? Hardly—they tell us nothing. Likewise Dasher and Prancer have no connection with any of the suspects. Dr. Manners might be a Vixen and White could be a Cupid, but Sturgess couldn't expect the police to spot such a nebulous thing. No, dad, the reindeer clue had to be something so obvious the killer was forced to alter it."

"That's why you asked Dr. Manners if she was a dancer!"

"Exactly. It's doubtful that the limping Bernard White or the overweight Captain Mike are notable as dancers, and once I ruled Dr. Manners out as well, that left only one name on the list."

"Comet!"

"Yes, dad. The most famous reindeer of all might be Rudolph, but the most famous comet of all is surely Halley's Comet."

"Captain Mike Halley! Somebody grab him!"

112

Moments later as the struggling Halley was being led away, Bernard White said, "But he was our only handler! We're ready to open the gates and who's going to look after the children?"

Ellery glanced at his father and smiled broadly. "Maybe I can help out. After all, it's Christmas," he said.

22

TOP MAN

Jonathan Craig

I HADN'T BELIEVED it the first time I heard it, and I still didn't believe it. But the boys kept saying it—that is, the boys up in the States kept saying it, and the boys down here in Rio kept repeating it—and I was beginning to wonder if there just might be something to it after all. A lot of wild things were happening in the States these days, and some of the old-timers were saying that it reminded them of the way it was back in Chicago when Big Al was going so good.

Capone was long before my time, of course; I'd come into the outfit after the machine-gun days and the one-way rides. In fact, I'd come in as a bookkeeper in a numbers shop. I'd had almost two years at Hanley Miller High School—which is why they call me the Scholar—and if I'd kept my nose a little cleaner I'd still be up there where the action is, instead of down here with the rest of the expatriates, as they say.

There are a lot of us here in Rio, you know, and very few of us by choice. Not that we don't like Brazil; it's just that of all the good things about it the best is that it's a long way from the cops and the courts in the good old United States. A thing like that can be very important to certain people. You might even say it can make the difference between life and death.

But about this business I started to talk about, these rumors and hints we'd been getting from the States. It didn't seem possible, but what the boys up there were saying was that Benny the Booze was now the Top Man.

And that didn't make any sense at all, because Benny the Booze was too hard in the muscle and too soft in the head, and he didn't have any more moxie and boss-man ability than a high-class ape. But still, that's what they were saying, in the phone calls between here and there. And what's more, they were saying it like Benny's becoming Top Man was the funniest thing that had happened in the outfit since Arson Eddie burned himself up instead of the warehouse he was supposed to put the torch to for Fader Jake. That's all we had to go on—the phone calls. Nobody in the outfit writes letters, of course, because the Feds have a way of reading them first.

So there were all those rumors and hints on the phone, with the boys in the States pretty much amused by it, but nobody down here knew any of the details and it was driving us all right out of our skulls. We all get together once a week you see, in a private dining room at this hotel on Copacabana Beach, which we've pretty much made into an exile's club, as they say, and we maybe lift a few and cut up old times and try to keep up on what the boys in the States are doing these days.

But this thing about Benny the Booze now being Top Man of the outfit really had us going. The last any of us had heard, Tony Rock was Top Man, just like he'd been for the last dozen or so years. They didn't come any tougher or smarter than Tony, and how a wet-brain like Benny the Booze could have taken over from Tony Rock was more than any of us could figure.

And then there were, like they say, the lieutenants, the guy next in line after Tony. Rough boys like Fat Felix and Angie Aces and Kay-Cee Matcher and Little Vincent. To be Top Man, Benny the Booze would have had to knock off not only Tony Rock but Fat Felix and the three others as well. But the boys in the States said it, and kept saying it: Benny the Booze was the Top Man.

So when we heard that Country Boy was going to be in Rio that Friday night, and that he was going to join us at our little weekly get-together at the hotel, we all made the scene, and we made it early. Country Boy was the first one to come in from the States since the rumors had started, and if anybody would know the real straight dope, he was the one. Like I say, we were all there: Johnny the Knock and Fig Lip and Millie from Milwaukee and Charley One and Charley Two and Preacher and Seldom Seen and the Indian and all the rest.

Country Boy was a little late getting there, and when he finally did show he looked like he might have stopped off at a few places along the way to see whether his elbow action was still in good working order. That meant he was taking a vacation, because when he's working, Country Boy doesn't drink at all. He's a real pro, one of the best hit men in the business—some say *the* best. He'd been a top torpedo before I was born, and a legend in his time, as they say. He wasn't really *in* the outfit, though; he was a free-lance, and always had been; but since he was such a good man, and a big favorite with Tony Rock, he worked mostly for the outfit.

He looked just like he had the first time I'd ever seen him, and I was pretty sure he was still wearing the same suit he'd been wearing then, and maybe even the same tie. He always wore old-fashioned double-breasted suits with wide stripes and wide lapels and flowery neckties about as wide as your hand with big splashy flowers on them. He had a long skinny face, and when he laughed he opened his mouth about as wide as it would go, without making a sound, so that every time he laughed half of his face disappeared.

He didn't look like much, but he was the best. And he never carried a gun. He was an icepick man, and an artist in every sense of the word.

He would stand in a crowded elevator, put his icepick just beneath the base of a mark's skull, and walk out at the next floor, with everybody thinking the guy had dropped dead of a heart attack. And he had a way of following marks into movie houses and taking the seat just behind them. When the action on the screen got interesting enough, he'd sort of lean forward a little, and even the people sitting on each side of the mark never suspected that he has suddenly lost all interest in the movie and everything else, permanently.

Like I say, Country Boy was a real artist, and it was no wonder he'd stood so high with Tony Rock, the Top Man—unless the rumors about Benny the Booze being the *new* Top Man were true after all.

Well, Country Boy must have been clued in by somebody that we were all pretty hot to know the score, but he just sat there at the guest of honor's place at the table, squinching up his little eyes behind those gold-rimmed cheaters of his and telling us all how good we looked and how nice it was to see us again. He had a lot of news for us, all right, and he didn't stop talking for a second. But not one word about Benny the Booze being the new Top Man.

He must have run on that way about half an hour, with everybody getting more irritated and frustrated every second, and some of the looks he was getting, especially from Millie from Milwaukee, would've knocked most guys right out of their chair.

Finally Millie from Milwaukee couldn't stand it any longer. She sort of eased herself about halfway up out of her chair—which wasn't easy for her, since she hits the Fairbanks at about 340—and gave Country Boy a hard focus and said, "All right, Country. You've got your kicks by now, so give with the news on Benny the Booze. Is he, or isn't he, the Top Man?"

Country Boy looked at her for a while, and then he took off his cheaters and wiped them on that big flowery tie of his, and put the specs back on and looked at her some more.

"It's a fact," he said, slow and solemn. "Benny the Booze is the Top Man."

Everybody around the table made some kind of noise—grunts and gasps and so on—to show they could hardly believe it. Hell, who *could* believe it?

"What happened to Tony Rock?" Charley One asked. "How come *he* isn't still the Top Man?"

"Good old Tony," Country Boy said shaking his head sadly. "A wonderful guy. A sweet, wonderful guy. One of the grandest men I ever knew."

"Yeah, but what about Benny the Booze?" Charley Two said. "Talk it up, Country. What do you want to keep us hung up like this for?"

"It's a real sad story," Country Boy said. "There was even some violence connected with it. Quite a bit, in fact." He paused. "I guess you all know how much Benny the Booze *wanted* to be Top Man."

Everybody around the table made sounds to show they knew.

"Well," Country Boy said, "Benny figured there were five boys between him and the Top Man job—Kay-Cee Matcher, Little Vincent, Angie Aces, Fat Felix, and the Top Man himself, Tony Rock. So he looked around for somebody to help him eliminate them, so he could be Top Man himself."

"*All* of them?" Fig Lip asked, amazed.

"Every one," Country Boy said. "And he was lucky, because he was able to hire the best hit man in the business to help him out." He smiled modestly. "When I say the best hit man, I know I don't have to name any names for you to know who I mean. Right?"

We all made sounds to let him know we knew who the best hit man was.

"I *understand* the price for the entire contract was fifty G's," Country Boy said. "Cash in advance. People in a position to know tell me that's a record. But there were a couple of riders. First, all those boys had to be hit the same night. Second, Benny the Booze had to see for sure they'd been hit; he had to inspect them, one by one, as they arrived."

Country Boy paused, frowning. "And there was one more thing—something this hit man figured was beneath his dignity. And that thing was that Benny the Booze insisted the hit man dig a grave deep enough for all the boys, *and dig it himself.* You can imagine how the hit man felt about *that.*"

He looked around the table for the sympathy and understanding he knew was coming to him, and we all looked back at him the way we were supposed to. What a thing! Asking an artist like Country Boy to dig a hole in the ground!

"But as I was saying," Country Boy went on, "the price was right—it was a record contract for one night's work. And so this hit man did it. He dug a grave deep enough for all five of 'em. Oh, sure, he hated himself for it, but he did it. And then he made a few arrangements and supplied himself with a few choice icepicks from a collection of such items which he seems to keep, and got out his old battered last year's Cadillac and went to work. He was a man of his word. He'd made a contract with Benny the Booze to help Benny be Top Man, and that was exactly what he was going to do."

"All in one night?" the Indian asked, not doing too good a job of keeping the astonishment out of his voice. "All in *one night,* Country?"

Country Boy laughed that wide open-mouthed laugh that made half of his face disappear.

"Naturally," he said. "This hit man wasn't only the best, he was the fastest too. First he went calling on Kay-Cee Matcher. About an hour later there's old Kay-Cee, with no more problems, face down in the bottom of that fine new grave."

"And so where was Benny the Booze all this time?" Seldom Seen wanted to know.

"Parked behind some trees about fifty feet away." Country Boy said. "After this hit man heaved Kay-Cee in the grave, here came Benny on the double and shined a flashlight down in the hole to see for sure it's Kay-Cee, and then beat it back to his car again. Didn't say a word."

"All right for Kay-Cee," Millie from Milwaukee said. "Who was next?"

"This hit man was sort of working his way up the chain of command," Country Boy said. "He wasn't only good and fast but . . . ." He broke off and looked down the table at me and raised an eyebrow questioningly.

"Methodical," I said.

"Right," Country Boy said, smiling. "Methodical. Thank you, Scholar."

I was pleased, of course. It was one of those little things that you can look back on in later life, after you're past 40.

"The next man up," Country Boy began, and then laughed. "Or maybe I'd better say the next man *down,* was Little Vincent. Right in the ground, no trouble at all. And Benny the Booze races back and forth with his flashlight, making sure this hit man isn't throwing in any ringers on him."

"And next?" Preacher asked.

"Angie Aces," Country Boy said. "Angie gave this hit man a little trouble. He was kind of hard to find, and even harder to get into the car; but it all worked out fine, and pretty soon Angie was down in there with the rest of them. And of course Benny the Booze makes his two-way sprint with his flashlight, just to make sure it's really Angie.''

''That's three,'' Millie from Milwaukee counted.

''Number four was Fat Felix,'' Country Boy said. ''And they never called that boy Fat Felix for nothing, believe me. Getting old Felix in that hole was more work than all the others put together.''

''And that left only the Top Man himself,'' Johnny the Knock said, awed. ''Tony Rock.''

Country Boy let out a long sigh. ''Ah, yes,'' he said. ''Tony Rock. One of the sweetest guys that ever lived.''

There was a long silence all the way around the table. You know the kind of silence I mean; it's the kind that's loud enough to break your eardrums. I don't know how the others felt; me, I felt like I'd been hit with a sledge hammer. Tony Rock! The toughest, brainiest boy that had ever taken over the outfit. It left me feeling numb all over.

Country Boy sighed again. ''But a contract is a contract, and I'm a man of my word, as is well known. Am I right?''

Some of us nodded, but nobody said anything. He was right. A contract is a contract, and when you make one you keep it.

''Anyhow,'' Country Boy said, ''as soon as Fat Felix was in the hole, here comes Benny the Booze out of the trees again and shines his flashlight down on Felix's face and grunts and says, 'Four down and one to go, and then I'll be Top Man,' and then this hit man says, 'Right,' and puts his icepick into Benny where he figures it'll do the most good.''

Nobody said anything; I don't think anybody *could* have.

Country Boy looked around the table. ''Like I told you,'' he said, ''this hit man had made a few arrangements before he started out—like calling Tony Rock for an okay on what he was going to do.'' He paused, and I could see that crazy silent laugh of his beginning to build itself up again.

''And so that's how Benny the Booze got to be Top Man,'' he said. ''The last boy to go in that hole, right on top of all the other boys stacked up in it was Benny. This hit man had told him he'd make him Top Man, and he had—Top Man in the grave.''

23

CREATURE OF HABIT

William Campbell Gault

WITHOUT THE FRIDAY nights he might have gone on and on. He had his own world, after office hours, his printed world, and adversity troubled him very little.

But always on Friday nights Bertha would be waiting in front of Bloom's, her two hundred and seventeen pounds outlined by the white store behind her. She'd be smiling. She was always smiling.

What the hell was so funny?

Two hundred and seventeen pounds, an even hundred more than Fred weighed, and her hand would be out and he'd put the week's wages in that, and she'd shove it into her tiny purse.

When they were first married Bertha had been young, shapely and romantic. Now she was still romantic and the Friday evenings were a must. In the interests of peace. Not that she'd scream, but she'd pout. A two-hundred-and-seventeen-pound pout is a horrible sight, and Fred avoided it by meeting her in front of Bloom's at 5:08 each Friday evening.

At the long counter in Bloom's Bertha would have a Double Banana Royale. Fred would have a sandwich and coffee.

Then the movie. Very few movies interested Fred; none failed to enchant Bertha. She held his hand all through the double feature. He loathed its damp capaciousness; he loathed Bertha.

One hundred and seventeen pounds and two hundred and seventeen pounds. People would turn as they walked by, would smile at them. Fred was sensitive, being the lighter one. Bertha? Who knows?

The street is so busy in front of Bloom's. There are so many people. Some are men, tall and superior. Some are women, beautiful and young. Smiling at Fred and Bertha.

121

One of Fred's favorite writers was the minor-league philosopher, Ramsay Elleson. In one of the thin books Ramsay published—infrequently and at his own expense—Ramsay got going on Hell.

Eternity, itself, Ramsay claimed, was Hell, though it would be a personal matter. For the author, Hell would be an eternal seat at an eternal football game, Ramsay being an intellectual (self-proclaimed). For football fans Hell would be an eternity in the library of Ramsay Elleson. And so on.

Fred gave the matter some thought and his personal view of Hell would be an eternity with Bertha. Eternity is only a word; he'd actually gone through most of it already. Twenty-two years of Friday nights. Twenty-two years of the Hollywood product for a man who could enjoy the profundity of Ramsay Elleson.

Only a little less than twenty-two years of—avoirdupois.

Eternity can end. It can be brought violently to a stop. With determination and fortitude and something heavy to swing, a man can establish a better destiny than an eternity with Bertha.

Fred had this thought on a Wednesday night, while working out a cryptogram. He looked over at Bertha, monumental and placid under a reading lamp, and waited for the thought to go away.

The thought didn't go away.

He slept with it. He carried it, along with his lunch, to work the next day. The figures in his ledgers seemed to dance and form strange shapes, leering at him. He left early, his head aching.

At home, Bertha said, "Honey, you're sick. . . ."

"What makes you think I'm sick. . . ."

"You're home early. And you look sick, Honey."

"I'm not sick. I'm just a little tired. I didn't sleep very well last night." He rubbed the back of his neck with a trembling hand. "I'm going down to look at the furnace."

It was July.

She stared at him.

He said irritably, "Well, I can look at it, can't I? Damn it!"

She said soothingly, "Of course you can. I'll make some tea. I'll have it ready for you."

The floor in the cellar was dirt. It was a cheap house. He paid more rent for it than it was worth. But the floor was dirt, which suited his present purpose.

After a little while, she called, "Honey, the tea is ready."

He didn't answer.

"Fred?"

He didn't answer.

"Fred—answer me!"

He didn't answer, and she started down the stairs. . . .

It was a restless, fretful night. Well, it was done; nothing could change that. He'd grown weary, digging, and had covered her very skimpily. But he could finish that tonight. He could use the time they usually wasted in the movie.

He ate his breakfast at a coffee shop near the office. He spent the day rereading meaningless figures. Ahead of him stretched a Berthaless Elysium; to hell with figures, today.

Then, around five, one figure jumped to the front of his consciousness and burned a hole in his brain. It was the figure on his desk calendar.

Today was the 21st of July.

Today was the day the gas man read the meter in the cellar, using the duplicate key Bertha thoughtfully left for him under the rear-door mat.

Fred stood up, his stomach filled with flying birds. He stood up and saw the men talking to Mr. Pritchard at the front of the office. One was obviously a detective. The other was a blue-uniformed patrolman.

Mr. Pritchard was indicating Fred now, and both officers started his way. Their faces were grave, watchful and ominous.

Fred didn't wait for his hat. There was a door at the rear, and old wooden steps going down to the alley. Fred bolted.

He saw the startled faces of the other employees and heard the shouted, "Stop, in the name of the law! Stop that man!"

Now Fred was through the door and going down the steps. From the head of the steps, as he was halfway down, he heard the "Stop!" again. He heard the single deafening shot.

One shot—that missed. He was in the alley, running. He came out of the alley on Eighth and turned north. He was still running, and no more commands reached his ears.

Eight to Grand and down Grand.

And then, suddenly, he stopped without the command. Stopped to stare, stopped to realize that single shot *hadn't* missed.

For there, outlined against the front of Bloom's, Bertha was waiting. Smiling, holding her purse, but her hand wasn't out for his wages.

What need was there for money—where they were?

24

WEEDS

Charlene Weir

EMMA TRASK QUIETLY closed her kitchen door and stepped out into the frail light of dawn. She glanced anxiously at the brick house next door. Nothing stirred. Curtains covered the windows.

"Please, please," Emma whispered, "let Mattie still be asleep." She bolted past the open space between the two houses and into the shelter of her garden. She knelt in the soil and viciously yanked the weeds threatening the tiny pansies. Such pretty little faces the pansies had. She caressed one with a fingertip.

Mattie's like a weed, Emma thought with sudden insight. Steadily infiltrating and spreading.

Raising her head, Emma looked back at her little house. The early morning sun brushed the white wood with a delicate rosy hue. Emma caught her breath in a sob. The house had seemed so perfect when she first saw it. A perfect little pearl. But it was the garden—oh, the lovely garden—that captured her heart. All her life Emma had yearned for just such a garden. It seemed to cry out to her. *Come, come and live here. This is where you belong*.

It spoke plainly of neglect and her hands longed to set it right. To tear out the weeds choking the flowers and crawling over the pebbled paths. To neaten the straggly bushes and prune the roses and shape the fruit trees. The beautiful fruit trees—an apple and a peach and a lemon—meant to bear fruit just for her.

Yes, Emma knew immediately, this was the house to buy. From this garden of her dreams she would grow masses of flowers and fill every room in the house. Her hand shook when she signed the papers that would make the house her own.

125

During the following days she barely ate and she slept poorly in her anxiety that something would happen to prevent the sale. When she caught herself daydreaming over the garden, picturing the roses in bloom and apples on the tree, she went cold with dread that some malicious fate would snatch it all away.

But her fears proved foolish and at last she received the key to the house. She clutched it tightly in her hand, her heart pounding. The garden was truly hers. Anytime she liked she could work in her own garden—all day if she wanted. And she could have flowers. Flowers everywhere. Every kind and every color, in vases all over her house. Joy bubbled in her throat with such pressure that tears filled her eyes.

Then she met Mattie.

On the very day Emma moved in, she met Mattie. The moving men had unloaded her belongings and departed. Packing boxes crowded the rooms. Mama's dainty furniture sat askew and looked offended at finding itself removed from the elegant city apartment and dumped in this plain little house in the suburbs. Emma clasped her thin hands together, feeling such happiness she had to sing. She darted from box to box, reading her neatly printed labels until she found the one she wanted.

Unpacking it lovingly, she caressed each shiny new garden tool as she took it out—trowel, pruning shears, clippers, something that looked like a metal claw, the garden books collected over the years and until now used only for pleasant reading. She was leafing through one when the doorbell rang.

On the porch stood a plump middle-aged woman with short blonde hair and a wide smile that bared such large strong teeth that for a moment Emma was frightened.

"I'm Mattie," the woman said. "From next door." Her voice was loud and positive and she swept in. "I've been watching the movers. I thought I'd come over and lend you a hand." She looked around at the disorder and dusted her hands together. "On second thought, I'd better lend you both of them."

"Oh, that's nice of you," Emma said. "But actually I thought I'd do a little work in the garden. You see, this is my very first garden and I'm so excited—"

"It's no trouble at all," Mattie said. "I like to keep busy. I know you must feel you'll never get this mess cleared up, but don't worry. I'm here to help." She seized a carton and ripped it open. "Kitchen things. I don't have

126

to ask where you want these. In no time, we'll have everything straight.''

''But there's no hurry,'' Emma protested.

Mattie paid no attention. She hefted the carton and marched to the kitchen.

Emma sighed, supposing the woman was right, that it would be better to get the house settled before starting on the garden. But it was *her* house and *her* garden. Emma felt ashamed of her annoyance. Mattie was just being neighborly. And it *was* nice of her to help. After one longing glance out of the window, Emma opened another box and stacked the towels and sheets out of it into the linen closet.

As order began to appear out of chaos Emma began to feel grateful to Mattie—so much was being accomplished so quickly. But although Mattie worked hard, she talked in a loud voice all about herself. About being a widow, about her husband dying after a lingering illness, about having no children. About living alone in the big brick house next door that was much too big for her.

After several hours Emma, exhausted from the unpacking and limp from Mattie's voice booming at her, talked simply to keep that voice from pounding her eardrums. At first she spoke of general things like the weather and the number of closets in the house, but Mattie asked so many eager questions that Emma found it difficult to keep anything back. Soon she was talking about herself, about her life, about the apartment, and about Mama dying.

''I know just how you feel,'' Mattie said sympathetically. ''It's so hard when you lose someone you love.'' She sighed gustily. ''We're both all alone in the world.''

Alone? Well, yes, Emma knew she was alone. But it wasn't a sad thing the way Mattie seemed to think. Emma was happy to be alone and free to do what she wanted instead of what Mama wanted. Free to move from the apartment she disliked so much to her own house. Free to have a garden and flowers. Because of Mama's allergies, Emma couldn't have any flowers or plants in the apartment. Not even so much as an African violet on her window-sill.

Mama. Always doing things, playing cards, going to parties, entertaining friends and having them in for tea. And of course she wanted Emma to share it all with her. And to pour the tea from the silver teapot. Even if Emma wanted to stay home and read a book, Mama always insisted that Emma come with her.

''I'm so glad you moved here,'' Mattie said. ''I already feel that we're good friends. Now we have each other and neither one of us will be alone.'

Emma was startled and vaguely uneasy. She remembered Mama saying over the years, "We only have each other now that Daddy's gone."

The next morning Emma got up early. As she sipped a cup of spiced tea, she looked around at her tidy kitchen and thought that Mattie was right. How nice to have everything unpacked and put away where it belonged and the boxes all flattened and set out for the trashmen to pick up.

And today she could spend the whole day in the garden. She would start on the weeds. By the end of the day she should have one whole flower bed free of those strangling weeds—

A brisk rat-a-tat sounded on the door, the knob turned, and Mattie came in.

"So you're an early riser too," Mattie said. "Good. If there's one thing I can't stand it's people who stay in bed half the day. I just made some doughnuts. Have one before they get cold."

Emma felt a sharp prick of annoyance as she made tea for Mattie. The doughnuts were delicious and it was kind of Mattie to bring them, but Emma had already had breakfast and she wanted to get an early start in the garden. Well, perhaps she wouldn't stay long.

"Now," Mattie said after draining her cup, "are you ready? We won't get anything done sitting here."

"Oh, but there's nothing left to do."

"The rest of the boxes need unpacking."

"Oh, no, you see—"

All the boxes had already been unpacked except those with Mama's silver and china. Emma meant to leave that packed and the boxes stacked in the extra bedroom out of the way. Silver was so much trouble, having to be polished all the time, and the fragile china collected dust and needed such careful washing.

"Of *course* you want this unpacked," Mattie said, tearing open a carton. "You can't leave all these beautiful things in boxes. They need to be out where you can see them."

They unpacked the china, carefully washed and dried each piece, and placed it in the china cabinet where it had sat for so many years. They took out the silver and polished it all, the teapot and the bowls and the platters and the candlesticks. By the time they finished, there was very little daylight left and Emma was too tired to work in the garden anyway.

Every day after that Mattie came, uninvited, often early in the morning and sometimes not leaving until after dark. With no more unpacking to do, Mattie started cleaning until every inch of the house had been scrubbed until it shone.

They painted one bedroom because Mattie convinced Emma that lavendar walls made the room too dark and white would be better. The paint fumes gave Emma a headache, but Mattie smiled with her large horse teeth and said, "Isn't this fun? I'm so glad you're here. Now we have each other."

Emma felt a chill.

The house was spotless and Emma had to admit it looked lovely. But she hadn't made much headway in the garden. The flower beds remained choked with weeds, the shrubbery was still shaggy, and she hadn't yet planted the herbs she had bought. Headaches started to plague her, occurring more and more often, the pain more severe with each one.

When not scrubbing or painting, Mattie went places and insisted Emma go with her—shopping or out for lunch or to a movie or meetings or lectures. "Now," Mattie would say when Emma protested, "I'm not going to leave you all alone to start brooding and grieving for your mother. Remember, I'm here now. You're not alone anymore."

"But the garden," Emma protested.

"That's no good. Gardening keeps your hands busy, but it leaves your mind free to feel sorry for yourself."

Emma got up earlier and earlier to have some quiet time in her garden before Mattie came. She couldn't sleep at night, worrying whether she'd beat Mattie to a precious hour or two alone in her garden. But Mattie got up earlier to join Emma in the garden. She gave Emma a pair of gloves and urged her to wear them so her hands wouldn't get stained with dirt.

Emma hated the gloves. They were clumsy things that made her hands awkward and her fingers unable to feel the tender plants. Always too thin, she got even thinner and her headaches got worse.

Mattie insisted the weight loss and headaches were because Emma worked too hard in the garden. She brought over a bottle of weed killer. "There's no sense in killing yourself trying to pull out all those weeds. Just dose them with this."

"Oh, but I don't like to use this sort of thing. It's not good for—"

"There are some weeds you just have to use weed killer on."

Emma accepted the bottle, but so many warnings covered the label she was frightened of it and she put it under the sink and never used it.

If only, Emma thought in despair. If only she could tell Mattie to leave her alone. If only she could keep her door locked and not answer her phone. If only Mattie would just go away.

But Emma couldn't. Mama had taught her to be a lady, to be meek and docile. She couldn't bring herself to be rude no matter how much she wanted to. She could only smile and be agreeable and listen to Mattie's booming voice.

She did try to escape a few times. When Mattie told her they were going somewhere at a certain time, Emma went off for a walk. But Mattie looked at her so oddly and made such pointed comments about forgetfulness and senility and speaking to a doctor that Emma gave it up.

Emma had a recurring dream that she and Mattie were daisies, side by side in the flower bed. The daisy that was herself shriveled and shrunk little by little while the daisy that was Mattie got bigger and stronger, and then dropped its petal disguise and revealed itself as a monstrous weed. It grabbed Emma by the roots and squeezed the life out of her.

Each time Emma woke up sweating and with her heart pounding. She would get up even earlier then and go out to the garden for reassurance.

There were mornings, however, when she tried to escape Mattie by staying in bed late. She kept her doors locked and, pretending to be asleep, didn't answer the phone though it rang and rang until she thought she would scream.

But nothing kept Mattie away. One morning she called the fire department and insisted they break the lock because Emma might be dying.

And Emma, lying in bed in her nightgown, wanted to die of shame when strange men came into her bedroom.

Her face grew hot just remembering.

Emma dropped a handful of weeds in her basket. "There now," she murmured to the pansies. "That's better, isn't it?" She fancied that the flower faces looked happier already.

"Yoo-hoo," Mattie called and a few seconds later her feet crunched firmly down the pebbled path.

Emma crouched over the flowers, her muscles tensing protectively.

"There you are," Mattie said. "I've been looking for you. You haven't forgotten, have you? We have appointments to have our hair done."

Emma smiled vaguely and shook her head. She felt the skin tighten on her scalp and pain stabbed her behind her eyes.

"You know," Mattie went on. "I've been thinking. You gave me such a fright last week, I'll never get over it. Don't you think it would be better if I moved in with you? Then we'd never be alone. I'd always be right here.''

"Oh dear," Emma moaned, rocking back and forth. The pain swelled in her head.

Mattie looked at her with concern. "Are you all right?" She put her hand on Emma's shoulder.

Emma drew back. "Yes." She squeezed her eyes shut for a moment. "I'm just a little stiff." She rose to her feet. The pain clouded her vision. She peeped at Mattie through the grey mist. Mattie's face faded, the features blurred, then sharpened into Mama's face, then blurred again. A breeze lifted the blonde hair and it waved around the face like the petals in a daisy mask.

"I'll have to change," Emma said. Her voice sounded far away. "Maybe you'd like a cup of tea while you wait." Emma started for the house.

Mattie followed. In her booming voice, she pointed out the advantages of living together. Emma didn't hear. The pain was so bad now that she could barely see.

She told Mattie to sit in the living room while she made the tea. She took down Mama's silver teapot and set it on the kitchen cabinet, then patted the sweat from her forehead. She bent, almost screaming from the pain, and took what she needed from the bottom cabinet.

Straightening, she grasped the edge of the cabinet. She swayed, pain crashing through her head. Strong, she thought, it must be very strong. She unscrewed the jar and poured a generous portion of weed killer in the silver teapot before filling it with spiced tea.

Some weeds you just have to use weed killer on.

25

SOMETHING VERY SPECIAL

Fletcher Flora

CLARA DEFOREST, MRS. Jason J. DeForest, was entertaining her minister, the Reverend Mr. Kenneth Culling, who conducted himself with a kind of practiced and professional reticence, faintly suggesting a reverent hush, that was appropriate to a house of bereavement. The situation, however, was delicate. In fact, the Reverend Mr. Culling was not at all certain that his visit, under the ticklish circumstances, was quite proper. So far as he could determine, there seemed to be no etiquette established for such occasions. But he had decided he could not afford to risk offending a parishioner as prominent as Clara DeForest, and that he must offer at least a tactful expression of sympathy. So here he was, with a teacup balanced on his knee and a small sweet cracker in his hand.

It was close to the time when he customarily fortified himself with a glass of sherry, and he wished wistfully that he were, at this instant, doing that very thing. He was unaware that Clara DeForest, who was also drinking tea and eating crackers, would have greatly preferred a glass or two of sherry, and would have happily supplied it. In short, the two were not quite in contact, and they were forced to suffer, consequently, the petty misery common to misunderstandings.

Clara DeForest's bereavement, to put it bluntly, was qualified. It was true that her husband Jason was gone, but he had gone of his own volition, aboard a jet headed for Mexico City, and not in the arms of angels headed for Heaven. At least, that was the rumor. It was also rumored that he had withdrawn his and Clara's joint checking account and sold some bonds, had helped himself to the most valuable pieces in Clara's jewelry box, and had been accompanied on the jet by a platinum blond. Clara made no effort to refute these charges. Neither did she confirm them. She merely made it clear, with a touch of pious stoicism, that she preferred to forgive and forget the treacheries of her errant husband, whatever they may have been precisely. Her marriage to Jason, twenty years her junior, had been under sentence from the beginning, and it was well over and done with. She was prepared, in short, to cut her losses. The Reverend Mr. Culling was vastly relieved and reassured to find her so nicely adjusted to her misfortune.

"I must say, Mrs. DeForest," he said, "that you are looking remarkably well."

"I feel well, thank you."

"Is there nothing that you need? Any small comfort that I may offer?"

"I am already quite comfortable. I appreciate your kindness, but I assure you that I need nothing."

"Your fortitude is admirable. A lesser woman would indulge herself in tears and recriminations."

"Not I. The truth is, I have no regrets whatever. Jason has deserted, and I am well rid of him."

"Do you feel no resentment, no anger? It would be perfectly understandable if you did."

The Reverend Mr. Culling looked at Clara hopefully. He would have been pleased to pray for the cleansing of Clara's heart. It would have given him something useful to do and made him feel useful. But Clara's heart, apparently, required no cleansing.

"None at all," she said. "Jason was a young scoundrel, but he was quite a charming one, and I am rather grateful to him than otherwise. He gave me three exciting years at a time of life when I had no reasonable expectation of them."

The nature of Clara's excitement took the shape of a vague vision in the minister's mind, and he tried without immediate success to divert his thoughts, which were hardly proper in connection with a woman of fifty, or any woman at all, however effectively preserved. He could not be blamed for noticing, however, that Clara was still capable of displaying a slender leg and neat ankle.

"There are unexpected compensations," he murmured with a vagueness equal to that of his vision.

"On the contrary, I did expect them, and I had them. I should hardly have married Jason for any other reason. He was poor. He was unscrupulous. He was rather stupid. He was pathetically transparent even in his attempts to kill me."

"What!" The Reverend Mr. Culling's voice escaped its discipline and jumped octaves into an expression of horror. "He made attempts on your life?"

"Twice, I believe. Once with something in a glass of warm milk he brought me at bedtime. Another with something in my medicine. He repeated, you see, the same basic technique. Jason, like all dull young men, had absolutely no imagination."

"But surely you reported these attempts to the police!"

"Not at all. What would have been the good? It would merely have destroyed our whole relationship, which still retained from my point of view, as I have indicated, much that was satisfactory."

The minister, feeling that he was somehow on trial, tried to restrain his emotions. "Do you mean that you did nothing whatever about it?"

"Oh, I did something, all right." Clara smiled tenderly, remembering what she had done. "I simply explained that I had disposed of my small fortune in such a way as to deprive him of any motive for killing me. Since he would receive no benefits from my death, there was no advantage in trying to rush what will occur, in any event, soon enough. He was like a child. So embarrassed at being detected!"

"Like a monster, I should say!" The Reverend Mr. Culling's restraint faltered for a moment, and he rattled his teacup in his saucer to show the height of his indignation. "I must admit, however, that your method was ingenious and effective."

"Was it? Not entirely." Clara's tender smile took on a touch of sadness. "It may have deprived him of any motive for killing me, but it also relieved him of any compelling reason for sticking around. Not, as I said, that I have regrets. At least, no serious ones. But I shall miss Jason. Yes, indeed, I shall miss him. I shall certainly keep some small memento around the house to keep my memory of him fresh and vivid. As one grows older, you know, one's memories fade without the help of mnemonics."

"He has only been gone for a week. Perhaps he'll return."

"I think not," Clara shook her head gently. "He left a note, you know, saying that he was leaving for good. Besides, he could, under the circumstances, hardly be sure of his reception. In a moment of pique, I destroyed the note. I regret now that I did. I should have kept it to read periodically. It would have served admirably to bring him back in spirit, if not in flesh."

"You are an astonishing woman, Mrs. DeForest. I am utterly overwhelmed by your incredible charity."

"Well, it is reputedly a Christian virtue, is it not?"

"Indeed it is. Faith, hope and charity, and the greatest of these . . ."

The minister's voice trailed off, not because the rest of the words had slipped his mind, but because he chose not to compete with the front doorbell, which had begun to ring. Clara DeForest, in response to the ringing, had stood up.

"Excuse me," she said, and left the room.

He heard her a moment later in the hall, speaking to someone at the door. He was disturbed and a little confused by her almost placid acceptance of what he considered a shameful and faithless act. He was, in fact, inclined to resent it as an excessive application of his own principles. After all, it was entirely possible to be too understanding and submissive. His head tended to reel with antic thoughts, and he leaned back in his chair and looked for something substantial on which to anchor them. His eyes centered on a vase on the mantle, which made him think of Keats' "Ode on a Grecian Urn." Odes and urns seeming safe and substantial enough, he began trying to recall the lines of the poem, but he could only remember the famous one about a thing of beauty being a joy forever, a contention which he privately considered extravagant and dubious. Clara DeForest returned to the room. She was carrying a package wrapped in brown paper and tied with string. Placing the package on a table, she went back to her chair.

"It was the postman," she explained. "Will you have more tea?"

"No, thank you. No more for me. I was just admiring the vase on your mantle. It's a lovely thing."

"Yes, isn't it?" Clara turned her head to look at the vase, her eyes lingering. "My brother Casper brought it to me last week when he drove up to see me."

"I heard that your brother was here. It's a great comfort to have a loved one near in a time of trouble."

"Yes, Casper came immediately when I told him by telephone that Jason had left me, but it was hardly necessary. I did not consider it a time of trouble, actually, and I was perfectly all right. I suppose he merely wanted to reassure himself. He only stayed over night. The next morning, he drove directly home again."

"I have never had the pleasure of meeting your brother. Is his home far away?"

"About two hundred miles. He lives in the resort area, you know. He's a potter by trade. He made the little vase you have been admiring."

"Really? How fascinating!"

"It's actually an art, not a trade, but Casper has developed it to the point where it is also a business. He started out years ago with a little shop where he sold his own wares, but they were so superbly done that the demand for them grew and grew, and he soon had to increase the size and numbers of his kilns to meet it. Now he supplies shops and department stores in all the larger cities of this area.''

"He must be very busy."

"Oh, yes, Yes, indeed. He was forced to hurry home last week because he had some urgent work to do. He has great artistic integrity, you see. He personally makes all his own vases. It limits his production, of course, but each piece is far more valuable because of it.''

"I know so little about the making of pottery. I must read up on it.''

"You will find it interesting, I'm sure. The pieces are baked, for instance, in intense heat. Do you have any idea of the temperature required to produce a piece of biscuit ware?''

"Biscuit ware?"

"That is what the pottery is called after the initial baking, before glazing.''

"Oh. No, I must confess I haven't the slightest idea.''

"An average temperature of 1,270 degrees.''

"Mercy!"

"Centrigrade, that is."

"Good heavens!"

"So, you see," Clara finished humorously, "my lovely vase had been put through quite an ordeal. Don't you agree it is worth it, though? It is too squat for most flowers, of course, but never mind. I shall keep it for something very special.''

Talk of such heat had prompted the Reverend Mr. Culling to think uneasily of Hell. He preferred talking of it to thinking of it, for silence increased its terrors, but it would hardly do as a topic for this polite conversation, which had continued, an any rate, long enough. He rose.

"Well, I must run along. I really must. I can't tell you how relieved I am to find you taking things so well.''

"You mustn't worry about me. I shall survive, I assure you.''

They walked together to the front door and said good-by.

"I'm so glad you called," said Clara. "Do come again soon.''

From the door, she watched him to his car at the curb, and then she turned and went back into the living room. At the table, she took up the package with an expression of annoyance. Really, Casper was simply too exasperating! It was well enough to be thrifty, but her dear brother was positively penurious. Not only was the package flimsy and insecurely tied, but it had been sent third class, just to save a few cents postage. Of course, one realized that postal employees rarely availed themselves of the right to open and inspect packages, but just suppose, in this instance, that one had! It would have been embarrassing, to say the least.

She took the lovely vase from the mantle and set it on the table beside the package. Her annoyance dissolved in a feeling of delicious companionship. Opening the package, she began to pour its contents into the vase.

26

SHATTERPROOF

Jack Ritchie

HE WAS A soft-faced man wearing rimless glasses, but he handled the automatic with unmistakable competence.

I was rather surprised at my calmness when I learned the reason for his presence. "It's a pity to die in ignorance," I said. "Who hired you to kill me?"

His voice was mild. "I could be an enemy in my own right."

I had been making a drink in my study when I heard him and turned. Now I finished pouring from the decanter. "I know the enemies I made and you are a stranger. Was it my wife?"

He smiled. "Quite correct. Her motive must be obvious."

"Yes," I said. "I have money and apparently she wants it. All of it."

He regarded me objectively. "Your age is?"

"Fifty-three."

"And your wife is?"

"Twenty-two."

He clicked his tongue. "You were foolish to expect anything permanent, Mr. Williams."

I sipped the whiskey. "I expected a divorce after a year or two and a painful settlement. But not death."

"Your wife is a beautiful woman, but greedy, Mr. Williams. I'm surprised that you never noticed."

My eyes went to the gun. "I assume you have killed before?"

"Yes."

"And obviously you enjoy it."

He nodded. "A morbid pleasure, I admit. But I do."

I watched him and waited. Finally I said, "You have been here more than two minutes and I am still alive."

"There is no hurry, Mr. Williams," he said softly.

"Ah, then the actual killing is not your greatest joy. You must savor the preceding moments."

"You have insight, Mr. Williams."

"And as long as I keep you entertained, in one manner or another, I remain alive?"

"Within a time limit, of course."

"Naturally. A drink, Mr. . . . . ?"

"Smith requires no strain on the memory. Yes, thank you. But please allow me to see what you are doing when you prepare it."

"It's hardly likely that I would have poison conveniently at hand for just such an occasion."

"Hardly likely, but still possible."

He watched me while I made his drink and then he took an easy chair.

I sat on the davenport. "Where would my wife be at this moment?"

"At a party, Mr. Williams. There will be a dozen people to swear that she never left their sight during the time of your murder."

"I will be shot by a burglar? An intruder?"

He put his drink on the cocktail table in front of him. "Yes. After I shoot you, I shall of course, wash this glass and return it to your liquor cabinet. And when I leave, I shall wipe all fingerprints from the doorknobs I've touched."

"You will take a few trifles with you? To make the burglar-intruder story more authentic?"

"That will not be necessary, Mr. Williams. The police will assume that the burglar panicked after he killed you and fled empty-handed."

"That picture on the east wall," I said. "It's worth thirty thousand."

His eyes went to it for a moment and then quickly returned to me. "It is tempting, Mr. Williams. But I desire to possess nothing that will even remotely link me to you. I appreciate art, and especially its monetary value, but not to the extent where I will risk the electric chair." Then he smiled. "Or were you perhaps offering me the painting? In exchange for your life?"

"It was a thought."

He shook his head. "I'm sorry, Mr. Williams. Once I accept a commission, I am not dissuaded. It is a matter of professional pride."

I put my drink on the table. "Are you waiting for me to show fear, Mr. Smith?"

"You will show it."

"And then you will kill me?"

His eyes flickered. "It is a strain, isn't it, Mr. Williams? To be afraid and not to dare show it."

"Do you expect your victims to beg?" I asked.

"They do. In one manner or another."

"They appeal to your humanity? And that is hopeless?"

"It is hopeless."

"They offer you money?"

"Very often."

"Is that hopeless, too?"

"So far it has been, Mr. Williams."

"Behind the picture I pointed out to you, Mr. Smith, there is a wall safe."

He gave the painting another brief glance. "Yes."

"It contains five thousand dollars."

"That is a lot of money, Mr. Williams."

I picked up my glass and went to the painting. I opened the safe, selected a brown envelope and then finished my drink. I put the empty glass in the safe and twirled the knob.

Smith's eyes were drawn to the envelope. "Bring that here, please."

I put the envelope on the cocktail table in front of him.

He looked at it for a few moments and then up at me. "Did you actually think you could buy your life?"

I lit a cigarette. "No. You are, shall we say, incorruptible."

He frowned slightly. "But still you brought me the five thousand?"

I picked up the envelope and tapped its contents out on the table. "Old receipts. All completely valueless to you."

He showed the color of irritation. "What do you think this has possibly gained you?"

"The opportunity to go to the safe and put your glass inside it."

His eyes flicked to the glass in front of him. "That was yours. Not mine."

I smiled. "That was your glass, Mr. Smith. And I imagine that the police will wonder what an empty glass is doing in my safe. I rather think, especially since this will be a case of murder, that they will have the intelligence to take fingerprints."

His eyes narrowed. "I haven't taken my eyes off you for a moment. You couldn't have switched our glasses."

"No? I seem to recall that at least twice you looked at the painting."

Automatically he looked in that direction again. "Only for a second or two."

"It was enough."

He was perspiring faintly. "I say it was impossible."

"Then I am afraid you will be greatly surprised when the police come for you. And after a little time, you will have the delightful opportunity of facing death in the electric chair. You will share your victims' anticipation of death with the addition of a great deal more time in which to let your imagination play with the topic. I'm sure you've read accounts of executions in the electric chair?"

His finger seemed to tighten on the trigger.

"I wonder how you'll go," I said. "You've probably pictured yourself meeting death with calmness and fortitude. But that is a common comforting delusion, Mr. Smith. You will more likely have to be dragged . . ."

His voice was level. "Open that safe or I'll kill you."

I laughed. "Really now, Mr. Smith, we both know that obviously you will kill me if I *do* open the safe."

A half a minute went by before he spoke. "What do you intend to do with the glass?"

"If you don't murder me—and I rather think you won't now—I will take it to a private detective agency and have your fingerprints reproduced. I will put them, along with a note containing pertinent information, inside a sealed envelope. And I will leave instructions that, in the event I die violently, even if the occurrence appears accidental, the envelope be forwarded to the police."

Smith stared at me and then he took a breath. "All that won't be necessary. I will leave now and you will never see me again."

I shook my head. "I prefer my plan. It provides protection for my future."

He was thoughtful. "Why don't you go direct to the police?"

"I have my reasons."

His eyes went down to his gun and then he put it in his pocket. An idea came to him. "Your wife could very easily hire someone else to kill you."

"Yes. She could do that."

"I would be accused of your death. I could go to the electric chair."

"I imagine so. Unless . . ."

Smith waited.

"Unless, of course, she were unable to hire anyone."

"But there are probably half dozen others . . ." He stopped.

I smiled. "Did my wife tell you where she is now?"

"Just that she'd be at a place called the Petersons'. She will leave at eleven."

"Eleven? A good time. It will be very dark tonight. Do you know the Petersons' address?"

He stared at me. "No."

"In Bridgehampton," I said, and I gave him the house number.

Our eyes held for half a minute.

"It's something you must do," I said softly. "For your own protection."

He buttoned his coat slowly. "And where will you be at eleven, Mr. Williams?"

"At my club, probably playing cards with five or six friends. They will no doubt commiserate with me when I receive word that my wife has been . . . shot?"

"It all depends on the circumstances and the opportunity." He smiled thinly. "Did you ever love her?"

I picked up a jade figurine and examined it. "I was extremely fond of this piece when I first bought it. Now it bores me. I will replace it with another."

When he was gone, there was just enough time to take the glass to a detective agency before I went on to the club.

Not the glass in the safe, of course. It held nothing but my own fingerprints.

I took the one Mr. Smith left on the cocktail table when he departed.

The prints of Mr. Smith's fingers developed quite clearly.

27

PROJECT MUSHROOM

Julie Smith

IT WAS JUNE 29, the day before the end of the fiscal year, and Carla looked awful. She was trying to cheer herself up with a puny little joke. "We've decided to kill Martin," she said. "Everyone in the office is going to strike a blow, like in that Agatha Christie novel. Do we count you in or not?"

I shook my head. "I guess I haven't been here long enough. I'm nowhere close to murder."

"Just wait. He gets to everybody."

In fact, I'd been on Project Mushroom only about a week. The project's purpose was to figure out ways to increase California's mushroom sales income by several zillion bucks. It was funded by the State and administered by the State Department of Food and Agriculture, and if it wanted to continue being funded it had to deliver a mountain of reports to Food and Ag by June 30th. Its director was Martin Larson, who did more to block advances in mushroom agriculture than anyone the Twentieth Century has yet produced.

The project was inspired by the current fancy-cooking fad. Some State Assemblyman noticed that dried morels cost more than three hundred dollars a pound and no one could keep them in stock. He thought that if California could figure out a cheap way to grow morels and other fancy fungi, the state would get richer. A lot of people thought that was ridiculous. I thought it was a good idea. I'm a botanist and the author of a children's book on mushrooms and I live in a tiny town in the San Joaquin Valley, about twenty miles from the tiny Valley town that housed Project Mushroom. Because of those three facts, Betty Castor, the head geneticist on the project, recruited me.

Betty reasoned that if I could write, I could edit, and she didn't think the project stood a chance of getting refunded unless someone translated the required mountain of reports into English before they were sent to Sacramento. Martin insisted on writing them all himself, and he wrote only in bureaucratese. So I joined the project to save it. One of the conditions of my employment was that I deal directly with Carla, the education director, and not with Martin.

Poor Carla got darker and darker circles under her eyes as the end of June drew nearer. The day she unveiled the joke murder plan I was in the office to pick up the last paper, planning to take it home to work on it. "Where," I asked her, "is the report on 'Options for Improving California's Mushroom Resources'?"

"Martin hasn't started it yet."

I began to see what she meant about the way he got to *everybody*. He phoned me at ten o'clock that night. "I don't think I'll be finished till very late. I'll put the report under your doormat, okay? It's got to be on a bus for Sacramento by two o'clock tomorrow and I've got to go over your edit and then we've got to have it typed. Do you think you could have it back to me by ten-thirty?"

I sighed. "I'll shoot for eleven."

It would mean getting up at 4:00 A.M., but so what? It would all be over a few hours after that and I could be back in bed by noon, with a check under my pillow that would pay the rent for the next three months.

The report was about fifty pages long, and apparently the work of the Cleveland Wrecking Company. By 9:30, I still had fifteen pages to go. I called Martin: "Come over and start looking at the part I've done. If you have questions, I'll be right here."

He didn't come over. He sent someone to pick up the report and take it back to his office—about a twenty-minute drive. But I couldn't worry about that. I was starting to panic. The last five pages were gibberish. They needed a complete rewrite, but I couldn't do it until I knew what Martin was trying to say. I would have to go in to the office and work with him—each page would have to be handed to the typist as we finished it.

I left at 10:30, forty-five minutes behind the messenger. Martin had gone through only about ten or twelve pages of my edit. Frantic last-minute activity whirred about him, but he seemed oblivious to the approaching deadline. He was sitting in his private office, utterly relaxed, agonizing happily over each comma. I'd never been in his office before. It was decorated with dried mushrooms, mounted and framed. At that moment, I'd love to have fed him his own big, loathsome specimen of *Amanita phalloides,* the most poisonous toadstool that grows in California.

He put down his pencil and gave me his full attention. He answered my questions slowly and deliberately, fully and completely—and then some. I was sweating with impatience by the time we'd finished.

I started the rewrite and he worked on the rest of my edit, interrupting me now and then. I answered as shortly as I could, but somehow he managed to work in a few questions about my background and whether I'd be available for future jobs—questions I really couldn't ignore without being horribly rude. And I didn't want to be rude, but it was getting on toward noon—we had only two hours to get the report on the bus. The typist came in, grabbed a sheaf of papers, and left. Carla came in in a panic. She had a bunch of color samples with her, in shades of mushroom tan, mushroom gray, and mushroom gray-green. "Martin," she said, "the man from the bindery is here. Pick the color for the cover—quick."

"Oops. Stop the presses," he said. "A lifetime decision." He began to pore over the samples. I resumed typing. Carla left.

"Katherine, what do you think?" He spread about twenty samples out in front of me. I picked a soft gray-green.

"I don't think so," he said. "I think this tan." He held it up.

"Great," I said.

"No, I'm not sure. I'm going to ask Bill." Bill was the art director.

He left to find Bill and I thankfully went back to the rewrite.

Martin came back in a few minutes, fingering a gray sample. "This is the one Bill likes. He thinks the black type'll look best on it. What do you think?"

"Take Bill's advice—it's what you're paying him for."

"The trouble with the world today is that everybody listens to the experts."

I shrugged and kept typing, trying not to think about the chunk of tax money that was paying for Bill, and me, and other unlistened to "experts" on Project Mushroom.

Carla came back in: "Martin, how about it? The guy from the bindery's getting impatient."

"Just a second, Carla. This is important."

Carla disappeared. Martin continued to stare at the samples. Finally, he picked another gray—at least it must have been another gray since it was on a different sample card. But it looked for all the world like the one Bill had picked. Martin covered it with a sample of black type, then put the sample on the gray Bill had picked. Sure enough, it showed up better on Bill's gray. Martin pointed to his own gray. "I think this is a much richer color, don't you?"

147

"I hardly see any difference at all." This time I couldn't keep the curtness out of my voice.

"I know what I'll do. I'll ask Betty." Martin picked up the phone and spoke to Betty: "Get your fanny in here. We've got a problem."

I kept typing. In a second, Betty whirled in, hair flying, arms full of papers, face frantic. "What's the problem?"

Martin explained—slowly. Betty told him to listen to Bill.

When she had left, Martin stared at the color cards some more. Finally, he stood up. "I'm going to have to flip a coin," he said. "Tails, we go with Bill's choice. Heads, we go with mine."

He flipped a quarter onto my typing table. It was tails.

"That's it," I said. "Go with Bill's gray."

"This is important, Katherine. It's got to be right."

"So go with your gray."

"I'm not sure. I'm just not sure."

He sat down and stared at the samples some more. Carla came in, red-faced: "Martin, for heaven's sake. We're paying this guy by the minute."

I guess she meant the man from the bindery. I didn't ask. Martin went out with her, and came back in about ten minutes, just as I was pulling the final page of the rewrite out of the typewriter. "We went with one of the tan ones."

"I'm sure it'll look very nice. Can you look this over? There's about fifteen minutes to get it read and typed."

Carla rushed in again. "We've got five typists standing by. Any pages yet?"

Martin waved her away. "Katherine," he said, "after this is over, could you give me some pointers on improving my writing style?"

"Sure. Tomorrow maybe."

"My main problem is I have so much to say, you know? I don't wany any of those guys at Food and Ag to miss anything. I think if we just—"

In my head, a clock ticked away. "Oh, dear!" I put my hand to my mouth. "I've just forgotten something. Martin, can you excuse me a second?"

I ran from the room and ducked into Carla's office. I picked up the phone and started dialing numbers at random, trying to look busy in case Martin followed me and tried to finish his sentence. I called my mother, my sister, and my boy friend, who was on a business trip in New York.

Finally I saw Martin burst out of his office, waving the rewrite pages. He raced over to the head typist's desk and said, "Type like the wind." He was smiling, clearly having the time of his life. The other four typists each rushed over and took a page. They typed like the wind. Carla stood by, playing with a set of keys, ready to race the finished report to the bindery.

I went to lunch with Betty. Two beers and a ham sandwich later I felt nearly normal again. I came back to the office with her to get directions to Bill's house, where a Project Mushroom New Fiscal Year Party was going to take place in a few hours. Betty was explaining how to get there when Carla came in, streaming tears: "I missed the bus."

Martin put an arm around her. "No big deal. I called Food and Ag yesterday—they gave us a day's grace."

Carla shoved him away and clomped out of the room, not looking at Martin, Betty, or me, simply getting out of the room quick. Martin apparently didn't notice. He turned to me: "Katherine, I went through your edit pretty quickly. I think we're going to have to do a few things over."

So I didn't go to the New Fiscal Year Party after all. I stayed home and worked. I'd been looking forward to the party, too. It was a potluck dinner, and everything on the menu had mushrooms in it. There were stuffed mushrooms for hors d'oeuvres and then mushroom soup and marinated mushrooms and mushroom crepes. Dessert was a cake in the shape of a mushroom.

I worked until 1:00 A.M. and then I took my edit of Martin's rewrite of my rewrite over to the project office and pushed it through the mail slot as arranged. After that, I went home, took the phone off the hook, and slept. I slept through most of the next day, getting up late in the afternoon to eat and read a little. Then I went back to bed and slept all night.

The headline in the next day's paper was PROJECT MUSHROOM DIRECTOR DIES OF MUSHROOM POISONING. The story told about the New Fiscal Year Party, and what had been on the menu, and said that Martin had been poisoned by an *Amanita phalloides*. No one else had been stricken. No one could explain how the *phalloides* had gotten into any of the dishes, as only domesticated mushrooms had been used.

It was a Saturday, so I knew no one would be at Project Mushroom. I went over and got the guard to let me in by saying I'd left a book in the office. Then I went into Martin's private office. His mushroom collection was still intact, except for the framed phalloides. Another specimen, an *Amanita muscaria*, had been hung in its place. I called Carla and told her the *phalloides* was missing. "What *phalloides*?" she said. "Martin never had a *phalloides* specimen."

I called Betty. She'd never seen the *phalloides*, either. Then I called Bill. Neither had he. Neither had the head typist.

So I decided not to mention the missing *phalloides* to the police. I didn't want to look like a crazy lady.

But if Martin's death was an accident, the news media pointed out, that meant it must be possible to buy a *phalloides* accidentally at the grocery store. They also questioned the need for anything called Project Mushroom in the first place, and went on quite a bit about frivolous programs that were using up tax money.

So far as I know, there was only the most cursory investigation of Martin's death. The police seemed to think it was surprising that only Martin had been stricken, but practically everyone on the staff was a mushroom expert and none of them thought it odd, so the cops went away cowed. Project Mushroom was not refunded.

I have no idea how those people did it. If I had to, I'd put my money on the crepes, which had to be made individually but I wouldn't rule out the soup or even the marinated mushrooms—a single portion of either could have been easily doctored. I also don't know if they all participated, or if one or two of them did it and the rest simply kept quiet about the missing specimen. All I know is that Martin Larson did more to block advances in mushroom agriculture than anyone the Twentieth Century has yet produced. In California, anyway.

28

TERROR IN THE NIGHT

Robert Bloch

IT MUST HAVE been about two o'clock when Barbara started shaking me.

She kept saying "Wake up!" over and over again, and tugging at my shoulder. Since I'm generally a pretty sound sleeper, it took me almost a minute to come to.

Then I noticed she had the lights on and she was sitting up in her bed.

"What's the matter?" I asked.

"There's somebody downstairs, pounding on the door. Can't you hear?"

I listened and I heard. It certainly sounded like the door was getting a workout.

"Who the devil would be showing up here at this hour?" I asked.

"Get up and find out," Barbara told me. Which was a sensible suggestion.

So I walked over to the window and looked down. Sure enough, I could see someone standing down there, but in the shadows it was hard to make out any details. I got the funniest notion that whoever it was, was wearing a white sheet.

Now the doorbell began to ring, insistently.

Barbara said, "Well?"

"I don't know," I told her. "Can't make out anything from up here. You stay where you are. I'll go down and see."

I went out of the bedroom and almost tripped on the stairs, because I forget about turning on the light. I still wasn't used to staying here in the summer place.

Of course I remembered where the hall light was, and when I got down there I switched it on. All the while the doorbell kept ringing.

Then I opened the door.

There was a woman standing on the porch. She wasn't wearing a sheet, but she had on the next thing to it—some kind of long white nightgown. Not lingerie, but a real old-fashioned nightgown that came way down to her ankles. Or used to. Now it was torn and there were stains on it; dirt or grease. Her hair hung down over her eyes and she was crying or panting, or both. For a minute I didn't recognize her, and then she said, "Bob!"

"Marjorie! Come in."

I turned my head and called up to Barbara, "Come on down, honey. It's Marjorie Kingston."

There wasn't time to say anything more. Marjorie was off the porch in nothing flat, and she hung onto me as if she were afraid of drowning. Her head was right against my chest, so that I could feel her shaking, and all the while she kept mumbling something I couldn't make out. At last I got it.

She was saying, "Shut the door, please. Shut the door!"

I closed the door and steered her into the front room. I turned on one of the lamps, and she looked at me and said, "Pull the shades, Bob."

She'd stopped crying and her breathing was a little more relaxed by the time Barbara came downstairs.

Barbara didn't say anything. She just walked over to Marjorie and put her arms around her, and that was the signal for her to really let go.

I finished pulling the shades and then ducked out to the kitchen. I couldn't find any soda, but when I came back I had three glasses and the bottle of Scotch I'd bought when I went into town on Monday.

The two of them were sitting on the sofa now, and Marjorie had calmed down a little. I didn't ask if anyone wanted a drink, just poured out three stiff slugs. I gave Marjorie her glass first, and she put the shot down like water.

Barbara took a sip as I sat down in the armchair, and then she looked at Marjorie and said, "What happened?"

"I ran away."

"Ran away?"

Marjorie brushed the hair out of her eyes and looked straight at her. "Oh, you needn't worry about pretending. You must have heard where I've been. At the asylum."

Barbara gave me a look but I didn't say anything. I remembered the day I bumped into Freddie Kingston at lunch in town and he told me about Marjorie. Said she'd had a nervous breakdown at school and they were sending her up to this private sanatorium at Elkdale. That must have been about three months ago. I hadn't seen him since to get any further details.

I stood up. Marjorie sucked in her breath. "What's the matter?" I asked.

"Don't go," she said. "Don't call anyone. Please, Bob. I'm begging you."

"How about Freddie? Shouldn't he know?"

"Not Freddie. Not anybody, but most of all not Freddie. You don't understand, do you?"

"Suppose you tell us," Barbara suggested.

"All right." Marjorie held out her glass. "Can I have another drink, first?"

I poured for her. When she lifted the glass up I could see her fingers. The nails had been bitten all the way down.

She drank, and then all at once she was talking, even before she took the glass away from her lips.

"You see, it wouldn't do any good to tell Freddie, because he sent me there in the first place and he must have known what it was like. He has this Mona Lester, and he thought they'd kill me and then he'd be free. I had plenty of time to figure things out and I can see that now. I mean, it makes sense, doesn't it?"

I tried to catch Barbara's eye but she wasn't looking at me. She kept staring at Marjorie. And then she said, very softly, "We heard you had a nervous breakdown, dear."

Marjorie nodded. "Oh, that part's true enough. It's been coming on for a long time, only nobody knew it. That's my fault, really. I was too proud to tell anyone. About Freddie, I mean."

"What about Freddie?"

"Freddie and this Mona Lester. She's a model. He met her last year, down at the studio. They've been living together ever since. When I found out, he just laughed. He said he wanted a divorce and he'd furnish me with all the evidence I needed. Glad to. But of course I don't believe in divorce. I tried everything—I argued with him, I pleaded with him, I went down on my hands and knees to him. Nothing did any good.

"He started to stay away night after night, and weekends, too. Then he'd come back and tell me about what he'd been doing with Mona, in detail, everything. You can't imagine the things he said, and the way he'd watch me while he told me. And he used to watch me at parties, too, when we had to go out together. He said he got a kick out of seeing me pretend that everything was all right. Because nobody knew about Mona. You didn't, did you? Freddie was too smart for that. Even then he must have been planning the whole thing. Yes, I know he must, because I remember now

153

what he said that one time—if I didn't divorce him he'd keep on until I went crazy and then he could do what he pleased." She paused for breath.

Barbara bit her lip. "Are you sure you want to talk about this?" she asked. "You mustn't get excited. . . ."

Marjorie made a sound. It took me a second to realize she was laughing, or trying to laugh. "Quit talking like a doctor," she said. "You don't have to humor me. I'm not crazy and I'm not psychotic. That's the word the doctors use, you know. Psychotic. Or when they talk to the relatives they say, 'mentally disturbed.' It isn't that way with me at all. When I broke down in class that day—English IV, my last afternoon class—it was just nerves. I had hysterics. God knows what the pupils thought. The principal had to come in and quiet me down. They sent me home and gave me a sedative, and the doctor came and he left some pills. Then Freddie came. He doped me up. I mean it. I was supposed to take two pills at the most. He gave me six. He kept on feeding me the stuff, all through the next week. When the other doctor came, and when he took me to see Corbel, and when we went to court. I was shot. By the time I came to, I was committed. He'd gotten the papers signed and everything. And I woke up in Corbel's little private asylum."

I didn't look at her. I couldn't. She went on talking, louder and louder.

"That was three months ago. I've kept track of the days. The hours, even. What else was there to do? Freddie has never come to see me. And nobody else has come, either. He has it fixed with Corbel not to let them. I tried to write, until I realized the letters weren't being mailed. And if I got any letters, Corbel saw to it they weren't allowed to reach me. That's the way he runs the place. That's why they pay him so much—to keep anyone from getting in, to keep anyone from getting out. It must be costing Freddie a fortune to have me there, but it's worth it to him. And to the others."

"What others?" Barbara asked.

"The other relatives. Of the other patients, I mean. Most of them are wealthy, you know. We've got some alcoholics and some drug addicts out there, but I wouldn't say any of them were really mental cases. At least they weren't when they arrived. But Corbel does his best to drive them crazy. You can have all the liquor and shots you want. He calls it therapy. What he's really trying to do is kill them off as fast as he can. Maybe he gets an extra fee that way. He must. Particularly with the old people. The sooner they die, the sooner the relatives inherit."

"This Corbel," I said. "He's a psychiatrist?"

"He's a murderer!" Marjorie leaned forward. "Go ahead, laugh at me—it's true! I can hear. I stay awake all night and listen. I heard him and

Leo beating old Mr. Scheinfarber to death two weeks ago in the hydro-therapy room. They never use it for hydrotherapy at all, you know. But when he was done screaming they dumped his body in the water and left him there. The next morning they said he'd been taking a treatment and slipped under—committed suicide. Corbel signed the certificate. I know what's going on! Poor old Mr. Scheinfarber, who only wanted to be left alone . . . And now that sneaky son and daughter-in-law of his get all the money. Leo almost admitted as much to me.''

"Who is Leo?" Barbara asked.

"One of the orderlies. Leo and Hugo. Leo's the worst; he's on night duty. He was after me from the beginning.''

"What for?''

"Can't you guess?" Marjorie made that laughing sound again. "He's after most of the women patients there. Once he locked Mrs. Matthews in isolation and stayed with her for two days. She couldn't dare do anything about it; he said he'd see to it she starved to death if she wouldn't let him.''

"I see," I said.

Marjorie looked at me. "You don't see. You think I'm lying to you. I can tell. But it's all true. I can prove it. That's why I ran away—to prove it. I want to get to the police. Not the sheriff or anyone around here; I think they're in cahoots with Corbel. Otherwise, how would he be able to fix things with the coroner and everyone so there isn't any fuss? But when I get to town maybe somebody will listen. We could force an investigation. That's all I want, Bob. Really it is. I don't even want to punish Freddie. I'm past that stage. I just want to help those people, those poor, hopeless people stuck away to rot and die. . . .''

Barbara reached over and patted her on the shoulder. "It's all right," she said. "It's all right. We believe you, don't we, Bob?''

"I know what it sounds like," Marjorie said, and she was calmer now. "You tell yourself such things can't happen in this day and age. And you see Doctor Corbel in town and he's such a kind, brilliant man. You go for a drive past the sanatorium and look at the building up on the hill, in among all those trees—you think it's a beautiful place, a wonderful rest-home for those who can afford it. You don't notice the bars, and you never get inside the soundproof part where you could hear the screams and the moans, or see the stains on the floor in isolation. The stains that won't wash off, the stains that never wash off—''

"Another drink?" I interrupted. I didn't want to give her another drink, but I had to stop her someway.

155

"No thanks. I'm all right now, really I am. You'll see. It's just all this running—"

"You need rest," Barbara nodded. "A good night's sleep before we decide anything."

"There's nothing to decide," Marjorie said. " I've made up my mind. I want you to drive me into the city tonight so that I can make a statement right away. I don't care if they believe me or not, just so they come out and investigate. Once they get inside, they'll find proof. I'll show them. All I'm asking you to do is drive me."

"I can't," I said. "The car's in the garage but the battery's out of whack. I'm having the garage man out to fix it in the morning."

"It may be too late then," Marjorie said. "They'll cover things up once they realize I'm liable to go to the authorities."

I took a deep breath. "How did you manage to get away?" I asked her.

Marjorie put her hands down in her lap and looked at them. Her voice was very low.

"For a long while I didn't even think about escaping. Everyone said it was impossible, and besides, even if I did, where could I go? Certainly not to Freddie or the local police. And how could I get to town safely without any money? Then I happened to remember that you folks had this summer place, and you'd be up here. It isn't too far from Elkdale. All I needed was a good start. So I knew the thing to do, then.

"I told you about this Leo, the night orderly—the one who was always after me? I kept fighting him off all the time; I'd never take sleeping pills or even doze off while he was on duty.

"Well, tonight Leo was drinking a little. I heard him coming around in the hall, and I asked him in. I even took a drink from him, just to get him started again. He had quite a few. And then . . . I let him."

She didn't say anything for almost a minute. Barbara and I waited.

"After he fell asleep, I got his keys. The rest was easy. At first I couldn't get my bearings, but then I remembered the creek running next to the highway. I kept close to the creek and waded in it at first. That was to throw them off the scent."

"Throw *who* off the scent?" Barbara asked.

Marjorie's eyes widened. "The bloodhounds."

"What?"

"Didn't you know? Corbel keeps bloodhounds out there. To track down the patients, in case they ever escape."

I stood up.

"Where are you going?"

156

"To fix your bed," I said.

"I won't sleep," Marjorie told me. "I can't. What if Leo woke up? What if he got Corbel and they called out the bloodhounds to look for me?"

"Don't you worry about a thing," I answered. "No bloodhounds can get in here. We won't let anyone harm you, Marjorie. You're overtired. You've got to rest and forget about—"

"The asylum! You're going to call Corbel!"

"Marjorie, please try—"

"I knew it! I knew it when you stood up, from the look on your face! You're going to send me back; you're going to let them kill me!"

She jumped up. Barbara reached for her and I started forward, but not in time. She hit Barbara in the face and ran. I tried to head her off from the hall, but she got there first and tugged the front door open. Then she was running, jumping off the porch and circling through the trees in back. I could see her white nightgown waving behind her. I called, but she didn't answer.

If the car had been working, I would have tried to follow her. But even so, there wouldn't have been much chance of catching up, because she wouldn't stick to the roads.

After a couple of minutes, I went back into the house and closed the door. Barbara took the glasses into the kitchen, but she didn't say anything, not even when we went upstairs. It wasn't until we switched off the light and settled down in bed that she spoke to me.

"Poor Marjorie," Barbara said. "I felt so sorry for her."

"Me, too."

"You know, for a while she almost had me believing her. Sometimes those crazy stories turn out to be true after all."

I grunted. "I know. But all that medieval stuff about killing patients in asylums—that's just delusions of persecution."

"Are you sure, Bob?"

"Of course I'm sure. I admit I had my doubts for a while, too. But you know what tipped the scales?"

"What?"

"When she got to that part about the bloodhounds. That did it for me. Only a nut would dream up an idea like that."

"It bothers me, though. Don't you think we ought to call the sheriff after all? Or this Doctor Corbel, or Freddie?"

"Why get mixed up in it?" I asked. "I mean, look at the mess we'd get into."

"But the poor girl, running around out there all alone . . ."

"Don't worry, they'll get her. And she'll be taken care of."

"I can't help thinking about what she said, though. Do you think the part about this Leo was true?"

"I told you, it's delusions of persecution, Barbara. The whole works; about Freddie and his woman, about the killings—everything. Now just forget it."

She was quiet for a minute and I was quite for a minute, and then we heard the noise. Faint and far away it was, but I recognized it.

"What's that?" Barbara asked.

I sat up in bed, listening to it, listening to it get closer and closer. I was still listening to it when it faded off in the distance again.

"What's that?" Barbara asked, again.

"Oh, just some damned dogs on the loose," I told her. "Lots of strays out here, you know."

But I was lying.

I'm a Southerner, born and bred, and if there's one thing I can recognize, it's the sound of bloodhounds. Bloodhounds, unleashed and on the scent.

29

DRUM BEAT

Stephen Marlowe

THE BIG MAN sitting next to me in the window seat of the turboprop that was flying from Duluth, Minnesota, to Washington, D.C., looked at his watch and said, "Ten after seven, Drum. We're halfway there. If I were running away and out over the ocean somewhere, they'd call it the point of no return."

"You're not running away, Mr. Heyn," I said.

He smiled a little and agreed. "No, I'm not running away."

And then the ticking started.

Heyn's eyes widened. He'd been living with uncertainty and fear too long. The physical response was instant: the widening of the eyes, the sudden rictus of the mouth, a hand clutching at my wrist on the armrest between us.

The wordless response said: You read the papers, don't you? This wouldn't be the first bomb planted aboard an air liner, would it? And I'm a marked man, you know I am. That's why you're here.

I stood up quite calmly, but a pulse had begun to hammer in my throat, as if in time to the ticking. For a moment I saw the deep blue of the sky beyond Heyn's head and then on the luggage rack over it I saw the attaché case. It wasn't Sam Heyn's. Heyn's was next to it, monogrammed.

The ticking came from the unmarked case. It was very loud, or maybe that was my imagination. It sounded almost like a drum—each beat drumming our lives away and the lives of forty other innocent people in the turboprop.

I looked at the attaché case. I didn't touch it. Time-rigged, sure; but who could tell what kind of a spit-and-string mechanism activated it? Maybe just lifting it from the rack would set it off.

A minute had passed. Heyn asked, "Find it?"

159

I nodded mutely. A little boy squirmed around in the seat in front of Heyn. "Mommy," he said, "I hear a clock."

Mommy heard it too. She gave Heyn and me a funny look. Just then a stewardess came by with a tray. She stopped in the aisle next to my seat, in a listening attitude.

"Is that yours?" Her smile was strained. "With a clock in it, I hope?"

"It's not mine." I squeezed near her in the narrow aisle. Close to her ear I said softly, "It may be a bomb, miss. That's Sam Heyn in the window seat."

Her back stiffened. That was all. Then she hurried forward to the pilot's compartment. Heyn looked at me. A moment later over the PA a man's voice said:

"Whoever owns the unmarked attaché case above seat seventeen, please claim it. This is the captain speaking. Whoever owns . . ."

I heard the ticking that was like a drum. Faces turned. There was talking in the cabin of the turboprop. No one claimed the attaché case.

Sweat beaded Heyn's forehead. "When, dammit?" he said. "When will it go off?"

The captain came back. He had one of those self-confident, impassive faces they all have. He looked at the attaché case and listened to it. A man across the aisle got up to speak to him.

"Sit down, please," the captain said.

Then a voice said: "Bomb . . ." and the passengers scrambled from their seats toward the front and rear of the cabin. In the confusion I told the captain quickly, "My name is Chet Drum. I'm a private investigator bringing Sam Heyn here to testify in Washington before the Hartsell Committee. If he can prove what the Truckers' Brotherhood's been up to in the Midwest, there's going to be trouble."

"I can prove it," Heyn muttered.

I stared at the attaché case. I heard the ticking. It didn't look as if he'd get the chance.

"We could unload it out the door," the captain told me.

"Cabin's pressurized, isn't it?"

"So?"

"Who the hell knows how it's rigged? Change of pressure could be enough to set it off."

The captain nodded. He raised his voice and shouted, "Will you please all resume your seats?" Then he said, "If we could land in a hurry . . ." His face brightened. "Jesus, wait a minute." He looked at his watch. "Seven-nineteen," he said. Nine minutes had passed since the ticking started. "All we need is four thousand feet of runway. There's a small airport near New Albany . . ."

He rushed forward. Seconds later we were told to fasten our seat belts for an emergency landing. The big turboprop whined into a steep glide.

The attaché case ticked and ticked.

We came in twice. The first time the wind was wrong, and the captain had to try it again. Buzzing the field, I saw a windsock tower, two small lonely hangars and three shiny black cars waiting on the apron of the runway.

Three black cars waiting for what?

I felt my facial muscles relax. I smiled idiotically at Sam Heyn. He frowned back at me, mopping sweat from his forehead. "Well, well, well," I said.

He almost jumped from his seat when I reached over his head and lifted down the ticking attaché case. The man across the aisle gasped. We were banking steeply for our second run at the field. I carried the attaché case forward and through the door to the crew compartment.

The copilot had the stick. The captain looked at me and the attaché case. "Are you nuts or something?"

"I almost was."

He just stared. The flaps were down. We were gliding in.

"Keep away from that field," I said. The copilot ignored me.

I did the only thing I could to make them listen. I smashed the attaché case against a bulkhead, breaking the lock. The captain had made a grab for me, missing. I opened the case. There was a quiet little clock inside, and a noisy big one. The little one had triggered the big one to start at seven-ten. That was all.

No bomb.

"They knew your route," I said. "They figured you wouldn't dare ditch a time bomb, knew you'd have to land here if you heard it ticking at seven-ten. Three shiny black cars waiting at an airport in the middle of nowhere. They're waiting for Heyn." I pointed. "If you radio down below, you can have them picked up by the cops."

It was seven-thirty. "I never want to live through another twenty minutes like that," the captain said.

Neither did I. But Sam Heyn would get to Washington on schedule.

30

INVITED WITNESS

George Harmon Coxe

"SPEAK YOUR PIECE, Charlie, and quit stallin'." Jack Wolfe leaned back in his chair and rolled a cigarette.

"I know what you want. I read that Sob Sister story in *The Record*. I'm a killer, eh? And you're being big-hearted—gonna give me a chance to tell my side of the story maybe."

Wolfe stuck the finished cigarette in one corner of his mouth, lighted it, and turned to face me.

For a moment or so I studied that thin, gray-eyed face with its pointed chin and almost lipless mouth. Then I could feel the flush that swept over my face. I dropped my eyes and picked at the brim of my dark hat.

I wasn't prepared for a direct attack. I had hoped to get around to the subject in a more diplomatic manner. Now he had me where I couldn't sidestep—not and get away with it.

"Something like that," I mumbled. "This Varelli was a family man and—"

"Yeah. He was. Had a wife and two kids. He drove a Packard and they were starving. All they got was a monthly beating. And Varelli had only killed two men. The last one was a bank messenger—was shot four times. Four times, Charlie, and the kid never had a gun. Think it over. I suppose it would have been better if I'd let Varelli make it three. But then I wouldn't be here to give you your story, would I, Charlie?"

Wolfe's voice was bantering but there was no smile on his face.

I didn't answer right away, couldn't think of anything to say. Jack Wolfe was Special Investigator for the District Attorney and he had the reputation of getting things done. He had all kinds of authority to back him up. He was practically independent as an operative, responsible only to the D.A. Yet he could call on the police if he needed help.

This Varelli had been a rat, a murderer—anyone could tell you that. And Wolfe had done a good job in knocking him off. But he had, nevertheless, the unsavory reputation of a killer. Most people left the "e" off his name—labeled him The Wolf, and public sentiment was against him.

And when this dame down at *The Record* had run wild on the Varelli story, the chief sent me down to see what I could get from Wolfe for *The Courier*. I looked up at him again. The half-smoked cigarette drooped from his mouth and there was a mocking twinkle in his eyes.

"Well," he said. "What about it?"

"Don't get me wrong," I replied. "I'm not saying you shouldn't've plugged Varelli. All I know is that you're quicker'n hell on the draw. The witnesses who saw it said you both yanked out your guns at the same time, but that you fired an instant before he did."

Wolfe laughed. "I'm quick on the draw—but we both drew at the same time. Then I can't be so quick, eh?"

"Well—" I stammered. "I don't know, I wasn't here. That's what I heard."

Wolfe sat upright with a jerky movement, tossed the cigarette away and pulled his coat sleeve up. Rolling up his shirt sleeve above the elbow, he showed me his arm. A yellowish scar showed on one side of the muscle, a larger scar on the other side.

"There's one," he snapped. "I got another one in my side. I didn't get 'em in Europe either. I got 'em right here in Boston. And I got both of 'em because I drew first—and didn't shoot."

He rolled down his sleeve. "Quick on the draw! That's a lot of bunk. It's got nothin' to do with it. There's plenty of guys in the grave that drew first."

"Well, then," I pressed, "what's the answer?"

"The answer's a state of mind." He waited a moment for his words to sink in. "When you go after a man you've got to know whether he's gonna shoot or not. And if he is going to shoot, you've got to be first—if you want to live.

"I've seen a cop with his gun drawn stop a guy who still had his rod in his pocket. Yet the cop was the one that got plugged. Why? Because he didn't think the other guy would shoot—while the guy himself knew he would.

"After this second nick I got, I made up my mind I wanted to live a while. Understand, I don't draw unless I have to. But when I draw on a killer now, I figure on shootin'.

"This Varelli thug is an example. He was a killer. I knew it, everybody knew it. I went in after him. Neither of us had a gun in our hand. When he went for his, I knew he meant business.''

Wolfe pulled out the makings and started another cigarette.

"Doesn't make a very good story, does it, Charlie?''

"Well—'' I hedged, "I guess it does, but I never thought of it that way before.''

"Then let it lay. I'll give you a ring in a couple days— if I'm lucky. If you want, I'll let you see for yourself.''

Wolfe kept his word and three days later I got the call. It was in the evening and I was down at his office about nine o'clock.

He was sitting indolently in his chair, one of his half-consumed, smoke-stained cigarettes in the corner of his mouth. It was a funny habit, that rolling his own. It must've been a hangover from his army days. I never saw him smoke anything else.

I waited for him to speak. I didn't know just what he was going to do or what he had in mind. He'd said he was going to let me see for myself. And without knowing how or why, there was a definite tingle to my skin and the palms of my hands were damp.

"All set, Charlie?'' he said, finally.

"Sure. What're we gonna do?''

"We're goin' after Shulz.''

I whistled and made no attempt to disguise my feelings. Shulz was the one they had been looking for on the baby killings. The fellow had a record a mile long but with surprisingly few convictions. He'd been up for murder twice and both times he had beaten the rap. And two weeks ago, in gunning out a rival, he had killed a little girl and crippled a boy.

I hadn't said anything to the chief about Wolfe's offer, but now I thought I'd better phone in. To tell the truth, I wasn't so sure I was coming back.

"Is it all right to call in and tell 'em what I'm on?'' I asked. "I'd like to have 'em get all the stuff out of the files and the morgue, so they'll be ready for it. Will it break by eleven?''

Wolfe looked at me with that poker face of his and his lips barely moved.

"It'll break by eleven. But I don't think you'd better call in. You may change your mind about it before you get through. And—we might not be successful.''

I knew what he meant by that last, so I sat back and watched him open the drawer of his desk and take out a long-barreled, light automatic. I was plenty surprised and I guess I showed it when I spoke.

"You're not going after Shulz with that, are you? Looks like a .22."

"It is." Wolfe fondled the gun, slipped out the clip. "And this isn't always what I use, Charlie."

He put the clip back in the .22, pulled back the slide to throw a bullet in the chamber, and laid it on the desk. Then taking a larger gun—a revolver—from the drawer, he inspected this also.

"This is the old stand-by. A .38 special. But sometimes I have use for the .22. It all depends on the job and what I've got to do."

He slipped this in his shoulder holster and picked up the .22 again.

"It's a funny thing, Charlie. They've got me down for a killer. A hardboiled murderer. Well, I've been on this job five years and I've killed just three men in that time—including Varelli. Not so many, is it, when you think of what I've been up against."

"But," I sputtered. "It seems like—"

"Nope." Wolfe interrupted and forestalled the thought I was about to express. "I've shot plenty, Charlie. That's what you're thinking of. I've shot plenty—wounded 'em enough so we could take 'em. But that doesn't make such a good story, does it?"

I kept still and he continued. "That's what the .22 is for. With the .38 I can generally put a quick shot in a three-inch circle at ordinary range. With the .22 I can make that a one-inch circle. It's almost as good as a rifle, Charlie. And sometimes it comes in handy."

Wolfe stood up and slipped the .22 in his coat pocket. "I guess we're set. And just remember, this is no picnic. You know Shulz's reputation. If he should get me, it might be sort of tough on you. I'll try to take care of you, but it's not too late to back out and I wouldn't blame you if you did."

I looked at the sharp-featured face, sized up the slim, wiry build. There was competence in every line of him.

"It's O.K. with me," I said.

We left the taxi at Columbus Avenue. "How do you know you'll find him?" I asked.

"I'll find him. That's what stoolies are for. He won't be in when we get there but we'll stick around till he comes.

"The house is almost down to the next block. I'll go down alone. You watch me. See where I go. Then follow me in about five minutes. I'll wait down in the hall for you."

Five minutes later I followed Wolfe down the depressing canyon of three and four storied, dirty brick apartment houses. There was a sordid atmosphere of decay about the neighborhood that quickened my footsteps. I was glad when I reached the house into which Wolfe had turned.

The door was unlocked and Wolfe was waiting inside.

I followed him up two flights of narrow, dimly lighted stairs and down a corridor to an entrance on the left. He tried the knob, then fished out a ring of keys. An instant later he pushed open the door and stepped inside. I followed and stood out of the way until he had closed the door.

The place seemed pitch black. And as I waited there in the darkness for him to speak, I was conscious that I was holding my breath, that the blood was thumping at my eardrums. It seemed as though we stood there for five minutes before he said:

"Just stand there a minute."

He snapped on a flashlight. A handkerchief was over the lens and the diffused light which came from the bulb cast an eerie glow over the room. I could see that it was garishly furnished, could make out a davenport, a table, some chairs.

Then the light went out. I could hear Wolfe fumbling with something in the room, heard him grunt.

"It won't be long now," he said. "I guess the best place for you to stand is right in that doorway. If things don't work out, you can beat it back there to the kitchen. Now we'd better keep still."

He snapped on the light again until I took up my station in the hall doorway, then he switched it off again. But I wanted to ask one more question and I did.

"How come you're after this guy alone. You know he's goin' to be here. Why not let the cops in on it?"

"Yeah. That's just it. If they knew about it, there'd be fifty cops around this place. They'd be so thick Shulz couldn't miss. This way is safer. Now shut up."

I don't know how much later it was, probably not more than ten minutes, when I heard the footsteps in the outside corridor. And if I was nervous before, I was tensed all over now. Maybe I was scared; I know I wasn't happy about it. I wished then that I'd found out if there was a back door.

Then a key clicked in the lock and I tried to put my thoughts together. Would Wolfe shoot Shulz down in the doorway? Would he give him a chance?

I watched the door swing slowly open. A narrow strip of yellow from the lighted hall crept across the floor, picked out the pattern in the rug, played tricks with the table and chair in its path. I glanced quickly toward the wall opposite the door to see if Wolfe could be seen. I couldn't pick him out.

Then I watched the tall, thick-set figure, silhouetted in the doorway; saw him step into the room and raise one hand along the wall.

A switch clicked. Nothing happened. I stiffened as the fellow by the door spat out a curse. That was what Wolfe had been fumbling with. He had unscrewed the light bulbs.

Then a conical beam of light shot out from a point directly opposite the door. Wolfe's flashlight. I couldn't see what was behind it. I shrank back in my doorway and looked at Shulz.

For a second or two he stood there as though transfixed. His fleshy, heavily jowled face looked ghastly white in the artificial light. His eyes seemed to recede under the puffy lids and a tongue licked out to wet his lips.

"Stick 'em up, Shulz!" Wolfe barked the command. Then it happened.

This was what I had come to see and here it was. My eyes were glued on that puffy face of Shulz. I saw it coming, that thing Wolfe had spoken about, that action of the brain that meant death.

His hand darted inside his coat and I knew what to expect when the gun came out. I wanted to yell at Wolfe, wanted him to shoot while he had time.

Shulz's automatic whipped into view and the instant it was free of his clothing a streak of flame stabbed the darkness and a roar shattered the quiet of the room.

The time between the first shot and the second couldn't have been more than a watch tick. But it was long enough for a weakness of fear to sweep over me with the realization that Wolfe must have been hit. But the conical sweep of the flashlight still held steady.

Then the second shot roared and by that time I couldn't have run if I'd wanted to. Then two jets of flame shot out from a spot about four feet from the flashlight. Two sharp, distinct cracks sounded, like a person slapping a mosquito on his hand.

Shulz's face twitched. His mouth dropped open and the automatic slid from a hand that showed red on the back. One knee sagged and he braced himself on the other leg to keep from falling.

Wolfe, the .22 in his right fist, stepped into the flashlight's rays, reached up and turned one of the light bulbs. The resulting glow showed the flashlight resting on the back of an overstuffed chair. Wolfe moved over to Shulz, who hadn't said a word, and picked up the fallen automatic.

Backing toward a wall phone he said, "Now you see where the .22 comes in, Charlie. The one in the forearm crippled his gun hand, the one in the knee makes him stick around. I didn't have to kill this guy because, for once, we got a case he can't beat."

He reached up for the receiver. "Of course, this may not give you the story you want. This wasn't a regular shooting contest. I tricked him with the flash, turned it on and stepped to one side. Maybe that don't count. But maybe you can see what would've happened to some conscientious cop standing there with a flashlight—maybe you can see how a real killer works.

"And if this ain't just what you want, Charlie, let it lay. There may be a time when I can take you out with a .38 instead of the .22."

31

POISON

Katherine Mansfield

THE POST WAS very late. When we came back from our walk after lunch it still had not arrived.

"*Pas encore, Madame,*" sang Annette, scurrying back to her cooking.

We carried our parcels into the dining-room. The table was laid. As always, the sight of the table laid for two people only—and yet so finished, so perfect, there was no possible room for a third, gave me a queer, quick thrill as though I'd been struck by that silver lightning that quivered over the white cloth, the brilliant glasses, the shallow bowl of freesias.

"Blow the old postman! Whatever can have happened to him?" said Beatrice. "Put those things down, dearest."

"Where would you like them . . . ?"

She raised her head; she smiled her sweet, teasing smile.

"Anywhere—Silly."

But I knew only too well that there was no such place for her, and I would have stood holding the squat liqueur bottle and the sweets for months, for years, rather than risk giving another tiny shock to her exquisite sense of order.

"Here—I'll take them." She plumped them down on the table with her long gloves and a basket of figs. "The Luncheon Table. Short story by—by—" She took my arm. "Let's go on to the terrace—" and I felt her shiver. "*Ca sent,*" she said faintly, "*de la cuisine. . . .*"

I had noticed lately—we had been living in the south for two months—that when she wished to speak of food or the climate, or, playfully, of her love for me, she always dropped into French.

We perched on the balustrade under the awning. Beatrice leaned over gazing down—down to the white road with its guard of cactus spears. The

171

beauty of her ear, just her ear, the marvel of it was so great that I could have turned from regarding it to all that sweep of glittering sea below and stammer: "You know—her ear! She has ears that are simply the most . . ."

She was dressed in white, with pearls round her throat and lilies-of-the-valley tucked into her belt. On the third finger of her left hand she wore one pearl ring—no wedding ring.

"Why should I *mon ami?* Why should we pretend? Who could possibly care?"

And of course I agreed, though privately, in the depths of my heart, I would have given my soul to have stood beside her in a large, yes, a large, fashionable church, crammed with people, with old reverend clergymen, with *The Voice that breathed o'er Eden,* with palms and the smell of scent, knowing there was a red carpet and confetti outside, and somewhere, a wedding-cake and champagne and a satin shoe to throw after the carriage— if I could have slipped our wedding-ring on to her finger.

Not because I cared for such horrible shows, but because I felt it might possibly perhaps lessen this ghastly feeling of absolute freedom, *her* absolute freedom, of course.

Oh, God! What torture happiness was—what anguish! I looked up at the villa, at the windows of our room hidden so mysteriously behind the green straw blinds. Was it possible that she ever came moving through the green light and smiling that secret smile, that languid, brilliant smile that was just for me? She put her arm round my neck; the other hand soflty, terribly, brushed back my hair.

"Who are you?" Who was she? She was—Woman.

. . . On the first warm evening in Spring, when lights shone like pearls through the lilac air and voices murmured in the fresh-flowering gardens, it was she who sang in the tall house with the tulle curtains. As one drove in the moonlight through the foreign city hers was the shadow that fell across the quivering gold of the shutters. When the lamp was lighted, in the newborn stillness her steps passed your door. And she looked out into the autumn twilight, pale in her furs, as the automobile swept by. . . .

In fact, to put it shortly, I was twenty-four at the time. And when she lay on her back, with the pearls slipped under chin, and sighed "I'm thirsty, dearest. *Donne moi un orange,*" I would gladly, willingly, have dived for an orange into the jaws of a crocodile—if crocodiles ate oranges.

> *Had I two little feathery wings*
> *And were a little feathery bird . . .*

sang Beatrice.

I seized her hand. "You wouldn't fly away?"

"Not far. Not farther than the bottom of the road."

"Why on earth there?"

She quoted: "He cometh not, she said . . ."

"Who? The silly old postman? But you're not expecting a letter."

"No, but it's maddening all the same. Ah!" Suddenly she laughed and leaned against me. "There he is—look—like a blue beetle."

And we pressed our cheeks together and watched the blue beetle beginning to climb.

"Dearest," breathed Beatrice. And the word seemed to linger in the air, to throb in the air like the note of a violin.

"What is it?"

"I don't know," she laughed softly. "A wave of—a wave of affection, I suppose."

I put my arm around her. "Then you wouldn't fly away?"

"And she said rapidly and softly: "No! No! Not for worlds. Not really. I love this place. I've loved being here. I could stay here for years, I believe. I've never been so happy as I have these last two months, and you've been so perfect to me, dearest, in every way."

This was such bliss—it was so extraordinary, so unprecedented, to hear her talk like this that I had to try to laugh it off.

"Don't! You sound as if you were saying good-bye."

"Oh, nonsense, nonsense. You mustn't say such things even in fun!" She slid her little hand under my white jacket and clutched my shoulder. "You've been happy haven't you?"

"Happy? Happy? Oh, God—if you knew what I feel at this moment . . . Happy! My Wonder! My joy!"

I dropped off the balustrade and embraced her, lifting her in my arms. And while I held her lifted I pressed my face in her breast and muttered: "You *are* mine?" And for the first time in all the desperate months I'd known her, even counting the last month of—surely—Heaven—I believed her absolutely when she answered:

"Yes, I am yours."

The creak of the gate and the postman's steps on the gravel drew us apart. I was dizzy for the moment. I simply stood there, smiling, I felt, rather stupidly. Beatrice walked over to the cane chairs.

"You go—go for the letters," said she.

I—well—I almost reeled away. But I was too late. Annette came running. *"Pas des lettres,"* said she.

My reckless smile in reply as she handed me the paper must have surprised her. I was wild with joy. I threw the paper up into the air and sang out:

"No letters, darling!" as I came over to where the beloved woman was lying in the long chair.

For a moment she did not reply. Then she said slowly as she tore off the newspaper wrapper: "The world forgetting, *by* the world forgot."

There are times when a cigarette is just the very one thing that will carry you over the moment. It is more than a confederate, even; it is a secret, perfect little friend who knows all about it and understands absolutely. While you smoke you look down at it—smile or frown, as the occasion demands; you inhale deeply and expel the smoke in a slow fan. This was one of those moments. I walked over to the magnolia and breathed my fill of it. Then I came back and leaned over her shoulder. But quickly she tossed the paper away on to the stone.

"There's nothing in it," said she. "Nothing. There's only some poison trial. Either some man did or didn't murder his wife, and twenty thousand people have sat in court every day and two million words have been wired all over the world after each proceeding."

"Silly world!" said I, flinging into another chair. I wanted to forget the paper, to return, but cautiously, of course, to that moment before the postman came. But when she answered I knew from her voice the moment was over for now. Never mind. I was content to wait—five hundred years, if need be—now that I knew.

"Not so very silly," said Beatrice. "After all it isn't only morbid curiosity on the part of the twenty thousand."

"What is it, darling?" Heaven knows I didn't care.

"Guilt!" she cried. "Guilt! Didn't you realize that? They're fascinated like sick people are fascinated by anything—any scrap of news about their own case. The man in the dock may be innocent enough, but the people in court are nearly all of them poisoners. Haven't you ever thought"—she was pale with excitement—"of the amount of poisoning that goes on? It's the exception to find married people who don't poison each other—married people and lovers. Oh," she cried, "the number of cups of tea, glasses of wine, cups of coffee that are just tainted. The number I've had myself, and drunk, either knowing or not knowing—and risked it. The only reason why so many couples"—she laughed—"*survive*, is because the one is frightened of giving the other the fatal dose. That dose takes nerve! But it's bound to come sooner or later. There's no going back once the first little dose has been given. It's the beginning of the end, really don't you agree? Don't you see what I mean?"

She didn't wait for me to answer. She unpinned the lilies-of-the-valley and lay back, drawing them across her eyes.

"Both my husbands poisoned me," said Beatrice. "My first husband gave me a huge dose almost immediately, but my second was really an artist in his way. Just a tiny pinch, now and again, cleverly disguised—Oh, so cleverly!—until one morning I woke up and in every single particle of me, to the ends of my fingers and toes, there was a tiny grain. I was just in time. . . ."

I hated to hear her mention her husbands so calmly, especially today. It hurt. I was going to speak, but suddenly she cried mournfully:

"Why! Why should it have happened to me? What have I done? Why have I been all my life singled out by . . . It's a conspiracy."

I tried to tell her it was because she was too perfect for this horrible world—too exquisite, too fine. It frightened people. I made a little joke.

"But I—I haven't tried to poison you."

Beatrice gave a queer small laugh and bit the end of a lily stem.

"You!" said she. "You wouldn't hurt a fly!"

Strange. That hurt, though. Most horribly.

Just then Annette ran out with our *apéritifs*. Beatrice leaned forward and took a glass from the tray and handed it to me. I noticed the gleam of the pearl on what I called her pearl finger. How could I be hurt at what she said?

"And you," I said, taking the glass, "you've never poisoned anybody."

That gave me an idea; I tried to explain. "You—you do just the opposite. What is the name for one like you who, instead of poisoning people, fills them—everybody, the postman, the man who drives us, our boatman, the flower-seller, me—with new life, with something of her own radiance, her beauty, her—"

Dreamily she smiled; dreamily she looked at me.

"What are you thinking of—my lovely darling?"

"I was wondering," she said, "whether, after lunch, you'd go down to the post-office and ask for the afternoon letters. Would you mind, dearest? Not that I'm expecting one—but—I just thought, perhaps—it's silly not to have the letters if they're there. Isn't it? Silly to wait till tomorrow." She twirled the stem of the glass in her fingers. Her beautiful head was bent. But I lifted my glass and drank, sipped rather—sipped slowly, deliberately, looking at that dark head and thinking of—postmen and blue beetles and farewells that were not farewells and . . .

Good God! Was it fancy? No, it wasn't fancy. The drink tasted chill, bitter, *queer*.

32

THE SCIENTIST AND THE VANISHED WEAPON

Arthur Porges

LIEUTENANT TRASK'S FACE was gray and haggard, not so much from fatigue—he'd had only four hours' sleep in the last two days, which was no more than usual—as from frustration, grief, and rage.

"This is the season of miracles," he said in a bitter voice. "Christmas, Peace on Earth, Love Thy Neighbor, and all the rest. But I didn't expect a teen-age killer to pull a miracle. Drucker had a wife and four children," he added, "and this punk Remick shot three slugs into poor Drucker before Tom even knew what was happening. It didn't have to be like that; the punk could've got out the back door easily; Drucker was big and slow. Brave—too damned brave—but slow. I told him a million times to stop taking chances—to have his gun out and to use it, but not Tom—always afraid he'd shoot a frightened kid. Now," Trask grated, "one shot him—three times over. He might've lived—probably would've, Doc says—if Remick hadn't fired twice more."

Cyriack Skinner Grey, sitting quietly in the wheelchair in which he was destined to stay for the rest of his life, felt a surge of affection and sympathy for the tired detective. The police often suffered from a bad image in the public eye, but there were thousands of fine men like Trask who killed themselves by inches—when they didn't die violently at the hands of criminals—trying to make life safer for the people of their communities.

Grey took a shot-glass from a recess in one arm of the chair, held it under a tiny tap, and pressed a button. Amber liquid flowed out in a thin stream. He held the drink up for his friend.

"Can't," Trask said regretfully. "I'm still on duty."

The older man cocked his head, shrugged, and drank the whiskey himself.

"In that case," he said, "how about some coffee?"

177

From another faucet he quickly produced hot, black, and fragrant brew, drawing it into a small handleless cup of fine bone china.

Trask shook his head in wonder, and accepted it.

"One of these days," he said, a little of the gloom leaving his face, "you'll haul a beautiful dancing girl out of that incredible contraption, and that's when I'll have myself tested for hallucinations!" He knew that Grey, formerly a top research scientist, who still had a fully equipped lab in this old house, had built a hundred gadgets into his wheelchair; yet the Lieutenant was surprised by a new one at least once a month. But it was because of the old man's flair for solving problems, first in the lab and now as a free-lance crime consultant, that Trask had come to see him.

"All right," Grey said, as the detective swallowed a third cupful. "Let's have it. What's all this about a miracle?"

"The miracle of the vanishing gun," Trask said. "I was licked at the scene, but I figured if anybody could counter a bad miracle with a good one, you're the man to do it."

He gave Grey the empty cup, and with hands clasped behind his back, paced the floor of the old man's study, speaking as he walked.

"It's like this. Tom Drucker caught the kid—Arnold Remick's his full name—inside Jack's Camera Exchange. The punk saw Tom first, and put three slugs into him; then he ran. Two of my men were in a cruiser not far away; they heard the shots and poured it on to get there. They spotted Remick going down an alley, and took after him. The punk hopped a fence, so they left the car to follow. The kid was running scared, I guess, because he ducked into a big apartment building and up the stairs. Fool thing to do really—no way out.

"Well, he sees an apartment with the door ajar, and slips in; but my two men, right behind, catch a glimpse, and know they have him boxed. "The kid was kill-crazy; he fired right through the door until he ran out of shells. That's my guess, anyhow—we don't have the gun yet, which is why I'm here. When he stopped shooting; my men crashed into the place and handcuffed him—there was no more fight left in the punk.

"Naturally, they looked for the gun first thing, but it just wasn't there. The window was open, the way the door had been, and for the same reason. The woman who lives there had something cooking in the oven, so she wanted to air the rooms out. Meanwhile she went downstairs to chew the fat with another woman.

"Not finding the gun in the apartment, the men figure Remick tossed it out the window—what good that would do, I don't think he stopped to consider. He should've known we'd find it below soon enough. That's what

I thought!'' Trask added bitterly. ''We combed that yard inch by inch, and every other area reachable from a third-floor window by a pro pitcher—nothing.

''Now you tell me,'' Trask concluded, jaw out, looking squarely at Grey, ''how a jerky kid with only seconds to spare can make a .38 automatic—that's what it was, judging from the bullets they dug out of poor Drucker—vanish. That's what I meant by a punk pulling a miracle.''

''Gun not in the apartment—you're sure?''

''Absolutely. Nobody could hide something that big so quickly where we couldn't find it. We tore that place wide open. The tenants didn't like us one bit.''

''Is the boy naturally clever or ingenious?''

''Just the opposite, damn it—that's what bugs me. He's a stupid drop-out punk of seventeen—can hardly put a sentence together, even in Basic English. And everything else he did that night shows stupidity—stupidity and hate. And another thing,'' the Lieutenant said in a thoughtful voice, ''it just came to me. I think Remick expected us to find the gun. When my man came back empty-handed Remick looked sort of surprised. Now why was that, I wonder?''

''Tell me about the yard.''

''Nothing to tell. Wouldn't be much of a sight even in summer—very little gardening done, I imagine. Right now, at this time of the year, it's just bare, except for the two grubby trees, the birdbath, and a barbecue covered with a plastic sheet. Oh, and a wooden table with built-on bench seats—you know the kind; like on a picnic ground.''

''You checked them all, of course?''

''You bet. Found exactly nothing. Even took the plastic off the barbecue, although the gun obviously didn't go through it—no hole. And the birdbath was just solid ice inside. Without that gun,'' he said sourly, ''we can't make a case, especially against a juvenile. The punk can claim he was just scared and running for fear of being accused. Sure, we can swear he fired from the room, and produce slugs similar to the ones that killed Tom, but you know juries and lawyers. They'll say: if this kid had a gun, where is it? Maybe it's just another cop frame-up—swearing away a boy's life because we let the real killer escape.''

''What about the area beyond the yard?'' Grey asked. He pressed a button; a humidor swung out and swiveled open. He took a thin, very black cigar from it, and the box disappeared with a snake-like glide.

Watching the scientist light the cheroot in a glowing disc set into one arm of the wheelchair, the detective said, ''Same story. All pretty bare. Dry fishpond; some scrubby dead grass; a few beat-up shrubs—no place where a gun could disappear.''

"Forgive me if I'm obvious," Grey said, smiling crookedly, "but couldn't somebody outside have simply picked it up and carried it away?''

·"I thought of that. But the yard is completely fenced in, and it was dark out, remember. A person after the gun would need eyes like an owl, and he'd have to move like a scalded cat, besides. My man got down there pretty fast, after that quick first check of the apartment. We guarded the area all night, and searched again this morning—but no luck.''

The scientist sat quietly in his chair, puffing on the cigar.

"I suppose," the detective said a little wistfully, "it's time to call in Edgar."

He meant Grey's puckish carrot-topped son, aged 14, who had an I.Q. of 180 and a genius for higher mathematics, especially topology. His father, who hated prigs, had made sure that Edgar developed both a sense of humor and a large bump of humility. As a widower and an intellectual, he knew the risk of raising his son single-handed but hoped—and planned—for the best. Edgar was the immobilized scientist's legs; he gathered data from which Grey extracted the key patterns that led to the solutions of his cases.

"No-o," Grey drawled. "I don't think that's necessary this time. If you've searched as carefully as you say, then sending Edgar to the scene wouldn't help. It seems to be a matter of pure reason at this point. Considering how quickly Remick must have acted, and assuming that your inference about his own surprise is valid, I can think of only one possible solution."

Trask was staring at him.

"Are you trying to tell me," he blurted, "that you already have it solved? That you know where the gun is?''

"I wouldn't be quite that dogmatic. But if your report was factual and complete, then my solution is at least highly probable. It was a cold night, I believe you said.''

"That's right," the detective replied, almost absently. "Damp-cold, with some freezing slush on the ground. Which, by the way, as I should have told you, also indicated that nobody else picked up the gun from the yard and took it away—no fresh footprints except our own. Now," he begged, "for the love of Pete, what's the answer? Where is the gun?''

"I would say," the old man drawled with maddening deliberation, "that the gun is at the bottom of the birdbath, under the ice.''

"Wha-a-t?" Trask exclaimed; then his face darkened, and he shook his head emphatically. "It can't be. This time, for once, you're wrong. Maybe it's my fault,'' he added quickly. "I didn't make the timing clear enough. After my men crashed the door, a fast once-over turned up nothing, so one of them ran down to the yard, while the other kept searching the apartment. Now, Ferber's a good cop; he checked the birdbath—remember this was less than ten minutes after Remick tossed out the gun, if he did. Well, there were six inches of solid ice in that birdbath—solid, as I said.''

He gave Grey a weak, lopsided smile. "I'm an old pond-skater from Vermont; I know how water freezes. First, a crust forms at the top; then the ice moves down to the bottom. But it takes quite a while, even in cold weather. Last night it was maybe twenty-eight or so. That birdbath couldn't possibly freeze completely in the few minutes after the kid ditched the gun. And if it broke through the crust, Ferber would have found it—he jabbed the ice, and it was frozen solid right through to the bottom. Besides, the hole the gun would have made going through the crust would show up different, even if it glazed over fast.''

"I take it the ice wasn't clear.''

"So Ferber couldn't see down to the bottom,'' Grey said placidly.

"No, but—''

"All right,'' the old man interrupted him, beginning to show impatience. "I see the point you've tried to make. Only it's not necessarily valid in this case. If your search was thorough, the gun's not anywhere in the apartment or on the ground outside. Therefore it must be in the birdbath.''

Grey raised one hand as Trask began to protest again. "Ever hear of supercooling? Last night the temperature dropped to below freezing— about twenty-eight, you suggested. Now ordinarily, water begins to solidify at thirty-two, with very little leeway. But occasionally, when the temperature drop is gradual and the liquid remains undisturbed, it stays unfrozen even with a fall to several degrees below thirty-two. Then, if you toss a pebble, a twig—or a gun—into the supercooled water, it suddenly freezes solid, in a flash, all the way to the bottom.

"I think that's what happened last night. The boy got panicky and tossed the gun out of the window, not knowing how else to get rid of it fast. He *did* expect you to find it, which is why he looked so surprised at your failure. He couldn't guess that it would fall into the supercooled water of the birdbath, triggering it instantaneously to ice. As an old pond-skater,'' he jibed, "I'm surprised you never noticed the phenomenon before. Anyhow, you'd have found the gun after the first thaw.''

Trask was wordless for a moment, then he said, "Not if somebody else—maybe a pal of Remick's tipped off to look around for what we missed—got there first.'' He wagged his head wonderingly. "Supercooled water—well, I'll be damned. The funny thing is," he said sheepishly, "that it comes back to me now. One night my dad actually showed us the stunt—made the whole pond on our farm freeze instantly by tossing in a stone. But I was only about nine, and didn't remember it till now. I'm almost afraid to check, in case you're wrong."

"If I am," Grey said, "then the boy is either a genuine miracle worker or your men are not very efficient. Why not go and find out," he suggested. "I'm rather curious myself."

"I'll just call Gaffney, who's watching the place," Trask said. "Then we'll know the truth in a hurry."

The answer came back by phone a few minutes later. The gun was there—a .38, and empty.

"It will match those slugs," the Lieutenant said, "so now we've got a case."

"Congratulations," the old man said in his driest voice. "And now I'll get back to my electronics."

He pressed a button. A motor hummed in the base of his wheelchair, and it rolled up a ramp toward the lab on the second floor. Trask watched for a moment, smiling, and then headed for the door. Suddenly the smile left his mouth. He still had to face Mrs. Drucker and Tom's four kids.

33

NIGHT-WALKER

Robert J. Randisi

HE SITS AT the dimly lit bar and listens to the conversations going on around him. He does not concentrate on any one conversation, but strains to catch at least a piece of each separate one within earshot. With a wave of his hand he orders a second drink and continues to listen. He is listening for a certain phrase to be spoken, at which time he will make his plans and act upon them.

The words, however, when spoken, do not come from any of the conversations going on around him, but from the bartender as he brings him his third drink.

"So, what do you think?" the bartender asks.

Glancing at the heavily built man behind the bar, he asks, "About what?"

Pointing to the far end of the bar the bartender says, "We was having an argument, about Ali and this new guy. I think the challenger is gonna get hurt pretty good, but those guys figure Ali is taking the guy too light. Me, I know Ali can beat a nobody like this bum. I mean, who is he, you know? He's a nobody!"

He stares at the overweight bartender for a few moments before telling the man, "Go back to your friends."

Frowning, the bartender starts to say something else, but thinks better of it and moves off . . .

Finishing his drink, he rises to leave, stopping only to ask the hatcheck girl, "What time does the bartender work until?"

"Midnight," she answers and, batting heavily made-up eyes at him, adds, "Why? Won't I do?"

Without answering, he leaves the bar and picks a spot outside.

The bartender leaves at five minutes past midnight. He turns right and

183

proceeds towards an alley. As he passes the alley he is grabbed by the neck from behind and dragged in. Although the attacker is smaller and thinner, his strength is sufficient to hold the bigger man until he chooses to release him, deeper into the alley. There he pushes the bartender against the building.

"What do you want?" the heavier man cries, eyes wide with fright. "I ain't got no money! What do you want?"

Slowly the smaller man takes a switchblade from his pocket and allows the four-and-a-half-inch blade to spring from the six-inch handle. Although at its widest the blade is a mere three-eighths of an inch it is a very effective weapon.

Rotating the knife slowly, he catches the frightened man's eyes with his own, then he plunges it swiftly into his belly. The man screams. He falls to the ground whimpering. The last words he hears before dying are "Everybody is somebody."

He rides the subway, listening to the conversations. Not to any one conversation, but to at least a part of every one he can.

He listens for a certain phrase.

From behind him he hears, "I wouldn't go out with Arnold on a bet. He's so short—a little fat nobody."

He turns to see who is speaking. The girl is young, not yet twenty, with blond hair and smooth skin. He watches closely to see where she gets off, and follows when she does.

It is late and he and the girl are the only two to leave the train. The girl gives him a brief and suspicious look, satisfying herself as to who got off with her and what he looks like. Apparently what she sees does not frighten her and she begins to walk towards the stairway to the street. He notices that there is no clerk in the change booth. He follows the girl closely and calls to her as she approaches the stairs. She turns, but does not see the blade in his hand. She does see his intense eyes when they catch hers and hold them.

"What is it? What do you—" she begins, her voice tinged now with fear. He steps in and, in one swift motion, plunges the thin blade into the girl. She falls to the floor clutching herself. The last words she hears before dying are "Everybody is somebody."

It is almost morning, almost daylight. He cannot function correctly in daylight. Somehow the sunlight inhibits him, makes him a different person. At night it's different. In the daytime, as a janitor in a high school, he is a nobody. He cleans floors, walls, the yard and locker rooms, the lunch room—everyone believing that, as a janitor, he is subject to their commands.

"Clean that up, Woodley."

"I dropped some milk, Woodley, mop it up, would you, please?"

"Who's that? Oh, just Woodley."

In the daytime he is Woodley the nobody.

But everybody is somebody, so at night when darkness falls, he is somebody.

34

THE INNOCENT ONE

Evan Hunter

IT WAS PABLO, poor bastard, who got it.

You must understand, first, that the sun was very hot on that day and Miguel had been working in it from just after dawn. He had eaten a hearty breakfast, and then had taken to the fields early, remembering what had to be done and wanting to do it quickly.

There were many rocks among the beans that day, and perhaps that is what started it all. When Miguel discovered the first rock, he reached down gingerly and tossed it over his shoulder to the rear of his neat rows of beans. The sun was still not high in the sky, and the earth had not yet begun to bake, and so a smile worked its way over his brown features as he heard the rock thud to the soft earth behind him. He started hoeing again, thinking of Maria and the night before.

He would never regret having married Maria. Ah, but she was a one! There was the passion of the tigress in her, and the energy of the rabbit. He thought again of her, straightening up abruptly, and feeling the ache in his back muscles.

That was when he saw the second rock.

He shrugged, thinking, *Madre de Dios, another one!*

He lifted it, threw it over his shoulder and began hoeing again. He was surprised when he came across more rocks. At first he thought someone had played a joke on him, and he pulled his black brows together, wondering who it could have been. Juan, that pig? Felipe, that animal with the slobbering lips? Pablo?

Then he remembered that it had rained the night before, and he realized that the waters had washed the soil clean, exposing the rocks, bringing them to the surface.

He cursed himself for not having thought to protect the beans in some way. Then he cursed the rocks. And since the sun was beginning to climb in the sky, he cursed that too, and got to work.

The rocks were not heavy. They were, in fact, rather small.

It was that there were very many of them. He picked them up painstakingly, tossing them over his shoulders. How could a man hoe his beans when the rows were full of rocks? He started to count them, stopping at ten because that was as far as he knew how to count, and then starting with one all over again.

The sun was very hot now. The hoe lay on the ground, the rich earth staining its long handle. He kept picking up the rocks, not looking up now, swearing softly, the sweat pouring down his neck and back. When a long shadow fell over the land before him, he almost didn't notice it.

Then a voice joined the shadow, and Miguel straightened his back and rubbed his earth-stained fingers on his white trousers.

"You are busy, Miguel?" the voice asked. The voice came through the speaker's nose rather than his mouth. It whined like the voice of the lamb. It was Felipe.

"No, I am not busy," Miguel said. "I was, at this very moment, lying on my back and counting the stars in the sky."

"But it is mornin . . ." Felipe started. Miguel's subtle humour struck him then, and he slapped his thigh and commenced to guffaw like the jackass he was. "Counting the stars!" he bellowed. "Counting the stars!"

Miguel was not amused. "You were perhaps on your way somewhere, *amigo*. If so, don't let me detain you."

"I was going nowhere, Miguel," Felipe said.

Miguel grunted and began picking up rocks again. He forgot how many tens he had counted thus far, so he started all over again.

"You are picking up rocks, Miguel?"

Miguel did not answer.

"I say you are picking up . . ."

"Yes!" Miguel said. "Yes, I am picking up rocks." He stood up and kneaded the small of his back, and Felipe grinned knowingly.

"The back, it hurts, eh?"

"Yes," Miguel said. He looked at Felipe. "Why do you nod?"

"Me? Nod? Who me?"

"Yes, you. Why do you stand there and nod your head like the wise snake who has swallowed the young chicken?"

Felipe grinned and nodded his head. "You must be mistaken, Miguel. I do not nod."

"I am not blind, *amigo*," Miguel said testily. "I say my back hurts, and you begin to nod your head. Why? Is it funny that my back hurts? Is it funny that there are rocks and stones among my beans?''

"No, Miguel. It is not funny."

"Then why do you nod?"

Felipe grinned. "Maria, eh?"

Miguel clenched his fists. "What about Maria, *amigo*? Maria who is my wife."

Felipe opened his eyes innocently. "Nothing, Miguel, nothing. Just . . . Maria."

"You refer to my back?"

"*Si.*"

"And you connect this somehow with Maria?"

"*Si.*"

"How?"

"This Maria . . . your wife, God bless her . . . she is a strong one, eh, Miguel?"

Miguel was beginning to get a little angry. He was not used to discussing his wife among the beans. "So? What do you mean she is a strong one?"

"You know. Much passion. Like the tigress."

"How do you know this?"

Felipe grinned. "It is known, Miguel."

Miguel's lips tightened into a narrow line. "How is it known?"

"I must go to town, Miguel," Felipe said hastily. "I see you soon."

"Just a moment. Felipe. How is it . . ."

"Good-bye, *amigo*."

Felipe turned his back, and Miguel stared at him as he walked towards the road. The dust rose about him, and he waved back at Miguel. Miguel did not return the wave. He stood there with the strong sun on his head, and the many rocks and stones at his feet.

How did this animal with the slobbering lips know of Maria's passion? Surely he had never spoken a word about it to any of the men. Then how did Felipe know?

The possibilites annoyed Miguel. He turned back to the rocks, and this time they seemed heavier, and the sun seemed stronger, and his back seemed to ache more.

How did Felipe know?

He was pondering this in an ill-temper when Juan came to stand beside him. Juan was darkly handsome, his white trousers and shirt bright in the powerful sunlight. Miguel looked up at him sourly and said, "So? Do you wish to pass the time with idle chatter also?"

189

Juan smiled, his teeth even and white against the ruddy brown of his face. "Did I offend you, Miguel?"

"No!" Miguel snapped.

"Then why do you leap at me like a tiger?"

"Do not mention this animal to me," Miguel said.

"No?"

"No! I have rocks to clear, and I want to clear them before lunch because Maria will be calling me then."

"Ahhh," Juan said, grinning.

Miguel stared at him for a moment. The grin was the same one Felipe had worn, except that Felipe was ugly and with slobbering lips—and Juan was perhaps the handsomest man in the village.

Miguel stared at him and wondered if it had been *he* who had told Felipe of Maria's great passion. And if so, how had Juan known?

"Why do you 'ahhhhh'?" he asked.

"Did I 'ahhhhh'?"

"You did. You did indeed. You made this very sound. Why?"

"I was not aware, *amigo*." Juan smiled again.

"Was it mention of lunch that evoked this sigh?"

"No. No, I do not think so."

"Then there remains only Maria."

Juan grinned and said nothing.

"I said . . ."

"I heard you, Miguel."

"What about Maria?"

Juan shrugged. "Who said anything about Maria?"

"You are saying it with your eyes," Miguel said heatedly. "What about her?"

"She is your wife, Miguel."

"I know she is my wife. I sleep with her, I . . ."

Juan was grinning again.

"What's funny about that, Juan? Why do you grin now?"

"I have nothing to say, *amigo*. Maria is your wife. God bless her."

"What does that mean?"

"It means . . . well, God bless her. She is a remarkable woman."

"How would you know?" Miguel shouted.

"That she is a remarkable woman? Why, Miguel . . ."

"You know what I mean! Why is my wife the sudden topic of conversation for the whole village? What is going on? Why do you all discuss her so intimately? What . . ."

"Intimately?"

"Yes! By God, Juan, if there is something . . ."

Juan smiled again. "But there is nothing, Miguel. Nothing."

"You are sure?"

"I must go to town now, my friend. Is there anything I can do there for you?"

"No!" Miguel snapped.

"Then, *adios, amigo.*"

He turned and walked off, shaking his head, and Miguel could have sworn he heard him mutter the word "tigress."

He went to work on the rocks with a fury. What was all this? Why Felipe? And now Juan?

What was going on with his wife?

He thought of her passion, her gleaming black hair, the way it trailed down the curve of her back, reaching her waist. He thought of the fluid muscles on that back, beneath the soft, firm skin. He thought of the long, graceful curve of her legs, the way the firelight played on her lifted breasts.

Too passionate, he thought. *Far too passionate*.

Far too passionate for one man. Far too passionate for simple Miguel who worked in the fields picking stones and hoeing beans. Yes, she was a woman who needed many men—many, many men.

Was that why Felipe had laughed with his dripping lips? Was that why Juan had smiled that superior, handsome smile? Miguel picked up his hoe and swung it at a large rock. The rock chipped, but it did not budge from the earth.

Was that it? Was Maria then making a cuckold of her simple Miguel? Was that why all the men in the village were snickering, smiling, laughing behind their hands? Or was it only the men from this village? Was it the adjoining village, too? Or did it go beyond that?

Did they pass her from hand to hand like a used wine-jug? Did they all drink of her, and was that why they laughed at Miguel now? Was that why they laughed behind their hands, laughed aloud with their mouths and their eyes?

The sun was hot, and the bowels of the earth stank, and the rocks and stones were plentiful, and Miguel chopped at them with the hoe, using the sharp blade like an axe.

I will show them, he thought. I will teach them to laugh! I will teach them to make the fool of Miguel de la Piaz!

It was then that Pablo strolled by. He had passed Miguel's house, and Maria had asked him to call her husband home for lunch. He was not a bright lad,

Pablo. He walked up close to Miguel, who furiously pounded the earth with his hoe, using it like an axe, the sharp blade striking sparks from the rocks. He tapped Miguel on the shoulder, smiled, and started to say, "Maria . . ."

Miguel whirled like an animal, the hoe raised high.

So you see, it was Pablo, poor bastard, who got it.

35

FUNNY YOU SHOULD ASK

Lawrence Block

ON WHAT A less original writer might deign to describe as a fateful day, young Robert Tillinghast approached the proprietor of a shop called Earth Forms. "Actually," he said, "I don't think I can buy anything today, but there's a question I'd like to ask you. It's been on my mind for the longest time. I was looking at those recycled jeans over by the far wall."

"I'll be getting a hundred pair in Monday afternoon," the proprietor said.

"Is that right?"

"It certainly is."

"A hundred pair," Robert marveled. "That's certainly quite a lot."

"It's the minimum order."

"Is that a fact? And they'll all be the same quality and condition as the ones you have on display over on the far wall?"

"Absolutely. Of course, I won't know what sizes I'll be getting."

"I guess that's just a matter of chance."

"It is. But they'll all be first-quality name brands, and they'll all be in good condition, broken in but not broken to bits. That's a sort of an expression I made up to describe them."

"I like it," said Robert, not too sincerely. "You know, there's a question that's been nagging at my mind for the longest time. Now you get six dollars a pair for the recycled jeans, is that right?" It was. "And it probably wouldn't be out of line to guess that they cost you about half that amount?" The proprietor, after a moment's reflection, agreed that it wouldn't be far out of line to make that estimate.

"Well, that's the whole thing," Robert said. "You notice the jeans I'm wearing?"

The proprietor glanced at them. They were nothing remarkable, a pair of oft-washed Lee Riders that were just beginning to go thin at the knees. "Very nice," the man said. "I'd get six dollars for them without a whole lot of trouble."

"But I wouldn't want to sell them."

"And of course not. Why should you? They're just getting to the comfortable stage."

"Exactly!" Robert grew intense, and his eyes bulged slightly. This was apt to happen when he grew intense, although he didn't know it, never having seen himself at such times. "Exactly," he repeated. "The recycled jeans you see in the shops, this shop and other shops, are just at the point where they're breaking in right. They're never really worn out. Unless you only put the better pairs on display?"

"No, they're all like that."

"That's what everybody says." Robert had had much the same conversation before in the course of his travels. "All top quality, all in excellent condition, and all in the same stage of wear."

"So?"

"So," Robert said in triumph, "who throws them out?"

"Oh."

"The company that sells them. Where do they get them from?"

"You know," the proprietor said, "it's funny you should ask. The same question's occurred to me. People buy these jeans because this is the way they want 'em. But who in the world sells them? That's what I'd like to know. Not that it would do me any good to have the answer, but the question preys on my mind. Who sells them? I could understand about young chldren's jeans that kids would outgrow them, but what about the adult sizes? Unless kids grow up and don't want to wear jeans anymore."

"I'll be wearing jeans as long as I live," Robert said recklessly. "I'll never get too old for jeans."

The proprietor seemed not to have heard. "Now maybe it's different out in the farm country." he said. "I buy these jeans from a firm in Rockford, Illinois—"

"I've heard of the firm," Robert said. "They seem to be the only people supplying recycled jeans."

"Only one I know of. Now maybe things are different in their area and people like brand-new jeans and once they break in somewhat they think of them as worn out. That's possible, don't you suppose?"

"I guess it's possible."

"Because it's the only explanation I can think of. After all, what could they afford to pay for the jeans? A dollar a pair? A dollar and a half at the outside? Who would sell 'em good condition jeans for that amount of money?'' The man shook his head. ''Funny you should ask a question that I've asked myself so many times and never put into words.''

''That Rockford firm,'' Robert said. ''That's another thing I don't understand. Why would they develop a sideline business like recycled jeans?''

''Well, you never know about that,'' the man said. ''Diversification is the keynote of American business these days. Take me, for example. I started out selling flowerpots, and now I sell flowerpots and guitar strings and recapped tires and recycled jeans. Now there are people who would call that an unusual combination.''

''I suppose there are,'' said Robert.

An obsession of the sort that gripped Robert is a curious thing. After a certain amount of time it is either metamorphosized into neurosis or it is tamed, surfacing periodically as a vehicle for casual conversation. Young Robert Tillinghast, neurotic enough in other respects, suppressed his curiosity on the subject of recycled jeans and only raised the question at times when is seemed particularly apropos.

And it did seem apropos often enough. Robert was touring the country, depending for his locomotion upon the kindness of passing motorists. As charitable as his hosts were, they were apt to insist upon a quid pro quo of conversation, and Robert had learned to converse extemporaneously upon a variety of subjects. One of these was that of recycled blue jeans, a subject close at once to his heart and his skin, and Robert's own jeans often served as the lead-in to this line of conversaton, being either funky and mellow or altogether disreputable, depending upon one's point of view, which in turn largely depended (it must be said) upon one's age.

One day in West Virginia, on that stretch of Interstate 79 leading from Morgantown down to Charleston, Robert thumbed a ride with a man who, though not many years older than himself, drove a late-model Cadillac. Robert, his backpack in the back seat and his body in the front, could not have been more pleased. He had come to feel that hitching a ride in an expensive car endowed one with all the privileges of ownership without the nuisance of making the payments.

Then, as the car cruised southward, Robert noticed that the driver was glancing repeatedly at his, which is to say Robert's, legs. Covert glances at that, sidelong and meaningful. Robert sighed inwardly. This, too, was part of the game, and had ceased to shock him. But he had so been looking forward to riding in this car and now he would have to get out.

The driver said, ''Just admiring your jeans.''

"I guess they're just beginning to break in," Robert said, relaxing now. "I've certainly had them a while."

"Well, they look just right now. Got a lot of wear left in them. I guess they'll last for years," Robert said. "With the proper treatment. You know, that brings up something I've been wondering about for a long time." And he went into his routine, which had become rather a little set piece by this time, ending with the question that had plagued him from the start. "So where on earth does that Rockford company get all these jeans? Who provides them?"

"Funny you should ask," the young man said. "I don't suppose you noticed my license plates before you got in?" Robert admitted he hadn't. "Few people do," the young man said. "Land of Lincoln is the slogan on them, and they're from Illinois. And I'm from Rockford. As a matter of fact, I'm with that very company."

"But that's incredible! For the longest time I've wanted to know the answers to my questions, and now at long last—" He broke off. "Why are we leaving the Interstate?"

"Bypass some traffic approaching Charleston. There's construction ahead and it can be a real bottleneck. Yes, I'm with the company."

"In sales, I suppose? Servicing accounts? You certainly have enough accounts. Why, it seems every store in the country buys recycled jeans from you people."

"Our distribution is rather good," the young man said, "and our sales force does a good job. But I'm in Acquisitions, myself. I go out and round up the jeans. Then in Rockford they're washed to clean and sterilize them, patched if they need it and—"

"You're actually in Acquisitions?"

"That's a fact."

"Well, this *is* my lucky day," Robert exclaimed. "You're just the man to give me all the answers. Where do you get the jeans? Who sells them to you? What do you pay for them? What sort of person sells perfectly good jeans?"

"That's a whole lot of questions at once."

Robert laughed, happy with himself, his host, and the world. "I just don't know where to start and it's got me rattled. Say, this bypass is a small road, isn't it? I guess not many people know about it and that's why there's no other traffic on it. Poor saps'll all get tangled in traffic going into Charleston."

"We'll miss all that."

"That's good luck. Let's see, where can I begin? All right, here's the big question and I've always been puzzled by this one. What's a company like yours doing in the recycled jeans business?"

"Well," said the young man, "diversification is the keynote of American business these days."

"But a company like yours," Robert said. "Rockford Dog Food, Inc. How did you ever think to get into the business in the first place?"

"Funny you should ask," said the young man, braking the car smoothly to a stop.

36

CASTLE IN SPAIN

Julian Symons

SAN AVALO IS a dot on the map of Spain some twenty miles from Corunna, in the northwest corner of Galicia. Don Easton went there because a friend said that it was the most beautiful village in Spain, and added contemptuously that no travel agent had ever heard of it.

Don's tendency to wanderlust was aroused, and his pride as a travel agent was stung. Within a month he was on his way to Galicia, which the Spaniards used to call Finisterre, or world's end.

Galicia may not be the world's end, but it is certainly not easily accessible. The nearest big airport is at Lisbon, three hundred miles away, and the sea route to Vigo is used mostly by ships that lack tourist accommodation. Don took the train to the French-Spanish frontier and then changed to the bus, which is often the quickest way of getting about in Spain. He had already decided that if San Avalo was to figure on the Easitravel list it must be as part of a coach tour. Traveling by bus, he might well see other good stopping places.

He sat in the bus station at Bilbao, reading a day-old English paper. There was not much news in it—a mother had left her month-old baby on the steps of the Soviet Embassy with a note asking the Russians to take care of it, Mel Charles had been declared unfit to play for Arsenal, a financier named Richard Baker had jumped his bail on a fraud charge. He put down the paper with pleasure at the sound of English voices.

A tall dark young man and a short, fair girl came in. The young man carried a heavy suitcase, the girl a lighter one.

"Has the bus for Santader gone?" the young man asked an attendant in atrocious Spanish.

Don answered him. "I'm catching it myself. And here it is." He took the

199

case out of the girl's hand and lifted it onto the bus. The label was old and torn. It bore the name Boyd, with an address scratched out but still visible: EL CASTILLO DE ORO, SAN AVALO.

"You know San Avalo?"

A quick look, of some indecipherable kind, passed between the two. Then the girl spoke.

"I don't know it, but Roly does. He says it's nice."

"Rugged but beautiful. My uncle Justin lives out there, and I went out to see him once last July. He lives in a castle."

"The golden castle," Don said. "A nice name."

"It looks golden, too, with the sun shining on the turrets. But my word, it's cold and dank in the winter."

"Are you out here on business?"

"Sort of a holiday," the little woman said. She chirped like a bird. "March isn't just the time you'd choose for a holiday on this coast, but Roly's got a new job—he's an engineer—and they gave him a few days before he started."

"So you're going to stay with your uncle?"

"You'd better ask Roly. He says we're not. By the way, my name's Jenny Boyd, and this is my husband." She added demurely, "I'd love to see the castle."

"You don't know what you're saying, darling." Her husband shivered. He was perhaps in his early thirties, a hungry-looking man with a hard mouth but a ready smile. "Once was enough. Uncle Justin's eccentric, and I mean eccentric. He lives in this great barracks, with some old crone of a housekeeper. Doesn't smoke, doesn't drink, never looks at an English newspaper. He's no fun, let me tell you."

"That's enough about us," Jenny said, adding with a curiosity so childlike that one couldn't take offense at it, "What do you do, Mr.—?"

"Easton." Don told them what he did, and said that he was breaking his journey in several places, but would reach San Avalo eventually. Should he look up Uncle Justin?

Roly laughed. "Do, by all means, but I can't vouch for your reception. He keeps a shotgun handy to discourage strangers if he's feeling inhospitable."

There was something odd about the conversation, but Don couldn't think what it was. They parted in Santander, and within half an hour he had forgotten them.

He remembered again, and remembered the oddity, when he came down into the valley where San Avalo nestled, on a day rawly cold but beautifully sunny. The village was as pretty as a picture postcard, with its single street and three shady plazas, and the Hotel España, with a restaurant terrace overlooking the sea, and steps down to a private beach, was delightful. Don did some hard bargaining with the proprietor, Señor Mendoza, and made a block booking for July in the following year. Then he mentioned the castle.

"El Castillo de Oro," Mendoza said. He took Don out to the terrace and waved a hand. The castle stood on a promontory above the village. At this moment, with the sunlight gleaming on its towers, the place really looked as though it were made of gold.

Don described the Boyds. Mendoza had not seen them, but he knew their uncle, the Englishman who was *loco*, an old man with a beard, who sometimes shut himself up for weeks in the castle.

"For weeks? What about food?"

What indeed, Mendoza said rhetorically. Certain it was that at these times neither he nor the housekeeper he had brought out from England came down to the village. At these times, the villagers believed, he was not merely *loco*, harmlessly mad, but *dementi, maniaco, furioso*. A demon no doubt possessed him. At such times the village girls who worked at the castle were told not to go there. More than this, there were ghosts in the castle.

"Ghosts? What sort of ghosts?"

That Mendoza could not say, but certain it was that Juanita, one of the village girls, had heard voices speaking in some of the rooms, young voices, not those of the mad Englishman.

Don brooded over this information, and over the oddity that had struck him, while he ate an excellent paella. He made a telephone call to Martin Burns, his assistant in London, partly to confirm that he had made the San Avalo booking, but chiefly to ask for some information. An hour later Martin rang him back. Don had been playing a hunch, and the hunch was right. He left the hotel, called at the office of the Guardia Civil, and walked up to the castle.

He took the main road out of the village, walked along it for a mile, and then turned onto a rough track. The castle loomed ahead of him. As he walked the sun died, the sky darkened. The castle's color changed from gold to black. It looked less romantic than sinister as he walked past a big iron gate into a courtyard. Around him the place was still. He walked toward the big iron door.

"Stop." The voice was rusty, like an unused key in a lock, but unmistakably English. "Stop, or I shoot."

The voice came from above. Don looked up. A fierce old man with a long and dirty beard glared at him out of a narrow window. The rifle in his hand was steady. Don stopped.

"Who are you? What do you want?"

"My name is Easton. I met your nephew, and he suggested I should call on you." It was not quite the truth, but it would serve.

"The worthless scoundrel has not even called on me," the old man said, but he lowered the rifle.

"It is a long way from the village."

"Wait." Don stood in the courtyard until he heard a creak of bolts. The old man said, "Come in."

The hall he entered was so dark that for a moment he could not distinguish more than the outlines of the figure who faced him. Then he saw the matted white hair, the intense stare of dark eyes. He followed down a corridor into a room where oil lamps and a meager wood fire gave a minimum of light and heat.

"I am a recluse, Mr. Easton, but I do not wish to appear inhospitable. Will you take a glass of wine?"

"Thank you."

The old man went to the door. "Henrietta," he suddenly bawled. "Wine."

A little old woman entered the room, a black shawl over her head and black gloves on her hands, so bent that it was hard to see her face. She carried a silver tray with a decanter and glasses on it.

The old man poured the wine. "This is a friend of my nephew Roland. He came here last summer."

She muttered something. Don said, "And you have seen nothing of him this time? Or of his wife?"

"Nothing. It was his only visit." The eyes glared fiercely. "And what is the news of the world? We see nothing, hear nothing."

"You haven't a radio?" Don sipped the wine. It was strong and sweet.

"I abominate them. What do I read or hear but filth? Theft and adultery, display of the body, children deserted and given away to the godless—"

His voice died away. The old woman cackled. Don said quietly, "It's not good. Give it up."

"What do you mean?"

"You've made too many mistakes. I know who you are."

The old man said in a high voice, "I am Justin Boyd."

"Justin Boyd never existed, nor his housekeeper. Your name is Richard Baker, and you are wanted for fraud charges in England."

There was a small pistol in the woman's hand.

"It's no good," Don repeated. "I've talked to London on the telephone and got a description of you both. You're his wife. And I told the Guardia Civil I was coming up here, and who you were. They'll be coming to look for me."

"There'll be no violence," the man said. He put his hand over the woman's wrist, and twisted. She cried out and dropped the pistol. "I never really thought we could get away with it."

The housekeeper straightened up and took off the shawl, revealing bright fair hair. She said in the chirping voice of Jenny Boyd, "Of course we could have got away with it if he hadn't stuck his nose in. You should have fired that rifle."

"It would have made no difference," Don said. "It was an ingenious idea, to create a separate identity out here in Spain, ready for a getaway, so that Richard Baker and his wife turned into Justin Boyd and his house-keeper, but you made too many mistakes. First, leaving the label on the suitcase, then telling me that you'd only visited your uncle once, in July, and saying in the next breath that the castle was cold and dank in winter."

The man stripped off the wig and pulled away the beard, to reveal the darkly handsome face of Roland Boyd. "That was a mistake."

"When I came here and learned that the mad Englishman shut himself up for weeks at a time without seeing anybody, I had a hunch that at these times you might not be there at all. When I heard that there were ghosts speaking in different voices I guessed somebody might be masquerading as Uncle Justin. But the worst mistake of all was the one you made just now."

"What was that?"

"When you mentioned the child given away to the godless. I read about the baby deposited on the steps of the Soviet Embassy two days ago. How could you know about it if you never saw a paper and had no radio?"

"All right," Roland Boyd or Richard Baker said hopelessly. "All right."

"But you were foolish from the start," Don said. "Relying for your hideout on a castle in Spain."

37

PROPOSAL PERILOUS

Morris Hershman

MISS HARRIET KING of Philadelphia, Pennsylvania, U.S.A., in Paris on urgent business, had received her first proposal of marriage from a man she'd known a very short time. She had not clasped her hands together joyfully, accepted him on the spot, or done any of the million things a young girl would have done.

Miss King was not a young girl. Though her friends valiantly insisted that you'd never think it to look at her, Miss King was fifty-three years of age.

Her first proposal! Even now, as her patent-leather oxfords thudded harshly on the sidewalk of a typical Parisian boulevard, she experienced the same chill of doubt she'd had when he asked her. She realized once more that she would have to tell him—inside of an hour now, for the decision had been promised today—that she was fond of Henri (dearest Henri) but she had thought it over carefully and decided not to marry him.

If she'd been twenty-three instead of fifty-three, Miss King's decision would have been the same. After all, she wasn't tied down. In what she sometimes thought of as her shockingly restricted circle, not one marriage that she knew of had turned out quite well for both the man and the woman involved.

As she grew older, the idea of losing her freedom and going to the bed of a virtual stranger appalled her. She ought to have known somehow that a man like Henri wouldn't feel the same way she did about marriage, but the proposal had taken her completely unawares.

"Give me a little time," she had pleaded, running her hands through her hair in desperation.

"Ma petite 'arriette, when?"

"A week, Henri, You'll know in a week."

Even though it was now October of 1915, and things were not shaping up too well for France and her chief ally, England, Miss King had come to Paris because she was afraid not of the Germans but of her conscience. An elderly aunt of hers who'd never cared much for Harriet during her lifetime had requested in her will that "my beloved niece, Harriet" come to France "in order to act as one of my executors."

When the old woman passed away in the early part of July, Harriet had spoken to her brother about going. Aided by innumerable aunts and uncles, they all talked it over among themselves and decided for her that if she, Harriet, did refuse to go, she'd always regret the injustice to a dearly loved relative. Harriet, therefore, booked passage on the first available liner.

And she had met Henri. He was a dealer in used furniture, which he was buying on speculation. He claimed that the price of used furniture would skyrocket just as soon as the war was over, next year perhaps, because the factories, geared as they were to munitions making, would find it long and costly to convert to peacetime production.

Short and stout, with large black eyebrows and a fine beard which he industriously pomaded three times a week, Henri conformed in every way to the average tourist's conception of the *petit bourgeois*. He had an economical turn of mind as well and he'd once shown her a pocket-sized memorandum book in which he noted his daily expenses in a handwriting so small that his words fitted comfortably between the ruled lines.

And in a few short days, Henri had proposed.

"So far as money is concerned, *ma petite,* I have the business, which even now is bringing me a substantial income. There are no children from previous marriages to arouse antagonism on one side or the other. God be thanked, there are no in-laws! Since we are both middle-aged people, you will not have to endure the chasing around after young girls on my part. At this time I want most of all a devoted helpmate."

He had a charming villa out of town where they could live together. From the enthusiastic descriptions he gave, Miss King would have had no difficulty in finding her way through the house and garden with her eyes closed.

And she was going to refuse him. Though she might never have another chance at a husband, she was going to refuse him. . . .

Usually, Miss King traveled with a Baedeker in her pocketbook and noted her surroundings carefully, as if she expected to come across a stray monument on the very next block. She was indefatigable. Nothing daunted her. Having paid out good money for a trip, Miss King didn't want the time to be wasted. But the problem of what exact words to use in telling Henri of her decision preyed on her mind to such an extent that she'd hardly seen where she was going.

Turning off the boulevard into a pitch-black side street, however, Miss King became aware of her surroundings for the first time. With the night everything had taken on a brownish tinge along the narrow thoroughfare, so that walking on it was like walking in a bottle of beer.

Her eyes rested casually on a shop window in front of which a group of small boys crouched, playing marbles, and halted apprehensively before a row of semi-private houses.

She wished she knew in which one of those houses Henri lodged. He'd written the number down for her on the back of an envelope, nearly forgetting it himself because he stayed there so infrequently when he came to Paris; and she had put it away somewhere and promptly lost it. The house was on this street, beyond question—but was it Number 51 or 67 that Miss King wanted?

She had just made up her mind to ask the concierge of each house when she saw Henri himself peering out anxiously from an upstairs window. He caught sight of her in a moment. He waved boyishly, his head vanished and the window was closed after him.

The house she'd been looking for, Number 67, was no better and no worse than any of the others. A thin, T-shaped gravel path bisected a small garden that obviously hadn't been cared for in years, but the house itself had been repainted a few months ago and it looked comfortable.

Once inside, Miss King walked up a flight of stairs and knocked at his door.

Henri had dressed rapidly and was in a state of high excitement as he welcomed her with bows and apologies. "You insist upon coming to see this room. *Voila!* I 'ope you are not too disappointed."

"I'm not at all disappointed," she answered in French. Next to the uncurtained window she had seen downstairs, Miss King was confronted with a large mahogany chest of drawers. At her right was an old-fashioned four-poster bed, at her left a gramophone and a small table piled with magazines. Stiff-backed chairs had been placed in every corner and Miss King sat down on the nearest one. Henri sat down with a flourish. "I am charmed by it all, Monsieur—"

"I should like you to call me Henri," he interposed.

There was a silence. Henri leaned forward attentively.

"Henri, I have considered your proposal"—half-forgotten words Miss King had not even thought of since the turn of the century came back to her—"and while I am deeply sensible of the honor, I am unable to—"

His eyes widened. *"Voyons, ma petite 'arriette—"*

"It would never work out, Henri. The whole arrangement is impossible. You and I belong to different worlds. You have a business here and your friends and your home. Everything I have is in America."

He nodded.

"Don't forget that I am fifty-three years old, Henri, and a creature of habit. I don't really want to give up those habits. A great many things that I'm used to I couldn't possibly give up for any man. You see, it's not as if we could either of us go ahead and sacrifice all for love."

"But why not?" he pleaded. "I am willing to."

She interrupted him again. "Take into consideration the fact that France is at war now, Henri. The Germans may conceivably enter Paris at any time, tomorrow or the day after. My family will be worried to death about me."

"Your family?"

"My brothers, Henri. I live with them and they have control of my income, small though it is. For sentimental reasons alone, I wouldn't want to be married without their approval."

"I had not realized," he said after a pause, "that it would be so difficult."

They gazed at each other for a moment.

"Perhaps I had better go now," said Miss King, when she felt that the silence was becoming intolerable. She was a little shocked to hear him agree.

"I do not see why we have to prolong it myself." Sighing audibly, he pushed back his chair and stood up. "Too, my concierge is a very inquisitive woman."

He went to the door with her. Miss King reflected that he would probably never know just how eased she was by his calm acceptance of the news. She was a little tired, too, since it was all over and done with.

Framed in the doorway at the head of the stairs, it occurred to Miss King that she would remember this day as long as she remembered anything. In a weary or disgruntled state of mind, she would tell herself that it was no more than she deserved. *Why didn't you stay in France with Henri? He loved you. He wanted you.* As long as she remembered anything she would remember this.

If there had been someone for her to talk it over with—if they'd both been younger! Fifty-three—fifty-three.

Henri took her hand, kissing it gravely.

"Shall we go downstairs together?"

" Thank you, but it's only one flight."

"There's no reason for me to inquire"—he was obviously holding his breath—"I don't suppose you've changed your mind?"

"No."

"Then we have only to say good-bye and it is over."

"Good-bye, Henri, I'll always remember you."

A door opened somewhere on the ground level and the inquisitive concierge Henri had complained of peered up the badly lighted staircase at them, their arms akimbo.

Very formally Henri said, "Good-bye, Mademoiselle King."

Very formally she echoed, "Good-bye—good-bye, Monsieur Landru." . . .

Some five years later, in a wide rambling stone cottage on the outskirts of Philadelphia, Miss Harriet King sat frowning distractedly at her needle-work.

At precisely three-fifteen the door opened. One of her brothers came in, holding a rumpled newspaper under his arm. Laying aside what she earnestly hoped to make a scarf out of in less than a week, Miss King glanced at the headlines. The black print stared at her.

PARIS BLUEBEARD ARRESTED
LANDRU CHARGED WITH FOUR MURDERS

She drew in her breath sharply. For a moment, the newspaper crinkled and shuddered in her trembling hands. She remembered suddenly the vital importance of controlling herself and made a tight little ball of her fingers.

She heard her brother's voice coming from a great distance. "Can you imagine it, Harriet?" His voice seemed to drip with pure scorn. "This Landru used to marry friendless women and kill 'em for whatever they had."

"It's terrible," Miss King said, hardly recognizing her own voice, so aged and coarse was it. "Simply terrible."

"You were on the other side a few years back, as I recall." Her brother cleared his throat embarrassedly. "Could have run into him for all you know. It's fortunate that you had—ahem!—the family to get home to—hm! Yes. I hate to think what might have happened otherwise."

When her brother had left, closing the door behind him with an earsplitting thud, Harriet King stared at the newspaper for a long time.

She picked up her needlework again. *He loved you—He wanted you.*

''I wonder,'' she thought, looking down with bitter resentment at the clacking needles in her hand. ''I wonder just how fortunate I've been.''

38

THE CROOKED PICTURE

John Lutz

THE ROOM WAS a mess. The three of them, Paul Eastmont, his wife, Laura, and his brother, Cuthbert, were sitting rigidly and morosely. They were waiting for Louis Bratten.

"But just who is this Bratten?" Laura Eastmont asked in a shaking voice. She was a very beautiful woman, on the edge of middle age.

Cuthbert, recently of several large eastern universities, said, "A drunken, insolent sot."

"And he's a genius," Paul Eastmont added, "in his own peculiar way. More importantly, he's my friend." He placed a hand on his wife's wrist. "Bratten is the most discreet man I know."

Laura shivered. "I hope so, Paul."

Cuthbert rolled his king-size cigarette between thumb and forefinger, an annoyed look on his young, aquiline face. "I don't see why you put such stock in the man, Paul. He's run the gamut of alcoholic degeneration. From chief of homicide to—what? If I remember correctly, you told me some time ago that they'd taken away his private investigator's license."

He saw that he was upsetting hs sister-in-law even more and shrugged his thin shoulders. "My point is that he's hardly the sort of man to be confided in concerning *this*." He looked thoughtful. "On the other hand, half of what he says is known to be untrue anyway."

The butler knocked lightly, pushed one of the den's double doors open, and Louie Bratten entered. He was a blocky, paunchy little man of about forty, with a perpetual squint in one eye. His coarse, dark hair was mussed, his suit was rumpled, and his unclasped tie hung crookedly outside one lapel. He looked as if he'd just stepped out of a hurricane.

"Bratten!" Paul Eastmont said in warm greeting. "You don't know how glad I am to have you in on this!"

Cuthbert nodded coldly. "Mr. Bratten."

Laura stared intently at her hands, which were folded in her lap.

"Give me a drink," Bratten said.

Paul crossed to the portable bar and poured him a straight scotch, no ice.

Bratten sipped the scotch, smacked his lips in satisfaction, and then slouched in the most comfortable leather armchair in the den.

"Now, what's bugging you, Paul?" he asked.

Cuthbert stood and leaned on the mantel. "It's hardly a matter to be taken lightly," he said coldly.

"How in hell can I take it lightly," Bratten asked, "when I don't even know what the matter is?"

Paul raised a hand for silence. "Let me explain briefly. Several years ago, before Laura and I had met, a picture was taken of her in a very— compromising pose. This photo fell into the hands of a blackmailer named Hays, who has been milking us for two hundred dollars a month for the past four years. Recently Hays needed some cash badly. He offered to give me the photo for five thousand dollars."

Paul Eastmont glanced protectively at his embarrassed wife. "Naturally I agreed, and the deal was made. The negative, incidentally was destroyed long ago, and I happen to know that the photo wasn't reproduced at any time since by taking a picture of it. That was part of the original blackmail arrangement. It's the only picture in existence, an eight-by-ten glossy."

"Interesting," Bratten said.

"But Hays turned out to be a stubborn sort," Paul went on. "He gave me the photograph yesterday, and like a fool I didn't destroy it. He saw me put it in my wall safe. Last night he broke in here and tried to steal it back."

"And did he?"

"We don't know. Clark, the butler, sleeps in that part of the house, and he heard Hays tinkering about. He surprised him as he ran in here."

"Terrific scotch," Bratten said. "Did you have the photo?"

"Yes. It wasn't in the wall safe. As you can see, he hurriedly rummaged about the room, lifting cushions, knocking over the lamp, we think looking for a place to hide the photo. Then he leaped out the window."

"Caught?"

"Hurt himself when he landed and couldn't run fast enough. Shot dead by the police just outside the gate. And he didn't have the photo on his body, nor was it on the grounds."

"Hays was a smart blackmailer," Bratten said. He squinted at Paul. "You left the room as it was?"

Paul nodded. "I know your peculiar way of working. But the photo must be in this room. We looked everywhere, but we didn't disturb anything, put everything back exactly the way we found it.''

''Ah, that's good,'' Bratten said, either of the scotch or of the Eastmonts' actions. ''Another drink, if you please.'' He handed the empty glass up to Cuthbert, who was the only one standing.

''Really,'' Cuthbert said, grabbing the glass. ''If I had my way we wouldn't have confided this to you.''

''We never did hit it off, did we?'' Bratten laughed. ''That's probably because you have too much education. Ruins a man sometimes. Restricts his thinking.''

Cuthbert reluctantly gave Bratten his fresh drink. ''You should be an expert on ruination.''

''Touch. That means touché in English.'' Bratten leaned back and ran his tongue over his lips. ''This puts me in mind of another case. One about ten years ago. There was this locked-room-type murder—''

''What on earth does a locked room murder have to do with this case?'' Cuthbert interrupted in agitation.

''Everything, you idiot.''

Paul motioned for Cuthbert to be silent, and Bratten continued.

''Like they say,'' Bratten said, ''there's a parallel here.'' He took a sip of scotch and nonchalantly hung one leg over an arm of his chair. ''There were these four brothers, rich, well-bred—like Cuthbert here, only with savvy. They'd made their pile on some cheap real estate development out West. The point is, the business was set up so one of the brothers controlled most of the money, and they didn't get along too well to start off with.''

He raised his glass and made a mock bow to Cuthbert. ''In language you'd understand, it was a classic sibling rivalry intensified by economic inequality. What it all meant was that if this one brother was dead, the other three would profit a hell of a lot. And lo and behold, this one brother did somehow get dead. That's when I was called into the case by a friend of mine, a local sheriff in Illinois.

''Seems one of the brothers had bought a big old house up in a remote wooded area, and six months later the four of them met up there for a business conference or something. The three surviving brothers' story was simply that their brother had gone into this room, locked the door, and never came out. Naturally not, lying in the middle of the floor with a knife in his chest.''

''I fail to see any parallel whatever so far,'' Cuthbert said.

''The thing of it was, this room was locked from the inside with a sliding bolt and a key still in the keyhole. The one window that opened was locked and there wasn't a mark on the sill. It was summer, and the ground was hard, but I don't think we would have found anything outside anyway."

"Secret panel, no doubt," Cuthbert said.

"Nope. It did happen to be a paneled room, though. We went over that room from wall to wall, ceiling to floor. There was no way out but the door or the window. And to make the thing really confusing, the knife was wiped clean of prints, and there was nothing nearby the dying man could have used to do that, even if he'd been crazy enough to want to for some reason. There was no sign of a struggle, or of any blood other than what had soaked into the rug around the body.

"Without question the corpse was lying where it fell. On the seat of a chair was an open book, and on an end table was a half-empty cup of coffee with the dead man's prints on it. But there was one other thing in the room that caught my attention."

"Well, get it over with and get to the business at hand," Cuthbert said, trying to conceal his interest. "Who was it and how was it done?"

"Another drink," Bratten said, handing up his glass. "Now here was the situation: dead man in a locked room, three suspects with good motives who were in the same house at the time of the murder, and a knife without prints. The coroner's inquest could come to no conclusion but suicide unless the way the murderer left the room was explained. Without that explanation, no jury could convict."

Bratten paused to take a long pull of scotch. "The authorities thought they were licked, and my sheriff friend and I were walking around the outside of the house, talking about how hopeless things were, when I found it."

"The solution?" Cuthbert asked.

"No. A nail. And a shiny one."

"Good Lord," Cuthbert said.

"Doesn't that suggest something to you?"

"It suggests somebody dropped a nail," Cuthbert said furiously.

"Well, I tied that in with what had caught my attention inside the room," Bratten said, "and like they say, everything fell into place. We contacted the former owners of the house, who were in Europe, snooped around a bit, and that was that. We got a confession right away."

Cuthbert was incredulous. "Because of a nail?"

"Not entirely," Bratten said. "How about another drink, while you're up?"

Cuthbert turned to Paul. "How do you expect this sot to help us if he's dead drunk?"

"Give him another," Paul said, "and let him finish."

His face livid, Cuthbert poured Bratten another glass of scotch. "What was it you saw in the room that you connected with the nail you found?"

"A picture," Bratten said. "It was hanging crooked, though everything else in the room was in order. It's things like that that bring first daylight to a case." He looked at Cuthbert as if he were observing some kind of odd animal life. "You still don't get it?"

"No," Cuthbert said, controlling himself. "And as I first suspected, there is no parallel whatsoever with our problem."

Bratten shrugged. "What the brothers did was this: through their business, they gathered the materials secretly over a period of time and got things ready. When the time was right, they got their victim to go there with them and stabbed him on the spot, then wiped the knife handle clean. They had the concrete block foundation, the floor, the roof and all but one of the walls up. They built an L of the big house so there were only two walls to bother with. They even had the rug and furniture down and ready.

"After the victim was dead, they quickly put up the last wall, already paneled like the rest on the inside and shingled with matching shingles on the outside, and called the police. In short, the locked room was pre-fabricated and built around the body."

Cuthbert's mouth was open. "Unbelievable!"

"Not really," Bratten said. "No one would think to check and see how many rooms the house had, and they did a real good job on the one they built. Of course on close examination you could tell. The heating duct was a dummy, and the half of the molding that fitted against the last wall had dummy nail heads in it.

"But from the outside the room was perfect. The shingles matched and the metal corner flashing was a worn piece taken from another part of the house. The trouble was they didn't think to use old nails, and they didn't want to leave the inside of that last wall bare when they fit it in place."

"An amusing story, I admit," Cuthbert said. "True or not. Now if you'll be so kind as to point out this damned parallel you keep talking about . . ."

Bratten looked surprised. "Why, the picture, you imbecile! The crooked picture on the last wall!" He pointed to a cheap oil painting that hung on the Eastmonts' wall.

"But that picture is straight!" Cuthbert yelled in frustration. "It is immaculately straight!"

"Exactly, you jackass. It's the only thing in this fouled-up room besides my drink that is immaculately straight. And I suspect if you look between the painting and cardboard backing, you'll find your photograph."

They did.

39

THE LADY, OR THE TIGER

Frank R. Stockton

IN THE VERY olden time there lived a semi-barbaric king, a man of exuberant fancy, and of an authority so irresistible that, at his will, he turned his varied fancies into facts. He was greatly given to self-communing; and, when he and himself agreed upon anything, the thing was done. When his domestic and political systems moved smoothly, his nature was bland and genial; but whenever there was a little hitch, he was blander and more genial still, for nothing pleased him so much as to make the crooked straight, and crush down uneven places—as in the public arena, by exhibitions of manly and beastly valor. The arena of the king, with its encircling galleries, its mysterious vaults, and its unseen passages, was an agent of poetic justice, in which crime was punished, or virtue rewarded, by the decrees of an impartial and incorruptible chance.

When a subject was accused of a crime of sufficient importance to interest the king, public notice was given that on an appointed day the fate of the accused person would be decided in the king's arena. When all the people had assembled in the galleries, and the king, surrounded by his court, sat high up on his throne of royal state on one side of the arena, he gave a signal, a door beneath him opened, and the accused subject stepped out into the amphitheater. Directly opposite him, on the other side of the enclosed space, were two doors, exactly alike and side by side. It was the duty and the privilege of the person on trial, to walk directly to these doors and open one of them. He could open either door he pleased: he was subject to no guidance or influence but that of impartial and incorruptible chance.

If he opened the one, there came out of it a hungry tiger, the fiercest and most cruel that could be procured, which immediately sprang upon him, and tore him to pieces, as a punishment for his guilt. The moment that the case of the criminal was thus decided, doleful iron bells were clanged,

217

great wails went up from the hired mourners posted on the outer rim of the arena, and the vast audience, with bowed heads and downcast hearts, wended slowly their homeward way, mourning greatly that one so young and fair, or old and respected, should have merited so dire a fate.

But, if the accused person opened the other door, there came forth from it a lady, the most suitable to his years and station that his majesty could select among his fair subjects; and to this lady he was immediately married, as a reward of his innocence. It mattered not that he might already possess a wife and family, or that his affections might be engaged upon an object of his own selection: the king allowed no such subordinate arrangements to interfere with his great scheme of retribution and reward. The exercises took place immediately, and in the arena. Another door opened beneath the king, and a priest, followed by a band of choristers, and dancing maidens blowing joyous airs on golden horns, advanced to where the pair stood, side by side; and the wedding was promptly and cheerily solemnized. Then the gay brass bells rang forth their merry peals, the people shouted glad hurrahs, and the innocent man, preceded by children strewing flowers on his path, led his bride to his home.

This was the king's semi-barbaric method of administering justice. Its perfect fairness is obvious. The criminal could not know out of which door would come the lady: he opened either he pleased, without having the slightest idea whether, in the next instant, he was to be devoured or married. On some occasions the tiger came out of one door, and on some out of the other. The decisions of this tribunal were not only fair, they were positively determinate: the accused person was instantly punished if he found himself guilty; and, if innocent, he was rewarded on the spot, whether he liked it or not.

There was no escape from the judgments of the king's arena.

The institution was a very popular one. When the people gathered together on one of the great trial days, they never knew whether they were to witness a bloody slaughter or a hilarious wedding. This element of uncertainty lent an interest to the occasion which it could not otherwise have attained. Thus, the masses were entertained and pleased, and the thinking part of the community could bring no charge of unfairness against this plan; for did not the accused person have the whole matter in his own hands?

This semi-barbaric king had a daughter as blooming as his most florid fancies, and with a soul as fervent and imperious as his own. As is usual in such cases, she was the apple of his eye, and loved by him above all humanity. Among his courtiers was a young man of that fineness of blood

218

and lowness of station common to the conventional heroes of romance who love royal maidens. This royal maiden was well satisfied with her lover, for he was handsome and brave to a degree unsurpassed in all this kingdom; and she loved him with an ardor that had enough of barbarism in it to make it exceedingly warm and strong.

This love affair moved on happily for many months, until one day the king happened to discover its existence. He did not hesitate nor waver in regard to his duty in the premises. The youth was immediately cast into prison, and a day was appointed for his trial in the king's arena. This, of course, was an especially important occasion; and his majesty, as well as all the people, was greatly interested in the workings and development of this trial. Never before had such a case occurred; never before had a subject dared to love the daughter of a king.

The tiger-cages of the kingdom were searched for the most savage and relentless beasts, from which the fiercest monster might be selected for the arena; and the ranks of maiden youth and beauty throughout the land were carefully surveyed by competent judges, in order that the young man might have a fitting bride in case fate did not determine for him a different destiny. Of course, everybody knew that the deed with which the accused was charged had been done. He had loved the princess, and neither he, she, nor anyone else thought of denying the fact. But the king would not think of allowing any fact of this kind to interfere with the workings of the tribunal, in which he took such great delight and satisfaction. No matter how the affair turned out, the youth would be disposed of; and the king would take an esthetic pleasure in watching the course of events, which would determine whether or not the young man had done wrong in allowing himself to love the princess.

The appointed day arrived. From far and near the people gathered, and thronged the great galleries of the arena; and crowds, unable to gain admittance, massed themselves against its outside walls. The king and his court were in their places, opposite the twin doors—those fateful portals, so terrible in their similarity. All was ready. The signal was given.

A door beneath the royal party opened, and the lover of the princess walked into the arena. Tall, beautiful, fair, his appearance was greeted with a low hum of admiration and anxiety. Half the audience had not known so grand a youth had lived among them. No wonder the princess loved him! What a terrible thing for him to be there!

As the youth advanced into the arena, he turned, as the custom was, to bow to the king. But he did not think at all of that royal personage—his eyes were fixed upon the princess, who sat to the right of her father.

Had it not been for the barbarism in her nature, it is probable that lady would not have been there; but her intense and fervid soul would not allow her to be absent on an occasion in which she was so terribly interested. From the moment that the decree had gone forth, that her lover should decide his fate in the king's arena, she had thought of nothing, night or day, but this great event and the various subjects connected with it. Possessed of more power, influence, and force of character than anyone who had ever before been interested in such a case, she had done what no other person had done—she had possessed herself of the secret of the doors. She knew in which of the two rooms, that lay behind those doors, stood the cage of the tiger, with its open front, and in which waited the lady. Through these thick doors, heavily curtained with skins on the inside, it was impossible that any noise or suggestion should come from within to the person who should approach to raise the latch of one of them; but gold, and the power of a woman's will, had brought the secret to the princess.

And not only did she know in which room stood the lady ready to emerge, all blushing and radiant, should her door be opened, but she knew who the lady was. It was one of the fairest and loveliest of the damsels of the court who had been selected as the reward of the accused youth, should he be proved innocent of the crime of aspiring to one so far above him; and the princess hated her. Often had she seen, or imagined that she had seen, this fair creature throwing glances of admiration upon the person of her lover, and sometimes she thought these glances were perceived and even returned. Now and then she had seen them talking together. It was but for a moment or two, but much can be said in a brief space; it may have been on most unimportant topics, but how could she know that? The girl was lovely, but she had dared to raise her eyes to the loved one of the princess; and, with all the intensity of the savage blood transmitted to her through long lines of wholly barbaric ancestors, she hated the woman who blushed and trembled behind that silent door.

When her lover turned and looked at her, and his eye met hers as she sat there paler and whiter than anyone in the vast ocean of anxious faces about her, he saw, by that power of quick perception which is given to those whose souls are one, that she knew behind which door crouched the tiger, and behind which stood the lady. He had expected her to know it. He understood her nature, and his soul was assured that she would never rest until she made plain to herself this thing, hidden to all other lookers-on, even to the king. The only hope for the youth in which there was an element of certainty was based upon the success of the princess in discovering this mystery: and the moment he looked upon her, he saw she had succeeded, as in his soul he knew she would succeed.

Then it was that his quick and anxious glance asked the question: *Which?*

It was as plain to her as if he shouted it from where he stood. There was not an instant to be lost. The question was asked in a flash; it must be answered in another.

Her right arm lay on the cushioned parapet before her. She raised her hand, and made a slight, quick movement toward her right. No one but her lover saw her. Every eye but his was fixed on the man in the arena.

He turned and with a firm and rapid step he walked across the empty space.

Every heart stopped beating, every breath was held, every eye was fixed immovably upon that man.

Without the slightest hesitation, he went to the door on the right, and opened it.

Now, the point of the story is this: *Did the tiger come out of that door, or did the lady?*

The more we reflect upon this question, the harder it is to answer. It involves a study of the human heart which leads us through devious mazes of passion, out of which it is difficult of find our way. Think of it, fair reader, not as if the decision of the question depended upon yourself, but upon that hot-blooded, semi-barbaric princess, her soul at a white heat beneath the combined fires of despair and jealousy. She had lost him, but who should have him?

How often, in her waking hours and in her dreams, had she started in wild horror, and covered her face with her hands as she thought of her lover opening the door on the other side which waited the cruel fangs of the tiger!

But how much oftener had she seen him at the other door! How in her grievous reveries had she gnashed her teeth, and torn her hair, when she saw his start of rapturous delight as he opened the door of the lady! How her soul had burned in agony when she had seen him rush to meet that woman, with her flushing cheek and sparkling eye of triumph; when she had seen him lead her forth, his whole frame kindled with the joy of recovered life; when she had heard the glad shouts from the multitude, and the wild ringing of the happy bells; when she had seen the priest, with his joyous followers, advance to the couple, and make them man and wife before her very eyes; and when she had seen them walk away together upon their path of flowers, followed by the tremendous shouts of the hilarious multitude, in which her one despairing shriek was lost and drowned!

Would it not be better for him to die at once, and go to wait for her in the blessed regions of semi-barbaric futurity?

And yet, that awful tiger, those shrieks, that blood!

Her decision had been indicated in an instant, but it had been made after days and nights of anguished deliberation. She had known she would be asked, she had decided what she would answer, and, without the slightest hesitation, she had moved her hand to the right.

The question of her decision is one not to be lightly considered, and it is not for me to presume to set myself up as the one person able to answer it. And so I leave it with all of you:

Which came out of the opened door,—the lady, or the tiger?

40

THIS ONE'S ON ME

Edward Hunsburger

SAM BANNER PAUSED in the doorway to knock a thick frosting of powdered snow from his boots. As Green River's Chief of Police, he knew it was important not to "track up" the scene of a crime. It made no difference to Sam that the crime was a minor one which had already been solved or that the cafe's worn, brown linoleum floor obviously held no clues. He liked to do things by the book.

Banner was a big, broad-shouldered man with a sand-colored beard and a head as smooth and hairless as a riverbed rock. He pulled an old Dunhill pipe and a tobacco pouch out of the pocket of his sheepskin coat, and began to load the briar. "Well, Tom," he asked. "What happened here?"

Tom DeBaer grinned. "Just what I told you on the phone, Chief. It's a clear-cut case: assault with intent to rob." He pointed to a thin stranger in a shabby overcoat who was sitting at the counter with his hands cuffed behind his back. "I was just coming in the door, when the suspect practically fell into my arms. He had socked Mr. Panzer on the head, scooped up a handful of coins, and he was fleeing the scene when he ran right into me. It couldn't have been any neater if I planned it myself."

Sam looked at DeBaer with bewilderment. "Mr. Panzer? Coins? You mean to tell me that this man committed assault for a handful of change?"

DeBaer's grin widened. He was really enjoying himself. "Not just ordinary coins, Chief. *Rare* coins. Mr. Panzer is a rare coin dealer from St. Paul."

Now Sam understood. "Nice work, DeBaer."

"Thanks, Chief. But it was just luck, to be honest."

Sam bit into the stem of his pipe. He wished DeBaer wouldn't call him Chief. It got on his nerves. Everyone else, from the mayor on down, called him Sam. But DeBaer was new to the force, in fact new to Green River

223

itself. He had left the Chicago Police to come to work in Green River, a town of less than 10,000 people. That was two years ago. Since the day of his arrival, DeBaer had made Sam uncomfortable. Time hadn't helped the situation. Sam could fire him, but DeBaer was a good cop and Sam was a fair man. You didn't fire a man just because he made you uncomfortable.

"How about witnesses?" Sam asked.

"Jake was coming out of the kitchen when it happened. He saw the whole thing. Then, of course, there's the victim himself."

The two men looked across the empty cafe to the rear booth where Jake, the owner, was carrying on a low-voiced conversation with a well-dressed, elderly man.

"That's Panzer, Chief. I'll have to take him down to the station so that he can file a complaint. I hope he doesn't mind riding in the same car as the prisoner."

The old man seemed to sense that he was being talked about. He slid out of the booth and hurried over to where Sam and DeBaer were standing.

"Lock the door! Don't let anyone out," he shouted. His whole body was literally dancing with agitation. "The Lafayette Eagle is missing!"

Sam laid a restraining hand on the old man's arm. "Calm down, Mr. Panzer."

"I will not calm down!" He looked at DeBaer. "Officer, I insist that you lock that door immediately."

"Mr. Panzer," Sam began, "I'm Sam Banner, the local chief of police. I don't know how it is in your part of the country, but in Green River you don't order my men around. Now, what seems to be the problem?"

The admonishment had the effect of a cold shower on Panzer. He slumped into the nearest booth and looked at the two men pleadingly.

"I'm sorry, Chief Banner. I guess I got carried away. I thought I had recovered all of the coins involved in the incident. But I was mistaken. My Lafayette Eagle is still missing, and it has to be somewhere in this room."

Sam nodded to DeBaer, who went over and locked the front door. "From your excitement, I take it the coin is a valuable one?"

The old man paled visibly. "Valuable? The Lafayette Eagle is one of the rarest coins I've ever had the pleasure of handling and I've been in the business for over 40 years."

"What makes this particular coin so valuable?" Sam asked.

"The Lafayette Eagle is unique. The coin was minted by Henry Voigt, the chief coiner of the U.S. Mint, in 1794. It's a small gold piece with an eagle on one side and a profile of the Marquis de Lafayette on the other. Only six coins were ever minted."

224

"Why only six?" Sam asked with growing interest.

"Politics," Panzer grumbled. "What else? When the coin was struck, the French were at the midway point in their ten-year revolution. President Washington had declared a position of neutrality in 1789, but popular sentiment was strong, both for and against the French cause. Voight minted the Lafayette Eagle to honor a hero of *our* revolution. What he didn't realize was that Lafayette was no longer a hero in France. He tried to advocate moderation to the mobs and was forced to flee to Flanders for his life. So, in the interest of diplomacy, the coin was never minted for circulation. Of the six gem specimens struck, only two are known to be in existence today, and one of them is in this room."

Sam relit his pipe. He had been so engrossed in the tale that he hadn't noticed it go out. "Mr. Panzer, you say the coin is valuable. Just how valuable?"

Panzer took a deep breath. "I was carrying the Eagle with me because I was on my way to sell it to a client for two hundred thousand dollars."

"Two hundred thousand dollars!"

The voice, like an echo, seemed to come from the second row of booths along the opposite wall. Everyone turned toward the area.

A red-faced man sat slowly upright and blinked his eyes. "Morning, all. Did I just hear someone mention a rather large sum of money?"

"What are you doing here?" Sam demanded.

Carl Stranger, reporter for the Green River *Sentinel*, smiled. "I felt a touch of vertigo after eating one of Jake's blue plate specials so I just stretched out for a little nap. What's going on, Sam?"

"Vertigo, my foot," Jake growled. "I thought he had walked out without paying again."

Sam laid a restraining hand on Jake's shoulder. The reporter's presence was going to make the search for the missing coin just that much harder. Sam always thought of Carl Stranger as a part of Green River's local color. He drank a little too much, gambled a little to much, and went around getting people's backs up far too much. Basically he wasn't a bad man, he just rubbed people the wrong way. Sam took him aside and briefly explained the situation.

"That's terrific," Stranger said after Sam had finished the story. "It's the first scoop I've had since the mayor's wife brained him with the Christmas tree last year. I'd better phone it right in."

"Hold it, Carl. I'm afraid I can't let you do that just yet. If you phone the paper there's going to be a mob down here within minutes. If, on the other hand, we keep this quiet for a few hours, we can conduct the search without

225

being disturbed. Either way, you still get your scoop. Okay?''

Stranger looked wistfully at the old wooden phone booth in front of the cafe and then back at Sam. ''Okay, provided that I get to help with this glorified egg hunt.''

Sam nodded his agreement. He asked Jake to pull down the shades and put the ''closed'' sign in the front window. Everyone gathered around Green River's Chief of Police, except for the prisoner, who had fallen asleep with his head resting on the lunch counter.

''I think we all have an interest in helping Mr. Panzer recover his missing coin. If any one of you doesn't want to help with the search, he can leave . . . after he's been thoroughly searched by Tom and myself.'' Sam paused to let the words sink in. After a moment of silence everyone agreed to help look for the missing Eagle.

Sam looked at the elderly coin dealer. ''Mr. Panzer, it might make things easier if you told us exactly what happened.''

''Well, I was sitting in the back booth with Mr. Lyons,'' he nodded in Jake's direction, ''showing him a few items I thought he might be interested in . . .''

''I didn't know you collected coins, Jake,'' Sam interrupted.

''Only in a small way, Sam.''

Mr. Panzer cleared his throat. ''As I was saying . . . I was showing Mr. Lyons some coins. I had about a dozen out of the envelopes and spread out on a small velvet examining board I use, when the thief walked by the table on his way to use the restroom. Foolishly, I mentioned the Lafayette Eagle to Mr. Lyons. I guess when you make the acquisition of a lifetime it's difficult not to boast about it. He asked to see it, and I saw no reason not to show it to him. I had just placed it on the board when,'' Mr. Panzer glared at his slumbering aggressor, ''that man tried to rob me.''

''How exactly did he go about it?'' Sam asked.

''He stepped out of the restroom and hit me on the head with his fist. Mr. Lyons jumped up, the man shoved him back in the booth. Then he scooped up the coins from the board and bolted for the front door, where,'' the old man smiled, ''he ran right into Officer DeBaer.''

''And then?'' Sam prompted.

''Your officer realized the situation immediately and grabbed the man. During the scuffle the thief dropped the coins. By the time Officer DeBaer had the man handcuffed, Mr. Lyons and I were sufficiently recovered to pick up the scattered coins. We brought the coins back to the table while Officer DeBaer phoned you. I didn't realize the Eagle was still missing until you arrived.''

Sam looked at Jake who nodded agreement. "One other thing," Sam said. "Has anyone entered or left here since the incident took place?"

"Only you, Chief," DeBaer said, smiling.

"Okay, it's probably someplace up front. Let's divide up that area and start looking."

The search lasted for a little over three hours. It yielded an overdue library book, four pocket combs, a cigarette lighter, and fourteen coins. All of the coins were contemporary and they amounted to a dollar and fourteen cents. The Lafayette Eagle was still missing.

"Well, we covered every inch of this place twice over." Sam said. "If it's all right with you, Jake, I'd like to try again tomorrow."

"Can you make it tomorrow morning? I'd like to be able to open by ten if I can."

"Sure, Jake. I'll bring my men over around seven." Sam made an elaborate ritual out of loading and lighting his pipe. What he had to say next he wanted to get right. It wasn't an easy thing to say.

"Except for Mr. Panzer," he began, "I've known most of you a long time. I don't want anyone to take this the wrong way. I think you're all honest men, but the fact of the matter is that the coin is missing. Before we leave we'll all have to search each other, myself included."

There was a murmur of protest from the group, but finally everyone agreed. "While we're at it," Jake said, "would anyone like a cup of coffee?"

"On the house?" DeBaer asked quickly.

"Yes, on the house, Tom." Jake served coffee to everyone, including the prisoner, who had been awakened for the personal search.

The "on the house" business was another thing about DeBaer that irritated Sam. Sam respected a man who knew the value of money, but Tom DeBaer was so tight-fisted it made Sam angry. He never socialized with the other men on the force or contributed so much as a quarter to the department's camp program for underprivileged kids. Sam had even known him to go out of his way just to save a dime. Still, it was up to DeBaer to do what he wanted with his own money.

It took almost an hour to search everyone thoroughly. Sam watched as Jake locked the cafe door behind them. That coin, Sam thought, is somewhere inside that room. Why can't we find it?

At ten o'clock that night, Sam was sitting in his oversized easy chair trying to relax. He had a bourbon and water on the sidetable and a book of Conrad's sea stories on his lap. But it just wouldn't work. Every time he started to read he would end up thinking about the missing coin.

There were too many possibilities. Any one of the men could have rehidden the Eagle in an area that had already been searched. Any one of them could have swallowed it with his coffee. Or two of them could have gotten together and passed it back and forth during the personal search.

What about motive? Two hundred thousand dollars was enough to tempt the most honest man. DeBaer liked money too much not to try it. Stranger, with his gambling and drinking, was always in debt. Jake collected coins and he was the one who suggested the coffee. Sam didn't know Mr. Panzer very well, but the coin was insured. So if he could collect on the insurance money and later sell the coin on the quiet? Then there was Bradford, the prisoner. He tried to steal it in the first place; why not again? If there was only a clue that pointed in one direction.

The phone rang and Sam answered it. It was Jake checking to make sure Sam would be there tomorrow morning at seven. Sam assured him that he would and hung up, irritated at having his chain of thought interrupted.

Sam picked up the book again and started to read. Then suddenly, he had the answer. He tossed the book down and headed for the door.

The sound of someone breaking the back door lock came at 3:10. Sam slipped his luminous dial wristwatch off and put it in his pocket. His legs were cramped from over four hours of sitting almost motionless in the back booth of Jake's cafe. He rechecked the position of his gun and flashlight on the table and then sat back to wait for the thief's next move.

A small pen flashlight went on at the other end of the darkened room. After a few minutes Sam heard the sound of metal against metal, then a snapping noise as something gave way, followed by the jingle of coins. He smiled to himself, took up his gun and flashlight, and started across the room.''

''Okay, don't make any sudden moves!'' As Sam spoke he clicked on the flashlight. The glare blinded Tom DeBaer as he stood in the phone booth with the coin box in his gloved hands.

''What . . . how . . . ,'' DeBaer sputtered.

''Just put the box down and hand over your gun and badge. You know me well enough not to try anything funny.''

DeBaer complied silently. Sam handcuffed him and told him to sit down in one of the booths. He went over and brought the coin box back to the table.

''I don't understand how you figured it out,'' DeBaer said quietly.

''It was easy.'' Sam emptied the box out on the table. In the pile of silver a small gold coin glowed. Sam inspected the Lafayette Eagle and then slipped it into his shirt pocket. "You gave yourself away," he said, after a moment's silence.

"But how?"

"You're a tightwad, DeBaer. You never spend a dime on anything you don't have to. But you did today. You called me without leaving this room. You used the pay phone in here when you could have walked out to the curb and called me for free on your car radio."

"I want to talk to a lawyer."

"Sure, you can phone from here if you want to." Sam reached into his pocket and pulled out a dime. He slid it across the table to DeBaer. "Go ahead. This one's on me."

41

TO STRIKE A MATCH

Erle Stanley Gardner

THE LOVE OF Loyalty Road in Canton is a wide thoroughfare cut ruthlessly through the congested district in order to modernize the city. Occasional side streets feed the traffic of automobiles and rickshaws into it, but back of these streets one enters the truly congested areas, where people live like sardines in a tin.

The Street of the Wild Chicken is so wide that one may travel down it in a rickshaw. But within a hundred feet of the intersection of The Street of the Wild Chicken and The Love of Loyalty Road, one comes to *Tien Mah Hong,* which, being translated, means The Alley of the Sky Horse. And in *Tien Mah Hong* there is no room for even rickshaw traffic. Two pedestrians wearing side-brimmed hats must tilt their heads as they meet, so that the brims would not scrape as the wearers pass each other shoulder to shoulder.

Houses on each side of *Tien Mah Hong*, with balconies and windows abutting directly on The Alley of the Sky Horse, give but little opportunity for privacy. The lives of neighbors are laid bare with an intimacy of detail which would be inconceivable in a less congested community or a more occidental atmosphere. At night the peddlers of bean cakes, walking through The Alley of the Sky Horse, beat little drums to attract attention, and shout their wares with a cry which is like the howl of a wolf.

Leung Fah walked down The Alley of the Sky Horse with downcast eyes, as befitted a modest woman of the coolie class. Her face was utterly without expression. Not even the shrewdest student of human nature could have told from her outward appearance the thoughts which were seething within her breast.

It had been less than a month before that Leung Fah had clasped to her breast a morsel of humanity which represented all life's happiness, a warm, ragged bundle, a child without a father, a secret outlet for her mother love.

Then one night there had been a scream of sirens, a panic-stricken helterskelter rush of shouting inhabitants, and, over all, the ominous, steady roar of airplane engines, a hideous undertone of sound which mounted until it became as the hum of a million metallic bees.

It is easy enough to advocate fleeing to a place of safety, but the narrow roads of Canton admit of no swift handling of crowds. And there are no places of safety. Moreover, the temperament of the Chinese makes it difficult to carry out any semblance of an air-defense program. Death in one form or another is always jeering at their elbows. Why dignify one particular form of death by going to such great lengths so far as precautions are concerned?

The devil's eggs began to fall from the sky in a screaming hail. Anti-aircraft guns roared a reply. Machine guns sputtered away hysterically. Through all the turmoil the enemy flyers went calmly about their business of murder, ignoring the frenzied, nervous attempts of an unprepared city to make some semblance of defense.

With fierce mother instinct Leung Fah had held her baby to her breast, shielding it with her frail body, as though interposing a layer of flesh and bone would be of any avail against the "civilized" warfare which rained down from the skies.

The earth had rocked with a series of detonations, and then suddenly Leung Fah had been surrounded by a terrific noise, by splintered timbers, dust and debris.

When she had wiped her eyes and looked at the little morsel of humanity in her arms, she had screamed in terrified anguish.

No one had known of Leung Fah's girl. Because she had no husband, she had kept her offspring as a secret; and because she slept in one of the poorest sections of the city, where people are as numerous and as transient as bats in a cave, she had been able to maintain her secret.

Since no one had known of her child, no one had known of her loss. Night after night she had gone about her work, morsel of humanity in her arms, she had screamed in terror—her face an expressionless mask.

Sahm Seuh, the man who had only three fingers on his right hand, and whose eyes were cunning, moving as smoothly moist in their sockets as the tongue of a snake, had noticed her going about her work, and of late had had become exceedingly solicitous. She was not looking well. Was she perhaps sick? She no longer laughed, or paused to gossip in loud tones with the slave girls in the early morning hours before daylight. Was it perhaps that the money she was making was not sufficient? . . . Sahm Seuh's oily eyes slithered expressively. Perhaps that too could be remedied.

Because she had said nothing, because she had stared at him with eyes that saw not and ears that heard not, her soul numbed by an anguish which made her as one who walks in sleep at the hour of the rat, Sahm Seuh grew bold.

Did she need money? Lots of money—gold money? Not the paper money of China, but gold which would enable her to be independent? *Aiii-ahhh*. It was simple. As simple as the striking of a match. And Sahm Seuh flipped his wrist in a quick motion and scratched a match into flame to illustrate his meaning. He went away then, leaving her to think the matter over.

That night, as she moved through the narrow thoroughfares of the city, her mind brooded on the words of Seuh . . .

Canton is a sleepless city of noise. At times, during the summer months, there comes a slight ebb of activity during the first few hours after midnight, but it is an ebb which is barely perceptible to occidental ears. In the large Chinese cities people sleep in shifts because there is not enough room to accommodate them all at one time in houses. Those who are off-shift roam the streets, and because Chinese ears are impervious to noise, just as Chinese nostrils are immune to smells, the hubbub of conversation continues unabated.

Daylight was dawning, a murky, humid dawn which brought renewed heat to a city already steeped in its own emanations—a city of silent-winged mosquitoes, oppressive and sweltering heat, unevaporated perspiration, and those odors which cling to China as an aura.

Sahm Seuh stood suddenly before her.

"That gold?" he asked. "Do you wish it?"

"I would strike a match," she said tonelessly.

"Meet me," Sahm Seuh said, "at the house in The Alley of the Sky Horse where three candles burn. Open the door and climb the stairs. The time is tonight, at the last minute of the hour of the dog."

And so, as one in a daze, Leung Fah turned down The Alley of the Sky Horse and shuffled along with leaden feet, her eyes utterly without expression, set in a face of wood. . . .

Night found her turning into The Alley of the Sky Horse.

In a house on the left a girl was playing a metallic-sounding Chinese harp. Ten steps back of her a bean peddler raised his voice in a long, howling "*o-w-w-w-w-e-o-o-o-o*." Fifty feet ahead, a family sought to scatter evil spirits by flinging lighted firecrackers from the balcony.

Leung Fah plodded on, circling a bonfire where paper imitation money, a model sedan chair, and slaves in effigy were being sent by means of fire to

233

join the spirits of ancestors. Three candles flickered on the sidewalk in the heavy air of the hot night.

Leung Fah opened the door and climbed stairs. There was darkness ahead, only darkness. She entered a room and sensed that others were present. She could hear their breathing, the restless motions of their bodies, the rustle of clothes, occasionally a nervous cough. The hour struck—the passing of the hour of the dog, and the beginning of the hour of the boar.

The voice of Sahm Seuh came from the darkness. "Let everyone here close his eyes and become blind. He who opens his eyes will be judged a traitor. It is given to only one man to see those who are gathered in this room. Any prying eyes will receive the kiss of a hot iron, that what they have seen may be sealed into the brain."

Leung Fah, seated on the floor, her feet doubled under her, her eyes closed tightly, sensed that men were moving around the room, examining the faces of those who were present by the aid of a flashlight which stabbed its beam into each of the faces. And she could feel heat on her cheeks, which made her realize that a man with a white-hot iron stood nearby ready to plunge the iron into any which might show signs of curiosity.

"She is strange to me," a voice said, a voice which spoke with the hissing sound of the *yut boen gwiee*—the ghosts of the sunrise.

"She is mine," the voice of Sahm Seuh said, and the light ceased to illuminate her closed eyelids. The hot iron passed by.

She heard a sudden scream, the sizzling of a hot iron, a yell of mortal anguish, and the sound of a body as it thudded to the floor. She did not open her eyes. Life, in China, is cheap.

At length the silent roll call had been completed. The voice of Sahm Seuh said, "Eyes may now open."

Leung Fah opened her eyes. The room was black with darkness.

"Shortly before the dawn," Sahm Seuh said, "there will be the roar of many motors in the sky. Each of you will be given a red flare and matches. To each of you will be whispered the name of the place where the red flare is to be placed. When you hear the roar of motors, you will crouch over the flare, as though kneeling on the ground in terror. When the motors reach the eastern end of the city, you will hold a match in your fingers.

"There will be none to watch, because people will be intent on their own safety. When the planes are overhead, you will set fire to the red flares, and then you will run very rapidly. You will return most quickly to this place; you will receive plenty gold.

"It is, however, imperative that you come to this place quickly. The bombing will last until just before daylight. You must be here before the bombing is finished. You will receive your gold. In the confusion you will flee to the river. A boat will be waiting. It will be necessary that you hide for some time, because an investigation will be made. There are spies who spy on us, and one cannot explain the possession of gold. You will be hidden until there is more work to be done.''

Once more there was a period of silence, broken only by the shuffling of men and of whispered orders. Leung Fah felt a round wooden object thrust into her hands. A moment later, a box of matches was pushed into her fingers. A man bent over her, so close that his voice breathed a thought directly into her ears, almost without the aid of sound.

''The house of the Commissioner of Public Safety,'' he said.

The shuffling ceased. The voice of Sahm Seuh said, ''That is all. Go, and wait at the appointed places. Hurry back and there will be much gold. In order to avoid suspicion you will leave here one at a time, at intervals of five minutes. A man at the door will control your passing. There will be no lights, no conversation.''

Leung Fah stood in the darkness, packed with people whom she did not know, reeking in the stench of stale perspiration. At intervals she heard a whispered command. After each whisper the door would open and one of the persons in that narrow crowded staircase would slip from the suffocating atmosphere into the relative coolness of the street.

At length the door was in front of her. Hands pushed against her. The door swung open and she found herself once more in The Alley of the Sky Horse, shuffling along with demure eyes downcast, and a face which was the face of a sleepwalker.

Leung Fah went only so far as the house where the sacrifices were being offered to the spirit of the departed. The ashes of the sacrificial fire were still smoldering in the narrow street, drifting about in vagrant gusts of wind. Leung Fah knew that in this house there would be mourners, that any who were of the faith and desired to join in sending thought waves to the Ancestor in the Beyond would be welcome.

She climbed the stairs and heard chanting. Around the table were grouped seven nuns with heads as bald as a sharp razor could make them. At another table, flickering peanut-oil lamps illuminated a painting of the ancestor who had in turn joined his ancestors. The table was laden with sacrifices. There were some twenty people in the room who intermittently joined in chanting prayers.

Leung Fah unostentatiously joined this group. Shortly thereafter she moved quietly to the stairs which gave to the roof, and within a half hour had worked her way back to the roof of the house of the three candles. She sought a deep shadow, merged herself within it, and became motionless.

Slowly the hours of the night wore away. Leung Fah began to listen. Her ears, strained toward the east, then heard a peculiar sound. It was like distant thunder over the mountains, a thunder which rumbles ominously.

With terrifying rapidity the murmur of sound in the east grew into a roar. She could hear the screams of people in the streets below, could hear babies, aroused from their sleep as they were snatched up by frantic parents, crying fretfully.

Still Leung Fah remained motionless. The planes swept by overhead. Here and there in the city bright red flares suddenly blossomed into blood-red pools of crimson. And wherever there was a flare, an enemy plane swooped down, and a moment later a mushroom of flame rose up against the night sky, followed by a reverberating report which shook the very foundations of the city.

Leung Fah crept ot the edge of the roof where she might peer over and watch The Alley of the Sky Horse. She saw surreptitious figures darting from shadow to shadow, slipping through the portals of the house of three candles.

At length a shadow, more bulky than the rest, the shadow of a fat man running on noiseless feet, crossed the street and was swallowed up in the entrance of the house of three candles. The planes still roared overhead.

Leung Fah placed her box of red fire on the roof and tore off the paper. With calm, untrembling hands, she struck a match to flame, the flame to the flare.

In the crimson pool of light which illuminated all the housetops, Leung Fah fled from one rooftop to another. And yet it seemed she had only been running a few seconds when a giant plane materialized overhead and came roaring down out of the sky. She heard the scream of a torpedo. The entire street rocked under the impact of a stupendous explosion.

Leung Fah was flung to her knees. Her eardrums seemed shattered, her eyes about to burst from their sockets under the enormous rush of pressure which swept along with the blast.

Day was dawning when she recovered enough to limp down to The Alley of the Sky Horse. The roar of the planes was receding into the distance.

Leung Fah hobbled slowly and painfully to the place where the house of the three candles had stood. There was now a deep hole in The Alley of the Sky Horse, a hole surrounded by bits of wreckage and torn bodies.

A blackened torso lay almost at her feet. She examined it intently. It was all that was left of Sahm Seuh.

She turned and limped back up The Alley of the Sky Horse, her eyes downcast and expressionless, her face as though it had been carved of wood.

The sun rose in the east, and the inhabitants of Canton, long since accustomed to having the grim presence of death at their side, prepared to clear away the bodies and debris, to resume once more their daily course of ceaseless activity.

Leung Fah lifted the bamboo yoke to her sore shoulders. *Aiii ah-h-h* it was painful, but one must work if one would eat.

42

HUSH-A-BYE, MY BABY

Anton Chekhov

NIGHT. VARKA, THE little nurse, a girl of thirteen, is rocking the cradle and humming hardly audibly:

> *Hush-a-bye, my baby wee,*
> *While I sing a song for thee.*

A little green lamp is burning before the ikon; there is a string stretched from one end of the room to the other, on which baby clothes and a pair of big black trousers are hanging. There is a big patch of green on the ceiling from the ikon lamp, and the baby clothes and the trousers throw long shadows on the stove, on the cradle, and on Varka. . . . When the lamp begins to flicker, the green patch and the shadows come to life, and are set in motion, as though by the wind. It is stuffy. There is a smell of cabbage soup, and of the inside of a shoe store.

The baby is crying. For a long while he has been hoarse and exhausted with crying; but he still goes on screaming, and there is no knowing when he will stop. And Varka is sleepy. Her eyes are glued together, her head droops, her neck aches. She cannot move her eyelids or her lips, and she feels as though her face is dried and wooden, as though her head has become as small as the head of a pin.

"Hush-a-bye, my baby wee," she hums, "while I cook the groats for thee . . ."

A cricket is churring in the stove. Through the door in the next room the master and the apprentice Afanasy are snoring . . . The cradle creaks plaintively, Varka murmurs—and it all blends into that soothing music of the night to which it is so sweet to listen, when one is lying in bed. Now that music is merely irritating and oppressive, because it goads her to sleep; and

239

she must not sleep; if Varka—God forbid!—should fall asleep, her master and mistress would beat her.

The lamp flickers. The patch of green and the shadows are set in motion, forcing themselves on Varka's fixed, half-opened eyes, and in her half-slumbering brain the shadows are fashioned into misty visions. She sees dark clouds chasing one another over the sky, and screaming like the baby. But then the wind blows, the clouds are gone, and Varka sees a broad highroad covered with liquid mud; along the highroad stretch files of wagons, while people with wallets on their backs are trudging along the shadows flit backward and forward; on both sides she can see forests through the cold harsh mist. All at once the people with their wallets and their shadows fall on the ground in the liquid mud. "What is that for?" Varka asks. "To sleep, to sleep!" they answer her. And they fall sound asleep, and sleep sweetly, while crows and magpies sit on the telegraph wires, scream like the baby, and try to wake them.

"Hush-a-bye, my baby wee, and I will sing a song to thee," murmurs Varka, and now she sees herself in a dark stuffy hut.

Her dead father, Yefim Stepanov, is tossing from side to side on the floor. She does not see him, but she hears him moaning and rolling on the floor from pain. "His guts have burst," as he says; the pain is so violent that he cannot utter a single word, and can only draw in his breath and clack his teeth like the rattling of a drum "Boo—boo—boo—boo . . ."

Her mother, Pelageya, has run to the master's house to say that Yefim is dying. She has been gone a long time, and ought to be back. Varka lies awake on the stove, and hears her father's "Boo—boo—boo—" And then she hears someone who has driven up to the hut. It is the young doctor from the town, who has been sent from the big house where he is staying on a visit. The doctor comes into the hut; he cannot be seen in the darkness, but he can be heard rattling the door.

"Light a candle," he says.

"Boo—boo—" answers Yefim.

Pelageya rushes to the stove and begins looking for the broken pot with the matches. A minute passes in silence. The doctor, feeling in his pocket, lights a match.

"In a minute, sir, in a minute," says Pelageya. She rushes out of the hut, and soon afterward comes back with a bit of candle.

Yefim's cheeks are rosy and his eyes are shining, and there is a peculiar keenness in his glance, as though he were seeing right through the hut and the doctor.

"Come, what is it? What are you thinking about?" says the doctor, bending down to him. "Aha! Have you had this long?"

"What? Dying, your honor, my hour has come . . . I am not to stay among the living . . ."

"Nonsense! We will cure you."

The doctor spends a quarter of an hour over Yefim, then he gets up.

"I can do nothing. You must go into the hospital, there they will operate on you. Go at once . . . You must go! It's rather late, they will all be asleep at the hospital, but that doesn't matter, I will give you a note. Do you hear?"

"Kind sir, but when can he go in?" said Pelageya. "We have no horse."

"Never mind. I'll ask your master, he'll let you have a horse."

The doctor goes away, the candle goes out, and again there is the sound of "Boo—boo—boo—" Half an hour later someone drives up to the hut. A cart has been sent to take Yefim to the hospital. He gets ready and goes . . .

But now it is a clear bright morning. Pelageya is not at home; she has gone to the hospital to find what is being done to Yefim. Somewhere there is a baby crying, and Varka hears someone singing with her own voice:

"Hush-a-bye, my baby wee, I will sing a song to thee."

Pelageya comes back; she crosses herself and whispers:

"They put him to rights in the night, but toward morning he gave up his soul to God . . . The Kingdom of Heaven be his and peace everlasting . . . They say he was brought too late . . . He ought to have gone sooner . . ."

Varka goes out into the road and cries there, but all at once someone hits her on the back of the head so hard that her forehead knocks against a birch tree. She raises her eyes, and sees facing her, her master, the shoemaker.

"What are you about, you scabby slut?" he says. "The child is crying and you are asleep!"

He gives her a sharp slap behind the ear, and she shakes her head, rocks the cradle, and murmurs her song. The green patch and the shadows from the trousers and the baby clothes move up and down, nod to her, and soon take possession of her brain again.

Again she sees the highroad covered with liquid mud. The people with wallets on their backs and the shadows have laid down and are fast asleep. Looking at them, Varka has a passionate longing for sleep; she would lie down with enjoyment, but her mother Pelageya is walking beside her, hurrying her on.

"Give the baby here!" a familiar voice cries. "Give the baby here!" the same voice repeats, this time harshly and angrily. "Are you asleep, you wretched girl?"

Varka jumps up, and looking round grasps what is the matter: there is no highroad, no Pelageya, no people meeting them; there is only her mistress, who has come to feed the baby, and is standing in the middle of the room. While the stout broad-shouldered woman nurses the child and soothes it, Varka stands looking at her and waiting till she has done. And outside the windows the air is already turning blue, the shadows and the green patch on the ceiling are visibly growing pale, it will soon be morning.

"Take him," says her mistress, buttoning up her chemise over her bosom. "He is crying. He must be bewitched."

Varka takes the baby, puts him in the cradle, and begins rocking it again. The green patch and the shadows gradually disappear, and now there is nothing to force itself on her eyes and cloud her brain. But she is as sleepy as before—fearfully sleepy! Varka lays her head on the edge of the cradle and rocks her whole body to overcome her sleepiness, but yet her eyes are glued together, and her head is heavy.

"Varka, heat the stove!" she hears the master's voice through the door.

So it is time to get up and set to work. Varka leaves the cradle and runs to the shed for firewood. She is glad. When one moves and runs about, one is not so sleepy as when one is sitting down. She brings the wood, heats the stove, and feels that her wooden face is getting supple again, her thoughts are clearer.

"Varka, get the samovar!" shouts her mistress.

Varka splits a piece of wood, but has scarcely time to light the splinters and put them in the samovar, when she hears a fresh order:

"Varka, wash the steps outside! I am ashamed for customers to see them!"

Varka washes the steps, sweeps and dusts the rooms, then heats another stove and runs to the shop. There is a great deal of work: she hasn't one minute free.

But nothing is so hard as standing in the same place at the kitchen table peeling potatoes. Her head droops over the table, the potatoes dance before her eyes, the knife tumbles out of her hand while her fat angry mistress is moving about near her with her sleevs tucked up, talking so loud that it makes a ringing in Varka's ears. It is agonizing, too, to wait at dinner, to wash, to sew; there are minutes when she longs to flop onto the floor regardless of everything, and to sleep.

The day passes. Seeing the windows getting dark, Varka presses her temples that feel as though they were made of wood, and smiles, though she does not know why. The dusk of evening caresses her eyes that will hardly keep open, and promises her sound sleep soon. In the evening, visitors come.

"Varka, set the samovar!" shouts her mistress.

The samovar is a little one, and before visitors have drunk all the tea they want, she has to heat it five times. After tea Varka stands for the whole hour on the same spot, looking at the visitors, and waiting for orders.

"Varka, fetch some vodka! Varka, where's the corkscrew? Varka, clean a herring!"

But now, at last, the visitors have gone. The lights are put out, the master and mistress go to bed.

"Varka, rock the baby!"

The cricket churrs in the stove; the green patch on the ceiling and the shadows from the trousers and the baby clothes force themselves on Varka's half-opened eyes again, wink at her and cloud her mind.

"Hush-a-bye, my baby wee," she murmurs, "and I will sing a song to thee."

And the baby screams, and is worn out with screaming. Again Varka sees the muddy highroad, the people with wallets, her mother Pelageya, her father Yefim. She understands everything, she recognizes everyone, but through her half sleep she cannot understand the force which binds her, hand and foot, weighs upon her, and prevents her from living. She looks round, searches for that force that she may escape from it, but she cannot find it.

At last, tired to death, she does her very utmost, strains her eyes, looks up at the flickering green patch, and listening to the screaming, finds the foe who will not let her live. That foe is the baby.

She laughs. It seems strange to her that she has failed to grasp such a simple thing before. The green patch, the shadows, and the cricket seem to laugh and wonder too.

The hallucination takes possession of Varka. She gets up from her stool, and walks up and down the room. She feels pleased and tickled at the thought that she will be rid of the baby that binds her hand and foot . . . Kill the baby and then sleep, sleep, sleep . . .

Laughing and winking and shaking her fingers at the green patch, Varka steals up to the cradle and bends over the baby. When she has strangled him, she quickly lies down on the floor, laughs with delight that she can sleep, and in a minute is sleeping as sound as the dead.

43

BECAUSE THE CONSTABLE BLUNDERED

Francis M. Nevins, Jr.

AT LONG LAST the procedural delays were over and the date of the trial was announced. Gilmore heard the news on the car radio while trapped and sweltering in the daily traffic jam out of the city. He swung the car off the boulevard at the next corner, making a right and then another right, heading back downtown to Headquarters.

The announcer of the six o'clock news recapped the headlines —Eisenhower takes history's first presidential helicopter ride, plans completed for nationwide civil defense exercise, Aga Khan dies—but Gilmore wasn't listening. He gunned the car up the ramp to the rooftop parking deck for high Department officials, locked the car doors, jogged across oil-stained concrete to the elevators.

In his own cedar-paneled office he pulled out the MO sheet on Bugs Ruber (having decided a week ago that Ruber would be the best one to use) and reread it over and over, puffing on a cigar as he did so, until every detail had become a part of him. Then he transferred the necessary equipment from his bottom desk drawer to his jacket and rode the elevator back to the roof.

The traffic had thinned and he made good time to the northwest corner of the city. He parked five blocks from his destination, across the street from a run-down neighborhood theater, and looked up curiously at the already lighted marquee. Two Westerns were playing tonight. He liked Western films. You could always tell who was good and who was bad in them.

He walked the five blocks, passing few people since it was suppertime, and turned in at a shabby red-brick residence that had been converted into four apartments. Tom Stroud had the top rear, Gilmore knew. He used a skeleton key on his ring to bypass the vestibule's buzzer system, mounted the work stairs to the second floor, and pressed the bell with a knuckle and waited. On the third ring the door opened the width of the chain latch.

Gilmore thrust his card through the aperture. "Official business," he said brusquely.

Stroud fumbled with the chain and stepped back to let his visitor in. Gilmore briefly studied the man, a tall, lean, crew-cut, pleasant-faced fellow wearing a T-shirt and chino slacks, his face and arms glistening from the July heat. A whirring fan in the corner of the untidy livingroom pushed humid air around the apartment. A blue patrolman's uniform hung on a wire hanger from the top edge of a closet door, swaying in the air current.

"Sorry to disturb you when you're off duty, Stroud," Gilmore began, "but if you heard the evening news you'll know what I'm here about." He nodded in the direction of a tacky small-screen TV cater-cornered against a wall junction.

"I didn't," the young partolman said. "I just got up a little while ago. I have the 12-to-8 this week." Gilmore knew that already. He could see rumpled bedclothes through the doorway into the next room.

"Your wife isn't around?"

"We've separated, sir," Stroud explained.

Gilmore knew that too. "Sorry to hear it," he lied. "Well, the reason I had to see you is that Jackson Coy is definitely not going to cop a plea. He's sticking to his guns and the trial is on for three weeks from tomorrow. When you go on duty tonight you're probably going to find a message to report to the prosecutor's office in the morning. I just wanted to, well, go over with you what you're going to say to the prosecutor."

Stroud's face took on a quizzical expression, as if he couldn't quite see the point. "All right, sir, if you say so. Why don't you take off your jacket and make yourself comfortable? I'll get us some iced tea. In this heat we can use a cold drink."

"I'll leave the jacket on," Gilmore said. "No thanks on the tea." He walked across a cheap imitation-Persian rug to the sagging mohair couch and sat erect in a corner while Stroud padded to the kitchen. The patrolman poured a tall glass of iced tea from a pitcher in the refrigerator and took a long swallow, then crossed the room and took a seat at the opposite corner of the couch, setting down his glass on a coffee table marred with the residue of countless wet rings.

"If you'll excuse my saying so, sir, I don't see anything in the Jackson Coy case that's important enough for a visit from . . ." He glanced down at the card he had taken from Gilmore at the door. ". . . from a deputy assistant commissioner."

"We do want to win this one," Gilmore said, pinching an end of his steel-gray moustache between two fingers. "These imputed-malice cases can be tricky."

"Well, I'm not a lawyer, but I remember what we were told about felony murder and imputed malice when I took that refresher course at the Police Academy last year," Stroud said. "I thought the courts in this state have ruled that whenever anyone dies in the course of a felony, the premeditation that's necessary for first-degree murder is sort of carried over from the felony and imputed to all the people involved so that they can all be charged with Murder One and sentenced to the chair if they're convicted. It doesn't matter whether any of the felons did the killing themselves."

"That's about right," Gilmore agreed. The hard mohair surface of the couch was like fine quills against his back. "We've had cases where an officer accidentally shot an innocent bystander in a gun battle with some thieves, and one where a robbery victim resisted and shot one of the two guys who were robbing him, and where two fellows were committing arson and one of them managed to burn himself to a cinder as well as the building. We got murder convictions against the surviving felons in all three cases and the state supreme court upheld them all on appeal. This imputed-malice theory is a great deterrent to anyone who's tempted to commit a felony. If there's any death as a result, no matter how it comes about, they can be hit with Murder One. The Department," Gilmore said solemnly, "wants the law to stay that way."

"So do I, sir," the young patrolman replied earnestly.

"So let's go over the facts," Gilmore suggested.

Stroud leaned back in his corner of the couch and drank more tea. "It was about nine months ago, the first week in October. Jim Noonan and I were out in our squad car on the 12-to-8 trick. We'd been teamed up off and on for about three years, ever since I got back from Korea."

"You joined the force five years ago, around '51, didn't you?" Gilmore interrupted.

"Right." Stroud displayed a lopsided boyish grin. "Then a few months after I'd graduated from the Academy and gotten married, my Reserve unit was called up for Korea duty. When I got back I joined the force again and was assigned to a car. Jim was my partner, oh, about half the time all told." His face fell and the light faded from his deep brown eyes. "Poor Jim. That night in October was his last."

Gilmore tried to prod him out of his brooding silence. "You got a call on the squawk box that a burglary was in progress . . . ."

"Right. About three in the morning. It was raining and overcast and visibility was terrible. We got a squawk there was a burglary in progress over on Webster Avenue. We were the nearest car and got there in a couple of minutes. It was an old store front divided in two, one side a pawnshop and the other a rug dealer with a funny name.''

"Nalabindian," Gilmore supplied absently.

Stroud's eyes widened in surprise.

"The Department is *very* interested in this case," Gilmore said. "Go on with your story, Officer."

"Yes, sir. We got out of the squad car and started to close in on the store just the way it says to do in the book. We'd only taken a few steps across the sidewalk when the guy looting the store opened up on us with a .45. We split up. I took cover behind the hood of the squad car and Jim ran for the doorway and hit the deck. We returned fire. It was dark and noisy as hell and the whole thing was over in less than a minute. Twelve or fifteen shots fired, the burglar in the pawnshop howling his head off with a bullet in his leg, and poor Jim Noonan dead in the doorway of Nalabindian's rug store. More cars came up then, and they grabbed the suspect and hauled him downtown, and called an ambulance for Jim even though we knew he was dead.''

He paused a moment in his recital. "You know who it was in the pawnshop, of course—Jackson Coy, with a knife scar across his cheek and a record a mile long. Jim was my buddy and it was damn tough to lose him that way. If you haven't come up through the ranks I don't know if you can realize how tough a thing like that can be."

Gilmore said nothing for a full minute. It was like the traditional sixty seconds of silence for one who has died. Then he fingered his moustache again and looked down at his wristwatch. It was getting late.

"The worst of it came later, I suppose," he ventured. "When the autopsy report came in."

"I almost quit the force when I heard," Stroud said, his voice falling to a near-whisper.

"Coy had been firing a .45 at you and Noonan," the official recounted, "but the autopsy showed that the bullet that killed Noonan came from a .38. The Police Positive caliber. Since he obviously hadn't shot himself, then it must have been one of your shots that hit him in the darkness and confusion when he was edging out of that doorway."

"Do you have to go over it?" Stroud demanded. He seemed to be fighting to hold back tears. "Don't you think I've done that often enough to myself?"

"And then to top it off, your wife left you a couple of weeks later," Gilmore said, almost gently.

"She couldn't take it. I told her I'd killed a lot of people in Korea and that never bothered her, but somehow this was different for her. Too close to home, I guess."

"Naturally," Gilmore pointed out, "Jackson Coy and his lawyer don't know yet that it wasn't Coy's bullet that killed Noonan. The prosecutor tried to get him to cop a plea to second-degree murder but it was no go. Coy's a crapshooter from way back. He's going to go for broke, stand trial for first degree and hope something will come up that will get him a hung jury or better."

He paused.

"The fact that it was your shot that killed Noonan," he went on quietly, "may just do the trick for Coy. When we go to trial that will have to come out."

Stroud pushed himself to his feet, paced parallel to the ring-marred coffee table as if its length were that of a prison cell. "But so what?" he demanded. His voice was on the verge of breaking, his T-shirt drenched with sweat. "Under the imputed-malice cases he's still guilty of first-degree murder, isn't he? It's just like that case where the officer accidentally killed the innocent bystander. That guy was convicted."

"There's a difference," Gilmore said.

Stroud stood still. His head jerked to face the deputy assistant commissioner. He kept silent and the sweat kept pouring down him.

"You know what the difference is," Gilmore said.

"I'm not a lawyer . . . ." the young patrolman began.

"But you damn well remembered the law you were taught in that refresher course at the Academy!" Gilmore spat out the words from between taut lips. "You found out that Noonan had been shacking up with your wife the whole time you were in the service and afterward too. I don't think you found out until shortly before the night of the shooting. You're not the type that could sit calmly in a patrol car night after night with a guy who was making time with your wife. You found out she and Noonan had a thing going and your refresher course gave you the idea what to do about it. All you had to do was wait till the next call came in that would put you and him in a gun battle. In a city like this, that wouldn't be a long time. In the confusion of the gunfight you pump a slug into Noonan, and under the imputed-malice rule the poor slob who was committing the original crime gets the chair for first-degree murder. That's why your wife left you, wasn't it? *She* knew it wasn't just an accident that you had shot the guy she was making it with."

"You can't prove any of this," Stroud began defiantly.

"Come off it," the other growled. "Why do you think I'm here? Your wife talked to Captain Logan of the Confidential Squad two months ago. Logan talked to the commissioner and the commissioner talked to me. In a technical sense you're right, I haven't enough proof to get you indicted for murder, and we don't dare bring departmental charges against you for what you did because then the truth comes out and Jackson Coy gets off the hook, and we want that boy put away. But what do you think is going to happen now that there has to be a trial? What do you think Coy's lawyer—and he's been assigned a good one—is going to do when the autopsy surgeon testifies that your bullet killed Noonan? He's going to do some investigating, and find out what I found out when I talked to a few of your neighbors over the past week: that Noonan visited here every chance he could get when you were on duty and he was off. The judge will instruct the jury that under the imputed-malice cases it doesn't matter how Noonan died, Coy is still legally responsible, but maybe the jury will balk and acquit him anyway, or maybe they'll find him guilty and on appeal the supreme court will reverse it and may just knock out a good part of the imputed-malice theory at the same time, because that theory was never intended to shield a cop who commits cold-blooded murder behind it. So thanks to you, Stroud, we stand a good chance of losing a damned effective deterrent against the commission of felonies.''

Stroud stood silent, drenched in his own sweat.

''Get into your uniform,'' Gilmore ordered. ''You're going downtown with me.''

Stroud did not move toward the blue uniform swaying gently in the breeze from the fan.

''Move!'' Gilmore shouted.

The patrolman jerked around like a robot, turned his back on the official and began taking hesitant steps toward the open closet door.

Gilmore caught up to him in two strides. He pulled out the crowbar taped to the lining of his jacket and smashed it against the back of Stroud's head with all his strength, then again, and again. Stroud crumpled in a heap. His blood and brains crawled onto the faded rug.

Gilmore moved rapidly now, retrieving his official card, wiping his prints from the weapon and dropping it beside the body, opening a rear window and breaking an upper pane from the outside, leaving other traces around the apartment that conformed to Bugs Ruber's modus operandi which Gilmore had mastered so completely. It took him no more than five minutes. Then he let himself out cautiously by the front door and softly descended the worn oak staircase to the street door and walked back the five blocks to where he had parked his car.

One of his favorite sayings kept going though his mind as he walked, a statement of a wise judge many years before. *Why should the criminal escape because the constable blundered?* Gilmore had never been able to think of a single reason why.

It had been a good evening's work, he told himself as he lit another cigar, one that he could never officially report nor even hint at off the record to anyone else in the Department, but a good evening's work nevertheless. He had avenged a cold-blooded killing, taken care of a legally unpunishable murderer, removed a bad cop from the force without even a whisper of adverse publicity for the Department, left open at least a fighting chance that Coy would be convicted on the theory that Stroud's shooting of Noonan had been an accident for which Coy was legally responsible, and had even hung a rap around the neck of Bugs Ruber, who was a dangerous character and a threat to decent citizens.

The double feature across the street was letting out. Gilmore turned the car into the stream of others driven by moviegoers departing from the pair of Western films and became indistinguishable from them.

44

CLOAK AND DIGGER

John Jakes

ROGER GUESSED THAT the opposite side had got on to his mission when a black Citroen roared into the street and three men armed with Sten guns leaped out and began shooting at him simultaneously.

Bullets lacerated the stones of the cafe wall. Roger's head had been in front of this spot a moment before. As the slugs whined murderously in the twilight air, Roger crawled on hands and knees between the hems of the checked tablecloths.

He heard a great crashing above his own panicky breath. French curses, liquid and rapid, punctuated the bursts of gunfire. Spasmodically the shooting stopped twenty seconds after it had begun.

But by that time Roger had already crawled into the shadows of the cafe, bowled over the mustached proprietor and raced up rickety stairs to the second floor. He went out through a trapdoor to the slate roof.

Clinging dizzily to a chimneypot, he looked down. A flock of geese which had been strolling through the cobbled main street of the tiny village of St. Vign flew every which way, honking at the Citroen which nearly ran over them as it gathered speed and rolled away. Then, with a tightlipped gasp of relief, Roger located the source of the crash which had saved him—an overturned vintner's cart. He vaguely remembered the cart being unloaded before the shooting started, as he sat sipping Coca-Cola, reading the pamphlet in his pocket, *A New Glossary of Interesting Americanisms,* and trying to look like a tame philologist in horn-rimmed spectacles.

He had failed miserably, he thought. In the disguise, that is. But then, the opposite side always had first-rate intelligence. Lucky the vintner's cart had gotten in the line of fire. The poor vintner was drawing a crowd of people as he sobbed over his dribbling and bullet-riddled casks and cursed off would-be drinkers. The whine of the Citroen had died altogether.

It was chilly, hanging on the chimneypot in the wind. Below in the street a nun in the crowd pointed up at Roger. Quickly he scrambled down the slates. He leaped to the adjoining roof in the amber dusk.

As he went skulking across the rooftops, one thought came up paramount in his mind after his shock and surprise had passed: his still-urgent need to get aboard *The Silver Mistral Express* which was scheduled to go through St. Vign on its way to Paris in—Roger consulted his shockproof watch while resting on the roof of a laundry—exactly forty-eight minutes.

His first task was to reach the railway station, hoping the assassins would be frightened off making another attempt on him because of the notoriety their first failure caused. Sliding, Roger dropped into an alley and began to run through the grape-fragrant French twilight.

As he ran he heard a number of whistles and saw several gendarmes pedalling frantically on bicycles. Good, he thought, puffing. Wonderful. If they keep the Citroen holed up in some garage for—again the watch—thirty-two minutes, I'll make it.

Reaching the depot without incident, he paced restlessly along the platform, trying to read his pamphlet. At least, up the track, a light shone and an air horn cried out stridently.

When the crack train from the south of France pulled to a hissing halt in response to the ticket seller's signal lantern, Roger leaped aboard with the pamphlet of Americanisms still clutched in one hand. The conductor badgered him in French for disturbing the schedule as the express began to roll. Roger ignored him. He held up the pamphlet in the vestibule light. On the inside front cover a car and compartment number had been noted in ballpoint. Roger turned to the right, stepped through a velvet padded door, then hastily backed out again. He had gone the wrong way. The private saloon car was filled with men and women in formal clothes, opera capes and evening gowns.

"What's that?" Roger asked the trainman sourly. "A masked ball?"

"An opera troupe, *Anglais*. Returning from a triumphant engagement in the South," replied the trainman, kissing his fingertips. Then he scowled. "Let me see your ticket, please."

Roger handed it over.

"How far is compartment seven, car eleven-twelve?"

"Four cars to the rear," said the trainman without interest, turning his back on Roger and beginning to whistle an operatic aria. Roger kicked open the door on his left. He hurried, walking as fast as he dared. The cars were dimly lit, most of the doors closed. The wheels of the train clicked eerily from the shadows. Roger shivered. He felt for his automatic under his coat.

Finally he found the right car. Putting his pamphlet in his pocket, Roger knocked at compartment seven.

"Dozier? Open up."

Mouth close to the wood, Roger whispered it again:

"Dozier! For God's sake, man, open—"

With a start Roger realized the sliding door was unlocked.

He stepped quickly into the darkened carriage, blinked, and uttered a sigh of disgust. He might have known.

Wasn't this precisely why he had been sent to board the train in such haste? Because the agent—some agent, Roger thought, staring at the compartment's lone occupant—was one of the worst bunglers in the trade. An IBM machine had slipped a cog or something, dispensing the wrong punch card when the escort was being selected for the vital mission of accompanying Sir Stafford Runes from Cairo to Paris. At the last moment, higher-ups had caught the error and dispatched Roger by 707 to catch the train at St. Vign and see that no fatal damage had been done.

The agent in question, actually a coder from London who doubled in ladies' ready-to-wear, and who had no business at all in the field, was a fat, pot-bellied bald man with the first name Herschel. At the moment he was snoring contentedly with his hands twined over his Harris-tweeded paunch. Roger shook him.

"Dozier, wake up. Do you hear me? What's the matter with you, Dozier?"

Sniffing, Roger realized dismally that brandy had aided Herschel Dozier's slumber. With each valuable minute spent attempting to wake the slumbering cow-like fellow, Sir Stafford Runes sat alone, undoubtedly in the next compartment. Disgusted, Roger slid back into the corridor.

Which compartment, right or left?

He tried the one on the right, tapping softly. A feminine giggle came back, together with some sounds which indicated that if an archaeologist was inside, he was a young, lively archaeologist, not the red-haired, vain, aging Runes.

Moving back along the carpeted corridor to the other door, Roger hesitated, his knuckles an inch from the panel.

The compartment door stood open perhaps a thirty-second of an inch, allowing a hairline of light to fall across Roger's loafers.

Sweat came cold on his palm. He drew his automatic.

Was someone from the opposite side in there?

Runes, on an underground exploration in the vicinity of Nisapur, had unearthed what headquarters described only as a "vital plan" belonging to the opposite side. The plan, apparently, was so important that higher-ups had ordered Runes to discontinue his valuable roll as a double agent at once and return to home base as fast as he could while still avoiding danger. Now Roger smelled danger like burning insulation on a wire.

Drawing a tight breath, he cursed the faulty IBM machine, gripped the door handle, and yanked.

The first thing he saw was the corpse of Sir Stafford Runes.

It sprawled doll-fashion on the seat, an ivory knife-hilt poking from the waistcoat. Against the talcumed whiteness of the dead man's puffy old features, the carrot brightness of his thick red hair looked gruesome.

Then Roger's eyes were torn to the tall man who stood calmly in the center of the compartment, eyeing him with a stainless-steel gaze from under the rim of a shining top hat. From the man's lean shoulders fell the shimmering folds of an opera cape, which showed a flashing hint of blood-red satin lining as he raised one white-gloved hand in a vicious little salute. Roger slammed the door shut as the man said:

"Is it really you, Roger?" His voice was clipped, educated. "I'd thought they took care of you in St. Vign."

"No such luck."

Covering the gaunt man with his automatic, Roger nodded down at the dead body. The express train's horn howled in the night.

"So you did this, you rotten bastard. Just the way you ran over Jerry Pitts with the road-grader in Liberia and fed Mag Busby that lye soup in Soho." A vein in Roger's temple began to hammer. "You rotten bastard," he repeated. "Someone should have squashed you a long time ago. But what are you doing in that get-up, Victor? Travelling with that opera company?"

"Of course, dear boy," the other purred. "I'm representing them on this tour. I schedule performances wherever duty calls. Such as in Paris. Most convenient." A white glove indicated the speeding motion of the train, but for all the man's casualness there was glacial chill in his calculating eyes. "It appears that this time, however, with you as relief man, I've landed in a spot of trouble. I'd thought all I had to worry about was that fool asleep next door."

"This time, Foxe-Craft," Roger said quietly, "you've got a bullet to worry about."

"A bullet?" The urbane man's eyebrow lifted. "Oh, now, really, old chap, so *brutal?*"

"Did you think about brutality when you fed Mag the lye soup? Listen, mister, for ten years we've wanted you. You and your fancy gloves and your code name.'' A line of derision twisted Roger's wirelike mouth. ''*Elevenfingers*. Proud of that name, aren't you? One up on the rest of us, and all that. Well, tonight, I think I'll take those fingers off. One at a time.''

With a stab of satisfaction Roger saw a dollop of sweat break out on Foxe-Craft's upper lip. Roger made a sharp gesture with the automatic.

''All right, Elevenfingers—''

''Don't make it sound cheap,'' Foxe-Craft said, dangerously soft. ''Not theatrical, I warn you.''

''Where's the folio Runes was carrying?''

Hastily Roger searched the archaeologist's corpse. He performed the same action on the person of his enemy, a shred of doubt beginning to worry him as he completed the task, unsuccessfully. Apart from the usual innocuous card cases, visas, anti-personnel fountain pen bombs and other personal effects, neither dead researcher nor live agent possessed a single item remotely resembling the flat, eight-and-a-half by eleven series of sheets, blank to the eye but inked invisibly, which Runes was carrying back from Nisapur. Roger raised the automatic again.

''Take a long look down the muzzle, friend. See the message? I can put some bullets in places that'll hurt like hell. And I don't care if I wake the whole damned train doing it. But you're going to tell me where the folio is. You're going to give it to me, or I'll blow you into an assortment of pieces no doctor on the Continent can put together.'' Desperate, angry, Roger added: ''In five seconds.''

Foxe-Craft shrugged.

''Very well.''

As Foxe-Craft consulted a timetable card riveted to the compartment wall his eyes glinted maliciously for a moment. Then the toe of his dancing pump scraped a worn place in the carpeting. Looking at his wristwatch, the man who liked to call himself Elevenfingers said: ''You're an American. Look under the rug.''

''I'll just do that.''

Carefully Roger knelt, keeping the automatic in a position to fire at the slightest sign of movement in the corner of his eyes. Roger probed at the frayed edges of the hole in the carpeting. And at that precise instant, the game turned against him; *The Silver Mistral Express* whipped around a curve and into a tunnel.

There was a scream of horn, a sudden roar of wheels racketing off walls. Roger swayed, off balance.

257

A tasselled pump caught him in the jaw, exploding roman candles behind his eyes a moment after he caught a fragmentary glimpse of traces of ash beneath the carpet.

Foxe-Craft *couldn't* have burned the folio, Roger thought wildly as he fell backward, flailing. I didn't smell anything—and that means *Runes* burned it because he knew they were on to us, but why did he burn the only copy in existence—?

No answer came except the roar of wheels and another brutal smash of a pump instep on his jaw, smacking Roger's head against the side of the compartment, sending him to oblivion.

Through his pain he had dim recollections of the next hour—hands lifting him, a fall through space, a jolt, the *clacka-clacka-clacka* of wheels gathering speed, then the chirruping of night insects. And silence.

Bruised, disappointed, briar-scratched and burr-decorated, Roger woke sometime before dawn, lying in a ditch a few hundred yards south of another railway depot, this one bearing a signboard naming the town as St. Yar.

Roger picked himself up and tried to wipe the humiliation of failure from his mind. In another two hours Foxe-Craft—and the train—would be in Paris, doubtless with the vital material in his hands.

Roger felt, somehow, that it still existed; that Elevenfingers had tricked him. But how? Starting off, Roger noticed his ubiquitous pamphlet in the weeds. He stared at it dully, finally putting it back in his pocket as he passed a sign pointing the way to a French military aerodrome two kilometres away.

Trudging into the village, Roger located an inn and ordered a glass of wine. The proprietor treated him with the respect given by all Frenchmen to those who look like confirmed alcoholics—torn clothes and hangdog expression. Dispiritedly Roger sat at a street-side table as the sun rose. Bells chimed in the cathedral. A French jet lanced the sky overhead.

To kill the futility of it all, Roger bought a paper at a kiosk and sat by a fountain reading. At a town quite a distance south, the wet-inked lead story ran, an unidentified bald man had been found in a ditch by railway inspectors.

Poor Herschel Dozier, Roger thought. It would be just like Elevenfingers to finish the sleeping agent, just for amusement. Another knife in the guts from nothing . . .

When he had finished the paper, he dragged out the pamphlet to try to dull his mind.

"What the hell do *I* care about Interesting Americanisms?" he said, blinking in the sun. And then, as pigeons cooed around his feet and a postcard-seller passed by hawking indecent views, the depth of his blunder made itself known.

Foxe-Craft's remark flashed like a bomb. With a whoop, Roger leaped up and ran to the cafe.

"Where can I get a taxi to the military aerodrome? I have to get a helicopter to Paris right away!"

The baffled proprietor gave him directions. Roger's identification papers, concealed in his heels, served him well. Within an hour he stood on the noisy platform as *The Silver Mistral Express* chugged in along the arrival track.

Roger felt for the automatic in his pocket, grinning tensely. Of *course* Runes had burned the folio. Too obvious. But if Roger was right, there was another copy—*had* to be!

Down the platform trouped the formally-dressed opera company, Foxe-Craft in their midst. When he saw Roger he turned and tried to walk in the opposite direction. Roger raced after him. He gouged the automatic in the agent's ribs.

"*Really,* old fellow—" Foxe-Craft began.

"Shut up," Roger said. "You egotistical bastard. Think you're so damn clever. One up. Well, you shouldn't have opened your precise mouth, Elevenfingers, because now you're going to be tagged with a killing. I thought it was Dozier in the ditch. But it wasn't. It was Runes. Bald, vain Runes."

Roger dug into the writing agent's pocket, came up with his prize, carrot-red.

"First we'll go wake up Dozier. Probably he's still asleep."

Roger turned his find over, noted minute markings which looked like ink on the inner, rather burlap-like surface.

"Then," Roger added, gagging his captive, "we'll have the lab blow up the stuff that's written here. Inside old Sir Stafford's—"

A crowd began to gather. The divas and tenors of Elevenfinger's now-defunct opera troup clucked curiously. Roger held up the carrot-colored wig and finished:

"—inside, or under—as we Americans say—his rug."

45

TO AVOID A SCANDAL

Talmage Powell

MY DEAR FELLOW, it's all perfectly simple and clear. I detest discussing such a gory thing, but I must do so. Otherwise, I fear you'll receive your only knowledge of the episode from those lurid newspaper accounts, which are written for scandal-hungry human animals of the lowest order. I shudder even to reflect upon the workings of such minds. And I should rather die than endure scandal.

This attitude of mine is the result of generations of breeding, I assure you. It is as much a part of me as the cells of my blood. I trace my ancestry back two hundred years on this continent. From that time—until the present moment—scandal has never touched my family. I come from a line of college professors and doctors, on my father's side, and social workers and genteel poets on my mother's. I was taught the appreciation of the finer things quite young. My dear mother impressed upon me that the family name I bore, Croyden, was a cherished possession which I must never sully.

The accident, you say? You saw the picture in the paper of my little wife lying on the concrete completely destroyed? Really, I feel a trifle faint just thinking of that picture. I fail to see why the photographer put such great store by it. Some things, I maintain, are simply not meant for the public eye.

I shall tell you about the accident, and it was all an accident from start to finish. You have my word, sir, the word of a Croyden. But first you must see how simple and clear it all really was.

Now I've already told you something about my background. With a little exercise of the imagination you can see my home, where everything was in perfect taste, where my mother played Chopin and Schubert on the grand piano.

261

I didn't take to the piano, as she had hoped I would. I couldn't imagine myself a pianist, because I never could have exposed myself to public view.

Even had I forced myself, I could never have been a good pianist. It was my nature to be too precise. I was precise in everything. I, from earliest years, always tied my shoes so the laces were exactly even, hung my trousers with the creases just so. Our maid used to complain that my room didn't look like a child's room at all. In fact, said she, you'd never know anyone lived in it. She was, of course, a big, blousy woman who lost her temper every now and then. I supposed she was none too bright and felt rather sorry for her.

While I was attending college, my dear parents died within six months of each other. They did it gently, in their beds, in excellent taste, without ostentation.

When the estate was settled, I found I must seek employment rather than continue my education. There was a very fine, old banking family in our town whose roots went deeply in the history of our section. I was fortunate enough to secure employment with them as a bookkeeper.

I loved my job. I ached with delight over the rows of precise figures. The months and years rolled rapidly away. As I advanced I was very careful about those whom I eventually came to employ. Scandal of a personal nature would reflect against the bank. I was careful never to hire anyone without background and breeding. I tried to seek out those like myself, though it was not always easy.

I had never given much thought to women. I was content to dote over my rows of figures, to live in my orderly apartment where not even a stickpin was out of place, and to indulge my hobbies. I had two such diversions. I collected stamps and I worked ciphers.

The only woman who ever interested me was Althea. A gentle, quiet slip of a thing, I met her at my employer's home one evening when I had gone there for some overtime work. She served us tea when the task was finished, and she gave me a gentle smile. She was not beautiful in the usual sense, but I found her most attractive. She had a small, quiet face, soft blue eyes, and dark brown hair. She was my employer's cousin.

Althea and I experienced a brief courtship. We dined together quietly. We sat in my employer's home of an evening and watched the better TV shows. We took in a concert. We strolled in the park on a Sunday afternoon.

My poor hobbies suffered from all this lack of attention. I had no less than five codes to which I had given no attention. In the drawing room of my employer's home, I asked Althea to marry me.

She threw her arms about my neck and squealed. She kissed me wetly.

She wept. I was taken aback. It was so unlike her. Seeing the strange new animation in her eyes, I felt hesitant.

She accepted my proposal very quickly.

As I walked home, I was so taken up with the problem of whether or not I had acted wisely that I forgot to stop for my evening newspaper. I knew there were depths in people that different circumstances sometimes bring to light, and I had glimpsed a new Althea this evening. A bit animal, a bit too vivacious for good taste.

However, before I could gracefully withdraw my proposal, she had announced the engagement. What dreadful scandal had I called it off then! So we went through with the wedding, quietly, with only her immediate family and a very few friends present.

We set up housekeeping in my apartment. From the first moment I knew that it was not going to work. Her habits were despicable. She appeared for breakfast in a flimsy negligee over her pajamas. She shopped without a list of purchases to be made. She was often as much as thirty minutes late with dinner. She was definitely not the gentle, timid Althea that I thought I had married.

And she was entirely too foolish and ignorant to understand my hobbies. She took no interest in them. She was jealous of them.

I felt like a desperate man at bay, sir. No longer was the apartment a beckoning climax to each perfect day at my place of employment. I felt as if I had been expelled from a wonderful dream of life to a nightmare caricature of life. What could I do? To what haven could I flee? There was none, sir, and I became utterly miserable.

At the bank, naturally, I kept up a graceful front. No other course ever occurred to me. So far as any of them knew, everything in my life was still perfect.

I considered the matter more and more gravely. And the afternoon she destroyed my codes, I knew I could endure it no longer.

I could hear her humming as I approached the apartment door. I closed my eyes and leaned against the wall for a moment of weariness. Then I opened the door, and stood speechless, riven to the spot with repugnance.

The apartment was up-ended, with new furniture all over the place. It smote my eyes. It lashed against my brain. Such furniture, in bright colors and garish modern design.

''Hello, darling,'' she lilted. ''How do you like—?''

''What ever are you doing, Althea?'' I asked in a controlled voice.

''Why, I'm re-doing the apartment, darling,'' she said.

''I see,'' I said.

263

I stumbled toward the little room I'd so long ago—in that other beautiful lifetime—fixed into a den. I assure you that the blood vessels in my head almost burst when I reached the door of the den. Her horrible depredations had reached even there! Gone was my beloved desk, gone my walnut book shelves neatly stacked with ciphers.

"Althea, Althea," I demanded of her, "what have you done here?"

"Why, I'm lightening up the place a bit, darling. That old fashioned lamp you had wasn't good for the eyes and the furniture was positively depressing."

"And my codes?"

"Those old papers?" she said. "Oh, I threw them out, dear. Are you ill, Horace?"

Of course I was. In a way she would never know, could never understand. I staggered away from the door of the den, shook off her arm. Her touch was revolting. I wished I had never seen her. I wished she would just vanish—like a puff of vile smoke in an otherwise perfect day.

"Perhaps you'd better lie down, darling." I heard her say.

I looked up at her. Somehow I'd sat down in the living room on one of the horrid striped chairs.

"No," I said coolly, "I'm feeling quite well now."

"You're sure?"

"I wouldn't have said it unless I were!" I retorted.

She rattled on, until I thought her voice would drive me over the brink of madness.

There was a little balcony outside the apartment. I had never used it. Now, as she chirped on, she picked up four thin pillows with plastic coverings.

"Open the door for me, Horace?" she said, holding the pillows with both arms.

As I opened the double doors leading to the balcony, I saw that she had furnished it with a round wrought iron table and four matching chairs. The pillows were for the chairs, of course.

I remember that I glanced overhead. A jet plane, very high and leaving a vapor trail, was glinting like a silver speck in the rays of the late sun. From far below came the muted sounds of the city. To my right, I saw a few cars on the street and a newsboy on the sidewalk.

Everything outside was so normal. But my world was gone. And I knew it could be restored in only one way.

She had finished putting the pillows on the chairs. She stood back to appraise the balcony's altered appearance. She was quite close to the rail.

It was four stories down, to a concrete alley.

I strolled over beside her.

Then I grabbed her and threw her over.

Her thin, scream cut her away from life. From me. From the terrible ruin she had brought to my life.

Dear me, the joyous sense of relief I experienced! Of course, I couldn't let it be apparent. I had a part to play now, but I knew I could get through the trying days that were sure to come because the reward would be so great. I could hold on because afterwards the apartment would be as if she had never been in it. Once again it would be orderly and neat. My life would be beautiful.

I rushed into the hallway with a hoarse cry. Several doors opened, framing the staring faces of neighbors.

"My poor wife," I moaned. "She has fallen. From the balcony . . ."

Then I collapsed.

They carried me into the apartment. They patted my face with water. They yelled instructions at each other. Get a doctor. Get an ambulance. Call the police. How senselessly ineffectual they were! It was all I could do to keep from showing my contempt for them.

After a time, a rough, uncouth fellow in a policeman's uniform shoved his way through the ring of neighbors.

"You Croyden?" he said to me.

"Yes," I said, sitting on the edge of the divan. "I'm Horace Croyden."

"Then get on your feet!" he ordered.

"Officer," I said looking up at him, "I've suffered a most acute shock. You've no right . . ."

"I've got every right, bub," he said. "I guess you claim she fell."

"Of course she did."

"Why, you little liar," he looked at me as if he wanted to spit with disgust. "You threw her right off that balcony. There was a jet plane passing overhead. And a kid down on the street selling papers; tells me you happen to be one of his regular customers. Like most kids, them jet planes get to him. He was neglecting business for a minute, see? So he could look at that jet plane and think what it must be like up there and how maybe he'd pilot one of them babies one of these days. And he seen you. He seen every bit of it."

The apartment was suddenly hushed. I sat appalled. Positively appalled.

"Why'd you do it?" the cop demanded.

"She—she was ruining my life," I said.

"Then why didn't you just leave her?"

It was obvious to me that here was a lout who could never understand. And suddenly all the faces surrounding me were like the cop's, totally devoid of feeling or comprehension.

"Leave her?" I heard myself ask, aghast. "Leave her—and risk the horrid scandal of a divorce?"

46

THE PREVALENCE OF MONSTERS

Thomas B. Dewey

ELLEN MACDONALD WAS roused from a dream of midsummer madness to hear Robbie, her five-year-old son, screaming his head off. Her throat was dry and twisted with longing. Her dream in that short afternoon nap had centered on a mountain of ice cream (fresh peach) topped by a veritable lava flow of sauce (maple walnut), rigorously forbidden in reality, but now all hers just as soon as she could make her way to the table. The table had seemed at first to be in her own kitchen, and then, curiously, it had shifted to the farthest corner of the student union, on a campus she had not seen for eight years.

The screen door banged heavily and she whimpered at the shock. She managed to get her feet on the floor as Robbie hurled himself at her. She interpreted his gasped explanation to mean that her older son Dean, eight, had tried to force Robbie to go into the boathouse.

"—and there's—a—*monster* in there!"

"There's no such thing as a monster," she said sharply.

"There is so a monster in the boathouse!"

"Well, you don't have to go in the boathouse if you don't want to."

By the time he had quieted down, it was a quarter to five and she had to hurry her bath, as usual, then fly to get their dinners and something for the babysitter, who would be there at six. Then she would have to dress hastily, not knowing for sure that everyting was in place, properly hooked. All this in order to meet Betty Quillan and Patricia Dorn at the mailbox, so they could drive over to Nancy Caldwell's cottage for the weekly meeting of "The Castaways"—the wives of men who worked in the city and sent their families to the Lake for the summer.

Not that she really wanted to go, but the group had been formed to provide some solidarity for the city wives and she felt a certain loyalty. If only it weren't for Nancy Caldwell's annoying habit of posing her "hypo-thetical problems"— Some of those nasty, penetrating questions might be all right in the security of the full home, in winter; but how they were upsetting, even hair-raising, in the summer dog days.

Tonight, for instance, they were nearly finished with dessert and coffee when Nancy said, "Let's just face it, what would you do? Say you have to go into town unexpectedly; it's long after working hours, you let yourself into the apartment, and there he is, that great god guy of yours from Olympus to whom you've given the best years of your life, wrapped in the arms of some tantalizing bit of blonde fluff with nothing in the world to do but provide female companionship for lonely males. What would you do? Really and truly. Let's take turns."

One by one, according to their inclinations, they made shift to answer. Waiting for her turn, Ellen brooded. She was tired and she had an uncom-fortable, stuffed feeling, mingled with guilt, from the rich, forbidden dessert.

Why do I let myself get trapped, she thought, into doing so many things I don't want to do? I hate these scratchy hen parties. I hate coming to the Lake, having to cope with children and dead fish, while Bill stays in the city in an air-conditioned office with his bright, unencumbered secretary—

"Ellen?" Nancy was saying. "It's your turn. What would *you* do?"

"I'd—I think I'd kill him," Ellen said.

A hush fell, deep and embarrassing.

Trapped again, she thought, and she wanted to slap at the sly smile on Nancy's face . . .

Ellen got back at 11:15 and heard Robbie whimpering in the bedroom.

"What's the matter with him?" she asked.

"I don't know," the babysitter said. "I read to him—but he keeps on talking about monsters."

When the babysitter had gone, Ellen fixed warm milk for Robbie and stayed with him till he fell asleep. Then she woke up Dean and marched him to the kitchen.

"Repeat after me," she said. "There is no such thing as a monster."

He rubbed his eyes, mumbling, "Therenoschthinsamonster."

"Say it again, and this time slowly, distinctly."

He stared at her.

"There is no such thing as a monster," he said.

"All right. Now go back to bed and don't let me hear you scaring Robbie again with that nonsense."

He lingered a moment, hurt and confused, and she turned away because she had begun to cry. By the time she got to bed it was 1:30 and her body felt like a knotted rope.

"It isn't fair!" she said through her teeth.

She groped for the telephone beside the bed, got the local operator, and put in a call to their city apartment. She let them ring at least twenty times before she finally hung up.

Almost two in the morning, she thought, and he's always in the office by nine. Where would he be at two in the morning? And what would he be doing?

The next day was hot, the Lake glassy calm. At four in the afternoon she called Betty Quillan, who had two children Robbie's and Dean's age.

"Sure, send them over," Betty said.

"I may be late, you know the trains—"

"I'll put them up in the bunks. Don't hurry, and have yourself a good time."

"Thanks, Betty. I'll do the same for you—"

She caught the 5:15, which got her to the city at 7:30. She took a taxi to the apartment and let herself in at five minutes after eight.

Everything seemed orderly enough, except for some debris on the coffee table—three cocktail glasses and some crumpled napkins. But one of the glasses bore lipstick stains, as did one of the napkins.

She carried the tray to the kitchen and was sick at her stomach in the sink. She washed her face, turned out the lights, and sat in the dark living room—waiting.

At ten she dragged herself out of a sour-smelling stupor and went to the bedroom. The bed was neatly made, and everything hung in place. She could see Nancy Caldwell's face smirking at her.

But he's *always* neat, she thought desperately.

In the bathroom she found a couple of discarded tissues, stained a bright pink. She wadded them into a ball and flushed them out of sight. She had begun to cry and her throat was pinched and dry. Braced on both hands over the lavatory, she forced out words as if spitting.

"You will not do this to me—"

On tiptoe, stretching, she groped on the high closet shelf, dislodging shoe boxes and bundles of obsolete accessories. Finally she found the gun—a small .25 caliber pistol that Bill had taught her how to use—"just in case of possible prowlers." It was loaded and she carried it to the bed, sat there with it in her lap, and tried to ignore the pain in her stomach, the buzzing in her ears.

The telephone rang four times before she realized what the sound was. There was a man's voice, briefly nonplused. Then—

"Oh—you would be Mrs. MacDonald. Sorry to call so late—this is George Reamer. Just wanted to tell Bill that I signed the contract with Mr. Devlin."

"I see—" Ellen said.

"Sorry you couldn't be with us—afraid we kept your husband up till all hours. The wife and I enjoyed ourselves very much. Great guy you've got there—glad he'll be on the account. If you'll tell him—"

Over the voice and the buzzing in her head she heard the front door of the apartment.

"Yes, I'll tell him," she said.

The gun slipped from her lap and she barely had time to pick it up and push it under the pillow before the bedroom door opened and Bill came in.

Thank you, Mr. Reamer, whoever you are—thank you for assuming that I'm Mrs. MacDonald—

"Baby, baby, baby!" Bill was saying, pulling her down beside him on the bed. "Am I glad to see you! How did you know to come home tonight? I got great news—a big new account—"

"Yes," she said, "Mr. Reamer just called—"

"What a couple, those Reamers! Cleaned us out of gin in thirty minutes. But listen, I've got some ice cream out there, your favorite, and some maple walnut sauce—"

"Yes—yes, darling."

Later, bathed and cool, the ache in her throat melted away with the ice cream, and she looked at the familiar ceiling while Bill got ready for bed.

"On account of inflation," he said, "five cents for your thoughts."

Under the pillow she could feel the hard lump of the gun she hadn't yet had a chance to hide away.

"Not worth it," she said drowsily. "But if you want to be a spend-thrift—I was just thinking—"

She let it trail off.

"Come on," Bill nudged, "you made a deal."

"—about the prevalence of monsters."

47

THE NINE MILE WALK

Harry Kemelman

I HAD MADE an ass of myself in a speech I had given at the Good Government Association dinner, and Nicky Welt had cornered me at breakfast at
the Blue Moon, where we both ate occasionally, for the pleasure of rubbing
it in. I had made the mistake of departing from my prepared speech to
criticize a statement my predecessor in the office of County Attorney had
made to the press. I had drawn a number of inferences from his statement
and had thus left myself open to a rebuttal which he had promptly made and
which had the effect of making me appear intellectually dishonest. I was
new to this political game, having but a few months before left the Law
School faculty to become the Reform Party candidate for County Attorney.
I said as much in extenuation, but Nicholas Welt, who would never drop his
pedagogical manner (he was Snowdon Professor of English Language and
Literature), replied in much the same tone that he would dismiss a request
from a sophomore for an extension on a term paper, "That's no excuse."

Although he is only two or three years older than I, in his late forties, he
always treats me like a schoolmaster hectoring a stupid pupil. And I,
perhaps because he looks so much older with his white hair and lined,
gnomelike face, suffer it.

"They were perfectly logical inferences," I pleaded.

"My dear boy," he purred, "although human intercourse is well-nigh
impossible without inference, most inferences are usually wrong. The
percentage of error is particularly high in the legal profession where the
intention is not to discover what the speaker wishes to convey, but rather
what he wishes to conceal."

I picked up my check and eased out from behind the table.

"I suppose you are referring to cross-examination of witnesses in court.

Well, there's always an opposing counsel who will object if the inference is illogical.''

"Who said anything about logic?" he retorted. "An inference can be logical and still not be true."

He followed me down the aisle to the cashier's booth. I paid my check and waited impatiently while he searched in an old-fashioned change purse, fishing out coins one by one and placing them on the counter beside his check, only to discover that the total was insufficient. He slid them back into his purse and with a tiny sigh extracted a bill from another compartment of the purse and handed it to the cashier.

"Give me any sentence of ten or twelve words," he said, "and I'll build you a logical chain of inferences that you never dreamed of when you framed the sentence."

Other customers were coming in, and since the space in front of the cashier's booth was small, I decided to wait outside until Nicky completed his transaction with the cashier. I remember being mildly amused at the idea that he probably thought I was still at his elbow and was going right ahead with his discourse.

When he joined me on the sidewalk I said, "A nine mile walk is no joke, especially in the rain."

"No, I shouldn't think it would be," he agreed absently. Then he stopped in his stride and looked at me sharply. "What the devil are you talking about?"

"It's a sentence and it has eleven words," I insisted. And I repeated the sentence, ticking off the words on my fingers.

"What about it?"

"You said that given a sentence of ten or twelve words—"

"Oh, yes." He looked at me suspiciously. "Where did you get it?"

"It just popped into my head. Come on now, build your inferences."

"You're serious about this?" he asked, his little blue eyes glittering with amusement. "You really want me to?"

It was just like him to issue a challenge and then to appear amused when I accepted it. And it made me angry.

"Put up or shut up," I said.

"All right," he said mildly. "No need to be huffy. I'll play. Hm-m, let me see, how did the sentence go? 'A nine mile walk is no joke, especially in the rain.' Not much to go on there."

"Its more than ten words." I rejoined.

"Very well." His voice became crisp as he mentally squared off to the problem. "First inference: the speaker is aggrieved."

"I'll grant that," I said, "although it hardly seems to be an inference. It's really implicit in the statement."

He nodded impatiently. "Next inference: the rain was unforeseen, otherwise he would have said, 'A nine mile walk in the rain is no joke,' instead of using the 'especially' phrase as an afterthought."

"I'll allow that," I said, "although it's pretty obvious."

"First inferences should be obvious," said Nick tartly.

I let it go at that. He seemed to be floundering and I didn't want to rub it in.

"Next inference: the speaker is not an athlete or an outdoors man."

"You'll have to explain that one," I said.

"It's the 'especially' phrase again," he said. "The speaker does not say that a nine mile walk in the rain is no joke, but merely the walk—just the distance, mind you—is no joke. Now, nine miles is not such a terribly long distance. You walk more than half that in eighteen holes of golf—and golf is an old man's game," he added slyly. *I* play golf.

"Well, that would be all right under ordinary circumstances," I said, "but there are other possibilities. The speaker might be a soldier in the jungle, in which case nine miles would be a pretty good hike, rain or no rain."

"Yes," and Nicky was sarcastic, "and the speaker might be one-legged. For that matter, the speaker might be a graduate student writing a Ph.D. thesis on humor and starting by listing all the things that are not funny. See here, I'll have to make a couple of assumptions before I continue."

"How do you mean?" I asked, suspiciously.

"Remember, I'm taking this sentence *in vacuo*, as it were. I don't know who said it or what the occasion was. Normally a sentence belongs in the framework of a situation."

"I see. What assumptions do you want to make?"

"For one thing, I want to assume that the intention was not frivolous, that the speaker is referring to a walk that was actually taken, and that the purpose of the walk was not to win a bet or something of that sort."

"That seems reasonable enough," I said.

"And I also want to assume that the locale of the walk is here."

"You mean here in Fairfield?"

"Not necessarily. I mean in this general section of the country."

"Fair enough."

"Then, if you grant those assumptions, you'll have to accept my last inference that the speaker is no athlete or outdoors man."

"Well, all right, go on."

"Then my next inference is that the walk was taken very late at night or

273

very early in the morning—say, between midnight and five or six in the morning.''

''How do you figure that one?'' I asked.

''Consider the distance, nine miles. We're in a fairly well-populated section. Take any road and you'll find a community of some sort in less than nine miles. Hadley is five miles away, Hadley Falls is seven and a half, Goreton is eleven, but East Goreton is only eight and you strike East Goreton before you come to Goreton. There is local train service along the Goreton road and bus service along the others. All the highways are pretty well traveled. Would anyone have to walk nine miles in a rain unless it were late at night when no buses or trains were running and when the few automobiles that were out would hesitate to pick up a stranger on the highway?''

''He might not have wanted to be seen,'' I suggested.

Nicky smiled pityingly. ''You think he would be less noticeable trudging along the highway than he would be riding in a public conveyance where everyone is usually absorbed in his newspaper?''

''Well, I won't press the point,'' I said brusquely.

''Then try this one: he was walking toward a town rather than away from one.''

I nodded. ''It is more likely, I suppose. If he were in a town, he could probably arrange for some sort of transportation. Is that the basis for your inference?''

''Partly that,'' said Nicky, ''but there is also an inference to be drawn from the distance. Remember, it's a *nine* mile walk and nine is out of the exact numbers.''

''I'm afraid I don't understand.''

That exasperated schoolteacher-look appeared on Nicky's face again. ''Suppose you say, 'I took a ten mile walk' or 'a hundred mile drive'; I would assume that you actually walked anywhere from eight to a dozen miles, or that you rode between ninety and a hundred and ten miles. In other works, *ten* and *hundred* are round numbers. You might have walked *exactly* ten miles or just as likely you might have walked *approximately* ten miles. But when you speak of walking *nine* miles, I have a right to assume that you have named an exact figure. Now, we are far more likely to know the distance of the city from a given point than we are to know the distance of a given point from the city. That is, ask anyone in the city how far out Farmer Brown lives, and if he knows him, he will say, 'Three or four miles.' But ask Farmer Brown how far he lives from the city and he will tell you. 'Three and six-tenths miles—measured it on my speedometer many a time.' "

"It's weak, Nicky," I said.

"But in conjunction with your own suggestion that he would have arranged transportation if he had been in a city—"

"Yes, that would do it," I said. "I'll pass it. Any more?"

"I've just begun to hit my stride," he boasted. "My next inference is that he was going to a definite destination and that he had to be there at a particular time. It was not a case of going off to get help because his car broke down or his wife was going to have a baby or somebody was trying to break into his house."

"Oh, come now," I said, "the car breaking down is really the most likely situation. He could have known the exact distance from having checked the mileage just as he was leaving the town."

Nicky shook his head. "Rather than walk nine miles in the rain, he would have curled up on the back seat and gone to sleep, or at least stayed by his car and tried to flag another motorist. Remember, it's nine miles. What would be the least it would take him to hike it?"

"Four hours," I offered.

He nodded. "Certainly no less, considering the rain. We've agreed that it happened very late at night or very early in the morning. Suppose he had his breakdown at one o'clock in the morning. It would be five o'clock before he would arrive. That's daybreak. You begin to see a lot of cars on the road. The buses start just a little later. In fact, the first buses hit Fairfield around five-thirty. Besides, if he were going for help, he would not have to go all the way to town—only as far as the nearest telephone. No, he had a definite appointment, and it was in a town, and it was for some time before five-thirty."

"Then why couldn't he have got there earlier and waited?" I asked. "He could have taken the last bus, arrived around one o'clock, and waited until his appointment. He walks nine miles in the rain instead, and you said he was no athlete."

We had arrived at the Municipal Building where my office is. Normally, any arguments begun at the Blue Moon ended at the entrance to the Municipal Building. But I was interested in Nicky's demonstration and I suggested that he come up for a few minutes.

When we were seated I said, "How about it, Nicky, why couldn't he have arrived early and waited?"

"He could have," Nicky retorted. "But since he did not, we must assume that he was either detained until after the last bus left, or that he had to wait where he was for a signal of some sort, perhaps a telephone call.''

"Then according to you, he had an appointment some time between midnight and five-thirty—''

"We can draw it much finer than that. Remember, it takes him four hours to walk the distance. The last bus stops at twelve-thirty A.M. If he doesn't take that, but starts at the same time, he won't arrive at his destination until four-thirty. On the other hand, if he takes the first bus in the morning, he will arrive around five-thirty. That would mean that his appointment was for some time between four-thirty and five-thirty.''

"You mean that if his appointment was earlier than four-thirty, he would have taken the last night bus, and if it was later than five-thirty, he would have taken the first morning bus?''

"Precisely. And another thing: if he was waiting for a signal or a phone call, it must have come not much later than one o'clock.''

"Yes, I see that,'' I said. "If his appointment is around five o'clock and it takes him four hours to walk the distance, he'd have to start around one.''

He nodded, silent and thoughtful. For some queer reason I could not explain, I did not feel like interrupting his thoughts. On the wall was a large map of the county and I walked over to it and began to study it.

"You're right, Nicky,'' I remarked over my shoulder, "there's no place as far as nine miles away from Fairfield that doesn't hit another town first. Fairfield is right in the middle of a bunch of smaller towns.''

He joined me at the map. "It doesn't have to be Fairfield, you know,'' he said quietly. "It was probably one of the outlying towns he had to reach. Try Hadley.''

"Why Hadley? What would anyone want in Hadley at five o'clock in the morning?''

"The Washington Flyer stops there to take on water about that time,'' he said quietly.

"That's right, too,'' I said. "I've heard that train many a night when I couldn't sleep. I'd hear it pulling in and then a minute or two later I'd hear the clock on the Methodist Church banging out five.'' I went back to my desk for a timetable. "The flyer leaves Washington at twelve forty-seven A.M. and gets into Boston at eight A.M.

Nicky was still at the map measuring distances with a pencil.

"Exactly nine miles from Hadley is the Old Sumter Inn,'' he announced.

"Old Sumter Inn,'' I echoed. "But that upsets the whole theory. You can arrange for transportation there as easily as you can in a town.''

He shook his head. ''The cars are kept in an enclosure and you have to get an attendant to check you through the gate. The attendant would remember anyone taking out his car at a strange hour. It's a pretty conservative place. He could have waited in his room until he got a call from Washington about someone on the Flyer—maybe the number of the car and the berth. Then he could just slip out of the hotel and walk to Hadley.''

I stared at him, hypnotized.

''It wouldn't be difficult to slip aboard while the train was taking on water, and then if he knew the car number and the berth—''

''Nicky,' I said portentously, ''as the Reform District Attorney who campaigned on an economy program, I am going to waste the taxpayer's money and call Boston long distance. It's ridiculous, it's insane—but I'm going to do it!''

His little blue eyes glittered and he moistened his lips with the tip of his tongue.

''Go ahead,'' he said hoarsely.

I replaced the telephone in its cradle.

''Nicky,'' I said, ''this is probably the most remarkable coincidence in the history of criminal investigation: *a man was found murdered in his berth on last night's twelve-forty-seven from Washington!* He'd been dead about three hours, which would make it exactly right for Hadley.''

''I thought it was something like that,'' said Nicky. ''But you're wrong about its being a coincidence. It can't be. Where did you get that sentence?''

''It was just a sentence. It simply popped into my head.''

''It couldn't have! It's not the sort of sentence that pops into one's head. If you had taught composition as long as I have, you'd know that when you ask someone for a sentence of ten words or so, you get an ordinary statement such as 'I like milk'—with the other words made up by a modifying clause like, 'because it is good for my health.' The sentence you offered related to a *particular situation*.''

''But I tell you I talked to no one this morning. And I was alone with you at the Blue Moon.''

''You weren't with me all the time I paid my check,'' he said sharply. ''Did you meet anyone while you were waiting on the sidewalk for me to come out of the Blue Moon?''

I shook my head. ''I was outside for less than a minute before you joined me. You see, a couple of men came in while you were digging out your change and one of them bumped me, so I thought I'd wait—''

''Did you ever see them before?''

''Who?''

''The two men who came in,'' he said, the note of exasperation creeping into his voice again.

''Why, no—they weren't anyone I knew.''

''Were they talking?''

''I guess so. Yes, they were. Quite absorbed in their conversation, as a matter of fact—otherwise, they would have noticed me and I would not have been bumped.''

''Not many strangers come into the Blue Moon,'' he remarked.

''Do you think it was they?'' I asked eagerly. ''I think I'd know them again if I saw them.''

Nicky's eyes narrowed. ''It's possible. There had to be two—one to trail the victim in Washington and ascertain his berth number, the other to wait here and do the job. The Washington man would be likely to come down here afterwards. If there was theft as well as murder, it would be to divide the spoils. If it was just murder, he would probably have to come down to pay off his confederate.''

I reached for the telephone.

''We've been gone less than half an hour,'' Nicky went on. ''They were just coming in and service is slow at the Blue Moon. The one who walked all the way to Hadley must certainly be hungry and the other probably drove all night from Washington.''

''Call me immediately if you make an arrest,'' I said into the phone and hung up.

Neither of us spoke a word while we waited. We paced the floor, avoiding each other almost as though we had done something we were ashamed of.

The telephone rang at last. I picked it up and listened. Then I said, ''O.K.'' and turned to Nicky.

''One of them tried to escape through the kitchen but Winn had someone stationed at the back and they got him.''

''That would seem to prove it,'' said Nicky with a frosty little smile.

I nodded agreement.

He glanced at his watch. ''Gracious,'' he exclaimed, ''I wanted to make an early start on my work this morning, and here I've already wasted all this time talking with you.''

I let him get to the door. ''Oh, Nicky,'' I called, ''what was it you set out to prove?''

"That a chain of inferences could be logical and still not be true," he said.

"Oh."

"What are you laughing at?" he asked snappishly. And then he laughed too.

48

THE PULQUE VENDOR

Hal Ellson

THE GREAT BRONZE bell in the old Cathedral was tolling the hour. Luis Mendoza, the pulque-vendor, lifted his head, counted eleven strokes and felt the stillness move in on the deserted plaza. Time for the deadly appointment.

He arose from the bench, half-expecting to feel the wooden yoke on his neck and the weight of the two huge jars of pulque which he carried through the streets of the city from sun-up till the hungry shadows of night struck from the desert. Across the plaza he moved, striding rapidly through the shadows cast by sour-orange trees heavy with fruit, past the fountain, then directly across the gutter toward the Municipal Building, dark and mute in its crumbling splendor. A half-dozen police motorcycles stood at the curb in front of Police Headquarters. Inside, a ragged beggar stood bare-headed at a desk, pleading with the officer on duty. Another beggar lay curled on a bench behind the wooden bars of a tiny cell. Mendoza frowned and moved on, rounding the corner into a narrow street, where the shadows swallowed him. He emerged on a large plaza, more desolate than its counterpart, crossed it and vanished into another narrow street much like the one where he lived. Its houses were crumbling and silent, windows dark and barred, and not a single light to indicate the existence of tenants.

Halfway down the street, he stopped abruptly and glanced back. The walk was shadowed and empty. No one had tracked him, and none but the three inside the house where he stood knew of the meeting. For the moment he hesitated, wondering if he could go through with the task. The odds were against him. Others had failed dismally and lay in their graves, shot down by the General's gunmen.

Suddenly he made up his mind and entered the house. Three men awaited him in a small patio barely lit by the pale yellow light of an oil lamp.

281

Greetings were exchanged. Mendoza remained standing and looked from one to the other of the three men. One was old, with white hair and a pale gaunt face. The other two were younger, dark like himself, with the same soft eyes that belied the anger smoldering in them.

The old man was Don Gonzalo Aponte, professor without students, aristocrat without funds. Indirectly, General Macia had deprived him of his post at the university, relieved him of the family hacienda, a proud but crumbling ruin, and appropriated the land surrounding it. The order had been signed by the Governor, who was no more than a puppet. The intent of the General was clear, to break the spirit of Don Gonzalo Aponte.

Aponte's spirit was far from broken, but he was old and weak. To strike back on his own was impossible. Still, there were others who hated the General. Some had been brave enough to join with Aponte, an even dozen men—and nine were already dead, slaughtered by the General's gunmen in three bungled attempts at assassination. Bandits, the newspapers called them, preventing the truth at the request of the General.

Thinking of the dead who'd been buried in the desert where they'd been shot, Aponte nodded to Mendoza. "So you came," he said, measuring the wiry frame of the pulque-vendor.

"I said I'd be here," Mendoza replied with a shrug.

Aponte nodded to the young man on his right. "Your friend, Estaban, recommended you. You know the risk?"

"I know it well."

"Nine men have already died."

"They were unfortunate."

"Death is always unfortunate. If you wish to withdraw . . ."

"I wish no such thing."

A faint smile lit the old man's face. "There are few, if any, who would say that, but a question. Why are you willing to risk so much?"

"Because I am poor, Señor. I have use for the money."

"Many are poor, but . . ."

"Perhaps they like being miserable."

"Then your only concern is the money?"

Mendoza frowned, then shook his head. "The General is evil, the gunmen are animals. One kills them without feeling. Especially Pancho Negron, who murdered my friend. He has to die."

Aponte nodded and clasped his hands. A diamond ring flashed light. "You are ready?"

"Yes, Señor."

"Then it is tomorrow. You know the Mayor's residence?"

282

"I know it."

"At noon three cars will be there, and the gunmen. The center car will be for the General. The gunmen will be guarding the street. One will escort the General from the Mayor's residence to the car. A dozen men, all armed." A dry hacking cough wracked the old man. With his fist against his lips, he stemmed the attack and looked at Mendoza. "A dozen men," he repeated.

"I understand," said Mendoza.

"You will have no help. The odds are completely against you."

"It's a gamble," Mendoza conceded. "Twelve against one, but I still possess an advantage."

Aponte failed to see it and asked to be enlightened.

"It's very simple. I am only one man, a poor pulque-vendor," Mendoza explained. "The gunmen will hardly expect trouble from me, and so the element of surprise will be on my side. Besides, I have a plan."

"Which is?"

Mendoza smiled faintly. "That is something I prefer to keep to myself. If it succeeds, or doesn't, you will know about it tomorrow."

Aponte looked at the two younger men beside him and shrugged. "As you wish," he said, turning back to Mendoza.

"And now about the payment?" said the pulque-vendor.

"I see you haven't forgotten that."

"Nor my family," replied Mendoza. "I am doing this for them."

Aponte nodded gravely. "Tomorrow morning at the Cantina of the Matadors you will have your money. As for your mission, I wish you the best of luck."

"I'll need more than that," Mendoza shrugged. "Say a prayer for me." With that, he turned on his heels and left.

As the door closed after him, Aponte shook his head. "A brave fellow, a fool, or . . ."

"Or what" said Estaban.

"Perhaps he is one of them."

"No, he's all right."

"Perhaps, but if it's money he wants, he may go to the General. It would be worth his while to betray us."

"I've vouched for him. He won't betray us."

Aponte nodded. "Perhaps not. Tomorrow will tell, but I wonder about his plan."

"Whatever it is, it's a gamble. He may kill the General, but he won't survive the gunmen."

"Perhaps he wishes to die."

"No," said Estaban. "But he's poor, and the poor are always desperate."

"He appeared very calm," said Aponte, rising slowly from his chair. His thin face was gaunt with fatigue, his hands had begun to tremble. The two younger men noticed and prepared to leave. As they said good—night and moved toward the door, Aponte halted them. "About the payment," he said to Estaban. "I suggest you leave the money with the barman, properly packaged, just in case. . . ."

"I trust Mendoza. I will give it to him myself," said Estaban.

It was still early, the city awake, clamorous and vibrating with life after the black stillness of sleep. As the bronze bell in the Cathedral crashed out the hour, Mendoza crossed the plaza and stopped before the huge main door with its carved figures worm-eaten and scarred by dry-rot to a point of semi-obliteration. A step brought him beyond the door into the dim interior. At first it appeared empty, but a black-shawled figure knelt on the floor; a sibilant whispering came to him, candles flickered palely on the altar. To the left a dim chapel appeared like a grotto. Entering it, he felt the chill motionless air. The flames of half a dozen candles burned like white jewels and lighted the smooth cheekbones of a dark saint of his own blood. He knelt before the statue and began to pray.

With the long morning still before him, Mendoza returned home. Suddenly he felt tired and went to bed. His eyes were barely closed when he heard a familiar sound that brought a smile to his face. His granddaughter had come in from next door. Her small bare feet padded through the house and into the patio, where she greeted and nuzzled his son's pet lamb, which was tethered to a stake.

Back into the house she came, straight to Mendoza's bed to demand her morning kiss, then went off and he fell asleep with a smile on his face. Soon she returned, chewing fritto and bearing a cup of steaming coffee. She shared it with him and carried away the empty cup. Again he fell asleep and awakened to the voice of his daughter calling him to the kitchen table for breakfast—tortillas, with hot sauce and coffee. When his daughter returned to her own house, he lit a cigaret and stepped into the patio. A rare cold spell a month back had killed off the tops of the avocado and orange trees. Thought of the disaster made him frown, but tender new leaves were already appearing on the lower limbs in the heat of the morning. He smiled to himself and saw in this revival the fruits of his own loins, daughter, son and granddaughter. You die, but they live on for you, he thought in joy and sadness.

A moment later his son, Julio, stepped onto the patio. His skin was dark bronze like his father's; his black hair glistened.

"You ate?" said Mendoza.

The boy nodded.

"Good," Mendoza went to a raffish shed in back of the patio where the lamb was tethered and lifted a wooden yoke to his shoulders. Two huge jars attached to it balanced each other. The boy brought him his sombrero.

"Let's go," he said and off they went, the man with his heavy burden, the bare-footed boy holding a cup before him.

The sun was well up now, the streets hot. Mendoza felt the yoke and the weight of the jars. Sweat dripped like water from his face, salt stung his eyes. He had no complaint. It was good to be alive, to hear his son's sharp cry—"Ay, pulque! Ay, pulque!" But now it was a lament, piercing the streets, the sun and his heart—an innocent and terrible announcement of the imminence of disaster.

They rounded the plaza and moved on to the fly-ridden market with its stench, crossed a bridge to a devastated area of shacks and crumbling adobes where goats wandered in the rutted streets. At eleven they recrossed the bridge, sat on their haunches at a market stall, ate tortillas and a thin corn soup, then moved off to the Cantina of the Matadors.

Here Mendoza put down the ever-growing weight of the jars and stepped through the front door beneath a sign that proclaimed this to be the "Entrance of the Bulls." Estaban awaited him within. Over a bottle of beer the money was passed. Mendoza left through a side door, where another sign stated the legend—"Where Dead Bulls Go." Round the corner his son awaited him. Handing him the money, which was wrapped carelessly in a soiled piece of brown paper, he said, "Whatever happens, don't lose this. Put it inside your blouse."

"What is it?" asked Julio.

"Never mind. It is for you, your sister and the little one."

The boy put the money inside his blouse, and Mendoza placed the yoke on his shoulders. I may die, but they will have money, he thought, and nodded to his son.

"Ay, pulque! Ay, pulque!" cried the boy as they moved off.

It was very hot now, the streets almost deserted. At one minute of noon Mendoza and his son rounded the corner of the block where the Mayor's residence stood. Three cars were parked in front of the house, an ornate affair of white stucco, red tile and ornamental iron. Nine of the gunmen, including Pancho Negron, stood on the sidewalk. Three sat at the wheels of the cars. No one else was about.

"Ay, pulque!" Julio cried out, and suddenly Mendoza felt the yoke on his neck, the weight of the jars. One for pulque, and one for death, he thought, and the boy called out again.

A short man with broad shoulders and a pockmarked face, Pancho Negron's alert eyes riveted on Mendoza and his son. The others stood at ease, for the pulque-vendor and boy posed no threat.

"Listen to me," Mendoza whispered to Julio. "When I tell you to run, make certain to run as fast as you can."

The boy was puzzled, but asked no question. Again he cried out, and Mendoza glanced at the Mayor's house. No sign of the General. He slowed his steps, finally stopped before Negron and put down his burden.

"A drink, Señor?" he said, taking the cup from his son.

Negron made a face and shook his head. "From that filthy cup which everyone in the city has put his lips to?" The gunman spat to show his distaste.

Shrugging, Mendoza put a cigaret to his lips and, from the corner of his eye, saw the Mayor's door swing open, the General step from the house. Immediately the gunmen came alert; one hurried toward him to escort him to the car. Mendoza crushed his empty cigaret pack and said to Julio: "Get me another pack at the corner. Run."

The boy hesitated. A stinging slap across the face sent him off. The gunmen laughed. Bare feet padded on the walk as Julio fled. Mendoza heard them and gritted his teeth, then turned and saw the General ten feet from him, squat and ugly, his round face with its two small eyes set deep under his bulging forehead. The face was a brute's, the small eyes belonged to a reptile.

Casually, Mendoza lit his cigaret and held the match. In the burning sun its flame was barely visible, a pale innocuous flare that fell from his fingers into one of the jars as the General stooped awkwardly to enter his car. A terrible explosion shattered the scene and rocked the area for blocks around.

Deadly silence followed the blast. Then the Cathedral bell began to toll wildly above a medley of confused cries. Mendoza, the pulque–vendor, had fulfilled his trust.

49

DEATH THREAT

Susan Dunlap

"DON'T GIVE ME excuses. Do it right, damn it! What do you think I'm paying you for?" Wynne slammed down the phone.

I stood in the doorway, amazed at my sister's authority though I had seen her control situations for nearly 40 years. Even lying here in the hospital, she was still the executive, the first woman in the state to have become senior vice president of a major company. I wondered if it was Chuck or some other harried assistant who had felt the sting of her tongue.

As she looked at me her expression changed from irritation to concern. "Lynne, why are you lurking in the doorway? You're shaking. Come in and tell me what's the matter."

I walked in unsteadily and sat on the plastic chair next to the bed. "It happend again."

"What this time?"

I swallowed, holding my hands one on top of the other on my lap, trying to calm myself enough to be coherent.

The room was bare—hospital-green curtain pulled back against hospital-green walls. Wynne sat propped up in bed. I looked at her face, at the fragile smile that used to be strong. Funny, our features were so similar, almost exact, but no one had ever mixed us up. Wynne's compact body had always looked forceful, and mine had merely seemed small.

Then she changed so suddenly when she'd become ill months ago. It was as if her underpinnings had been jerked loose and she had sped past me on the way to old age. But even now, from a distance we were indistinguishable. But the way it looked; within six months we would both be dead.

"Lynne, I'm really worried about you," she said with an anxiety in her voice I hadn't heard in a long time. "What happened?"

"Another shot at me. It just missed my head. If I hadn't stumbled—" My hands were shaking.

Wynne put her hand over them, steadying them with her own calm. "Have you notified the police?"

"They're no help. They take a report and then—nothing. I don't think they believe me. Another hysterical middle-aged woman."

Wynne nodded. "Let's go through the whole thing again. I'm used to handling problems. It gives me something to think about when I'm on the dialysis machine."

It sounded cold, but it was just Wynne's way. She didn't want me to feel I was imposing.

"Someone shot at me three times. If I weren't always tripping and turning my ankle—"

"And you have no idea who it might be?"

"None. Who would want to kill me? Why? Really, what difference would it make if I died? Who would care?"

"I would." Her hand pressed mine. "You're all I have. You don't know how I look forward to your visits."

I swallowed. "Wynne, you shouldn't cut yourself off from your office. Why don't you let Chuck come to see you?"

"No," she snapped. "I can't let him see me like this."

She looked all right to me—better than I was likely to look if I didn't find out who was shooting at me.

Wynne must have divined my thought for she said irritably, "You don't show someone who's after your job how sick you are. I've never told any of them that I'm on the dialysis machine." She shook her head as if to dismiss an unacceptable thought. "I told them it was just one kidney that failed, that I was having it removed." Her face moved into a tenuous grin. "I know all the details from your own operation. So don't say you never did anything for me."

I didn't know how to answer. Could Wynne really hide the fact that she was dying? Chuck had been her assistant for ten years. He'd taken over her job as acting senior vice president. I had assumed they were friends, but I guess I didn't understand the nature of friendship in business.

Impatiently Wynne motioned me to go on.

Swallowing my annoyance, I reminded myself that Wynne was used to giving orders and now she had no one to order around but me. Still, I didn't know where to begin. I was too ordinary—a middle-aged first-grade teacher—to make enemies. If it had been Wynne—

"Well," she said, "we'll have to consider all the possibilities."

I shook my head. "I don't have any money, no insurance other than the teachers' association policy."

"And that goes to Michael?"

"Yes, but Michael's not going to come all the way from Los Angeles to shoot his mother so he can inherit two thousand dollars and an old clapboard house."

"I didn't mean that." She looked hurt. "I was just listing all the possibilities. You have to do that. You can't let sentiment stand in the way of your goal. I had to learn that long ago. There are plenty of people who have wanted me out of the way."

"But they weren't trying to murder you!

"Wynne, I'm the one they're trying to kill. No one would kill you now. I mean, not when you're—so sick." I didn't want to say dying. But maybe no one knew Wynne was dying. Chuck, at least, had been kept in the dark, or so Wynne thought. I was beginning to wonder if she herself had accepted it. "I mean you're not working. You don't have any active connection with the company now. How could you be a threat to anyone?"

The lines in her face hardened. "I know things. When I get out of here, I'm going back. I'll find out who's been out to get me. I'll take care of them! I'm too valuable for the company to just forget!"

I felt angry and guilty at the same time. Wynne had shoved the death threat to me aside—it was less important than her past business vendettas. I looked down at her hands, held one on top of the other on her lap. Just as mine were when I was nervous. In many ways we were so alike.

"Who, particularly," I asked, "would want to kill you?"

She didn't answer.

"Chuck? Would he really kill to keep your job? Would he mistake me for you?"

She looked at me in amazement, as if the possibility were too fantastic to believe. "Lynne, anyone—Chuck especially—who would take the trouble and the risk involved in murder would be more careful than that."

"But maybe they don't know you have an identical twin."

She sighed, her jaw settling back in the tired frown. "They know. When you've held as important a position as I have, they know." She paused, then said, "Lynne, I'm afraid you haven't made much of a case. I don't want to sound unsympathetic, but the truth is you've always leaned on me. Are you sure this death thing isn't just a reaction to my own condition? It does happen in twins."

"No, I think not. I've been through years of therapy. Our bodies may be identical, but my mind is finally my own!"

She sat silent.

The awkwardness grew. "Listen Wynne, I know you have business to take care of. I interrupted your phone call when I came in, so I'll see you tomorrow."

She nodded, a tired sorrow showing in her eyes. But I wasn't out of the room before she picked up the phone.

As I walked down the hall, I thought again what an amazing person she was. Dying from kidney failure, and she was still barking at subordinates. I wondered about Chuck—did he allow her to run things from her hospital room? Did he believe Wynne's story about her condition? Could he think I was she coming for treatment? Not likely. If Chuck were anything like Wynne, by now he would have a solid grip on the vice presidency. He would have removed any trace of Wynne and she'd have to fight *him* for the job.

Still, I stopped by the door, afraid to go out.

But if Wynne wasn't giving orders to Chuck or some other subordinate, who was she yelling at? "What do you think I'm paying you for?" she had demanded.

She wasn't paying anyone at the company. She wasn't paying any expenses at the hospital—she had full insurance coverage. There was nothing she needed.

Or was there?

My hand went around back to my kidney.

50

BY THE SEA, BY THE SEA

Hal Dresner

From the journal of Guy Dance:

Thursday, April 5

8 AM. A lovely morning spoiled before it began. Up at dawn, heavy with new thoughts squirming to be born. Coffee on the veranda. Cotton clouds swabbing sky with gentian violet. Pink mist rolling back to sea. Both reefs bared liked bleached bull's horns.

Walked along shore toward St. Croix. Sand salted with gold dust. Thoughts of Aurelia in Chapter VI. Should she mention R.G. or wait till party? Imagined entire ballroom shimmering on face of sea.

Then disaster! At far edge of shore where sand was still glazed by tide, body of precious silver fish, still sweetly odorous. A crescent of lovely breast torn away by savage turtle jaws. Barbaric!

10:30 PM. Impossible to write after horror of morning. Light lunch. Read Rimbaud in garden. Isobel pruning bougainvillea; orchids need new bedding.

Excellent dinner by Edgar Sam, Guacamole; sautéed fish meunière. But with reason: Isobel promised him week's holiday tomorrow, without my approval! Now it is too late to get another boy. Very poor planning for former private secretary. In punishment, no playing tonight. Listened to two *Brandenburgs* alone in study. Tried to capture Aurelia's opinion for scene with L.V. Overtaken by throbbing headache. Opened bottle of Barolo, '52; fair.

Friday, April 6

2:15 PM. Woke late. Fitful night, dream of silver fish. No appetite for breakfast, work.

Read Racine's *Cinna* on terrace. Maximus is overdrawn. Sky, pitiless blue; air clear. Mainland of St. Thomas is profile of Nephthys—but desecrated by crown of that tourist hotel. Isobel says they are building more. Soon those noxious jets will be preying on us like rocs. Animals know it. Odd stillness in underbrush lately; they have withdrawn to depths. No herons near beach in weeks. How long till this fragile beast shall also be flushed from his cloister?

Ironic to think that today. House a tomb. Edgar Sam gone; Isobel to Charlotte Amalie for shopping and "bargain hunting." Absurd after all these years. Yet she thrives on such activity. Look of unwilling exile in her eyes.

11:30 PM. Irony compounded; predilection of intrusion has come true. Guests tonight; first since Bronson and that cretinous producer. And just when secret of Chapter VI was near! Could have garroted Isobel when she came up walk with them. Mr. and Mrs. Pross ("Phil and Dotty") from Des Moines, Iowa. Tourists! Isobel met her in market floundering with college French. An imbecile but with a bright *sang-froid* charm. Slender; pale walnut hair; dazzling teeth.

But he! The Dim American from Chapter III in flesh. A living vegetable. Bland egg face, olive pit eyes, anchovy smile, everything! Like conversing with my own creation. State College. Sells Insurance. Follows Baseball. Reads Condensed Books. Wary of Island Water. Suggested barbeque pit in our garden!

Dinner on terrace, an atrocity: burned gigot, gelatinous bechamel sauce. Isobel is helpless without Edgar Sam. Lush night, too. Diaphanous moon; pearl waves scuttling up shore like crabs; symphonic wind through palms. All wasted save for one lyrical moment: In silhouette, head raised, sea breeze spreading her hair like gossamer, "Dotty" (that *cannot* be her given name!) looked for an instant like Aurelia standing on cliffs at Whitford. Strange.

Opened a bottle of Chablis, '54; bad. Pross loved it. Wrote name in black memo book. Torpid conversation. He relates every topic to insurance. In desperation, played. Beethoven: *Sonata Operas 109, 110;* Chopin's *Concerto 1*. Superb in tonal changes. Women appreciative. But then too late for trip back to mainland. With luck they will be gone by luncheon.

Saturday, April 7

3 PM. Uninspired day. Opal sky, stratus clouds. Ocean placid to peak of reefs, where waves froth like porpoises. Prosses swimming; Isobel, a proud mother, watches from shore. She is wearing that ochre playsuit!

Useless to try work while they are here. Gambol about like monkeys. Luggage still unpacked in hall. Agreed to for Isobel's sake. Seems so hungry for "outside news"; more alive than in months. "Dotty" helped her make lunch. *Saucisson en croute;* good. If their combined talents equal one half Edgar Sam, week may be bearable. Should talk to Pross for dialogue, but he is *too* dull. Isobel shouldering burden; feigning great interest in insurance. But that leaves "Dotty" casting warm glances here. Preposterous to imagine that—must discontinue. My collegiate siren approaches, slick from her swim in Tyrrhenian. Her suit is slightly immodest. *11:45* PM. Her name is Dorothea. Thank God! Has read all my books. Did not mention it before because she "supposed everybody had." Charming, impressionable intellect. Discussed Redon, Bresdin, Fragonard all afternoon. Father owned gallery for time; mother a fashion model.

Pleasant evening due to her dinner: chicken and rice; good. Wore stunning lemon voile. She is tanning peach. Isobel (in mauve crepe) contributed salad; salty. Opened incomparable bottle of Auslesen, '48. Breeze from sea was eau de Coeur-Joie. Played Schumann's *Fantasiestucke* with variations. Dorothea enraptured; Pross requested "Stardust." Their marriage is inconceivable.

Sunday, April 9

1 PM. Up at seven, exhilarated. Amethyst sky; gulls wheeling like scythes. Reworked five lines in Chapter IV. Croissants for breakfast.

Suggested tour of islet. Pross too painfully sunburnt (He is fuchsia!); Isobel cooking. Walked with Dorothea to Boar's Head. Wore blue slacks, sleeveless blouse. Arms like willows. Talked of *Proud Voyage.* She identified with Lise. Wrote college theme on Garden of Eden symbol. Incisive understanding. Compared my status to Mann, H. James. J. Joyce and several others.

Returned inland route. Parrots, trogans in trees. Native boys hunting agouti. Victoria cruziana blossoming on Button Pond. Dorothea called them "green pancake plants." Discussed my work in relation to Conrad, Dinesen, Hughes. Her eyes are liquid sienna.

10:30 PM. Languid afternoon. Fragrant wind rippling curtains of sea. Read Shelley aloud on terrace. *Prometheus Unbound; Epipsychidon; Song.* Pross slept; Isobel cooked; Dorothea folded at my feet like dawn.

Isobel's dinner unspeakable. Pross raved. Bridge saved evening. Dorothea's playing daring, imaginative. In beautiful contrast we soared like flames. Unconquerable vulnerability. Pross and Isobel in stodgy, cautious partials.

Monday, April 10

11:15 AM. Restless night. Isobel breathing like hornet. Up at eight. Bleak sky; sea fresh. May rain tonight. Breakfast alone in study. Changed Aurelia's description in Chapter II, more use of "serene" (Dorothea's favorite word).

Pross and Isobel into Charlotte Amalie for shopping; Dorothea still sleeping. Her window is open. Will awaken her by playing Grieg. One of her favorites, and mine.

10 PM. Day of rapture! Lunch on terrace. Cold chicken; nice Montrachet. Read Dorothea first chapters of book. Enthralled; says it will be "most important novel in 300 yrs." Wore white shorts, exquisite striped jersey. Sea wind tangling her hair, prickling her golden skin. Feeling of time embalmed in sunset.

Then at six, a rainstorm. Sky black, palm fronds lashing at French windows. As we frantically closed down, Isobel called from mainland. Storm ravenous there. Impossible to return till morning.

Hilarious dinner of uncooked fish, burnt potatoes. Finished magnum of marvellous Bollinger Brut, '55. Played Moussorgsky in fugue to lightning. Both wildly drunk. Watched ocean from terrace. Snarling gray beast gnashing teeth on rocks. Embraced like tides. Her mouth brandy: Grand Marnier.

Now bathed and scented, she awaits in her bed. Rain is ceaseless. God's blessing on us.

Tuesday, April 11

Noon. Dorothea is Aurelia. Vainglory not to have seen it from the first. Through study window, she is visible on terrace. In beige shorts, her thighs white as birth; beneath lime sweater, her breasts are quail. Torment to see and not touch her!

Pross sprawled like moss on chaise longue, going on about automobiles, supermarkets, electric saws. He is an electric saw. A more civilized society would have him dismantled. Now he drones insurance again. And Isobel listens attentively, paying premium to his policy.

The returned at ten in a fortunate abundance of noise. Scurried like Pan

294

from my love's bed. An embarrassed breakfast. Isobel garrulous about accommodations at Paradiso. An adventure for her!

Will remain here until dinner reading Blake. (''My silks and fine array/ My smiles and languish'd air/By love are driv'n away.'')

10:30 PM. A dreadful evening. Light salad for dinner. We had no appetite but for love; Pross and Isobel still gorged from yesterday's feast at hotel. Small favor, he is not possessive. Sat with her on terrace and talked publicly but our hands touched! Behind us, in their suburban minds, Pross and Isobel chattered like macaws. Sea was a ribbon begging to be tightened about Isobel's neck. Wind keened and mocked us.

Impossible to sleep knowing he shared my Aurelia's bed.

Wednesday, April 12

2 PM. Luck! Isobel and Pross took walk about islet. No doubt he will sell some poor native an endowment policy. We waited till they were past reef.

Love is no less sweet for being fleeting. Sugarbirds sang in choirs; sunlight clothed my Aurelia in lamé.

She wants to leave Pross. But what of Isobel? In her inanity she has served me well. It was my bad choice not hers. Divorce would be slow death to her. A shameful return to family. Stuttering explanations. Forced admissions of inadequacy. It is inhuman to even suggest it. She lacks strength to survive. She would go mad. Also it is not unthinkable to imagine she would make demands.

Yet to forsake all for this private secretary convenience saw me marry? Would not Art be better served with Aurelia? She understands my work; shares my purpose. More than honing pencils, she ministers to my soul. Decision is agony.

Chiffonade salad for lunch; a bottle of Moselle, '57; fair.

9:45 PM. They returned at four babbling banalities. We were on beach reading Landor; *The Hamadryad*. Could not bear seeing her with him; retired to room. Slept till eight. No taste for dinner. Read some Hazlitt in den. Spoke to no one.

Thursday, April 13

5 AM. Tortured night, no sleep. Walked in garden. Orchids Isobel planted staring plaintively. She has tended them with all the love she has, yet their color lacks rarity. She has transformed nobility in commonplace. So also

295

with this soul's flower. In her care it may grow but never blossom. A new gardener is needed.

3:30 PM. Has sacred moment with Aurelia. Told her killing Isobel is only solution. Agreeable. She will wait decent interval before divorce, return here. Intimated healthy dowry of alimony. My beloved!

Lunch by Pross. Surprise brought from Charlotte Amalie; franks and beans. Indigestible. How long, O Lord?

6:15 PM. Introspective day. Planning. Aurelia sunbathed; Pross read lurid best seller; Isobel sketched. Drowning is best way. Tide shall bear her away. Must be done while they are here. Better.

11:30 PM. News! Over bridge Pross related plans to leave Saturday. And Edgar Sam returns tomorrow! Had forgotten. So it must be done tomorrow morning. Weather looks promising. Velvet sky; diamond stars. Chill breeze from the singing sea.

Too excited to write more. Do not recall dinner.

Friday, April 14

10 AM. They are all upstairs dressing for beach. It is arranged with Aurelia. She will take Pross near north reef, out of sight. Sea is perfect. Crystal blue darkening to royal. Around south reef serpentine currents beat waves to spray; sky is streaked with crimson.

Had no breakfast. Must hurry into my suit now.

10:45 AM. Dazed, feeling faint. But must record this while possible. Feeling thoughts receding. Too horrible.

Led Isobel by hand into wilderness of sea. Waves crowding about us like children. Aurelia, Pross, undefinable on far side of north reef. Swam toward rocks, beckoning Isobel to follow. Water darkening; undertow growing. Isobel flailing desperately, face delighted. Waited for her within yards of reef. Between waves, rocks rising like headstones. Took her by waist, guided her gently into current. Water towering in dark horns. Isobel frightened. Held her shoulders, smiling. Closed eyes. Under.

Thrashing! Struggling! Invisible strands drawing emerald world about us. Felt stone peaks beneath feet. Surfaced, breathed, then with current, lashed her head against rocks.

Calm. Tide returning to ocean. Isobel with it. Swam toward shore. Thought of Swinburne; *Ballad of Death*.

"From brows wherein the sad blood failed of red
 And temples drained of purple and full of death
 Her curled hair had the wave of sea-water

And the sea's gold in it.''

Breathless, quivering, started toward north reef. Phrased declaration of horror:

"Help! Help! She's drowning!"

Across white fire of beach, saw Pross running toward me. But not to help. He had not yet heard me for he was shouting also. The same words! And in the same shrill rehearsed way!

Must tell Edgar Sam to put some beer on ice for police.

51

THE NIGHT RUNNER

Nedra Tyre

HUGH WAS RUNNING through the early morning dark. He wasn't running as fast as he used to, stumbling, sometimes sprawling in his exuberance over having once more got by without the slightest danger of being caught. His gait now was about the same as the jogger a block ahead of him.

Everything was all right. Nothing bothered him. You're okay, Hugh, he assured himself.

Hugh liked his name. He had given it to himself. He'd had lots of names given to him by other people, mostly foster mothers. Foster fathers worked all day and at night bellowed for you to be quiet, for God's sake, and they didn't call you anything. But foster mothers were hell on names. You remind me of Uncle Charles. You don't mind if I call you Charles, do you? What could he say? How could he object? And then before he knew it, he was Charlie or Chuck.

But not for long, because nobody wanted him. Sullen they would call him to his face, or he doesn't appreciate a thing anybody does for him, they would say when they complained to the social worker. She would come to get him and he'd be whisked off to another place where he was Christopher because that was Papa's name and if the foster mother had ever been able to have a son—and tears spilled down her blouse—she would have named him Christopher for papa. But Christopher didn't stay Christopher—it was Chris before the first day was over and every now and then it was Christy. At the next place the foster mother had said, you're as bull-headed as cousin Rudolph, and then he would be Rudy or Dolphie for a while.

Even as a kid he liked to prowl around the neighborhoods or venture into town and most people on the streets or in the stores or poolrooms called him You. Come here, You, or You put that back, or listen, You, let me give you a good piece of advice, unless you straighten out and change your ways you'll end up a hardened criminal. He didn't like being called You, and then he realized that Hugh was very close to You and couldn't be chopped in half or turned into something that sounded creepy like Dolphie or Christy. So when he was finally rid of foster mothers and on his own at 15, yet lying that he was 18 and getting away with it because he was so tall, he told everyone his name was Hugh.

As he jogged along he almost missed her because he had been thinking about his name. He stopped and retraced a few steps, then turned the corner and raced to catch up. The rest was simple. She didn't know what had hit her, but Hugh had struck her hard enough to knock her to the pavement, and when she became aware of the attack all she thought of was her shoulder bag. She grasped it to her bosom as if she held a baby about to be snatched from her. He didn't want the bag or any of the junk crammed inside—for God's sake he earned good money and didn't want a penny from creeps like her.

He struck her again when she squirmed to get up, and he left her. He had rounded the corner when he heard her begin to scream. Well, she ought to save her breath. He could tell her that no one would come to answer her call of distress. People were still asleep or in the kitchen making coffee or in the bathroom, and radios and TVs were turned on high. Or if anyone did hear her he or she would say, that's some drunk screaming and even if it's somebody being mugged or murdered, it's none of my business.

Hugh religiously checked the papers—maybe he was like athletes who wanted to read about their exploits. Sometimes during his early months in Lexington he hadn't been aware of exactly where he had been and he had given himself credit for attacks that someone else had made, but not any longer. Now he knew every nook and cranny of the city, every house by number, what potholes threatened, and the bus schedules that deposited easy prey on dark corners.

When he read the names of the women he had attacked he was pleased. Well, well, he would think, it's nice to be formally introduced. I didn't catch your name at first but there was something about you, about any woman walking by herself that reminds me of my foster mothers. I never had the chance to get even with them, but this goes a long way to make up for what I should have done to them.

There hadn't been anything even resembling a close call. No one was interested in what happened to women out alone in the early morning. Not that the time of day had much to do with it. Streets in certain neighborhoods could be as empty at high noon as in the early morning or late at night.

Only one incident had ever jolted him, and even now his breath grew short when he thought of it. He wanted to brace himself against the siding of a house or hold onto a porch railing or even sit down on a curb when he realized what might so easily have happened. He could have killed Ruth. He could have snuffed out her life. Oh, he wasn't a murderer, he just wanted to give women a scare that they'd never forget. But Ruth seemed so frail and delicate to him, though she insisted she was average size.

Ruth. He liked that name. He liked it as much as he liked the name of Hugh. He was glad she was named Ruth and called Ruth, not like the other girls he'd briefly known who called themselves Candy or Julie or Debbie or Merry or Jinks or Deedee or Mimi or some ridiculous name that was suitable only for a poodle or a chihuahua or a budgie.

It had been the dead of winter when 6:30 in the morning was as dark as midnight and he had seen her and had jogged to catch up with her. Another four steps and he would have grabbed her, but she dropped something and looked back to see him almost upon her and he reversed his plans and had stooped down and handed her the book she was grappling for. She had thanked him. They were beneath a street lamp and he looked closely at her and became angry at what could have happened, at what had almost hapened. He became stern. "You shouldn't be out alone. It's not safe."

"I know," she said. "But I've been lucky, at least so far."

Hugh wondered where she had come from and where she was going. This was his neighborhood. He had a room four blocks to the east at the Y and he worked in a bar called Frank's Place three blocks to the north. There was a hospital only a short distance away. Didn't he remember glimpsing white shoes and white stockings? She was wearing a heavy coat with a hood pushed far back that revealed hair cropped close or perhaps it was long and combed neatly to her skull. Obviously she worked in the hospital.

She didn't realize what danger she was in because she could put him in danger. He must be wary of another encounter with her. Coming upon her in the darkness he must not attack her, now that she had seen his face and could identify him. She had to be out of the way and in the hospital before he could safely begin his prowling. He must know exactly where she was. Perhaps she drove to work and parked her car as near the hospital as she could find a place. Or she might live nearby since the whole area was filled with roominghouses and apartment buildings in poor repair. For several mornings Hugh searched the neighborhood hoping he would see her leave her residence. On Friday he was lucky.

She recognized him immediately, as he had known she would, but she didn't greet him and left it up to him to justify his presence.

"Let me walk with you to work."

"I like walking alone."

Anyway, she didn't dismiss him and he walked along with her, and though their paces matched, the entire width of the sidewalk separated them.

At the hospital entrance she took no formal leave but gave a small wave and rushed up the steps through the swinging doors, and he knew that he was now free to jog down the street on his own exploits.

One morning he was surprised at his reaction when she didn't appear. It occurred to him that she might have left town forever, and instead of being reassured by the likelihood of her permanent absence he thought how nice it was to wait for her and to walk with her to the hospital.

The next day she was back but offered no explanation for her absence. They didn't talk during their walk together and it was many weeks before she even told him her name.

Not long after she had said her name was Ruth she invited him to supper. "You've been so nice to look after me and I want to show my appreciation. Please come to supper some night—that is, if you'd like to."

"I work every night. I can't come to supper."

"Oh," she had answered. He couldn't tell whether she was sorry or not.

But two days later she told him that she had every other Sunday off and couldn't he come to lunch some Sunday.

"Sure," he had answered, "any Sunday you say."

A few minutes later when he had left her at the hospital entrance he had run slowly for two blocks and had seen a woman walking alone on a side street. He caught up with her easily and knelt briefly at her ankles as if he were tying his shoelace, then he jerked her feet from beneath her and she fell on her face.

Hugh and Ruth were married in June, and Millie Watts, a nurse's aide like Ruth, and Joe Farmer, a waiter at the bar, were their witnesses. Nothing had ever been further from Hugh's mind than marriage, yet there he was, full partner in a Mr. and Mrs. team. Ruth gave up sharing a flat with Millie and Hugh moved out of the Y. They rented a small back apartment which they repainted light yellow—it took three coats—but they couldn't do anything about the stains in the bathtub or the uneven floors. Anyhow, they liked staying in the neighborhood they were used to and being within walking distance of their jobs—five blocks from the hospital and two from the bar. As always, Hugh walked to work with Ruth.

They weren't together a great deal as Ruth worked in the daytime and Hugh worked at night.

Even when they were together, Ruth and Hugh didn't have much to say to each other. Ruth was an only child, born late in her parents' marriage after they had given up hope of having a baby. Her father and mother were both dead. Her mother had been a little frail but not really sick a day in her life, yet she died a week after Ruth's father—she couldn't live without him.

"And you, Hugh, what about your family?"

"I never had one—just lots of foster homes."

"Poor Hugh."

No one had ever called him "poor Hugh" before and he didn't answer Ruth because he didn't know how to answer her.

At first Ruth had told Hugh a little about her patients, but he didn't encourage her—the last thing in the world he wanted to hear about was sick people. Ruth remarked almost apologetically, as if it were a failing, that she had liked to take care of people ever since she was a little girl. Something drew her to the helpless. Her grandmother had become feeble and needed constant attention, and after she had died Ruth's father had a stroke. Her mother was squeamish about tending him, so Ruth had quit school to look after him. That and the lack of money was why she was a nurse's aide instead of a nurse. No matter, there was plenty of time and she intended to take night courses to finish high school and then begin nurse's training. Not that there was any hurry—she was happy as she was. Hugh had no words to reply to that last remark. His answer was a kiss.

Living with Ruth hadn't changed Hugh except to make him feel more alert and alive. He enjoyed his jogging exploits more than ever and his quiet existence with Ruth made him more daring. Until after his marriage he had never followed a woman inside an apartment house because there wasn't any telling what he might face. Some other tenant might enter or leave and there would be a witness to his attack. But every now and then, as a special act of daring, he attempted it, and always with complete success. On occasion he was even bold enough to attack someone in the daylight. Sometimes after their early supper, while Ruth did the dishes and some laundry or wanted to watch TV, Hugh left the house to spend an exhilarating hour or so before he reported for work.

Ruth was always asleep when Hugh got home from the bar. He could look at TV, take a shower—nothing bothered her at all. She didn't even turn when he climbed into bed beside her. Knowing that she wasn't waiting anxiously for him, he sometimes took a long walk after work. He was giddy from all the noise and talk and smoke and the rush during the last half hour. The exercise always restored him and it was especially satisfying when he came upon a woman all alone. At 1:30 in the morning she damned well deserved what she got.

They didn't bring their work home with them. Ruth didn't tell him about the emergencies or deaths at the hospital and he didn't talk about the bar patrons. Every now and then Ruth phoned the hospital about the condition of a patient, and one night when he was leaving for work she had called about a Mrs. Moore. Then when she saw that Hugh had put on his jacket she set the receiver down and kissed him goodbye.

Ruth's patients meant nothing to Hugh. He got enough of other people's trouble at the bar, not that he let it bother him. He didn't pay much attention. Well, maybe he shook his head or mumbled that's tough, but he didn't intend to get involved just because a guy had bought a bottle of beer or a shot or two of bourbon. He didn't give one faint damn about what had happened to them.

One night he and Ted were leaning against the counter while all the customers were occupied with their drinks.

"Go on, Hugh," Ted said. "Let me take care of this. Take as long a break as you want. I owe it to you for handling it all by yourself the other night."

Hugh thanked Ted and left by the back door, and at once he was in his element. He liked the dark streets, whether in the early morning or at night. He liked running in the long stretches of darkness between the dim street light. It made him feel strong and adventurous. There was lots of talk in the bar about robbery and muggings, and the talk was shot by indignation. "This poor guy—did you read about it?—murdered and all for seventy-nine cents. That's all the guy had on him."

The customers were welcome to get sentimental over what happened to others. Hugh hadn't once felt any regret for his actions. Those women had demanded what they got. They shouldn't be out alone, flaunting themselves, making targets of themselves.

Ahead of him tonight a woman was walking her dog. When Hugh read crime prevention pieces saying that dogs were good protection against attack he snorted. Any fool dog would lick the hand of anyone, mugger or not. And sure enough the dog just stood aside with his tongue hanging out when Hugh slowed his pace to shove the woman. It wasn't much of a shove, just hard enough to make her realize she had been hit.

He returned to jogging speed until he reached Steward Street when he stopped to get his breath and to enjoy the exhilaration he always felt after making an attack. Well, Hugh, he said to himself, you've had your fun for tonight. You might as well get back to the bar.

Then he saw a woman some distance away going up the steps of an apartment house. She was picking her way carefully like someone walking on ice. The steps must be broken. Then she entered the hall and closed the door behind her. She seemed unsure of herself. Venturing inside was dangerous, Hugh realized, but it was heady stuff and he couldn't resist.

He crossed the threshold and watched her knock on a door. The dim globe that was the only light flickered and went out. After a long interval it came back on and Hugh saw the woman begin to mount the stairway. When she got to the top she might turn toward the front of the house and if she did, she'd be sure to see him. He had to reach her before then. He rushed up the steps and the light flickered off, but she was easily within his grasp. He had her by the throat but his hands were slack, and her elbows jabbed sharply against his chest, and her right heel lashed out at his shins.

Hugh hadn't ever encountered resistance before. His other victims had given in almost as if they were hypnotized. Occasionally he had wondered what he would do if a woman put up a fight, and now he knew—rage and uncontrollable fury overwhelmed him and he knocked her to the floor. The light must have gone out for good. Everything was dark and very quiet as he tiptoed down the stairs. Then just as he opened the front door the light flickered on again and threw his shadow across the split uneven floor of the narrow porch.

He leaped across it and then ran to the bar. When he reached it he lingered outside beneath the defective neon sign that announced FRA K'S P ACE. A wave of power and peace seemed to have entered his bloodstream and to pervade the air he slowly inhaled. He had never felt so sure of himself or so proud and confident.

Business had picked up when Hugh joined Ted behind the bar.

''You didn't stay long,'' Ted said.

The customers looked especially friendly, but they usually were a well-behaved crowd. In the three years that Hugh had worked at Frank's Place he could count on the fingers of one hand the times they had had to call the cops. Tonight everyone was genial and the voices weren't loud, and then with the next round of drinks the atmosphere got a little raucous, not enough to annoy anyone, but more like a Friday or Saturday crowd than a midweek one. As usual he and Ted worked frantically as if they were trying to put out brush fires in the last minutes of serving final drinks.

Then the night's work was over, the lights were turned out, the sign that leaned in the front window was switched from OPEN to CLOSED.

Hugh was more tired than he could remember as he walked toward home. The two blocks seemed to stretch to the distance of a marathon, and he wanted Ruth more than he had ever wanted her.

At last his key was in the lock, and he felt a welcome as he always did when he entered their apartment. Ruth was a good housekeeper and he liked the neat way she kept everything. It was nice, too, that she had such pretty pot plants—she said she got her green thumb from her grandmother.

He walked into the bedroom expecting to see Ruth lying in the bed, but she wasn't there. The bed had an appalling smoothness—the covers hadn't even been turned down. She must have been called back to the hospital on an emergency. Anyway, she couldn't have left without letting him know.

He hurried to the kitchen to look at the bulletin board where they left messages and instructions for each other, and as he untacked the note he took pride in Ruth's small precise handwriting.

> Darling, my patient Mrs. Moore just phoned. She's upset because the baby sitter got sick suddenly and had to go home. The children are alone and Mrs. Moore threatened to leave the hospital to go take care of them. I told her I'd be glad to look after them. Don't worry, worrywart. It's only a short distance from here and I'll be careful. Anyway, I know how to protect myself. But if it will make you happy you can come by tomorrow morning to walk with me to work as usual. The address is 1199 Stewart—I forgot to ask about the apartment number, so I'll have to check when I get there. Mrs. Moore says something is wrong with the hall light and the front porch and steps are rickety. So don't risk your neck. Just wait out front for me.
>
> Bless you. Love you. XXX
Ruth

52

THE LITTLE OLD LADY FROM CRICKET CREEK

Len Gray

ART BOWEN AND I were trying to analyze performance evaluations when
Penny Thorpe, my secretary, walked into the office.

"Yeah, Penny. What's up?"

"Mr. Cummings, there's a woman out in the lobby. She's applying for
the file clerk's job." Penny walked over and laid the application form on
my desk.

"Good, good. I sure hope she's not one of those high-school drop-outs
we've been getting—" I stopped, staring at the form. "Age fifty-five!" I
roared. "What the hell are we running around here? A playground for
Whistler's mother?"

Art put his Roman nose in it. "Now, Ralph, let's take it easy. Maybe the
old gal's a good worker. We can't kick 'em out of the building just because
they've been around a few years. How's the app?" Good old Art. The
peacemaker. With about as much sense as a lost Cub Scout.

"Well," I said doubtfully, "it says her name is Mabel Jumpstone.
That's right. Jumpstone. Good experience. Seems qualified. *If* she checks
out. You game for an interview?"

"Sure. Why not? Let's do one together," which is against the company
policy of Great Riveroak Insurance Company. All personnel interviewers
are to conduct separate interviews and make individual decisions—at least
that's what we're supposed to do. Usually we double up and save time.

Penny remained standing in front of my desk, tapping her pencil on the
glass top. "Well?" she asked haughtily, which sums up her dispositon
perfectly.

"Okay, Penny. Send Mrs. Jumpstone in."

She came shuffling into the office, smiling and nodding her head like an
old gray mare. Her black outfit looked like pre—World War I. She had on a

307

purple hat with pink plastic flowers around the brim. She reminded me of Ida Crabtree, my housekeeper, whose one passion in life is running over stray cats in her yellow Packard.

She sat down in the wooden chair and said, "Hello there!" Her voice was almost a bellow.

I looked at Art who was leaning forward in his chair, his mouth open, his eyes round.

"Ugh . . . Mrs. Jumpstone," I began.

"Mabel. Please."

"Okay, Mabel. This is Mr. Bowen, my associate." I waved a hand at Art, who mumbled something inappropriate.

"This is a very interesting application, Mabel. It says here you were born in Cricket Creek, California."

"That's right, young man. Home of John and Mary Jackson." She smiled at me, proud of the information.

Art bent over, scratching his wrist. "John and Mary Jackson?"

"Oh, yes," she replied, "the gladiola growers."

He tried to smile. I'll give him credit. "The—the—oh, yes, of course. It must have slipped my mind. Let me see that application, Ralph." He grabbed it from the desk and took a few minutes to study it thoroughly.

Mabel and I sat and watched each other. Every once in a while she'd wink. I tried looking at the ceiling.

Art glanced up and snapped, "You worked at Upstate California Insurance for ten years. Why did you quit?" Sharp-thinking Art. He made a career of trying to catch people off guard. I'd never seen him do it yet.

Mabel shrugged her tiny shoulders. "Young man, have you ever lived up north? It's another world. Cold and foggy. I just had to leave. I told Harry—that's my husband who passed away recently, God rest his soul— that we had to come down here. Mr. Bowen, you wouldn't believe how much I enjoy the sun. Of course, you've never been in Cricket Creek," she added, which was true, of course. I doubted very much if Art had ever *heard* of Cricket Creek.

Art looked as if he wanted to hide. Mabel smiled brightly at him, nodding her head pleasantly.

"Mabel," I said, "the job we have open entails keeping our personnel files up to date. Quite a bit of work, you know, in an office this size."

"Really?"

"Really. Even requires a bit of typing. You *can* type?"

"Oh, heavens, yes. Would you like me to take a test?"

"Uh . . . yes, that might be a good idea. Let's go find a typewriter. Coming, Art?"

He grinned. "Wouldn't miss it for the world."

We walked out of the office. Art whispered in my ear, "Maybe ten words a minute would be my guess."

It turned out to be more like ninety. I handed Mabel one of our surveys on employee retention and told her to have a go at it. She handled the typewriter like a machine gun. The carriage kept clicking back and forth so fast that Art almost got himself a sore neck watching the keys fly.

Our applicant handed me three pages. I couldn't find a single error. Art looked over each page as if he were examining the paper for fingerprints. He finally gave up, shaking his head.

Mabel went back to my office. Art and I walked over to a corner, Art holding the typed sheets.

"Well, what do you think?" he asked.

"She's the best typist in the building. Without a doubt."

"She's different. But you're right. Check her references."

"And if they check out?"

He shrugged. "Let's hire ourselves a little old lady from Cricket Creek."

Art poked his head in my door the next day. "What about our typewriter whiz?"

"I just called her. Application checked out perfectly."

He laughed. "I bet she raises a few eyebrows," which wasn't a bad prediction at all.

Within two months Mabel Jumpstone was the most popular employee in the building. Anytime someone had a birthday she brought in a cake and served it during the afternoon break. She never failed to make an announcement over the company P.A. system when she learned about new benefits. People with problems started coming to Mabel. She arrived early each morning and stayed late. She never missed a day of work. Not one.

Six months after we hired her, Art walked slowly into my office. His eyes were glassy and his mouth was slack. He plunked down heavily in a chair.

"What's the matter with you?" I asked.

"The cash mail," he groaned. We receive quite a lot of cash from our customers. Once a week, on Friday, we take it to the bank. It was Friday.

"What about the cash mail, Art? Come on, what's the matter?"

He looked at me, his eyes blinking. "Harvey was taking it to the bank.

He called ten minutes ago. He was robbed. Conked. Knocked out. And guess who did it?''

"Who?''

"Mabel. Mabel Jumpstone. Our little old lady.''

"You're kidding. You've got to be *kidding*, Art.''

He shook his head. "Harvey said she wanted a lift to the bank. After they got going she took a pistol out of her handbag and told him to pull over. Harvey said it looked like a cannon. The gun, I mean. He just woke up. The money and Harvey's car are gone. So's Mabel.''

I stared at him. "I can't believe it!'

"It's true. Every word. What are we going to do?''

I snapped my fingers. "The application! Come on.''

We ran to the file cabinets and opened the one labeled *Employees*. The application was gone, of course. There was a single sheet inside her manila folder. It was typed very neatly. "I resign. Sincerely yours, Mabel.'' The name had been typed, too. There was no handwritten signature. Mabel had never written anything. She always insisted on everything being typed.

Art stared at me. "Do you remember anything on the application? Anything? The references?'' He was pleading.

"For Pete's sake, Art, it was six months ago!'' I paused for a moment. "I can remember *one* thing. Just one.''

"What?''

"She came from Cricket Creek. I wonder if there *is* a Cricket Creek?''

We checked.

There wasn't.

I finally got home to my two-bedroom bachelor apartment late that evening. The police had been sympathetic. Real nice to us. They didn't even laugh when we told them they were after a little old lady of fifty-five. They asked for a photograph or a sample of handwriting.

We didn't have either.

I opened a can of beer and then walked into one of the bedrooms.

Mabel was sitting on the bed, neatly counting the $78,000 into separate piles.

I looked at her, smiled, and said, "Hi, Mom.''

53

HAPPY BIRTHDAY, DARLING

Joyce Harrington

IT ISN'T SO much that one really *wants* to be reminded that another year has gone down the drain or up the spout or however you want to put it. At any rate, kaput. I can live quite nicely, thank you, without singeing my eyebrows on all those candles. And there's no sane reason for making a public spectacle of the event, only to suffer the well-meant congratulations of friends, compliments that somehow turn into stinging nettles that itch and burn the tender sensibilities of the aging celebrant. I can hear them now.

"Darling, you don't look a day over twenty-nine."

"Here's to the birthday girl! I'd offer you a drink, my child, but first you have to prove you're of age."

". . . but, of course, you don't remember that." This one is obligatory whenever the speaker has been reminiscing and the nostalgia game has churned up the Great Depression, the Lone Ranger on radio, Orphan Annie mugs, the Battle of the Bulge, or the conquest of Mount Everest. You are caught in a cleft stick. If you admit remembering, you instantly date yourself, and if you agree that you are much too young for any personal recollection, everyone knows you are lying.

And, of course, and inevitably, "You're not getting older, you're getter better." Mixed blessings on the advertising whiz kid who invented that line.

Birthdays! Who needs them?

How clever of the Russians, or whoever it was, who celebrated name days. You were named after a saint and thenceforth, throughout your life, you had a day of your own on which to be congratulated with no smarmy nonsense about the years that had slipped away. No embarrassing overlook-

311

ing of the stray gray hair or the additional "laugh lines," as we ruefully call them nowadays, for all those Elizavetas and Ekaterinas of the past. I wonder what the Soviets celebrate in place of name days now that the saints have all been banished to some Siberian kind of limbo.

But can you imagine the pantheon of saints we would need, given our current practices in the naming of the young, to provide a name day for everyone, should we decide to eliminate the detestable birthday celebration? For myself, it would be no problem. I am plain Joan. A flashy kind of saint to be sure, given to hearing disembodied voices and dressing up in men's clothing, but one whose day I would be happy to adopt as my own providing all flaming objects such as candles, stakes, and banana flambées were kept well under control.

But what about all those up-and-coming Samanthas and Fluers and Cleos, not to mention the Jasons and Todds and the inevitable crop of Elvises? Every day of the year would have to be dedicated to a name, possibly to two or three names in the case of those that have achieved less than national popularity. Envision, if you will, celebrations in remote outposts on the day devoted to all the Mortimers, Mabels, and Aramintas under the sun. Of course, the whole thing would have to be subject to Federal regulation, lest the ever-popular Susans and Johns form power blocs and contrive to have their name days designated in the balmy spring or dramatic fall months, leaving the dog-days of summer and the gloom-days of winter to the unfortunate Gertrudes and Homers.

Personally, it doesn't matter a whit to me when St. Joan's day falls. Perhaps I'll look it up sometime and treat myself to a new outfit or a day at Elizabeth Arden's or a soppy, maudlin solitary binge on that day each year. But name day or birthday, it would be all the same to Alexander. Unremarkable and unremarked.

Aha, you say. Now we come to the crux of it. I've just had a birthday, you say, and no one noticed. Not precisely. Actually my birthday was weeks and weeks ago, and there was a gratifying flurry of cards and a few well-chosen gifts from friends and relatives. Much appreciated, although evoking an astonishing array of feeling. Another year gone by and I haven't paid that visit to my sister and her brood in Denver. Guilt. How kind of Rachel to remember me, and her husband dead not six months. Sadness. A funny card from an old boy friend whose birthday is the same as mine. He never forgets and I always do. Regret? A heavy book from a feminist friend and a light one from my scatty cousin who has laughed her way through four divorces and is about, she announces in the enclosed card, to marry number five. I will read both some day and perhaps be spurred to change my life. But in which direction?

And from Alexander? Well, Alex, you see, is very busy. (And when is Alexander's day? There must be one, if not for a saint, at least for the Czar of that name, or for the one called the Great. I'll have to look it up.) Alexander Clark Hemming, who would like to be called the Great, is a very busy man. He has an office at which he spends long hours every day and often much of the night. He has a secretary who types his terse commanding memos and diverts all unnecessary phone calls. In order to be considered necessary, I now have to declare a state of emergency, and lately I have been required to state the nature of the emergency.

"Mr. Hemming is in conference. He cannot be disturbed."

"Miss Wanderley, this is an emergency."

"May I tell him the nature of the emergency?"

"No, you may not."

"Then, I'm sorry, Mrs. Hemming. He left strict orders."

Bite your tongue, Wanderley. I know you in all your dreams and ambitions. You haven't been the first and you're a long shot from being the last. And even if you should, by some strange quirk of fate (accident, suicide, swift or lingering disease), take my place, do you think you would fare any better? Don't you know that you would be succeeded by a long string of Wanderleys, all pantingly eager to work long hours and provide consoling coffee breaks to the prince of industry? Haven't you ever noticed, Wanderley, that when the coffee is cold and you rise from the cushiony depths of that oversized sofa I chose for his office, it's back to the IBM Executive for you? Think about it, Wanderley. I do.

Wanderley, of course, is English. Cool, blonde, and efficient. Armored in the rote pronouncement of protective formulas. Intimidating to the unprepared.

"Do you have an appointment?"

"Mr. Hemming does not accept unsolicited proposals."

But I am not intimidated, Wanderley. I have been prepared by 15 years of watching Alex Hemming rise to the top. Fifteen years of Christmas presents selected at the last moment by you and your predecessors. Don't you remember?

"Miss Wanderley, run around to Tiffany's and pick out something for my wife. And charge a little something for yourself."

I have quite a nice collection of empty Tiffany boxes on a shelf in one of my closets. How about you? But what happened to my birthdays,

Wanderley? In your cool, efficient way how could you let him overlook the birthdays? Or did he simply never include them on your agenda of secretarial services, other things being more important? Shame on you, Wanderley.

On the other hand I will not forget *his* birthday. You're going to love it, Wanderley. Well, maybe not love it exactly, but I'm sure you'll be thrilled to pieces at your little part in commemorating Alex. He's already told me that he'll be staying in town all week (how nice for you, Wanderley)—the trade show, the difficult Japanese matter, the labor trouble in the Milan factory, the countless major and minor crises requiring the hand of the master. And I have already told him that I will be busy all week organizing the Art Show for the benefit of St. Hilda's Home for Unwed Mothers. He does so like for my name (actually his name—Mrs. Alexander Clark Hemming) to appear on programs and in publicity. It's good for business and it keeps me out of trouble. I've never been a mother, unwed or otherwise.

So he won't be expecting any kind of celebration on his birthday. Which is tomorrow. This afternoon I will telephone Wanderley, and the conversation will go something like this.

"Miss Wanderley, this is not an emergency."

"How may I help you, Mrs. Hemming?"

"Yes. That's it, exactly. I need your help. I'm going to enlist your aid as a conspirator, shall we say."

"How exciting." With all the enthusiasm of a jellied eel.

"Yes, it is, rather." I always find myself adopting Englishisms when bandying words with Wanderley. "Tomorrow is Mr. Hemming's birthday and since we can't celebrate it together, I would like to arrange for some small remembrance to be delivered to him at the office. Of course, I'll need your help, indeed, your active participation for it to be successful."

"Really." She has an uncanny knack of expanding the word by a couple of supercilious syllables. "What did you have in mind?"

"Nothing much, really. You know how fond he is of Sacher Torte." She could know nothing of the kind because he isn't, but sharing a supposed bit of inside information might enlist her more firmly in my plan.

"Of course." Oh, Wanderley, you are mine.

"Well, I've ordered one to be appropriately inscribed, you know, *Happy Birthday, Dear Alex,* and delivered at four o'clock tomorrow afternoon. It will come complete with candles and a card from me. All you have to do is light the candles and carry it in to him at an opportune moment. Perhaps when he takes his late afternoon coffee."

"Mrs. Hemming, how sweetly thoughtful of you. I'll be glad to serve as your emissary."

I'll just bet you will, you little twit.

"And I'm sure Mr. Hemming will enjoy his birthday cake."

Was there a hint of condescension in that so refined voice?

"Thank you, my dear. I hope you both get a big bang out of it."

Volunteer work has its rewards and they are not all in heaven. The unwed mothers are, by and large, a scruffy lot. Some of them are downright silly; others are earnest and highly principled. Yet others are radical young women with connections of an explosive sort.

It was through one of these that I acquired ten very innocent-looking birthday candles, one for each decade up to 40 and one for the supplier, since the candles would be used to attack a highly visible symbol of Amerikan kapitalism. It cost me three of my Tiffany Christmas presents. Cheap at the price.

Tomorrow evening, after I officiate at the opening of the Art Show, extolling the courage and fortitude of the unwed mothers, I shall hurry to my lovely suburban home, alone as usual, pour myself a solitary glass of champagne, and celebrate all birthdays, past, present, and future. I shall watch the television news. With any luck at all, the FALN will leap in to take credit for my simple celebration.

Happy birthday, darling.

54

ONE WILL TOO MANY

Joe L. Hensley

MARK WILHELM WAS what has come to be known within the legal profession as an "office lawyer." He had little ability for the fiery displays that help make the personality of a good courtroom tactician. He considered his mind to be too calculating and orderly for feigned heat and loud oratory. He was fairly adept at intricacies, at detail work, and so he existed well on settling estates, on minor tax work, and on abstracting titles to real estate.

He had certain abilities, certain faults. Among the former was his rather distinguished looks when he was dressed in his fine, dark clothes. Those looks made it possible for him to hold closely the attention of a widow when one visited his office, making each female client think that he regarded her as a more-than-friend. And, if sometimes the taste in his mouth was sour, still it was a living.

His practice was centered in a large Midwestern town. He liked the town, but it grew cold there in the winter. Very cold. Mark Wilhelm hated cold. He liked to spend those cold months in Florida, but vacation this year had been delayed by lack of funds and other reasons.

The most important reason was with him now on long-distance telephone.

"We haven't seen you. You've owed us more than forty thousand for almost a year," said the smooth voice that brought remembrance of daiquiris and suntans and horses that ran fast, but not fast enough. "When can we expect to get it? I rather dislike making these calls and I don't intend to call *you* again."

Mark's hands were wet and slippery as he held the phone.

"You know very well that gambling debts aren't legally collectible," he said weakly.

"Maybe they aren't in your business, but I'd hate to think they weren't in

317

mine,'' the voice said, small slivers of steel beginning to show.

''Are you threatening me?'' Mark asked, trying to raise the temperature of his voice with small success.

''Of course,'' the voice said. ''That's exactly what I'm doing.''

Mark started to hang up the telephone and got it all of an inch from his ear when resolve faded and fear came on. ''I've got to have some time to raise that kind of money.''

''I'll give you thirty days. If you don't have it then, I believe I'll assume you're never going to have it and proceed accordingly. One of my associates will call thirty days from today. Have the money ready for him.''

Mark hung up the phone carefully and sat at his oversize desk thinking. He did not dislike himself for his compulsion to gamble. When you spent your working days around an office trying to make old women happy so you could write their wills and settle their estates when they died, a man deserved some bright lights and excitement when vacationing in Florida.

But last year he'd really gone off the deep end. Forty thousand dollars—

The opportunity offered itself the very next day. Mrs. Belle Rivera, a widow with cold, clutching hands, who had more money than the rest of Mark's menage together, died. And the nice part was that he didn't even have to help her along, as he'd done once or twice with other clients. Not really murder them, of course. Just leave a bottle of sleeping pills close when they were in pain, or that one time when he'd stolen Mrs. Jaymon's heart medicine.

Mrs. Rivera, Mark remembered well, was an eccentric lady with no close relatives who had doted strongly on Mark. He, in turn, had held her hand and his breath and waxed eloquent for her for years. And she'd trusted him.

Mark's main fault was that he was dishonest. It was a compelling dishonesty that would seldom allow him to complete a transaction without getting something that was not his.

In Mrs. Rivera's estate the fee for settlement, he computed, would be almost enough to pay his gambling debt, but it would leave nothing for another trip to Florida. The weather was growing cold and he longed for the warmth of the southern sun. Besides, he wouldn't be able to draw against the attorney's fee for at least six months. The probate commissioner was very strict about that. Also he owed the bank a great deal of money, and they'd move in on the major part of the fee.

He sat in his office thinking for a long time. Finally the idea came.

First of all he called her bank and his, the one that he usually worked with, and asked to speak to John Sims.

"Mrs. Rivera died this morning," he said to Sims. "Terrible loss. I've her will here in my office. She named your bank as executor and myself as attorney. I trust that's satisfactory?"

Sims happily assured him that the bank would be most willing to work with him in the matter.

"I'll probate her will this afternoon," Mark told him. "There were two copies and I've retained both of them here in my office."

"That's unusual," Sims said.

"She trusted me implicitly," Mark said, putting a little ice in his voice. "She felt her will would be safer in my office than at her home. As you may know, she had become increasingly deaf and her sight was poor, and she was afraid that her servants might try to pry into her affairs."

"I see," Sims said, his voice satisfied.

Mark hung up the phone with relief, that part accomplished. What he'd said was perfectly true. Mrs. Rivera had left both copies of her will in his office. Now to change that will. But first he would have to contact his old associate, Alvin Light.

Alvin would be perfect for the idea he had in mind.

He told his idiot office girl he'd be out the rest of the morning and left.

The office girl had been chosen for two reasons. She was ugly and made none of his old lady friends jealous. Secondly, she was stupid and never noticed any of Mark's mistakes.

He found Alvin in a third-class bar doing what he was best at since he'd been disbarred—drinking. Outside the bar, though, before he went in, he watched with interest as an ambulance pulled up and loaded an old bum who lay tattered and supine in the gutter. None of the other bums paid much attention.

Mark heard one ambulance attendant grumble to the other: "Dead. This cold weather really gets to them."

The scene caught at something in his mind, an addition to the original idea. He stood thinking for a moment, then went into the bar. Alvin was holding drunken court in the back of the bar, but he shooed the bums away when Mark appeared.

Before Alvin's downfall for bribing a member of a petit jury and getting caught at it, the two had sliced up many a client between them. And even though Alvin was now a vile-smelling alcoholic, intelligence still showed dimly in his eyes.

Mark got him away from the bar and into the car.

"How'd you like to make fifty thousand dollars?" he asked.

Alvin's red eyes flickered. "I'd like it. Not for me so much. I'm smart enough to know what I am. But I'd like it for my boy. He hates my guts, but he's still my son. He's in medical school now, in California. He's married with a couple of kids I've never seen. He hasn't got any money, and he's going to have to drop out of school and go to work when this year is over. Enough money would see him through; the rest should buy me enough whiskey to finish killing me."

He looked up at Mark sharply. "What have you got going, Mark? I have to admire you, you know. I was a crook because I thought it was smart. You're dishonest because you're completely amoral—everything revolves around you." He sighed. "You've been luckier than I—a long time being caught."

Mark ignored the comment and went to the point, "You used to do Mrs. Rivera's work, didn't you?"

Alvin nodded. "She was a client of mine before you came along with your phony charm."

"She died," Mark said softly. "What if there was a bequest for a hundred thousand dollars to you in her will?"

"You mean there is one?"

"Not yet," Mark said, smiling. "But I have all copies of the will in my office and no one has seen them but me."

"I get fifty?"

"Same way we always went. Fifty-fifty." It was easy to say it. But there would be no split.

"How about witnesses to the will?"

"I was one. The other was my office girl. I didn't pick her for her brains. She's so dumb she has trouble remembering her own name. Besides, I typed the will and all she ever saw was the last page."

Alvin eyed him shrewdly and nodded. "Fifty thousand dollars is more than I'll ever need. Why so much for me? I might have gone for less."

"We've always gotten along at the even split," Mark said smoothly.

Alvin smiled. "Don't try to cross me on this, Mark. I need that money for my boy."

The rest was easy.

All he had to do was carefully take the staples out of the will, align the paper and insert, at the bottom of a page, among Mrs. Rivera's long list of specific bequests, a hundred-thousand-dollar one to Alvin Light, for "his past services to me and his present necessity." He would have preferred leaving it to himself, but that would be illegal, since he had drawn up and witnessed the will.

320

Then he probated the will.

The next four weeks went very smoothly. Mark lost himself in the intricacies of Mrs. Rivera's various problems. Final state and federal returns, inheritance tax schedules, waivers, inventories—nice detail work of the type in which he excelled.

Because Mrs. Rivera had died with a great deal of money and no close relatives, none of her heirs questioned her bequests. There was plenty for all. John Sims, probate officer at the bank, raised an eyebrow at Mark when he read the bequest to Alvin Light, but Mark pretended not to notice.

And so on the beautiful, but now very cold twenty-ninth day after Mark's long-distance telephone call, Alvin, armed with a check properly signed by John Sims, cashed that check, while Mark waited outside around the corner. Alvin was gone for a long time, but Mark was patient, if nervous.

When it was done they went back to Mark's office with a satchel containing a hundred thousand dollars and Mark got out a bottle of very good Bourbon and poured two drinks. He said: "This is the kind of day to be in Florida. Cold!" He shivered. "Drink some of this to warm you."

Alvin eyed the whiskey and Mark dubiously. "Just the one," he said.

"Of course," Mark said, and then watched while the one became two and then ten and conversation moved from old stories to monosyllables.

Everything went as planned. Mark thought of the whole hundred thousand and warm climates. He rationalized by realizing that Alvin couldn't be trusted. Alvin was an alcoholic and vain and sooner or later an alcoholic would part with any secret. And fifty thousand saved is an enormous saving.

After Alvin was suitably besotted Mark put him in the car, first carefully removing the money in Alvin's battered briefcase. He put most of this in his safe to pay the emissary of the gamblers and for his own future use. A few bills he kept for further use during the night.

He took Alvin to an even worse neighborhood than the one he'd originally visited the old lawyer in—a neighborhood known for muggings and knifings and doctored whiskey—and, of course, dead bums in the alleys.

Once, on the way, Alvin's eyes opened a little and Mark heard him whisper: 'Don't cross me—the will—'' and some gibberish following that.

Mark smiled and stopped his car in a deserted place and poured more whiskey down the weak old throat. Then he drove on. It was very cold outside and a light snow was falling. The car's heater could barely compensate. It was the kind of night to be heading south.

He dumped the older man in a little-used alley. This was the difficult and dangerous part, but Mark had been over the neighborhood thoroughly, figuring his chances, knowing they were good. He poured water he'd brought from the office over Alvin's sodden body, watchfully listening to distant street noises, careful and alert.

Alvin did not move when the water cascaded down. The snow was falling in a near blizzard now and the weather was very cold. He dragged Alvin behind a group of garbage cans and boxes. Twice more, during the night, he came back with more water, but the second trip was unnecessary. Alvin was dead.

Of course, there would be a furor about the hundred thousand dollars, but not the kind that a murder brings. Mark rehearsed his lines in his mind: 'I told him to leave it with me or put it in a bank, but he was drunk. After all, he's been taking care of himself for a long time.''

The hundred thousand could easily have been stolen by one of the toughs in the neighborhood. Mark scattered a few bills he'd kept for that purpose underneath the body and in Alvin's pockets.

The man from the Miami gambler came at eleven the next day. Mark had purposely let his office girl, "Dumb Dora," have the morning off.

The man was a nervous little wreck with a tic under his right eye and the face of a fallen saint. Mark smiled and escorted him to the inner office.

"You've got the money?" the little man asked.

Mark nodded and opened the safe and began counting it out in neat piles, hurrying, wanting to get this part done quickly.

"Good man," the nervous one said. "They were sure you weren't going to be able to come up with it. I'll have to get to a phone and call a certain number very soon now."

Mark increased the speed of his counting.

The interruption came then. Mark's door opened.

John Sims, the bank probate officer, was there. He had one of the uniformed guards with him.

"Sorry to break in, but there wasn't anyone in the outer office." Sims nodded apologetically at the little gambler's emissary. "This is important. They found poor Alvin Light's body in an alley a little while ago. Poor man had frozen to death."

Mark nodded, maintaining his composure. "Drinking too damned much."

Sims looked down at the desk, seeing the neat piles of money, and his face became curious. "I'm carrying out instructions. Alvin left a will with me yesterday when he picked up the money. Named the bank executor and you as attorney. He had me copy down all of the numbers and mark the wrappers of money I gave him yesterday. He stated in the will that if he should die suddenly I should come to you for the money immediately, that you would have it.''

Sims looked down at the desk again and his face went blank. ''Why, that looks like some of it there! I recognize the wrappers. You weren't going to use it, were you?'' He picked up the neat bundles and handed them to the guard. ''Alvin left the money to his son.''

The nervous little man with the lost eyes sidled out of the office, while Sims and the guard gathered the money from the desk and safe. Mark tried to say something, to think of something.

Nothing came. Nothing at all.

Not *that* day anyway.

55

THE DISPATCHING OF GEORGE FERRIS

Jack Foxx

MRS. BERESFORD AND Mrs. Lenhart were sitting together in the parlor, knitting and discussing recipes for fruit cobbler, when Mr. Pascotti came hurrying in. "There's big news," he said. "Mr. Ferris is dead."

A gleam came into Mrs. Beresford's eyes. She loked at Mrs. Lenhart, noted a similar gleam, and said to Mr. Pascotti, "You did say dead, didn't you?"

"Dead. Murdered."

"Murdered? Are you sure?"

"Well," Mr. Pascotti said, "he's lying on the floor of his room all over blood, with a big knife sticking in his chest. What else would you call it?"

"Oh, yes," Mrs. Lenhart agreed. "Definitely murder."

Mrs. Beresford laid down her knitting and folded her hands across her shelflike bosom. "How did you happen to find him, Mr. Pascotti?"

"By accident. I was on my way down to the john—"

"Lavatory," Mrs. Lenhart said.

"—and I noticed his door was open. He never leaves his door open, not when he's here and not when he's not here. So I'm a good neighbor. I peeked inside to see if something was wrong, and there he was, all over blood."

Mrs. Beresford did some reflecting. George Ferris had been a resident of their roominghouse for six months, during which time he had managed to create havoc in what had formerly been a peaceful and pleasant environment. She and the other residents had complained to the landlord, but the landlord lived elsewhere and chose not to give credence to what he termed "petty differences among neighbors." He also seemed to like Mr. Ferris, with whom he had had minor business dealings before Ferris' retirement and who he considered to possess a sparkling sense of humor. This flaw in

325

his judgment of human nature made him a minority of one, but in this case the minority's opinion was law.

The problem with Mr. Ferris was that he had been a practical joker. Not just an occasional practical joker; oh, no. A constant, unending, remorseless practical joker. A *Practical Joker* with capitals and in italics. Sugar in the salt shaker; ground black pepper in the tea. Softboiled eggs substituted for hardboiled eggs. Kitchen cleanser substituted for denture powder. Four white rats let loose in the dining room during supper. Photographs of naked ladies pasted inside old Mr. Tipton's *Natural History* magazine. Whoopee cushions, water glasses that dribbled, fuzzy spiders and rubber-legged centipedes all over the walls and furniture. These and a hundred other indignities—a deluge, an avalanche of witless and childish pranks.

Was it any wonder, Mrs. Beresford thought, that somebody had finally done him in? No, it was not. The dispatching of George Ferris, the joker, was in fact an act of great mercy.

"Who could have done it?" Mrs. Lenhart asked after a time.

"Anybody who lives here," Mr. Pascotti said. "Anybody who ever spent ten minutes with that lunatic."

"You don't suppose it was possibly an intruder?"

"Who would want to intrude in this place? No, my guess is it was one of us."

"You don't mean one of *us*?"

"What, you or Mrs. Beresford? Nice widow ladies like you? The thought never crossed my mind, believe me."

"Why, thank you, Mr. Pascotti."

"For what?"

"The compliment. You said we were nice widow ladies."

Mr. Pascotti, who had been a bachelor for nearly seven decades, looked somewhat uncomfortable. "You don't have to worry—the police won't suspect you, either. They'd have to be crazy. Policemen today are funny, but they're not crazy."

"They might suspect you, though," Mrs. Beresford said.

"Me? That's ridiculous. All I did was find him on my way to the john—"

"Lavatory," Mrs. Lenhart said.

"All I did was find him. I didn't make him all over blood."

"But they might think you did," Mrs. Beresford said.

"Not a chance. Ferris was ten years younger than me and I've got arthritis so bad I can't even knock loud on a door. So how could I stick a big knife in his chest?"

Mrs. Lenhart adjusted the drape of her shawl. "You know, I really can't imagine anybody here doing such a thing. Can you, Irma?"

"As a matter of fact." Mrs. Beresford said, "I can. We all have hidden strengths and capacities, but we don't realize it until we're driven to the point of having or needing to use them."

"That's very profound."

"Sure it is," Mr. Pascotti said. "It's also true."

"Oh, I'm sure it is. But I still prefer to think it was an intruder who sent Mr. Ferris on to his reward, whatever that may be."

Mr. Pascotti gestured toward the parlor windows and the sunshine streaming in through them. "It's broad daylight," he said. "Do intruders intrude in broad daylight?"

"Sometimes they do," Mrs. Lenhart said. "Remember last year, when the police questioned everybody about strangers in the neighborhood? There were a series of daylight burglaries right over on Hawthorn Boulevard."

"So it could have been an intruder, I'll admit it. We'll tell the police that's what we think. Why should any of us have to suffer for making that lunatic dead?"

"Isn't it time we did?" Mrs. Beresford asked.

"Did? Did what?"

"Tell the police what we think. After we tell them Mr. Ferris is lying up in his room with a knife in his chest."

"You're right," Mr. Pascotti said, "it is time. Past time. A warm day like this, things happen to dead bodies after a while."

He turned and started over to the telephone. But before he got to it there was a sudden eruption of noise from out in the front hallway. At first it sounded to Mrs. Beresford like a series of odd snorts, wheezes, coughs, and gasps. When all these sounds coalesced into a recognizable bellow, however, she realized that what she was hearing was wild laughter.

Then George Ferris walked into the room.

He was wearing an old sweatshirt and a pair of old dungarees, both of which were, as Mr. Pascotti had said, all over blood. In his left hand he carried a wicked-looking and also very bloody knife. His chubby face was contorted into an expression of mirth bordering on ecstasy and he was laughing so hard that tears flowed down both cheeks.

Mrs. Beresford stared at him with her mouth open. So did Mrs. Lenhard and Mr. Pascotti. Ferris looked back at each of them and what he saw sent him into even greater convulsions.

The noise lasted for fifteen seconds or so, subsided into more snorts, wheezes, and gasps, and finally ceased altogether. Ferris wiped his damp face and got his breathing under control. Then he pointed to the crimson stains on his clothing. "Chicken blood," he said. He pointed to the weapon clutched in his left hand. "Trick knife," he said.

"A joke," Mr. Pascotti said. "It was all a joke."

"Another joke," Mrs. Lenhart said.

"Another indignity," Mrs. Beresford said.

"And you fell for it," Ferris reminded them. "Oh, boy, did you fall for it! You should have seen your faces when I walked in." He began to cackle again. "My best one yet," he said, "no question about it. My best one *ever*. Why, by golly, I don't think I'll live to pull off a better one."

Mrs. Beresford looked at Mrs. Lenhart. Then she looked at Mr. Pascotti. Then she picked up one of her knitting needles and looked at the pudgy joker across its sharp glittering point.

"Neither do we, Mr. Ferris," she said. "Neither do we."

56

THE JOKER

Betty Ren Wright

THE TINY MICROPHONE just fit into a hollow in the low terrace wall. Harry stepped back and told himself, with a kind of anguish, that there was no danger of its being noticed. Anyone concerned about eavesdroppers would be looking toward the door into the house, not at the wall with its forty-foot drop to the sea.

He stared over the wall into the deep, foaming pool that had undercut the cliff and polished the walls of the cove to unmarred smoothness. He was terrified by water—Greta was, too—but the lashing of the waves suited his mood tonight. There was the same uneasy surge beneath the surface, the same sudden furious thrusts. The water reflected a Harry that no one—except perhaps Greta—had ever seen.

He really had to smile a little at the idea of Greta and his secret self. He had hidden his fear of being deserted, of being left all alone in an indifferent world, by marrying the kind of woman who would be desired and pursued by other men always.

It was an interesting trick, he thought. One of his best. And if Greta, more perceptive than most people, had recognized her limited role and resented it, he couldn't help that. Confidence, trust, frankness were expensive toys for a privileged few. He had learned to get along without them.

He shivered, and called himself a fool for being nervous. After all, no one would suspect him of malice in putting the tape recorder on the terrace. His jokes had never been vicious. This time it would appear that for once he had been caught in his own trap. People would talk about it for a long time and pity him, and though he regretted the pity, he relished the talk. There were other ways in which he might have killed Greta (he'd use one of them if this didn't work out tonight), but in none of them would her friends have seen her so clearly for what she really was. That was important. He hated

329

her now, with the same shattering intensity with which he had wanted her five years ago.

The doorbell rang.

"I'll get it." Harry stood at the French doors and watched her come down the last few stairs and cross to the foyer. She was small, straight, auburn, like a fall candle, and tonight she would make all the cameo-skinned, elegant females at the party wish they had been born with red hair and freckles. He could be quite objective about her now—could marvel at what no longer belonged to him—had apparently *never* belonged to him. (And that was the bad part—the wound that was not going to heal. She had been Peter Buckley's girl before their marriage; for the last six months she had been seeing him regularly again. The two facts invalidated all that had happened between.)

It was, predictably, Peter Buckley arriving first. Harry greeted him too loudly, toned it down, fixed him a drink, and went back to the door to meet the next arrivals. During the hour that followed he welcomed at least twenty more people, asked them how their work was going, whether their vacations had been exciting, how they liked their new houses, cars, and spouses. He showed first-time guests around—the fireplace made with not-quite-genuine fossils, the mirror that took your picture when you turned on the light over it, the mounted muskie that inflated while he described what a fight it had taken to land it. He mixed a great many drinks, told a great many stories. And all of this it seemed he accomplished without once taking his eyes from Greta and Peter. Every word they spoke to each other, every casual gesture, every smile was in some curious way a symptom of the disease that was destroying him. He felt like an invalid making bright conversation while at the same time he took his own pulse and found it dangerously irregular.

When Greta and Peter finally went out on the terrace together, closing the door behind them, he was actually relieved. If they had *not* wanted to be alone, it would have proved nothing except that they were inclined to caution now, when caution was ridiculous. Harry thought of the overheard, whispered phone calls in which she had arranged to meet Peter, the times he had seen them driving together—the bitter afternoon when, coming home early along the shore road, he had seen them driving up from Buckley's beach cottage. Greta was supposed to be in the city that afternoon; when he asked her, she described in detail where she had eaten, whom she had seen, the antique sale at which, not surprisingly, she had seen nothing worth buying.

"—so marvelous," a voice screamed in his ear. "Like living in an eagle's nest. You two must adore the water!"

"Adore looking at it," Harry corrected with a smile. It was Joe Herman's wife—a shrill, peevish kind of woman who embodied all the things Greta was not. Ugly, he thought, still smiling at her—ugly, malicious, domineering, and loyal. She might treat poor old Joe like dirt but nobody else had better try it.

June Herman's face turned red, as though some unexpected acumen let her read the thought behind his smile. "A man with a wife who looks like Greta *ought* to keep her in an eagle's nest," she said viciously. Harry turned, looking for an explanation for her anger, and saw Joe talking to Greta with obvious enjoyment.

The party dragged by, like a hundred others before it. He had been careful to add a few of the ingredients his guests had learned to expect: one of the "gelatin" molds of the buffet was made of rubber; the woman in the painting over the fireplace smiled at people who stopped to admire her, the new bearskin rug growled when Joe Herman stooped to pat its head. "Marvelous," everyone said when he finally left, and he knew exactly what they were thinking, *Good old corny old Harry—he'll never change*. Not one of them knew he existed apart from his jokes.

Peter Buckley and the Hermans were the last to leave. "Thank goodness," Greta said when the door closed behind them. Harry looked at her sharply, but her expression was as innocent as her tone. She yawned and, as if on cue, crossed to the terrace door and went out into the silver light. He followed. As he crossed the room he seemed to leave his state of fevered alertness and enter into a kind of dull automatism. He did not have to think about what was going to happen next. It was set, inevitable.

"I'm tired," Greta said. Her face was very white. The yellow dress was subdued fire against the darkness of the sea. Far below her the water lashed against the floor of the cliff.

"You had a terrible time tonight," she said when he walked over beside her. "Why do you bother with jokes when you're feeling this lousy? Why don't you tell me what's worrying you?"

She had the knack, he thought. She should have gone on the stage; it was wonderful the way she delivered those small lines. *Tell the little woman all about it,* he thought savagely, aping the sense if not the tone of her plea. He moved a few steps along the wall, picked up the microphone, and waited until she looked at him.

"What's that?"

"Another joke," he said and waited again, but she didn't seem to recognize what he held. "It's the microphone of the tape recorder," he said carefully. "I had it set up out here to get an hour or two of private-type conversations. Ought to be good for some laughs."

Awareness came slowly, just as he had imagined it would. in the long, painful night-hours of planning. And now, it was *her* voice that was careful, controlled, as she asked, "You had it—out here?"

He nodded.

She took it well, considering the depth of the pit that had suddenly opened up before her. "You ought to be ashamed of yourself," she said. "Funny jokes are one thing, but that—that's cheap and ugly."

He pretended to be startled. "You have a pretty poor opinion of our friends," he said. "What do you think we're going to hear, for heaven's sake? A lot of small talk about how pretty the ocean is in the moonlight and isn't it a dull party and wouldn't you think that joker would get tired of his little games after a while . . . that's all it'll be. We can play it at the next party if things are slow . . ." Without looking at her he lifted the tape recorder from behind the column of greenery in the corner and set it on the wall. "Sit down," he said. "Might as well listen to it before we go to bed."

She moved then, gliding along the wall so swiftly that he had only a fraction of a second to get ready. Her hands were on the tape recorder, pushing wildly, when he caught her around the hips and lifted her over the wall. One moment he was thrusting her away from him into space, the next his hands were empty. Her scream was cut short when she hit the water.

He had tried to prepare himself for the moments right afterward. Horror was what he expected, and it came, a wild trembling, a violent nausea as he stared down into the water. Doubt, fear, remorse because now he was a murderer and would know himself to be one forever. But he hadn't expected the overwhelming loneliness which, when it struck, drove every other feeling out of him. With his own hands he had done it, had rendered himself alone in a world that thought he was a very funny man indeed. She was the only one who hadn't laughed.

Later he thought that he might have followed her over the wall in that moment, might have ended it right then, if the doorbell hadn't rung. After the third or fourth ring he recognized the sound. And he knew he had to go ahead with the plan.

When he opened the door Joe Herman stepped inside, pulling his wife behind him. "Damn tire," he snarled and grabbed the telephone in the

entry. "That's the second one this week—I don't even have a spare . . . "
He looked at Harry more closely. "What's the matter—too much party?
You oughtta cut out all that cute stuff."

"Call the police," Harry said. "Call somebody. Greta just jumped off
the terrace. She's killed herself."

He didn't have to pretend the sobs that shook him when he actually said
the words.

The Hermans stared. "Look, funny boy," Joe said, but something
apparently convinced him it was not a joke, for he ran across to the terrace
and his wife followed him.

"The cliff walls are smooth as marble for a hundred yards around the
cove." Harry said harshly from the terrace door. He watched them stare
over the edge, seeing the churning blackness himself though he didn't leave
the lighted living room. "That was one of the reasons we built here—
privacy, no beach parties, nobody peeking in the windows."

He went back to the phone and called the police himself. When he was
through the Hermans were behind him, their faces white and curiously
hungry as they struggled to believe the worst. "You—you *wouldn't* joke
about a thing like this." Joe said uncertainly. "I don't believe you would.
But why would Greta—do that?"

Harry saw then that they were the right people to have here when the
police came. They both knew him as The Joker; Joe had been involved in
several of the best. They would believe the picture of the clown and the joke
that backfired. They would want to believe it, would want the police to
believe it. They would feel, in a way they would not even admit to
themselves, that he had it coming.

"I don't understand it myself," he said simply. "We were just talking—
you know, after-the-party talk. I mentioned that I had had the tape
recorder turned on out on the terrace this evening. She looked strange—
kind of sick—I asked her if she was feeling all right—she said yes, but then
she started to cry and when I switched on the re-wind she started to moan
and then she ran across the terrace and just—jumped."

They looked at him.

"Poor kid," Joe said. "I wonder why . . ."

"What about the tape recorder?" June asked eagerly. "Why don't
you play it now and see if there was something on it that might have upset
her?"

He knew he didn't have to let them hear the tape. June Herman knew the
whole story already, or thought she did; he had watched her eyes widen

when he mentioned the recorder, had seen the eager twitching of lips as she tasted the story she would have to tell.

"Greta never had anything to hide," he said stiffly "That's a lousy thing to say."

Joe shook his head and his wife made a small, protesting sound. "Of course not," she said soothingly. "But just the same, Harry, you ought to listen to the tape before the police come. You just ought to."

He thought it over, then shrugged as if he were too tired to argue. The recorder was still out on the terrace; he got it quickly and brought it back in. He knew he was taking a chance, but not a big one; there had been no doubt that Greta had not wanted him to hear the tape. And June Herman was the right one, the absolutely right one, to hear the whole story.

He pushed the re-wind button and waited, while the tape whirred innocently to the other spool. Then the room was full of the sound of waves. Loneliness came back as he listened; he was powerless before it, though he reminded himself that he had lost nothing, that he couldn't lose something he had never really had. Still he strained to hear Greta's voice, wanting the sound of it once more, regardless of the words it spoke.

Joe Herman leaned forward and turned up the volume of the recorder. There was the sound of footsteps on stone and then a giggle. Harry didn't recognize the voice but he could tell June was cataloging this, too, for future investigation. There followed a long pause with nothing but the splash of waves, and then, suddenly and sweetly, there was Greta's voice.

"It's more than a joke now, Petey," she said. "He hasn't trusted me from the very first, and lately we've been farther apart than ever. At first it just seemed as if it would be fun to turn the tables on him—once. Now it's much more. At first I had no intention of frightening him—now I feel as if shock is the only thing that might bring him back . . ."

"You're wonderful," Peter said. "I think I've mentioned that before. When are you going to do it?"

The Hermans frowned, trying hard to follow the conversation. As the tape whirled on, their faces seemed to move farther away, leaving Harry alone on a small island surrounded by Greta's voice.

"Soon," the voice said. "I'm not quite sure how I'll do it, but I can tell you this, Petey—I'll plan it so he thinks he's lost me. For a minute or two or maybe more he's going to face up to how much he needs me—he's going to value me as a person and not just as part of his pretty little stage set here on the cliff. I want him to wish to heaven he had one more chance to make our marriage work. I want him to know exactly what it's like to love someone terribly, as I love him, and not be able to reach him . . .'' She took a deep breath. ''And I do thank you Petey, for making it possible.''

The entry door opened. Joe saw it first; with a real effort he tore his eyes from the tape recorder and got up clumsily. ''It's the police—'' he said and then suddenly stopped.

Harry did not move. In the mirror over the couch he could see two figures neatly framed in gold, a picture to carry with him the rest of his life. Here the tall policeman, puzzled, frowning, and there, just beside him, the small, freckled, red-headed girl in a drenched yellow dress. They had come together in the darkness behind them; the policeman would have seen her somewhere on the beach beyond the smooth walls of the cove, walking slowly across the sand, trying to believe the thing that had happened.

Well, he thought, *I certainly found out what she wanted me to*. And then he began to laugh, because somebody's joke had backfired, and if he didn't laugh now he was going to cry. He laughed for himself, for the wife he had had, and for Pete Buckley who must have spent a good share of the last six months teaching Greta how to swim. He was still laughing when the policeman put the handcuffs on him and led him out of the house.

57

SCHEDULE FOR AN ASSASSINATION

Robert Edmond Alter

THE HIGHROAD SNAKED up to the very rim of the steep hill. From their car window the two assassins could look straight down to the blue floor of the cliff-girt harbor, where the little Mediterranean city—all whitewashed and slate-roofed—squatted like a broken angel food cake. They could see the tiny fishing boats moored in the pumice-white water, and the little ant-like people moving about the quays and squares.

Katov—the man who had actually fired the shot that had killed the visiting politician—drummed his fingertips nervously on the dashboard, and when he spoke his eyes and voice were edged with anger.

"All right, all right. They're not after us yet. Let's get on."

Vologin, who dated his term of service back to the Spanish Civil War, grunted and ground the gears. His physical appearance—short and swarthy—matched exactly with his temper and disposition.

"They better not come after us. I'll give them something—"

Katov looked at him, exasperated by his surly bravado. "Shut up, can't you?" he snapped. "Of course they'll come after us. They'll phone ahead, and the police will be out . . . probably the army too."

Vologin was a driver who fought the wheel instead of steering with it. He swerved away from a boy driving a sledge ox along the shoulder. The boy shouted after him, and Vologin shouted back and put on speed.

"Stop complaining," he said to Katov. "I've outwitted the *bourgeois* for twenty-four years. We'll be down at the villa in an hour."

"If we miss the roadblocks."

"By the time they get their roadblocks up, we'll be playing *vingt-et-un* at the villa and I shall be winning your money."

Vologin skinned past an oncoming Mercedes-Benz, almost forcing it

337

from the road. A horn hooted indignantly. "Fat swine!" Vologin muttered darkly.

"But we're two hours ahead of schedule," Katov fretted. "The yacht won't come for us until four."

Vologin looked ahead and then dodged a pothole in the road, making the tires whine. "That couldn't be helped," he said shortly. "Our orders were to shoot him when he landed. It was their fault, not ours, that the government yacht was two hours ahead of time."

"Yes, but *we'll* pay for it."

An old man walking the road missed death by an inch. Vologin didn't spare him a glance. "Why must you always be a worrier?" he wondered. "Why must you be one?"

Katov didn't know. He was, but he couldn't help it. For two days they had sat in the greasy little rented room overlooking the quay . . . and he'd worried. Then the government yacht had arrived and had tied up at the buoy, and then the politician had come ashore with a flock of minor visiting dignitaries.

Secret servicemen and uniformed policemen had been pushing everywhere and everyone on the quay, and Vologin, scowling out the window, had snarled, "Lackeys—all of them. I'd like to give them something in the neck to remember me by."

Damp with nervous sweat, agitated, Katov had pushed him aside and aimed the rifle out the window, picturing his victim in the scope. It had brought the politician in as clear and lifelike as an actor on a theater screen. Katov had set the fixed reticules on the man's chest . . . then he'd stalled.

"I don't think we should do it," he'd whispered. "We're too far ahead of schedule. We'll be stuck in that deserted villa for two hours while the police are searching for us."

"What do you mean *not do it?*" Vologin had gasped. "We're not private individuals who can call the turn. We have no choice. Our orders are to shoot him when he lands. Here, give me the gun if you've lost your nerve."

But Katov had no qualms about killing. He turned back to the window and put the politician in the scope again. The man was still standing down there, shaking hands, laughing; Katov could see his lips moving . . .

And then he'd squeezed the trigger, with one convulsive movement.

As they had fled the building, they'd bumped into a woman heavy with child, coming up the stairs. Vologin had slammed by her rudely, but Katov had been careful not to touch her, had murmered, "Pardon me," in passing.

When they'd piled into the waiting car, Vologin had said, "We should have shot her, too. She'll give them our description."

But Katov had said nothing. He'd thought how odd it was that he'd just killed a man, and then immediately had bumped into a woman who was bringing a new life into the world. *I suppose that's what makes the balance,* he'd thought. But Vologin had been right. They should have killed her. And then he really began to worry.

Forty-five minutes later the road was still on the rise. The mountains were sparse, pumice-streaked, and with blotches of shrubbery like a green leprosy. Katov was sick with suspense. Beyond each new curve he expected to see a roadblock confronting them, and he kept his right hand inside his jacket fingering the butt of the Mauser that was holstered under his armpit.

Vologin was gripping the wheel as though he were thinking of an enemy's throat, but he smiled when he glanced at the worried Katov.

"You see? Like I said—no trouble. We'll be down at the villa in fifteen minutes or so."

Right then the left rear went *PLAM!* and the car veered wildly toward the edge of the cliff, Vologin fighting the wheel savagely, and Katov shouting, "Keep your foot off the brake!"

The car lurched to a jarring halt and Katov put a trembling hand to his face to wipe at his mouth. Having to shoot the politician ahead of schedule had been the first mishap; then meeting the woman with child and not killing her; and now this. *What's coming next?* He wondered. *Something is . . . I can feel it.*

Vologin swore viciously, and poked his head out the window to look back at the defunct tire.

"Would you believe it?" he muttered. "That's the first blowout I've had since the war."

Katov looked around at the mountains with a cold glow of desperation. There was a green-choked cut leading off to his right. He eyed it reflectively, tasting his lips.

Vologin turned from the window. "Well," he said decisively, "it doesn't matter. We're way ahead of our schedule anyhow. Ten minutes to change the tire won't hurt us."

"A roadblock can be erected in ten munutes also. And *that'll* hurt."

"Worry about it when we get to it, will you? Give me a hand."

But Katov's creed was caution. He'd had enough. He opened the door and let himself out. "They're looking for two men in a car," he said.

"Perhaps you can get through by yourself. I'm going to cut across country."

Vologin was stunned. "Are you mad? They'll pick you up on foot like a rabbit with a broken hindleg. Come back here!"

Katov shook his head and turned away.

"I'll meet you at the villa," he called. "Providing we both get through. Luck, good luck!"

"Katov—you're insane!"

Katov ignored the announcement. He dashed across the road and dodged into the shelter of the bushy ravine. He'd lasted ten years in the world's riskiest business; he wasn't going to throw himself away now by walking blindly into a trap. Caution, caution. Vologin was a fool who left too much to chance.

He created a dry wake of billowing dust as he worked his way down the ravine and into a shallow valley. The place was lifeless and fallow. Its agriculture had deteriorated years ago with the invasion of the Axis powers.

Katov hurried across a dead checkerboard that had once produced olives, grapes, and grain. The abandoned peasant huts were gaping ruins with tumbled-in roofs, over-grown with burdocks, splotchy with rust and decay. It suited him fine; being observed was the one thing he didn't want, right now.

He cleared the silent valley and started up the barren hills. Overhead the hazy sun smouldered like a branding iron and everything was dry dust and slipping shale. He paused, fighting for breath, and looked at his wrist watch. 3:00. It was going to be a near thing. He simply had to reach the deserted villa by four. From experience he knew that those in the yacht wouldn't wait. He cursed softly and started climbing again. At that moment he felt very underpaid and put upon, and wished that he'd gone into another profession. Something with security to it.

He stumbled onto a shaggy plain and was confronted by a great sprawling ruin—a palace once, long before the coming of Christianity. But history—other than that which concerned the organization for which he labored—meant nothing to Katov. He could see a road running below the ruins, and to save time he decided to cut through the old palace. He walked across a spoiled courtyard, up broad steps and under an archway.

He tramped heedlessly down stilled corridors, through a queen's suite and sunken baths, into chambers pock-marked and ringed with mammoth black pillars . . .

Suddenly he was lost.

He scowled, looking around at the tortuous arrangement of endless rooms and corridors. He was in a labyrinth. Silly, he said. Retrace yourself. Well . . . turn right? No, that wasn't familiar. All right, go left then. He looked at his watch. 3:20. Bad. Very bad indeed. He started walking fast. He walked for three minutes and came into a chamber with black pillars. Back to his starting point.

Katov looked at the lichenous walls desperately, tasting a sharp irony when he reminded himself that he was the man who never walked blindly into a trap.

Something incongruous to the dusty stillness of the four-thousand-year-old ruin sounded in the air. Katov started, turning his head, then recognized the sound. Car brakes squealing on the road. He heard the muted, distant slam of a car door, and he started to shout.

A voice—not too far off—answered. "Where are you?"

"Here! I can't find my way out."

"Continue to call!"

Katov went toward the voice, his right hand inside his jacket and resting on the Mauser-butt. The stranger had a car, and that was something Katov needed. He rounded a corner and almost ran full-front into a uniformed policeman.

For a dead moment they appeared to belong in the ruin as two forgotten statues. Then the policeman said, "Who are you? What are you doing in here?"

"I—I'm a tourist. I got lost."

"How did you get up here? I saw no car on the road."

Katov swallowed and managed to work out a smile. "I hiked up from the village . . . I'm staying there."

"What village? Do you mean Vikiros?"

Katov grabbed at it. "Yes."

The policeman put a hand to the top of his holster, casually.

"I'd better see your papers," he suggested. "Vikiros has been an abandoned ruin since '42."

Katov retained his smile, nodded slowly, saying, "I've got them right here, officer."

The Mauser's explosion let loose a thunder of running echoes.

The policeman went over backwards as though struck by the blast of a grenade. He was dead when he hit the aged flagstones. Only his hands continued to twitch, as if seeking something.

The man in the uniform who left the ruin and cut through the weeds down to the police car waiting on the dirt road, walked with a grim smile. The time was 3:45. That gave Katov fifteen minutes to drive to the deserted villa. Ample time. He opened the car door, slid in, and paused to adjust the officer's cap on his head. He checked his appearance in the rearview mirror. Very satisfactory. He really couldn't help chuckling as he started the engine.

The old villa was at the end of a promontory, clinging tenaciously in decay to the rocky shore. Katov drove down the wooded drive with complete confidence. He rounded a bend and saw the glimmer of limestone walls through the latticework of greenery. He was wondering if Vologin had also managed to get through when he heard a shot.

He jammed the brakes, grabbed his pistol, opened the door and crouched down in the road, looking around at the shrubbery. And then he saw another police car drawn up in the weeded drive before the old villa. A gun crashed again, somewhere.

He stalled, wondering. They couldn't be after him, not in this uniform. And they couldn't have found out about the dead policeman, because he'd hidden the body in the ruins only ten minutes ago.

Vologin must have reached the villa then, was here somewhere waiting for him. But he hadn't come alone. Somewhere along the road Vologin had picked up the law.

I knew it, Katov raged. *The careless fool! He can't keep out of trouble. And now I'll have to help him.* He went at the shrubs in a running crouch and worked his way up closer to the walls of the old villa. Then he paused catching his breath, and looked around.

He saw an armed policeman standing behind a pine tree. The officer was waving at him to get down. "I've chased one of those assassins in here," he called to Katov. "He's in that patio somewhere. Now that you're here we can circle him."

Katov nodded numbly, wishing that the policeman wasn't so far off and that he might risk a shot at him. But he couldn't afford to tip his hand until he was certain of success. Then he had an inspiration; he would pretend to capture Vologin, and when the policeman lowered his guard . . .

Katov waved and started slipping through the shrubbery around to the north end of the crumbling patio wall. He heard Vologin trade a shot with the policeman, and grinned. What a surprise this was going to be for his friend.

He edged up to the wall and raised his head to look into the patio. It was a great, wildly unkempt place, like a secret garden in a fairy tale. He saw Vologin's hunched back sixty yards away. Vologin was crouching behind an old marble statue, peering out at the shrubbery in the tense posture of a man looking for a shot.

Katov, still watching him, started to scramble over the wall. He saw Vologin straighten up suddenly and start to raise his pistol . . . but the policeman was quicker. A shot whacked out of the shrubbery, and Vologin's head snapped back. He spun around grotesquely, got twisted in his own legs and sprawled headlong onto the flagstones.

Katov couldn't believe it. Just when everything was going his way. That impetuous trigger-crazy Vologin! Still—the game wasn't over yet. Perhaps Vologin wasn't dead. But no matter, the important thing was to get close to the policeman when his guard was down and let him have it.

He started picking his way through the tangled growth hurriedly.

Vologin, blood dribbling from his mouth, raised his head and looked at Katov coming for him. He was going out in the same manner he'd lived—hating.

Katov didn't even get a chance to call before Vologin's bullet hit him high in the chest.

He slammed into the ground, tried to raise himself, tried to shout at his distant friend, but his arms turned to liquid, and the only thing that came from his mouth was a warm, briny liquid. As from far away he heard Vologin shout:

"There's something to remember me by . . . you capitalist lackey!"

58

A TASTE FOR MURDER

Jack Ritchie

"IT'S MY BELIEF that the sausage is one of the noblest inventions of mankind," Henry Chandler said. "And presented in the form of a sandwich, it is not only nourishing, but also so practical. One can conduct the process of eating without undue preoccupation. One may read, or watch, or hold a gun."

On the wall, the electric clock showed fifteen minutes after twelve noon, and except for Chandler and me, the offices were empty. He bit into the sandwich, he chewed, and he swallowed. Then he smiled. "You and my wife were discreet, Mr. Davis. Exceptionally discreet, and that now works to my advantage. I will, of course, arrange matters to make it appear that you have taken your own life. But should the police not be deceived and decide a murder has been committed, they will still be at a loss for a motive. There is nothing obvious to link you and me beyond the fact that you employ me . . . and twenty others."

I placed my cold fingers on the desk top. "Your wife will know. She'll go to the police."

"Really? I doubt it. A woman may do a great deal for her lover . . . when he is alive. But once he is dead, it is another matter. Women are intensely practical, Mr. Davis. And there is the fact that she will only *suspect* that I may have murdered you. She will not *know*. And this uncertainty, if nothing else, will prevent her from going to the police. She will tell herself, quite reasonably, that there is no reason to bring her affair with you into the open. Perhaps there are dozens of people besides me who might want you dead."

Desperation was apparent in my voice. "The police will check on everyone. They'll discover that you stayed up here after the others left."

He shook his head. "I don't think so. No one knows I'm here. I left when

345

the others did, but I returned when I knew you were alone." He chewed for a moment or two. "I decided that it would be wisest to kill you during the lunch period, Mr. Davis. That is the time in which the police would have the most difficulty in placing anyone. People eat, they wander about, or shop, and eventually they return to their work. It is almost impossible to verify . . . or disprove . . . where they claim to have been."

He reached into the brown-paper bag again. "Ordinarily I eat in any of the number of cafeterias in this neighborhood. But I am not the type who is noticed—or missed. For two weeks, Mr. Davis, I have been waiting for you to linger after the others left." He smiled. "And then this morning I noticed that you brought your lunch to the office. Did you decide that you would be too busy to go out and eat?"

I licked my lips. "Yes."

He raised the top half of the sandwich and peered at the two small sausages. "The human body reacts in peculiar ways. I understand that in moments of stress—grief, fear, anger—it often responds with hunger. And at this moment, Mr. Davis, I find myself ravenously hungry." He smiled. "Are you positive you wouldn't care for a sandwich? After all, they are yours."

I said nothing.

He wiped his lips with a paper napkin. "In his present state of evolution, man still requires meat. However, from the point of view of one with my sensitivity, there are certain obstacles to enjoying its consumption. When I am presented with a steak, for instance, I approach it timidly. Did you know that should I bite into just one morsel of gristle, I am immediately so shattered that I cannot finish the meal?"

He studied me. "Perhaps you think that I am a bit hysterical to be discussing food at a time like this?" Then he nodded almost to himself. "I don't know why I don't shoot you this instant. Is it because I enjoy these moments and wish to prolong them? Or is it because I really dread the final act?" He shrugged. "But even if I *do* dread it, let me assure you that I have every intention of going through with this."

I took my eyes off the paper bag and reached for the pack of cigarets on the desk. "Do you know where Helen is now?"

"Did you want to say goodby? Or try to have her persuade me not to do this? I'm sorry I can't arrange that, Mr. Davis. Helen left on Thursday to spend a week with her sister."

I lit a cigaret and inhaled deeply. "I have no regrets about dying. I think I'm quite even with the world and the people in it."

He tilted his head slightly, not understanding.

346

"It's happened three times," I said. "Three times. Before Helen there was Beatrice, and before Beatrice there was Dorothy."

He smiled suddenly. "Are you talking to gain time? But that will do you no actual good, Mr. Davis. I have locked the outer doors to the corridor. Should anyone return before one o'clock—which I doubt—he cannot enter. And if he is persistent and knocks, I will merely shoot you and leave by the back way."

I stared at my cigaret. "I loved Dorothy and I was certain that she loved me. We would be married. I had planned upon it. I had *expected* it. But at the last moment, she told me that she didn't love me. That she never had."

Chandler smiled and bit into the sandwich.

I listened for a moment to the street traffic outside. "I couldn't have her, but no one else could either." I looked at Chandler. "I killed her."

He blinked and stared at me. "Why are you telling me this?"

"What difference does it make now?" I dragged on the cigaret. "I killed her, but that wasn't *enough*. Do you understand, Chandler? It wasn't *enough*. I hated her. *Hated* her."

I ground out the cigaret and spoke quietly. "I brought a knife and a hacksaw. And when I was through I weighted the bag with stones and I dropped the pieces into the river."

Chandler's face had paled.

I glared at the butt in the ashtray. "And two years later I met Beatrice. She was married, but we went out together. For six months. I thought that she loved me as I loved her. But when I asked her to divorce her husband . . . to come with me . . . she laughed. She *laughed*."

Chandler had backed away a step.

I could feel perspiration on my face. "This time the hacksaw and the knife weren't enough. That wouldn't satisfy me." I leaned forward. "It was night when I took the bag to the animals. Moonlight. And I watched as they growled and tore and waited at the bars for more."

Chandler's eyes were wide.

I got up slowly. I touched the sandwich he had left on my desk and lifted up the top slice of bread. Then I smiled. "Pork casings come packed in salt, Chandler. Did you know that? In a little round carton. Fifty feet of casings for eighty-eight cents."

I put the slice of bread back in place. "Did you know that a sausage stuffer costs thirty-five dollars?"

I stared past him and smiled. "First you bone the meat and then you cut it into convenient-sized pieces. The lean, the fat, the gristle."

I met his eyes. "Your wife would not leave you, Chandler. She had been toying with me. I loved her and I hated her. More than I had ever hated anyone in the world. And I remembered the cats and how much they had enjoyed every . . .''

I looked into Chandler's horror-filled eyes. ''Where do you think Helen *really* is now?''

And then I extended the half-eaten sandwich toward him.

After the funeral, I helped Helen back to the car. When we were alone, she turned to me. ''I'm positive Henry didn't know anything about us. I just can't understand why he should kill himself, and in your office.''

I drove out of the cemetery gates and smiled. ''I don't know. Maybe it was something he ate.''

59

THE GIRL WHO JUMPED IN THE RIVER

Arthur Moore

IT WAS AFTER dark when I came along the Redding Bridge, going home from work. I was late. Usually I get out earlier, but if I had I wouldn't have met her. I only saw her because I was on the walkway right beside the railing.

She was on an iron crossbeam, just out of the water, and she was soaking wet. I figured she had tried to end it all and had got cold feet at the last minute. You see those things in the papers all the time. Anyway it sure surprised me, seeing her. I got over the rail and down there in a second and grabbed her. There wasn't anybody around. A few cars passed, crossing the bridge as I hauled her over the railing, but nobody stopped.

When I had her safe, I said, "What'd you try that for?"

She glared at me like I had something to do with it, "I like swimming," she said with a lot of sarcasm. "What'd you think?"

So I shut up. I knew she hadn't gone swimming. It was way too chilly for that.

My name is Ralph Callicut and I work across the bridge at the Ender Hardware plant, which is a wholesale place. I don't have a car, so I walk back and forth across the bridge except when the weather is bad, then I take the bus.

Well, her teeth began to chatter, of course, because she was sopping and in a very bad way. I asked her where she lived and she said in Minneapolis, which was a long way off, so I figured she meant she was a stranger in town.

What do you think? I ended up taking her to my apartment so she could get dry. By the time we got there she was a worse mess, hair all stringy and her disposition very edgy. I got the heater going; she shucked her clothes in

349

the bedroom, put on my old bathrobe and stood in front of the heater with her clothes spread out to dry.

"Jeez, Ralph," she said, "can't you make this thing hotter?"

I said it only got so hot and that was it. It was, too. I had already told her my name. She said hers was Louise, and she was hungry. I said I could make her some soup and she sighed like it would have to do.

She was looking at me very close. "I thought you were older."

"I'm twenty-three."

"Yeah? So am I. What d'you do?"

I told her I work for a hardware company. She wanted to know what I make and I told her a hundred and four take-home every week, but with a chance of advancement.

She said, "Yeah?"

So I went in and fixed her the soup. I had already eaten at Joe's Place. While the soup was heating she came in and looked around the kitchen. It is not big. I have a small pad; livingroom, bedroom and kitchen. The landlord is going to paint next year, he says.

She looked at the soup and the peanut butter on the shelves. "Is that all you eat, soup and peanut butter?"

"You want some? I got bread, too."

"No, thanks."

She had combed her hair a little. It was slightly curly with frizzy ends, a little darker than blonde. Her face was shiny and raw-looking, with lines because she was tired. With no makeup she was on the seedy side. I wondered if she had run off from a husband, but I didn't ask her. She had a snappy way of talking; she bit at you, sort of. I guessed she'd had a bad time, having to jump into the river and all.

Louise ate the soup. I made her some toast and she ate that too, even with peanut butter. She was hungrier than she thought. Then she smoked a cigarette and stared at me. "Don't you have any coffee?"

I said sure, and boiled some water and made instant.

I wasn't used to having a girl around. I never did get married, and I don't have a steady girlfirend. Girls like me OK, but I'm not pushy, you know what I mean? When I ask them for a second date they usually say, "Oh gee, Ralph, why didn't you ask me sooner? I got something to do tonight." Like that.

While we had coffee, Louise turned all her clothes over and let them dry on the other side. She smoked most of my pack and kept staring at me. She was a very rumpled doll, but I didn't say so.

Then she told me she had a suitcase.

I asked, "Where?"

"It's at a guy's house. He's keeping it for me."

"Where's the house?"

She told me. It was about a mile away. She wanted to go over and get it. She got up and said, "Why don't we go over and get it?"

I said, "OK," and we went. About halfway there I began to wonder why I was going with her, but I couldn't back out then. We walked all the way and she found the house easy. It was a tall flat; we went in and up the stairs. She knocked at a door on the second floor. A guy opened it and frowned at her. He was about my size and had a pencil behind his ear.

She said, "I came for my bag, Charlie."

I was surprised, because he had it waiting for her right by the door. He just shoved it with his foot and she looked at me, so I stepped in and picked it up. Charlie stared at me too, but he didn't say anything at all, only I kind of thought he smiled a little bit. When I backed out he slammed the door.

"He was just keeping it for me," Louise said as we went down to the street.

It was on my mind to ask her, "What next?" but she marched us right back to my pad like that was the only place to go. I didn't know what to say.

When we got inside she went right into the bedroom and flopped on the bed. "Jeez, you made me walk the whole way. My feet're killing me."

I said, "You want to go to bed?" I guess I had ideas.

She looked at me then with a kind of funny stare. "Yeah, why don't you sleep on the couch, Ralph?"

So I said, "Sure, OK." Well, what the crackers—just for one night.

In the morning, instead of eating at Joe's again, I had to rush out for milk, eggs and some bacon. Louise said she liked bacon. "Get some marmalade too, Ralph."

While we were eating she asked me what my hours were and I told her, then I asked her, "What you going to do today?" I thought maybe she had someplace to go. "You going someplace?"

She said, "Nowhere. I guess I'll stay here."

I figured she had to think things over. I gave her a couple of bucks in case she needed to get something—you know. Then I slid out.

That night when I got off, I was sure surprised to see Louise coming across the bridge to meet me. It gave me a funny feeling having a sort of pretty girl interested in me. I guess I'm not a Don Juan or anything, really.

She was looking me over when we met. She said, "Don't slouch over that way, Ralph."

I said I wouldn't and we walked back to the apartment. I hoped she had made dinner, but she hadn't. She said she thought we were going out somewhere, which was funny because I hadn't mentioned nothing. Anyhow, I took her to a beanery where they have pretty good stuff, but she didn't think too much of it. They used too much salt in everything, she said.

I asked her what she did all day and she said she slept most of the time. "Except you can't sleep real good because of all that street racket under the window."

I said I was sorry.

When I turned on the TV set, she said, "How come you still got a black and white, huh?"

After a while I made some more coffee, and when it got late I realized she was going to stay there that night, too.

So I slept on the couch again.

I thought a lot about it the next day, but when I got home that night the apartment was all changed around. Louise had gone out and bought new curtains and charged them to me at the neighborhood center where they know me. Also she got me a new pillow for the couch. "It's better for you than those two little ones."

She had a fifth of gin too, and a couple of boxes of cookies. Later, when I saw the bottle, it was down by half and the cookies were all gone.

The next time she came across the bridge to meet me after work she said the stores were still open and that she really needed a new dress because she only had one. So I took her shopping. She bought a dress, panty hose, a pair of shoes and some underwear.

"I'll get the rest later," she said.

On the way back to the bridge she noticed Manny's Hofbrau Cafe, which is a kind of ritzy spot in the little park at the end of the bridge. I had never been there. Louise said it looked a lot better than the beanery.

Dinner cost me eleven bucks; just the dinner alone. Her martinis cost a buck eighty.

That really started me thinking.

I am sort of an easygoing guy, not pushy at all. I've never been pushy with dames. But by this time I was beginning to figure that if I was letting her sleep in my bed, with me on the old lumpy couch, and buying her expensive dinners and gin and cigarettes and clothes, especially underwear, that maybe I ought to have something going *my* way. You know what I mean? It occurs to a guy. Things like that, they occur to a guy.

So, later on, when we got home and she was in the bed and I was on the old, lumpy couch—well, I got up and went into the bedroom.

Louise turned over and said, "Hey, what you doing in here?"

"I thought . . . er . . . it seemed to me—"

"Hey, Ralph, you just knock off with those ideas."

"But . . . b—but—"

"No buts. We don't hardly know each other."

So I went back to the couch and thought about that. It was sort of true. Only it did seem to me that we could speed up the learning.

I kept on thinking about it. In the morning I got up and made both breakfasts, then thought about it all the way to work. At lunch time I had to borrow a buck because I had given Louise all my dough.

When I got home she was watching TV. She had bought another bottle of gin and more cookies. After I cooked dinner and was washing up, I asked her about the gin and she bit at me again, so I didn't say nothing more. The house was in a kind of mess, so I mopped and dusted a little and she complained that I was making her sneeze.

She said, "Why don't you do that on Saturdays?"

I said, "*You* could do a little something . . . "

She looked at me and snapped, "Hey, we're not married, Ralph."

Yeah. That was true, all right.

The next day a new bed was delivered—some surprise when I got home! My old one was gone. The new one had a pinkish coverlet on it and some of those cute little rag dolls sitting at the corners. There were frilly yellow and pink curtains on the two bedroom windows.

"That old bed was saggy in the middle, Ralph."

"Oh?" I hadn't noticed that. I said I hadn't noticed it.

"You don't notice anything, Ralph. I had my hair done, too."

Then I saw it; and I also noticed the bills that were piling up. She had put them under my new pillow on the couch. They added up to a lot more than I make in a week; one bill was for two more bottles of gin.

One evening the apartment house manager stopped me in the hall and asked about something. I was edgy because I thought he'd want to raise the rent because Louise was there, but he didn't say nothing, which surprised me. He is the snappy-dresser kind of sport who plays the ponies and is very tight with a buck if the buck happened to be his. It sure surprised me, him not adding a little something to the rent. He asked me when I was going to work late next. That was all.

I happened to ask Louise if she had met him and she said, "Why don't you fix yourself up a little bit, Ralph? You don't always have to look like a grape picker."

I said, using her comeback, "Ha—ha, we're not married."

"Ha—ha, you bet. You sure are a smart aleck, Ralph."

Then the guy in the grocery store mentioned her the next time I went in, and when I left he said, "Say hello to Louise, pal. Tell her Freddie said hello."

I had been trading there a year and I didn't even know his name was Freddie.

The telephone bill was forty-seven bucks because of long-distance calls to Chicago. When I yelled, Louise said she didn't make them. She didn't know anybody in Chicago. I called the operator and she gave me a rundown when I complained.

"They were made to a party named Kostivich, sir."

I told her that was their trouble. They had made a mistake and got my phone calls mixed up with the manager's. *His* name was Kostivich, not mine. She gave me an argument, then called the supervisor who said they didn't make them kind of mistakes. I didn't get anywhere with them.

Louise said, "Jeez, don't make a big stink, Ralph."

So all this stuff was making me think more and more. I'm not dumb, you know.

Then there was the neighborhood saloon near my apartment. I hardly ever went into it, but one night I did, just to sort of have a beer and think. You know.

The bartender said, "Hey, aren't you Ralph What's-his-name?"

I said, "Yeah, why?"

He leaned an elbow on the bar and looked at me with funny little fish eyes. "Oh, nothin'." Then he moved away.

When I went out, he said, "Hey, Ralph, say hello to Louise, huh? From Butchy."

I said, "Sure, Butchy." He glowered at me.

That was one more thing that made a guy wonder.

On Friday night Louise met me outside the hardware plant when I got off work. She was wearing a new dress and shoes and looked pretty good. "You never take me nowhere, Ralph," she said. "How about us going to Manny's Hofbrau for dinner?"

I said, looking at her new stuff, "I can't afford it."

She sniffed. "Jeez, Ralph, you sure are a cheapskate."

Well, I took her, and it cost me fourteen bucks this time. She went for the Wiener-something-or-other and two martinis. Man, did she sop up the gin!

354

I had just about done all my thinking by then. I don't go off half-cocked or anything.

It was dark when we got out of the cafe and strolled back across the bridge. There wasn't any traffic at all, so I threw her over the railing into the river and went on home.

60

THE DIAMOND OF KALI

O. Henry

THE ORIGINAL NEWS item concerning the diamond of the goddess Kali was handed in to the city editor. He smiled and held it for a moment above the wastebasket. Then he laid it back on his desk and said: "Try the Sunday people; they might work something out if it."

The Sunday editor glanced the item over and said: 'H'm!'' Afterward he sent for a reporter and expanded his comment.

"You might see General Ludlow," he said, "and make a story out of this if you can. Diamond stories are a drug; but this one is big enough to be found by a scrubwoman wrapped up in a piece of newspaper and tucked under the corner of the hall linoleum. Find out first if the General has a daughter who intends to go on the stage. If not, you can go ahead with the story. Run cuts of the Kohinoor and J.P. Morgan's collection, and work in pictures of the Kimberley mines and Barney Barnato. Fill in with a tabulated comparison of the values of diamonds, radium, and veal cutlets since the meat strike; and let it run to a half page."

On the following day the reporter turned in his story. The Sunday editor let his eye sprint along its lines. "H'm!" he said again. This time the copy went into the waste-basket with scarcely a flutter.

The reporter stiffened a little around the lips; but he was whistling softly and contentedly between his teeth when I went over to talk with him about an hour later.

"I don't blame the 'old man,' " said he, magnanimously, "for cutting it out. It did sound like funny business; but it happened exactly as I wrote it. Say, why don't you fish that story out of the w.-b., and use it? Seems to me it's as good as the tommyrot you write."

I accepted the tip, and if you read further you will learn the facts about the diamond of the goddess Kali as vouched for by one of the most reliable reporters on the staff.

Gen. Marcellus B. Ludlow lives in one of those decaying but venerated old red-brick mansions in the West Twenties. The General is a member of an old New York family that does not advertise. He is a globe-trotter by birth, a gentleman by predilection, a millionaire by the mercy of Heaven, and a connoisseur of precious stones by occupation.

The reporter was admitted promptly when he made himself known at the General's residence at about eight thirty on the evening that he received the assignment. In the magnificent library he was greeted by the distinguished traveller and connoisseur, a tall, erect gentleman in the early fifties, with a nearly white mustache, and a bearing so soldierly that one perceived in him scarcely a trace of the national Guardsman. His weather-beaten countenance lit up with a charming smile of interest when the reporter made known his errand.

"Ah, you have heard of my latest find. I shall be glad to show you what I conceive to be one of the six most valuable blue diamonds in existence."

The General opened a small safe in the corner of the library and brought forth a plush-covered box. Opening this, he exposed to the reporter's bewildered gaze a huge and brilliant diamond—nearly as large as a hailstone.

"This stone," said the General, "is something more than a mere jewel. It once formed the central eye of the three-eyed goddess Kali, who is worshipped by one of the fiercest and most fanatical tribes of India. If you will arrange yourself comfortably I will give you a brief history of it for your paper."

General Ludlow brought a decanter of whisky and glasses from a cabinet, and set a comfortable armchair for the lucky scribe.

"The Phansigars, or Thugs, of India," began the General, "are the most dangerous and dreaded of the tribes of North India. They are extremists in religion, and worship the horrid Goddess Kali in the form of images. Their rites are interesting and bloody. The robbing and murdering of travellers are taught as a worthy and obligatory deed by their strange religious code. Their worship of the three-eyed goddess Kali is conducted so secretly that no traveller has ever heretofore had the honor of witnessing the ceremonies. That distinction was reserved for myself.

"While at Sakaranpur, between Delhi and Khelat, I used to explore the jungle in every direction in hope of learning something new about these mysterious Phansigars.

"One evening at twilight I was making my way through a teakwood forest, when I came upon a deep circular depression in an open space, in the centre of which was a rude stone temple. I was sure this was one of the temples of the Thugs, so I concealed myself in the undergrowth to watch.

"When the moon rose the depression in the clearing was suddenly filled with hundreds of shadowy, swiftly gliding forms. Then a door opened in the temple, exposing a brightly illuminated image of the goddess Kali, before which a white-robed priest began a barbarous incantation, while the tribe of worshippers prostrated themselves upon the earth.

"But what interested me the most was the central eye of the huge wooden idol. I could see by its flashing brilliancy that it was an immense diamond of the purest water.

"After the rites were concluded the Thugs slipped away into the forest as silently as they had come. The priest stood for a few minutes in the door of the temple enjoying the cool of the night before closing his rather warm quarters. Suddenly a dark, lithe shadow slipped down into the hollow, leaped upon the priest, and struck him down with a glittering knife. Then the murderer sprang at the image of the goddess like a cat and pried out the glowing central eye of Kali with his weapon. Straight toward me he ran with his royal prize. When he was within two paces I rose to my feet and struck him with all my force between the eyes. He rolled over senseless and the magnificent jewel fell from his hand. That is the splendid blue diamond you have just seen—a stone worthy of a monarch's crown."

"That's a corking story," said the reporter. "That decanter is exactly like the one that John W. Gates always sets out during an interview."

"Pardon me," said General Ludlow, "for forgetting hospitality in the excitement of my narrative. Help yourself."

"Here's looking at you," said the reporter.

"What I am afraid of now," said the General, lowering his voice, "is that I may be robbed of the diamond. The jewel that formed the eye of their goddess is their most sacred symbol. Somehow the tribe suspected me of having it; and members of the band have followed me half around the earth. They are the most cunning and cruel fanatics in the world, and their religious vows would compel them to assassinate the unbeliever who has desecrated their sacred treasure.

"Once in Lucknow three of their agents, disguised as servants in a hotel, endeavored to strangle me with a twisted cloth. Again, in London, two Thugs, made up as street musicians, climbed into my window at night and attacked me. They have even tracked me to this country. My life is never safe. A month ago, while I was at a hotel in the Berkshires, three of them sprang upon me from the roadside weeds. I saved myself by my knowledge of their customs.''

"How was that, General?'' asked the reporter.

"There was a cow grazing near by,'' said General Ludlow, "a gentle Jersey cow. I ran to her side and stood. The three Thugs ceased their attack, knelt and struck the ground thrice with their foreheads. Then, after many respectful salaams, they departed.''

"Afraid the cow would hook?'' asked the reporter.

"No; the cow is a sacred animal to the Phansigars. Next to their goddess they worship the cow. They have never been known to commit any deed of violence in the presence of the animal they reverence.''

"It's a mighty interesting story,'' said the reporter. "If you don't mind I'll take another drink, and then a few notes.'

"I will join you,'' said General Ludlow, with a courteous wave of his hand

"If I were you,'' advised the reporter, "I'd take that sparkler to Texas. Get on a cow ranch there, and the Pharisees—''

"Phansigars,'' corrected the General.

"Oh yes; the fancy guys would run up against a long horn every time they made a break.''

General Ludlow closed the diamond case and thrust it into his bosom.

"The spies of the tribe have found me out in New York,'' he said, straightening his tall figure. "I'm familiar with the East Indian cast of countenance, and I know that my every movement is watched. They will undoubtedly attempt to rob and murder me here.''

"Here?'' exclaimed the reporter, seizing the decanter and pouring out a liberal amount of its contents.

"At any moment,'' said the General. "But as a soldier and a connoisseur I shall sell my life and my diamond as dearly as I can.''

At this point of the reporter's story there is a certain vagueness, but it can be gathered that there was a loud crashing at the rear of the house they were in. General Ludlow buttoned his coat closely and sprang for the door. But the reporter clutched him firmly with one hand, while he held the decanter with the other.

"Tell me before we fly,'' he urged, in a voice thick with inward turmoil, "do any of your daughters contemplate going on the stage?''

"I have no daughters—fly for your life—the Phansigars are upon us!'' cried the General.

The two men dashed out of the front door of the house.

The hour was late. As their feet struck the sidewalk strange men of dark and forbidding appearance seemed to rise up out of the earth and encompass them. One with Asiatic features pressed close to the General and droned in a terrible voice:

"Buy cast clo'!"

Another, dark-whiskered and sinister, sped lithely to his side and began in a whining voice:

"Say, miser, have yer got a dime fer a poor feller what—"

They hurried on, but only into the arms of a black-eyed, dusky-browed being, who held out his hat under their noses while a confederate of Oriental hue turned the handle of a street organ nearby.

Twenty steps farther on General Ludlow and the reporter found themselves in the midst of a half dozen villainous-looking men with high-turned coat collars and faces bristling with unshaven beards.

"Run for it!" hissed the General. "They have discovered the possessor of the diamond of the goddess Kali."

The two men took to their heels. The avengers of the goddess pursued.

"Oh, Lordy!" groaned the reporter, "There isn't a cow this side of Brooklyn. We're lost!"

When near the corner they both fell over an iron object that rose from the sidewalk close to the gutter. Clinging to it desperately, they awaited their fate.

"If I only had a cow!" moaned the reporter—"or another nip from that decanter, General!"

As soon as the pursuers observed where their victims had found refuse they suddenly fell back and retreated to a considerable distance.

"They are waiting for reinforcements in order to attack us," said General Ludlow.

But the reporter emitted a ringing laugh, and hurled his hat triumphantly into the air.

"Guess again," he shouted, and leaned heavily upon the iron object. "You old fancy guys or thugs, whatever you call 'em, are up to date. Dear General, this is a pump we're stranded upon—same as a cow in New York (hic!) see? Thas'h why the 'nfuriated smoked guys don't attack us—see? Sacred an'mal, the pump in N' York, my dear General!"

But further down in the shadows of Twenty-eighth Street the maurauders were holding a parley.

"Come on, Reddy," said one. "Let's go frisk the old 'un. He's been showin' a sparkler as big as a hen egg all around Eighth Avenue for two weeks past."

"Not on your silhouette," decided Reddy. "You see 'em rallyin' round The Pump? They're friends of Bill's. Bill won't stand for nothin' of this kind in his district since he got that bid to Esopus."

This exhausts the facts concerning the Kali diamond. But it is deemed not inconsequent to close with the following brief (paid) item that appeared two days later in a morning paper.

"It is rumored that a niece of Gen. Marcellus B. Ludlow, of New York City, will appear on the stage next season.

"Her diamonds are said to be extremely valuable and of much historic interest."

61

THE PERFECT TIME FOR THE PERFECT CRIME

R. L. Stevens

"THERE IS, OF course, no such thing as a really *perfect* crime," Wadsworth was saying in that positive tone of voice that Billings had found more and more irritating the past ten years.

"I wouldn't go so far as to say that," Billings objected, deliberately stuffing his pipe once again. "Perfect crimes happen every day of the week."

"Come now, Billings, you've been reading mystery stories again!" Wadsworth shifted in the overstuffed chair like a little toad limbering up for the spring. "Do you really think it's a perfect crime simply because someone hasn't been arrested for it?"

Billings lit his pipe, still trying to keep the conversation pleasant. "Some writers on the subject claim that the really perfect crime would be the simple murder of a stranger on a dark street. Muggings, robbery—they happen all the time. Men die, and no one ever seems to be arrested."

"But those crimes are far from *perfect,*" Wadsworth insisted, "chiefly because the victim is unknown to the murderer. He only happens along at the proper time. My ideal of a really perfect crime would be one in which victim and killer know each other and in which there is a real motive for the crime. A *real* motive, not merely gain through robbery."

"Well," Billings said, "what are the real motives, other than gain? Only fear and hatred, I believe." He put down his pipe for a moment and rose to pour another bit of brandy into Wadsworth's glass. It seemed sometimes that they'd been sitting there arguing, discussing, debating all their lives. It seemed—at least, to Billings—that the center of his universe had become these Tuesday evening dinners and disagreements with this man who was no longer really his friend, who had not been his friend for a long time.

Billings wondered, when he thought about it, just how long things could

363

go on like this. Forever? They were both in their late forties. He hated to think ahead to another twenty years of Tuesday night bickerings.

"Fear!" Wadsworth snorted. "A person who kills out of fear can never commit a perfect crime! No, hatred is the only true motive that demands perfection. The hatred of a man for his wife, of a woman for her husband, or . . ."

"Yes, hatred—deep, festering hatred. But such murders happen all the time," Billings said coldly.

"All the time—but hardly in a perfect manner."

"A husband kills his wife in another man's arms; the jury frees him—the unwritten law. Perfect!"

But Wadsworth only gave another of his annoying snorts. "Far from it! an unplanned act of anger, that's all."

"But the jury frees him," Billings insisted.

"A perfect crime is not one that depends for its success on the whim of a jury."

"What about a supposedly accidental shooting—say, a hunting accident. And suppose no one can prove premeditation."

"Same objection. You must stand trial—at least, go before a grand jury. Again there is nothing certain about the outcome."

"Pretended self-defense?"

"Same objection."

"But perfect crimes *are* committed!" Billings insisted, his voice cold again.

Wadsworth only tapped a short, fat finger on the table. *"Not* deliberately. They are accidental flukes compounded by poor police work or just plain luck on the part of the murderer. I say it is impossible to plan in advance and successfully execute a cold-blooded murder so perfectly that the murderer will never even be brought to trial and will be able to continue living a normal life."

For a long time Billings was silent, deep in thought. When he finally spoke, his voice was very low. "I think, perhaps, that it's all a matter of timing, my friend. There may not be any such thing as a perfect crime, but I believe there might very well be a perfect *time*."

"A what?"

"A perfect time."

"What are you talking about?"

Billings smiled. "Let me think about it some more. We'll continue this discussion next Tuesday evening."

Wadsworth lifted himself to his feet. "That's fine by me. I have to be getting home anyway. I'll see you at the usual time."

Billings watched him go down the street. "Yes," he said, "at the usual time."

The following Tuesday was damp and stormy, with a rising wind and a promise of all-night rain. They met for dinner at the little Swiss restaurant which they had long ago agreed on for alternate Tuesdays, and then made their way along the rain-swept streets to Wadsworth's apartment.

"Out of brandy," Wadsworth said when they had settled in their chairs. "Have a little port?"

"Anything to warm me," Billings said unhappily. He'd been looking forward to the brandy. Now he'd have to wait till his own return home.

Wadsworth came in with two glasses. He looked more than ever like a toad. "Given any more thought to last week's discussion? About the perfect crime?"

"I've given it some thought."

"Decided to commit one?" Wadsworth asked, chuckling as he poured the wine from an amber bottle.

"As a matter of fact, yes."

Wadsworth kept chuckling. "That would be one way of convincing me." He put down the bottle. "I'll visit you in jail."

"I think not. I expect to be successful."

"And how soon is this great event going to take place? This week?"

"Come now, a really perfect crime takes time. Let's see—this is November fifteenth. Suppose we say within six months. Suppose we say that I will commit a perfect crime—"

"A perfect *murder*."

"—a perfect murder on or before May fifteenth of next year."

Wadsworth was laughing now. "This is getting better and better! You agree to my other conditions—that the victim must be someone you know, someone you hate?"

Billings stared hard at him over the rim of his glass. "Of course."

"And the murder must be committed under circumstances that will make you absolutely immune from prosecution?"

"Correct."

"We must have another drink on this! My, my—this will give us conversation for six months of Tuesday night sessions."

Billings watched him carefully, and nodded.

But as autumn yielded to winter, and the snow began to collect on the sidewalk, the Tuesday evening meetings grew less frequent. Billings had a cold, Billings was busy, Billings was out of town. And when Wadsworth at last took to dropping in at Billings' house unexpectedly, he found his friend deep in a mass of thick medical books, poring over pages of tiny type.

"Look," Wadsworth said at last, when spring was almost around the corner, "what in hell's the matter with you lately? All winter you've been moping around with those books."

"I have things to learn," Billings answered.

"Not about that foolish perfect–crime business! I thought you'd forgotten about it. My God, I do believe you're trying to find some unknown poison! All those books—you'd better stop this, boy—this withdrawing from reality."

But the worst was yet to come.

The following week Billings resigned from his job at the bank and seemed to withdraw into himself and away from real life even more. Wadsworth learned that his friend had been visiting a psychiatrist, and his fears for the man increased.

Then, early in April, came the final blow. One day Billings had gone completely to pieces in the psychiatrist's office, and had been committed to an institution.

The first time Wadsworth went to see Billings he could hardly believe what he saw. The doctor merely shook his head and said it was a form of schizophrenia, and that Billings would need a great deal of rest and care.

"But does he always have to stay in that room?" Wadsworth asked.

The other blinked his eyes kindly. "When the weather is better he can walk outside. Maybe in another month."

Wadsworth talked to his old friend briefly and then went away, promising to return in a few weeks.

The next time things were a bit better, and the time after that the doctor announced that Billings could accompany Wadsworth on a stroll around the grounds. It was a lovely spring day, with birds overhead and a good sampling of leaves already on the trees. Other patients were out too, seemingly unbothered by the high wall that surrounded the place, or the occasional guards that passed on the walks.

Finally, after they'd taken a path that led to the rear of the main building and into a little grove of trees, Wadsworth said, "What do you say we rest on that bench a bit? Mustn't overdo it, you know."

"What?" Billings stared around blankly. "Oh, surely. The bench."

They sat down, and Wadsworth said after an awkward silence, "Whatever happened to you, anyway? What made you go off the deep end? Was it all that medical reading you were doing?''

''I suppose so,'' Billings said, looking at his visitor steadily, his eyes and voice cold.

''Well, I'm glad to see you're better today.''

''Yes, I'm better,'' Billings answered. ''But it's a day late. I was expecting you yesterday.''

''Yesterday?''

''Today is the sixteenth of May,'' Billings said, his voice quiet now.

''Yes . . . You're not still remembering those crazy conversations we had, are you? About the perfect murder?''

Billings smiled, and there was something terrifying about it. ''I am not only remembering, but I have succeeded in it, my friend.''

''Succeeded in committing a perfect murder?''

''A perfect murder.'' Billings leaned forward, as if to tell his secret. ''Those medical books I spent so many months over—I was merely learning everything I could about schizophrenia and related mental disorders. Learning it for only one reason—so I could fake all this!''

''Fake? Fake what?'' Wadsworth pulled back a bit on the bench.

''Fake this insanity, of course. I spoke to you of the perfect time, didn't I? Well, this it it! The perfect time to commit the perfect murder is when you're confined to an institution and certified legally insane.''

Wadsworth opened his mouth—but no words came out.

Billings leaned closer and said, ''They can't even try me for it. And in a year or so I'll suddenly begin to show signs of recovery. Shortly after that I'll be released, free as a bird—and I'll have committed the perfect crime!''

Wadsworth started to rise, but already Billings' left hand was pulling him down.

''Who are you going to kill?'' Wadsworth asked, his voice shaky.

Billings' other hand shot out from under his jacket. The hand was holding a stained and weathered knife whose blade was narrow from prolonged sharpening.

''Why, you, of course,'' Billings said with almost a chuckle. ''I thought you knew.''

Wadsworth twisted away. ''Where did you get that knife?''

''I stole it from the craft shop. I've had a long time to plan this—a long time for my hatred.''

The knife glistened suddenly as the sun caught the sweep and thrust of the blade.

* * *

The doctor shook his head sadly and looked away. "A terrible thing, terrible! And I thought he was coming along so well!"

They were sitting in the doctor's office, waiting for the police to arrive, with the bloodstained knife on the desk between them. "Don't you think we should have left the knife in the body, Doctor?"

"You needn't worry," the doctor answered reassuringly. "The police won't even press charges when they hear what happened. After all, Billings was legally insane when they brought him here."

"Still, it's an awful thing to kill a man."

"But it was self-defense. You had no choice, Mr. Wadsworth."

Wadsworth nodded sadly, all the time thinking how much simpler the knife had made things. It hadn't even been necessary to use the gun he had brought along—to satisfy his own long-festering hatred.

62

"YOU LISTEN!"

Norbert Davis and Dwight V. Babcock

HE WAS A small man, not old and not young, either, with a look of shadowy, indefinable vagueness about him. He sat down in the big chair in front of the desk and smiled uncertainly, while his eyes stayed round and worried and a little embarrassed. He took a worn wallet from his hip pocket, extracted three worn dollar bills, and pushed them across the desk with nervous little jerks.

"That—that's right?"

Chalmers Boone slowly nodded his head. It was a long, aristocratic head that went with his broad shoulders and his straight, tall body. His eyes were a deep, shadowy blue, and they were calculating and knowing and wise in many things.

"Three dollars is right," he said softly. "That is my fee, and for it you may talk for an hour on whatever subject you wish. Anything you say will be held confidential."

"About that, I wouldn't care," said the small man glumly. "Nobody wants to hear my troubles, even if they could. Otherwise, would I be paying you to listen? No. Everybody else I try to tell my troubles to, and what happens? So as soon as I start, they start telling me *their* troubles! Do I want to hear about somebody else's troubles? Ha! They should hear *mine* once!" He stopped and looked suspiciously at Chalmers Boone. "*You* ain't got no troubles you want I should hear, have you?"

Chalmers Boone smiled faintly, and the lines around his mouth became deep, hard semi-circles. "No. None that I want to tell you about."

"Good!" said the small man. He drew a deep breath, and his voice took on a dolorous, whining note. "So my name is Jacob Watt. I own an apartment building down on the east side, and until you got yourself an apartment building you wouldn't know nothing about troubles. Them tenants! I tear my hair when I even think about it. Tenants! There should be a law! And if it ain't them it's taxes and assessments and street improvements and water pipes leaking and the Fire Department yelling about the fire escapes and the Health Department yelling about air space. And murders!''

"Murders?" Chalmers Boone inquired politely.

"Isn't it enough troubles I got collecting my rent from a bunch of no-good property-destroying tenants, without they get murdered, too, and give my place a worse name than it's got now?''

"Someone was murdered in your apartment house?''

"Hah! I should tell you! In the papers, all over the front pages, with pictures! In 205 they live, them two Schaffers. So old you'd think maybe they was a couple of mummies on the loose. And tight like a can of sardines! What screaming they would scream when I collect the rent, and me losing money on the deal. So old man Schaffer, he finally dies as nice and peaceful as pie, and what does he leave his wife?''

"What?" Boone asked.

"Twenty-five thousand dollars worth of insurance is what! And would she invest in some nice stock I got which I would personally guarantee? No! She laughs and slams the door in my face! But that ain't enough she could do. Oh, no! She won't put the money in a bank on account she don't trust them, so she gets murdered and gets it stolen!''

Chalmers Boone moved slightly in his chair. "Have the police found the person who murdered her and stole her money?''

"Hah!" said Jacob Watt eloquently. "Them bums! They couldn't find who did it was he lit up like a neon sign. No! All they can do is make dirty cracks and push me around. And it ain't enough that out of all the places in the city she has to pick mine to get murdered in! On top of that, she gets me sued!''

"Sued?" Boone repeated.

"Yup. With papers served on me. Look, across the hall lives a weasel by the name of Pickering. Mrs. Schaffer, she's so tight that she won't even buy a paper—her with twenty-five thousand dollars!—and so she sneaks his every morning and reads it and puts it back. Only she don't always fold it right, and this weasel of a Pickering suspects. So he watches and sees. So he won't pay for his paper!''

"What has that to do with you getting sued?" Boone asked.

"I'm telling you! I put in his subscription, so now they tell me if he don't pay, then I got to. They sue me in the Small Claims Court!''

370

"Pickering is primarily liable, I should think," Boone said. "How can he prove that Mrs. Schaffer read his paper?"

"He can do that too, the weasel. The morning before she was killed, she takes it and tears a piece out of it before she puts it back. Pickering, he's got that torn paper, and he says that proves it on account it destroyed the paper's value to him and on account he will prove it by her fingerprints on it. He won't pay. Fifteen dollars he owes! A whole year's subscritption!"

Jacob Watt sank back, looking drearily exhausted. He made a discouraged gesture.

"So it's all said now, and I thought it would maybe give me some relief in the head. But it's only worse on account it sounds more terrible to me when I'm saying it."

"Haven't you got any more troubles?"

Jacob Watt stared, aghast. "More! *More!* You want I should have more than I already got?"

"No. But you've only used a part of your hour." Boone hesitated, tapping his long, strong fingers on the desk top. "Your story about Pickering and the Schaffers has interested me. Suppose, instead of merely wasting the rest of this fee you paid me, I go down and call on Mr. Pickering. Perhaps a third party, like myself, could make him see reason. After all, although it must have been irritating to have Mrs. Schaffer reading his paper on the sly, it hasn't hurt him any. He got the use of the paper, too. I'll talk to him for a few moments this evening."

"You could talk," said Jacob Watt gloomily, "but it won't do no good. That Pickering is nothing but a snake in the weeds.

There was a light at the top of the stairs—one round yellow dusty globe that looked as old as the walls and as mouldy as the strip of brownish carpet that ran raggedly back into the crawling shadows of the hall. Boone's feet creaked a little on the top step, and his nostrils seemed to pinch themselves together, trying instinctively to shut out the close thickness of the air, heavy with the odors of many years and many people.

He had to lean close to find the numerals on the faded door, and then he tapped lightly with his knuckles. While he waited, he took off his leather gloves and kneaded the long, strong fingers of his right hand, the muscular pad of his palm.

The door opened a cautious inch.

"Mr. Pickering?" Boone said.

"Uh. What d'you want?"

"My name is Boone. I came to speak to you about the paper."

The door didn't open further.

"Ain't no use talkin'. I ain't gonna pay."

"If I could come in for a moment I'm sure what I have to say would interest you."

"Uh." The voice was unwilling and unconvinced, but the door slid back jerkily. "All right. Come on."

The one room was indescribably littered and filthy, with the covers on the bed in a grayish-dirty pile and a scummy milk bottle thrown unheedingly in one corner. There was the thickly pungent smell of dirty clothes.

"Well?" said Pickering. "Well?"

He was a thin, bent man, and he had the same grayish look of uncleanliness as the rest of the room. He was wearing a shirt that was opened at its stained collar and at its black trousers. His feet were bare, and his scanty hair stuck up in a tuft on top of his head. Behind steel-rimmed spectacles, his eyes were small and bright and shiftily malicious.

Boone leaned his back against the closed door. "The woman who was murdered—Mrs. Schaffer—lived across the hall?"

Pickering squinted suspiciously. "Yeah. So what?"

"You were here the night she was killed?"

"Yeah."

"You didn't hear anything or see anything suspicious?"

"No! I told the police that."

Boone nodded slowly and put his gloves in his coat pocket. "I can understand your claim she had been stealing your paper and reading it. Can you prove that?"

"Sure." Pickering jerked his thumb to indicate a newspaper folded carefully in the midst of the litter on the dresser top. "Right there. It's got a piece tore out of it, and her fingerprints will be on it. I can prove it all right, if I have to. And I ain't gonna pay for the paper!"

"No," said Boone. "You're not."

His fist shot up in an incredibly quick, expert arc. The sound of it hitting Pickering's jaw was a sharp slap. He half turned with his arms sawing out wildly fell sprawling across the bed, and Boone knelt on him, holding him with his knees, pushing his head down into the wadded disorder of the covers. Pickering's legs threshed wildly and vainly, and the long, smooth fingers of Boone's right hand slid around the corded scrawniness of his neck and squeezed very slowly.

"That's all," said a voice. "Get up, Boone."

Boone turned his head and saw Jacob Watt standing in the open doorway into the hall. He still was as small as before, but he no longer gave the impression of smallness, nor vagueness, either, and there was a blunt, thick-cylindered police revolver in his right hand.

"Get up," he said.

Boone got slowly to his feet. His hands were hanging loose at his sides with the fingers moving just a little. Pickering made choking noises, twisting his head painfully.

"Sorry," Watt said to him. "He moved too fast, even if I was expecting it."

Boone slid one foot forward. "I don't know—" he murmured. His fingers were twitching, and he was watching the gun in Jacob Watt's hand with deadly concentration.

"Quit it," said Jacob Watt. "You're quick, but a bullet is a lot quicker. My name is still Jacob Watt but now I'm a detective on the Homicide Squad, and I'm arresting you for the murder of Mrs. Heinrich Schaffer,"

Boone said thickly: "You can't—"

"Shut up," Jacob Watt ordered. "This is one time you listen without getting paid for it. Mrs. Schaffer came to you to ask you to listen to her troubles. You heard about the twenty-five thousand and how she was afraid of banks. That was your chance, and you took it. You killed her and got the money. You cleaned up pretty well afterward. You knew how she had come to call on you. She showed you your advertisement, torn out of a newspaper. You took that back when you killed her. But you never thought that she might have torn the ad out of someone else's paper. When I told you, you knew you had to get the rest of that paper, because the rest gave you away just as much as the ad itself did. You knew the police would be interested if they heard. Well—they heard."

Boone didn't say anything.

Jacob Watt watched him closely.

"Yeah. This time, Boone, you ran up against some expert competition. The police were acting as Professional Listeners before anyone else ever thought of doing it."

63

THE MYSTERY OF CHANCE

Melville Davisson Post

IT WAS A night like a pit. The rain fell steadily. Now and then a gust of wind rattled the shutters, and the tavern sign, painted with the features of George the Third, now damaged by musket-balls and with the eyes burned out, creaked.

The tavern sat on the bank of the Ohio. Below lay the river and the long, flat island, where the ill-starred Blennerhasset had set up his feudal tenure. Flood water covered the island and spread everywhere—a vast sea of yellow that enveloped the meadow-lands and plucked at the fringe of the forest.

The scenes in the tavern were in striking contrast. The place boomed with mirth, shouts of laughter, ribald tales and songs. The whole crew of the *Eldorado* of New Orleans banqueted in the guest-room of the tavern. This was the guest-room for the public. Beyond it and facing the river was the guest-room for the gentry, with its floor scrubbed with sand, its high-boy in veneered mahogany, its polished andirons and its various pretensions to a hostelry of substance.

At a table in this room, unmindful of the bedlam beyond him, a man sat reading a pamphlet. He leaned over on the table, between two tall brass candlesticks, his elbows on the board, his thumb marking the page. He had the dress and manner of a gentleman—excellent cloth in his coat, a rich stock and imported linen. On the table sat a top hat of the time, and in the corner by the driftwood fire was a portmanteau with silver buckles, strapped up as for a journey. The man was under forty, his features regular and clean-cut; his dark brows joined above eyes big and blue and wholly out of place in the olive skin.

Now and then he got up, went over to the window and looked out, but he was unable to see anything, for the rain continued and the puffs of wind. He seemed disturbed and uneasy. He drummed on the sill with his fingers, and then, with a glance at his portmanteau, returned to his chair between the two big tallow candles.

From time to time the tavern-keeper looked in at the door with some servile inquiry. This interruption annoyed the guest.

"Damme, man," he said, "are you forever at the door?"

"Shall I give the crew rum, sir?" the landlord asked.

"No," replied the man; "I will not pay your extortions for imported liquor."

"They wish it, sir."

The man looked up from his pamphlet.

"They wish it, eh," he said with nice enunciation. "Well, Mr. Castoe, I do not!"

The soft voice dwelt on the "Mr. Castoe" with ironical emphasis. The mobile upper lip, shadowed with a silken mustache, lifted along the teeth with a curious feline menace.

The man was hardly over his table before the door opened again. He turned abruptly, like a panther, but when he saw who stood in the door, he arose with a formal courtesy.

"You are a day early, Abner," he said. "Are the Virginia wagons in for their salt and iron?"

"They will arrive tomorrow," replied my uncle; "the roads are washed out with the rains."

The man looked at my uncle, his hat and his greatcoat splashed with mud.

"How did you come?" he asked.

"Along the river," replied my uncle, "I thought to find you on the *Eldorado*."

"On the *Eldorado!*" cried the man. "On such a night, when the Tavern of George the Third has a log fire and kegs in the cellar!"

My uncle entered, closed the door, took off his greatcoat and hat, and sat down by the hearth.

"The boat looked deserted," he said.

"To the last nigger," said the man. "I could not take the comforts of the tavern and deny them to the crew."

My uncle warmed his hands over the snapping fire.

"A considerate heart, Byrd," he said, with some deliberation, "is a fine quality in a man. But how about the owners of your cargo, and the company that insures your boat?"

"The cargo, Abner," replied the man, "is in Benton's warehouse, unloaded for your wagons. The boat is tied up in the back-water. No log can strike it.''

He paused and stroked his clean-cut aristocratic jaw.

"The journey down from Fort Pitt was damnable,'' he added, ''—miles of flood water, yellow and running with an accursed current. It was no pleasure voyage, believe me, Abner. There was the current running logs, and when we got in near the shore, the settlers fired on us. A careless desperado, your settler, Abner!''

"More careless, Byrd, do you think,'' replied my uncle, ''than the river captain who overturns the half-submerged cabins with the wash of his boat?''

"The river,'' said the man, ''is the steamboat's highway.''

"And the cabin,'' replied my uncle, ''is the settler's home.''

"One would think,'' said Byrd, ''that this home was a palace and the swamp land a garden of the Hesperides, and your settler a King of the Golden Mountains. My stacks are full of bullet holes.''

My uncle was thoughtful by the fire.

"This thing will run into a river war,'' he said. ''There will be violence and murder done.''

"A war, eh!'' echoed the man. ''I had not thought of that, and yet, I had but now an ultimatum. When we swung in tonight, a big backwoodsman came out in a canoe and delivered an oration. I have forgotten the periods, Abner, but he would burn me at the stake, I think, and send the boat to Satan, unless I dropped down the river and came in below the settlement.''

He paused and stroked his jaw again with that curious gesture.

"But for the creature's command,'' he added, ''I would have made the detour. But when he threatened, I ran in as I liked and the creature got a ducking for his pains. His canoe went bottom upward, and if he had not been a man of oak, he would have gone himself to Satan.''

"And what damage did you do?'' inquired my uncle.

"Why, no damage, as it happened,'' said the man. ''Some cabins swayed, but not one of them went over. I looked, Abner, for a skirmish in your war. There was more than one rifle at a window. If I were going to follow the river,'' he continued, ''I would mount a six-pounder.''

"You will quit the river, then,'' remarked my uncle.

"It is a dog's life, Abner,'' said the man. ''To make a gain in these days of Yankee trading, the owner must travel with his boat. Captains are a trifle too susceptible to bribe. I do not mean goldpieces, slipped into the hand, but the hospitalities of the shopkeeper. Your Yankee, Abner, sees no difference in men, or he will waive it for a sixpence in his till. The captain is banqueted at his house, and the cargo is put on shore. One cannot sit in comfort at New Orleans and trade along the Ohio.''

"Is one, then, so happy in New Orleans?" asked my uncle.

"In New Orleans, no," replied the man, "but New Orleans is not the world. The world is in Piccadilly, where one can live among his fellows like a gentleman, and see something of life—a Venetian dancer, ladies of fashion, and men who dice for something more than a trader's greasy shillings.''

Byrd again got up and went to the window. The rain and gusts of wind continued. His anxiety seemed visibly to increase.

My uncle arose and stood with his back to the driftwood fire, his hands spread out to the flame. He glanced at Byrd and at the pamphlet on the table, and the firm muscles of his mouth hardened into an ironical smile.

"Mr. Evlyn Byrd," he said, "what do you read?"

The man came back to the table. He sat down and crossed one elegant knee over the other.

"It is an essay by the Englishman, Mill," he said, "reprinted in the press that Benjamin Franklin set up at Philadelphia. I agree with Lord Fairfax where the estimable Benjamin is concerned: 'Damn his little maxims! They smack too much of New England!' But his press gives now and then an English thing worth while.''

"And why is this English essay worth while?" asked my uncle.

"Because, Abner, in its ultimate conclusions, it is a justification of a gentleman's most interesting vice. 'Chance,' Mr. Mill demonstrates, 'is not only at the end of all our knowledge, but it is also at the beginning of all our postulates.' We begin with it, Abner, and we end with it. The structure of all our philosophy is laid down on the sills of chance and roofed over with the rafters of it.''

"The Providence of God, then," said my uncle, "does not come into Mr. Mill's admirable essay.''

Mr. Evlyn Byrd laughed.

"It does not, Abner," he said. "Things happen in this world by chance, and this chance is no aide-de-camp of your God. It happens unconcernedly to all men. It has no rogue to ruin and no good churchman, pattering his prayers, to save. A man lays his plans according to the scope and grasp of his intelligence, and his chance comes by to help him or to harm him, as it may happen, with no concern about his little morals, and with no divine intent.''

"And so you leave God out," said my uncle, with no comment.

"And why not, Abner?" replied the man. "Is there any place in this scheme of nature for His intervention? Why, sir, the intelligence of man that your Scriptures so despise can easily put His little plan of rewards and punishments out of joint. Not the good, Abner, but the intelligent, possess the earth. The man who sees on all sides of his plan, and hedges it about with wise precaution, brings it to success. Every day the foresight of men outwits your God.''

My uncle lifted his chin above his wet stock. He looked at the window with the night banked behind it, and then down at the refined and elegant gentleman in the chair beside the table, and then at the strapped-up portmanteau in the corner. His great jaw moved out under the massive chin. From his face, from his manner, he seemed about to approach some business of vital import. Then, suddenly, from the room beyond there came a great boom of curses, a cry that the dice had fallen against a platter, a blow and a gust of obscenities and oaths.

My uncle extended his arm toward the room.

''Your gentleman's vice,'' he said; ''eh, Mr. Byrd!''

The man put out a jeweled hand and snuffed the candles.

''The vice, Abner, but not the gentlemen.''

Mr. Byrd flicked a bit of soot from his immaculate sleeve. Then he made a careless gesture.

''These beasts,'' he said, ''are the scum of New Orleans. They would bring any practice into disrepute. One cannot illustrate a theory by such creatures. Gaming, Abner, is the diversion of a gentleman; it depends on chance, even as all trading does. The Bishop of London has been unable to point out wherein it is immoral.''

''Then,'' said Abner, ''the Bishop does little credit to his intelligence.''

''It has been discussed in the coffee-houses of New Orleans,'' replied Mr. Byrd, ''and no worthy objection found.''

''I think I can give you one,'' replied my uncle.

''And what is your objection, Abner?'' asked the man.

''It has this objection, if no other,'' replied my uncle, ''it encourages a hope of reward without labor, and it is this hope, Byrd, that fills the jail house with weak men, and sets strong ones to dangerous ventures.''

He looked down at the man before him, and again his iron jaw moved.

''Byrd,'' he said, ''under the wisdom of God, labor alone can save the world. It is everywhere before all benefits that we could enjoy. Every man must till the earth before he can eat of its fruits. He must fell the forest and let in the sun before his grain will ripen. He must spin and weave. And in his trading he must labor to carry his surplus stuff to foreign people, and to bring back what he needs from their abundance. Labor is the great condition

379

of reward. And your gentleman's vice, Byrd, would annul it and overturn the world.''

But the man was not listening to Abner's words. He was on his feet and again before the window. He had his jaw gathered into his hand. The man swore softly, ''What disturbs you, Byrd?'' said my uncle.

He stood unmoving before the fire, his hands to the flame.

The man turned quickly.

''It is the night, Abner—wind and driving rain. The devil has it!''

''The weather, Byrd,'' replied my uncle, ''happens in your philosophy by chance, so be content with what it brings you, for this chance regards, as you tell me, no man's plans; neither the wise man nor the fool hath any favor of it.''

''Nor the just nor the unjust, Abner.''

My uncle looked down at the floor. He locked his great bronze fingers behind his massive back.

''And so you believe, Byrd,'' he said. ''Well, I take issue with you. I think this thing you call 'chance' is the Providence of God, and I think it favors the just.''

''Abner,'' cried the man, now turning from the window, ''if you believe that, you believe it without proof.''

''Why, no,'' replied my uncle; ''I have got the proof on this very night.''

He paused a moment; then he went on.

''I was riding with the Virginia wagons,'' he said, ''on the journey here. It was my plan to come on slowly with them, arriving on the morrow. But these rains fell; the road on this side of the Hills was heavy; and I determined to leave the wagons and ride in tonight.

''Now, call this what you like—this unforeseen condition of the road, this change of plan. Call it 'chance,' Byrd!''

Again he paused and his big jaw tightened.

''But it is no chance, sir, nor any accidental happening that Madison of Virginia, Simon Carroll of Maryland and my brother Rufus are upright men, honorable in their dealings and fair before the world.

''Now, sir, if this chance, this chance of my coming on tonight before the Virginia wagons, this accidental happening, favored Madison, Simon Carroll and my brother Rufus as though with a direct and obvious intent, as though with a clear and preconceived design, you will allow it to me as a proof, or, at least, Mr. Evlyn Byrd, as a bit of evidence, as a sort of indisputable sign, that honorable men, men who deal fairly with their fellows, have some favor of these inscrutable events.''

380

The man was listening now with a careful attention. He came away from the window and stood beside the table, his clenched fingers resting on the board.

"What do you drive at, Abner?" he asked.

My uncle lifted his chin above the big wet stock.

"A proof of my contention, Byrd," he answered.

"But your story, Abner? What happened?"

My uncle looked down at the man.

"There is no hurry, Byrd," he said; "the night is but half advanced and you will not now go forward on your journey."

"My journey!" echoed the man. "What do you mean?"

"Why, this," replied my uncle: "that you would be setting out for Piccadilly, I imagine, and the dancing women, and the gentlemen who live by chance. But as you do not go now, we have ample leisure for our talk."

"Abner," cried Mr. Byrd, "what is this riddle?"

My uncle moved a little in his place before the fire.

"I left the Virginia wagons at midday," he went on; "night fell in the flat land; I could hardly get on; the mud was deep and the rains blew. The whole world was like the pit.

"It is a common belief that a horse can see on any night, however dark, but this belief is error, like that which attributes supernatural perception to the beast. My horse went into the trees and the fence; now and then there was a candle in a window, but it did not lighten the world; it served only to accentuate the darkness. It seemed impossible to go forward on a strange road, now flooded. I thought more than once to stop in at some settler's cabin. But mark you, Byrd, I came on. Why? I cannot say. 'Chance,' Mr. Evlyn Byrd, if you like. I would call it otherwise. But no matter."

He paused a moment, and then continued:

"I came in by the river. It was all dark like the kingdom of Satan. Then, suddenly, I saw a light and your boat tied up. This light seemed somewhere inside, and its flame puzzled me. I got down from my horse and went onto the steamboat. I found no one, but I found the light. It was a fire just gathering under way. A carpenter had been at work; he had left some shavings and bits of candle, and in this line of rubbish the fire had started."

The man sat down in his chair beside the two tallow candles.

"Fire!" he said. "Yes, there was a carpenter at work in my office cabin today. He left shavings, and perhaps bits of candle, it is likely. Was it in my office cabin?"

"Along the floor there," replied my uncle, "beginning to flame up."

"Along the floor!" repeated Mr. Byrd. "Then nothing in my cabin was burned? The wall desk, Abner, with the long mahogany drawer—it was not burned?"

He spoke with an eager interest.

"It was not burned," replied my uncle. "Did it contain things of value?"

"Of great value," returned the man.

"You leave, then, things of value strangely unprotected," replied my uncle. "The door was open."

"But not the desk, Abner. It was securely locked. I had that lock from Sheffield. No key would turn it but my own."

Byrd sat for some moments unmoving, his delicate hand fingering his chin, his lips parted. Then as with an effort, he got back his genial manner.

"I thank you, Abner," he said. "You have saved my boat. And it was a strange coincidence that brought you there to do it."

Then he flung back in his big chair with a laugh.

"But your theory, Abner? This chance event does not support it. It is not the good or Christian that this coincidence has benefited. It is I, Abner, who am neither good nor Christian."

My uncle did not reply. His face remained set and reflective.

The rain beat on the window-pane, and the drunken feast went on in the room beyond him.

"Byrd," he said, "how do you think that fire was set? A half-burned cigar dropped by a careless hand, or an enemy?"

"An enemy, Abner," replied the man. "It will be the work of these damned settlers. Did not their envoy threaten if I should come in, to the peril of their cabins? I gave them no concern then, but I was wrong in that. I should have looked out for their venom. Still, they threaten with such ease and with no hand behind it that one comes, in time, to take no notice of their words."

He paused and looked up at the big man above him.

"What do you think, Abner? Was the fire set?"

"One cannot tell from the burning rubbish," replied my uncle.

"But your opinion, Abner?" said the man. "What is your opinion?"

"The fire was set," replied my uncle.

Byrd got up at that, and his clenched hand crashed on the table.

"Then, by the kingdom of Satan, I will overturn every settler's cabin when the boat goes out tomorrow."

My uncle gave no attention to the man's violence.

"You would do wanton injury to innocent men," he said. "The settlers did not fire your boat."

"How can you know that, Abner?"

My uncle changed. Vigor and energy and an iron will got into his body and his face.

"Byrd," he said, "we had an argument just now; let me recall it to your attention. You said 'chance' happened equally to all, and I that the Providence of God directs it. If I had failed to come on tonight, the boat would have burned. The settlers would have taken blame for it. And Madison of Virginia, Simon Carroll of Maryland and my brother Rufus, whose company at Baltimore insure your boat, would have met a loss they can ill afford."

His voice was hard and level like a sheet of light.

"Not you, Byrd, who, as you tell me, are neither good nor Christian, but these men, who are, would have settled for this loss. Is it the truth—eh, Mr. Evlyn Byrd?"

The man's big blue eyes widened in his olive skin.

"I should have claimed the insurance, of course, as I had the right to do," he said coldly, for he was not in fear. "But, Abner—"

"Precisely!" replied my uncle. "And now, Mr. Evlyn Byrd, let us go on. We had a further argument. You thought a man in his intelligence could outwit God. And, sir, you undertook to do it! With your crew drunken here, the boat deserted, the settlers to bear suspicion and your portmanteau packed up for your journey overland to Baltimore, you watched at that window to see the flames burst out."

The man's blue eyes—strange, incredible eyes in that olive skin—were now hard and expressionless as glass. His lips moved, and his hand crept up toward a bulging pocket of his satin waistcoat.

Grim, hard as iron, inevitable, my uncle went on:

"But you failed, Byrd! God outwitted you! When I put that fire out in the rubbish, the cabin was dark, and in the dark, Byrd, there, I saw a gleam of light shining through the keyhole of your wall desk—the desk that you alone can open, that you keep so securely locked. Three bits of candle were burning in that empty drawer."

The man's white hand approached the bulging pocket.

And my uncle's voice rang as over a plate of steel.

"Outwit God!" he cried. "Why, Byrd, you had forgotten a thing that any schoolboy could have told you. You had forgotten that a bit of candle in a drawer, for lack of air, burns more slowly than a bit outside. Your pieces set to fire the rubbish were consumed, but your pieces set in that locked drawer to make sure—to outwit God, if, by chance, the others failed—were burning when I burst the lid off.''

The man's nimble hand, lithe like a snake, whipped a derringer out of his bulging pocket.

But, quicker than that motion, quicker than light, quicker than the eye, my uncle was upon him. The derringer fell harmless to the floor. The bones of the man's slender fingers snapped in an iron palm.. And my uncle's voice, big, echoing like a trumpet, rang above the storm and the drunken shouting:

''Outwit God! Why, Mr. Evlyn Byrd, you cannot outwit me, who am the feeblest of His creatures!''

64

THE MAN WHO SWALLOWED A HORSE

Craig Rice

"THE MAN WAS killed," John J. Malone, the famous criminal lawyer, said, "in a particularly vicious manner. Mr. Duck was scared to death by his psychiatrist."

"Nonsense," Homicide Captain von Flanagan growled. He paused. They looked at the late Mr. Duck, who had just been moved from the operating room. Where is Dr. Nash, anyway?"

"He's lying down," the white-faced nurse said. "The shock—" she gulped. "Of course we knew Mr. Duck had a bad heart, but no one thought—it was really just a harmless little joke. I mean, it was meant to be one."

She added, "Mrs. Duck is in the doctor's office with him."

The little attorney and von Flanagan took a last glance at the dead Mr. Duck. He had been a portly man with a broad face that had once been red and thick-veined. A small incision had been made in his abdomen, hardly more than a scratch.

"He just suddenly gasped and died," the nurse said. Her eyes narrowed. "Dr. Nash and Mrs. Duck are great friends."

Malone looked her over. A pretty little thing she was, with reddish gold hair and a sweet mouth.

"Let's go into the office," von Flanagan said. "Malone, how did you get into this?"

"Mr. Duck was my client," Malone said. He told me he was going to this psychiatrist his wife recommended. For an operation. Because he'd swallowed a horse."

"Malone," the police officer said sharply, "you've been drinking."

"Mr. Duck was positive he'd swallowed a horse," the little counselor-at-law said stubbornly. He added reminiscently, "I remember once when you thought you had a mouse in your mouth."

Von Flanagan growled and pushed open the door to the office. Dr. Nash was supine on the couch, his handsome face pale. Mrs. Duck sat beside him, holding his hand.

She jumped up, startled, and cried out, "It wasn't anyone's fault."

The doctor said, "Mr. Duck was convinced he had swallowed a horse. We decided to practice a harmless little deception. We put him under anesthesia, made a slight incision, and before he came to, we led a horse into the operating room. Hardly conventional procedure, but—well, I explained to him we'd operated and extracted the horse, and he would be as good as new. Mr Duck took one look at the horse and—just died."

"It was murder," Malone said. "You knew about his heart—you knew the slightest shock would kill him. And if I'm not mistaken, you and the charming Mrs. Duck have plans for the future."

"Prove it," Mrs. Duck said angrily.

"I can," Malone said. "He told me all about it in a letter . . . all about this ailment and the planned operation. What he didn't know about was the gimmick you had in mind. That was what murdered him."

Later, sitting in Joe the Angel's City Hall Bar, von Flanagan growled, "I still think you made it all up."

"Naturally," Malone said, signaling for two more gins. "But it scared Dr. Nash, who isn't such a stable character, into breaking down and telling you the truth. A signed confession, no less. And you pay for the next drink."

"If he changes his mind," the police officer said gloomily, "It's going to be hell selling this story to a jury." He scowled into his glass. "Tell me the truth, Malone, or you pay for the next drink."

"Mr. Duck really did think he'd swallowed a horse," Malone told him. "He really did have a fixation. And he did think that the operation was going to make him as good as new."

"But why did he drop dead the minute he looked at the horse?" von Flanagan demanded.

"Because," Malone said patiently, "the horse in the operating room was a white horse. The horse Mr. Duck thought he'd swallowed was a black one."

65

THE PROMISE

Marilyn Granbeck

HERBIE LOVED THE car. With a car like this, he could go anywhere. With a car like this, no one would laugh at him. The boys on the street would stop talking, and look at him. Even the girls would want to know him.

He hunched over the wheel, his eyes intent on a spot just beyond the smooth curve of the hood. His foot pressed the accelerator, and he let his eyes flick across the instrument panel for an instant. Deep in his throat he made a rumbling sound to imitate the engine of the big car. Joy raced through him.

Vroom! Herbie heard the roar of the exhaust as he gunned the motor. This car could make him free! This car could take him—

"Herbie!"

He yanked his foot from the gas pedal and slammed it on the brake, then focused his eyes on the garage wall directly in front of him until his stepfather spoke again.

"Get out!" Steve jerked the car door and motioned angrily. His face was red, and Herbie knew Steve was mad. He stepped out onto the garage floor. He looked down, trying to wish himself someplace else, anyplace where he wouldn't have to listen to Steve yell at him.

"How many times have I told you to stay away from that car? I warned you last time. *Stay away from my car,* I said. You told me you understood, didn't you?"

Herbie nodded. He had understood, too. He'd meant it when he promised not to play in the car, but somehow he forgot again. He didn't want to make Steve angry or see the hurt look on Momma's face. More than anything, Herbie wanted everyone to be happy.

Steve slammed the car door. "You and your promises! I should have known better than to believe you'd remember." He pulled open the basement door and shoved Herbie up the stairs ahead of him. "Upstairs! We're going to settle this once and for all."

Herbie stumbled and almost fell. He grabbed the rail, hoping Steve wouldn't notice and start yelling about how clumsy he was. It was just that when he got nervous, things seemed to go wrong.

"Upstairs," Steve ordered again.

Herbie concentrated on his feet. *Please*, he begged his body, *don't be clumsy*.

In the kitchen, Momma turned from the stove and smiled at him. He forgot about Steve for a second and felt warm and comfortable in his mother's love. Steve closed the basement door and came to stand next to him. The pleasant feeling disappeared, and Herbie felt heavy and cold.

"Grace, we have to talk."

Momma's smile faded. She looked at Herbie, then at Steve, and back at Herbie again. Herbie wanted to reach out and touch her to make her smile again, but he didn't dare. He stood very still and waited.

"He was in the car again, Grace. After all the promises," Steve frowned at her.

Momma didn't take her eyes from Herbie.

"I've had it," Steve said in an ugly voice. "When I married you I said I'd try living with him around. I've tried for three months now, and it doesn't work. I can't stay in the same house with this—overgrown moron!"

Momma's face went white. "How can you be so cruel?"

"You're the one that's being cruel," Steve shouted. "Herbie should be put— He should be with his own kind."

Herbie's stomach tightened to a hard knot. He wanted to put his hands in his pockets, but his fingers felt big and clumsy and wouldn't find the openings.

Momma looked like she was going to cry. "Herbie, please go to your room. I'll come in a little while."

Herbie started to obey, but Steve grabbed his arm. "Let him stay. He's got to know sooner or later."

"I don't want to talk in front of him," Momma said. "You know how it upsets him."

"What about the way he upsets me?" Steve demanded. "Do you care about that? I've told him time after time to stay away from that car, but it doesn't sink through that thick skull of his."

"Steve!"

"Face the truth, Grace. Herbie has the body of a man of twenty but the mind of a five-year-old kid—and not a very bright one at that. He should have been sent away years ago. Everyone would have been better off."

Tears were running down his mother's cheeks now, and Herbie felt somehow it was his fault because he forgot about the car.

"Steve, please. Let me talk to him. I think I can make him understand. I'll watch him so he doesn't play in the car again." She wiped at the tears quickly. "I'll keep the garage locked."

Steve shook his head, but Momma went on. "Please? Give him another chance. You know I can't send him away."

"You said the same thing last week. I gave him a chance, and it didn't work. It's no use, Grace. He's got to go."

"Please? It isn't as though he hurts anything. I mean, he just sits in the car and pretends."

Steve's face got red again. "That car is mine," he said, "I don't want him touching it!"

"I'll watch him. I'll make him understand and promise—"

"I promise," Herbie said quickly.

Steve didn't seem to believe him, so Herbie repeated his offer. "I promise, Steve. I won't forget again, honest." He wanted Steve to be happy. The room was quiet for a long time. Herbie held his breath and waited.

Finally Steve said, "Okay, but this is really the last time. Understand? The last time. If that— If Herbie touches my car again, he goes or I go." He turned and walked out of the kitchen.

Herbie let his breath out. Momma must have been holding her breath, too, because he heard it escape like a small gust of wind against a window screen.

"Herbie, do you really understand?" she asked. "Steve was very angry. You mustn't touch the car, ever again."

"I just sat in it, Momma. I didn't break anything."

"I know, dear, but you mustn't ever go in the garage again. You don't want to make Steve angry, do you?"

Herbie shook his head. So many things made Steve angry, but the car was the worst, he knew that. This time he wouldn't forget.

For three day Herbie remembered. Each morning Momma reminded him about the car before he went outside. She told him again at lunch and again at supper. Every time Herbie passed the locked garage he remembered his promise.

On Saturday, Momma was talking on the telephone when Herbie finished his breakfast. He carefully scraped the bread crusts and a few crisp edges of fried egg into the garbage and placed the dirty dishes in the sink. Then he put on his heavy jacket, zipping it carefully, and pulled the hood over his ears. He went out the back door.

The air was cold and felt stiff as he breathed it. He walked around the block, counting the cracks in the sidewalk. They zigged and zagged or cut across the cement in straight lines, and they reminded him of the maze of wires under the hood of Steve's car. He got mixed up when he got to fifteen, but it didn't matter. He just began again.

Once he stopped to look into a yard where a cat huddled on a step. She looked cold, and Herbie wanted to pick her up and slip her inside his jacket to warm her, but the cat stared at him with eyes that seemed to go right through him. Somehow they reminded him of Steve's eyes when he was angry, and Herbie hurried home.

Herbie stopped in front of the big garage door. From inside, he heard the running motor and the clink of Steve's tools, but the garage door wasn't locked. Instead of touching the driveway, it was open a few inches, resting on a large hose. Herbie knew it shouldn't be under the door that way. Steve would get mad at Momma if he knew she forgot about keeping the door locked, so Herbie carefully slipped his fingers through the handle and lifted. With his shoe he kicked the hose until it disappeared behind the edge of the door. Then he let the big door down gently. It made only a tiny noise as the lock clicked into place.

Herbie stood up and smiled. Now Steve wouldn't get mad at Momma. Herbie had remembered. He went to his room and looked at his collection of stones for a long time. They were pretty, some round and smooth, others rough and sharp. Herbie thought they were like people—some scowling and angry, their sharp edges ready to slash him. He set these in the bottom of the box. Gradually he covered them with the happy rocks that curved into smiles.

When he heard Momma call, he pushed the box back ino the closet and went downstairs. The table was set for lunch.

"Herbie, will you please go downstairs and tell Steve that lunch is ready and on the table?"

Herbie frowned. "I don't want him to get mad at me. I haven't gone near the car at all, honest."

Momma patted his arm. "All right," she said softly, "I'll go." She started down the stairs and Herbie followed her. He stayed in the doorway when she opened the garage. The air smelled warm and dry, almost sweet.

"Lunch is ready, Steve," she called.

There was no answer except the steady throb of the engine. Herbie saw

Steve bent over the motor under the open hood, but he wasn't working. A wrench lay on the fender just beyond his fingertips and his other hand dangled loosely.

"Steve!" Momma screamed, and she ran around the car and grabbed Steve's shoulder. He slid sideways, and Herbie saw his face. It was dark red—redder than Herbie had ever seen it before.

Herbie backed out of the doorway. Steve was mad because he'd come down here. But he hadn't touched the car! He'd kept his promise!

Herbie heard his mother moving quickly in the garage. The engine stopped and she came back to the basement door, holding the piece of hose in her hand. Her eyes filled with tears.

"I didn't go in, honest. Tell Steve I didn't go in."

"Herbie—"

"Don't let him be mad, Momma. I closed the door so he wouldn't get mad. I remembered. Tell him I remembered." Herbie's hands felt cold and his legs shook.

Tears ran down Momma's cheeks as she took his hand and started up the stairs. Her voice sounded hollow when she spoke. "Steve isn't mad at you. He's . . . Steve won't get mad anymore, Herbie."

Herbie looked at her. He didn't understand.

His mother blinked at the tears and said, "Steve's . . . going away."

Herbie still didn't understand, but he believed her. He thought about his stepfather going away. "Will he take the car?" he asked.

She shook her head and pressed her hand against her mouth. She told Herbie to sit on a chair, and she picked up the telephone.

Herbie waited until she hung up before he spoke again. "Momma, if Steve doesn't take the car, will I be able to play in it now?"

Momma didn't answer because she was crying again.

66

DIAMONDS IN PARADISE

Ellery Queen

MAYBE LILI MINX was THE GIRL of your dreams, too. It's nothing to be ashamed of. Lili caused more insomnia in her day than all the midnight maatjes herring consumed on Broadway and 51st street on all the opening nights put together since Jenny Lind scared the gulls off the roof of Castle Garden.

It wasn't just Lili's face and figure, either, although she could have drifted out on a bare stage before a two-bit vaudeville flat and stood there for two hours and twenty minutes just looking at you, and you'd have headed for your herring mumbling "smash hit." It wasn't even her voice, which made every other set of female pipes on Broadway sound like something ground out of a box with a monkey on it. It was the trick she had of making every male within eyeshot and mike range feel that he was alone with her in a dreamboat.

Of course there was a catch, as the seven yachtsmen she married found out. With all her wonderful equipment, Lili was a mixed-up kid. She was a hopelessly incurable gambler, and she was hipped on diamonds. And the two things didn't seem to go together. Let the psychologists explain it, but the fact is money didn't mean a thing to her. She could drop ten grand at the roulette wheel and yawn like a lady. Diamonds were another story. Let her temporarily mislay a single chip from her jewel box and she went into hysterics. Her press agent swore that she checked her inventory every night before going to bed like a kid casing his marbles.

Naturally, Lili's collection was the target of every itch-fingers out of the jug. But Lili was no pushover. When it came to her diamonds, she was like Javert in the sewers of Paris; she never gave up. The police were kept busy. They didn't mind. With La Minx on the broadcasting end of a complaint,

393

every cop with a front porch and asthma felt like No-Hips Lancelot, the Terror of the Underworld.

Lili's favorite gambling hell, while it lasted, was Paradise Gardens. Those were the days when New York was wide open and everything went, usually before you could come back for more. Paradise Gardens had a longer run than most. It operated behind a frowsy old brownstone front off Fifth Avenue, in the Frolicking Fifties.

The ceiling was a menace to healthy eyesight, with its glittering stars and sequinned angels; you swallowed your buffalo steaks and cougar juice among tropical flowers under papier-mâché trees with wax apples tied onto them; and you were served by tired ex-showgirltype waitresses wearing imitation fig leaves. So it was a relief to go upstairs where there was no mullarkey about gardens or Edens—just nice business décor and green baize-covered tables at which the management allowed you to lose your shirt or bra, as the case might be.

On this particular evening Lili Minx, being between husbands, was alone. She drifted in, pale and perfect in white velvet and ermine, unapproachable as the nearest star and tasty-looking as a charlotte russe. On each little pink ear glowed a cold green fire, like a radioactive pea, La Minx's only jewelry tonight. They were the famous mumtaz green-diamond earrings, once the property of Shah Jahan's favorite wife, which had been clipped to Lili's lobes by the trembling hands of an Iraqi millionaire, who was running hard at the time in the sixth race of La Minx Handicap. Lili prized her green diamonds at least as highly as the ears to which they were attached.

Everything stopped as Lili posed in the archway for her usual moment of tribute; then life went on, and Lili bought a stack of hundred-dollar chips at the cashier's cage and made for the roulette table.

An hour later, her second stack was in the croupier's bank. Lili laughed and drifted toward the ladies' lounge. No one spoke to her.

The trim French maid in the lounge came forward swiftly. "Madame has the headache?"

"Yes."

"Perhaps a cold compress?"

"Please."

Lili lay down on a chaise longue and closed her eyes. At the cool touch of the wrapped ice bag on her forehead she bestowed a smile. The maid adjusted the pillow about her head deftly, in sympathetic silence. It was quiet in the deserted lounge, and Lili floated off into her own world of dreams.

She awoke a few minutes later, put the ice bag aside, and rose from the chaise. The maid had discreetly vanished. Lili went to a vanity and sat down to fix her hair. . . .

And at that exact moment the gambling rooms of Paradise Gardens went berserk. Women shrieked, their escorts scuttled about like trapped crabs, the housemen struggled with their nefarious tools, and the massive door gave way under the axheads of the police.

"Hold it!" An elderly man with a gray mustache hopped nimbly onto a crap table and held up his arms for silence. "I'm Inspector Queen of police headquarters on special gambling detail. This is a raid, ladies and gentlemen. No sense trying to make a break; evey exit is covered. Now if you'll all please line up along the walls while these officers get going—"

And that was when Lili Minx burst from the ladies' lounge like one of the Furies, screaming, "My diamond earrings! I been robbed!"

So immediately what had begun as a gambling raid turned into a robbery investigation. La Minx was in top form, and Inspector Queen did her bidding as meekly as a rookie cop. She had often enough disturbed his dreams, too.

As the axes rose and fell and the equipment flew apart, the Inspector was crooning, "Now don't you worry your pretty head, Miss Minx. We'll find your earrings—"

"And that creep of a maid!" stormed La Minx. "She's the only one who touched me, Inspector Queen. I want that maid clobbered, too!"

"She can't get away, Lili," soothed the Inspector, patting the lovely hand. "We've had the Paradise surrounded for an hour, getting set for the jump, and not a soul got out. So she has to be here . . . Well, Velie?" he barked, as the big Sergeant came loping from the ladies' lounge, furtively feeling his tie. "Where is the woman?"

"Right here," said Sergeant Velie, looking at Lili like a homesick Newfoundland. And he thrust into Inspector Queen's hands, blindly, a maid's uniform, a starched cap and apron, a pair of high-heeled shoes, two sheer stockings, and a wig. "Dumped in the broom closet."

"What does this mean?" cried Lili, staring at the wig.

"Why, it's Harry the Actor," said the Inspector, pleased. "A clever character at female impersonation, Lili—he's made his finest hauls as a French maid. So Harry's tried it on you, as he? You just wait here, my dear," and the Inspector began to march along the lineup like a small gray Fate, followed by La Minx, who waited for no one.

"And here he is," said the Inspector cheerily, stopping before a short slender man with boyish cheeks which were very pale at the moment.

"Tough luck, Harry—about the raid, I mean. Suppose we try this on for size, shall we?" and he clapped the wig on the little man's head.

"That's the one," said Lili Minx in a throbbing voice, and the little man turned a shade paler. She stepped up to him and looked deep into his eyes. "You give me back my diamond earrings, or—" She mentioned several alternatives.

"Get her away from me, get her out of here," quavered Harry the Actor in his girlish treble, trying to burrow into the wall.

"Search him, Velie," said Inspector Queen sternly.

A half hour later, in the manager's office, with the drapes drawn before the window, Harry the Actor stood shivering. On the desk lay his clothes and everything taken from his person—a wallet containing several hundred dollars, a pocketful of loose change, a ball of hard candy, a yellow pencil, a racing form, a pair of battered old dice, a crumpled cigarette pack and a booklet of matches, a tiny vial of French perfume, a lipstick, a compact, a handkerchief smeared with make-up and a box of Kiss-Mee, the Magic Breath-Sweetener. Everything in parts had been disassembled. The cigarettes had been shredded. The hard candy had been smashed. Harry's clothing had been gone over stitch by stitch. His shoes had been tapped for hidden compartments. His mouth and hair had been probed. Various other indignities had been visited upon his person. Even the maid's outfit had been examined.

And no green-diamond earrings.

"All right," muttered the Inspector, "get dressed."

And all the while, from the other side of the manager's door, Lili's creamy voice kept promising Harry what was in store for him as soon as she could get her little hands on him.

And it drove the thief at last to a desperate folly. In the midst of stuffing his belongings back in his pockets, he leaped over the desk, stiff-armed the officer before the window, and plunged headfirst through the drapes like a goat. It was a hard-luck night for Harry the Actor all around. The railing of the fire escape was rotted through with rust. His momentum took him into space, carrying the railing with him.

They heard the railing land on the concrete of the back yard three stories below, then Harry.

The officers posted in the yard were shaking their heads over the little man when Inspector Queen and Sergeant Velie dropped off the fire-escape ladder, followed—inevitably—by Lili.

If the thief had had any hope of cheating fate, one glazed look at the furious beauty glaring down at him destroyed it. Either way he was a goner, and he knew it.

"Harry," said Inspector Queen, tapping the swollen cheek gently. "You're checking out. If you want a fair shake Upstairs, you'd better talk fast. Where did you stash 'em?"

Harry's eye rolled. Then his tongue came out and he said thickly, "Diamonds . . . in . . . the Paradise . . ."

"In the Paradise *what*, Harry?" asked the Inspector frantically, as Harry stopped. "In the Paradise *where?*"

But Harry had had it.

Ellery always said that, if it wasn't his greatest case, it was certainly his shortest.

He first learned about it when his father staggered home at breakfast time. Ellery got some coffee into the old man and extracted the maddening details.

"And I tell you, son," raved the Inspector, "we went back into that joint and tore it apart. It was rotten luck that Harry died before he could tell us just where in the Paradise Gardens he'd hidden Lili's diamonds. They had to be in the building somewhere, either in something or on someone. We still hadn't let anyone go from the raid. We not only took the Paradise apart piece by piece, we body-searched every mother's son and daughter on the premises, thinking Harry might have passed the earrings to an accomplice. Well, we didn't find them!" The Inspector sounded as if he were going to cry. "I don't know what I'll say to that lovely child."

"Diamonds speak louder than words," said Ellery briskly. "At least— from all I hear—in the case of Lili Minx."

"You mean . . . ?" said his father. "But how *can* you know where the Actor hid them?" he cried. "You weren't even there!"

"You told me. Harry was putting his belongings away in his pockets when he made his sudden break. Where is Harry now, Dad?"

"Harry? In the Morgue!"

"Then the Morgue is where Lili's earrings are."

"They were *on* him? But Ellery, we searched Harry outside and—and in!"

"Tell me again," said Ellery, "what he had in his pockets."

"Money, a dirty handkerchief, women's cosmetics, a hard candy, a racing form, cigarettes, a pair of dice, a pencil—"

"I quote you quoting the late Actor's dying statement," said Ellery. " 'Diamonds—in Paradise.' "

"Paradise . . . " The Inspector's jaw wiggled. *"Pair o' dice!* His dice were just shells—*they're in the dice!"*

"So if you'll phone the Morgue property clerk, Dad—"

"Inspector Queen turned feebly from the phone. "But Ellery, it did sound just like the Paradise. . . . "

"What do you expect from a dying man," asked Ellery reasonably, "elocution lessons?"

67

THE ART OF DEDUCTION

Robert L. Fish

WE HAD JUST come back from having some food in a greasy spoon when the call came through, or at least that's when we first heard it. The dispatcher sounded irked, but he usually sounded irked.

"Car 63! Car 63!"

"That's us," I said.

"Too true," Joe Rouse said—he's my partner—and pushed a button. "Car 63," he said.

The dispatcher came on, querulous. "Where you guys been?"

"Having lunch," Joe said. "We always do. Why?"

"We got a bank job here," the dispatcher said. "City Farmers Trust. They got away with eighteen thousand and change in an overnight bag. We think they may be heading your way."

Joe was busy scribbling notes while I started the engine and got ready to roll. Joe paused and looked at the car speaker. "How long ago?"

"Roughly thirty minutes," the dispatcher said. "Time to get to your area if they're headed that way."

Joe jerked his thumb at me; I knew what he meant and headed for the nearest entrance to the turnpike. Joe nodded his agreement and went back to the car speaker. "What kind of car?"

This time the dispatcher's voice was more disgusted then irked.

"We got three witnesses, so of course we got three descriptions. One says it was a dark green Ford, practically new; another says it was dark blue, not green, and he's almost positive it was a Pontiac four, five years old, because his brother-in-law's got one just like it; while the third simply says it was black and he has no notion as to what make or year. About all they agree on," the dispatcher added sourly, "is that it wasn't a polkadot striped staton wagon."

399

"Normal," Joe said. "Did anyone at least notice was it a two-door or a four?"

"One guy said two, one said four, and the third didn't notice."

"I'm beginning to like the third guy best," Joe said. "Did anyone bother to notice how many guys were in on the job?"

"Witnesses say they couldn't tell if there were two or three in the car; it was too far away. People in the bank say only one guy did the stickup there, and there was the driver, but there could have been others inside the car."

"That's fine," Joe said, and sighed. "With witnesses like you got, they could drop people off, pick 'em up, switch cars, anything. With witnesses like you got, they could even park the car, take a bus, split the dough, and give the bus driver a cut."

"What do you want from me?" the dispatcher asked.

"Sympathy," I said, leaning over and getting into the act.

"Who's that, Fenner? You got it," the dispatcher said, and for the first time he sounded happy. "The captain says you guys got to stay on patrol until further notice. Or until the bank robbers are caught, whichever comes first. I think maybe he's got stock in the bank. Heh, heh!" And the speaker went dead.

"That four-letter word!" I said bitterly, "or a couple of them! And I got a heavy date for tonight!" I jammed on the accelerator in frustration, angled into the turnpike entrance with a squeal, speeded up, and managed to edge into traffic without being sideswiped. "Of all times!"

"Don't worry about it," Joe said, not impressed, and jerked his thumb toward the shoulder of the highway. "You trying to race them to the border, Fenner? Pull over!"

"Oh! Yeah," I said a bit shamefacedly, and pulled from the turnpike, bumping to a halt on the shoulder, but keeping the car engine running. I stared out at the hundreds of cars that flashed by, trying to pick out a blue one, or a green one, or a black one, or the two-door or four-door ones, or the ones with two guys or maybe three guys or maybe more guys in them, and I wondered what we were doing here when we had no idea if the bank robbers were even heading our way, or what color car they were driving, or the make or model, or how many passengers were in it. And if I knew the captain, we'd still be sitting here at midnight if the guys weren't picked up somewhere before then, or if they didn't just drive into some station and confess!

Suddenly Joe leaned forward, his eyes narrowing almost to slits as they do when he gets to thinking hard. His big hand came out, squeezing my leg above the knee painfully.

"Let's go, Fenner! Move!"

I stepped on the gas, as much out of reflex to that painful grip as to his yell, spurting onto the road between a semi-trailer and a big truck, barely missing being squooshed, buffeted by the backlash of the wind from the semi and the blast of an outraged horn from the truck, swaying wildly a moment to get control, and finally settling down between the two monsters speeding along just under 70. I glanced over at Joe.

"Where we going?"

"Just stay behind that semi!" he said grimly.

"Right!" I said, mystified, and then suddenly had to touch my brakes as the trailer's directional lights flashed on and the huge semi pulled to the left to pass a car.

"There!" Joe said, pointing. "That dark sedan! Let's get them!"

I put on the flasher and siren and at the same time cut sharply in front of the sedan, forcing it to brake and spin onto the shoulder, twisting, almost into the guard-rail before it came to a shuddering stop, the truck shooting by us, its horn blaring, almost taking off my tail. I wondered what on earth had come over Joe, but he was already out of the car and had his gun on the men in the sedan before they could begin to recover from the shock of being stopped so suddenly. And when they did I was there on the other side of the car and the three were climbing down and lining up, leaning against the side of the sedan while Joe frisked them.

We found the money wedged under the back seat, $18,000 plus in an overnight bag, and we brought it in with our three prisoners. But I still couldn't understand how Joe had spotted the car. Joe explained when we went out for a shot and a beer, which he properly felt we had earned.

"Man!" he said wonderingly. "Who goes 55 miles per hour on a highway today? You go 55 and you better have a ramp on top of your car so they can go over you, because otherwise they'll go right through you!"

"True," I said, still puzzled, "but—"

"The only guys going 55 are guys who don't want to be stopped, can't afford to be stopped, can't take a chance of being stopped," Joe said. "So when I see this car just ambling along, staying inside the limit—"

He shrugged. "And you notice the car was gray, not green or blue or black? And it was a Chevy? Witnesses!" he said with a grimace, and raised his glass.

68

CATTAILS

Marcia Muller

WE CAME AROUND the lake, Frances and I, heading toward the picnic ground. I was lugging the basket and when the going got rough, like where the path narrowed to a ledge of rock, I would set it down a minute before braving the uneven ground.

All the while I was seeing us as if we were in a movie—something I do more and more the older I get.

They come around the lake, an old couple of seventy, on a picnic. The woman strides ahead, still slender and active, her red scarf fluttering in the breeze. He follows, carrying the wicker basket, a stooped gray-headed man who moves hesitantly, as if he is a little afraid.

Drama, I thought. We're more and more prone to it as the real thing fades from our lives. We make ourselves stars in scenarios that are at best boring. Ah, well, it's a way to keep going. I have my little dramas; Frances has her spiritualism and séances. And, thinking of keeping going, I must or Frances will tell me I'm good for nothing, not even carrying the basket to the picnic ground.

Frances had already arrived there by the time I reached the meadow. I set the basket down once more and mopped my damp brow. She motioned impatiently to me and, with a muttered "Yes, dear," I went on. It was the same place we always came for our annual outing. The same sunlight glinted coldly on the water; the same chill wind blew up from the shore; the same dampness saturated the ground.

January. A hell of a time for a picnic, even here in the hills of Northern California. I knew why she insisted on it. Who would know better than I? And yet I wondered—was there more to it than that? Was the fool woman trying to kill me with these damned outings?

She spread the plaid blanket on the ground in front of the log we always

403

used as a backrest. I lowered myself onto it, groaning. Yes, the ground was damp as ever. Soon it would seep through the blanket and into my clothes. Frances unpacked the big wicker basket, portioning out food like she did at home. It was a nice basket, with real plates and silverware, all held in their own little niches. Frances had even packed cloth napkins—leave it to her not to forget. The basket was the kind you saw advertised nowadays in catalogs for rich people to buy, but it hadn't cost us very much. I'd made the niches myself and outfitted it with what was left of our first set of dishes and flatware. That was back in the days when I liked doing handy projects, before . . .

"Charles, you're not eating." Frances thrust my plate into my hands.

Ham sandwich. On rye. With mustard. Pickle, garlic dill. Potato salad, Frances's special recipe. The same as always.

"Don't you think next year we could have something different?" I asked.

Frances looked at me with an expression close to hatred. "You know we can't."

"Guess not." I bit into the sandwich.

Frances opened a beer for me. Bud. I'm not supposed to drink, not since the last seizure, and I've been good, damned good. But on these yearly picnics it's different. It's got to be.

Frances poured herself some wine. We ate in silence, staring at the cattails along the shore of the lake.

When we finished what was on our plates, Frances opened another beer for me and took out the birthday cake. It was chocolate with darker chocolate icing. I knew that without looking.

"He would have been twenty-nine," she said.

"Yes."

"Twenty-nine. A man."

"Yes," I said again, with mental reservations.

"Poor Richie. He was such a beautiful baby."

I was silent, watching the cattails.

"Do you remember, Charles? What a beautiful baby he was?"

"Yes."

That had been in Detroit. Back when the auto industry was going great guns and jobs on the assembly line were a dime a dozen. We'd had a red-brick house in a surburb called Royal Oak. And a green Ford—that's where I'd worked, Ford's, the River Rouge plant—and a yard with big maple trees. And, unexpectedly, we'd had Richie.

"He was such a good baby, too. He never cried."

404

"No, he didn't."

Richie never cried. He'd been unusually silent, watching us. And I'd started to drink more. I'd come home and see them, mother and the change-of-life baby she'd never wanted, beneath the big maple trees. And I'd go to the kitchen for a beer.

I lost the job at Ford's. Our furniture was sold. The house went on the market. And then we headed west in the green car. To Chicago.

Now Frances handed me another beer.

"I shouldn't." I wasn't used to drinking anymore and I already felt drunk.

"Drink it."

I shrugged and tilted the can.

Chicago had been miserable. There we'd lived in a railroad flat in an old dark brick building. It was always cold in the flat, and in the Polish butcher shop where I clerked. Frances started talking about going to work, but I wouldn't let her. Richie needed her. Needed watching.

The beer was making me feel sleepy.

In Chicago, the snow had drifted and covered the front stoop. I would come home in the dark, carrying meat that the butcher shop was going to throw out—chicken backs and nearly spoiled pork and sometimes a soupbone. I'd take them to the kitchen, passing through the front room where Richie's playpen was, and set them on the drainboard. And then I'd go to the pantry for a shot or two of something to warm me. It was winter when the green Ford died. It was winter when I lost the job at the butcher shop. A snowstorm was howling in off Lake Michigan when we got on the Greyhound for Texas. I'd heard of work in Midland.

Beside me, Frances leaned back against the log. I set my empty beer can down and lay on my side.

"That's right, Charles, go to sleep." Her voice shook with controlled anger, as always.

I closed my eyes, traveling back to Texas.

Roughnecking the oil rigs hadn't been easy. It was hard work, dirty work, and for a newcomer, the midnight shift was the only one available. But times hadn't been any better for Frances and Richie. In the winter, the northers blew through every crack in the little box of a house we'd rented. And summer's heat turned the place into an oven. Frances never complained. Richie did, but, then, Richie complained about everything.

Summer nights in Midland were the only good times. We'd sit outside, sometimes alone, sometimes with neighbors, drinking beer and talking. Once in a while we'd go to a roadhouse, if we could find someone to take care of Richie. That wasn't often, though. It was hard to find someone to stay with such a difficult child. And then I fell off the oil rig and broke my leg. When it healed, we boarded another bus, this time for New Mexico.

I jerked suddenly. Must have dozed off. Frances sat beside me, clutching some cattails she'd picked from the edge of the lake while I slept. She set them down and took out the blue candles and started sticking them on the birthday cake.

"Do you remember that birthday of Richie's in New Mexico?" She began lighting the candles, all twenty-nine of them.

"Yes."

"We gave him that red plastic music box? Like an organ grinder's? With the fuzzy monkey on top that went up and down when you turned the handle?"

"Yes." I looked away from the candles to the cattails and the lake beyond. The monkey had gone up and down when you turned the handle— until Richie had stomped on the toy and smashed it to bits.

In Roswell we'd had a small stucco house, nicer than the one in Midland. Our garden had been westernized—that's what they call pebbles instead of grass, cacti instead of shrubs. Not that I spent a lot of time there. I worked long hours in the clothing mill.

Frances picked up the cattails and began pulling them apart, scattering their fuzzy insides. The breeze blew most of the fluff away across the meadow, but some stuck to the icing on the cake.

"He loved that monkey, didn't he?"

"Yes," I lied.

"And the tune the music box played—what was it?"

" 'Pop Goes the Weasel.' " But she knew that.

"Of course. 'Pop Goes the Weasel.'" The fuzz continued to drift through her fingers. The wind from the lake blew some of it against my nose. It tickled.

"Roswell was where I met Linda," Frances added. "Do you remember her?"

"There's nothing wrong with my memory."

"She foretold it all."

"Some of it."

"All."

I let her have the last word. Frances was a stubborn woman.

Linda. Roswell was where Frances had gotten interested in spiritualism, foretelling the future, that sort of stuff. I hadn't liked it, but, hell, it gave Frances something to do. And there was little enough to do, stuck out there in the desert. I had to hand it to Linda—she foretold my losing the job at the clothing mill. And our next move, to Los Angeles.

Frances was almost done with the cattails. Soon she'd ask me to get her some more.

Los Angeles. A haze always hanging over the city. Tall palms that were nothing but poles with sickly wisps of leaves at the top. And for me, job after job, each worse, until I was clerking at the Orange Julius for minimum wage. For Frances and Richie it wasn't so bad, though. We lived in Santa Monica, near the beach. Nothing fancy, but she could take him there and he'd play in the surf. It kept him out of trouble—he'd taken to stealing candy and little objects from the stores. When they went to the beach on weekends I stayed home and drank.

"I need some more cattails, Charles."

"Soon."

Was the Orange Julius the last job in L.A.? Funny how they all blended together. But it had to be—I was fired from there after Richie lifted twenty dollars from the cash register while visiting me. By then we'd scraped together enough money from Frances's baby-sitting wages to buy an old car—a white Nash Rambler. It took us all the way to San Francisco and these East Bay hills where we were sitting today.

"Charles, the cattails."

"Soon."

The wind was blowing off the lake. The cattails at the shore moved, beckoning me. The cake was covered with white fuzz. The candles guttered, dripping blue wax.

"Linda," Frances said. "Do you remember when she came to stay with us in Oakland?"

"Yes."

"We had the seance."

"Yes."

I didn't believe in the damned things, but I'd gone along with it. Linda had set up chairs around the dining-room table in our little shingles house. The room had been too small for the number of people there and Linda had made cutting remarks. That hurt. It was all we could afford. I was on disability then because of the accident at the chemical plant. I'd been worrying about Richie's adjustment problems in school and my inattention on the job had caused an explosion.

"That was my first experience with those who have gone beyond." Frances said now.

"Yes."

407

"You didn't like it."

"No, I didn't."

There had been rapping noises. And chill drafts. A dish had fallen off a shelf. Linda said afterward it had been a young spirit we had contacted. She claimed young spirits were easier to raise.

I still didn't believe in any of it. Not a damned bit!

"Charles, the cattails."

I stood up.

Linda had promised to return to Oakland the next summer. We would all conduct more "fun" experiments. By the time she did, Frances was an expert in those experiments. She'd gone to every charlatan in town after that day in January, here at the lake. She'd gone because on that unseasonably warm day, during his birthday picnic at this very meadow, Richie had drowned while fetching cattails from the shore. Died by drowning, just as Linda had prophesied in New Mexico. Some said it had been my fault because I'd been drunk and had fallen asleep and failed to watch him. Frances seemed to think so. But Frances had been wandering around in the woods or somewhere and hadn't watched him either.

I started down toward the lake. The wind had come up and the overripe cattails were breaking open, their white fuzz trailing like fog.

Funny. They had never done that before.

I looked back at Frances. She motioned impatiently.

I continued down to the lakeside.

Frances had gone to the mediums for years, hoping to make contact with Richie's spirit. When that hadn't worked, she went less and spiritualism became merely a hobby for her. But one thing she still insisted on was coming here every year to reenact the fatal picnic. Even though it was usually cold in January, even though others would have stayed away from the place where their child had died, she came and went through the ritual. Why? Anger at me, I supposed. Anger because I'd been drunk and asleep that day . . . .

The cattail fuzz was thicker now. I stopped. The lake was obscured by it. Turning, I realized I could barely see Frances.

Shapes seemed to be forming in the mist.

The shape of Richie. A bad child.

The shape of Frances. An unhappy mother.

"Daddy, help!"

The cry seemed to come out of the mist at the water's edge. I froze for a moment, then started down there. The mist got thicker. Confused, I stopped. Had I heard something? Or was it only in my head?

Drama, I thought. Drama . . . .

The old man stands enveloped in the swirling mist, shaking his gray head. Gradually his sight returns. He peers around, searching for the shapes. He cocks his head, listening for another cry. There is no sound, but the shapes emerge . . . .

A shape picking cattails. And then another, coming through the mist, arm outstretched. Then pushing. Then holding the other shape down. Doing the thing the old man has always suspected but refused to accept.

The mist began to settle. I turned, looked back up the slope. Frances was there, coming at me. Her mouth was set; I hadn't returned with the cattails.

Don't come down here, Frances, I thought. It's dangerous down here now that I've seen those shapes and the mist has cleared. Don't come down.

Frances came on toward me. She was going to bawl me out for not bringing the catttails. I waited.

One of these days, I thought, it might happen. Maybe not this year, maybe not next, but someday it might. Someday I might drown *you,* Frances, just as—maybe—you drowned our poor, unloved son Richie that day so long ago . . . .

69

AN EXERCISE IN INSURANCE

James Holding

WHEN THREE MASKED men walked into the bank with sawed-off shotguns that afternoon and calmly began to clean out the tellers' cash drawers, I wasn't even nervous. I was sure they weren't going to get away with it. I was perfectly certain that five straight-shooting policemen, strategically placed, would be waiting for the robbers outside the bank door when they emerged.

That's the way it would have happened, too, if it hadn't been for Miss Coe, Robbsville's leading milliner.

As proprietress and sole employee of a hat shop, just around the corner from the bank and felicitously called *Miss Coe's Chapeux*, Miss Coe fabricated fetching hats for many of the town's discriminating ladies. She was an excellent designer, whose products exhibited a fashionable flair, faintly French, that more than justified her use of the French word in her shop name.

Miss Coe was middle-aged, sweet, pretty, methodical and utterly reliable. Indeed, her dependability was often the subject of admiring comment from local ladies who had become somewhat disillusioned by the unreliability of other tradesmen. "You can always count on Miss Coe," they frequently told each other. "If she says she'll have the hat ready on Tuesday at eleven, she'll have it ready. She'll be putting in the last stitch as you come in the door." I had even heard remarks of this kind at my own dinner table, since my wife was one of Miss Coe's steady customers.

But perhaps you are wondering what Miss Coe, a milliner—reliable and methodical as she undoubtedly was—could possibly have to do with the robbery of our bank?

Well, you may remember that some years ago, several of the companies that insured banks against robbery agreed to reduce the premium rates on

411

such insurance if the insured bank was willing to conform to a certain security arrangement.

This meant, simply, that to win the lower insurance rate, a bank must maintain a robbery alarm system somewhere outside the bank itself; that in the event of a robbery, a warning bell or buzzer must sound elsewhere so that police could be instantly alerted without interference, and arrive on the scene in time to prevent the robbery and even, hopefully, to capture the bandits in the act.

In those days of rather primitive electrical wiring, the insurance companies did not insist that, to meet this security requirement, the outside alarm be necessarily installed in the police station itself. Any other location where the ringing of the alarm would unfailingly initiate instant action would serve as well.

The potential savings on insurance premiums made possible in this way were quite substantial. Our bank accordingly decided to take advantage of them. As Cashier, I was entrusted with the job of selecting a suitable outside alarm site, preferably somewhere near the bank, since the installation charges would thus be minimal.

After some thought, and with the memory of my wife's recent words to a bridge partner, "You'll find Miss Coe utterly dependable," fresh in my mind, I went around to see the milliner on my lunch hour one day.

After introducing myself I explained to her that the bank intended to install an alarm buzzer somewhere in the neighborhood. I explained the alarm's purpose. Then I went on diplomatically, "Miss Coe, I have never heard you referred to among the ladies of my acquaintance without some warm testimonial to your complete reliability, to your calm, methodical turn of mind."

"How nice," she murmured, pleased. "I do try to be precise and methodical about things, it's true. I find life less complicated that way."

"Yes. And that's exactly why I am going to ask you to permit us to install our alarm buzzer in your shop."

"Here?"

"Right here. You are always in your shop during banking hours, are you not?"

"Of course. I carry my lunch, so I'm not even away at lunch time."

"Good. With your penchant for doing exactly what is needed at exactly the right time, I am certain that our alarm buzzer, although placing a new responsibility on your shoulders in the unlikely event of a bank robbery, will in no way discommode or harm you. And I might add that the bank will naturally expect to pay you a small stipend for your cooperation."

She flushed with pleasure. ''What would I have to do?'' she asked.

''If the alarm buzzer should ever ring, you merely go at once to your telephone there, Miss Coe . . . '' I indicated her telephone on a counter at the back of the shop, '' . . . and place an emergency call to the police, giving them a prearranged signal. That is all. Your responsibility then ceases. You see, it's very simple.''

''I'm sure I could do that, if that's all there is to it,'' Miss Coe said, glancing at her wall clock a little guiltily, as though she feared she were three stitches late on a hat promised a customer one minute from then. ''And I won't say that a bit of extra income won't be more than welcome.''

By the end of the week the buzzer was installed in her shop. The system was thoroughly tested, and it worked perfectly. On our first ''dry run,'' the squad of police arrived at the bank just four minutes from the time they received their telephone call from Miss Coe. The insurance people, satisfied with their inspection of the system and my recommendation of Miss Coe, granted us the lower insurance rate forthwith.

Since a daily test of the wiring circuit, to assure its constant readiness, was specified in our insurance agreement, I arranged with Miss Coe that at exactly three o'clock each day, I would press the button under my desk at the bank and ring the buzzer in her shop. That was as far as the daily test needed to go; it was expected that Miss Coe's telephone would always be operative but if, in the event it were out of order or in use when the buzzer should ring, Miss Coe could merely nip into the shop next door and telephone the police from there.

For two years it seemed that Miss Coe would never be called upon to display her reliability in behalf of the bank's depositors. We had no bank robbery, nor even an attempted one. I tested the alarm buzzer each day at three; Miss Coe continued to make fetching hats for Robbsville's ladies undisturbed; and each month I mailed her a small check for her participation in the bank's alarm system.

You can readily see now, I am sure, why I had no qualms whatever when our bank robbery finally did occur. This was the event for which the police, Miss Coe and I had so carefully prepared. This was the actual happening that our rehearsals had merely simulated. I knew that our outside robbery alarm was in perfect working order. I knew that Miss Coe was in her shop, ready to act, as dependable and unfailing as the stars in the heavens.

So, far from being startled or apprehensive, I really felt a certain pleasurable excitement when I looked up from my desk just before closing time that afternoon, and saw the three masked bandits presenting their weapons to our staff and terrified patrons. In common with the other occupants of the banking room, I slowly raised my hands over my head at the robbers' command. Simultaneously and unnoticed, however, I also pressed my knee against the alarm button under my desk.

I could picture clearly the exact sequence of events that would be set in train by that movement of my knee. Miss Coe's buzzer would sound. She would perhaps sit immobile for a shocked second at her worktable. She would drop the hat she was working on, and cross speedily to her telephone. She would place her emergency call to the police with splendid calm. And then she would wait confidently for the news from me that our bank robbers had been circumvented or captured.

Unfortunately, as I found out later, Miss Coe did none of these things.

What she did do, when the alarm buzzer sounded in her shop, was merely to glance at the clock on her wall, rise impatiently from her sewing stool and cross the room, and there, (bless her methodical heart!) push the minute hand of the wall clock ahead ten minutes so that it pointed to exactly three o'clock.

70

THE SECRET OF
FORT BAYARD

Georges Simenon

WE MISSED THE most terrible part of this adventure, G.7 and I. But the case remains my most vivid nightmare. The most sinister prison seems to me a delightful spot compared with Fort Bayard.

This fort is on an islet off La Rochelle. Two large islands, Re and Oleron, here lie parallel to the coast, thus enclosing a magnificent roadstead which was formerly of strategic importance. Napoleon, among others, bestrewed it with forts which still stand amid the waves. The best known of these is Fort Bayard.

In the center of the roadstead, hardly a mile from Bayard, lies the island of Aix, on which a hundred or so inhabitants live—mostly on fish and particularly on oysters.

The setting is a harsh one, even in the summer season. In November it is sinister. The ocean roars and surges, and the people of Aix are sometimes cut off from the mainland for weeks.

When we arrived, the excitement aroused by the affair had not yet died down, but the worst was over. We landed on the island of Aix one foggy noonday. The gasoline lamps were already lit in the houses. You could believe that it was twilight.

G.7 had George's house pointed out to him. This George was the only fisherman on the island who had his own small cutter to haul his net. We found him at home, before the fireplace, surrounded by his wife and three children. He was a man of about forty, large, strong, rough-looking, but with a disconcerting calm about him.

Despite which, public opinion had accused him of the most hideous crime. The woman's eyes seemed to me dead and lightless. Even the children seemed crushed by the atmosphere of suspicion that pressed down on the house.

The dialogue was brief:

"Will you take us to the fort?"

George didn't stir. "Now?"

"Yes, now." G.7 showed his badge.

The man rose, took down his oilskin from a hook, threw it around his shoulders, and changed his wooden shoes for hip boots. For a moment he looked at us in our city clothes, then shrugged as though to say, "So much the worse for you. . . ."

A quarter of an hour later, we were on the bridge of the cutter, clinging to the rigging as we pitched unceasingly, our eyes fixed on the black walls of Fort Bayard.

It's a dangerous spot, full of rocks. The fishermen never go there unless for some very good reason. The crumbling walls are a danger, too. Though there is a narrow opening through which you can get into what's left of the fort, no one ever had the curiosity to do so, for fear of a blow on the head from one of the rocks that fall from time to time.

The yachting party were strangers to the district and lacked the natives' prudence. That is how they came to make their monstrous discovery.

There was a being living in the fort. A human being. *A woman.*

You'd have to see the place to realize how much those words mean. The papers are fond of sob-stuff about the hard lot of the lighthouse-keepers, isolated out in the ocean. But lighthouses are livable. At least other men come there occasionally. At Fort Bayard, the wind whirls in through a hundred holes. The rain pours down through a roof that is now nothing but a few beams.

The woman was naked. When she saw strangers, her first movement was to flee.

And now, while we were sailing to what had been her prison, she was in a mental sanitarium in La Rochelle, surrounded by doctors.

She was eighteen. A girl.

But what a girl . . . ! Knowing nothing of human speech, casting frightened glances about her like a hunted animal, hurling herself avidly upon her food. . . .

As I said at first, we arrived only when the case was almost over. The photograph of the girl had appeared in all the papers. And already a man had come from Amsterdam who had recognized her, who had given a name to that enigmatic face: Clara Van Gindertael.

"Here! Grab the ladder!"

George held tight to the helm. We had reached the fort. The surf could shatter our boat against it. G.7 grasped an iron rung and passed a mooring rope over it.

So this was the examination of the scene of the crime. What should one call it? A prison? But even prisons have roofs. . . .

Four ancient walls. Loose rocks. Seaweed. Rubble and rubbish of all kinds. I could imagine the girl crouching in some corner. . . .

I tried to imagine the man who must have brought her food regularly. Mechanically I turned to George, who seemed calmly detached from all that lay around us.

When the yachting party had found Clara Van Gindertael, there had been a stock of provisions for her not more than a month old. Public rumor accused the fisherman. People remembered that he was the only man who ever dared the dangers of this region and dragged his net near the fort.

I examined his features. I asked myself if it were possible that this man, whom I'd just seen at home with his children, could have been coming here for thirteen years, bringing monthly provisions for a human being.

Thirteen years! Clara was five then. Much the same age as George's children. . . . It was horrible. I felt unhappy. I was impatient to get away from this accursed fort.

The magistrates had already questioned the fisherman.

His answers had cast no light on the problem: ''I don't know anything. I never saw the woman you're talking about. I used to fish around the fort, but I never set foot inside. . . .''

He ended his deposition with a question which embarrassed his examiners: ''Where am I supposed to have picked up this little girl?''

The fact is that she was kidnaped in Paris, where George had never been. G.7 had showed me an old newspaper clipping:

> A mysterious abduction took place yesterday in a hotel in the Avenue Friedland.
>
> For some days a Dutchman, M. Pieter Claessens, had been occupying a suite on the first floor of this hotel, which he shared with his five-year-old niece, Clara Van Gindertael, the child heiress, whose guardian he is, since she is an orphan.
>
> His personal valet looked after the child.
>
> Yesterday then, while M. Claessens was out, this servant went down to the kitchens where he remained about an hour, leaving the child alone in the suite. When he returned, she had disappeared.
>
> The description of the little girl is as follows: rather large for her age, slender, fair hair, blue eyes, wearing a white silk dress, white socks, and black patent-leather shoes.
>
> The police have begun an investigation.

Pieter Claessens had arrived at La Rochelle three days after the discovery of the girl who was still known only, in the phrase of the press, as "the Fort Bayard Unknown." He read in the papers the account of the yachtsmen's find. There was a photograph of the girl. And there was the statement that she had on her left wrist the scar of an old burn.

This was what clinched the identification for her guardian. He said that she had received the burn when she was only four, from the explosion of an alcohol heater.

That was as far as the affair had gone. You can imagine the many questions that arose:

Who had kidnaped Clara Van Gindertael thirteen years ago?

Why had she been taken to Fort Bayars?

Who had regularly brought her provisions?

What interests were at work behind this maddening drama?

The one most concerned, the victim herself, could not speak a word. According to the doctors, it would take many years to make a normal human being of her. Some specialists doubted that it could ever be done.

Reporters argued furiously over Fort Bayard. Photographs of the spot had appeared in all the dailies. The most unlikely hypotheses had been seriously considered.

It was a wonder that George was still at liberty. I knew myself that this was at the express order of G.7, who had telegraphed from Paris to La Rochelle as soon as he got wind of the affair.

What was his own opinion? And why had our first step been to visit the fort, though it has seemed more logical to me to start off by seeing the victim herself, especially since we had to come through La Rochelle?

I had no idea.

G.7 was as calm as the fisherman.

The two men were not without certain points of resemblance. One was as niggardly with words as the other. They both had the same clear eyes, the same imposing figure.

Was their silence with each other a sort of challenge?

I was ill at ease. I wandered clumsily around the square enclosure, my feet slipping on the seaweed. The empty food containers had a more sinister significance here than elsewhere.

There was a mountain of them.

It was beginning to get dark all around us, though it was only three o'clock. We heard the prow of the boat striking against the wall with every wave.

As for G.7, he paced up and down with long slow strides, his head lowered.

"You've been married how long?" he asked suddenly, turning toward George.

The fisherman started, then answered promptly: "Eighteen years."

"You . . . you love your wife?"

I saw his Adam's apple quiver. It was some moments before he spoke. At last I heard a dull murmur: ". . . and the kids . . ."

"Let's go!" G.7 concluded unexpectedly. He turned toward the only break in the walls through which we could get back to the cutter. He took my arm. And he whispered, while George hoisted the sails, "The affair has only begun!"

I heard the rest of his speech in snatches. There was a storm coming up. I kept my eyes riveted on George, who sat motionless in the stern, wrapped up in his oilskin, the helm between his legs, his attention fixed on the swelling of the sail.

"The guilty man," G.7 said, "betrayed himself, you see. Reread that clipping I gave you. Reread the description of the child. The point at that time was to give the most complete description possible, wasn't it? A description that would help find her? It lists the details of shoes, even socks. And it doesn't say a word about the burn on the wrist. Why? *Because that burn didn't as yet exist!* Thanks to that, I knew the truth even before we came here. . . .

"Or listen: Pieter Claessens has no fortune of his own. But he's the uncle and guardian of Clara, who is very rich in her own right. At the same time he is the child's heir. . . .

"Is he afraid to commit, strictly speaking, a crime? . . . Does he fear that he'll be accused. . . I don't know. . . . At any rate he shuts up Clara, or has her shut up, in Fort Bayard and there abandons her to her fate. . . . She is sure to die there. . .

"After the delays of legal formalities, he inherits. He returns to his own country. He doesn't think of the child again. . . .

"Then why, suddenly, after thirteen years, does he feel this intense need of knowing what's become of her, of making sure that she's really dead? I'll bet anything you please that he had his eye on an inheritance which only the girl herself could receive. . . .

"Claessens tells himself that she may be alive, that people may have picked her up. . . . He comes back secretly to see. . . . At Fort Bayard, he finds her. . . .

"But still he has to find her *officially*. There still has to be his official *identification*. Merely a resemblance, after so many years, wouldn't do for the courts. . . . Some identifying mark is better. . . . a scar, for example. . . . He has only to burn the girl's wrist. . . .

"Claessens returns to Holland and waits long enough for the scar to seem reasonably old. The girl's exposed life would help there. His accomplices play out the comedy of the yacht and the discovery. The papers announce the find. He rushes to the spot—too fast, in fact. Beforehand he spreads the story of the scar. . . .

"There was the slip! I repeat, if that scar had existed at the time of the kidnaping, it *must* have appeared in the description. . . .

"Do you understand now that the affair has only begun? That man thinks himself safe, free from all suspicion. . . . Another man has been accused."

"George?" I asked.

G. 7 glanced at the fisherman and lowered his voice. "And George won't talk. . . . He hid his discovery for motives that I can't explain to myself too clearly. . . . These simple people can sometimes have horribly complicated souls. Was he afraid that they'd think his story was a myth? That his wife might suspect him of palming off as a foundling a child of his own? Again, I don't know. . . . He fed the child. Little by little she became a woman. . . . Now do you begin to see? It is monstrous, I know. They say that Clara, despite her strange life, is beautiful. . . ."

Up till then I had never stopped looking at George. Now I turned abruptly to the sea. It was a relief to lose myself in the tumult of the raging elements.

71

SWEET, SWEET MURDER

H. A. DeRosso

I DON'T KNOW why everyone thinks we Smedleys are unusual. We're like everybody else, with two arms and two legs and a head and a body. And our brains are always working. I remember my great-uncle Simeon, who was the intellect of the family and cleaned up after horses in the days before automobiles, well, he took up yoga or something and while in suspended animation thought up a whole book and wrote it down afterwards in Greek. Anyway, that's what every publisher he sent it to said it was. And people think my cousin Albert is strange because he walks around at night with a lighted flashlight, looking for dew-worms. It isn't his fault he's allergic to night air and has to look for dewies in his living room. And take me—I like peanuts salted in the shell. I throw the peanuts away and eat the salted shells because I like them, and how else are you going to get salted shells except with peanuts? Everybody has their little idiosyncrasies. But people just seem to make more fuss over those adopted by the Smedleys.

This brings me quite naturally to Uncle Phil. Eveyone else in our family thinks of Uncle Phl as the black sheep, but to me he always was and still is a great man. Unfortunately, he was born ahead of his time, and what he did, I am sure, would have found favor in a later era. In a way, he was a pioneer, and pioneers always have tough going. Look at the Donner party that was caught in the Sierra Nevadas in the middle of winter, but that's another story.

To get back to Uncle Phil, he was the only one who ever understood me. Maybe that's why I can sympathize with him. When two people are just about outcasts, they tend to lean on each other for understanding and compassion. It was like that with me and Uncle Phil, though he was thirty years older than me. Still, there was a rapport between us, if you know what I mean, a feeling of *muy simpático* or *lebensraum* or something.

421

Anyway, this closeness, this mutual sympathy, developed when Grandmother Smedley died. The rest of the family—the brothers, the sisters, the aunts, the uncles, the cousins and second-cousins, the nieces, the nephews—were all somewhat scandalized by his attitude. I was the only one, young as I was, to realize that he was only being philosophical and practical about her death.

Neither Uncle Phil nor I had hated Grandmother Smedley. Oh, I'd had my differences with her, but I realized that she was old and crabby because she couldn't help being either, and so I tried my best to be tolerant. Even when she killed my pet mosquito, Annabelle, a week before she died, I kept myself from hating her. I told myself that her eyesight wasn't too good, I think she had cataracts or something, and so she hadn't recognized Annabelle and squashed her with one well-aimed slap. Of course, she would never believe that I had trained poor Annabelle not to bite people. Afterwards, I tried to find another pet mosquito, but I never could find one quite like Annabelle.

Well, the relatives came from far and near for Grandmother Smedley's funeral. With all that company it seemed like a holiday to me, but Mother and Father didn't approve of my attitude. Only Uncle Phil agreed, because he felt the same way.

You could hardly blame Uncle Phil. He worked in the iron-ore mines, deep underground, ten hours a day and six days a week. This was before unions; so there was no such thing as holidays with pay or vacations with pay. There were no vacations, period. Not only that, but if a miner missed a shift, he'd get fired. So it came as a welcome relief, an answer to a prayer, when Uncle Phil was allowed to take three days off from work, without pay, for the mourning and the funeral, and without jeopardizing his job.

That was why he understood the way I felt and I understood the way he felt. He found me after Mother had given me a severe talking-to and I'd run off to sulk behind the woodshed. I was working off my spite, hanging a grasshopper, when Uncle Phil walked up.

He hunkered down on his heels and watched the grasshopper kicking for a while, then he reached over and adjusted the noose better. Then he watched a few moments more and nodded approval. After that, he turned his pale blue eyes on me. They always looked soft and wet, as though great sorrows were constantly tormenting him, even though he was usually smiling.

"I heard your mother, Paul," he said to me, "but don't mind her. She doesn't understand people like you and me. You know how she picks on me just because she's my sister. She, all of them, have the wrong attitude about death. Look at them up in the house, talking in hushed voices, sighing, twittering, crying. What did they expect, Grandmother to live forever?''

He prodded the grasshopper, which had stopped kicking, with a finger, and nodded, satisfied, when it didn't move.

"This is really a break for me. Grandmother couldn't have picked a better time to die—middle of summer with the sun shining and all that. You don't know what it means to me to be able to walk around in the sun. Do you realize in the winter I go to work before daylight and come home after dark? What kind of a life is that? A man should be entitled to some time off from his job once in a while. Grandmother must have understood. That's why she took it upon herself to pass away now, so on these days off I can enjoy the sun and the outdoors. She made me a gift. Should I cry over that? Am I an outlaw because I don't feel like joining the others in their mourning and weeping?''

His eyes were wet, but, like I said, they always looked that way. He smiled brightly at me. ''Let's go for a walk, hey, Paul? We're buddies, me and you. . . . ''

I still sigh when I think of that walk. A feeling of peace and contentment came over me as we walked through the fields. The sun shone in a deep blue sky; a couple of fluffy white clouds drifted by. The air was rich with the smell of ripening timothy and clover, and sweet with the singing of birds. It was the most comforting feeling I'd ever know.

I caught a frog, and me and Uncle Phil hanged it. Then we did some other interesting things. I really had a wonderful time on that walk, and I know Uncle Phil did, too.

''Am I going to hate going back to work day after tomorrow,'' he said on our way home, and sighed deeply. ''What the miners ought to have is a five-and-half-day week.'' Tomorrow was Grandmother's funeral. ''It's so nice having a vacation.''

''Maybe Aunt Selma will die,'' I said, trying to comfort him, because for once he wasn't smiling, and really looked like he was ready to cry. ''She looks pretty old, and I heard her coughing something terrible.''

''It's that corncob,'' Uncle Phil said, almost absently, and I could tell his mind was on something else. 'She should switch to another kind of pipe.''

''Maybe she'll die anyway,'' I said, trying to cheer him up, ''and you'll have another vacation.''

He looked at me for the first and only time with disapproval. ''Hush now, Paul,'' he said. ''You mustn't say things like that.''

That hurt and made me mad. ''You sound just like Mother,'' I said, and ran off, crying.

Well, we buried Grandmother, and that brings up Cousin Newfry. He was Uncle Phil's nephew, like me, but he was grown up. I never liked him because he was all-fired bossy. I remember that in church I couldn't help myself, and got a giggling jag. Mother tried to shush me, and though I got a belly-ache for my efforts, I couldn't quit giggling. So Cousin Newfry, who was in the pew behind me, rapped me one on the skull real hard, and that made me bust out crying, right out loud. That was when they took me out of the church and really gave me something to cry about.

The only one to understand and show me sympathy was Uncle Phil. "I hate Cousin Newfry," I told Uncle Phil between sobs, "I'd like to hang him right from the belfry."

He didn't swat me one like the others would have done. He just tousled my hair and nodded thoughtfully. I took care to stay next to Uncle Phil throughout the rest of the doings. He was the only protection I had.

Uncle Newfry lived in the southern part of the state, and I could hardly wait for him to go home. I thought he'd leave right after the funeral or the next day, but he hung around. There was something about a will, I think, and the way I got it from Uncle Phil, it was Cousin Newfry causing all the trouble—which didn't surprise me any.

What did surprise me was how Uncle Phil suddenly started playing up to Cousin Newfry. It also disgusted me very much. Here I thought I was Uncle Phil's favorite nephew, and all at once he starts preferring Cousin Newfry to everyone else.

He invited Cousin Newfry to stay at his house. And two weeks later, on a Sunday, the only day off he had from the mine, he took Cousin Newfry fishing with him. I ran off and hid in the woods and just bawled when Uncle Phil didn't ask me to go along. I looked around for something to hang, and when I couldn't find anything, I cried harder than ever.

Well, it happened that Uncle Phil and Cousin Newfry went out on the lake in a boat, and somehow the plug in the bottom came out, and the boat sank. Uncle Phil said he just barely made it to shore, but Cousin Newfry, who couldn't swim, drowned.

I tell you, I didn't shed any tears for Cousin Newfry. I went around with a hand over my mouth to keep from laughing out loud, and that got me plenty of dirty looks from all the Smedleys, who had gathered again, and a good whipping from Father. I was behind the woodshed hanging a chipmunk when Uncle Phil found me this time, but he cut the chipmunk down before it was dead, and I stared at him. For once he didn't make any sense to me.

"Paul," he said gently, "you've got to realize that people can't understand why you act the way you do. Just like the big boss at the mine not understanding me when I spoke up for all the miners not getting enough time off. I understand you, yes, but no one else does, and so you've got to act the way they expect you to.''

"But I'm glad Cousin Newfry is dead," I said, "Aren't you glad, too?"

His eyes watered more than ever. "Newfry was a guest in my house. He was my sister's son. How can I be glad?"

"You got another vacation and—"

He clapped a hand over my mouth and looked around. "Leave us not say what our hearts feel," he said solemnly, sounding just like the minister. "It is possible to rejoice within and mourn without. Do you follow me, Paul?"

"Sure, Uncle Phil," I whispered when he took his hand away, awed by all his wisdom. "I follow you. . . ."

By being kind and reasonable he taught me a lesson I never forgot. Uncle Phil had a way about him with children, and it's too bad he never had any of his own, although I heard Mother often say thank God for that. I have to disagree with her, however. All she and Father thought was necessary to teach me something was with the back of a hand or the front of a stick. Uncle Phil was different. He used psychology, which is why I've never forgotten the things he taught me. That is why I say my Uncle Phil was a great man, with some shortcomings.

Anyway, I learned how to behave when people were dead, and that came in handy the following summer, when, in a period of perfect weather in July, Aunt Donora died.

Now, Aunt Donora was Uncle Phil's wife. They seemed to get along real good, though Uncle Phil let his hair down with me a few times, but to everyone else he pretended everything was just fine between him and Aunt Donora. He would say, "Yes, dear" and "Right away, dear" and "Certainly, dear" and "You're ever so right, dear." But that was for public consumption. To me, his only confident, he related the miserable life he was living.

"It isn't that I don't love Donora, Paul," he said, "but if she'd only quit nagging. She's always finding fault. I don't know why, because I never do anything wrong. Yet she nags me for putting ketchup in my soup and gravy on my salad. She nags me for picking between my toes. All I'm trying to do is have perfectly clean feet. I sleep better then." He sighed deeply, and my heart went out to him. "I have a cross to bear, Paul, I really have."

Well, anyway, that July he had just bought a car, one of those Model T's with the shift pedals in the floor. I could never figure out which pedal was which. I only knew they made the car go. They sure were confusing. You had to have the emergency on, I think, to get it in low, and then leave the pedal out for it to go into high, or something like that. It really was confusing, and that was how Aunt Donora was killed.

Uncle Phil really wasn't used to the shift pedals yet, having just bought the car. I know he was having trouble with the pedals, mixing up the low-and-high one with the reverse, and that's how it happened. He took Aunt Donora for a ride out in the country, and the car got stuck or something, and Aunt Donora got out to push, with Uncle Phil driving, and he accidentally stepped on the wrong pedal, putting the car in reverse and runing over poor Aunt Donora.

Of course, Uncle Phil got to have another vacation, no argument at all from the big boss down at the mine, since Aunt Donora was Uncle Phil's wife. Uncle Phil even cried real tears, he was so broken up. I remembered what he had taught me, about how to act when people are dead, and I tell you, I didn't do any smiling or laughing, and I behaved very well all through the services and afterwards at the cemetery. When it was all over, Uncle Phil patted me on the head and said I had learned real well.

"I sure hate to think of going back to work in the morning," he told me when we were alone. "But I suppose, under the circumstances, it will be good for me to get out of the house for a few hours. Too many memories here. Poor Donora." And he sniffled for real again.

By now I was starting to catch on, and so I began to play a little game, trying to figure out who it would be the next time Uncle Phil got the urge to have a vacation from the mine. The summer wore on, and autumn came. I figured that Uncle Phil would wait until next spring, at the earliest, because he liked his vacations when the weather was nice. But he fooled me. He picked the fall, bird season.

Uncle Jarvis—he was my uncle because he was Aunt Donora's brother and Uncle Phil's brother-in-law—anyway, Uncle Jarvis brought up something about some insurance Aunt Donora had that peeved Uncle Phil a little. But Uncle Phil wasn't one to quarrel with anybody. I don't think he spoke a single word in anger in all his life. He was gentle that way. He sure believed in live and let live. Anyway, he listened to what Uncle Jarvis had to say, and then they had a long discussion, and everything got patched up so that Uncle Phil and Uncel Jarvis were the best of friends that day late in October when they went hunting partridge.

The way this one happened was that somehow the barrel of Uncle Jarvis's twelve-gauge got plugged up with mud, and when the went to shoot a partridge, the twelve-gauge exploded in Uncle Jarvis' face. That didn't surprise me at all. The surprise came when the sheriff interrupted Uncle Phil's vacation and arrested him.

I don't care what they say, but I'll bet they gave poor Uncle Phil the third degree to make him talk. They say they found the same kind of mud that had exploded the twelve-gauge on Uncle Phil's clothes and under his fingernails. Maybe, but how come Uncle Phil confessed to killing Cousin Newfry and Aunt Donora, too, just so he could have vacations from the mine? Don't tell me they didn't give Uncle Phil the third degree.

Anyway, just because Uncle Phil said he killed those people to get time off from his job, they sent him away to the state hospital at Winnebago. All the Smedleys thought this was something terrible, and none of them ever spoke Uncle Phil's name again. I did a few times, at first, and promptly got licked each time.

I'll never forget Uncle Phil. Like I said, he was a pioneer. He was the first in these parts to feel that a working man is entitled to some time off from his job and to do something about it. I'll admit he was a little selfish, thinking mainly about a vacation for himself, but none of us are perfect.

Anyway, the unions finally came to the mines, and now that the miners are organized, they have their vacations every year, and with pay besides. But there are still some stubborn people who don't think that it's right for anyone to get time off from a job and be paid for it. Mr. Self, who owned the hardware and appliance store where I work, was one of these.

Mr. Self never did give in to our demands for a union. He fought it all along, because he wanted us to work six days a week, fifty-two weeks a year. We had to like it or lose our jobs. Well, we finally got a few days off, because when me and Mr. Self were delivering a refrigerator to a second-floor apartment, the dolly to which the refrigerator was strapped slipped from my grip, and the refrigerator fell smack on top of Mr. Self and killed him.

72

ONE DOWN

Ed McBain

SHE LEANED BACK against the cushions of the bed, and there was that lazy, contented smile on her face as she took a drag on her cigarette. The smoke spiralled around her face, and she closed her eyes sleepily. I remembered how I had once liked that sleepy look of hers. I did not like it now.

"It's good when you're home, Ben," she said.

"Uh huh," I murmured. I took a cigarette from the box on the night table, lighted it, and blew out a stream of smoke.

"Yes, yes, it's really good." She drew on her cigarette, and I watched the heave of her breasts, somehow no longer terribly interested.

"I hate your job," she said suddenly.

"Do you?"

"Yes," she said, pouting. "It's like a . . . a wall between us. When you're gone, I sit here and just curse your job and pray that you'll be home again soon. I hate it, Ben. I really do."

"Well," I said drily, "we have to eat, you know."

"Couldn't you get another job?" she asked. It was only about the hundredth time she'd asked that same question.

"I suppose," I said wearily.

"Then why don't you?" She sat up suddenly. "Why don't you, Ben?"

"I like travelling," I said. I was so tired of this, so damned tired of the same thing every time I was here. All I could think of now was what I had to do. I wanted to do it and get it over with.

She grinned coyly. "Do you miss me when you're on the road?"

"Sure," I said.

She cupped her hands behind my neck and trailed her lips across my jaw line. I felt nothing.

"Very much?"

She kissed my ear, shivered a little, and came closer to me.

"Yes, I miss you very much," I said.

She drew away from me suddenly. "Do you like the house, Ben? I did just what you said. I moved out of the apartment as soon as I got your letter. You should have told me sooner, Ben. I had no idea you didn't like the city."

"The neighbors were too snoopy," I said. "This is better. Out in the country like this."

"But it's so lonely. I've been here a week already, and I don't know a soul yet." She giggled. "There's hardly a soul *to* know."

"Good," I said.

"Good?" Her face grew puzzled. "What do you mean, Ben?"

"Adele," I told her, "you talk too much."

I pulled her face up to mine and clamped my mouth onto hers, just to shut her up. She brought her arms up around my neck immediately, tightening them there, bringing her body close to mine. I tried to move her away from me gently, but my arms were full of her, and her lips were moist and eager. Her eyes closed tightly, and I sighed inwardly and listened to the lonely chirp of the crickets outside the window.

"Do you love me?" she asked later.

"Yes."

"Really, Ben? Really and truly?"

"Really and truly."

"How much do you love me?"

"A whole lot, Adele."

"But do you . . . where are you going, Ben?"

"Something I want to get from my jacket."

"Oh, all right." She stopped talking, thinking for a moment. "Ben, if you had to do it all over again, would you marry me? Would you still choose me as your wife?"

"Of course." I walked to the closet and opened the door. I knew just where I'd left it. In the righthand jacket pocket.

"What is it you're getting, Ben? A present?" She sat up against the pillows again. "Is it a present for me?"

"In a way," I said. I closed my fist around it and turned abruptly. Her eyes opened wide.

"Ben! A gun. What . . . what are you doing with a gun?"

I didn't answer. I grinned, and she saw something in my eyes, and her mouth went slack.

"Ben, no!" she said.

"Yes, Adele."

"Ben, I'm your wife. Ben, you're joking. Tell me you're joking."

"No, Adele, I'm quite serious."

She swung her legs over the side of the bed, the covers snatching at the thin material of her gown, pulling it over her thighs.

"Ben, why? Why are you . . . Ben, please. Please!"

She was cringing against the wall now, her eyes saucered with fear.

I raised the gun.

"Ben!"

I fired twice, and both bullets caught her over her heart. I watched the blood appear on the front of her gown, like red mud slung at a clean, white wall. She toppled forward suddenly, her eyes blank. I put the gun away, dressed, and packed my suitcase.

It took me two days to get there. I opened the screen door and walked into the kitchen. There was the smell of meat and potatoes frying, a smell I had come to dislike intensely. The radio was blaring, the way it always was when I arrived. I grimaced.

"Anybody home?" I called.

"Ben?" Her voice was surprised, anxious. "Is that you, Ben?"

"Hello, Betty," I said tonelessly. She rushed to the front door and threw herself into my arms. Her hair was in curlers, and she smelled of frying fat.

"Ben, Ben darling, you're back. Oh, Ben, how I missed you."

"Did you?"

"Ben, let me look at you." She held me away from her and then lifted her face and took my mouth hungrily. I could still smell the frying fat aroma.

I pushed her away from me gently. "Hey," I said, "cut it out. Way you're behaving, people would never guess we've been married for three years already."

She sighed deeply. "You know, Ben," she said, "I hate your job."

431

73

A HOME AWAY FROM HOME

Robert Bloch

THE TRAIN WAS late, and it must have been past nine o'clock when Natalie found herself standing, all alone, on the platform before Hightower Station.

The station itself was obviously closed for the night—it was only a way-stop, really, for there was no town here—and Natalie wasn't quite sure what to do. She had taken it for granted that Dr. Bracegirdle would be on hand to meet her. Before leaving London, she'd sent her uncle a wire giving him the time of her arrival. But since the train had been delayed, perhaps he'd come and gone.

Natalie glanced around uncertainly, then noticed the phonebooth which provided her with a solution. Dr. Bracegirdle's last letter was in her purse, and it contained both his address and his phone number. She had fumbled through her bag and found it by the time she walked over to the booth.

Ringing him up proved a bit of a problem; there seemed to be an interminable delay before the operator made the connection, and there was a great deal of buzzing on the line. A glimpse of the hills beyond the station, through the glass wall of the booth, suggested the reason for the difficulty. After all, Natalie reminded herself, this was West Country. Conditions might be a bit primitive—

"Hello, hello!"

The woman's voice came over the line, fairly shouting above the din. There was no buzzing noise now, and the sound in the background suggested a babble of voices all intermingled. Natalie bent forward and spoke directly and distinctly into the mouthpiece.

"This is Natalie Rivers," she said. "Is Dr. Bracegirdle there?"

"Whom did you say was calling?"

"Natalie Rivers. I'm his niece."

"His what, Miss?"

"Niece," Natalie repeated. "May I speak to him, please?"

"Just a moment."

There was a pause, during which the sound of voices in the background seemed amplified, and then Natalie heard the resonant masculine tones, so much easier to separate from the indistinct murmuring.

"Dr. Bracegirdle here. My dear Natalie, this is an unexpected pleasure!"

"Unexpected? But I sent you a 'gram from London this afternoon." Natalie checked herself as she realized the slight edge of impatience which had crept into her voice. "Didn't it arrive?"

"I'm afraid service is not of the best around here," Dr. Bracegirdle told her, with an apologetic chuckle. "No, your wire didn't arrive. But apparently you did." He chuckled again. "Where are you, my dear?"

"At Hightower Station."

"Oh, dear. It's in exactly the opposite direction."

"Opposite direction?"

"From Peterby's. They rang me up just before you called. Some silly nonsense about an appendix—probably nothing but an upset stomach. But I promised to stop round directly, just in case."

"Don't tell me they still call you for general practice?"

"Emergencies, my dear. There aren't many physicians in these parts. Fortunately, there aren't many patients either." Dr. Bracegirdle started to chuckle, then sobered. "Look now. You say you're at the station. I'll just send Miss Plummer down to fetch you in the wagon. Have you much luggage?"

"Only my travel-case. The rest is coming with the household goods, by boat."

"Boat?"

"Didn't I mention it when I wrote?"

"Yes, that's right, you did. Well, no matter. Miss Plummer will be along for you directly."

"I'll be waiting in front of the platform."

"What was that? Speak up, I can hardly hear you."

"I said I'll be waiting in front of the platform."

"Oh." Dr. Bracegirdle chuckled again. "Bit of a party going on here."

"Shan't I be intruding? I mean, since you weren't expecting me—"

"Not at all! They'll be leaving before long. You wait for Plummer."

The phone clicked off and Natalie returned to the platform. In a surprisingly short time, the station-wagon appeared and skidded off the road to halt at the very edge of the tracks. A tall, thin, gray-haired woman, wearing a somewhat rumpled white uniform, emerged and beckoned to Natalie.

"Come along, my dear," she called. "Here, I'll just pop this in back." Scooping up the bag, she tossed it into the rear of the wagon. "Now, in with you—and off we go!"

Scarcely waiting for Natalie to close the door after her, Miss Plummer gunned the motor and the car plunged back onto the road.

The speedometer immediately shot up to seventy, and Natalie flinched. Miss Plummer noticed her agitation at once.

"Sorry," she said. "With Doctor out on call, I can't be away too long."

"Oh yes, the house-guests. He told me."

"Did he now?" Miss Plummer took a sharp turn at a crossroads and the tires screeched in protest, but to no avail. Natalie decided to drown apprehension in conversation.

"What sort of a man is my uncle?" she asked.

"Have you never met him?"

"No. My parents moved to Australia when I was quite young. This is my first trip to England. In fact, it's the first time I've left Canberra."

"Folks with you?"

"They were in a motor smashup two months ago," Natalie said. "Didn't the Doctor tell you?"

"I'm afraid not—you see, I haven't been with him very long." Miss Plummer uttered a short bark and the car swerved wildly across the road. "Motor smashup, eh? Some people have no business behind the wheel. That's what Doctor says."

She turned and peered at Natalie. "I take it you've come to stay, then?"

"Yes, of course. He wrote me when he was appointed my guardian. That's why I was wondering what he might be like. It's so hard to tell from letters." The thin-faced woman nodded silently, but Natalie had an urge to confide. "To tell the truth, I'm just a little bit edgy. I mean, I've never met a psychiatrist before."

"Haven't you, now?" Miss Plummer shrugged. "You're quite fortunate. I've seen a few in my time. A bit on the know-it-all side, if you ask me. Though I must say, Dr. Bracegirdle is one of the best. Permissive, you know."

"I understand he has quite a practice."

"There's no lack of patients for *that* sort of thing," Miss Plummer observed. "Particularly amongst the well-to-do. I'd say your uncle has done himself handsomely. The house and all—but you'll see." Once again the wagon whirled into a sickening swerve and sped forward between the imposing gates of a huge driveway which led towards an enormous house set amidst a grove of trees in the distance. Through the shuttered windows Natalie caught sight of a faint beam of light—just enough to help reveal the ornate facade of her uncle's home.

"Oh, dear," she muttered, half to herself.

"What is it?"

"The guests—and it's Saturday night. And here I am, all mussed from travel."

"Don't give it another thought," Miss Plummer assured her. "There's no formality here. That's what Doctor told me when I came. It's a home away from home."

Miss Plummer barked and braked simultaneously, and the station-wagon came to an abrupt stop just behind an imposing black limousine.

"Out with you now!" With brisk efficiency, Miss Plummer lifted the bag from the rear seat and carried it up the steps, beckoning Natalie forward with a nod over her shoulder. She halted at the door and fumbled for a key.

"No sense knocking," she said. "They'd never hear me." As the door swung open her observation was amply confirmed. The background noise which Natalie had noted over the telephone now formed a formidable foreground. She stood there, hesitant, as Miss Plummer swept forward across the threshold.

"Come along, come along!"

Obediently, Natalie entered, and as Miss Plummer shut the door behind her, she blinked with eyes unaccustomed to the brightness of the interior.

She found herself standing in a long, somewhat bare hallway. Directly ahead of her was a large staircase; at an angle between the railing and the wall was a desk and chair. To her left was a dark panelled door—evidently leading to Dr. Bracegirdle's private office, for a small brass plate was affixed to it, bearing his name. To her right was a huge open parlor, its windows heavily curtained and shuttered against the night. It was from here that the sounds of sociability echoed.

Natalie started down the hall toward the stairs. As she did so, she caught a glimpse of the parlor. Fully a dozen guests eddied about a large table, talking and gesturing with the animation of close acquaintance—with one another, and with the contents of the lavish array of bottles gracing the tabletop. A sudden whoop of laughter indicated that at least one guest had abused the Doctor's hospitality.

Natalie passed the entry hastily, so as not to be observed, then glanced behind her to make sure that Miss Plummer was following with her bag. Miss Plummer was indeed following, but her hands were empty. And as Natalie reached the stairs, Miss Plummer shook her head.

"You didn't mean to go up now, did you?" she murmured. "Come in and introduce yourself."

"I thought I might freshen up a bit first."

"Let me go on ahead and get your room in order. Doctor didn't give me notice, you know."

"Really, it's not necessary. I could do with a wash—"

"Doctor should be back any moment now. Do wait for him." Miss Plummer grasped Natalie's arm, and with the same speed and expedition she had bestowed on driving, she steered the girl forward into the lighted room.

"Here's Doctor's niece," she announced. "Miss Natalie Rivers, from Australia."

Several heads turned in Natalie's direction, though Miss Plummer's voice had scarcely penetrated the general conversational din. A short, jolly-looking fat man bobbed toward Natalie, waving a half-empty glass.

"All the way from Australia, eh?" He extended his goblet. "You must be thirsty. Here, take this, I'll get another." And before Natalie could reply, he turned and plunged back into the group around the table.

"Major Hamilton," Miss Plummer whispered. "A dear soul, really. Though I'm afraid he's just a wee bit squiffy."

As Miss Plummer moved away, Natalie glanced uncertainly at the glass in her hand. She was not quite sure where to dispose of it.

"Allow me." A tall, gray-haired and quite distinguished-looking man with a black mustache moved forward and took the stemware from between her fingers.

"Thank you."

"Not at all. I'm afraid you'll have to excuse the major. The party spirit, you know." He nodded, indicating a woman in extreme décolletage chattering animatedly to a group of three laughing men. "But since it's by way of being a farewell celebration—"

"Ah, there you are!" The short man whom Miss Plummer had identified as Major Hamilton bounced back into orbit around Natalie, a fresh drink in his hand and a fresh smile on his ruddy face. "I'm back again," he announced. "Just like a boomerang, eh?"

He laughed explosively, then paused. "I say, you *do* have boomerangs in Australia? Saw quite a bit of you Aussies at Gallipoli. Of course that was some time ago, before *your* time, I daresay—"

"Please, Major." The tall man smiled at Natalie. There was something reassuring about his presence, and something oddly familiar too. Natalie wondered where she might have seen him before. She watched while he moved over to the Major and removed the drink from his hand.

"Now see here—" the major sputtered.

"You've had enough, old boy. And it's almost time for you to go."

"One for the road—" The Major glanced around, his hands waving in appeal. "Everyone *else* is drinking!" He made a lunge for his glass, but the tall man evaded him. Smiling at Natalie over his shoulder, he drew the Major to one side and began to mutter to him earnestly in low tones. The Major nodded exaggeratedly, drunkenly.

Natalie looked around the room. Nobody was paying the least attention to her except one elderly woman who sat quite alone on a stool before the piano. She regarded Natalie with a fixed stare that made her feel like an intruder on a gala scene. Natalie turned away hastily and again caught sight of the woman in décolletage. She suddenly remembered her own desire to change her clothing and peered at the doorway, seeking Miss Plummer. But Miss Plummer was nowhere to be seen.

Walking back into the hall, she peered up the staircase.

"Miss Plummer!" she called.

There was no response.

Then from out of the corner of her eye, she noted that the door of the room across the hallway was ajar. In fact, it was opening now, quite rapidly, and as Natalie stared, Miss Plummer came backing out of the room, carrying a pair of scissors in her hand. Before Natalie could call out again and attract her attention, Miss Plummer had scurried off in the other direction.

The people here, Natalie told herself, certainly seemed odd. But wasn't that always the case with people at parties? She crossed before the stairs, meaning to follow Miss Plummer, but found herself halting before the open doorway.

She gazed in curiously at what was obviously her uncle's consultation room. It was a cozy, book-lined study with heavy, leather-covered furniture grouped before the shelves. The psychiatric couch rested in one corner near the wall and near it was a large mahogany desk. The top of the desk was quite bare, save for a cradle telephone, and a thin brown loop snaking out from it.

Something about the loop disturbed Natalie and before she was conscious of her movement she was inside the room looking down at the desk-top and the brown cord from the phone.

And then she realized what had bothered her. The end of the cord had been neatly severed from its connection in the wall.

"Miss Plummer!" Natalie murmured, remembering the pair of scissors she'd seen her holding. *But why would she have cut the phone cord?*

Natalie turned just in time to observe the tall, distinguished-looking man enter the doorway behind her.

"The phone won't be needed," he said, as if he'd read her thoughts. "After all, I *did* tell you it was a farewell celebration." And he gave a little chuckle.

Again Natalie sensed something strangely familiar about him, and this time it came to her. She'd heard the same chuckle over the phone, when she'd called from the station.

"You must be playing a joke!" she exclaimed. "You're Dr. Bracegirdle, aren't you?"

"No, my dear." He shook his head as he moved past her across the room. "It's just that no one expected you. We were about to leave when your call came. So we had to say *some*thing."

There was a moment of silence. Then, "Where *is* my uncle?" Natalie asked at last.

"Over here."

Natalie found herself standing beside the tall man, gazing down at what lay in a space between the couch and the wall. An instant was all she could bear.

"Messy," the tall man nodded. "Of course it was all so sudden, the opportunity, I mean. And then they *would* get into the liquor—"

His voice echoed hollowly in the room and Natalie realized the sounds of the party had died away. She glanced up to see them all standing there in the doorway, watching.

Then their ranks parted and Miss Plummer came quickly into the room, wearing an incongruous fur wrap over the rumpled, ill-fitting uniform.

"Oh, my!" she gasped. "So you found him!"

Natalie nodded and took a step forward. "You've got to do something," she said. "Please!"

"Of course, you didn't see the others," Miss Plummer said, "since they're upstairs. The Doctor's staff. Gruesome sight."

The men and women had crowded into the room behind Miss Plummer, staring silently.

Natalie turned to them in appeal. "Why, it's the work of a madman!" she cried. "He belongs in an asylum!"

"My dear child," murmured Miss Plummer, as she quickly closed and locked the door and the silent starers moved forward. "This *is* an asylum . . ."

74

THE BLUE WASH MYSTERY

Anna Katharine Green

ONE SUMMER DAY, several years ago now, a gentleman was walking down Broadway, when he encountered Mr. Hardy of the firm of Hanson, Gregg & Hardy, House Painters and Decorators. Being friends, they both stopped.

"Well met," cried the former. "I am just on my way to spend a couple of weeks with my family at Lake George, and your face reminds me of a pleasant surprise I can give my wife upon our return. Our front parlor needs to be freshly frescoed and painted, or so she has been saying for the last six months. Now if it could be done while I am gone, her wishes would be gratified and I would escape a confounded nuisance. What do you think about it? Can you manage to do it at such short notice?"

"Yes," was the sturdy reply, "if you let us into the house today. I have two men on hand waiting for orders this morning. If I could make use of them I think there would be no difficulty about the matter."

"But I haven't the key—I gave it to Henry, who is going to sleep in the house while I am gone, and he went to Newark this morning and won't be home till midnight. Won't tomorrow do? Or stay, I have an idea. Our house is a corner one as you know, and my room looks out on G——— Street. If your men will put a ladder up on that side of the house, they can get in through the farther window on the second floor. I left it up this morning with injunctions to Henry to close it when he came home tonight. Won't that do? The furniture you can put in the back room, the carpet you can cover up—anything so my wife gets her surprise."

"Well, we'll try."

And the gentlemen parted.

Now to you lady readers, the mystery will be that any man in his sane mind would dare to order his parlor furniture removed and the ceiling torn over a first-class axminster carpet, without warning his wife of the destruction that loomed over her favorite property. But that is not the mystery of this tale. The mystery of this story is one that a man can comprehend, even a boy, I think. So listen and be patient while I relate a few further facts.

Well, then, Mr. Hardy, who was of a prompt and energetic disposition, went immediately to his store and notified his two men of what he wanted done. Being fully engaged that morning, he could not go with them himself, but he told them expressly where the house was and by what means they were to enter, adding that he would be with them by noon when he hoped they would have the walls scraped and the blue wash on, ready for whatever final coloring he should decide upon employing.

"Remember," said he, "the large double-house on the northeast corner of G——— Street and Seventh Avenue. You cannot mistake it as there is but one house of that sort on the block." And conscious of having displayed the efficiency of his character, he left the store to attend to the business more immediately demanding his attention.

The men started. Pushing before them their hand-cart with its long ladder, they proceeded slowly uptown, and arriving at G——— Street, turned down toward the Seventh Avenue. Soon they came to a corner on which was a large double-house. Looking up, they saw it was closed, all but the one window on the second floor which they had expected to find open.

Stopping, they put up their ladder, entered the house, made their way unmolested to the parlor, carried out the furniture into the back room, tore up the carpet and laid it in a heap in the center. Then they scraped the walls and having put on the blue wash as had been ordered, went upstairs to look out of the window by which they had entered, in order to see if Mr. Hardy was coming. He was. He was just passing the corner. Without a glance in their direction, he was going quickly by, when one of the men whistled. That made him stop. Astonished, almost aghast, he looked up.

"What are you doing here?" cried he, coming hastily to the foot of the ladder.

"Scraping the walls as you ordered," exclaimed the man, alarmed at the expression on the face that met his gaze from below.

"But this is not the house!" cried Mr. Hardy. "I told you the large double-house on the corner of Seventh Avenue. This is Sixth!"

It was true. The men, misled by the appearance of things, had failed to notice what avenue they were on and had stopped one block short of their real destination.

Shaking the ladder in his wrath, Mr. Hardy cried, "Have you scraped the walls?"

The man nodded.

"Good heavens! And put on the blue wash?"

"Yes, sir."

"Thunder and lightning!—and I don't even know the name of the man who lives here. Is the house empty?"

"Yes, sir, empty, and ready to be swept," said the workman. "Sweep it then, you idiots, and put things back in their place, while I go and see what can be done."

He went to one of the neighbors, a man he knew, and told him of the mistake his men had made, and asked who lived in the house thus invaded. He was told:

"A Mr. Crippens, sir. The bitterest old curmudgeon and the worst man to irritate you ever saw. Once let him know that anyone has dared to invade his premises and do what you have done, and no amount of apology—no, nor damages either—would ever appease him. He would hound you and hinder you and get into your way all the rest of your life. Nothing is too mean for him to do, nothing too much trouble. You might as well rouse the Evil One himself."

"But what is to be done, then?" exclaimed Mr. Hardy in dismay.

"Nothing. Take off your men, shut up the house, and keep quiet. The neighbors are all away but myself and you may be sure he will learn nothing from me. Let him stamp his feet and howl over the matter if he will. 'Twill ease his mind and do him just as much good as if he spent time and money in ruining the business of a respectable man."

And Mr. Hardy partially followed this advice. He had the carpet put back and the furniture restored to its place, left a suitable sum of money on the mantel, but beyond that did nothing by way of explanation or remedy for the havoc he had caused.

And now what is the mystery? The mystery is this. What did that same old curmudgeon and his family think when they returned to their home and found the walls of their parlor denuded of every particle of paint? What explanation were they ever able to make to themselves of this startling occurrence? And if any of them are living yet, what do they think today when they remember the surprise of that moment and how the long years have passed without offering them any solution to the enigma?

75

THE CANDIDATE

Henry Slesar

A MAN'S WORTH can be judged by the calibre of his enemies. Burton Grunzer, encoutering the phrase in a pocket-sized biography he had purchased at a newsstand, put the book in his lap and stared reflectively from the murky window of the commuter train. Darkness silvered the glass and gave him nothing to look at but his own image, but it seemed appropriate to his line of thought. How many people were enemies of that face, of the eyes narrowed by the myopic squint denied by vanity the correction of spectacles, of the nose he secretly called patrician, of the mouth that was soft in relaxation and hard when animated by speech or smiles or frowns? How many enemies? Grunzer mused. A few he could name, others he could guess. But it was their calibre that was important. Men like Whitman Hayes, for instance; there was a 24-carat opponent for you. Grunzer smiled, darting a sidelong glance at the seat-sharer beside him, not wanting to be caught indulging in a secret thought. Grunzer was thirty-four; Hayes was twice as old, his white hairs synonymous with experience, an enemy to be proud of. Hayes knew the food business, all right, knew it from every angle; he'd been a wagon jobber for six years, a broker for ten, a food company executive for twenty before the old man had brought him into the organization to sit on his right hand. Pinning Hayes to the mat wasn't easy, and that made Grunzer's small but increasing triumphs all the sweeter. He congratulated himself. He had twisted Hayes's advantages into drawbacks, had made his long years seem tantamount to senility and outlived usefulness; in meetings, he had concentrated his questions on the new supermarket and suburbia phenomena to demonstrate to the old man that times had changed, that the past was dead, that new merchandising tactics were needed, and that only a younger man could supply them. . . .

Suddenly, he was depressed. His enjoyment of remembered victories

445

seemed tasteless. Yes, he'd won a minor battle or two in the company conference room; he'd made Hayes's ruddy face go crimson, and seen the old man's parchment skin wrinkle in a sly grin. But what had been accomplished? Hayes seemed more self-assured than ever, and the old man more dependent upon his advice. . . .

When he arrived home, later than usual, his wife Jean didn't ask questions. After eight years of a marriage in which, childless, she knew her husband almost too well, she wisely offered nothing more than a quiet greeting, a hot meal, and the day's mail. Grunzer flipped though the bills and circulars, and found an unmarked letter. He slipped it into his hip pocket, reserving it for private perusal, and finished the meal in silence.

After dinner, Jean suggested a movie and he agreed; he had a passion for violent action movies. But first, he locked himself in the bathroom and opened the letter. Its heading was cryptic: *Society for United Action*. The return address was a post office box. It read:

> Dear Mr. Grunzer:
> Your name has been suggested to us by a mutual acquaintance. Our organization has an unusual mission which cannot be described in this letter, but which you may find of exceeding interest. We would be gratified by a private discussion at your earliest convenience. If I do not hear from you to the contrary in the next few days, I will take the liberty of calling you at your office.

It was signed, *Carl Tucker, Secretary*. A thin line at the bottom of the page read: *A Nonprofit Organization*.

His first reaction was a defensive one; he suspected an oblique attack on his pocketbook. His second was curiosity: he went to the bedroom and located the telephone directory, but found no organization listed by the letterhead name. *Okay, Mr. Tucker,* he thought wryly, *I'll bite.*

When no call came in the next three days, his curiosity was increased. But when Friday arrived, he forgot the letter's promise in the crush of office affairs. The old man called a meeting with the bakery products division. Grunzer sat opposite Whitman Hayes at the conference table, poised to pounce on fallacies in his statements. He almost had him once, but Eckhardt, the bakery products manager, spoke up in defense of Hayes's views. Eckhardt had only been with the company a year, but he had evidently chosen sides already. Grunzer glared at him, and reserved a place for Echkardt in the hate chamber of his mind.

At three o'clock, Carl Tucker called.

"Mr. Grunzer?" The voice was friendly, even cheery. "I haven't heard from you, so I assume you don't mind my calling today. Is there a chance we can get together sometime?"

"Well, if you could give me some idea, Mr. Tucker—"

The chuckle was resonant. "We're not a charity organization, Mr. Grunzer, in case you got that notion. Nor do we sell anything. We're more or less a voluntary service group: our membership is over a thousand at present."

"To tell you the truth," Grunzer frowned, "I never heard of you."

"No, you haven't, and that's one of the assets. I think you'll understand when I tell you about us. I can be over at your office in fifteen minutes, unless you want to make it another day."

Grunzer glanced at his calendar. "Okay, Mr. Tucker. Best time for me is right now."

"Fine! I'll be right over."

Tucker was prompt. When he walked into the office, Grunzer's eyes went dismayed at the officious briefcase in the man's right hand. But he felt better when Tucker, a florid man in his early sixties with small, pleasant features, began talking.

"Nice of you to take the time, Mr. Grunzer. And believe me, I'm not here to sell you insurance or razor blades. Couldn't if I tried; I'm a semi-retired broker. However, the subject I want to discuss is rather— intimate, so I'll have to ask you to bear with me or a certain point. May I close the door?"

"Sure," Grunzer said, mystified.

Tucker closed it, hitched his chair closer and said:

"The point is this. What I have to say must remain in the strictest confidence. If you betray that confidence, if you publicize our society in any way, the consequences could be most unpleasant. Is that agreeable?"

Grunzer, frowning, nodded.

"Fine!" The visitor snapped open the briefcase and produced a stapled manuscript. "Now, the society has prepared this little spiel about our basic philosophy, but I'm not going to bore you with it. I'm going to go straight to the heart of our agreement. You may not agree with our first principle at all, and I'd like to know that now."

"How do you mean, first principle?"

"Well . . ." Tucker flushed slightly. "Put in the crudest form, Mr. Grunzer, the Society for United Action believes that—*some* people are just not fit to live." He looked up quickly, as if anxious to gauge the immediate reaction. "There, I've said it," he laughed, somewhat in relief. "Some of our members don't believe in my direct approach; they feel the argument has to be broached more discreetly. But frankly, I've gotten excellent results in this rather crude manner. How do you feel about what I've said, Mr. Grunzer?"

"I don't know. Guess I never thought about it much."

"Were you in the war, Mr. Grunzer?"

"Yes, Navy." Grunzer rubbed his jaw. "I didn't think the Japs were fit to live, back then. I guess maybe there are other cases. I mean, you take capital punishment, I believe in that. Murderers, rape-artists, perverts, hell, I certainly don't think *they're* fit to live."

"Ah," Tucker said. "So you really accept our first principle. It's a question of category, isn't it?"

"I guess you could say that."

"Good. So now I'll try another blunt question. Have you—personally— ever wished someone dead? Oh, I don't mean those casual, fleeting wishes everybody has. I mean a real, deep-down, uncomplicated wish for the death of someone *you* thought was unfit to live. Have you?"

"Sure," Grunzer said frankly. "I guess I have."

"There are times, in your opinion, when the removal of someone from this earth would be beneficial?"

Grunzer smiled. "Hey, what is this? You from Murder, Incorporated or something?"

Tucker grinned back. "Hardly, Mr. Grunzer, hardly. There is absolutely no criminal aspect to our aims or our methods. I'll admit we're a 'secret' society, but we're no Black Hand. You'd be amazed at the quality of our membership; it even includes members of the legal profession. But suppose I tell you how the society came into being?

"It began with two men; I can't reveal their names just now. The year was 1949, and one of these men was a lawyer attached to the district attorney's office. The other man was a state psychiatrist. Both of them were involved in a rather sensational trial, concerning a man accused of a hideous crime against two small boys. In their opinion, the man was unquestionably guilty, but an unusually persuasive defense counsel, and a highly suggestible jury, gave him his freedom. When the shocking verdict was announced, these two, who were personal friends as well as colleagues, were thunderstruck and furious. They felt a great wrong had been committed, and they were helpless to right it. . . .

"But I should explain something about this psychiatrist. For some years, he had made studies in a field which might be called anthropological psychiatry. One of those researches related to the voodoo practice of certain groups, the Haitian in particular. You've probably heard a great deal about voodoo, or Obeah as they call it in Jamaica, but I won't dwell on the subject lest you think we hold tribal rites and stick pins in dolls. . . . But the chief feature of his study was the uncanny *success* of certain strange practices. Naturally, as a scientist, he rejected the supernatural explanation and sought the rational one. And of course, there was only one answer. When the *vodun* priest decreed the punishment or death of a malefactor, it was the malefactor's own convictions concerning the efficacy of the death wish, his own faith in the voodoo power, that eventually made the wish come true. Sometimes, the process was organic—his body reacted psychosomatically to the voodoo curse, and he would sicken and die. Sometimes, he would die by 'accident'—an accident prompted by the secret belief that once cursed, he *must* die. Eerie, isn't it?''

"No doubt," Grunzer said, dry-lipped.

"Anyway, our friend, the psychiatrist, began wondering aloud if *any* of us have advanced so far along the civilized path that we couldn't be subject to this same sort of 'suggested' punishment. He proposed that they experiment on this choice subject, just to see.

"How they did it was simple," he said. "They went to see this man, and they announced their intentions. They told him they were going to *wish him dead*. They explained how and why the wish would become reality, and while he laughed at their proposal, they could see the look of superstitious fear cross his face. They promised him that regularly, every day, they would be wishing for his death, until he could no longer stop the negative juggernaut that would make the wish come true."

Grunzer shivered suddenly, and clenched his fist. "That's pretty silly," he said softly.

"The man died of a heart attack two months later."

"Of course. I knew you'd say that. But there's such a thing as coincidence."

"Naturally. And our friends, while intrigued, weren't satisfied. *So they tried it again.*"

"Again?"

"Yes, again. I won't recount who the victim was, but I will tell you that this time they enlisted the aid of four associates. This little band of pioneers was the nucleus of the society I represent today."

Grunzer shook his head. "And you mean to tell me there's a *thousand* now?"

"Yes, a thousand and more, all over the country. A society whose one function is to *wish people dead*. At first, membership was purely voluntary, but now we have a system. Each new member of the Society for United Action joins on the basis of submitting one potential victim. Naturally, the society investigates to determine whether the victim is deserving of his fate. If the case is a good one, the *entire* membership then sets about to *wish him dead*. Once the task has been accomplished, naturally, the new member must take part in all future concerted action. That and a small yearly fee, is the price of membership.''

Carl Tucker grinned.

''And in case you think I'm not serious, Mr. Grunzer—'' He dipped into the briefcase again, this time producing a blue-bound volume of telephone directory thickness. ''Here are the facts. To date, two hundred and twenty-nine victims were named by our selection committee. Of those, *one hundred and four* are no longer alive. Coincidence, Mr. Grunzer?''

''As for the remaining one hundred and twenty-five—perhaps that indicates that our method is not infallible. We're the first to admit that. But new techniques are being developed all this time. I assure you, Mr. Grunzer, *we will get them all*.''

He flipped through the blue-bound book.

''Our members are listed in this book, Mr. Grunzer. I'm going to give you the option to call one, ten or a hundred of them. Call them and see if I'm not telling the truth.''

He flipped the manuscript toward Grunzer's desk. It landed on the blotter with a thud. Grunzer picked it up.

''Well?'' Tucker said. ''Want to call them?''

''No.'' He licked his lips. ''I'm willing to take your word for it, Mr. Tucker. It's incredible, but I can see how it works. Just *knowing* that a thousand people are wishing you dead is enough to shake hell out of you.'' His eyes narrowed. ''But there's one question. You talked about a 'small' fee—''

''It's fifty dollars, Mr. Grunzer.''

''Fifty, huh? Fifty times a thousand, that's pretty good money, isn't it?''

''I assure you, the organization is not motivated by profit. Not the kind you mean. The dues merely cover expenses, committee work, research and the like. Surely you can understand that?''

''I guess so,'' he grunted.

''Then you find it interesting?''

Grunzer swiveled his chair about to face the window.

God! he thought.

God! if it *really* worked!

But how could it? If wishes became deeds, he could have slaughtered

450

dozens in his lifetime. Yet, that was different. His wishes were always secret things, hidden where no man could know them. But this method was different, more practical, more terrifying. Yes, he could see how it might work. He could visualize a thousand minds burning with the single wish of death, see the victim sneering in disbelief at first, and then slowly, gradually, surely succumbing to the tightening, constricting chain of fear that it *might* work, that so many deadly thoughts could indeed emit a mystical, malevolent ray that destroyed life.

Suddenly, ghostlike, he saw the ruddy face of Whitman Hayes before him.

He wheeled about and said:

"But the victim has to *know* all this, of course? He has to know the society exists, and has succeeded, and is wishing for *his* death? That's essential, isn't it?"

"Absolutely essential," Tucker said, replacing the manuscripts in his briefcase. "You've touched on the vital point, Mr. Grunzer. The victim must be informed, and that, precisely, is what I have done." He looked at his watch. "Your death wish began at noon today. The society has begun to work. I'm very sorry."

At the doorway, he turned and lifted both hat and briefcase in one departing salute.

"Goodbye, Mr. Grunzer," he said.

76

THE BOOSTER

Percy Spurlark Parker

I SLIPPED THE evening gloves in my purse as the sales clerk turned to get a few other pairs off the shelf. She laid them on the counter with the others she had already laid out.

"How are these, Miss?" she asked, her voice a little tired.

I frowned and picked though the gloves. "No, I'm afraid not. Thanks anyway."

I walked away, smiling to myself. I had kept her occupied for a good fifteen minutes, had made her totally confused about what she was doing, and had gotten away with a twenty-dollar pair of gloves.

There were eight floors in the department store, and so far I'd made a score on the first five. Thank heaven for large shoulder bags. I'd actually gotten a four-slice toaster into mine once, but it didn't leave room for much else.

It was Saturday and the store was pretty full—not so packed that you bumped into someone every two minutes, but full enough to lose yourself in the crowd. It was the ideal condition for a "booster"—or shoplifter in plain language—as long as you kept an eye on the security personnel. The store had both uniformed and plainclothes security people. Sometimes, like the guy standing at the elevators with his hands behind his back, the plainclothesmen are more obvious than those in uniform.

"Oh, Miss."

I turned, expecting to see the sales clerk with a security guard, but instead a white-haired gentleman was smiling at me.

"Yes?"

He stepped closer, speaking in a low tone. "That was really a very clumsy effort back there."

Maybe he was from store security and I'd been caught after all.

"Look—" I started.

"Don't raise your voice. You don't want to make a scene."

"What do you want?"

"To help," he said. "You're a pretty girl, but that's not going to do you any good behind bars. And believe me, young woman, the way you're going at it jail's the only thing ahead for you. Look at yourself—jeans, a fatigue jacket. And that shoulder bag's a dead givaway. That clerk would have had you back there if she hadn't been totally blind."

"Look, do you work security for this store or what?"

The smile broadened across his smooth face. "Not hardly, my dear."

"Then bug off."

He held up a hand, still smiling. "I said I wanted to help you,. I know what I'm doing—now just watch me."

He looked around, and headed for the cosmetic department. There were several displays of cologne and perfume standing free of the cosmetic counters. He mixed with the customers and made a pass by one of the displays. If he hadn't told me to watch him I wouldn't have caught it. It was one of the most fluid moves I've ever seen. When he started back toward me he had pocketed two bottles of cologne.

"Now do you believe I know what I'm talking about? I was making a living at this long before you got out of diapers. I usually don't display my talents this way, but you are a lovely girl and I'm curious to see what you look like in a proper dress. Would you join me for dinner tonight? I can teach you a great deal."

I pulled out my I.D., which stated that I was an operative for the Elton Detective Agency. I specialize in running security checks on retail operations, identifying the weak spots and confirming those that are strong. But I'd never had a booster hand himself over to me before. This was going to be good for at least a couple of days off, with pay.

77

WHO HAS SEEN THE WIND?

Michael Gilbert

To Superintendent Haxtell, education was something you dodged at school and picked up afterward as you went along.

"All I need in my job," he would say, "I learned in the street."

And he would glare down at Detective Petrella, whom he had once found improving his mind with Dr. Bentley's *Dissertation on Fallacies* at a time when he should have been thumbing his way through the current number of *Hue & Cry*.

Petrella was, of course, an unusual Detective Constable. He spoke three languages—one of them was Arabic, for he had been brought up in Egypt; he knew about subjects like viniculture and the theory of the five-lever lock; and he had an endlessly inquiring mind.

The Superintendent approved of that. "Curiosity," he said. "Know your people. If you don't know, ask questions. Find out. It's better than book learning."

Petrella accepted the rebuke in good part. There was a lot of truth in it. Most police work was knowledge—knowledge of an infinity of small everday facts, unimportant by themselves, deadly when taken together.

Nevertheless, and in spite of the Superintendent, Petrella retained an obstinate conviction that there were other things as well, deeper things and finer things: colors, shapes, and sounds of absolute beauty, unconnected with the world of small people in small houses in gray streets. And while in one pocket of his old raincoat he might carry Moriarty's *Police Law,* in the other would lie, dog-eared with use, the *Golden Treasury* of Palgrave.

"She walks in beauty, like the night Of cloudless climes and starry skies," said Petrella, and, "That car's been there a long time. If it's still there when I come back it might be worth looking into."

He was on his way to Lavender Alley to see a man called Parkoff about a missing bicycle. It was as he was walking down Barnaby Passage that he forgot poetry and remembered he was a policeman.

For something was missing. Something as closely connected with Barnaby Passage as mild with bitter or bacon with eggs. The noise of the Harrington children at play.

There were six of them, and Barnaby Passage, which ran alongside their back garden, was their stamping ground. On the last occasion that Petrella had walked through it, a well-aimed potato had carried away his hat, and he had turned in time to see the elfin fact of Mickey Harrington disappear behind a row of dustbins. He had done nothing about it, first because it did not befit the dignity of a plainclothes detective to chase a small boy, and secondly because he would not have had the smallest chance of catching him.

Even when not making themselves felt, the Harrington family could always be heard. Were they at school? No, too late. In bed? Much too early. Away somewhere? The Harrington family rarely went away. And if by any chance they had moved, that was something he ought to know about, for they were part of his charge.

Six months ago he had helped to arrest Tim Harrington. It had taken three of them to do it. Tim had fought because he knew what was coming to him. It was third time unlucky and he was due for a full stretch.

Mrs. Harrington had shown only token resentment at this sudden removal of her husband for a certain nine and a possible twelve years. He was a man who took a belt to his children and a boot to his women. Not only when he was drunk, which would have been natural, if not forgivable, but with cold ferocity when sober.

Petrella paused at the corner where the blank walls of Barnaby Passage opened out into Barnaby Row. It was at that moment that a line of Rossetti came into his head. *Who has seen the wind?* he murmured to himself. *Neither you nor I.*

A casement rattled up and an old woman pushed out her head. "Lookin' for someone?"

"Er, good evening, Mrs. Minter," said Petrella politely. "I wasn't going to—that's to say, I wondered what had happened to Mrs. Harrington. You can usually hear her family."

"Noisy little beggars," said Mrs. Minter. But she said it without feeling. Children and flies, hope and despair and dirt and love and death: she had seen them all from her little window.

"I wondered if they'd gone away."

"They're home," said Mrs. Minter. "And Mrs. Harrington." Her eyes were button-bright.

As Petrella turned away he heard the window slamming down and the click of the catch.

He climbed the steps. Signs of calamity were all about him: the brass dolphin knocker unpolished, the steps unwhited. A lace curtain twitched in the front window, and behind the curtain something stirred.

Petrella knocked. He had lifted the knocker a second time when it was snatched out of his hand by the sudden opening of the door, and Mrs. Harrington stood there.

She was still the ghost of the pretty girl Tim Harrington had married ten years before, but life and rough usage had sandpapered her down to something finer and smaller than nature had ever intended. Her fair hair was drawn tightly over her head and all her girl's curves were turning into planes and angles.

Usually she managed a smile for Petrella, but today there was nothing behind her eyes but emptiness.

"Can I come in?" he asked.

"Well—yes, all right."

She made no move. Only when Petrella actually stepped toward her did she half turn to let him past her, up the dark narrow hall.

"How are the children?" he asked—and saw for himself. The six Harrington children were all in the front room, and all silent. The oldest boy and girl were making a pretense of reading books, but the four younger ones were just sitting and staring.

"You're very quiet," he said. "Has the scissor man come along and cut all your tongues out?"

The oldest boy tried out a grin. It wasn't a very convincing grin, but it lasted long enough for Petrella to see some freshly dried blood inside the lip.

I can smell tiger, he thought. The brute's here all right. He must have made his break this afternoon. If it had been any earlier, the news would have reached the station before I left it.

"I'd like a word with you," he said. "Perhaps you could ask the children to clear out for a moment." He looked at the door which led, as he knew, into the kitchen.

"Not in there" she said quickly. "Out into the hall."

Now that he knew, it was obvious. The smallest boy had his eyes glued to the kitchen door in a sort of dumb horror.

They shuffled out into the hall. Petrella said softly, "I'm not sure you shouldn't go too. There's going to be trouble."

She looked at him with sudden understanding. Then she said, in a loud rough voice, "I don't know what you're talking about. If you've got anything to say, say it and get out. I got my work to do."

"All right," said Petrella. "If you want to play it that way."

He was moving as he spoke. The door to the kitchen was a fragile thing. He ran at it, at the last moment swinging his boot up so that the sole of his heavy shoe landed flat and hard, an inch below the handle.

The door jumped backward, hit something that was behind it, and checked. Petrella slid through the opening.

Tim Harrington was on his knees on the floor. The door edge had cut open his head, and on his stupid face he had the look of a boxer when the ring gets up and hits him.

Petrella fell on top of him. He was giving away too much in weight and strength and fighting experience for any sort of finesse. Under his weight Harrington flattened for a moment, then braced himself, and bucked.

Petrella had his right arm in a lock round the man's neck, and hung on. Steel fingers tore at his arm, plucked it away, and the lumpy body jerked again, and straightened. Next moment they were both on their feet, glaring at each other.

In the front room the woman was screaming steadily, and a growing clamor showed that the street was astir. But in the tiny kitchen it was still a private fight.

Harrington swung on his heel and made for the window into the garden. For a moment Petrella was tempted. Then he jumped for the big man's legs, and they were down on the floor again, squirming and fighting and groping.

There was only one end to that. The bigger man carried all the guns. First he got Petrella by the hair and thumped his head on the linoleum. Then he shambled to his feet and, as Petrella turned onto his knees, swung a boot.

If it had landed squarely, that would have been the end of Petrella as a policeman, and maybe as a man as well; but he saw it coming and rolled to avoid it. And in the moment that it missed him, he plucked at the other foot. Harrington came down and in his fall brought the kitchen table with him. A bowl of drippings rolled onto the floor, spilling its brown contents in a slow and loving circle. Petrella, on his knees, watched it, fascinated.

Then he realized that he was alone.

His mind was working well enough to bring him to his feet but his legs seemed to have an existence of their own. They took him out into the front room, which was empty, and then into the hall.

He was dimly aware of the children, all staring at him, all silent. The door was open. In the street footsteps, running.

"You won't catch him now," said Mrs. Harrington.

He turned his head to look at her, and the sudden movement seemed to clear his brain. "I'm going after him," he said. "Ring the police."

Then he was out in the street, and running. Mrs. Minter shouted, "Down there, Mister," and pointed. He stumbled, and righted himself. Harrington was already disappearing round the corner. Petrella shambled after him.

When he got to the corner there was one car in the road ahead of him and no one in sight. The car was moving, accelerating, a big blue four-door sedan. Too far away to see the license number.

"Gone away!"

A second car drew up behind him, and a voice said politely, "Is there anything wrong?"

Petrella became aware that he was standing, swaying, in the middle of the road. Behind him, its hood inches from his back, was a neat little sports car in two shades of green, driven by a fat young man with fair hair and a Brigade-of-Guards mustache.

"Police," said Petrella. "Got to get that car. It's stolen."

The blue sedan was turning into High Street now. "Move over. I'll drive."

"Hop in," said the young man. "You don't look too fit. I'd better do the driving. It's a tricky little bus, this, till you get the hang of it."

"All right," muttered Petrella. "but quick."

The young man took him at his word. The little car jumped forward like a horse at the touch of a spur. They cornered into High Street, under the nose of a bus, and shot down the middle of the crowded road.

The young man hardly seemed to have moved in his seat. He handled his car like a craftsman, insolently exact, both careful and careless at the same time.

"Right fork ahead. He's going up to the Heath, I think."

"His neck'll be for sale if he does much more of *that*," said the young man calmly. The blue sedan had pulled out, charged past a bus, and only just got back again ahead of the oncoming truck.

"I say," said Petrella, "you can drive."

"Done a good deal of it," said the man. "Rally stuff mostly, a bit on the track. Name of Blech."

459

Petrella placed him then.

Time came, and time went, and they were off the Heath and making for the maze of small streets which fills the triangle between Hampstead, Regent's Park, and Camden Town.

"I'm a bit too light to ram him," said Blech. "No need, really. All we have to do is keep in sight. He'll do himself soon."

It happened as he was speaking. The road went up in a hump over the Canal. The blue sedan hit the rise so fast that it almost took off, came down threshing and screaming, went into a long sideways skid, hit the low parapet, and toppled over.

Blech came neatly to a halt, and Petrella was out, and running again.

The blue car was standing on its nose in three feet of water and mud, sinking ponderously. Petrella got the rear door open, and pulled. Behind him, Blech pulled. As the car fell away, the bulk of Tim Harrington tumbled back on top of them.

Petrella seized him by the hair and hammered his head on the towpath.

He felt a restraining hand on his arm, and the mists cleared again for a moment. "I think," said Blech, "that you're being rather too—er—vigorous with him. What he wants is first aid, really."

"Sorry," said Petrella. "Not thinking very straight. Fact is, I think I'm bit concussed myself."

"That makes two of you. If you helped, we might get him into my car."

They did this, between them. The street slept in a timeless summer's evening doze. From first to last no other person appeared on the scene.

"Where to now?"

Petrella tried to think. Harrington was out cold. There was a big purple bruise on one side of his forehead, and an occasional bubble formed in the corner of his open mouth. He was a hospital case. But no hospital would take him in without explanations. Nor would any other police station.

"Home," he said. "The way we came. It'll be quicker in the long run."

They drove home decorously, back up onto the Heath, and west, with the setting sun in their eyes. For a few seconds Petrella dozed. That wouldn't do. No time to sleep. Job not finished. Better talk and keep awake.

"It's very good of you," he said, "to take all this trouble."

"Enjoyed it," said Blech. "What is he?"

"He's an escaped convict," said Petrella. "Named Harrington. Not exactly a pleasant character."

"How did you cotton on to him?"

How had he? It was so many years ago. A great gale was singing through

460

his head, a mighty diapason of sound that came and went. "It was Rossetti put me on to him," he said, as the gale dropped for a moment.

"Rossetti? *The Blessed Damozel*—"

"Not Dante Gabriel, Christina. *Who has seen the wind? Neither you nor I: But when the trees bow down their heads The wind is passing by.* Fork left here."

"That's nice," said Blech. "Is there any more of it?"

"Who has seen the wind? Neither I nor you: But when the leaves hang trembling The wind is passing through." That was it. Hang trembling. It was the children that had made him certain. Sitting there like drugged mice.

"I must remember that," said Blech. "Here we are, I think. You'd better get some help to carry out our passenger. And then you ought to lie down, I think."

Superintendent Haxtell reckoned that he was beyond surprise, but the events of that evening tried him hard. First, there came two stalwart constables, supporting the drooping figure of a convict of whose escape in transit from one prison to another he had only just been notified; secondly, a diffident figure, whose face he vaguely recognized from the columns of the popular press; and, bringing up the rear, his shirt torn open to the waist, his face rimmed with blood and dried dripping, Detective Petrella.

When he had sorted things out a bit, he sat down to make his report.

Plainly it was a case that reflected the greatest credit on all concerned. And a lot of it must, and should go to Petrella. And, according to Petrella, Blech had behaved very well. A foreigner, but a good chap. So far so good.

But what the Superintendent couldn't make out was exactly what credit was to be given to a person named Rossetti. Sounded like some sort of Italian. Some further inquiries needed there. His pen scratched busily . . .

78

DEATHBED

Frank Sisk

THE DOCTOR AND the nurse emerged from George Painter's room just after 4 P.M. They conferred for a long minute in the upper hallway, voices low, before moving to the head of the circular staircase. At the foot, fretfully waiting, Coral hadn't been able to make out a word that was said.

Why, she wondered, are members of the medical profession always whispering to each other? Why must they treat death and adenoids with similar secrecy? Even orderlies conceal the result of a thermometer reading as if it were privileged information. Charlatans, most of them. They certainly weren't fooling George Painter with their mysterious muttering, always a bit out of earshot. That old crock has known for at least a month that he's on the last lap. What's more, the idea of death doesn't seem to faze him at all. Lately his rare smile has grown sly. As his strength ebbs he looks each day more like a wily old gambler with an ace up his sleeve, a final card with which he plans to trump, for a moment at least, death itself.

Dr. Wolff and Miss Suratt were descending the stairs, he a stocky figure in gray tweed, she a slender figure in white nylon, their downward progress soundless on the thick gold carpet.

Coral slipped a dolorous mask over her tanned face. This morning she had played tennis with Otis and a little before lunch they had made love. She was still feeling keenly alive, almost youthful—not a bit like a prospective widow—but she wore the sad mask well.

"How is he doing, Doctor?" Into her own whisper she wove the correct amount of tension. "Is he still alert?"

"Very much so," Wolff whispered back. "He's a remarkable man. Remarkable."

"Is he able to speak?"

"Yes, indeed. Not with any of his erstwhile vigor, of course, but his mind is quite clear. Quite clear."

"Exuse me if you will," Miss Suratt whispered. "I simply must go to the kitchen for my cup of tea."

"Phone me at once if there's a critical change." Wolff said.

"And have Glenda fix you something to eat," Coral said.

"Yes, thanks," Miss Suratt said, on her way.

"Please be frank with me, Doctor," Coral said. "How long does George really have?"

Wolff expelled a tiny hiss of air through crooked teeth. "My dear lady, I try not to prophesy in these terminal cases. A patient with a will of iron may battle a long time after that last faint spark of life should have flickered out. Your husband is that kind of person. A man of very strong will, very strong indeed."

"I'm only asking for an educated guess, Doctor."

"I hesitate to give it."

"You're an experienced physician. I understand you've been treating my husband for at least ten years. You must know what to expect. Roughly."

"I do. Very roughly."

"Will he last through the night?"

"I believe that's safe to say. Yes, through the night."

"Through the week?"

"Ah now, my dear lady." Wolff raised a defensive hand.

"Well, may I see him now? Is he well enough for that?"

"Certainly. As a matter of fact, he asked me to send you up. But I do advise you to keep the visit brief. He's already had a rather busy afternoon. Yes, rather busy."

You can say that again, Coral thought.

First, at 1:30, the densely bewhiskered priest from the Greek Orthodox Church had appeared for the third time in as many days. His name was Mikos Gavros. He arrived as usual in a dusty old limousine, his black-garbed bulk occupying most of the tonneau. The chaffeur was his seventeen-year-old son Teddy, the eldest of what Coral understood to be a big brood. Father Gavros' patriarchy wasn't confined to the spirit alone.

Teddy, a runner-up in the hirsute category to his old man, hurried his own bearded face around the car to open the rear door. Father Gavros squeezed out. They entered the foyer together. Coral was there to receive the priest's greeting, one of oily unction that parted his peppery whiskers in the middle, exposing lips of liverish hue.

Was he seeking a new convert? Coral wondered.

While he was closeted upstairs with the dying man, whose name had been legally changed long ago from Pantopoulous to Painter, Coral was left with Teddy, who seemed to have a rather salacious eye. She led him to the library, where she'd twice before abandoned him, and abandoned him again.

Norman Yard arrived an hour later, a few minutes after the departure of Gavros and son. The habitual smile of semiamusement lurked beneath his clipped gray moustache, the slender brown attaché case grew from his left arm like a prosthetic device. Coral's opinion of lawyers, never worshipful at best, had been dropping steadily with each of Yard's frequent visits this last month. She detested that know-it-all smirk of his. Smirking once more, Yard hastily ascended the stairs to consult with his richest client.

Yes, old George Painter had indeed had a busy afternoon.

She entered the enormous bedchamber for the first time in a week. The windows were closed against the late October chill, the great brocaded drapes were drawn. The air was heavy with an odor which she would always associate with George—Turkish cigarette smoke; and there was an odor of something else now, something repugnantly dry and stale. The room was a place of silent dusk except for a nimbus of light centered around a lamp on a bedside table. George sat propped up like a bloodless puppet, so thin that his body hardly raised the thermal blanket covering him, and he was smoking a cigarette; the gray tendrils curling slowly round the lampshade were the only signs of life.

"Hello, George," Coral said nervously as she approached the foot of the king-size bed.

The dying man's face was skeletal but the dark eyes imbedded in that face burned like coals of fire. Coral felt almost literally scorched by his gaze.

"I just left Dr. Wolff. He says you're doing fine."

With brown, bony fingers the man removed the cigarette from his dry lips. "You are a natural liar," he said in a thin, hoarse voice.

"He told me you wanted to see me," Coral said.

"I said I wanted to see—" A thin hacking cough dimmed his eyes for a moment. "Yes, I said I wanted to see that slut without conscience who calls herself my wife. And here you are."

"George, this is hardly the time—"

"Hold your tongue, Coral. Listen." Again that throat-scraping cough. "Pour me a glass of water."

Concealing the disgust that this man aroused in her, she went to the bedside and reached for the pitcher. How had she ever managed to endure these sickening years? Money. Was the money really worth it? It had better be.

"I nurtured no illusions when we married," he was saying. "A tennis bum, your first husband. You outgrew him. Understandable. I outgrew a few previous wives when I was young. You wanted a little luxury for a change. I wanted somebody—" the cough was like a rasp across cartilage "—somebody to keep me warm the last years of my life. Not love—the gesture of attention. A fair trade."

"Do you think you should be talking so much?" She held out the glass of water.

"I should talk. You should listen." He took a sip of water and set the glass on the table. "So listen."

"I'll try."

"It will open your deceitful eyes, what I have to say."

"*Please*. No more of that."

"Almost from the beginning you broke our personal deal."

"What did you expect?"

"Just that. It was no surprise. A healthy young trollop tied to a sick old goat. The horns were inevitable. As long as you were discreet I was tolerant. My pride was not touched. But then you finally threw discretion to the winds. Your gross infidelities became common knowledge. You made me the butt of sad dirty jokes. Even then . . . yes, even then I—" The cough was phlegmy this time and he gave it thoughtful concentration. "Even then I rationalized the situation. But when you seduced my nephew Otis under this roof and flaunted the affair, that was just too much. I decided to take drastic steps."

"I don't know what you can do about it now."

"At this moment Otis is on a plane to Athens where his father, my brother, will welcome him. Already I have done that."

"Impossible. We had lunch together and—"

"He failed to mention the journey. In Greek the name Otis means keen-eared. A few days ago my nephew listened well to Norman Yard, who outlined certain financial arrangements that could improve his future."

"Why, you interfering old buzzard!"

"Wait till you hear what I have in store for you, Coral."

"Well, you can't disinherit me, George. I'm you legal wife. You have no children. Even if you die intestate I'm entitled to half of what you leave."

That rare, sly smile tightened his dry lips. "You know the state law well.

So you may as well see what you will inherit half of.'' From his bathrobe pocket he took a thin sheaf of greenbacks. ''A hundred thousand, ten bills of ten thousand each. My entire estate as of today.''

''You're not kidding me, George,'' Coral said nonchalantly.

''You'll see soon enough. All my other assets have become part of the ecological Painter Foundation. What I have here is all that's left of my personal wealth.''

Stunned, Coral watched the disgusting old man take one of the bills and tear it into a dozen small pieces.

''What in hell are you doing?''

Reaching for the glass of water, he crammed the shredded paper into his mouth and washed it down with a gulping swallow. ''I'm taking it with me,'' he said as he began tearing up another bill.

''Why, you crazy old bugger,'' she screamed, grasping his scrawny throat with her strong tennis-playing hands. He died so quickly that she couldn't believe it. She looked at the greenback clutched in his hand. It was transparently bogus. Of course. The government hadn't printed $10,000 bills in years.

''What have you done to him?'' asked a voice at her shoulder. It was Miss Suratt.

''What have I done to him?'' She raised the murdering hands to her eyes. ''What has he done to me? What has *he* done to *me?*''

79

THE DEVIL BEHIND YOU

Richard A. Moore

HE SAT UNDER the tree in the dark and stared at the illuminated stained-glass windows of the church. A few late arrivals were hurrying from the parking lot. A pair of high heels clicked up the sidewalk, the last of the faithful sounding off the final seconds. The door swung open, letting a shaft of light pierce the darkness, and then pneumatically hissed shut. The night service was beginning.

"Praise God from whom all blessings flow," the chant began, with the choir leading the way.

He watched all this from the edge of the woods, in his usual Sunday-night seat. He stood and automatically wiped the pants of his new blue suit. It would be an hour now before the service would end and his mother would be back to pick him up.

It was much darker under the trees and the pine-needle carpet muffled his footsteps. He could hear the whir of traffic on the highway beyond the church and a dog barking among the houses across the highway. The only nearby sounds were the twigs sharply protesting his steps.

He moved deeper into the woods toward a small stream where he liked to pass the time. It wasn't a great pleasure, sitting on the cool bank listening to the many sounds of the brook, but it was so much better than the inside of the glaringly lighted church.

Going to church was the only social activity in the dreary village, and the main service in the morning was enough contact for most of the congregation. Many made their living from the poor soil and the rest worked at the nearby state prison. It was a simple hard life, and most preferred to contemplate it in solitude.

The eight-year-old boy dreaded the lonely Sunday ordeal, but he had stopped questioning his mother's absense. He was shunned by the other church members and he knew it concerned his mother's past and the father he never had. At times he sat through the sermon, but the fear and tension that traveled through the crowd as they listened to the red-faced preacher frightened him. He dimly grasped the teaching of an ever-present danger of hell and damnation, but his young mind sometimes rebelled and he sought the quiet forest.

He could hear the breeze rustling the few remaining stubborn leaves. An occasional chill reminded him of the winter to come.

"Are you lost?"

The sudden voice shattered the quiet darkness and pricked the boy's heart into a racing flutter. He turned quickly and stared upward at the looming silhouette. The figure knelt, seeming to telescope back to normal size after its early exaggerated hugeness.

A round face, impossibly round, with eyes yielding space enough for several noses, although one was not immediately apparent in that vast area, leaned toward him. A mouth, large beyond belief as if it served double duty because of the minute nose, curved across the face like the world's last river after all else has eroded to pale desert.

"I say, are you lost, boy?"

Clenching bits of twigs and crushed leaves in his fists, the boy attempted to answer, but for the moment could only stammer. The gibbous face nodded with lips stretching another inch in smile.

"Where do you belong?"

The boy found his voice at last but it sounded awkward. "The church. I was at church." He pointed back over the hill from where the distant rumble of the preacher could still be heard working steadily toward the meat of the sermon.

Heavy deliberate laughter came slowly from the crouched figure, as if much more was imprisoned in the barrel chest but only a carefully measured portion was allowed to escape through those awful lips.

"Slipped away from church, eh? Slipped away to the woods." The man gazed about the dark forest. "Couldn't stand to be cooped up, I'll bet. I can understand that. You'd rather visit with me than listen to the preacher go at it. Well, you found a kindred soul. I can't stand those Bible thumpers or close quarters either."

The man's huge face seemed to blot out the small amount of night light that filtered through the trees. The boy tried to stand, but the man put a thick hand on his shoulder and held him firmly to earth.

"Now where do you think you're going?"

The boy stared at the bulging forearm inches from his face. For a moment he seemed to be counting the coarse black hairs that with the movement of the breeze appeared to be crawling along the arm.

"I have to go back now. They'll be missing me."

The man laughed again. "No, son, you've made your choice. They wanted you and instead you came here to me and here you'll stay. I can't let you go now. We haven't got to know each other. I didn't ask for you, but maybe you can be of help." He tightened his grip on the boy's shoulder. "I hope so, boy, I really hope so."

All of the boy's suspicions were aroused. A terrible possibility occurred to him. When he spoke, his voice was tiny, made small by fear.

"Who are you? What can I do?"

The man settled himself, facing the boy, and moved his hand to grip a leg just above the ankle. "You tell me, boy. Who do you think you've found here in the woods?"

His leg felt like a small rope in the man's grip, but the boy spoke his heart. "I think you're the Devil." He trembled again. "I skipped church and you got me."

The last words were drowned in the man's laughter, louder this time. "The Devil!" He chuckled again. "I like that. You figured that out all by yourself in a minute of seeing me when it's taken others quite some time before they called me by that name."

He shook the boy's leg. "What do you think of this outfit?"

The boy stared closely at the man's clothing for the first time. He could see a loosely fitting white shirt and pants with a faded blue stripe along the legs. The dark shape of a pistol butt protruded from the waistline. "That's like what they wear at the state prison."

The man shook the leg in congratulation. "Right again. You are a wonder, boy. I've been in there visiting friends." The laughter returned. "Yes, sir, I was just visiting with some good old buddies of mine who followed in my steps. Just visiting."

He leaned closer to the tiny figure. "But there comes a time to leave and my time came. As enjoyable as the company was to me, you can't expect me to stay there a lifetime. Sure you can't, but others might have different ideas. So here I am moving along at night and running into you.

"Now as to your help, boy. Well, I don't know right offhand but it will come. It will come. You keep real quiet and let's look at this church you left to find me."

The man retained a tight clasp on one arm, but he let the boy lead him to the edge of the forest. The stared across the lake of asphalt that surrounded the church. The light from the stained-glass windows revealed only a few

471

dozen cars huddled close to the building. Sunday evening services were attended only by the elderly, the newly converted, and a handful of the always faithful.

It was hard for the boy to believe that minutes earlier he had purposely left such a safe warm place. He wanted to cry, but his fright was beyond tears. His small brow wrinkled with effort as he sought to radiate promises of everlasting goodness in the future for a bit of help in the present.

The man squatted beside him while the strangely emotional voice from inside the church washed over them unheard. Even when the man spoke an inch from his ear, the boy could not look at him.

"A pretty little church. Pretty. Not too large, but large enough for the faithful in a town this size. And large enough for me to find what I need to leave this place forever. I see some stairs there in the back, my boy. Do you know where they lead?"

The boy thought for a moment. "It's a little room for the singers, the choir. That's where they put on their robes."

The man tightened his grip on the boy's arm. "Perfect. Exactly as I thought, but it needed you to be sure. A nice little choir room where they ready themselves to sing thanksgiving. Do you remember seeing ladies' pocketbooks there? Purses, boy, where they keep their money and car keys?"

When the boy nodded, the man embraced him quickly before turning the child to face him directly. Inches apart, the boy could not see both the man's eyes without turning his head. The breath from the wormlike lips was overpowering. He quivered in the man's arms ready to faint, but the man shook him to attention.

"Now listen carefully boy, for your life depends on you hearing and obeying what I'm about to ask of you." He turned his head slightly toward the church, as if to keep one eye there while the other remained tightly on the boy's white features. "Think of a lady in that choir, sitting just now behind the preacher, her hands in her lap waiting for the next hymn to be sung. Think of one in particular for me, boy, one who drives a nice big car you couldn't help but remember."

The man turned the boy back to face the knot of cars. "Maybe she drives that green one there or the black one next to it. Just pick out one that belongs to some nice lady you're certain is in the choir."

The boy thought for a moment before answering. "The black one. The big one. It belongs to the lady who plays the organ. But she dresses with the singers too."

"That will do nicely, boy. She doesn't have to sing. I'll sing for both of us for miles and miles. Now you, my little friend, must slip across to the church, up those stairs, and find the organ-lady's purse. Don't try to bring it all back. All I need are the keys. Her little fold of money would be a nice present, but that's just a suggestion. The keys are the thing.''

The boy could not think. His mind swam with indecision while his body ached to curl on the ground and rest.

The man shook him with impatience. "You've got to do it! If you don't, I'll send you to Hell in a minute and you'll never see your dear mother again. Ah, what we do to little boys when we get them there! But I don't want to frighten you with that. Do this for me and I'll let you go back. You're a tough little one, I could see that right off, and smart. A little girl I wouldn't trust with this job. But you can do it and live to tell about it. The time you helped the Devil himself.''

He turned the boy to face him again and that wide mouth folded into a line of determination. "You see this pistol, don't you, boy? Yes, I knew you had. As sure as I'm the Devil himself, I can pop your little skull with this gun and send you to Hell right now.''

Tears blurred the boy's vision but he wiped them on his sleeve. "I'll do it. Just let me do it and go away. I won't ever skip church—''

The man interrupted. "Now that's all right. You do this little thing for me and you'll have the Devil behind you. Just don't bang about and get yourself caught. No excuses. If you don't come back, I'll carry you away to where the sun never shines and little boys cry for all eternity.''

After one final look at that terrible smile the boy lunged from the forest toward the church. He could hear the low laughter over the soft padding of his feet and the quick gasps of his lungs. The wind cut through his thin clothing to damp skin, chilling him thoroughly. He felt no relief as the distance from the strange awful man increased. The terrible, lonely responsibility was worse than the grip of certain death.

He hesitated a second at the bottom of the steps, listening under the preacher's loud exhortations for the sounds of other adults. Hearing none, he climbed quickly and slipped into the small room. Coats, sweaters, and hats dotted a score of folding metal chairs. He found the purses grouped together in a corner. It took just a moment to find the one he sought, a green leather one large enough to hold a small dog. A frantic digging uncovered the keys and he was quickly out the door and down the stairs.

He stopped at the edge of the woods, unable to see the man in the darkness. After a few tentative steps he listened carefully, but could hear only the night sounds of the forest. Relief was a moment from flooding his mind when he turned slightly and his eyes focused on the man sitting just to one side of the path. The boy was more shaken by the silent discovery than he would have been from a sudden gesture or noise. For an eternity of seconds they stared at each other without movement. The boy raised an arm, unclasped a fist, and displayed the keys.

A long even row of teeth appeared in the dark face. ''Ah, the keys. Well done, my boy, well done. Now we must give them a try. And quickly, for this silence no doubt means the prayer at the end of the sermon. That leaves a verse or two of hymn, a benediction, and then swift sure discovery of your little theft.''

He rose and stepped to the boy's side. ''Perhaps we'll be lucky and a few lost ones will choose this moment to step down the aisle and prompt another verse or two.''

''I can't go with you. You said if I—''

The man grabbed the boy by both arms. ''No, now. I know what I said. Just come with me to the edge of town. If I free you now, your hallelujahs might embarrass me in front of the congregation.''

The man tucked the boy under his arm and his free hand kept all screams and cries from escaping. As they crossed the parking lot, the boy, half choked and dazed with fear, ceased to struggle.

The car started easily and the man edged it slowly away from the church toward the highway. In a few moments the town was behind them and the man sighed with noise and apparent relish.

He watched the edges of the highway carefully. ''Need a little road—a nice quiet road for us to conclude our deal.''

The boy stirred in the front seat as the car left the highway and bounced in the ruts of a dirt road. His eye fell on the black grip of the pistol peeking out from the loose clothing, and a desperate hope was born. The man did not stop until the road ended at the ruins of a burned homestead. A bleached chimney tottered over the weeds.

The man turned toward the boy and sighed again. ''You know, I make a pretty poor Devil. Up till now I've done my best with the role.'' He shook his head. ''But I have to admit temptation came my way at last. I mean, boy, I was actually tempted for a moment to let you go.''

The boy crouched in a corner as far from the massive figure as possible. His fright was bottled up and put away. His body tingled with alertness. One small hand slipped from a jacket pocket and crawled along the seat.

When he spoke, the boy didn't recognize his own voice. ''You promised.''

The man suppressed a laugh. ''Sometimes I promise too much, boy. I did threaten to send you to Hell.'' The dark figure moved across the seat. ''But since you were such a good little fellow, I'll send you to Heaven instead.''

At the moment the boy deftly snatched the pistol and pointed it at the massive head. He saw the startled look on that hideous face as his finger searched for the trigger that was not there. Not understanding, he jerked back against the window, and in the moonlight stared with horror at the crudely carved piece of wood, covered with black shoe polish. The same moonlight gave him one final glimpse of that wide awful smile.

80

COUNTERPLOT

Francis M. Nevins, Jr.

THE WEEKEND ICE storm made the motel cleaning woman late for work on Monday morning. The woman assigned to the rooms at the end of the west wing gave a ritual tap of the door of 114, then used her passkey and stepped in. When she saw what lay on the green shag carpet she shrieked and went careening down the corridor in terror. The Cody police arrived ten minutes later. When the fingerprint report came back from F.B.I. headquarters the next day, they knew a part of the story. The rest they never learned, and would not have believed if someone had told them.

She followed instructions precisely. The Northwest jet touched down at Billings just before 5:00 P.M. on Friday, and by 5:30 she had rented a car from the Budget booth near the baggage-claim area. As the sun dropped over the awesomely close mountaintops she was crossing the Montana border into Wyoming. The two-lane blacktop rose and fell and wound among the magnificent mountains like a scenic railway, bringing her to the edge of Cody around 8:00.

She'd been told there would be a reservation for her at the Great Western Motel in the name of Ann Chambers. There was. She checked in, unpacked the two smaller suitcases, left the large gray Samsonite case at the back of the room closet, locked. Then she bathed, changed to a blue jumpsuit, turned on the TV, and settled in to wait. Until Monday morning if necessary. Those were the instructions.

Friday passed, and Saturday, and Sunday. She heard the harsh sound of frozen rain falling on the streets, the screech of brakes, the dull whine of car motors refusing to start. The storm didn't affect her. She stayed in the room, watching local television and reading a pile of paperback romances she had brought with her. Three times a day she would stride down the corridor to the coffee shop for a hasty meal. The only other customers were a handful of pickup-truck cowboys who kept their outsized Stetsons on as they ate flamboyantly. None of them could be the man she was waiting for. She wondered if the storm would keep him from coming.

At 10:00 P.M. on Sunday, while she was sitting on the bed bundled in blankets, boredly watching a local TV newscast, a quick triple knock sounded on her door. She sprang up, smoothed the bedcovers, undid the chain bolt, and opened two inches. "Yes?"

"Software man." The words were exactly what she expected.

"Hardware's here," she replied as instructed, and cautiously drew back the door to let him in. He was heavy-set and rugged-looking, about 40, wearing a three-quarter-length tan suede jacket with sheepskin collar. When he took off his mitten cap she saw he was partially bald. He threw his jacket on the bed and inspected her.

"You sure ain't Frank Bolish," he said. "So who are you?"

"Arlene Carver. One of Frank's assistants." She held out her hand to him and took a chance. "If you read his columns you've probably seen my name mentioned. I do investigative work for him."

"Never read his columns," the man grunted. "I don't think news-papermen should be allowed to attack public officials the way Bolish does. Prove who your are." His accent was heavily Western, almost like Gary Cooper's but too soft and whispery as if he had a sore throat. Taking small steps, she backed toward the formica-topped round table at the room's far end where her oversized handbag lay.

"Hold it right there," the man ordered. "I'll find your ID myself." He strode long-legged across the room, passing her cautiously, reached for the bag, and shook its contents out on the bed.

"There's no gun," she told him, trying to control the irritation she was beginning to feel, "and the money's not there either. Do you think I'm a fool?"

He pawed through her alligator wallet, studying the array of plastic cards in their window envelopes. "Okay, so your name's Arlene Carver and you live in Bethesda, Maryland. That's close enough to Washington all right, but what tells me you're with Bolish?"

"How do I know you're Paxton?" she demanded. "I was told he was a skinny guy with thick gray hair. You're two hundred pounds and could use a toupee."

"I never claimed I was Paxton." He tugged a bulging pigskin wallet from his hip pocket and passed her a business card. "Ted Gorman, from

Cheyenne. Private investigator. Paxton got cold feet Friday, hired me to drive up to Cody and make the delivery for him.'' He took a long careful breath. ''He said either Bolish himself or his chief assistant Marty Lanning would pick it up.''

''Frank has to be on a TV show tomorrow morning and Marty's down with flu,'' she said.

He gazed coldly at her. She knew he was trying to decide if she was genuine or an impostor. ''Come *on,* man!'' she told him impatiently. ''I knew the stupid password and I knew what Paxton looks like. Give me the damn videotape!''

''Not yet.'' He perched himself on the round table and pointed a finger at her. ''If you're with Bolish you'll know what's supposed to be on the tape. Tell me.''

''The way Frank said Paxton described it over the phone,'' she answered slowly, ''it's a videocassette made with a hidden camera at Vito Carbone's condo in Miami Beach. It shows Senator Vega taking a $100,000 payoff from Carbone and agreeing to sponsor some amendments to the Federal Criminal Code that the Mob wants.'' She paused and looked at him.

''More,'' he demanded.

''The videocassette was made for Angelo Generoso,'' she went on. ''His family and the Carbones have been in an undeclared war for years. Paxton was the low-level torpedo the Generosos sent to Carbone's pad to dismantle the equipment and bring back the cassettes when it was all over. Only Paxton found out what was on that one tape, saw a chance to get rich, and disappeared with the thing instead. He'd grown up in rural Wyoming, so he came back out here to hole up till the heat died down. Then he phoned Frank in Washington and offered him the cassette for $25,000.''

''Okay.'' The bald man nodded slightly. ''That's the same story Paxton tells. You got the money?''

''Yes. You have the cassette?''

''Hold still a minute.'' He strode across the room and out into the corridor, leaving the door slightly ajar. She watched him enter the alcove down the hall that held the soft-drink machine. There was the sound of a lid being lifted, then the rumble of ice cubes being displaced. He re-entered the room rubbing the moist white protective jacket of the cassette against his shirt. ''Ice machine didn't do it any harm,'' he said. ''Let's see the money.''

She bent over the bureau, pulled out the bottom drawer, and removed the Gideon Bible. Then she shook the Bible out over the bed. Twenty-five

$1000 bills fluttered down from the pages onto the rumpled blanket. She picked them up and arranged them in a neat stack but did not hold them out to him.

"They could be counterfeit," the bald man muttered.

"Oh, for God's sake! This is throwaway money for Frank Bolish. Now give me the damn cassette!"

Hesitantly he placed it on the blanket beside the bills, then perched on the edge of the formica again, while she rebolted the chain lock. She then dragged the large gray Samsonite suitcase out of the closet, lifted it to the bed, and unlocked it. She took out the videocassette player, set it down on the bureau top, and used a tiny screwdriver to connect its wires with certain wires of the room television. When the player was ready she flipped the ON switch, took the cassette out of its protective jacket, and inserted it into the machine. Then she depressed the PLAY button and turned on the TV to watch the images from the cassette.

The tape ran for about twelve minutes. Its technical quality was poor, which was natural considering the secrecy in which it was made. It showed a quiet conference between two men in shirtsleeves. The older she recognized—Vito, lion of the Carbones. The younger—tall, slender, hypnotic-voiced—certainly looked like Senator Vega. The hidden camera caught the quick transfer of an envelope, the counting of the money, the careful repetition of what the senator must do in return for the gift.

She hit the STOP button before the scene had ended. "I don't like it," she said. "There's something stage-looking about that payoff. One of them's an actor, maybe both of them." She chewed her underlip nervously and turned her back for a second to switch off the TV.

When she faced him again, he was holding a small .25 aimed at her middle.

"You took a gamble and lost, lady," the bald man said. "It happens I do read Bolish's column every day, and I got a real good memory for names. He's never mentioned you in any of his material. Now, who the hell are you?"

She took another long deep breath to gain time. "All right," she told him then. "I—guess I gave myself away with what I said about that tape. My name is Arlene Carver but I don't work for Bolish. I'm a troubleshooter for Senator Vega. We heard rumors about a plot to smear him with a phony videotape, and then when Paxton offered the tape to Bolish one of Bolish's staff leaked the story to us. My partner managed to sidetrack the man Bolish sent out to make the pickup and I came on in his place. Look, what do you and Paxton care who pays you? The tape's a phony, but the media could crucify the senator with it, so we're willing to pay to keep it under wraps.''

"Sure it's a phony. All you true believers who think Jorge Vega can pull together that good old Sixties coalition of the Hispanics and the blacks and the feminists and the Indians and the kids, you'll all swear till you're blue in the face the tape's a phony so your boy can become President in '84. Only if the tape gets out, it's Vega's finish, and you know it.''

"It's no use talking politics with you," she said icily. "Take the money and leave this room, right now.''

"Not quite yet." He waggled the .25 at her lazily. "You see, I still don't know who you are, lady, but I surely know who you're not. You don't work for Jorge Vega. *But I do.*''

Consternation flushed her face, and she jerked back as though he had struck her.

"Paxton didn't just make one long-distance call to Washington about that cassette," the man explained. "He offered it to Vega for the same price he wanted from Bolish. I'm a Wyoming boy, so the senator took me off my other work on his staff and asked me to get the tape from Paxton. I did. Didn't use money, just muscle. But then I decided to keep Paxton's date with Bolish, hoping I could find out what Bolish planned to print about the senator. Now, you're not with Bolish and you're not with Vega, so before I get angry and ask you the hard way, you tell me who you are and what your game is.''

He took two slow steps toward her, his fingers tightening on the .25 as he moved.

"Put that toy away," she told him calmly, "before you find yourself in deep trouble." She reached inside her blouse with careful motions, pulled out a hinged leather cardholder, opened it, and held it out so he could see the gold shield and identification.

"Oh, hell," he mumbled, and gently set down the gun on the dresser top. "Why didn't you say you were F.B.I.?''

"Well, your loyalties weren't exactly displayed on a billboard," she told him. "The Bureau heard rumors about that cassette too, and my job was to run them down. A woman on Bolish's staff leaked it to the Bureau when Paxton made him the offer. I told the truth when I said my partner intercepted Bolish's messenger and I came on in his place. Another two minutes and I would have been reading you your rights. Depending on whether that tape is real or a phony, either Vega's going to be charged with taking a brige or some big bananas in the Mob are going to face extortion charges. I don't think you broke any Federal laws by hijacking the cassette from Paxton, but I'll keep the tape from this point on.''

"I'm not so sure of that." He grinned at her, reached down to his oversized cowboy belt buckle, and disconnected it from its leather strap. From the interior of the hollow buckle he extracted a leather cardholder of his own and flipped it at her. "Damndest thing I've seen in fifteen years with the Bureau," he laughed. "Two agents playing cat and mouse with each other like this. Yeah, I've been working the case from the other side. Picked up Paxton in Laramie on Friday night and decided to keep his appointment with Bolish's messenger on the off chance I'd get something we could use against Bolish. He's written a lot of columns the Bureau doesn't appreciate."

"Nice job," she said. "You fooled me all the way. I never would have guessed you were with the Bureau." She came toward him slowly, almost seductively, until she was two steps from the corner of the dresser that held his gun.

She leaped for the .25 at the same moment his hands leaped for her throat.

Late the next morning, when she entered to clean Room 114, the cleaning woman found the two intertwined bodies—the man shot with a .25 at point-blank range, the woman strangled to death. The police quickly determined what had happened but had no idea why they had killed each other, nor could they make sense of the inordinate number of artifacts of identify found in the room, all of them turning out to be spurious.

The F.B.I. report on the two sets of fingerprints, however, proved to be helpful. The man was identified as a pistolero for the Carbone organized-crime family and the woman as an enforcer for the more progressive and affirmative-action-oriented Generosos.

81

RANSOM DEMAND

Jeffrey M. Wallmann

FRANCES BARTLETT SAT in her husband's easy chair, her big hands clasped loosely in her lap, a plumpish auburn-haired woman in her late thirties, wearing a quilted robe over her pink nightgown. She was watching the *Today* show on television after having packed the children off to school, but this particular morning she wasn't relaxing as she usually did. She was worried.

She wanted to know what had happened to Paul.

Her husband was supposed to have been home sometime after 2 A.M. last night, after his flight from Chicago landed. Frances had awakened at three-thirty from the instinct bred of ten years' marriage to a sales manager, and had tossed and fretted in the dark for an hour before calling the airlines. A clerk at the check-in counter told her the plane had arrived on time, but that she'd have to wait until the business office opened to learn if her husband's name was on the passenger manifest or if he had transferred flights. Sorry. Touched slightly by hysteria, Frances had phoned long distance to the hotel at which Paul had been staying; he had checked out the previous evening without leaving any messages. Sorry . . .

She hadn't been able to sleep the rest of the night.

At least there hadn't been a crash, she told herself as she sat watching the television. She'd have heard about it if there had been, and surely she'd have been notified if there'd been an accident or Paul had gotten sick and was in a hospital. It was probably nothing, a mix-up of some kind. But it wasn't like Paul not to let her know. Where was he? Oh God, where was Paul?

She glanced at her wrist-watch. Another hour and she'd phone the airlines office, and if they couldn't help her, she'd wait until the next flight from Chicago, and if he wasn't on that, she'd . . . Frances shivered, not wanting to think about what she would have to do then. The police, Paul's boss, the publicity and questions and embarrassment; the prospect seemed too dreadful for words.

A commercial began, and she went to the kitchen for another cup of coffee. She was stirring it absently when the phone rang. She set the cup down and hurriedly picked up the receiver of the extension phone near her.

"H-Hello?"

"Mrs. Bartlett? Mrs. Paul Bartlett?"

"Yes. Who is this?"

"We have your husband, Mrs. Bartlett."

"What?" she said blankly. "What?"

"We have your husband," the voice repeated.

"What? You have Paul? How?"

"This is a ransom demand. Now do you understand?"

"Oh, my God . . . !" Frances sucked in her breath, trying to steady herself with her free hand. She knocked over the cup, coffee spilling across the counter; she never noticed it. "Paul, is he all right?"

"He's fine. He'll stay that way only if you do what I tell you."

"Let me speak to him. Please, let me—"

"No. Listen to me, Mrs. Bartlett, and listen closely." The man's voice was low and flat. "We want ten thousand dollars in unmarked bills, nothing over a twenty. Is that clear?"

"Yes, but I don't have—"

"Hock your jewels if you have to, but get ten thousand together by noon if you want to see your husband alive again. Take the money in a lunch pail—the old kind with the round top—to McKinley Park. You know where that is?"

"Downtown," she answered quickly. "It's downtown."

"Right. There's a statue of McKinley in the middle of it. At exactly twelve-thirty, walk along the north path and put the pail beside the third bench from the statue. Got that? Third bench, north side."

"I—I'm afraid I don't know which is north."

"The side facing Woolworth's. Then keep on going and don't look back."

"I won't. Twelve-fifteen, third bench, facing Woolworth's," she recited numbly. "When do I . . . I see Paul?"

"Tomorrow night."

"That long? Can't you . . . ?"

"Don't call the police, Mrs. Bartlett. We'll be watching you, and if you try to double-cross us, you'll never get another chance."

"I understand. But can't you let him go sooner? Please, can't you?" And then she realized that she was talking into a dead receiver; the man had hung up. She stood holding the phone for another moment, still stunned, and then slowly replaced it with mechanical deliberation.

"No," she cried out to her still, empty house. *"No!"*

Frances had been unable to sit still since she'd returned from McKinley Park. Now, with school over and her children playing in the yard, she paced aimlessly thorugh the house, the phone serving as the base of her wanderings. She would walk to the living-room window and move the drapes aside to peer out; then let them drop to pace through the hall and up the stairs, gazing abstractedly into her bedroom, hers and Paul's; down to smoke a cigarette and drink a cup of coffee, only to leave it half finished; return once more to stare at the phone, occasionally touching its bright plastic.

She knew she would carry this day alive and painfully fresh in her mind for a long time. She wouldn't forget her initial panic, when she'd almost called the police, followed by her longer, cold dread of the chance she'd be taking if she did. She wouldn't forget how frantic she'd been at the bank, closing out the accounts and cashing most of their bonds, or how acutely she'd had to control herself when she'd left the pail and simply kept on walking. Or now, despairing, hoping she'd done right and praying Paul would be released unharmed. She kept asking herself why? They weren't rich or famous—only an average, middle-class family like millions of others. Why had they been picked?

The phone rang again. She ran to it, clutching it.

"Hello? Hello?"

"Honey?

Paul!" Tears of relief welled, blurring her vision. "Oh, Paul, are you all right?"

"A little tired, but otherwise I'm okay. What's the matter?"

"Where are you?"

"Philadelphia."

"Philadelphia?"

"Sure. The meeting just broke up; it lasted longer than I thought."

"Meeting?" Frances felt dazed and bewildered. "Paul, I-I don't understand. What meeting?"

"This new accounts thing that came up at the last minute. I tried calling you last night to tell you I had to go, but the line was always busy, as usual. Didn't you get my wire?"

"No, I didn't. You mean you're all right?"

"I told you, I'm okay. Just what's going on, anyway?"

"You mean . . . you weren't kidnaped?"

"Kidnaped!" Her husband laughed. "What makes you think I was kidnaped, for God's sake?"

Frances thought about the phone call and the ransom demand—then she thought about the ten thousand dollars and she fainted.

Lew Sieberts lounged in his swivel chair, tapping his thick fingers on the battered oak desk, impatient for his shift to be over. He was still amazed how smoothly the job had gone, and every once in a while he'd have to look in the third drawer of his desk just to be sure the pailful of money he'd picked up on his lunch hour wasn't a figment of his imagination. Man, if he had to get fired, this was the kind of severance pay to leave with; the job was proving to be the best he'd ever had, even if the shortest. He'd stick around to pocket his regular severance tomorrow morning, but then he was getting out of town before that Bartlett guy returned. To New York City, maybe—it had the action, and he could get so lost there he'd never be caught. Yeah, New York sounded real good . . .

The teletype across the room began to chatter. When its bell ran, Sieberts went over to it and tore off the flimsy. It read:

BLTMR XLT1960 JS DL PD KANSAS CITY MO 6/21 340P XXX CAROLE WILSON 424 MAXWELL CT BLTMR MD 467 9073 XXXX MUST GO TO SPRINGFIELD FOR TWO DAYS STOP UNEXPECTED BUSINESS SORRY STOP DONT WORRY LOVE PETER STOP END XXXX

Sieberts sat down again, studying the message. It was very similar to the wire Bartlett had sent yesterday. He leaned back until he could see out of the dusty window of the telegraph office and smiled faintly, wondering if he could pull the same trick twice in a row. Well, twenty grand was twice as much as he had now . . .

He swiveled around and picked up the phone, dialing the number printed on the telegram. The line buzzed and then a woman's voice answered.

"Mrs. Wilson? Mrs. Peter Wilson?" he said to her. "We have your husband . . ."

82

LETTER TO THE EDITOR

Morris Hershman

DEAR MR. HITCHCOCK:

I'm writing to you because I've heard of you and I want your advice about something. My friends say I ought to be a real writer, anyhow. I write letters very good.

What I figure, though, is that maybe you can tell me if I ought to be as scared as I am.

Like I say, this thing really happened. If you want to make a story out of it maybe I could collaborate with you on it. I've got the story; all you'd have to do is write it up.

Anyhow, this happened to me on Brighton Beach. In Coney Island, you know, in Brooklyn.

When I go out there I usually bring a blanket in a paper bag, unroll it on the sand, take off my pants and shirt and, with my bathing suit already on instead of shorts, try to catch me a little sun. I park myself near the peeling wooden sign that says Bay 2. A lot of people near my own age come out there, in the twenties and thirties. I can lie on the sand and look up at the boardwalk. Though it's plastered with signs saying that you need shirt and pants to go walking up there, that doesn't really matter.

It happened just this afternoon, the thing I want to tell you about. You know what it's been like in the city: 93 in the shade, people dropping like flies. Even on the beach today, the sand was like needles under your feet.

When I'd waited for half an hour and none of my friends showed up, I went into the water. Usually I walk in up to my ankles, then dive in to get the rest of me good and wet.

Well, I swam out past the first buoy. Like all the rest of them, it's red on top and with what looks like barnacles on the sides. All of a sudden I saw a guy coming almost head on into me. About twenty feet or so away I heard another man yell, "Sam!" and then there was the sound of bubbles.

The fellow had disappeared (the guy I'd been looking at call him number one so you won't get confused) and then he showed up above water with the crook of his arm on the other guy's neck, pulling him in.

"This man's hurt!" he shouted.

I can scream pretty good, too. "Give 'em room!"

On the shore they tried artificial respiration. I went along to watch the hefty lifeguard in his white shirt, the victim's legs between his, jumping up and down like clockwork. I won't forget it as long as I live.

How long that's going to be, maybe you can guess.

Anyway, this fellow who'd brought him in stood off to one side. He wore a bright-red rubber cap and a bathing suit with white stripes at the sides. He was a beanpole of a guy, the kind who probably never stops eating, though. His large brown eyes stared right past me.

"Poor guy, whoever he was," Beanpole said to anybody who'd listen. Then he stopped and pointed. "Look!"

I did, but all I saw was the usual beach scene: the kids selling ice cream or tin-bottomed paper cartons of orange drink or cans of cold chocolate, or cellophane bags with potato knishes inside. You can always recognize the sellers because they wear white sun helmets like in movies about big-game hunters in Africa.

At my left a guy wandered from girl to girl, trying to strike up a talk—"operating," it's called nowadays. A lot of acquaintances run into each other at Bay 2 because they've mostly been to the same summer places: White Roe, Banner Lodge, Tamiment, Lehman, whatever you like.

At one blanket, people gathered around a uke player who was picking out "Blue-Tail Fly." He stopped to tell a singer something about one of the downtown social clubs for older unmarried people. "I'm going down for a dance tonight at the change-of-life club," he said.

Then I saw what Beanpole had been pointing at. Two men, clearing a path for themselves, inched their way along the lines of blankets. Between them they carried what looked like a white gauze pad folded in two. It turned out to be a stretcher. They covered up the guy with a sheet over his face, so he couldn't even breathe.

"I guess they're taking him to the first-aid station," I said to a small blonde next to me, remembering the wooden shack on Bay 6 or 7 that looks like it was on stilts and with a spiral staircase that takes you up to the dispensary.

The blonde shook her head slowly. "No, it's the ambulance for him and then the morgue. I saw him earlier in the day. He was a very good swimmer.''

At my side the Beanpole nodded. ''He must'a gotten cramps or something. We were way out, past the fourth marker. Nobody in sight except . . .'' And he turned to me like he'd just noticed I was there.

I introduced myself. He mumbled that he was glad to know me, but he didn't mention his name. His eyes were hard and bright.

''How much of it did you see?'' he asked quietly.

''I saw you practically on top of him and trying to get a grip on him. You did a hero's job out there. Nothing to be ashamed of, believe me!''

I had made up mind not to go in swimming today, and when my friends came around a little later, I told them what I'd seen and spent the afernoon lying in the sun.

Once I felt somebody's eyes on me. I looked up and there was Beanpole, not too far away. He was asking a girl the name of the book she was reading, but every so often he glanced in my direction. I lay back and closed my eyes and forgot it.

But when I was going home by way of the Brighton local, I started to ask myself questions. Once I remember I looked up at my reflection in a subway window glass; I might have been a skeleton.

Well, as soon as I got home to Snyder Avenue, where I live, I started writing this letter to you. I was supposed to take a shower and go down to a State of Israel bond rally at Twenty-third and Madison, but I don't think I will. Not tonight. For all I know, maybe I'll never go to a rally again in my life.

It's this way: the blond girl at the beach told me that the dead guy was a good swimmer. If he'd been in trouble, well, any old hand at swimming knows enough to float around till he can save himself. I'd heard the victim calling, ''Sam!'' before he went under, like Sam was right near; but Beanpole said he never knew the dead guy.

The idea I've got explains why Beanpole behaved like he did, the way he kept looking at me. I've been thinking hard, and now what I saw looks completely different. I had told Beanpole, ''I saw you practically on top of him.'' The way I remember it now, Beanpole was holding the guy *under* water, not saving him. Beanpole kept him under water till it made no difference one way or the other.

But maybe I'm wrong. Maybe Beanpole is a right guy, after all. Maybe.

I figure it like this, though: I'm the only one who saw it happen, and he knows that.

Like I say, maybe I'm all wrong. Beanpole could have gotten so bollixed

489

up trying to save the guy he went around afterwards like he'd flipped his lid. He looked calm to me, but maybe some guys carry all their feelings inside them, like a guy does if he's worked up to kill somebody.

Well, that shows what you can think about in the morning. It's almost morning here, and I can look out the window and see dawn touch the rooftops across the street.

I guess I'm all wrong, crazy with the heat or whatever you'd call it.

But it'd be so easy for Beanpole to find me. After all, he knows my name and it's in the phone book. All he has to do is come in right now and shoot the top of my head off.

But even if he did the truth would come out. This letter alone is sure to do it. If I hear anybody coming, I'll stop writing and hide it as quick as I can. It'd be found by the police, afterwards. I'm sure Beanpole's name and address were taken this afternoon, and plenty of people got a good look at him.

Anyhow, that's all of it, and like I said at the beginning I want your advice about whether I'm right to be as scared as I am. Should I go to the police and tell them all this?''

To show you the way a guy can get nervous; just this minute I could have sworn I felt a draught on the back of my neck, like the door had been quietly opened by somebody, and

83

FIRST MAN AT THE FUNERAL

Dion Henderson

WE WERE UP in the Erickson north forty with my old dog, and the Sheriff had just missed the prettiest double on quail you ever saw when the jailer came panting and wheezing through the sedge.

"Sheriff," he hollered. "There's been a death."

"Not here there ain't, dang it," the Sheriff said, blowing smoke out of the barrels of his double gun. "I shot under the left bird and I was a mile behind the right one."

"No, no," the jailer hollered, even though he was right close to us by then. "I mean there's a man dead."

The Sheriff looked relieved.

"Well," he said. "The way I'm shooting today, I'm better off back in town hunting criminals."

"Hold on a minute," the jailer was getting red in the face again, not from running this time. "I'm trying to tell you there ain't any criminals. It's just that old man Pembroke got flung from his horse and killed."

The Sheriff took off his hat.

"There goes the last man in Andrew Jackson County," he said reverently, "to own a good singles dog."

"Amen," the jailer said. "Doc though you'd want to know right away."

Being the game warden and something of a bird dog man myself, I had figured out by this time what they were talking about. There used to be a saying that you take a bird dog that was certain sure on hunting coveys of quail, and you catch his owner on the verge of starvation, you might buy that dog for money. But you take a dog that could mark down and find the scattered singles from a wild flushed covey, and the way you got that dog was to be first man at his owner's funeral. Even then, the saying went, you

491

might have to take on the support of seven minor children to get the dog away from the widow.

The Sheriff was safe enough there. Old man Pembroke didn't have any widow, and no children. No anything, except a nephew who'd come down lately from the city. And that singles dog, of course. There hadn't been much chance of anybody getting that dog before, because rich as he was, old man Pembroke would've been the last man in Jackson County to starve if famine hit.

"Let's get back to town," the Sheriff said.

We drove on in and stopped at Doc's furniture store, which he was running when he wasn't occupied with the undertaking business. Being the only undertaker around, Doc was the county coroner too, naturally.

"Poor feller," Doc said, meaning old man Pembroke. "Probably put his horse over that log a hundred times. Probably got flung off twenty times out of the hundred, the way he rode. But this time he landed square on a rock and bashed in his head."

"Right sad," the Sheriff said. "You reckon I ought to go up and investigate, it being a violent death and all?"

"I reckoned you would," Doc said, a mite tartly, "or I wouldn't have been in such an all-fired hurry to tell you about it."

"Well," the Sheriff said. "It being about supper time now, and out of consideration for the feelings of the bereaved, I'll wait until tomorrow."

"If that nephew ain't any more bereaved than he sounded when he called me," Doc said, "there ain't a whole lot to consider."

"How'd he sound?"

"Rich," Doc said. "How the heck do you think a man'd sound, his only relative setting about to die and leaving a million dollars, thereabouts, to you?"

"I'll get over there in a day or so," the Sheriff said.

"Young Pembroke sounded to me," Doc said, "like a man who didn't know a singles dog from a single tree, and what's more didn't aim to learn."

"Tomorrow," the Sheriff said firmly. "First thing. You want to come along," he said to me, "in your official capacity as game warden?"

"Sure," I said. "Seeing as how you've been hunting birds over my dogs for the last eight, ten years, I got quite an interest in seeing you get a dog of your own."

We let it go at that. But next morning the Sheriff stopped for me and we went on up to the Pembroke place. The farmstead, where the tenant who cropped the place lived with his family, was right close to the road. Then you took the drive that wound up into the piney woods along the sedge fields and the buckwheat patches that old man Pembroke kept just for a shooting preserve. And presently you came to the old mansion, kind of tumbled down, and the stable for the riding horses, and the kennels. The tenant's wife came up and gave the house a lick and a promise a couple of times a week, but old man Pembroke took care of the dogs himself.

Young Pembroke came out to meet us. There was another fellow, the one who came down from the city with him, kind of hanging around in the background. In my calling, you get to make pretty fast judgments, and I wouldn't have trusted either one of them up a tree, especially up the same tree.

The Sheriff was talking about how it was all too bad, and young Pembroke said it certainly was, he felt real depressed, especially because he didn't get to spend much time with his poor old uncle.

Out in the kennels the dogs heard us and started up a ruckus and I walked back there. The sheriff and young Pembroke followed along. I noticed all the water dishes were empty and when I could get a word in between them two soft-soaping one another, I asked whether the dogs had been fed.

Young Pembroke looked kind of startled and said he didn't know much about dogs, he'd forgotten all about it. So the Sheriff and I went to work, and I tell you a yardful of dogs can get middling hungry in a couple of days.

We got to a run where a big white and lemon pointer was, and the Sheriff whispered to me, "This one's him, ain't it?"

I looked at that dog, the big smooth moving fellow that still showed in his marking that Lady Ferris and Mr. Fishel's dog were away back there in his pedigree, and I said, "It sure is."

Young Pembroke came up and the big white and lemon dog bristled and then he did something that made me think I'd lost my hearing. He showed his teeth at young Pembroke and backed up and opened his mouth like he was going to beller, but it came out like this:

"_____"

Just nothing—a bark that didn't make any noise at all.

Young Pembroke backed up a little, and the dog went:

"_____, _____"

The Sheriff stood there with a funny expression on his face.

"Say," he said. "Ain't that the dog your uncle used to keep in the house?"

"Not that I know of," young Pembroke said. "He's been out here with the others for the few weeks I've been visiting."

"That's funny," the Sheriff said. He scratched his head. We finished the dogs, then the Sheriff said to young Pembroke:

"Mind if we look over the scene where your uncle was killed? Just routine, but I got to make out a report."

"Not at all," young Pembroke said. "I'll show you. but if you don't mind, I'd rather not go down there. You know how it is."

"I reckon," the Sheriff said. "Say, before we do that I wonder if I could talk to you about buying this here dog. That's what I really came for, to be honest with you."

Young Pembroke looked at him and then laughed. The other fellow showed up from somewhere and he laughed too.

"Shucks, Sheriff," young Pembroke said. "You can have him to recollect my uncle by, if you want. You can have all the dogs. I don't know much about dogs."

"Yuh," the Sheriff said. "Well, that's settled. Now, me and the game warden will just mosey on over to the scene of the dyin'."

The log jump was just a little ways past the stables, the path showing it was a favorite ride for the old man. The jump was right at the edge of the woods and on the far side of it there was a low place gouged out from all the horses landing there through the years. It was partly churned up from hooves and partly in grass. There was no mistaking the rock that killed the old man, either. It was off to one side and there still was blood on it. The Sheriff turned it over with his toe, but only some grass was under it.

"I reckon that's enough," the Sheriff said. He looked kind of serious, so we didn't talk much on the way back. He opened the kennel run and the big white and lemon dog came out, tail wagging a little. The Sheriff snapped a leash on him and we walked around to the front of the house. Young Pembroke and the other fellow were standing there beside their car. They came to meet us. When they were about twenty feet off, the white and lemon dog kind of bunched himself and opened his mouth and said, "——" and jumped straight for young Pembroke.

"That dog doesn't like me," young Pembroke said.

"Doesn't surprise me none," the Sheriff said. "You expect him to be in love with the fellers that beat his master to death?"

Young Pembroke said, "You're kidding, Sheriff."

"Wish I was," the Sheriff said. "Sure wish I was. But when you lied to me about this dog being out in the kennels for a couple weeks, I figured you might have lied about some other things. The rock that killed your uncle, for instance. It wasn't lying there longer'n yesterday—the grass is still green under it. May even be some fingerprints on it. I'll bet you," the Sheriff said, "there won't even be any grass stains on your uncle's clothes, down in Doc's ice box."

Young Pembroke had turned as white as his friend was.

He said, "How in blazes did you know about the dog?"

"Hoarse," the Sheriff said. "Put a house dog out in a kennel, he'll bark himself hoarse in twenty-four hours. Then for a couple days he won't make a sound, but after that his voice comes back. Only then he don't bark any more because he ain't a house dog no longer, he's a kennel dog. You must have rassled this here dog outside yesterday morning, because he was trying to stave you off the old man."

The two of them started to run, going in opposite directions. The Sheriff took the leash in his left hand and unlimbered his .38. Young Pembroke was going to the left and the Sheriff hit him in the calf of the leg with the first shot. The other fellow went to the right and the Sheriff hit him in the hand with the second shot as he tried to get the keys into the car door. Then the Sheriff flipped open the cylinder of the revolver, blew smoke out of the barrel and looked at me.

"If you game wardens would let a man use a .38 on quail," he said, "I'd be all right, even on them going-away doubles."

84

AN ILLUSION IN RED AND WHITE

Stephen Crane

NIGHTS ON THE Cuban blockade were long, at times exciting, often dull. The men on the small leaping dispatch-boats became as intimate as if they had all been buried in the same coffin. Correspondents who, in New York, had passed as fairly good fellows sometimes turned out to be perfect rogues of vanity and selfishness, but still more often the conceited chumps of Park Row became the kindly and thoughtful men of the Cuban blockade. Also each correspondent told all he knew, and sometimes more. For this gentle tale I am indebted to one of the brightening stars of New York journalism.

"Now, this is how I imagine it happened. I don't say it happened this way, but this is how I imagine it happened. And it always struck me as being a very interesting story. I hadn't been on the paper very long, but just about long enough to get a good show, when the city editor suddenly gave me this sparkling murder assignment.

"It seems that up in one of the back counties of New York Sate a farmer had taken a dislike to his wife; and so he went into the kitchen with an axe, and in the presence of their four little children he just casually rapped his wife on the nape of the neck with the head of this axe. It was early in the morning, but he told the children they had better go to bed. Then he took his wife's body out in the woods and buried it.

"This farmer's name was Jones. The widower's eldest child was named Freddy. A week after the murder, one of the long-distance neighbors was rattling past the house in his buckboard when he saw Freddy playing in the road. He pulled up, and asked the boy about the welfare of the Jones family.

"'Oh, we're all right,' said Freddy, 'only ma—she ain't—she's dead.'

"'Why, when did she die?' cried the startled farmer. 'What did she die of?'

"'Oh,' answered Freddy, 'last week a man with red hair and a big white

497

teeth and real white hands came into the kitchen, and killed ma with an axe.'

"The farmer was indignant with the boy for telling him this strange childish nonsense, and drove off much disgruntled. But he recited the incident at a tavern that evening, and when people began to miss the familiar figure of Mrs. Jones at the Methodist Church on Sunday morning, they ended by having an investigation. The calm Jones was arrested for murder, and his wife's body was lifted from its grave in the woods and buried by her own family.

"The chief interest now centered upon the children. All four declared that they were in the kitchen at the time of the crime, and that the murderer had red hair. The hair of the virtuous Jones was grey. They said that the murderer's teeth were large and white. Jones only had about eight teeth, and these were small and brown. They said the murderer's hands were white. Jones's hands were the color of black walnuts. They lifted their dazed, innocent faces, and crying, simply because the mysterious excitement and their new quarters frightened them, they repeated their heroic legend without important deviation, and without the parroty sameness which would excite suspicion.

"Women came to the jail and wept over them, and made little frocks for the girls, and little breeches for the boys, and idiotic detectives questioned them at length. Always they upheld the theory of the murderer with red hair, big white teeth, and white hands. Jones sat in his cell, his chin sullenly on his first vest-button. He knew nothing about any murder, he said. He thought his wife had gone on a visit to some relatives. He had had a quarrel with her, and she had said that she was going to leave him for a time, so that he might have proper opportunities for cooling down. Had he seen the blood on the floor? Yes, he had seen the blood on the floor. But he had been cleaning and skinning a rabbit at that spot on the day of his wife's disappearance. He had thought nothing of it. What had his children said when he returned from the fields? They had told him that their mother had been killed by an axe in the hands of a man with red hair, big white teeth, and white hands. To questions as to why he had not informed the police of the county, he answered that he had not thought it a matter of sufficient importance. He had cordially hated his wife, anyhow, and he was glad to be rid of her. He decided afterward that she had run off; and he had never credited the fantastic tale of the children.

"Of course, there was very little doubt in the minds of the majority that Jones was gulty, but there was a fairly strong following who insisted that Jones was a course and brutal man, and perhaps weak in the head—yes—

but not a murderer. They pointed to the children and declared that children could never lie, and these kids, when asked, said the murder had been committed by a man with red hair, large white teeth, and white hands. I myself had a number of interviews with the children, and I was amazed at the convincing power of their little story. Shining in the depths of the limpid up-turned eyes, one could fairly see tiny mirrored images of men with red hair, big white teeth, and white hands.

"Now, I'll tell you how it happened—how I imagine it was done. Some time after burying his wife in the woods Jones strolled back into the house. Seeing nobody, he called out in the familiar fashion 'Mother!' Then the kids came out whimpering. 'Where is your mother?' said Jones. The children looked at him blankly. 'Why, pa,' said Freddy, 'you came in here, and hit ma with the axe; and then you sent us to bed.' 'Me?' cried Jones. 'I haven't been near the house since breakfast-time.'

"The children did not know how to reply. Their meager little sense informed them that their father had been the man with the axe, but he denied it, and to their minds everything was a mere great puzzle with no meaning whatever, save that it was mysteriously sad and made them cry.

" 'What kind of a looking man was it?' said Jones.

"Freddy hesitated. 'Now—he looked a good deal like you, pa.'

" 'Like me?' said Jones. 'Why, I thought you said he had red hair?'

" 'No, I didn't,' replied Freddy. 'I thought he had grey hair, like yours.'

" 'Well,' said Jones. 'I saw a man with kind of red hair going along the road up yonder, and I thought maybe that might have been him.'

"Little Lucy, the second child, here piped up with intense conviction. 'His hair was a little teeny bit red. I saw it.'

" 'No,' said Jones. 'The man I saw had very red hair. And what did his teeth look like? Were they big and white?'

" 'Yes,' answered Lucy, 'they were.'

"Even Freddy seemed to incline to think it. 'His teeth may have been big and white.'

"Jones said little more at that time. Later he intimated to the children that their mother had gone off on a visit, and although they were full of wonder, and sometimes wept because of the oppression of an incomprehensible feeling in the air, they said nothing. Jones did his chores. Everything was smooth.

"The morning after the day of the murder, Jones and his children had a breakfast of hominy and milk.

" 'Well, this man with red hair and big white teeth, Lucy,' said Jones. 'Did you notice anything else about him?'

"Lucy straightened in her chair, and showed the childish desire to come out with brilliant information which would gain her father's approval. 'He had white hands—hands all white—'

" 'How about you, Freddy?'

" 'I didn't look at them much, but I think they were white,' answered the boy.

" 'And what did little Martha notice?' cried the tender parent. 'Did she see the big bad man?'

"Martha, aged four, replied solemnly, 'His hair was all red, and his hand was white—all white.'

" 'That's the man I saw up the road,' said Jones to Freddy.

" 'Yes, sir, it seems like it must have been him,' said the boy, his brain now completely muddled.

"Again Jones allowed the suject of his wife's murder to lapse. The childen did not know that it was a murder, of course. Adults were always performing in a way to make children's heads swim. For instance, what could be more incomprehensible than that a man with two horses, dragging a queer thing, should walk all day, making the grass turn down and the earth turn up? And why did they cut the long grass and put it in a barn? And what was a cow for? Did the water in the well like to be there? All these actions and things were grand, because they were associated with the high estate of grown-up people, but they were deeply mysterious. If, then, a man with red hair, big white teeth, and white hands should hit their mother on the nape of the neck with an axe, it was merely a phenomenon of grown-up life. Little Henry, the baby, when he had a want, howled and pounded the table with a spoon. That was all of life to him. He was not concerned with the fact that his mother had been murdered.

"One day Jones said to his children suddenly, 'Look here: I wonder if you could have made a mistake. Are you absolutely sure that the man you saw had red hair, big white teeth, and white hands?'

"The children were indignant with their father. 'Why, of course, pa, we ain't made no mistake. We saw him as plain as day.'

"Later young Freddy's mind began to work like ketchup. His nights were haunted with terrible memories of the man with the red hair, big white teeth, and white hands, and the prolonged absence of his mother made him wonder and wonder. Presently he quite gratuitously developed the theory that his mother was dead. He knew about death. He had once seen a dead dog; also dead chickens, rabbits, and mice. One day he asked his father, 'Pa, is ma ever coming back?'

"Jones said: 'Well, no; I don't think she is.' This answer confirmed the boy in his theory. He knew that dead people did not come back.

"The attitude of Jones toward this descriptive legend of the man with the axe was very peculiar. He came to be in opposition to it. He protested against the convictions of the children, but could not move them. It was the one thing in their lives of which they were stonily and absolutely positive.

"Now that really ends the story. But I will continue for your amusement. The jury hung Jones as high as they could, and they were quite right: because Jones confessed before he died. Freddy is now a highly respected driver of a grocery wagon in Ogdensburg. When I was up there a good many years afterwards people told me that when he ever spoke of the tragedy at all he was certain to denounce the alleged confession as a lie. He considered his father a victim to the stupidity of juries, and some day he hopes to meet the man with the red hair, big white teeth, and white hands, whose image still remains so distinct in his memory that he could pick him out in a crowd of ten thousand."

85

GENTLEMEN'S AGREEMENT

Lawrence Block

THE BURGLAR, A slender and clean-cut chap just past thirty, was rifling a drawer in the bedside table when Archer Trebizond slipped into the bedroom. Trebizond's approach was as catfooted as if he himself were the burglar, a situation which was manifestly not the case. The burglar never did hear Trebizond, absorbed as he was in his perusal of the drawer's contents, and at length he sensed the other man's presence as a jungle beast senses the presence of a predator.

The analogy, let it be said, is scarcely accidental.

When the burglar turned his eyes on Archer Trebizond his heart fluttered and fluttered again, first at the mere fact of discovery, then at his own discovery of the gleaming revolver in Trebizond's hand. The revolver was pointed in his direction, and this the burglar found upsetting.

"Darn it all," said the burglar, approximately, "I could have sworn there was nobody home. I phoned, I rang the bell——"

"I just got here," Trebizond said.

"Just my luck. The whole week's been like that. I dented a fender on Tuesday afternoon, overturned my fish tank the night before last. An unbelievable mess all over the carpet, and I lost a mated pair of African mouthbreeders so rare they don't have a Latin name yet. I'd hate to tell you what I paid for them."

"Hard luck," Trebizond said.

"And just yesterday I was putting away a plate of fettucini and I bit the inside of my mouth. You ever done that? It's murder, and the worst part is you feel so stupid about it. And then you keep biting it over and over again because it sticks out while it's healing. At least I do." The burglar gulped a breath and ran a moist hand over a moister forehead. "And now this," he said.

503

"This could turn out to be worse than fenders and fish tanks," Trebizond said.

"Don't I know it. You know what I should have done? I should have spent the entire week in bed. I happen to know a safecracker who consults an astrologer before each and every job he pulls. If Jupiter's in the wrong place or Mars is squared with Uranus or something, he won't go in. It sounds ridiculous, doesn't it? And yet it's eight years now since anybody put a handcuff on that man. Now who do you know who's gone eight years without getting arrested?"

"I've never been arrested," Trebizond said.

"Well, you're not a crook."

"I'm a businessman."

The burglar thought of something but let it pass. "I'm going to get the name of his astrologer," he said. "That's just what I'm going to do. Just as soon as I get out of here."

"If you get out of here," Trebizond said. "Alive," Trebizond said.

The burglar's jaw trembled just the slightest bit. Trebizond smiled, and from the burglar's point of view Trebizond's smile seemed to enlarge the black hole in the muzzle of the revolver.

"I wish you'd point that thing somewhere else," he said nervously.

"There's nothing else I want to shoot."

"You don't want to shoot me."

"Oh?"

"You don't even want to call the cops," the burglar went on. "It's really not necessary. I'm sure we can work things out between us, two civilized men coming to a civilized agreement. I've some money on me. I'm an open-handed sort and would be pleased to make a small contribution to your favorite charity, whatever it might be. We don't need policemen to intrude into the private affairs of gentlemen."

The burglar studied Trebizond carefully. This little speech had always gone over rather well in the past, especially with men of substance. It was hard to tell how it was going over now, or if it was going over at all. "In any event," he ended somewhat lamely, "you certainly don't want to shoot me."

"Why not?"

"Oh, blood on the carpet, for a starter. Messy, wouldn't you say? Your wife would be upset. Just ask her and she'll tell you shooting me would be a ghastly idea."

"She's not at home. She'll be out for the next hour or so."

"All the same, you might consider her point of view. And shooting me would be illegal, you know? Not to mention immoral."

"Not illegal," Trebizond remarked.

"I beg your pardon?"

"You're a burglar," Trebizond reminded him. "An unlawful intruder on my property. You have broken and entered. You have invaded the sanctity of my home. I can shoot you where you stand and not get so much as a parking ticket for my trouble."

"Of course you can shoot me in self-defense—"

"Are we on *Candid Camera?*"

"No, but—"

"Is Allen Funt lurking in the shadows?"

"No, but I—"

"In your back pocket. That metal thing. What is it?"

"Just a pry bar."

"Take it out," Trebizond said. "Hand it over. Indeed. A weapon if I ever saw one. I'd state that you attacked me with it and I fired in self-defense. It would be my word against yours, and yours would remain unvoiced since you would be dead. Whom do you suppose the police would believe?"

The burglar said nothing. Trebizond smiled a satisfied smile and put the pry bar in his own pocket. It was a piece of nicely shaped steel and it had a nice heft to it. Trebizond rather liked it.

"Why would you want to kill me?"

"Perhaps I've never killed anyone. Perhaps I'd like to satisfy my curiosity. Or perhaps I got to enjoy killing in the war and have been yearning for another crack at it. There are endless possibilities."

"But—"

"The point is," said Trebizond, "you might be useful to me in that manner. As it is, you're not useful to me at all. And stop hinting about my favorite charity or other euphemisms. I don't want your money. Look about you. I've ample money of my own—that should be obvious. If I were a poor man you wouldn't have breached my threshold. How much money are you talking about, anyway? A couple of hundred dollars?"

"Five hundred," the burglar said.

"A pittance."

"I suppose. There's more at home, but you'd just call that a pittance too, wouldn't you?"

"Undoubtedly." Trebizond shifted the gun to his other hand. "I told you

I was a businessman," he said. "Now if there were any way in which you could be more useful to me alive than dead—"

"You're a businessman and I'm a burglar," the burglar said, brightening.

"Indeed."

"So I could steal something for you. A painting? A competitor's trade secrets? I'm really very good at what I do, as a matter of fact, although you wouldn't guess it by my performance tonight. I'm not saying I could whisk the *Mona Lisa* out of the Louvre, but I'm pretty good at your basic hole-and-corner job of everyday burglary. Just give me an assignment and let me show my stuff."

"Hmmmm," said Archer Trebizond.

"Name it and I'll swipe it."

"Hmmmm."

"A car, a mink coat, a diamond bracelet, a Persian carpet, a first edition, bearer bonds, incriminating evidence, eighteen and a half minutes of tape—"

"What was that last?"

"Just my little joke," said the burglar. "A coin collection, a stamp collection, psychiatric records, phonograph records, police records—"

"I get the point."

"I tend to prattle when I'm nervous."

"I've noticed."

"If you could point that thing elsewhere—"

Trebizond looked down at the gun in hand. The gun continued to point at the burglar.

"No," Trebizond said, with evident sadness. "No, I'm afraid it won't work."

"Why not?"

"In the first place, there's nothing I really need or want. Could you steal me a woman's heart? Hardly. And more to the point, how could I trust you?"

"You could trust me," the burglar said. "You have my word on that."

"My point exactly. I'd have to take your word that your word is good, and where does that lead us? Up the proverbial garden path, I'm afraid. No, once I let you out from under my roof I've lost my advantage. Even if I have a gun trained on you, once you're in the open I can't shoot you with impunity. So I'm afraid—"

"No!"

Trebizond shrugged. "Well, really," he said. "What use are you? What are you good for besides being killed? Can you do anything besides steal, sir?"

"I can make license plates."

"Hardly a valuable talent."

"I know," said the burglar sadly. "I've often wondered why the state bothered to teach me such a pointless trade. There's not even much call for counterfeit license plates, and they've got a monopoly on making the legitimate ones. What else can I do? I must be able to do something. I could shine your shoes, I could polish your car—"

"What do you do when you're not stealing?"

"Hang around," said the burglar. "Go out with ladies. Feed my fish, when they're not all over my rug. Drive my car when I'm not mangling its fenders. Play a few games of chess, drink a can or two of beer, make myself a sandwich—"

"Are you any good?"

"At making sandwiches?"

"At chess."

"I'm not bad."

"I'm serious about this."

"I believe you are," the burglar said. "I'm not your average wood-pusher, if that's what you want to know. I know the openings and I have a good sense of space. I don't have the patience for tournament play, but at the chess club downtown I win more games than I lose."

"You play at the club downtown?"

"Of course. I can't burgle seven nights a week, you know. Who could stand the pressure?"

"Then you *can* be of use to me," Trebizond said.

"You want to learn the game?"

"I know the game. I want you to play chess with me for an hour until my wife gets home. I'm bored, there's nothing in the house to read, I've never cared much for television, and it's hard for me to find an interesting opponent at the chess table."

"So you'll spare my life in order to play chess with me."

"That's right."

"Let me get this straight," the burglar said. "There's no catch to this, is there? I don't get shot if I lose the game or anything tricky like that, I hope."

"Certainly not. Chess is a game that ought to be above gimmickry."

"I couldn't agree more," said the burglar. He sighed a long sigh. "If I didn't play chess," he said, "you wouldn't have shot me, would you?"

"It's a question that occupies the mind, isn't it?"

"It is," said the burglar.

They played in the front room. The burglar drew the white pieces in the first game, opened king's pawn, and played what turned out to be a reasonably imaginative version of the Ruy Lopez. At the sixteenth move Trebizond forced the exchange of the knight for rook, and not too long afterward the burglar resigned.

In the second game the burglar played the black pieces and offered the Sicilian Defense. He played a variation that Trebizond wasn't familiar with. The game stayed remarkably even until in the end game the burglar succeeded in developing a passed pawn. When it was clear that he would be able to queen it, Trebizond tipped over his king, resigning.

"Nice game," the burglar offered.

"You play well."

"Thank you."

"Seem's a pity that . . . "

His voice trailed off. The burglar shot him an inquiring look. "That I'm wasting myself as a common criminal? Is that what you were going to say?"

"Let it go," Trebizond. "It doesn't matter."

They began setting up the pieces for the third game when a key slipped into a lock. The lock turned, the door opened, and Melissa Trebizond stepped into the foyer and through it to the living room.

Both men got to their feet. Mrs. Trebizond advanced, a vacant smile on her pretty face. "You found a new friend to play chess with. I'm happy for you."

Trebizond set his jaw. From his back pocket he drew the burglar's pry bar. It had an even nicer heft than he thought. "Melissa," he said. "I've no need to waste time with a recital of your sins. No doubt you know precisely why you deserve this."

She stared at him, obviously not having understood a word he had said to her, whereupon Archer Trebizond brought the pry bar down on the top of her skull. The first blow sent her to her knees. Quickly he struck her three more times, wielding the metal bar with all his strength, then turned to look into the wide eyes of the burglar.

"You've killed her," the burglar said.

"Nonsense," said Trebizond, taking the bright revolver from his pocket once again.

"Isn't she dead?"

"I hope and pray she is," Trebizond said, "but I haven't killed her. *You've* killed her."

"I don't understand."

"The police will understand," Trebizond said, and shot the burglar in the shoulder. Then he fired again, more satisfactorily this time, and the burglar sank to the floor with a hole in his heart.

Trebizond scooped the chess pieces into their box, swept up the board, and set about the business of arranging things. He suppressed an urge to whistle. He was, he decided, quite pleased with himself. Nothing was ever entirely useless, not to a man of resources. If fate sent you a lemon you made lemonade.

86

THE TERRARIUM PRINCIPLE

Bill Pronzini

ANDREA PARKER WAS on the back porch, working on her latest project—the planting of seeds in a bottle terrarium—when she heard Jerry's car in the driveway. She took off her gloves, brushed flecks of potting soil off her gardening shirt, and went into the kitchen to meet him as he opened the garage door.

There was a preoccupied scowl on Jerry's face. He looked rumpled, the way Columbo used to look on television. Which was unusual; her husband may have been a police lieutenant attached to the Homicide Division, but he definitely was not the Peter Falk type.

He brushed his lips over hers—not much of a kiss, Andrea thought—and said, "I could use a drink." He went straight to the refrigerator and began tugging out one of the ice trays.

"Rough day?" she asked him.

"You can say that again. Except that the operative word is frustrating. One of the most frustrating days I've ever spent."

"Why?"

"Because a man named Harding committed murder in a locked room this morning and I can't prove it. *That's* why."

"Want to talk about it?"

He made a face. But he said, "I might as well. It's going to be on my mind all evening anyway. You can help me brood."

Andrea took the ice tray away from him, shooed him into the living room, and made drinks for both of them. When she brought them in, Jerry was sitting on the couch with his legs crossed, elbow resting on one knee and chin cupped in his palm. He really did look like Columbo tonight. All he needed, she thought, was a trench coat and a cigar.

She handed him his drink and sat down beside him. "So why can't you

511

prove this man Harding committed murder? You did say it happened in a locked room, didn't you?''

''Well, more or less locked. And I can't prove it because we can't find the gun. Without it we just don't have a case.''

''What exactly happened?''

''It's a pretty simple story, except for the missing gun. The classic kind of simple, I mean. Harding's uncle, Philip Granger, has—or had—a house out in Roehampton Estates; wealthy guy, made a lot of money in oil stocks over the years. Harding, on the other hand, is your typical black-sheep nephew—drinks too much, can't hold down a job, has a penchant for fast women and slow horses.

''This morning Harding went out to his uncle's house to see him. The housekeeper let him in. According to her, Harding seemed upset about something, angry. Granger's lawyer, Martin Sampson, happened to be there at the time, preparing some papers for Granger to sign, and he confirms the housekeeper's impression that Harding was upset.

''So Harding went into his uncle's study and either he or Granger locked the door. Fifteen minutes later both Sampson and the housekeeper heard a gunshot. They were sure it came from the study; they both ran straight for that door. But the door was locked, as I said. They pounded and shouted, and inside Harding yelled back that somebody had shot his uncle. Only he didn't open the door right away. It took him eight and one-half minutes by Sampson's watch to get around to it.''

''Eight and a half minutes?'' Andrea said. ''What did he say he was doing all that time?''

''Looking out the window, first of all, for some sign of a phantom killer. Harding's claim is that window was open and Granger was shot through the window from outside; he says Sampson and the housekeeper must have been mistaken about where the shot came from. The rest of the time he was supposedly ministering to his uncle and didn't stop to open the door until the old man had died.''

''But you think he spent that time hiding the gun somewhere in the room?''

''I *know* that's what he was doing,'' Jerry said. ''His story is implausible and he'd had arguments with his uncle before, always over money and sometimes to the point of violence. He's guilty as sin—I'm sure of it!''

''Couldn't he have just thrown the gun out the window?''

''No. We searched the grounds; we'd have found the gun if it had been out there.''

"Well, maybe he climbed out the window, took it away somewhere, and hid it."

"No chance," Jerry said. "Remember the rain we had last night? There's a flower bed outside the study window and the ground there was muddy from the rain; nobody could have walked through it without leaving footprints. And it's too wide to jump over from the window sill. No, the gun is in that room. He managed to hide it somewhere during those eight and one-half minutes. His uncle's stereo unit was playing, fairly loud, and if he made any noise the music covered it—Sampson and the housekeeper didn't hear anything unusual."

"Didn't one of them go outdoors to look in through the study window?"

"Sampson did, yes. But Harding had drawn the drapes. In case the phantom killer came back, he said."

"What's the study like?" Andrea asked.

"Big room with a heavy masculine motif: hunting prints, a stag's head, a wall full of books, overstuffed leather furniture, a walk-in fireplace—"

"I guess you looked up the fireplace chimney," Andrea said.

He gave her a wry smile. "First thing. Nothing but soot."

"What else was in the room?"

"A desk that we went over from top to bottom. And model airplanes, a clipper ship-in-a-bottle, a miniature train layout—all kinds of model stuff scattered around."

"Oh?"

"Evidently Granger built models in his spare time, as a hobby. There was also a small workbench along one wall."

"I see."

"The only other thing in there was the stereo unit—radio, record player, tape deck. I thought Harding might have hidden the gun inside one of the speakers, but no soap."

Andrea was sitting very still, pondering. So still that Jerry frowned at her and then said, "What's the matter?"

"I just had an idea. Tell me, was there any strong glue on the workbench?"

"Glue?"

"Yes. The kind where you only need a few drops to make a bond and it dries instantly."

"I guess there was, sure. Why?"

"How about a glass cutter?"

"I suppose so. Andrea, what are you getting at?"

"I think I know what Harding was doing for those eight and a half

513

minutes," she said. "And I think I know just where he hid the gun."

Jerry sat up straight. "Are you serious?"

"Of course I'm serious. Come on, I want to show you something." She led him out through the kitchen, onto the rear porch. "See that terrarium?"

"What about it?"

"Well, it's a big glass jar with a small opening at one end, right? Like a bottle. There's nothing in it now except soil seeds, but pretty soon there'll be flowers and plants growing inside and people who don't know anything about terrariums will look at it and say, 'Now how in the world did you get those plants through that little opening?' It doesn't occur to them that you *didn't* put plants in there; you put seeds and they grew into plants."

"I don't see what that has to do with Harding—"

"But there's also a way to build a bottle terrarium using fullgrown plants," she went on, "that almost never occurs to anybody. All you have to do is slice off the bottom of the container with a glass cutter; then, when you've finished making your garden arrangement inside, you just glue the bottom back on. That's what some professional florists do. You can also heat the glass afterward, to smooth out the line so nobody can tell it's been cut, but that isn't really necessary. Hardly anyone looks that close."

A light was beginning to dawn in Jerry's eyes. "Like we didn't look close enough at a certain item in Granger's study."

"The ship-in-a-bottle," Andrea said, nodding. "I'll bet you that's where Harding put the gun—inside the ship that's inside the bottle."

"No bet," Jerry said. "If you're right, I'll buy you the fanciest steak dinner in town."

He hurried inside, no longer looking like Columbo, and telephoned police headquarters. When he was through talking he told Andrea that they would have word within an hour. And they did—exactly fifty-six minutes had passed when the telephone rang. Jerry took it, listened, then grinned.

"You were right," he said when he'd hung up. "The bottom of the bottle had been cut and glued back, the ship inside had been hollowed out, and the missing gun was inside the ship. We overlooked it because we automatically assumed nobody could put a gun through a bottle neck that small. It never occurred to us that Harding didn't *have* to put it through the neck to get it inside."

Andrea smiled. "The terrarium principle," she said.

"I guess that's a pretty good name for it. Come on, get your coat; we'll go have that steak dinner right now."

"With champagne, maybe?"

"Sweetheart," he said, "with a whole magnum."

87

DOCTOR'S ORDERS

John F. Suter

THIS PAIN, THE pain is everywhere. No, not everywhere, but I throb in the places where there is no real pain. And now it is only an ache and an exhaustion, but it seems as if there is no time, no space, nothing but this. But I am a little stronger than I was. So little. But I am stronger. I have to get well. I intend to get well. I will get well.

"Mr. Shaw, I think she'll come out of it all right. As you know, it was either your wife or the baby, for a while. But she's improved, I assure you. Of course, there will always be that weakness which we can't correct."

"I understand. Just to have her well again is all I care about."

I had better open my eyes. Jeff isn't here. I can't sense him. But I can stand the white room now. I no longer have a wish to die. Even though he didn't live. I could grieve and grieve and grieve, and I wanted to when Jeff first told me. But there is no strength in that sort of grief. I will get well.

"You did tell her that the baby died?"

"Yes, doctor. It was hard for her to take at first. Very hard. Then I told her that it had been a boy. That pleased her, in spite of—of what happened."

There. The world is back. So much sunshine in the room. So many flowers. I wonder if Jeff—"

"Did you tell her that the child is already buried?"

"Not yet. If you're sure that she's stronger, I'll tell her today."

"You don't think she'll hold it against you for going ahead with the funeral, Mr. Shaw?"

"Jessie is very level-headed, Doctor. She'll understand that we couldn't

515

wait. And—if you don't think it's out of style to say so—we love each other.''

I'm sure Jeff has done whatever is best. If only it—he—had lived until I could have seen him . . . How long have I been here? Where is Jeff? Is he being sensible, as I begged him to be? Is he at work, so that he won't endanger his job, the job that's so important to him? Oh, I do love him, and I do so want to give him fine children.

''Perhaps, then, Mr. Shaw, it would be better for you to tell her the rest of it than for me to do it. It might be easier for her to believe someone who loves her. Sometimes the patient thinks the doctor doesn't know as much as she herself does.''

''That part won't be easy.''

I hope the children will look like Jeff. I'm not ugly, but I'm so—plain. Jeff has the looks for both of us. That's one of the reasons they all said he was only after my money. But he's refused to let me help him. He's independent. He keeps working hard managing the sporting-goods department, when neither of us would ever have to work again, if we didn't want to. I must get well, for his sake. I will get well.

''Easy or hard, Mr. Shaw, it has to be done. Someone has to tell her. It will come best from you. She must never try to have a child again. Never. It will kill her. Make no mistake about it—having another child will kill her.''

''I'll take the responsibility, Doctor. You needn't say a thing to her. I think I can convince her. Perhaps I can even persuade her to move away for a while, so that old associations won't keep haunting her.''

I'm glad that I made my will in Jeff's favor before I came to the hospital. He doesn't know about it, and it wasn't necessary, as it turned out. But I'm glad. He's been so good to me that now I'm sure of him . . .

The door swung inward, silently. She turned her head, slowly, and a tired smile crept across her white face. A tall young man with crinkled blond hair was in the doorway.

''Jeff.''

He was at her bedside, kissing her palm, ''Jessie.''

When they both could speak, she gripped his fingers. ''Jeff, I've been lying here thinking. Everybody has troubles of some kind or other. We can overcome this. I'm going to get strong, fast. Then we're going to have another baby, just as quickly as we can. Aren't we?''

He smiled proudly. The truth was exactly the right answer.

''We certainly are, sweetheart. We certainly are.''

88

NEVER TRUST A WOMAN

Helen Nielsen

A MAN WHO is foolish enough to marry a woman named Prudence should know what to expect. A name like that is to a woman what certain names are to a man: she has to live it down. Now a man named Joseph Buckram, Sales Representative, Anderson Electronics, didn't have to live down a thing except a wife named Prudence, whom he's been careless enough to acquire on a trip to the coast—that could double as a honeymoon, if the head office never found out.

It was nearly eleven o'clock when they checked into the hotel on Hollywood Boulevard. Joe, who'd made the trip enough times to know his way around, took charge of the registration.

"We have a nice double with twin beds, Mr. Buckram."

"Are you crazy?" Joe said.

After he got that straightened out, he looked around for Prudence, who was shoulder high, built like a tomboy with a few, to be expected, differences, and had large brown eyes that hadn't missed a thing since she'd first hoisted herself eye-level with the play-pen about nineteen years earlier.

"The Fandango Room—gathering place of the stars," she said, quoting the wishful thinking from a sign directing guests to the bar and grill. "Joe, do you suppose—?"

Back in Kingman, Arizona, where Joe had found Prudence on the working side of a counter that served coconut cream pies like mother used to make before she got a television set, girls were apt to make a ta-do about celebrities. Joe was an understanding guy, but this was their wedding night.

"Propaganda," he said. "Movie stars couldn't eat in this hotel. It's too expensive."

"Is it too expensive for us?"

She gave Joe those big eyes and his hat shrank at the temples.

"Tonight nothing is too expensive for us," he said with expression, "absolutely nothing!"

Which was the kind of reckless talk that got them joined in holy matrimony, in the first place.

They could have had room service, though Joe wasn't hungry. They'd already had dinner in a cozy little place on the highway, where nobody tortured jazz out of an organ as it was now being done in the Fandango Room. And the smoke hadn't been so thick that he had to squint, as he was not doing to make sure it really was Prudence across the table in that upholstered booth. But it had to be Prudence; only the petite ones ate so much. When she tore into her steak, it occurred to him that if he ever married again it would be to some diet-conscious matron who never ate anything more expensive than water-cress. Then he found Prudence's hand through the smoke—the one that didn't have a fork in it—and was glad she wasn't matronly, even if he'd have to ask the boss for a raise.

Prudence peered at the shadowy figures around the bar.

"I wonder if Errol Flynn is bald on top," she mused.

"It's getting late," Joe said. "I've got a nine-o'clock appointment with Aero-Dynamics."

"No, that isn't him after all. Or is it he? I never remember."

"It's a hot night," Joe said. "Nobody important goes any place on a hot night. They stay home in their swimming pools."

But Prudence went on peering.

"There's a woman in that booth across the aisle who looks a little like—No, she's too old and too fat. Now, that's strange. Why do you suppose she's crying?"

"She's probably wants to go upstairs and turn in for the night," Joe said.

"Joe, be serious! . . . It's that man with her. He's making her cry. I don't like him at all. He's wearing a flashy suit, and he's got a sneaky face and a moustache."

"Men have hung for less," Joe said.

It was impolite to stare at people, especially at bars, but nothing would do but that he look where Prudence was looking. He finally located what held her attention—a woman, not old and fat, but thirtyish and well developed—and a glutton for punishment to be wearing a fur coat on such a warm night. With her, a man in a flashy suit who had a sneaky face and a moustache. The woman dabbed at her eyes with a handkerchief while the man pleaded with her across the table. It was impossible to hear what he was saying, for the organ had just broken into what sounded like a rock and roll arrangement of The Old Rugged Cross.

520

"Don't worry about it," Joe said. It's their anniversary and he's asked the organist to play their song."

"It's not that kind of crying," Prudence argued. "I think she's afraid of him."

Joe looked again.

"You're right," he said. "It's not that kind of crying. It's the 'one drink too many,' or 'I've had such a hard life' kind of crying, and she's too far gone to be afraid of anything."

"Maybe that's his scheme. Maybe that's why he's forcing drinks on her."

It was like forcing taxes on the government. The woman clutched her glass as if it were lifeboat in a stormy sea. For a moment, it required her complete and undivided attention.

"Look," Prudence cried. "Look at him now!"

The organ struck an exuberant passage that covered her outburst, but not before Joe involuntarily obeyed. What the man was doing was taking a quick, furtive peek at the contents of the purse his thirsty companion had left open on the table.

"That only proves it's their anniversay," Joe said. "When we've been married that long I'll probably have to hit you for enough to pay the check."

He said it tenderly, hoping to remind her of the vows they'd exchanged before a Justice of Peace a little after dawn.

"He's a thief!" Prudence insisted. "And they can't be married. They don't match."

It was as stupid an observation as Joe had heard, but he hadn't married Prudence for her brains. He tried to signal the waiter to get his check before she took such an interest in any of the other customers, and that was just when the lady with the big thirst suddenly took affront at what was being confided to her across the table.

"You called me a tramp!" she shrieked. "How dare you call me a tramp?"

The organist had run out of music. So this lady's outburst had an instant audience of every ear in the room.

"I won't sit with you when you talk to me that way! . . . And you can take your lousy coat back!"

"That's an awfully careless way to treat mink," Prudence observed.

It was rather careless, the way she peeled off the coat and draped it over the man's head, but that wasn't what made Joe uneasy. In the smoky darkness, he couldn't tell a mink from a French poodle. Maybe Kingman, Arizona, wasn't as remote as he'd imagined. That thought and all its disturbing implications upset him so much he almost missed the next round. Obviously, the man with the coat on his head wouldn't take it lying down. He was already on his way to the bar where his lady friend was beginning to free-lance.

"You called me a tramp—" she whined.

He wrapped the coat around her shoulders and whispered in her ear. It must have been mink. She didn't whine long. A few minutes later, she was staggering off to the powder room to replace her face, and the man, looking pleased with the world, was calling for his check.

Joe also looked pleased with the world.

"So you've seen a real night-life drama," he remarked, "complete with happy ending. Now we can go—"

Joe watched Prudence march off to the powder room, and now he wasn't pleased with the world at all. She'd never been so difficult before. Maybe it was the city that upset her—the lights and the noise and that lobby swarming with strangers. Prudence had never spent a night in a hotel before. And then Joe saw the light. She was nervous—the poor kid was nervous! The thought pleased him. He began to feel very proud and tolerant. No wonder she was making such a fuss over nothing. No girl wants to admit she's nervous when she's married a man of the world. Smiling over the thought, Joe lit a cigarette. After all, how did he want her to be— brazen, like on those ladies of the evening hovering around the bar?

The waiter brought the check and Joe signed with a flourish. Still smiling, he lit a cigarette. The waiter looked at him strangely and went away. Then the lady with the reclaimed mink emerged from the powder room and went out with her sneaky faced friend. She wasn't in condition to see much of anything, but he looked at Joe strangely they passed. Seconds later, Prudence returned. she looked at him strangely, too.

"Joe, why are you smoking two cigarettes?"

Joe coughed out both cigarettes and ground them into the ash tray.

"Have they gone?" Prudence asked. "She was awfully sick in there."

"And you nursed her, I suppose."

"I didn't go near her, but I could hear. She's still careless, too. She dropped her mink coat on the floor and left her purse lying open on the make-up table. Her name is Leona Muller."

"I thought you didn't go near her." And then Joe had a horrible thought. "You didn't—"

"It was just lying there open. The catch wasn't caught."

"But ransacking another woman's purse!"

"I didn't ransack anything. I just found the identification card and wrote it down for the police." Prudence had a small piece of pink paper in her hand. She held it under the table lamp and began to read: "Leona Muller, 1221—"

"The police?" Joe echoed.

"In case something terrible happens. I have a feeling, Joe. There's something wrong. That expensive mink coat and a shabby old purse—They don't match.

"So she likes to economize!"

"And I don't think she should go off with that man tonight. I don't trust him."

"Look, honey," Joe said. "I'm an understanding guy, but this has gone far enough. I'm your husband and I order you to forget Leona Muller, her mink coat, and all of this silly business once and for all. We're getting out of here right now!"

Gently, but masterfully, he grabbed her wrist. It ws the wrist of the hand that clutched the small slip of pink paper. He looked closely at the slip of pink paper. It had perforated edges.

"Prudence—"

Joe tried to hide the tremor in his voice.

"Just one question. Where did you get this paper to write the name and address on?"

Prudence looked at him unblinkingly.

"I looked in my purse, but I didn't have anything to write on. Only a pen—"

"So you took this slip of paper from Leona Muller's purse?"

"It's just a little piece."

It was just a little piece, until Joe took it from her hand and unfolded it. Pink, perforated edges—Yes, it had to be. Joe sat down again and buried his face in his hands. The little piece of pink paper was a check made out to Leona Muller for the sum of $28,000.

When a man has married a woman who steals $28,000 on her wedding night, he must take drastic action. Joe sat with his head in his hands for fifteen seconds. Then he stood up.

"Come on," he ordered.

"Are you going to call the police?" Prudence asked.

"Not unless you want to postpose our honeymoon for about ten years. Those two went out of the street door. They must have a car in the parking lot."

"But Joe—"

"And when we catch them, I do the talking understand? You *found* that check on the powder room floor—understand?"

"But Joe—"

Joe wasn't the top west coast representative of Anderson Electronics just so he could argue with a five foot brunette who couldn't keep her hands out of another woman's purse. He was practically dragging her behind him when they reached the street. The man and the woman had a start of several minutes on them, but with the woman in such a fluid state, they couldn't move very fast. The hotel parking lot was just around the corner of the building. The lights were burning brightly. About halfway down the center row of cars, a man in a plaid suit was trying to pour his female companion into the front seat of a light green midget sedan. At first Joe wasn't sure—

"You called me a tramp! I haven't forgotten you called me at tramp!"

Joe was sure then. He ran forward.

"Hey!" he yelled. "Hey—you!"

"Joe, be careful!" Prudence cried.

This was the one time she lived up to her name. The man had his mind on what he was doing—and both hands, until Joe came on the scene. He didn't seem to appreciate interference.

"Who asked you to butt in?" he demanded. "Can't a man have a fight with his wife, without a buttinsky butts in?"

"I'm not butting in," Joe said. "I've got something for you—"

"And I've got something for you!"

Joe didn't even have time to duck—much less explain. Sneaky face was in a terrible hurry. A fist had shot out of nowhere, a car door slammed, and above the plaintive wail—"You called me a tramp—" the midget motor sputtered alive. when Prudence reached him, Joe was seated in the middle of the asphalt drive and the little sedan was nosing its way toward the exit of the parking lot.

Joe muttered in an ancient tongue, native to boot camps and locker rooms.

"I told you not to trust that man," Prudence said.

Joe looked up at Prudence and, for one ghastly instant, he had a wild desire to slug her.

Never could Joe have done what he did then, if he hadn't been so angry. Nobody, but an exceedingly angry man, could pull a car out of a lot that fast, miss tearing off anybody's fenders, ignore the protests of a be-wildered brunette clinging to the edge of the seat, and make it to the street just as the little sedan was pulling away from the boulevard stop at the corner.

"Keep your eye on him!" Joe ordered. "Don't let him out your sight!"

"Joe, are you hurt?"

"A guy tries to do a guy a favor! A maniac like that shouldn't run loose!"

"Joe, the light—"

Joe didn't have times for lights. The only red he could see was in his own eyes, and the boulevard was nearly empty at this hour anyway. Up ahead, the tail-lights of the little sedan were bobbing over the pavement like a pair of skipping fireflies. Joe ground his foot against the gas pedal and the fireflies were a lot nearer.

"That motorized kiddy-car! I'll run it clear up on the sidewalk! I'll put it in the trash can!"

"Joe, there's another light—I mean, there was another light!"

It was a fine time for Prudence to be getting cautious. This was all her fault anyway. Joe hadn't forgotten that for a minute.

"Damn the lights!" he said. "I've got to get that idiot before he reaches the Freeway."

"But the police—"

"I told you, I don't want the police. I'm going to give Leona her $28,000 if I have to stuff it down her husband's throat!"

"I still say they aren't married," Prudence said.

Prudence didn't say any more. She never had a chance. By this time they had come alongside the little sedan, and Joe wasn't kidding about running it up the curb. He veered his car toward the midget; the midget veered toward the sidewalk. The man with the sneaky face yelled something out of the window and Joe yelled something back; and then, as Joe swung toward the little car again, it leaped the curbing, shuddered, and came to a stop in the doorway of a florist's shop.

The driver's door was open by the time Joe reached the sidewalk.

"You stay away from me!" the man yelled. "Stay away or I'll let you have it!"

Joe heard the words, but they didn't register. As far as he was concerned, he'd already had it. He had to slug somebody, and Prudence was too small. The man backed toward the shop window, one hand stuck out in front of him. The lights from the little car glinted off the object in his hand, but Joe was too far gone for caution. His fists began to whirl in front of him like a pair of crazy propellers. The gun clattered to the sidewalk as useless as a toy. Somebody screamed. There was a loud thudding sound, and the window shattered as if it had been struck by a heavy body—because it had been.

When the glass stopped tinkling, there was a moment of awful silence; then brakes screeched and a blinding light stabbed through the darkness. Joe whirled about, blinking.

"The police—" he gasped.

Prudence picked her way toward him across the broken glass.

"That's what I was trying to tell you in the car," she said, "when you ran the lights—"

Joe didn't say anything. He groaned.

It was nearly two o'clock when they got back to the hotel. The police were very understanding after Prudence explained everything. That was after they'd pulled the sneaky faced man out of the potted Camelias and throttled Leona Muller's wails when they took away her mink coat.

"Tha's my wedding present! We're goin' to Las Vegas to get married, an' tha's my wedding present!"

"You see!" Prudence said. "I knew they weren't married."

And then the policeman who was in charge of the sneaky faced man turned his flashlight on his sneaky face and said, "Well, if it isn't Duke McGinnis! Getting married again, Duke? Where did you steal the bait this time? And how much is the lady's dowry?"

"$28,000," Prudence said. "My husband has the check which I found in the powder room and we were only trying to return—"

"My house money!" Leona Muller exclaimed. "Tha's my house money!"

It was very confusing for awhile, especially after Leona finally realized that McGinnis had given her a hot mink and was only trying to marry her for the $28,000 check she'd just received for the sale of her old, run-down bungalow at the edge of Beverly Hills. It all had to be straightened out at the police station with the owner of the florist shop bawling about his broken window and uprooted Camelias, and the police looking at Joe and shaking their heads.

"'Your husband is an excitable man, Mrs. Buckram," the desk sergeant said.

"He's really very sweet, but tonight he's a little nervous. You see, we were only married this morning."

After that the police were very understanding.

Back in the hotel—in their own room at last—Joe had a few words to say.

"I'm not angry any more," he said. "I'm willing to forget the whole thing and never mention it again. I won't even ask if you knew that piece of pink paper was a check when you lifted it from the purse."

"No woman should carry anything that valuable around with her when she's out with a man who's deliberately trying to get her drunk," Prudence said.

"I won't," Joe added, "even ask if you knew that mink was stolen—"

"It didn't have any labels in it," Prudence explained. "I looked when I was in the powder room. If I had a real mink coat I'd have the furrier's label and my name embroidered in gold."

"—stolen," Joe repeated, "and given to Leona to lure her into a phoney marriage long enough for McGinnis to get her check cashed—"

"Imagine a flashy looking man like Mr. McGinnis going for a fat old woman like Leona Muller. They don't match!"

"Like the mink coat and the cheap handbag?"

"Exactly the handbag McGinnis couldn't keep his hands off because all he was really interested in the check tucked away inside. Joe—"

Prudence didn't have $28,000, but Joe had her in his arms. And he didn't want to hear any more explanations, or to be told how brave he was for knocking an armed man into the Camelias even if he had been too angry to recognize that it was a gun McGinnis had stuck in front of him, or to engage in any kind of conversation at all—because it was two o'clock in the morning, and he had an early appointment at Aero-Dynamics, and some people did match—perfectly.

Joe, finally, made this all clear to Prudence. And they were just getting cozy when a shrill, female voice drifted up from the parking lot below.

"You called me a bar-fly! You take your hands off me! You called me a bar-fly!"

Prudence raised up.

"Joe—listen!"

Joe was on his feet in an instant. He made it to the window in one leap and slammed down the sash.

"But, Joe, it'll get warm in here—"

Joe came back toward Prudence with a determined glint in his eye.

"I wouldn't be surprised," he said.

89

SOMEBODY ON THE PHONE

Cornell Woolrich

"I HEAR IT! Let it ring!" she snapped back at me. We were always snapping at each other. That's how you could tell we were brother and sister. But this snap had teeth in it. There was something frightened, tense, about it. And her face matched it—white, drawn, straining forward.

She was right in the room with it, sitting facing it in a big chair. She didn't make a move to go over and answer it. She just sat there listening to it, as if she'd never heard one before, as if she wanted to see how long it would keep up.

I happened to look at her hand on the arm of the chair. It was heel down, but the fingers were uptilted; they weren't touching the chair arm. And at each ring that sounded, I saw one press down, as if she were counting them to herself. The pinkie, then the ring finger, then the middle, then the index, then the thumb. Like someone practicing scales on a piano keyboard.

On the fifth ring, the thumb count, it quit. A moment's stop, as though the connection had been broken at the other end, and then it got under way again.

"You paralyzed?" I said. A whole layer of shaving cream was evaporating on me on account of this foolishness. But when she saw me step out to go over to the phone, she left her chair like something out of a slingshot, and backed up against it to keep from getting at it.

"No, Ken! Let it alone!" There was desperation in her voice. And then the ringing quit a second time, for good, and that ended it for her. But not for me.

"You're white as a ghost. Who was that? What's going on around here? A code too, eh? Maybe you think I missed that! You count the number of rings. The other end hangs up on five, then calls right back. If the coast is clear you answer. That's bad medicine. Maybe you think I didn't see you at

529

the Congo Club last Tuesday night with some guy who looked like a cardshark?''

She gave me a comet of a look—a white, startled flash.

"I didn't butt in," I said, "because you've always been very level-headed. You've always known your way around. One thing sure, it wasn't a social meeting. I watched the two of you. You weren't there for dancing or for drinking; you were there to talk business.''

She shivered as if the room were cold, but it was July. She tried to put a bold front on it. "Go ahead, cable Dad and Mother in London—all because I don't answer a phone call. You should be a scenario writer.''

I was shrugging into my coat. "I've got to make the bank before closing time. Tomorrow's payday at the firm. I want to talk to you some more about this when I get back. Stick around.''

"I'll stick around," she said. I couldn't get rid of that for years afterward: "I'll stick around.''

The teller handed back my check to me. "No funds, Mr. Hunter.''

I nearly went down on the marble floor. "Why, there was twenty thousand in that account on the first of last month!'' The office salaries and upkeep had to come out of it, and our living expenses; Dad had given both of us access to it when he went away.

"Not only that. You're overdrawn by another thousand. We called you about it yesterday, and Miss Hunter took the message.''

"Well, where's my statement? Show me the canceled checks? Who's been drawing on it?''

"We mailed that to you early in the week," he said. I thought: She must have intercepted it, then . . .

I went back and she was waiting for me as she'd said she would. She was dressed to go out, though. I grabbed her by the wrist and swung her all the way around.

"Who took you for a cleaning?" I said. "Who's been shaking you down? Where's the pearls Dad gave you for Christmas? Take off your glove—where's your diamond solitaire? You've been gambling again, haven't you?" Her head went down.

"And they found out who you were, found out we're well-heeled, knew that a scandal would kill Dad, and have been putting the screws on you ever since. Is that it?''

Her head went down a second time.

"That was what that call was, on the phone before, that frightened you so. Wasn't it?''

This time she spoke. "Yes, Ken, that was what that was.''

"Gimme the guy's name," I said.

"Oh, don't!" she begged. "It'll ruin all of us. Wait here a minute. I have a better way than that. Let me handle it my way. She went into her room and closed the door.

I paced back and forth. Finally I went over and rapped. "Jean," I said, "you coming out? I want to talk to you!"

Before she could answer, the doorbell rang and a sleepy-looking cop was standing there. "Hunter? Take it easy now, take it easy," he said for no apparent reason. "Your sister—"

I had no time to bother. "What d'you want? She's in her room."

"No, she isn't," he said. "She just fell fifteen stories down to the street. That's what I'm trying to tell you."

I knew almost at once what I was going to do, even while they were still asking me the routine questions.

"We were going out together," I said through my hands, "and she remembered she'd left the window open in her room. She went back a minute to close it. I guess she must have—"

Yes, they agreed sympathetically, she must have. And they went out and closed the door.

I'd had the gun, and the license for it, ever since that time we'd been burglarized at Great Neck, I got it out and made sure it was loaded. This was a sentence—here in my mind—that no clever lawyer could set side or whittle down to nothing. This was a sentence that smirched no names except mine. Oh, any excuse would do. I didn't like his necktie, or he'd stepped on my foot. This was a sentence from which there was no appeal. Because somebody had killed her—by calling her up on the phone. The law mightn't see it that way, but I did.

It might have seemed a funny place to go, that very night while she was broken and white and all alone with just flowers. The Congo Club, with its clatter and its rainbow spotlights. It didn't to me; it seemed the right place, the only place.

" . . . where that empty table is, inside that booth there. Last Tuesday night, with a very pretty girl." I killed my drink at this point, and it was all salty. "I want to know who the man was."

For a hundred dollars anyone'll remember anything. "That was Buck Franklin," the manager said. "He's the club owner himself. Some sort of private gambling place. He comes here quite a lot. I expect them both tonight again. He reserved that same table."

I squeezed my glass hard with one hand and got another drop out of it; the liquid would hardly go down my throat, though. Stuck in the middle. And the glass cracked and split in two pieces. "No, he won't be here tonight—with her," I said quietly. "That's why I've got to reach him. I've got a message for him—from her."

One of the hackmen that had the concession outside might know, he suggested. The third on line admitted he knew who the man was and had driven him home from here numerous times. He couldn't remember where, though. He said the man always gave him a five-dollar tip on each haul. I gave him fifty, and then he remembered where.

He took me to the apartment.

It was him all right, the same man who had been with her at the Congo Club. He was waiting for me by the open door, after I'd been announced and sent up. "You say you've got a message for me from Miss Jean Hunter?"

"You know her then, do you?"

"Sure I know her."

"Let's close the door and keep this just between us," I suggested. He closed it.

"I've been waiting to hear from her all evening," he said aggrievedly. "I've tried to reach her at her apartment, and she's not there."

"No, she's not there," I agreed, unbuttoning my jacket so I could get at my back pocket.

"I'm a busy man," he said. "I put myself out to do her a favor, because I feel sorry for her, and then she keeps me waiting—"

"That's her ring," I interrupted. He was breathing on a diamond solitaire he'd taken out of his vest pocket, and absentmindedly rubbing it on the back of his hand.

"She gave it to me as collateral for a loan. I'm not sure it's worth what I let her have, but I always was an easy mark for a femme in trouble. I suppose she's out right now trying to raise the rest of it. I hope she does for her sake."

"Loan? Is that what they're calling it now?" I said without heat. "I think you better turn around. The back is about the right place."

He didn't. He got out two words after the first shot. Two husky breaths that didn't touch his larynx walls at all. "What—for?"

"For Jean Hunter . . . Here's your code back again," I said above the noise, while I kept punching the trigger in and out. "Five times, then quit, then call back again."

He was down long before the last one, so I gave it to him on the floor. I took the ring back, but I threw the gun down beside him in exchange.

There was evidently no one there with him, and the place must have been soundproofed. No one seemed to have heard it outside in the hall when I went out there. On the way down I was going to tell the elevator operator, "I just shot that Franklin guy up there." But then I thought, "Aw, let them come over to my place after me, if they want me!" I went home.

The door was still closed, where she'd gone in that afternoon and never come out again.

"It's taken care of, Jean," I said quietly, as if she were still in there. "He won't be calling you up any—"

Just then it started to ring. *Brring!*—one. *Brring!*—two. *Brring!*—three. *Brring!*—four. *Brring*—five. Then it stopped for a minute.

Then it started in again.

90

THE PEPPERMINT-STRIPED GOODBY

Ron Goulart

1

THE DRIVE-IN, all harsh glass and stiff redwood and brittle aluminum and sharp No. 7 nails, stood on the oceanside of the bright road like some undecided suicide. My carhop had a look of frozen hopefulness and the flawed walk of a windup doll with a faulty gudgeon pin. Shifting in the seat of my late-model car, I eased the barrel of my stiff black .38 Police special so that it stopped cutting off the circulation in my left leg.

"Where's the town of San Mineo?" I asked the girl, my voice an echo of all the lost hopes of all of us.

"Back that way about twenty miles," she said.

I'd thought so. Sometimes the intricate labyrinth that is Southern California gets one up on me. But there is, as my once-wife used to point out, an intense, harsh, sun-dried stubbornness about Ross Pewter. She often talked like that.

It was stubborn of me to drive my late-model car, gunning it too much on the sharp death-edged curves of the road that wound by the sea, twenty miles in the wrong direction. I was thirty-six now and sometimes the harsh sun-dried motor trips through the fever-heat madness that is Southern California made me feel that time's winged chariot was behind me. Other times it was a lettuce truck. Nobody passed Ross Pewter on the road.

"Do you wish to see a menu?" the carhop asked. Her voice had the ring of too much laughter deferred in it.

"No," I told her. I backed out of the place, afraid of the already ghost-town look of it, and cannoned back toward San Mineo and my client.

"Pewter," I said aloud as my late-model car flashed like a dazed locust down the mirage of the state highway, "Pewter, some of these encounters you get into in the pursuit of a case seem to be without meaning."

I would have answered myself that life itself is at times, most times, meaningless. But a Highway Patrol cycle, its motor like the throaty cough of an old man who has come to Los Angeles from Ohio and found that his Social Security checks are being sent still to his Ohio address, started up behind me. The pursuit began and I had to ride the car hard to elude it.

2

The pillars that held up the porch of the big house reminded me of the detail of the capital and entablature of the Ionic temple at Fortuna Virilis at Rome. The entablature, cornice, and architrave were encrusted with carved ornament, a motif of formalized acanthus leaf enriching the design, and the scrolls terminated in rosettes.

I almost wished this were the house I was going to visit.

Sighing, and dislodging the barrel of my pistol from a tender part of my thigh, I crossed the rich moneyed street and approached the home of old Tro Bultitude. Decay seemed to drift all around, carried like pollen on the hot red wind of this late Southern California afternoon. Even the pilasters, the balustrades, and the cornices of the sprawling Bultitude mansion seemed decayed. It sat like the waiting wedding cake in that book by Charles Dickens.

The thought of it all filled me with a sadness and the actual pollen in the air started my hay fever going again.

The butler was a heavy-set man, all thick hair and musty black clothes, and there was about him the faint smell of Saturday matinees in small Midwestern movie theaters now renovated and made into supermarkets and coin laundries.

"Blow off, Jack," he said.

"The name is Pewter," I said. "Tell your boss I'm here to see him."

"Scram, Jacko. We got illness in the family. All the Colonel's unmarried daughters are down with nymphomania."

I didn't speak. I just showed him the barrel of my .38.

"What's that hanging on the end of it?" he asked.

I looked. "Some elastic from my shorts, it seems. Want to make a quip about it?"

"I'll quip you," said the butler, snarling. "You remind me of all the lonely self-abusing one-suited bill collectors that haunted the time-troubled corridors of my long-ago youth."

"I'll do the metaphors around here," I said and went for him. I got two nice chops at his jaw and he tumbled back like a condemned building that has just been hit by a runaway truck.

"Let's not waste any more time," called an old life-worn voice from inside.

I vaulted the fallen butler and found myself not in a hallway but at once in a giant white-walled room. As I looked on, steam began to come from jets low in the wall.

"The name is Pewter," I said to the crumbled old man who sat in a sunchair, wrapped in a towel as white as the flash of a .38 like mine. "You've got a problem?"

"Vachel Geesewand said you'd cleared up that business in Santa Monica," said Bultitude.

"I cleared up the whole damn town before I quit."

"Good. My problem," said the old man, "is simply this. About twenty-two years ago in Connecticut—the name of the town doesn't matter—a young man named Earl K. M. Hoseblender was riding a bicycle down East Thirty-fourth Street, heading for a hardware store."

"Go on," I said, interested now.

"My mind wanders," he admitted. "That isn't the right problem. That one the police will handle. What I want you to do is find my daughter, Alicia."

"I can do that."

"Alicia is a strange girl," said the old man. "For a long time she wore a false beard and hung out with the surfers at Zuma Beach. They drove around in an old ice-cream wagon they'd painted with peppermint stripes."

"Red and white stripes?"

"You've guessed it," said Tro Bultitude. "Then about a year ago there was an accident."

"What kind of an accident?"

"Alicia never told me. I do know that the bell fell off the ice-cream wagon; she's talked about that often. And a boy named Kip may have broken his left ankel. It was all a year ago, a long time ago for a twenty-year-old like Alicia.

"You see, Mr. Pewter, Alicia has not had an untroubled childhood. When she was four my first wife—the former Hazel Wadlow Whitney—fell unaccountably from the top of a Christmas tree and succumbed. Alicia was the only witness." He sighed a dry dead sigh, like leaves being swept up by a slipshod gardener. "At fourteen she was unavoidably involved in a bank robbery in Connecticut. The town will be nameless."

"Is it the same town Hoseblender was riding his bicycle in?"

"No," he admitted. "It's a different nameless town."

"Do you have any pictures of your daughter?"

"Yes, but you'll have to be careful who you show them to since they're pornographic. Another unfortunate moment in the poor child's past."

"When'd she leave?"

"The day after my fourth wife—the former Hazel Wadlow Whitney— fell off the cupola."

"I thought Hazel Wadlow Whitney was your first wife?"

"This is a different Hazel Wadlow Whitney. I have a tendency to marry women with that name. It has upset Alicia more than once. When she was fifteen she ran away to Topeka, Kansas, and was later arrested for trying to break the Menninger Brothers' windows."

"Any idea where she might be?"

"You might look for that candy-striped ice-cream wagon."

I scowled at his finished old lusterless eyes. "You're keeping something back from me."

"Very well," he said, making a feminine gesture. "She is not alone. There is a strong possibility she may be with her half brother. You see, fifteen years ago I discovered a foundling on my doorstep. He was nearly five years old at the time, and quite bright. The note pinned to him explained that he had an IQ of 185."

"How does that make him a half brother to Alicia?"

"I can't tell you that."

"A hundred dollars a day and expenses is my fee," I told him.

"Dawes will give you an envelope full of money, Mr. Pewter. If you'll excuse me I have to take a steam bath. I suffer from a malignant disease, and steam seems to be good for me."

The room, now that I noticed it, was as foggy as the 2900 block on Jackson Street in San Francisco. I said goodby and went out to find the butler and my money.

3

Something old Bultitude had said gave me a hunch and I took a jet to Connecticut as soon as I left him.

The night seems timeless when you are hurtling through it at a fast clip—like a marble in some pinball machine in a grease-and-chili-smelling place on some hot, dry side street on the underbelly of Southern California.

We all of us drag the past with us like one of those big silver trailers that clog the L.A. highways. Looking, all of us, for a place to pull off the road and park the damn thing but we never do it.

Spent time is somewhat like the bird in that poem by Coleridge and we carry it around our neck like a gift necktie that we have to wear to please the giver, who gave it to us like someobdy passing out the second-rate wine now that the guests, who sit around like numbed patients in some sort of cosmic dentist's waiting room, are too unsober to know or care.

I suppose you've felt like that when you're flying too.

4

The cops beat me up in Connecticut. They always do. But I found out what I wanted. By noon, on a hot, dry, sticky-90-and-climbing day, I was back at the drive-in I'd gone to by mistake.

The kitchen was like all the meals they made you eat as a lonely child. It smelled of oatmeal and fried foods and stale chocolate cake.

"You," I said to the frycook.

He was a pale youth of about twenty. His face had the worn look of one who has lost two falls out of three—lost too many battles with the dark side of himself.

"Don't bug me now, mister," he said. "I've got to fry three orders of oatmeal."

I picked a soft spot in his belly and gave him a stiff-fingered jab there. He fell over onto the stale chocolate cake, making the silent falling sound that a giant tree does when it topples alone in a distant wood.

"I know you're Albert B. Bultitude," I told the kid, jerking him to his feet. "Yesterday when I came in here I saw the overcoat."

"You weren't in this kitchen yesterday, mister."

"Don't mix me up while I'm trying to explain this case," I said. "They told me some things in Connecticut."

"Sure, they're a knowledgeable bunch in Connecticut. You take Westport, for instance; they have a great many gifted people there."

"Forget that," I told him. "I know who your mother is."

His eyes flickered like a cigaret lighter about to run out of fluid. "How did you guess?"

"She let the towel slip when she was in the steam bath and I figured it out."

539

"Well, you're right. Our mistake was keeping the past festering too long."

"It wasn't Hazel Wadlow Whitney who fell from the cupola; it was Tro Bultitude, pushed by you. I thought Dawes was too tough. He's really your Uncle Brewster from Maine. Still, the whole business about the silverware doesn't make sense to me."

"I never heard of any silverware."

"Good. Then I'll leave that part out."

"I guess you know about Alicia, too."

"There is no Alicia," I said. "There never was. Alicia is really Tony, your other half brother. He drove the car that time in Connecticut. The accident with the ice-cream wagon made him walk funny and then he decided to try the Alicia bit."

"It's odd how the past catches up with us," said Albert.

"The only thing is," I said, watching the oatmeal burn away to ashes, "I still don't see why your mother hired me at all. She's accomplished only the arrest of her son for the murder of her husband."

"Mother's been rather dotty since she fell off the Christmas tree that time."

I needed a lungful of fresh air. "Let's go, Albert. I know some cops in L.A. who aren't corrupt and I'm turning you over to them."

Outside, Albert stared at the bright, intense blue of the ocean. He hesitated for a long second and then waved boyishly at the mindless timeless water.

"Goodby," he called. "I don't think I'll be seeing the ocean again for a while."

He was right.

91

THE MAN OF THE KNIFE

Alexandre Dumas

THERE DWELLS IN Ferdj' Ouah a Sheik named Bou Akas en Achour. It is one of the most ancient names in the country, so we find it in the history of the dynasties of the Arabs and Berbers of Ibu Khaldoun.

Bou Akas is 49 years of age. He dresses like the Kabyles; that is, in a gandoura of wool girt with a leather belt, and fastened around the head with a slender cord. He carries a pair of pistols in his shoulder belt, at his left side the Kabyle flissa, and, hanging from his neck, a little black knife. Before him walks a Negro carrying his gun, and at his side bounds a large greyhound.

When a tribe in the vicinity of the twelve tribes over which he rules occasions him any loss, he deigns not to march against it, but is satisfied with sending his Negro to the principal village, where the Negro shows the gun of Bou Akas, and the injury is repaired.

There are in his pay two or three tolbas who read the Koran to the people. Every person passing by his dwelling on a pilgrimage to Mecca received three francs and at the Sheik's expense remains in Ferdj' Ouah as long as he pleases. But should Bou Akas learn that he has had to do with a false pilgrim, he sends emissaries to overtake the man wherever he may be, and they, on the spot, turn him over on his face, and give him twenty blows of the bastinado on the soles of his feet.

Bou Akas sometimes dines 300 persons, but instead of partaking of the repast he walks around among his guests with a stick in his hand, marshaling his domestics; then, if there is anything left, he eats, but the very last.

When the Governor of Constantina, the only man whose supremacy he acknowledges, sends him a traveler, according to whether the traveler is a man of note, or the recommendation is pressing, Bou Akas presents him with his gun, his dog, or his knife. If he presents his gun, the traveler shoulders it; if his dog, the traveler holds it in leash; if his knife, the traveler suspends it from his neck. With one or another of these talismans, each of which bears with it the degree of honor to be rendered, the traveler passes through the twelve tribes without incurring the slightest danger. Everywhere he is fed and lodged for nothing, for he is the guest of Bou Akas. When he leaves Ferdj' Ouah, it is sufficient for him to deliver the knife, the dog, or the gun to the first Arab that he meets. The Arab, if hunting, stops; if tilling the ground, he quits his plow; if in the bosom of his family, he departs; and taking the knife, the dog, or the gun, returns it to Bou Akas.

In fact, the little black-handled knife is very well known; so well known, that it has given its name to Bou Akas—Bou d'Jenoui, or The Man of the Knife. It is with this knife that Bou Akas cuts off people's heads when, for the sake of prompt justice, he thinks fit to decapitate with his own hand.

When Bou Akas succeeded to his possessions there were a great number of thieves in the country. He found means to exterminate them. He dressed himself like a simple merchant, then dropped a douro, taking care not to lose sight of it. A lost douro does not remain long on the ground. If he who picked it up pocketed it, Bou Akas made a sigh to his chiaous, disguised like himself, to arrest the culprit. The chiaous, knowing the Sheik's intention in regard to the culprit, beheaded him without more ado. The effect of this rigor is such that there is a saying among the Arabs that a child of twelve years of age wearing a golden crown could pass throught the tribes of Bou Akas without a finger's being raised to steal it . . .

One day Bou Akas heard mentioned that the Cadi of one of his twelve tribes rendered judgments worthy of King Solomon. Like another Haroun al Raschid, he wished to decide for himself the truth of the stories which were told him. Consequently he set out in the guise of an ordinary horseman, without the arms which usually distinguished him, without any emblem of rank, nor any followers and mounted on a blood-horse about which nothing betrayed that it belonged to so great a Chief.

It is chanced that on the day of his arrival at the thrice-happy city where the Cadi sat in judgment there was a Fair, and, in consequence of that, the Court was in session. It so chanced also—Mahomet watches over his servants in all things—that at the gate of the city Bou Akas met a cripple who, hanging upon his burnoose, as the poor man hung upon the cloak of St. Martin, asked him for alms. Bou Akas gave the alms, as behooves an honest Musselman to do, but the cripple continued to cling to him.

"What do you want?" asked Bou Akas. "You have solicited alms and I bestowed them on you."

"Yes," replied the cripple, "but the Law does not say only, 'Thou shalt bestow alms on thy brother,' but, in addition, 'Thou shalt do for thy brother all in thy power.' ''

''Well, what can I do for you?'' inquired Bou Akas.

''You can save me, poor wretch that I am, from being crushed under the feet of the men, the mules, and the camels, which will not fail to happen if I risk myself in the city.''

''And how can I prevent that?''

''By taking me up behind you, and carrying me to the marketplace, where I have business.''

''Be it so,'' said Bou Akas, and lifting up the cripple he helped him to mount behind. The operation was accomplished with some difficulty, but it was at last done. The two men on the single horse traversed the city, not without exciting general curiosity. They arrived at the marketplace.

''Is it here that you wished to go?'' inquired Bou Akas of the cripple.

''Yes.''

''Then dismount,'' said the Sheik.

''Dismount yourself.''

''To help you down, very well!''

''No, to let me have the horse.''

''Why? Wherefore should I let you have the horse?'' said the astonished Sheik:

''Because the horse is mine.''

''Ah, indeed! We shall soon see about that!''

''Listen, and consider,'' said the cripple.

''I am listening, and I will consider afterward.''

''We are in the city of the just Cadi.''

''I know it,'' assented the Sheik.

''You intend to prosecute me before him?''

''It is extremely probable.''

''Now, do you think that when he sees us two—you with your sturdy legs, which God has destined for walking and fatigue, me with my broken legs—think you, I say, that he will not decide that the horse belongs to the one of the two travelers who has the greater need of it?''

''If he say so,'' replied Bou Akas, ''he will no longer be the just Cadi, for his decision will be wrong.''

''They call him the just Cadi,'' rejoined the cripple, laughing, ''but they do not call him the infallible Cadi.''

''Upon my word!'' said Bou Akas to himself, ''here is a fine chance for me to judge the Judge.'' Then he said aloud, ''Come on, let us go before the Cadi.''

Bou Akas made his way through the throng, leading his horse, on whose back the cripple clung like an ape; and presented himself before the tribunal where the Judge, according to the custom in the East, publicly dispensed justice.

Another case was before the court, and of course it took precedence. Bou Akas obtained a place among the audience, and listened. The case was a suit between a taleb and a peasant—that is to say, a savant and a laborer. The point in question was in reference to the savant's wife, with whom the peasant had eloped, and whom he maintained to be his, in opposition to the savant who claimed her. The woman would not acknowledge either of the men to be her husband, or rather she acknowledged both; which circumstance rendered the affair embarrassing to the last degree.

The Judge heard both parties, reflected an instant, and said, "Leave the woman with me, and return tomorrow."

The savant and the laborer each bowed and withdrew.

It was now the turn of Bou Akas and the cripple.

"My lord Cadi," said Bou Akas, "I have just come from a distant city with the intention of buying goods at this mart. At the gate of the city I met this cripple, who at first asked me for alms, and finally begged me to allow him to mount behind me; telling me that, if he risked himself in the streets, he, poor wretch, feared he should be crushed under the feet of the men, the mules, and the camels. Thereupon I mounted him behind me. Having arrived at the marketplace, he would not alight, saying that the horse which I rode belonged to him; and when I threatened him with the law, 'Bah!'' he replied. 'The Cadi is too sensible a man not to know that the horse is the property of that one of us who cannot travel without a horse!' This is the affair, in all sincerity, my lord Cadi, I swear it by Mahomet."

"My lord Cadi," said the cripple, "I was going on business to the market of the city, mounted on this horse which is mine, when I saw, seated by the wayside, this man, who seemed about to expire. I approached him and inquired whether he had met with any accident. 'No accident has befallen me,' he replied, 'but I am overcome with fatigue, and if you are charitable you will convey me to the city where I have business. After reaching the marketplace I will dismount, praying Mahomet to bestow upon him who aided me all that he could desire.' I did as this man requested, but my astonishment was great when, having arrived at the marketplace, he bade me dismount, telling me that the horse was his. At this strange threat I brought him before you, that you might judge between us. This is the matter, in all sincerity, I swear by Mahomet."

The Cadi made each repeat his deposition, then having reflected an instant he said, "Leave the horse with me, and return tomorrow."

The horse was delivered to the Cadi, and Bou Akas and the cripple retired.

The next day, not only the parties immediately interested but also a great number of the curious were present in Court.

The Cadi followed the order of precedence observed the first day. The taleb and the peasant were summoned.

"Here," said the Cadi to the taleb, "here is your wife; take her away, she is really yours." Then turning toward his chiaous, and pointing out the peasant, he said, "Give that man fifty strokes on the soles of his feet."

The Sheik's case was now called, and Bou Akas and the cripple approached.

"Could you recognize your horse among twenty horses?" inquired the Judge of Bou Akas.

"Yes, my lord judge," replied Bou Akas and the cripple with one accord.

"Then come with me," said the Judge to Bou Akas, and they went out.

Bou Akas recognized his horse among twenty horses.

"Very well," said the Judge. "Go and wait in Court, and send me your adversary."

Bou Akas returned to the court, and awaited the Cadi's return.

The cripple went to the stable as quickly as his bad legs would allow him. As his eyes were good, he went straight up to the horse and pointed it out.

"Very well," said the Judge. "Rejoin me in Court."

The Cadi resumed his seat on his mat and everyone waited impatiently for the cripple, who in the course of five minutes returned out of breath.

"The horse is yours," said the Cadi to Bou Akas. "Go take it from the stable." Then addressing his chiaous and pointing out the cripple he said, "Give that man fifty strokes of the bastinado on the back."

On returning home the Cadi found Bou Akas waiting for him.

"Are you dissatisfied?" he inquired.

"No, the very reverse," answered the Sheik, "but I wished to see you, to ask by what inspiration you render justice, for I doubt not that your other decision was a correct as the one in my case."

"It is very simple, my lord," said the Judge. "You observed that I kept for one night the woman and the horse. At midnight I had the woman awakened and brought to me, and I said to her, 'Replenish my inkstand.' Then she, like a woman who had performed the same office a hundred times in her life, took my inkglass, washed it, replaced it in the stand, and poured fresh ink into it. I said to myself immediately, 'If you were the wife of the peasant you would not know how to clean an inkstand; therefore you are the taleb's wife.' ''

''Be it so,'' said Bou Akas. ''So much for the woman, but what about my horse?''

''Ah, that is another thing, and until this morning I was puzzled.''

''Then the cripple was not able to recognize the horse?'' suggested Bou Akas.

''Oh, yes, indeed, he recognized it.''

''Well?''

''By conducting each of you in turn to the stable I did not wish to ascertain which one would recognize the horse, but *which one the horse would recognize!* Now, when you approached the horse it neighed; when the cripple approached the horse it kicked. Then I said to myself, 'The horse belongs to him who has the good legs, and not to the cripple.' And I delivered it to you.''

Bou Akas pondered for a moment, and then said, ''The Lord is with you; it is you who should be in my place. I am sure, at least, that you are worthy to be Sheik, but I am not so sure that I am fit to be Cadi.''

92

A COOL SWIM
ON A HOT DAY

Fletcher Flora

SUDDENLY AWAKE, HE opened his eyes in a glare of morning sun. The glare was blinding and painful, and so he closed his eyes again quickly and lay without moving in the soft shadows behind his lids. He could hear a clock ticking in the room. He could hear a cardinal singing in the white light outside. Something seemed to be scratching at his brain. The remembrance of something.

And then he remembered. He remembered the night and the night's shame. The focus of the night was Ellen's face. The sound of the night was Ellen's voice. The face was cold and scornful, remote and strange. The clear and precise articulation of the voice was more appropriate to proud defiance than to a confession. Lying and remembering, fixed in despair, he held to the slender hope that he remembered a dream.

After a few minutes, needing to know, he got up and walked across the room and into a bathroom and through the bathroom into a room beyond. Ellen was lying on her bed in a gold sheath. He had put her there himself, he remembered, after shooting her. Ankles neatly together and one hand folded upon the other below her breasts. The hands covered with a definitive gesture of modesty, as if it were something intimate or obscene, the small hole through which her life had slipped out and away between her fingers. He had removed her shoes.

So it was not a dream. He had killed her indeed in the shameful night, and there on the floor where he had dropped it was the gun he had killed her with. He looked at the gun and back at her. *Oh, golden wanton. Oh, sweet and tender harlot wife*. Having killed her, having laid her out neatly on a quilted satin cover, he had gone to sleep in his clothes in his own room. But this was an oversimplification and therefore a distortion. He had not merely

547

gone to sleep. He had withdrawn, rather, into a deep and comforting darkness in which, if nothing was solved or made better, everything was at least suspended and grew no worse. He had slept soundly.

Now, of course, he was awake and faced with the necessity of doing something, and what he must do was perfectly apparent. The loaded gun was there, and he was there, and he had now, since last night, not only the negative motivation of not wanting particularly to live, but also the positive one of wanting and needing to die. But there was no urgency in it. He felt a kind of indolence in his bones, a remarkable lassitude. Walking over to the gun on the floor, he bent and picked it up and put it in a side pocket of his jacket, in which he had slept. He stood quietly, with an air of abstraction, watching Ellen on the bed. In his heart was a movement of pain which he fancied for a moment that he could hear faintly, like the dry rustle of cicada wings. Turning away, the gun in his pocket, he went out of the room and out of the house and began walking down the street in a tunnel of shade that breached the bright day.

He had no destination. He did not even have a particular purpose in leaving the house, except that he was not quite ready to die and felt compelled to do something, almost anything, until he was. He had a vague notion that he might walk into the country and kill himself there in some quiet spot, or perhaps, after a while, he might return to the house and kill himself in the room with Ellen, so that they might later be found together. This was an enormous problem, where finally to kill himself, and at the moment he felt in no way capable of coping with it. His mind was sluggish, still fixed in the gray despair to which he had wakened, and now, besides, his head was beginning to throb like a giant pulse, measuring the cadence of his heart.

It was a very hot day. A bright, white, hot day. Heat shimmered on the surface of the street in an illusion of water. The sun was approaching the meridian in the luminous sky. The shimmering heat had somehow entered his skull, and all at once he was very faint, hovering precariously on the verge of consciousness while the gaseous world shifted and wavered and threatened to fade away. He had left the tunnel of shade and was now hatless in white light, the sun beating down directly upon his head.

Still walking, he pressed a hand across his eyes, recovering in darkness, and when he removed his hand at last, looking down at his feet, he was filled with wonder to see that his feet were bare. On the tip of the big toe of the left foot was a small plastic bandage, signifying that the toe had been lately stubbed. The bare feet were making their way on a gray dirt road. The

dirt was hot and dry and powdery, rising in little puffs of dust at every step
and forming a kind of thin, gray scum on faded blue denim.

For a second or two he could not for the life of him remember where he
was or where he was going or how he had got there, but then it all came back
clearly—how he had been sitting under the big cottonwood in the side yard
at home, and how he had been thinking how good a swim in the creek would
feel on such a hot day, and how at last he had decided to walk out and have
the swim. So here he was, on the way, and everything was familiar again
after being momentarily strange. He had just crossed Chaffee's pasture to
reach the dirt road where it junctioned with another road at the northeast
corner of Mosher's old dairy, and there ahead was the stand of scrub timber
along the creek in which the swimming hole was.

With an odd feeling of comfort and assurance, he said softly to himself,
"I am Dewey Martin, and I'm going to have a cool swim in the creek on a
hot day."

It appeared to be only a short distance on to the creek, but it was farther
than it looked, nearly half a mile, beyond a cornfield and a pasture that were
part of Dugan's farm. Dewey left the road and crawled between two strands
of a barbed wire fence into the field. He walked around the edge of the field
to the other side, around the standing corn, and stopped there by the fence
and surveyed the pasture to see where Jupiter was. Jupiter was Dugan's
bull, and he was dangerous.

There he was, sure enough, down at one end of the pasture, a safe
distance away, and Dewey slipped through the fence and hurried across
before old Jupiter could make up his mind whether to chase him or not. The
creek was quite near now, no more than twenty yards away, but Dewey sat
down in the shade of a hickory tree to rest before going on. He was
curiously tired and still a little light-headed, and he was slightly disturbed
by being unable to recall anything between the time of leaving home and the
time of suddenly seeing his bare feet on the dusty road by Mosher's dairy.
he had a feeling of having come a long way from a strange place, but this was
surely nothing but a trick of the heat, the bright white light of the summer
sun. After a few minutes he quit thinking about it and went on to the creek
and stripped off naked and dived into the dark green water.

It was wonderfully cool in the water, and he stayed in it for about an hour
without getting out once, but then he got out and lay for quite a long time on
the bank in a patch of sunlight, his bare brown body shining like an acorn.
After that, when his flesh was full of clean white heat, he dived back into
the water, and it was cooler than ever by contrast, the purest and most

sensual pleasure that anyone could hope to have on earth. Altogether, he spent almost all the afternoon by himself at the creek, and he could tell by the position of the sun when he left that it was getting late, and that he would have to hurry on the long walk home.

It was not quite so hot going back. A light breeze came up, which helped, and he made it all the way to town without stopping to rest or feeling light in the head a single time. Cutting across several blocks to the street on which he lived, he started down this street in the direction of home, hearing as he walked the good and comforting sounds of mowers and sprinklers and the first cicadas, and smelling a supper now and then among flowers and cut grass.

Ahead of him, standing beside the walk, was a girl about his own age in a pink dress. It looked like a party dress, with a blue sash at the waist and a bit of lace at the throat. The girl had golden hair woven into two braids, and she was far and away the prettiest girl he had ever seen. As a matter of fact, he had instantly a notion that he had seen her before, although he couldn't remember where or when. This could not be true, however, for if he had seen her, pretty as she was, he would not have forgotten.

As he came abreast of her, she smiled and spoke.

"Hello," she said.

He stopped, watching her, and said hello.

"Do you live in this neighborhood?" she said.

"Down the street a few blocks."

"I live here. In this house. We just moved here yesterday."

"That's nice. I hope you like it."

"I don't know anyone yet. I'm a stranger. I may like it when I get to know someone. Would you come and talk with me sometime?"

"Sure. Maybe tomorrow."

He was painfully conscious of his dusty jeans and bare feet with the plastic bandage, somehow a survivor of swimming and walking, still stuck on the one big toe. He edged away and began to turn, lifting a hand in a brief, shy gesture of good-bye.

"What's your name?" she said.

"Dewey. Dewey Martin. What's yours?"

"My name is Ellen," she said.

The sound of it was like an echo in the fading afternoon as he hurried on his way, but he did not recognize it as a name that he had known in the future.

93

INSIDE OUT

Barry N. Malzberg

I'VE GOT TO start stacking them in the bedroom, now. The corpses, that is.

The living room, alas, is full. It was bound to happen sooner or later. Still, it is a shock to realize that the day of inevitability has come. There is simply no room anymore. Floor to ceiling, ceiling to floor, in four rows the bodies are stacked except for that little space in the corner I have left for my footrest and chair. Even the television set is gone. It was hard to sacrifice that but business is business. I put it at the foot of the bed, dreading the time when I would have to start putting the bodies where I slept. But I must face reality and the living room is finished. *Fini. Kaput* and *terminus.* Cheerlessly I accept my fate. If I am to go on murdering I will have to bring the bodies, as the abbess said to the bishop, into the boudoir. And I am, of course, going to go on murdering.

You betcha.

When I do away with Brown, the superintendent, tonight then, his corpse will go in the far corner, beside the dresser. Virgin territory so to speak . . . not that there is sexual undertone to this matter. None whatsoever. It is what it is. It is not a metaphor. It is not a symbol. It is the pure sad business of murder.

Brown rolls the emptied garbage cans across the lobby, filling my rooms with sounds from hell. He also refuses to clean the steps more than once a week. Time and again, I have asked him to desist from the one and perform the other, but the man is obdurate. He pretends not to learn English. He pretends not to hear and points to his left ear. He indicates other responsibilities. This morning I saw four disgusting orange peels on the third-floor landing, already turned brown. There is no way that a man of my disposition can deal with this anymore, but I am not able to move. For one thing, what would I do with the bodies? It would be *such* a job to transport them all.

Accordingly, Brown or what is left of him will repose in the bedroom tonight. *Au boudoir il couche.*

The murders are imaginary, of course. I am not actually a mass murderer. These are fictive murders, illusory corpses that have slowly filled these quarters since I began my difficult adjustment about a year ago. Abusive peddlers, disgusting street persons, noxious fellow employees in the Division. In my mind I act out intricate murders, in body I pantomime the matter of conveying the corpses, in my heart all of the dead dwell with me, mild and stoic in their condition. It is a fantasy that enables me to go on, just barely, in this disgusting urban existence: if I could not banish those who offend I would be unable to function. It is of course a perilous business, this fantasy, since I might plunge over the fine line someday and *actually* believe I have done away with these people, but it is the only way I can continue in circumstantial balance.

Giving the fantasy credence, however, demands discipline and a lot of so-called scut work. It is with regret that I have yielded all my living room but for chair and footrest, but also out of simple respect for will. If I were not to make reasonable sacrifices in order to propitiate this accord it would be meaningless. One cannot play the violin well (I do not, incidentally) without years of painful work with wrists and fingers, acquiring technique. One cannot be a proper employee of the Division (I am, I am) without careful study of its dismal and destructive procedures. One cannot be an imaginary mass murderer without taking responsibility for imaginary dead.

The derelict who wipes my windshield with a dirty rag at the bridge exit still is there, of course, although I murdered him six months ago. This morning he cursed me when I gave him only fifteen cents through a cautiously opened window. His rag hardly infiltrated my vision, his curses fell upon benign and smiling coutenance. How could I tell him after all, "Sir, you no longer exist. Since I did away with you half a year ago your real activities in the real world have made no impression upon me. Your rag is a blur, your curses song. I drove a sharp knife between your sixth and seventh ribs in this very street before witnesses, threw your body into the trunk, and conveyed it bloodless to my apartment where it now reposes. The essential *you* lies sandwiched in my apartment between the waitress from the Forum Diner who spilled a glass of ice water in my lap and the

medical social workers from the Division who said I had no grasp whatsoever of the nature of schizoid disassociation. You're finished, right?''

No. Wrong. I do not think he would understand. This miserable creature,
along with the waitress, the medical social workers, and so many others,
cannot appreciate the metaphysics of the situation.

I did away with Brown in his apartment two hours ago. ''Mr. Brown,'' I
said when he opened the door, ''I can't take this anymore. You're totally
irresponsbile. It's not only the orange peels, the hide-and-seek when the
toilet will not flush, and the terrible smells of disinfectant when you
occasionally wash the lobby. That would be enough, but it is your insolence
that degrades my spirit. You do not accept the fact that I am a human being
who has a right to simple services. By ignoring my needs, you have denied
my humanity.''

Ah, well. Then I shot him in the left temple with the delicate point
twenty-two I use for such extreme cases. The radio was playing the
Symphony Number One Hundred and One in D Major of Franz Joseph
Haydn loudly as I dragged him out of here, closing the door firmly behind. I
would not have suspected that he had a taste for classical music, but this
does not mitigate the situation. Besides, the second violin parts in the
Haydn symphonies are monstrous, lacking melody or reason. No wonder I
gave up the second violin years ago. Now Brown lies at the foot of my bed.
Intermittently he appears to sigh in the perfectitude of his perfect peace.

The medical social worker commented today during conference upon my ab-
stracted attitude and twice tapped me on the hand to make me attentive. I
know she feels something has reduced my caseworker's efficacy but how
could I possibly explain that the reason my attention lapses is that she was
smothered many weeks ago and has not drawn a breath, even in pantomime, since?

Brown's corpse is curiously odorous. Here is a new phenomenon. I am a
committed housekeeper and cannot abide smells of any kind in my apartment (other than pipe or rosin) and my corpses are aseptic. Brown's,
however, is not. It is increasingly foul. My sleep was disturbed last night.
Heavy sprays of the popular kitchen disinfectant do not work. The apartment was even worse when I came home tonight.

I *knew* it was a mistake starting disposal in the bedroom but what were
my choices? There is simply no room left outside of here and I will not have
corpses in the bathroom. I will absolutely not put them there. There are

limits. I will just have to do the best I can. After a while I'll either get used to this or the smell will dissipate on its own.

I should get rid of Brown's body—the smell is impossible—but I am reluctant to do so. It would set a dangerous precedent, it would break a pattern. If I were to dispose of his body he would not then be symbolically dead and if I did it with him might I not be then tempted to do it with one of the others? Or with succeeding victims? My project would become totally self-defeating and I would have accomplished nothing.

It has of course occurred to me to call the real Brown to help me dispose of the imaginary Brown but I am not going to do that either. It would be a pretty irony but one he would not understand. I will have to do the job myself or hold on.

Anyway, I haven't seen him around in days.

It is all too much. Too much, too much. I could not deal with it anymore and accordingly dragged Brown's body to the landing for pickup tomorrow morning. That should solve the problem, although I am concerned at the rupture of my pattern and also by the curious weight of his body as I lumbered with it, fireman-carry fashion, into the stairwell. He is the most unusually corporeal of all my victims. Even in imaginary death this lover of Haydn seems capable, typically, of making me miserable.

Two policemen at the door demand entrance to my apartment. Behind them I can see a circle of tenants.

There seems to be a problem.

At the first opportunity during this interview I intend to distract the police and kill them, thus putting an end to the harassment, but I have a feeling that won't work.

I should *never* have abandoned the living room as a mausoleum. That was my only mistake. I should have begun disposing of old corpses as they were replaced by the new. It would have been sufficient. It would have been good enough.

But it's too late now, the police say.

I think they're right.

94

WHO?

Michael Collins

MRS. PATRICK CONNORS was a tall woman with soft brown eyes and a thin face battered by thirty years of the wrong men.

"My son Boyd died yesterday, Mr. Fortune," she said in my office. "I want to know who killed him. I have money."

She held her handbag in both hands as if she expected I might grab it. She worked in the ticket booth of an all-night movie on 42nd Street, and a lost dollar bill was a very real tragedy for her. Boyd had been her only child.

"He was a pretty good boy," I said, which was a lie, but she was his mother. "How did it happen?"

"He was a wild boy with bad friends," Mrs. Connor said. "But he was my son, and he was still very young. What happened, I don't know. That's why I'm here."

"I mean, how was he killed?"

"I don't know, but he was. It was murder, Mr. Fortune."

That was when my missing arm began to tingle. It does that when I sense something wrong.

"What do the police say, Mrs. Connors?"

"The medical examiner says that Boyd died of a heart attack. The police won't even investigate. But I know it was murder."

My arm had been right, it usually is. There was a lot wrong. Medical examiners in New York don't make many mistakes, but how do you tell that to a distraught mother?

"Mrs. Connors," I said, "we've got the best medical examiners in the country here. They had to do an autopsy. They didn't guess."

"Boyd was twenty years old, Mr. Fortune. He lifted weights, had never been sick a day in his life. A healthy young boy."

It wasn't going to be easy. "There was a fourteen-year-old girl in San

Francisco who died last year of hardening of the arteries, Mrs. Connors. The autopsy proved it. It happens, I'm sorry.''

"A week ago," Mrs. Connors said, "Boyd enlisted in the air force. He asked to be flight crew. They examined him for two days. He was in perfect shape, they accepted him for flight training. He was to leave in a month.''

Could I tell her that doctors make mistakes? Which doctors? The air force doctors, or the medical examiner's doctors? Could I refuse even to look?

"I'll see what I can find," I said. "But the M.E. and the police know their work, Mrs. Connors.''

"This time, they're wrong," she said, opening her purse.

It took most of the afternoon before I cornered Sergeant Hamm in the precinct squad room. He swore at crazy old ladies, at his work load, and at me, but he took me over to see the M.E. who worked on Boyd Connors.

"Boyd Connors died of a natural heart attack," the M.E. said. "I'm sorry for the mother, but the autopsy proved it.''

"At twenty? Any signs of previous heart attacks? Any congenital weakness, hidden disease?''

"No. There sometimes isn't any, and more people die young of heart attacks than most know. It was his first, and his last, coronary.''

"He passed an air force physical for flight training a week ago," I said.

"A week ago?" The M.E. frowned. "Well, that makes it even more unusual, yes, but unusual or not, he died of a natural coronary attack, period. And in case you're wondering, I've certified more heart attack deaths than most doctors do common colds. All right?''

As we walked to Sergeant Hamm's car outside the East Side Morgue, Hamm said, "If you still have any crazy ideas about it being murder, like the mother says, I'll tell you that Boyd Connors was alone in his own room when he died. No way into that room except through the living room, no fire escape, and only Mrs. Connors herself in the living room. Okay?''

"Yeah," I said. "Swell.''

Hamm said, "Don't take the old woman for too much cash, Danny. Just humor her a little.''

After leaving Hamm, I went to the Connorses' apartment, a fifth-floor walkup. It was cheap and worn, but it was neat—a home. A pot of tea stood on the table as Mrs. Connors let me in. She poured me a cup. There was no one else there, Mr. Patrick Connors having gone to distant parts long ago.

I sat, drank my tea. "Tell me, just what happened?''

"Last night Boyd came home about eight o'clock," the mother said. "He looked angry, went into his room. Perhaps five minutes later I heard him cry out, a choked kind of cry. I heard him fall. I ran in, found him on the floor near his bureau. I called the police."

"He was alone in his room?"

"Yes, but they killed him somehow. His friends!"

"What friends?"

"A street gang—the Night Angels. Thieves and bums!"

"Where did he work, Mrs. Connors?"

He didn't have a job. Just the air force, soon."

"All right." I finished my tea. "Where's his room?"

It was a small room at the rear, with a narrow bed, a closet full of gaudy clothes, a set of barbells, and the usual litter of brushes, cologne, hair tonic, and after-shave on the bureau. There was no outside way into the room, and no way to reach it without passing through the living room; no signs of violence, nothing that looked to me like a possible weapon.

All that my searching and crawling got me was an empty box and wrapping paper from some drugstore, in the wastebasket, and an empty men's cologne bottle under the bureau. That and three matchbooks were under the same bureau, a tube of toothpaste under the bed, and some dirty underwear. Boyd Connors hadn't been neat.

I went back out to Mrs. Connors. "Where had Boyd been last night?" I asked.

"How do I know?" she said bitterly. "With that gang, probably. In some bars. Perhaps with his girlfriend, Anna Kazco. Maybe they had a fight, that's why he was angry."

"When did Boyd decide to join the air force?"

"About two weeks ago. I was surprised."

"All right," I said. "Where does this Anna Kazco live?"

She told me.

I left and went to the address Mrs. Connors had given me. An older woman opened the door. A bleached blonde, she eyed me until I told her what I wanted. Then she looked unhappy, but she let me in.

"I'm Grace Kazco," the blonde said, "Anna's mother. I'm sorry about Boyd Connors. I wanted better than him for my daughter, but I didn't know he was sick. Poor Anna feels terrible about it."

"How do you feel about it?" I asked.

Her eyes flashed at me. "Sorry, like I said, but I'm not at all busted up; Boyd Connors wasn't going to amount to a hill of beans. Now maybe Anne can—"

The girl came from an inner room. "What can Anne do?"

She was small and dark, a delicate girl whose eyes were puffed with crying.

"You can pay attention to Roger, that's what!" the mother snapped. "He'll make something of himself."

"There wasn't anything wrong with Boyd!"

"Except he was all talk and dream and do-nothing. A street-corner big shot! Roger works instead of dreaming."

"Who's this Roger?" I asked.

"Roger Tatum," the mother said. "A solid, hard working boy who likes Anna. He won't run off to any air force."

"After last night," Anna said, "maybe he won't be running here again, either."

"What happened last night?" I queried.

Anna sat down. "Boyd had a date with me, but Roger had dropped around first. He was here when Boyd came. They got mad at each other, Mother told Boyd to leave. She always sides with Roger. I was Boyd's date, Roger had no right to break in, but Mother got me so mad I told them both to get out. I was wrong. It made Boyd angry. Maybe that made the heart attack happen. Maybe I—"

"Stop that!" the mother said. "It wasn't your fault."

Under the bleached hair and the dictatorial manner, she was just a slum mother trying to do the best for her daughter.

"Did they get out when you told them?" I asked.

Anna nodded. "They left together. That was the last time I ever saw poor Boyd."

"What time was that?"

"About seven o'clock, I think."

"Where do I find this Roger Tatum? What does he do for a living?"

"He lives over on Greenwich Avenue, Number 110," Anna told me. "He works for Johnson's Pharmacy on Fifth Avenue. Cleans up, delivers, like that."

"It's only a temporary job," the mother said. "Roger has good offers he's considering."

The name of Johnson's Pharmacy struck a chord in my mind. Where had I heard the name? Or seen it?

Roger Tatum let me into his room. He was a small, thin youth who wore rimless glasses and had nice manners; the kind of boy mothers like—polite, nose to the grindstone. His single room was bare, except for books everywhere.

"I heard about Boyd," Tatum said. "Awful thing."

"You didn't like him too much, though, did you?"

"I had nothing against him. We just liked the same girl."

"Which one of you did Anna like?"

"Ask her," Tatum snapped.

"Not that it matters now, does it?" I said. "Boyd Connors is dead, the mother likes you, an inside track all the way."

"I suppose so," he said, watching me.

"What happened after you left the Kazco apartment with Boyd? You left together? Did you fight, maybe?"

"Nothing happened. We argued some on the sidewalk. He went off, I finished my deliveries. I'm not supposed to stop anywhere when I deliver, and I was late, so I had to hurry. When I finished delivering, I went back to the shop, then I came home. I was here all night after that."

"No fight on the street? Maybe knock Boyd Connors down? He could have been hurt more than you knew."

"Me knock down Boyd? He was twice my size."

"You were here alone the rest of the night?"

"Yes. You think I did somethng to Boyd?"

"I don't know what you did."

I left him standing there in his bare room with his plans for the future. Did he have a motive for murder? Not really; people don't murder over an eighteen-year-old girl that often. Besides, Boyd Connors had died of a heart attack.

I gave out the word in a few proper places that I'd like to talk to the Night Angels—five dollars in it, and no trouble. Maybe I'd reach them, maybe I wouldn't. There was nothing to do that I could think of, so I stopped for a few Irish whiskies, then went home to bed.

About noon the next day, a small, thin, acne-scarred boy with cold eyes and a hungry face came into my office. He wore the leather jacket and shabby jeans uniform, and the hunger in his face was the perpetual hunger of the lost street kid for a lot more than food. He looked seventeen, had the cool manner of twenty-seven with experience. His name was Carlo.

"Five bucks, you offered," Carlo said first.

I gave him five dollars. He didn't sit down.

"Boyd Connors' mother says Boyd was murdered," I said. "What do you say?"

"What's it to you?"

"I'm working for Mrs. Connors. The police say heart attack."

"We heard," Carlo said. He relaxed just a hair. "Boyd was sound as a dollar. It don't figure. Only what angle the fuzz got? We don' make it.''

"Was Boyd with you that night?''

"Early 'n late. He goes to see his girl. They had a battle, Boyd come around the candy store a while.''

"What time?''

"Maybe seven thirty. He don' stay long. Went home.''

"Because he didn't feel good?''

"No. He feel okay,'' Carlo said.

I saw the struggle on his face. His whole life, the experience learned over years when every day taught more than a month taught most kids, had conditioned him never to volunteer an answer without a direct question. But he had something to say, and as hard as he searched his mind for a trap, he couldn't find one. He decided to talk to me.

"Boyd, he had a package,'' Carlo finally said, tore it out of his thin mouth. "He took it on home.''

"Stolen?''

"He said no. He said he found it. He had a big laugh on it. Said he found it on the sidewalk, 'n the guy lost it could rot in trouble.''

That was when I remembered where I had seen the name of Johnson's Pharmacy.

"A package when he came home?'' Mrs. Connors said. "Well, I'm not sure, Mr. Fortune. He could have had.''

I went through the living room into Boyd Connors' bedroom. The wrapping paper was still in the wastebasket. Mrs. Connors was neglecting her housework, with the grief over Boyd. A Johnson's Pharmacy label was on the wrapping paper, and a handwritten address: 3 East 11th Street. The small, empty box told me nothing.

I checked all the cologne, after-shave and hair-tonic bottles—the box was about the size for them. They were all at least half full and old. I thought of the empty bottle under the bed, and got it; a good men's cologne—and empty. It had no top. I searched harder, found the top all the way across the room in a corner, as if it had been thrown. It was a quick-twist top, one sharp turn and it came off. I saw a faint stain on the rug as if something had been spilled, but a cologne is mostly alcohol, dries fast.

I touched the bottle gingerly, studied it. There was something odd about it; not to look at, no, more an impression, the *feel* of it. It felt different, heavier, than the other bottles, and the cap seemed more solid. Only a shade of difference, something I'd never have thought about if I hadn't been looking for answers.

I could even be wrong. When you're ready to find something suspicious, your mind can play tricks, find what it wants to find.

I decided to see Roger Tatum again. He was working over a book, writing notes when I arrived.

"Not working? Fired, maybe?"

"I don't go to work until one P.M.," he said. "Why would I be fired?"

"You lost a package you were supposed to deliver last night, didn't you?"

He stared at me. "Yes, but how did you know? And you think Mr. Johnson would fire me for that? It wasn't worth five dollars; Mr. Johnson didn't even make me pay. Just sent me back this morning with another bottle."

"Bottle of what?"

"Some men's cologne."

"When did you miss the package, notice that it was gone?"

"When I got to the address. It was gone. I guess I just dropped it."

"You dropped it," I said. "Did anything happen between the drugstore and Anna Kazco's place? Did you stop anywhere? Have an accident and drop the packages?"

"No. I went straight to Anna's place. I had all the packages when I left, I counted them."

"So you know you dropped the package after you left Anna Kazco's apartment."

"Yes, I'm sure."

My next stop was the Johnson Pharmacy on Fifth Avenue. Mr. Yvor Johnson was a tall, pale man. He blinked at me from behind his counter.

"The package Roger lost? I don't understand what your interest in it is, Mr. Fortune. A simpe bottle of cologne."

"Who was it going to?"

"Mr. Chalmers Padgett, a regular customer. He always buys his sundries here."

"Who is he? What does he do?"

"Mr. Padgett? Well, I believe he's the president of a large chemical company."

"Who ordered the cologne?"

"Mr. Padgett himself. He called earlier that day."

"Who packed the cologne? Wrapped it?"

"I did myself. Just before Roger took it out," he said slowly.

I showed him the empty bottle and the cap. He took them, looked at them. He looked at me.

"It looks like the bottle. A standard item. We sell hundreds of bottles."

"Is it the same bottle? You're sure? Feel it."

Johnson frowned, studied the bottle and the cap. He bent close over them, hefted the bottle, inspected the cap, hit the bottle lightly on his counter. He looked puzzled.

"That's strange. I'd almost say this bottle is a special glass, very strong. The cap, too. They seem the same; I'd not have noticed if you hadn't insisted, but they do seem stronger."

"After you packed the cologne for Mr. Padgett, how long before Roger Tatum took out his deliveries?"

"Perhaps fifteen minutes."

"Was anyone else in the store?"

"I think there were a few customers."

"Did you and Roger ever leave the packages he was to deliver unwatched?"

"No, they are on the shelf back here until Roger takes them, and—" He stopped, blinked. "Yes, wait. Roger took some trash out in back, and the man asked me if he could look at a vaporizer. I keep the bulky stock, like vaporizers, in the back. I went to get it. I was gone perhaps three minutes."

"The man? What man?"

"A big man, florid-faced. In a gray overcoat and gray hat. He didn't buy the vaporizer, I had to put it back. I was quite annoyed, I recall."

"Roger took the packages out right after that?"

"Yes, he did."

That conversation prompted me to visit Mr. Chalmers Padgett, president of P-S Chemical Corp. Not as large a company as Johnson had thought, and Dun & Bradstreet didn't list exactly what the company produced.

Padgett met me in his rich office down near Wall Street. He was a calm, pale man in a custom-made suit.

"Yes, Mr. Fortune, I ordered my usual cologne from Johnson a few days ago. Why?"

"Could anyone have known you ordered it?"

"I don't know, perhaps. I believe I called from the office here."

"Are you married?"

"I'm a widower. I live alone, if that's what you mean."

"What would you do when you got a bottle of cologne?"

"Do? Well, I'd use it, I suppose. I—" Padgett smiled at me. "That's very odd. I mean, that you would ask that. As a matter of fact I have something of a reflex habit—I smell things. Wines, cheeses, tobacco. I expect I'd have smelled the cologne almost at once. But you couldn't have known that."

"Who could have known it? About that habit?"

"Almost anyone who knows me. It's rather a joke."

"What does your company make, Mr. Padgett?"

His pale face closed up. "I'm sorry, much of our work is secret, for the government."

"Maybe Rauwolfia serpentina? Something like it?"

I had stopped at the library to do research. Chalmers Padgett looked at me with alarm and a lot of suspicion.

I said, "Do you have a heart condition, Mr. Padgett? A serious condition? Could you die of a heart attack—easily?"

He watched me. "Have you been investigating me, Mr. Fortune?"

"In a way," I said. "You *do* have a heart condition?"

"Yes. No danger if I'm careful, calm. but—"

"But if you died of a heart attack, no one would be surprised? No one would question it?"

"There would be no question," Chalmers Padgett said. He studied me. "One of our subsidiaries, very secret, does make some Rauwolfia serpentina, Mr. Fortune. For government use."

"Who would want you dead, Mr. Padgett?"

A half hour later, Mr. Padgett and I stopped for the drugstore owner, Mr. Johnson. Padgett rode in the back seat of the car with Sergeant Hamm and me.

"Rauwolfia serpentina," I said. "Did you ask the M.E.?"

"I asked," Sergeant Hamm said. "Related to common tranquilizers. Developed as a nerve gas for warfare before we supposedly gave up that line of study. Spray it on the skin, breath it, a man's dead in seconds. Depresses the central nervous system, stops the heart cold. Yeah, the M.E. told me about it. Says he never saw a case of its use, but he'd heard of cases. Seems it works almost instantly, and the autopsy will show nothing but a plain heart attack. A spy weapon, government assassins. No cop in New York ever heard of a case. Who can get any of it?"

"P-S Chemical has a subsidiary that makes some; very secret," I said. "Under pressure in a bottle, it spurts in the face of anyone who opens it to sniff. Dead of a heart attack. The bottle drops from the victim's hand, the pressure empties the bottle. No trace—unless you test the bottle very carefully, expertly."

"In my case," Chalmers Padgett said, "who would have tested the bottle? I die of a heart attack, there would be no thought of murder. Expected. I ordered the cologne, the bottle belonged in my apartment. No one would even have noticed the bottle."

We stopped at a Park Avenue apartment house and all went up to the tenth floor. The man who stood up in the elegant, sunken living room when the houseman led us into the apartment was big and florid-faced. Something happened to his arrogant eyes when he saw Chalmers Padgett.

"Yes," Mr. Johnson said, "that's the man who asked me to show him the vaporizer, who was alone in the store with the packages."

Chalmers Padgett said, "For some years we've disagreed on how to run our company. He won't sell his share to me, and he hasn't the cash to buy my share. He lives high. If I died, he would have the company, and a large survivor's insurance. He's the only one who would gain by my death. My partner, Samuel Seaver. He's the one."

I said, "Executive vice-president of P-S Chemical. One of the few people who could get Rouwalfia serpentina."

The big man, Samuel Seaver, seemed to sway where he stood and stared only at Chalmers Padgett. His eyes showed fear, yes, but confusion, too, and incredulity. He had planned a perfect murder. Chalmers Padgett's death would have been undetectable, no question of murder. No one would have noticed Seaver's lethal bottle, it *belonged* in Padgett's room.

However, Roger Tatum had dropped the package, Boyd Connors had taken it home and opened the bottle. Boyd Connors had no heart condition. Boyd Connors' mother did not believe the heart attack. The bottle had *not* belonged in Boyd's room.

Sergeant Hamm began to recite, "Samuel Seaver, you're under arrest for the murder of Boyd Connors. It's my duty to advise you that—"

"Who?" the big man, Samuel Seaver, said unwittingly. "Murder of who?"

95

THE ODOR OF MELTING

Edward D. Hoch

THE THING HE remembered most vividly from the last instant before the plane hit the cresting Atlantic waves was the odor of melting, the pungent wisp of a smell which told him the electric circuits had gone. Then there was no time for anything else—no time to reach the passenger compartment, no time for anything but a clawing endeavor to survive.

He couldn't have lived long in the freezing waters, but it seemed that he bobbed like Ishamel for days, the only survivor of this black disaster, clinging to one of the plane's seats until at last some unseen hands were lifting him. Perhaps he was bound for heaven, or for hell. He no longer cared. He merely slipped into a quiet slumber where the dreams were thick and deep, like the waters of the Atlantic . . .

When he opened his eyes, some time later, a man in white slacks and a white turtleneck sweater was bending over him. He was aware of the man's face, and of the coolness of the sheets against his naked body, and nothing more.

"How do you feel?" the man asked.

"I—I don't know. I expected to be dead. Where am I?"

The man smiled and felt the pilot's forehead. "We saw the crash and pulled you out of the water. You're very lucky. It's an awfully big ocean."

Now he was aware of the gentle swaying of the room, and he knew he was on a boat of some sort. "What ship is this?" he asked.

"The yacht *Indos*." The man smiled at the pilot's blank expression. "Owned by J. P. Galvan. Perhaps you've heard of him."

He tried to connect the name with something in his memory, and then suddenly everything else flooded back. "The President!" he gasped. "The President was on the plane! I must—"

He was struggling to get out of bed, but the man restrained him. "You were the only survivor. There is nothing you can do now."

"How long have I been here?"

"You've been sleeping. It's almost seven hours since we pulled you from the water."

"But . . . my God, I've got to get word to Washington!"

"That's been taken care of. They know you're here."

"But the President! I've got to tell them what happened. I was the pilot—it was my responsibility!"

"Rest for a while. Mr. Galvan will want to speak with you soon." The man turned and went out, perhaps to summon the owner of the yacht.

Alone between the cool white sheets, he ran over the whole thing again in his mind. He'd been the chief pilot of the presidential plane for only six months when the President of the United States decided on a flying trip to France and West Germany. The visit, and the high-level talks that accompanied it, had been most successful. The President and his advisors had been pleased when they finally boarded the plane in Paris for the return flight.

They were more than an hour out to sea when it happened, suddenly and without warning. An autumn storm blowing up from the tropics—perhaps an offshoot of some distant hurricane—had hurled a single lightning bolt at the plane, knocking out the radio and electrical systems. It was a freak accident that shouldn't have happened; but it did.

He remembered then the odor of melting as the plastic insulation began to go, remembered even seeing the yacht, a single speck on the vast expanse of storm-tossed waves. Suddenly the plane would no longer function. It was a dead thing, dead beneath his prodding hands.

He had screamed something at his copilot, frantically pressing every emergency button within reach. They'd got the auxiliary radio transmitter to function for a few seconds, but he'd only managed a brief gasping of words—"Going down, rush help!"—before that too fizzled into a spectrum of sparks.

He remembered the water, and then nothing else until now. "How long was I in there?" he asked the man in slacks when he returned. "It seemed like hours."

"We had you out in about twenty minutes."

"No one else?"

The man shook his head. "No one else." He offered him a cigarette and added, "Mr. Galvan is coming down to talk to you."

"Fine." The cigarette tasted good. "Are you Mr. Galvan's son?"

"Nothing so important. I'm only his secretary. You may call me—" he hesitated, then finished, "Martin."

The cabin door opened and a small, middle-aged man entered. He wore a dark-blue nautical jacket with brass buttons, and a captain's cap that seemed oddly out of place above his thin, pale features. "You would be John Harris, the pilot of the plane," he said without preliminaries. "I am J. P. Galvan."

He partly lifted himself from the bunk to shake the man's hand. Memory stirred again, and this time it was a magazine article he'd read some time back. J. P. Galvan, international banker, a man who gloried in the power to manipulate fortunes in world currency. "Thank you for saving me," he said.

"It was nothing. A stroke of luck on your part, that the plane came down so close to my yacht. But I was sorry for the others. Your President—a fine man."

"Do you have a radio I could listen to? I'd like to know what they're saying."

Galvan nodded and sat down beside the bunk. "All in due course. First, tell me what happened."

The yacht had begun a gentle rocking and Harris was aware for the first time that the engines had been cut. He wondered why. He wondered if they were perhaps preparing to shift him to a larger ship, possibly an American warship that had reached the search area.

"The electrical system failed," he told Galvan, going through the story as he remembered it, reliving once more the unexpected fury of the brief storm. "There was no chance to save the President, or even get off a radio message."

Galvan smiled slightly. "Oh, but you did get off a message, Mr. Harris."

"What?"

"Your new President—who has already been sworn into office—is under the impression that the plane was shot down by the Russians."

"*What!*" He sat up in the bunk again, this time with a sudden cold sweat forming over his body. "How could he think that?"

"They picked up a few garbled words. *Russians* was the only one they understood."

He thought back to that hasty final message. *Rush help* could have sounded like *Russians* in the static of the storm-swept airwaves. "But that's terrible! That could start a war!"

"Exactly," Galvan agreed.

"I've got to use your radio at once! I have to get the truth to Washington!"

But the small man restrained him. "There is plenty of time for that. Your new President took the oath of office almost immediately, even though the search for survivors still continues. I am most anxious to see how he handles the situation."

"How he handles it! We could be at war any minute now, and the President might be powerless to prevent a nuclear holocaust."

Galvan sighed. "Mr. Harris, my business is power. I have made a career out of the skillful manipulation of monkeys. Don't you see? I have in my hands now the greatest single power a man has ever had? I have the power to stop World War III, or to let it proceed."

Harris rolled over on the bunk, sweating freely now. "That's crazy talk! It couldn't have gone that far yet."

"No?" Galvan motioned to his secretary. "Turn on the speaker for the short-wave radio."

The secretary vanished for a moment and then reappeared as a hidden wall speaker suddenly came to life. " . . . no further word. Meanwhile, the great Atlantic search continues. A hundred aircraft and two dozen ships have now converged on the general area in which the President's plane went down. Some bits of wreckage *have* been sighted, but there is no trace of survivors at this hour. Meanwhile, in Washington, both houses of Congress have gone into an extraordinary all-night sessions to hear an urgent address by the new President. It is expected that the President will attempt to calm those who are calling for an immediate declaration of war with Russia. But on the basis of the presidential pilot's last words before the crash, it is becoming obvious that the pressure of an aroused public could plunge the United States and Russia into war within another twenty-four hours. Moscow has denied all knowledge of the missing plane, but it is known that Russian fishing boats were in the vicinity. Now for a direct report from . . ."

"We've got to stop them," Harris interrupted from the bunk. "We've got to—"

Galvan signaled the secretary to turn off the speaker. "You see, Mr. Harris, that is my problem. *Should* I stop them?"

For the first time he felt the fear—not only for the others, but for himself. "What do you mean? I can stop them if you won't. You told them you'd rescued me." Overhead somewhere, one of the search planes dipped low and then climbed again. It was the first one he'd heard. *"You did tell them, didn't you?"*

Galvan blinked and stepped closer to the bunk. "We have told them nothing, Mr. Harris. The crew does not understand English. Only the three of us know you are here. There has been no radio communication with the searchers."

The pilot slumped back on his pillow, knowing now, yet not quite knowing all of it. "What do you plan to do?"

"I have have been in touch with bankers in London, Rome, Rio, and Paris. There is much to be said for letting the war—this long-postponed confrontation—take place at last. Your Presidents have been men of peace, and even the Russians have shown no eagerness for world conflict. An event like this, today, is needed to plunge the world into chaos."

"You want that?"

"I do not know, Mr. Harris. It might be more profitable for me to buy and sell against the market, realizing that I could produce your evidence at the last possible moment—"

"But this *is* the last possible moment," he told Galvan. "Once the first missile is launched, by either side, it will be too late."

There was an insistent buzzing of a signal from somewhere, and the man in slacks went off to answer it, moving smoothly and silently out of view. When he returned, he spoke to Galvan in a language Harris couldn't understand.

The small man grunted and turned back to the bunk. "An American ship has hailed us—a bit sooner than I expected. I must tell them about you now, or not at all."

Looking up at Galvan, Harris already knew the decision. The owner of the yacht could not now allow him to live, to give even a hint to the waiting world of this fantastic conversation. "You're mad," he said, very quietly.

"Do you think those who are calling for war—do you think they are sane?"

"There's no money in it for you if the whole world goes up in smoke."

Galvan blinked and turned away. "Perhaps I am only tired of the indecision of it all."

"Or mad with the power of this moment." He waited no longer, but threw back the sheet and hurled himself across the cabin at the little man. He grabbed him by the neck and was tightening his grip on the wrinkled throat when the secretary drew a pistol and fired a single shot at close range.

Harris stumbled backward, seeing the two of them—the only two in the world who knew—suddenly tall above him, and he felt very tired as his life drained away. Again there came to him the unmistakable odor of melting, and he wondered if perhaps he was back in the dead plane, if all that went between had been but a drowning man's dream . . .

Or was this the way the earth smelled, as it died?

96

SHELL GAME

William Jeffrey

GLOVED HANDS THRUST into the pockets of his heavy tweed overcoat, Steve Blanchard entered the Midwestern National Exchange Bank a few minutes before three P.M. on a snowy Friday in December. A uniformed guard stood near the maintenance doors with a ring of keys in his hand, his eyes cast upward to the clock on a side wall, and Blanchard's steps echoed hollowly as he crossed the nearly-deserted lobby to the teller at window 4, the only one open at this late hour. He waited until a stout, gray-haired man had finished his transaction, and then moved up to the window.

A small bronze plaque positioned to the right indicated that the teller's name was James Cox. He was a thin, relaxed young man with dark eyes and sand-colored hair. He smiled at Blanchard, said, "Yes, sir, may I help you?"

Blanchard took the folded piece of paper from his coat pocket and slid it across the marble counter. The second hand on the wall clock made two full sweeps, half of a third, and then Blanchard turned and strode quickly away without looking back.

He had just passed through the entrance doors, was letting them swing closed behind him, when Cox shouted, "Stop that man! He just robbed me, Sam. Stop him!"

Blanchard halted on the snow-covered sidewalk outside and turned, his angular face a mask of surprise. The guard, a fat, florid man with mild blue eyes, remained motionless for a moment; then, like an activated robot, he pulled the doors open, stepped out, and grasped Blanchard by the coat with his left hand, his right fumbling the service revolver off his hip.

"What the hell's going on?" Blanchard asked.

The guard drew him roughly inside the bank, holding the revolver pressed tightly against Blanchard's ribs. The near funereal silence of three o'clock closing had dissolved now into excited murmurings, the scrape of chairs, and the slap of shoes on the marble flooring as the bank's employees surged away from their desks. Cox ran out from behind his teller's window, and the president of the Midwestern National Exchange Bank, Allard Hoffman, was at his heels. The teller held a piece of paper clenched in the fingers of his right hand, and his eyes were wide and excited; Hoffman looked angrily officious.

"He held me up," Cox said breathlessly as they reached Blanchard and the guard. "Every bill I had over a five."

Blanchard gave his head a small, numb shake. "I don't believe this," he said. He stared at Cox. "What's the matter with you? You know I didn't try to hold you up."

"Look in his overcoat pockets, Sam," Cox said. "That's where he put the money."

"You're crazy," Blanchard said incredulously.

"Go ahead, Sam, look in his pockets," Hoffman said.

The guard instructed Blanchard to turn around, and to keep his hands upraised. His eyes still wide with amazement, Blanchard obeyed. The guard patted his pockets, frowned, and then made a thorough, one-handed search. A moment later he stepped back, his forehead corrugated with bewilderment akin to that of Blanchard's; in his hand he held a thin pigskin wallet and seven rolls of pennies, nickels and dimes.

"This is all he's got on him" he said.

"What?" Cox exploded. "Listen, Sam, I *saw* him put that money into his overcoat pockets."

"Well, it's not there now."

"Of course it's not there," Blanchard said. He turned slightly, keeping his hands up, but his face was flushed with anger. "I told you I didn't commit any robbery."

Cox opened the folded piece of paper he held. "This is the note he gave me, Mr. Hoffman. Read it for yourself."

Hoffman took the note. It had been fashioned of letters cut from a newspaper and glued to a sheet of plain white paper, and it said: *Give me all your big bills, I have a gun. If you try any heroics, I'll kill you. I'm not kidding*. The bank president put voice to the message as he read it.

"He's not carrying any weapon, either," Sam said positively.

"I believed the note about that," Cox said, "but I made up my mind to shout nonetheless. I just couldn't stand by and watch him get away with the bank's money."

"I don't know where you got that note," Blanchard said to Cox, "but I didn't give it to you. I handed you a slip of paper, that's true enough, but it was just a list of those rolls of coins and you know it."

"You claim Cox gave them to you?" Hoffman asked him.

"Certainly he did. In exchange for twenty-eight dollars, mostly in singles."

"I didn't give him any coin rolls," Cox said with mounting exasperation. "I did exactly what it says in that note. I gave him every large bill I had in the cash drawer. The vault cart happened to be behind me too, since my cage was the only one open, and he told me to give him what was on that as well. He must have gotten twenty-five or thirty thousand altogether."

"You're a liar," Blanchard snapped.

"*You're* the only one who's lying!"

"I don't have your damned money. You've searched me and I don't have it. All I've got is about twenty-four dollars in my wallet."

"Well," Hoffman said darkly, "*somebody* has it."

At that moment two plainclothes detectives entered the bank, summoned by a hurried telephone call from one of the other Midwestern officials. They introduced themselves without preamble; one was named Salzberg, a lumbering and disheveled man with small, bright eyes; the other, named Flynn, was gray-mustached, the owner of a prominent veined nose.

Salzberg appeared to be the one in charge. He instructed the guard to lock the bank doors, and in a dog-eared notebook wrote Hoffman's and Cox's names, and Blanchard's, taken from the driver's license in the pigskin wallet. He took the holdup note from Cox, balancing it gingerly on the palm of his hand, then put it into an envelope which appeared from, and disappeared again into, an inside pocket of his rumpled suit.

He looked very surprised when Hoffman told him that Blanchard had been searched, and that the money had not been found on him. He said, "All right, let's hear what happened."

Cox related his version of the affair. Salzberg, writing laboriously in his notebook, didn't interrupt. When the teller had finished, Salzberg turned to Blanchard. "Now, what's your story?"

Blanchard told him about the rolls of coins. "I wanted them for a poker game some friends of mine and I set up for tonight." He made a wry mouth. "I'm supposed to be the banker."

"He also claims to have given Mr. Cox a list of what he wanted in the way of coins," Hoffman said.

"The only note he gave me was that holdup note," Cox said with thinly controlled anger. "He must have gotten those coins elsewhere, had them in his pocket when he came in here."

Blanchard's anger was just as thinly contained. He said to Salzberg, "Listen, why don't you check his cage? That list of mine has got to be around here somewhere." He glared at Cox. "Maybe you'll even find your damned missing money. I've heard stories of embezzling tellers trying to frame an innocent—"

"Are you suggesting that *I* stole the bank's money?" Cox shouted.

Hoffman looked astonished. "Mr. Cox has been a trusted, valued employee of Midwestern National for almost four years."

"Well, I've been a trusted, valued employee of Curtis Tool and Die for a hell of a lot longer," Blanchard snapped. "What does any of that prove?"

"All right, all right." Salzberg tapped his teeth with his pen, speculatively. After a moment he said, "Flynn, question the other employees; maybe one of them saw or heard something. Mr. Hoffman, I'd appreciate it if you'd detail someone to find out exactly how much money is missing, and whether or not this list Blanchard claims to have given can be found. You might as well have Mr. Cox's cage and possessions gone through too,"

Cox was disbelieving. "You mean you're taking this thief's word over mine?"

"I'm not taking anybody's word, Mr. Cox," Salzberg said calmly. "I'm just trying to find out what happened here today." He paused. "Would you mind emptying all your pockets for me?"

Purplish splotches appeared on Cox's cheeks, but his voice was icily controlled when he said, "No, I do not mind. I have nothing to hide."

It appeared that he hadn't, as far as his person went. He did not have either the list of coins of an appreciable amount of money.

Salzberg sighed. "Okay," he said, "let's go over it again . . . "

Some time later, Hoffman and Flynn rejoined the group. A check of receipts and records had revealed that a total of $35,100 was missing. No list of coins had been found in or about Cox's cage, and a careful audit of the rest of the bank's funds had failed to show an unexplained overage in another teller's cash supply. None of the employees Flynn had questioned had been able to shed any light on the matter; no one had been near Cox's cage at the time Blanchard had been there, and no one had had any idea that things were amiss until Cox shouted to the guard to stop Blanchard.

Salzberg looked pointedly at Blanchard. "Well, Mr. Cox doesn't seem to have the money, and it doesn't seem to be here in the bank. This alleged note of yours isn't here, either. How can you explain that?"

"I can't," Blanchard said. "I can only tell you what happened. I didn't steal that money!"

"Salzberg turned to the guard, Sam. "How far outside did he get before you collared him?"

"No more than a couple of steps."

"Did he have time to pass the money to an accomplice?"

"I doubt it. But I wasn't paying any attention to him until Mr. Cox yelled."

"I don't know much about big money," Blanchard said coldly, "but thirty-five thousand must be a lot of bills. I couldn't have passed that much to somebody in the couple of seconds I was outside the bank."

"He's got a point," Sam admitted.

"Why don't you search the guard?" Blanchard asked in a voice heavy with vitriol. "Maybe I passed the money to him."

"I was expecting this," Sam said. He stepped over to Flynn, raising his arms. "Shake me down and we'll get the idea I had anything to do with this out of everybody's mind."

Flynn searched him expertly and, not surprisingly, the guard was clean.

"What are we going to do?" Hoffman asked. "That money has to be somewhere, and this man Blanchard obviously knows where."

"Maybe," Salzberg said carefully. "Anyway, it looks like we'll have to take him downtown and see what we can do there about shaking his story."

"Go ahead, then," Blanchard snapped, "but I want a lawyer present while I'm questioned. And if charges are pressed against me, I'll sue you and the bank for false arrest."

They took him down to police headquarters and placed him in a small room, leaving him alone until a public defender could be summoned. Then he was subjected to an unending stream of questions, and through long hours he told the exact same story he had in the bank, vehemently proclaiming his innocence.

Shortly after eleven he was taken to Salzberg's office. The detective looked tired and grim as he explained that the three men with whom Blanchard was to have played poker that night had confirmed the game and the fact that he was to have been banker; that an investigation had borne out that Blanchard did not have a criminal record, had in fact never been arrested; that he was well-liked and respected by his neighbors and his co-workers at Curtis Tool and Die; that the holdup note had had only Cox's and Hoffman's fingerprints on it; that a search of Blanchard's apartment had revealed no evidence that he had manufactured the note; and, finally that another search of the bank had been undertaken—Cox and the guard and the other employees again questioned extensively—without anything new having been learned or the whereabouts of the missing money discovered.

Salzberg rotated his pen between his fingers, leaning back in his chair. He watched Blanchard for a moment, and then he said, "All right, you're free to go."

"You mean you finally believe I'm telling the truth?"

"No," Salzberg said, "I don't. I'm inclined to believe Cox, if you want the truth. We checked him out, too, as a matter of routine, and his background is even more spotless than yours. But it's his word against yours—two respectable citizens—and without the money we've simply got nothing to hold you on." He swung his body forward suddenly, his eyes cold and brightly hard. "But I'll tell you one thing, Blanchard: we'll be watching you—watching you very carefully."

"Watch all you like," Blanchard said exhaustedly. "I'm innocent."

On a night three weeks later, Blanchard knocked on the door of unit 9, the Beaverwood Motel, in a city sixteen miles distant. As soon as he had identified himself, the door opened and he was admitted. He took off his coat and grinned at the sandy-haired man who had let him in. "Hello, Cox," he said.

"Blanchard," the bankteller acknowledged. He moistened his lips. "You made sure you weren't followed here, didn't you?"

"Of course."

"But the police *are* still watching you?"

"Yes, but not nearly as closely as they were in the beginning." Blanchard cuffed him lightly on the shoulder. "Stop worrying, will you? The whole thing worked beautifully."

"Yes, it did, didn't it?

"Sure," Blanchard said. "Salzberg still thinks I passed the money to an accomplice somehow, but he can't prove it. Like he told me, it's your word against mine—and they're taking yours, just as we expected. They don't have an idea that it was actually *you* who passed the money, much less how it was done."

The room's third occupant—the stout, gray-haired man who had been at Cox's window when Blanchard entered the bank that evening—looked up from where he was pouring drinks at a sideboard. "Or that the money was already out of the bank, safely tucked into the inside pockets of my coat, when the two of you went into your little act."

Blanchard took one of the drinks from the gray-haired man and raised the glass high. "Well, here's to crime," he said. *"Perfect* crime, that is."

They laughed and drank, and then they sat down to split the $35,100 into three equal shares . . .

97

QUEASY DOES IT NOT

Jack Ritchie

I HAD BEEN just about to leave when my buzzer sounded.

She was about five feet six, had raven black hair, and I had never seen her before.

Her eyes seemed to calculate my apartment. "For two hundred twenty-five dollars, you are not lost. You have come to absolutely the right place."

"If your name is James Brannon, I have."

I took her wrap. "I'm sorry, but the apartment isn't for rent. If that's why you came up?"

"No. I'm here because the boy scouts find the darndest things." She took a seat on a divan. "You may call me Madelaine."

"Madelaine," I said, "it is the last thought in my mind to insult you, but nevertheless, in all fairness, I think I ought to mention that there are some things I do not play for. It is a principle of mine."

She smiled. "I don't go around knocking on strange doors for my living, James, if that's what you're thinking. As a matter of fact, I'm a school-teacher. Mathematics."

"Really," I said. "I'm rather good with figures myself."

"So the superintendent told me. We accidentally got around to discussing that while I pretended to be pricing apartments."

"Madelaine," I said, "all this must have a beginning. Could you start there?"

She nodded. "That would be in April on an old back road. It is a shortcut and I use it whenever I feel that I might be late for school. You see, I live with my parents in the country and I commute to the high school in Jefferson every day, which takes some planning."

I went about fixing two drinks.

"It is a one-lane road, hardly ever used, and you can imagine how

579

irritated I was to find another car blocking the way." She looked at me and smiled again. "I don't remember what model it was, but the car was large and expensive and empty. I blew my horn for perhaps ten minutes, but no one appeared. Finally I decided to take a chance and just managed to inch my car around it. I almost went into the ditch and it was the only time that semester I was late for school."

"Is Scotch all right?"

She nodded. "And now we come to this month of October and the boy scouts. It seems that Troop 181, Jefferson, was rooting about in the woods beside that particular road looking for arrowheads or mushrooms or whatever boys look for, when two of them noticed a depression in the ground. Their active imaginations told them it might be an Indian grave. And so the little ones dug, and what do you think they found?"

I gave her a glass. "A body, I'll bet."

"Exactly. Not Indian, of course. And through various gruesome means, the police identified it as that of Mrs. Irene Linton. She was last seen leaving her apartment in this city on April fourteenth. The police gave her husband a rather rough time, but eventually they decided he was innocent of her death. It does seem, though, that they suspect she was having an affair. However, she kept it so secret that they have been unable to find out who the man was."

Madelaine sipped her drink. "I took the trouble to check back in my school records, and I discovered that I'd been late on April fifteenth, the day after Mrs. Linton was last seen. Having established that, I drove to the license bureau, fluttered my eyes at a tall male clerk, and got the confidential information that license number P31416 belongs to one James Brannon."

I walked over to the fireplace. "And now you're going to tell me that the very big and very expensive car blocking the road on the morning of April fifteenth was mine? You have a remarkable memory, Madelane. You see a license number in Apirl and it remains with you until October? Or did you write it down for some reason at the time?"

"No. But as I said, I happen to be a mathematics teacher and the license number struck a note and remained in my memory. If you will recall your elementary arithmetic, you must remember that pi equals 3.1416," she said smugly.

"Madelaine," I said, "I have the strange feeling that you don't intend to go to the police with your information."

"Not unless I have to. I suppose you're bright enough to figure out what I mean by that?"

I took a poker out of the stand. "I've never been blackmailed before. But then I suppose there's a first time for everything."

Her eyes became wary. "This is apparently the ideal moment to remind you that I've taken the usual precautions. I've put all this into a letter, and if I should happen to depart this earth violently, or just disappear, it will naturally be forwarded to the police."

I examined the poker critically. "Washed this thoroughly after I whacked Mrs. Linton. Had to get a new rug, too."

She was curious. "Why did you kill her?"

"Just one of those things. Could happen to anybody. Women have a tendency to magnify what men would regard as basically casual." I sighed. "I don't often lose my temper to that extent, but I did have a headache and a screeching woman on my hands did not help to improve the situation."

I studied Madelaine. "You are a naughty blackmailer and I ought to call the police. But I will resist that temptation because I am magnanimous, generous and forgiving to a fault. I don't want to see you go to prison."

"How charming. But somehow I doubt your motive."

"Madelaine," I said, "you quite properly remembered the numerals on the license plate, but you should have paid a little more attention to the prefix P."

"Really? Why?"

"In this state," I said, "the prefix letters A and B are reserved for the month of January. They indicate that the license was issued in that month and expires in the same month the next year. C and D are reserved for February. E and F for March. And so on until we come to the letter P, which is reserved for August."

She didn't understand what I was driving at.

"Let me put it this way," I said. "In April you saw an automobile with the license number P31416. In other words, your murderer's license plates were due to expire in August of this year. They did. And he got another set of plates and another number. And since mine expire in August too, I happened to be in line when the bureau issued P31416."

I finished my drink. "When you fluttered your eyes at that tall clerk, Madelaine, you should have asked who had license number P31416 in *April*, not who happens to have it *now*."

It took her a few moments to accept that. "It wasn't your car? You didn't murder Mrs. Linton?"

"Of course not."

Her eyes became thoughtful.

"Madelaine," I said, "I suppose now you're going back to the license bureau and make you questions more specific? But perhaps your murderer is really a poor man. What profit is there in that?''

''You forget the very big and very expensive car.''

''You have a definite point to keep you interested, Madelaine. However, the license bureau is undoubtedly closed for the night and it's probably raining outside or something. There's no need to run away.''

I made two more drinks and brought her a glass.

She regarded me. ''It's a pity. I expected a rather profitable evening. You are the Brannon of Brannon Bakeries, aren't you?''

''The very same.'' I sat down beside her. ''Before you approach your murderer, Madelaine, would you do me one slight favor? Would you alter your letter to include his name instead of mine?''

''Oh, that,'' she said. ''There's no letter. I'm practical enough to know I can't enjoy revenge from the grave.''

I raised my glass in a silent toast to P31416.

It was a small conceit begun by my father and the license bureau has been cooperative. We have had the same number reserved for our family for fifteen years. The Brannon Bakeries were founded on the production of pie.

My eyes went to the poker.

No, *not now,* I thought. *Later.*

I moved closer to Madelaine and smiled.

98

THE EXPLOSIVES EXPERT

John Lutz

BILLY EDGEMORE, THE afternoon bartender, stood behind the long bar of the Last Stop Lounge and squinted through the dimness at the sunlight beyond the front window. He was a wiry man, taller than he appeared at first, and he looked like he should be a bartender, with his bald head, cheerfully seamed face and his brilliant red vest that was the bartender's uniform at the Last Stop. Behind him long rows of glistening bottles picked up the light on the mirrored backbar, the glinting clear gins and vodkas, the beautiful amber bourbons and lighter Scotches, the various hues of the assorted wines, brandies and liqueurs. The Last Stop's bar was well stocked.

Beyond the ferns that blocked the view out (and in) the front window, Billy saw a figure cross the small patch of light and turn to enter the stained-glass front door, the first customer he was to serve that day.

It was Sam Daniels. Sam was an employee of the Hulton Plant up the street, as were most of the customers of the Last Stop.

"Afternoon, Sam," Billy said, turning on his professional smile. "Kind of early today, aren't you?"

"Off work," Sam said, mounting a bar stool as if it were a horse. "Beer."

Billy drew a beer and set the wet schooner in front of Sam on the mahogany bar. "Didn't expect a customer for another two hours, when the plant lets out," Billy said.

"Guess not," Sam said, sipping his beer. He was a short man with a swarthy face, a head of curly hair, and a stomach paunch too big for a man in his early thirties—a man who liked his drinking.

"Figured you didn't go to work when I saw you weren't wearing your badge," Billy said. The Hulton Plant manufactured some secret government thing, a component for the hydrogen bomb, and each employee had to wear his small plastic badge with his name, number and photograph on it in order to enter or leave the plant.

"Regular Sherlock," Sam said, and jiggled the beer in his glass.

"You notice lots of things when you're a bartender," Billy said, wiping down the bar with a clean white towel. You notice things, Billy said to himself, and you get to know people, and when you get to know them, really get to know them, you've got to dislike them. "I guess I tended bar in the wrong places."

"What's that?" Sam Daniels asked.

"Just thinking out loud," Billy said, and hung the towel on its chrome rack. When Billy looked at his past he seemed to be peering down a long tunnel of empty bottles, drunks and hollow laughter; of curt orders, see-through stares and dreary conversations. He'd never liked his job, but it was all he'd known for the past thirty years.

"Wife's supposed to meet me here pretty soon," Sam said. "She's getting off work early." He winked at Billy. "Toothache."

Billy smiled his automatic smile and nodded. He never had liked Sam, who had a tendency to get loud and violent when he got drunk.

Within a few minutes Rita Daniels entered. She was a tall, pretty woman, somewhat younger than her husband. She had a good figure, dark eyes, and expensively bleached blonde hair that looked a bit stringy now from the heat outside.

"Coke and bourbon," she ordered, without looking at Billy. He served her the highball where she sat next to her husband at the bar.

No one spoke for a while as Rita sipped her drink. The faint sound of traffic, muffled through the thick door of the Last Stop, filled the silence. When a muted horn sounded, Rita said, "It's dead in here. Put a quarter in the jukebox."

Sam did as his wife said, and soft jazz immediately displaced the traffic sounds.

"You know I don't like jazz, Sam." Rita downed her drink quicker than she should have, then got down off the stool to go to the powder room.

"Saw Doug Baker last night," Billy said, picking up the empty glass. Doug Baker was a restaurant owner who lived on the other side of town, and it was no secret that he came to the Last Stop only to see Rita Daniels, though Rita was almost always with her husband.

"How 'bout that," Sam said. "Two more of the same."

Rita returned to her stool, and Billy put two highballs before her and her husband.

"I was drinking beer," Sam said in a loud voice.

"So you were," Billy answered, smiling his My Mistake smile. He shrugged and motioned toward the highballs. "On the house. Unless you'd rather have beer."

"No," Sam said, "think nothing of it."

That was how Billy thought Sam would answer. His cheapness was one of the things Billy disliked most about the man. It was one of the things he knew Rita disliked most in Sam Daniels too.

"How'd it go with the hydrogen bombs today?" Rita asked her husband. "Didn't go in at all, huh?"

Billy could see she was aggravated and was trying to nag him.

"No," Sam said, "and I don't make hydrogen bombs."

"Ha!" Rita laughed. "You oughta think about it. That's about all you can make." She turned away before Sam could answer. "Hey, Billy, you know anything about hydrogen bombs?"

"Naw," Billy said. "Your husband knows more about that than me."

"Yeah," Rita said, "the union rates him an expert. Some expert! Splices a few wires together."

"Five dollars an hour," Sam said, "and double time for overtime."

Rita whirled a braceleted arm above her head. "Wheee . . . "

Like many married couples, Sam and Rita never failed to bicker when they came into the Last Stop. Billy laughed. "The Friendly Daniels." Sam didn't laugh.

"Don't bug me today," Sam said to Rita. "I'm in a bad mood."

"Cheer up, Sam," Billy said. "It's a sign she loves you, or loves somebody, anyway."

Sam ignored Billy and finished his drink. "Where'd you go last night?" he asked his wife.

"You know I was at my sister's. I even stopped in here for about a half hour on the way. Billy can verify it."

"Right." Billy said.

"I thought you said Doug Baker was in here last night," Sam said to him, his eyes narrow.

"He was," Billy said. "He, uh, came in late." He turned to make more drinks, placing the glasses lip to lip and pouring bourbon into each in one deft stream without spilling a drop. He made them a little stronger this time, shooting in the soda expertly, jabbing swizzle sticks between the ice cubes and placing the glasses on the bar.

"You wouldn't be covering up or anything, would you, Billy?" Sam's voice had acquired a mean edge.

"Now *wait a minute!*" Rita said. "If you think I came in here last night to see Doug Baker, you're crazy!"

"Well," Sam stirred his drink viciously and took a sip, "Billy mentioned Baker was in here . . . "

"I said he came in late," Billy quickly.

"And he acted like he was covering up or something," Sam said, looking accusingly at Billy.

"*Covering up?*" Rita turned to Billy, her penciled eyebrows knitted in a frown. "Have you ever seen me with another man?"

"Naw," Billy said blandly, "of course not. You folks shouldn't fight."

Still indignant, Rita swiveled on her stool to face her husband. "Have I ever been unfaithful?"

"How the hell should I know?"

"Good point," Billy said with a forced laugh.

"It's not funny!" Rita snapped.

"Keep it light, folks," Billy said seriously. "You know we don't like trouble in here."

"Sorry, Rita said, but her voice was hurt. She swiveled back to face the bar and gulped angrily on her drink. Billy could see that the liquor was getting to her, was getting to them both.

There was silence for a while, then Rita said morosely "I *oughta* go out on you, Mr. Five-dollar-hydrogen-bomb-expert! You think I do anyway, and at least Doug Baker's got money."

Sam grabbed her wrist, making the bracelets jingle. She tried to jerk away but he held her arm so tightly that his knuckles were white. "You ever see Baker behind my back and I'll kill you both!" He almost spit the words out.

"Hey, now," Billy said gently, "don't talk like that, folks!" He placed his hand on Sam Daniels' arm and felt the muscles relax as Sam released his wife. She bent over silently on her stool and held the wrist as if it were broken. "Have one on the house," Billy said, taking up their almost empty glasses. "One to make up by."

"Make mine straight," Sam said. He was breathing hard and his face was red.

"*Damn you!*" Rita moaned. She half fell off the stool and walked quickly but staggeringly to the powder room again.

Billy began to mix the drinks deftly, speedily, as if there were a dozen people at the bar and they all demanded service. In the faint red glow from the beer-ad electric clock, he looked like an ancient alchemist before his rows of multicolored bottles. "You shouldn't be so hard on her," he said absently as he mixed. "Can't believe all the rumors you hear about a woman as pretty as Rita, and a harmless kiss in fun never hurt nobody."

"Rumors?" Sam leaned over the bar. "Kiss? What kiss? Did she kiss Baker last night?"

"Take it easy," Billy said. "I told you Baker came in late." The phone rang, as it always did during the fifteen minutes before the Hulton Plant let out, with wives leaving messages and asking for errant husbands. When Billy returned, Rita was back at the bar.

"Let's get out of here," she said. There were tear streaks in her makeup.

"Finish your drinks and go home happy, folks." Billy shot a glance at the door and set the glasses on the bar.

Rita drank hers slowly, but Sam tossed his drink down and stared straight ahead. Quietly, Billy put another full glass in front of him.

"I hear you *were* in here with Baker last night," Sam said in a low voice: "Somebody even saw you kissing him."

"You're *crazy!*" Rita's thickened voice was outraged.

Billy moved quickly toward them. "I didn't say that."

"I knew you were covering up!" Sam glared pure hate at him. "We'll see what Baker says, because I'm going to drive over to his place right now and bash his brains out!"

"*But I didn't even see Baker last night!*" Rita took a pull on her drink, trying to calm herself. Sam swung sharply around with his forearm, hitting Rita's chin and the highball glass at the same time. There was a clink as the glass hit her teeth and she fell backward off the stool.

Billy reached under the bar and his hand came up with a glinting chrome automatic that seemed to catch every ray of light in the place. It was a gentleman's gun, and standing there in his white shirt and red vest Billy looked like a gentleman holding it.

"Now, don't move folks." He aimed the gun directly at Sam's stomach. "You know we don't go for that kind of trouble in here." He looked down and saw blood seeping between Rita's fingers as she held her hand over her mouth. Billy wet a clean towel and tossed it to her, and she held it to her face and scooted backward to sit sobbing in the farthest booth.

Billy leaned close to Sam. "Listen," he said, his voice a sincere whisper, "I don't want to bring trouble on Baker, or on you for that matter, so I can't stand by and let you go over there and kill him and throw your own life away. It wasn't him she was in here with. He came in later."

"Wasn't him?" Sam asked in bewildered fury. "Who was it then?"

"I don't know," Billy said, still in a whisper so Rita couldn't hear. "He had a badge on, so he worked at the plant, but I don't know who he is and that's the truth."

"*Oh, no!*"

"Take it easy, Sam. She only kissed him in that booth there. And I'm not even sure I saw that. The booth was dark."

Sam tossed down the drink that was on the bar and moaned. He was staring at the automatic and Billy could see he wanted desperately to move.

A warm silence filled the bar, and then the phone rang shrilly, turning the silence to icicles.

"Now take it easy," Billy said, backing slowly down the bar toward the phone hung on the wall. "A kiss isn't anything." As the phone rang again he could almost see the shrill sound grate through Sam's tense body. Billy placed the automatic on the bar and took the last five steps to the phone. He let it ring once more before answering it.

"Naw," Billy said into the receiver, standing with his back to Sam and Rita, "he's not here." He stood for a long moment instead of hanging up, as if someone were still on the other end of the line.

The shot was a sudden angry bark.

Billy put the receiver on the hook and turned. Sam was standing slumped with a supporting hand on a bar stool. Rita was crumpled on the floor beneath the table of the booth she'd been sitting in, her eyes open, her blonde hair bright with blood.

His head still bowed, Sam began to shake.

Within minutes the police were there, led by a young plainclothes detective named Parks.

"You say they were arguing and he just up and shot her?" Parks was asking as his men led Sam outside.

"He accused her of running around," Billy said. "They were arguing, he hit her, and I was going to throw them out when the phone rang. I set the gun down for a moment when I went to answer the phone, and he grabbed it and shot."

"Uh-hm," Parks said efficiently, flashing a look toward where Rita's body had lain before they'd photographed it and taken it away. "Pretty simple, I guess. Daniels confessed as soon as we got here. In fact, we couldn't shut him up. Pretty broken."

"Who wouldn't be?" Billy said.

"Save some sympathy for the girl." Parks looked around. "Seems like a nice place. I don't know why there's so much trouble in here."

Billy shrugged. "In a dive, a class joint or a place like this, people are mostly the same."

Parks grinned. "You're probably right," he said, and started toward the door. Before pushing it open, he paused and turned. "If you see anything like this developing again, give us a call, huh?"

"Sure," Billy said, polishing a glass and holding it up to the fading afternoon light. "You know we don't like trouble in here."

99

NOT THE RUNNING TYPE

Henry Slesar

"HOW DUMB CAN you get!" Captain Ernest Fisher said, and slapped the desk blotter so hard that the calendar pad danced. Hogan, the bright-faced lieutenant of police, looked up from the standing files and asked a question with his eyebrows.

Fisher rattled the sheet in his hand. "I just got a look at this memo that came in last week—the one giving the names of parolees in the vicinity. It's got Milt Potter listed."

"Who's Milt Potter?"

"You mean I never told you about him?"

"No, sir."

"Take a look at the '46 file while you're there—under embezzlement. That's Milton Potter, spelled the way it sounds. Bring it over and I'll tell you the story."

Hogan slid shut the drawer he was investigating and obeyed the order. He brought the manila folder to the Captain's desk and flipped the cover to the first entry.

"Milton Potter," he read. "Age thirty-four; single; employment, Metro Investment Services, Inc. . . ."

"That's the man," Fisher nodded. He leaned back in the swivel chair and put his feet on the desk. "Tamest criminal you ever met in your life, or maybe the coolest. Walked off with two hundred thousand dollars of investors' money, easy as stealing fruit from a pushcart. But now he's a free man."

"Paroled?"

"Two days ago," Fisher scowled. "I had his release date on my calendar for twelve years—and then I don't watch the memos! But it won't make any difference. Two days, two weeks—I got Milt Potter's number."

591

The Captain lit a cigarette, then put the pack in front of him, readying himself for a siege of story-telling.

"It happened back in March of 1946. I was a looie like you then, and maybe even more of an eager beaver than you are now. I got called in when the Metro Investment discovered the shortage, but I didn't have any work to do. Milt Potter did it for me.

"Potter was a funny guy. He was short and kind of owlish-looking, with sad brown eyes like a cocker spaniel. He had worked for Metro Services since he got out of college, a total of thirteen years, and he was still making only sixty bucks a week. He had no family, and few friends. He was quiet, courteous, commonplace, and careful. Nobody could tell you anecdotes about him, or even describe him very well—we found that out when he showed up missing. He went about his duties without ever complaining or revealing the secret intention that must have burned inside his guts for years.

"Then it happened. One day Potter didn't report for work and nobody even cared very much. But when he didn't show up the next day, somebody thought it might be a good idea to call his home and see if he had broken a leg or something. There wasn't any answer. They didn't get *really* disturbed about it until three days after that, when Potter was still unreported. It took all that time to get suspicious—that's the kind of cookie Milt Potter was.

"Anyway, they finally came to their senses and made a quick check of Potter's books. They didn't even have to call in the auditors to determine that something wasn't on the up and up. There were great big obvious holes in Potter's accounting, and great big chunks of money missing, amounting to two hundred grand. Sure, Potter was the last guy in the world they would expect it from, but isn't it always that way?

"So at this point they got real frantic and hollered cop. The Chief put me on assignment, and I went down to talk to them. I made a check on Potter and it was pretty surprising. He wasn't at his rooming house, and his landlady didn't know his whereabouts, but he hadn't covered his trail worth a damn. His clothes and luggage were still in the room, and there were travel folders all over the place. Obviously, Potter had made plans for the money.

"I figured it wouldn't be too difficult a task to find him, but I never even got the chance to prove myself. I guess maybe that's why I was so upset over the case—the son of a gun cheated me out of my first big arrest! Because one day after Metro Services called in the police, Milton Potter walked into the precinct house and gave himself up.

"Well, maybe that wasn't so surprising at that—a lot of first-timers lose their nerve after a job is pulled. But Potter didn't look like a victim of the jitters. He was calm and rational, and all he said was, here I am, I took the money, do what you have to do.

"I grilled his for hours, but he stayed nice and cool all the time. Not cool the way some of these hoods you're dealing with are—a respectable kind of coolness. But the one point he wouldn't volunteer any information on was the location of the money. He clammed up tight every time I mentioned it. He was willing to go to jail for his crime, all right. But give up the dough? Uh-uh.

"Well, I really worked him over—in a legitimate way, of course. I told him that he was being a patsy, that it meant a fifteen- or twenty-year stretch for him if he kept up his attitude. I told him he would probably get off real light if he returned the dough—after all, it was his first offense. If he gave back the two hundred grand, both Metro and the insurance company would go easy on him. I practically promised it.

"But Milt Potter didn't see it that way; he stuck to his guns. He claimed he had taken the money because he thought he could get away with it, then realized he wasn't cut out to be a hunted criminal. He couldn't stand the idea of being hounded for the rest of his life—he just wasn't the running type. So he had given himself up. But what did he do with the money? That was a different story. He didn't care a hoot what we did to him—just so long as he didn't have to return the loot. That's the way he wanted it, and that's the way it turned out.

"The trial was short and sweet. He pleaded guilty, and got a fifteen-year sentence.

"I knew what he was up to, of course, and so did everybody else. He was making an investment—an investment of his time and his freedom in exchange for riches when he got out of prison. I guess he was a type that didn't mind prison life too much. He had spent five years in the army during the war, and the regimentation suited his personality to a T. He liked being told where to go and what to do; I tried to convince him that prison wasn't the same thing, but he didn't seem to care.

"That was back in '46, like I said. Potter was a model prisoner from the day he walked through the gates. He worked in the library most of the time, and did a lot of reading—travel books, mainly. He got three years clipped off his sentence for good behavior. Well, now he's got two days head start, but it won't matter."

Captain Fisher crushed out his third cigarette, and Hogan said:

"What happens now, Captain? Does he get away with the dough?'

Fisher shook his head sadly. "That's the tough part. He wouldn't believe me when I told him twelve years ago, but he's not going to profit from his investment. That two hundred grand doesn't belong to him, even if he thinks he earned it by a stretch in prison. I'm going to pay him a visit and tell him the facts of life."

"You mean you're going to see him today?"

"Sure," Fisher said. "I've had this appointment for a long time."

The address Captain Fisher obtained from the parole officials was a boarding house in the twenties, not far from Milt Potter's old neighborhood.

Potter was in his shirt sleeves when he answered the Captain's knock, and Fisher wondered if the dozen years had had so little effect on himself as it had on the ex-convict. He was still a short, owlish man with sad brown eyes, and the only marked inroads of time were a few light lines on his face and a patch of thinning hair on his head. He looked puzzled when he saw the Captain, and then distraught when recognition lit up his eyes.

"I'm Captain Ernest Fisher—you remember me, Mr. Potter?"

"Of course," Potter said nervously. "Come on in."

"Thanks. I was Lieutenant Fisher when we met the last time, Mr. Potter." He took a chair near the window and looked around the room casually. There was a closed suitcase on the wrought-iron bed.

"What was it you wanted, Captain?"

"Just to talk. It's been a long time, hasn't it?"

"Yes, it has."

"I understood you did pretty well in prison—nobody has any complaints about your conduct that I know about. Pays, doesn't it? Getting out sooner, I mean."

"Yes," Potter said, not looking at him. He went to the wash basin and rinsed his hands in cold water.

"I won't beat around the bush, Mr. Potter. I'm here for a reason, and I think you know what it is. There's still a matter of two hundred thousand dollars, and neither the police nor the insurance company are going to forget it. The fact that you served your sentence doesn't entitle you to the money, no matter what you think."

Potter didn't answer. He dried his hands on a thin towel and gazed out of the window towards the skyline. In the distance a ship blew its horn twice.

"There's no use being coy about it, Mr. Potter. It was obvious to everybody what your plan was. You thought you could earn that money with your time, but that's not the way these things are done. And I just wanted you to know that I'm making it my *personal* duty to see that you don't carry out your plan."

Fisher waited for Potter to say something. Finally, the parolee turned and answered, almost in a whisper.

"You have things all wrong, Captain."

"Really?"

"You have it all wrong about me. I know that's what everybody thinks, but they're wrong. I took that money because I wanted it, wanted it very much. I've always dreamed of traveling round the world, ever since I was a little boy, and I couldn't resist the temptation to take the money when it was so easily available. But after I took it, I realized that I wasn't the criminal type—not in the least."

He came over and sat in the chair opposite.

"I couldn't bear the idea of being hunted, living in fear all the time. Always jumping at shadows, always looking over my shoulder. Oh, maybe I had some wild idea about serving out my sentence and then running off with the money when I got out. But that would be exactly the same thing—running, afraid to live in the open, unable to enjoy any of the pleasures the money would bring me. I'm just not made that way, Captain."

Fisher stared at him.

"I thought prison wouldn't be hard to take, and in some ways it wasn't. But I had time to think everything out, and now I know what I have to do. So if you want the money, Captain, I'm ready to give it back."

"You're *what?*"

"All I want is to be let alone, Captain. All I want is to live in peace. Don't you understand?"

"Then where's the money?"

Potter swallowed.

"Right here—right here in this room."

He got up, went to the suitcase on the bed, and opened it. It was crammed with money.

The travel agent beamed when the short, owlish man walked into the office and said:

"I'm interested in a round-the-world cruise."

"Yes, sir!"

"But I want the best, understand? I don't care about the cost."

"I understand perfectly," the travel agent said.

Milt Potter sat down, gratefully. The last three days had been fatiguing. It had been an effort, visiting twenty city banks, signing twenty different names to twenty withdrawal slips. But the task was over, and he had his money. It wasn't a fortune, but it was more than he could have saved or even earned in the last twelve, tax-free, all expense-paid years. $84,000 interest, compounded over a dozen years on his capital investment.

100

E = MURDER

Ellery Queen

THE TITLE OF Ellery's lecture being *The Misadventures of Ellery Queen*, it was inevitable that one of the talks should be crowned by the greatest misadventure of all. It came to pass just after his stint at Bethesda University, in the neighborhood of Washington, D.C., where misadventures of all sorts are commonplace.

Ellery had scribbled the last autograph across the last coed's Humanities I notebook when the nearly empty auditorium resounded with a shot, almost a scream.

"Mr. Queen, wait! Don't go yet!"

The chancellors of great universities do not ordinarily charge down center aisles with blooded cheeks, uttering whoops; and Ellery felt the prickle of one of his infamous premonitions.

"Something wrong, Dr. Dunwoody?"

"Yes! I mean probably! I mean I don't know!" the head of Bethesda U. panted. "The President . . . Pentagon . . . General Carter . . . Dr. Agon doesn't—Oh, hell, Mr. Queen, come with me!"

Hurrying across the campus in the mild Maryland evening by Dr. Dunwoody's heaving side, Ellery managed to untangle the chancellorial verbiage. General Amos Carter, an old friend of Ellery's, had enlisted the services of Dr. Herbert Agon of Bethesda University, one of the world's leading physicists, in a top-secret experimental project for the Pentagon. The President of the United States himself received nightly reports from Dr. Agon by direct wire between the White House and the physicists's working quarters at the top of The Tower, Bethesda U.'s science citadel.

Tonight, at the routine hour, Dr. Agon had failed to telephone the President. The President had then called Agon, and Agon's phone had rung unanswered. A call to the Agon residence had elicited the information from the physicist's wife that, as far as she knew, her husband was working as usual in his laboratory in The Tower.

"That's when the President phoned General Carter," Dr. Dunwoody wailed. "It happens that the General was closeted with me in my office—a, well, a personal matter—and that's where the President reached him. When General Carter heard that you were on campus, Mr. Queen, he asked me to fetch you. He's gone ahead to The Tower."

Ellery accelerated. If Dr. Agon's experiments involved the President of the United States and General Amos Carter, any threat to the safety of the physicist would, like the shot fired by the rude bridge that arched the flood, echo round the world.

He found the entrance to the ten-story aluminum-and-glass Tower defended by a phalanx of campus police. But the lobby was occupied by three people: General Amos Carter; a harassed-looking stalwart in uniform, the special guard on Tower night duty; and a young woman of exceptional architecture whose pretty face was waxen and lifeless.

"But my husband," the young woman was saying, like a machine—a machine with a Continental accent. "You have no right, General. I must see my husband."

"Sorry, Mrs. Agon," General Carter said. "Oh, Ellery—"

"What's happened to Dr. Agon, General?"

"I found him dead. Murdered."

"*Murdered?*" The crimson in Chancellor Dunwoody's cheeks turned to ashes. "Pola. Pola, how dreadful."

General Carter stood like a wall. "It's dreadful in more ways than one, Doctor. All Agon's notes on his experiments have been stolen. Ellery, for the next few minutes I can use your advice."

"Of course, General. First, though, if I may . . . Mrs. Agon, I understand from Dr. Dunwoody that you're a scientist in your own right, a laboratory technician in Bethesda's physics department. Were you assisting your husband in his experiments?"

"I know nothing of them," Pola Agon's mechanical voice said. "I was a refugee, and although I am now a naturalized citizen and have security clearance, it is not for such high priority work as Herbert was doing."

Dr. Dunwoody patted the young widow's hand and she promptly burst into unscientific tears. The chancellor's arm sneaked about her. Ellery's brows went aloft. Then, abruptly, he turned to General Carter and the guard.

The top floor of The Tower, he learned, consisted of two rooms: the laboratory and the private office that housed Dr. Agon's secret project for the Pentagon. It was accessible by only one route, a self-service, nonstop elevator from the lobby.

"I suppose no one may use this elevator without identification and permission, Guard?"

"That's right, sir. My orders are to sign all visitors boud for the top floor in and out of this visitors' book. There's another book, just like it, in Dr. Agon's office, as a further check." The guard's voice lowered. "There was only one visitor tonight, sir. Take a look."

Ellery took the ledger. He counted 23 entries for the week. The last name—the only one dated and timed as of that evening—was James G. Dunwoody.

"You saw Dr. Agon tonight, Doctor?"

"Yes, Mr. Queen." The chancellor was perspiring. "It had nothing to do with his work, I assure you. I was with him only a few minutes. I left him alive—"

The General snapped, "Guard?" and the guard at once stepped over to block the lobby exit, feeling for his holster. "You go on up to Agon's office, Ellery, and see what it tells you—it's all right, I've locked the laboratory door." The General turned his grim glance on the head of Bethesda University and the murdered man's widow. "I'll be up in a minute."

General Carter stepped out of the elevator and said, "Well, Ellery?"

Ellery straightened up from the physicist's office desk. He had found Agon's body seated at the desk and slumped forward, a steel letter-knife sticking out of his back. The office was a shambles.

"Look at this, General."

"Where'd you find *that?*"

"In Agon's right fist, crumpled into a ball."

Ellery had smoothed it out. It was a small square memorandum slip, in the center of which something had been written in pencil. It looked like a script letter of the alphabet:

"E," General Carter said. "What the devil's that supposed to mean?"

Ellery's glance lifted. "Then it isn't a symbol connected with the project, General—code letter, anything like that?"

"No. You mean to tell me Agon wrote this before he died?"

"Apparently the stab wasn't immediately fatal, although Agon's killer might have thought it was. Agon must have revived, or played dead, until his killer left, and then, calling on his remaining strength, penciled this symbol. If it has no special meaning for you, General, then we're confronted with a dying message in the classic tradition—Agon's left a clue to his murderer's identity."

The General grunted at such outlandish notions. "Why couldn't he have just written the name?"

"The classic objection. The classic reply to which is that he was afraid his killer might come back, notice it, and destroy it," Ellery said unhappily, "which I'll admit has never really satisfied me." He was scowling at the symbol in great puzzlement.

General Carter fell back on orderly facts. "All I know is, only one person came up here tonight, and that was Dunwoody. I happen to know that Dunwoody's in love with Pola Agon. In fact, they had a blowup about it at the Agons' house last night—Agon himself told me about it, and that's why I was in Dunwoody's office this evening. I don't give a damn about these people's private lives, but Agon was important to the United States, and I couldn't have him upset. Dunwoody admits he lost his temper when Agon accused him of making a play for Mrs. Agon—called Agon a lot of nasty names. But he claims he cooled down overnight, and came up here tonight to apologize to Agon.

"For my money," the General went on grimly, "Dunwoody came up her tonight to kill Agon. It's my hunch that this Pola Agon is a cleverly planted enemy agent, out after Agon's experimental notes. She's played Mata Hari to Dunwoody—she's sexy enough!—and got him to do her dirty work. It wouldn't be the first time an old fool's turned traitor because of his hormones! But we'll find those notes—they haven't had time to get them away. Ellery, you listening?"

"E," Ellery said.

"What?"

"E," Ellery repeated. "It doesn't fit with the name James G. Dunwoody—or with Pola Agon, for that matter. Could it refer to Einstein's $E=mc^2$, where E stands for energy . . . ?" He broke off suddenly. "Well, well! Maybe it isn't an E after all, General!"

He had moved the memorandum slip a quarter turn clockwise. What General Carter now saw was:

"But turned that way it's an M!" the General exclaimed. "Who's M? There's no initial M in this either." He eyed the dead physicist's phone nervously. "Look, Ellery, thanks and all that, but I can't sit on this much longer. I've got to notify the President . . ."

"Wait," Ellery murmured. He had given the memo slip another quarter turn clockwise.

"Now it's a 3!"

"Does 3 mean anything to you or the project, General?"

"No more than the others."

"Visitor number 3 . . .? Let me see that check-in book of his." Ellery seized the duplicate visitors' book on the dead man's desk. "Agon's third visitor this week was . . ."

"Who?" General Carter rasped. "I'll have him picked up right away!"

"It was you, General," Ellery said. "Of course, I assume—"

"Of course," the General said, reddening. "Now what the deuce are you doing?"

Ellery was giving the memo sheet still another clockwise quarter turn. And now, astonishingly, it read:

"W?"

"No," Ellery said slowly. "I don't think it's a W . . . General, wasn't Agon of Greek extraction?"

"So what?"

"So Agon might well have intended this to stand for the Greek letter omega. The omega looks very like an English small script *w*."

"Omega. The end." The General snorted. "This was certainly Agon's end. Poetry yet!"

"I doubt if a scientist *in extremis* would be likely to think in poetic terms. Numbers would be more in character. And omega is the last letter of the twenty-four letter Greek alphabet. Number twenty-four, General. Doesn't something strike you?"

General Carter threw up his hands. "No! What?"

"Twenty-four's proximity to the number of visitors Agon actually received up here this week—which was twenty-three, you'll recall, Dr. Dunwoody tonight being the twenty-third. Surely that suggests that Agon meant to indicate a *twenty-fourth visitor*—someone who came after Dunwoody? And if that's true, Agon's killer was his twenty-fourth visitor. That's what Agon was trying to tell us!"

"It doesn't tell me a thing."

"It tells us why Agon didn't write his killer's name or initials. He denoted his visitor by number, not because he was afraid the killer might return and destroy the clue—a pretty far-fetched thought process for a man nine-tenths dead!—but because *he simply didn't know his murderer's name*."

General Carter's eyes narrowed. "But that would mean it was someone Agon knew only by sight!"

"Exactly," Ellery said. "And if you'll do a security recheck on the skunk, General, you'll find it's his loyalty to the United States, not Mrs. Agon's or Dunwoody's, that's been subverted."

"*What* skunk?" the General bellowed.

"The only skunk who could have got up here without signing in. That worried-looking night guard on duty in the lobby."

101

THE HOMICIDAL HICCUP

John D. MacDonald

YOU SAY YOU'VE been reading the series of articles in the Baker City *Journal* about how Mayor Willison cleaned up the city?

Brother, those articles are written for the sucker trade—meaning no offense, you understand.

Oh, I'll admit that the city is clean now—but not because of Willison. Willison is a cloth-head. He doesn't even know how Baker City got cleaned up. Being a politician, he's glad to jump in and take credit, naturally.

That's right. I know exactly how it happened, and it isn't going to be printed in any newspapers, even if I am a reporter. You spring for a few rounds of bourbon and I'll give it to you—just the way it happened.

You know about Johnny Howard. I don't pretend to understand him, or the guys like him. Maybe something happens when they're little kids, and by the time they get grown up, they have to run everything.

Nice-looking guy, in a way. Lean and dark and tall. But those gray eyes of his could look right through you and come out the other side. He came into town five, six years ago. Just discharged after three months in the Army. Heart or something. Twenty-six, he was then. Nice dresser. Sam Jorio and Buddy Winski were running the town between them. Anyway, Johnny Howard went to work for Sam Jorio. Two months later I hear talk that they're having some kind of trouble and that is ten days before Sam Jario, all alone in his car, goes off that cliff just south of town. Burned to nothing. Nobody can prove it isn't an accident, but there's lots of guessing.

With the boss gone, Buddy Winski tried to move in and take over Sam's boys. But he didn't figure on Johnny. He met Johnny at the bar of the Kit Club on Greentree Road and Johnny busted his beer bottle on the edge of the bar and turned Buddy Winski's face into hamburg. When Buddy got out of the hospital, he left town. There wasn't anything else to do. All his boys had teamed up with Johnny Howard.

Inside of a year Johnny not only had everything working smooth as glass in town, but he had things organized that Sam Jorio and Buddy Winski hadn't even thought of. Take a little thing like treasury pools. Syndicates are always trying to move in on a town this size. Buddy and Sam used to each have their own. Not Johnny. He folded up Sam's pool and Buddy's pool and let the syndicate come in. He gave them protection in return for two cents on every two-bit ticket. He made more out of it than Winski and Jorio ever thought of.

Another thing. No flashy cars for Johnny. No, sir. A little old black sedan with special plates in the body and special glass in the windows. That was Johnny. No going into the clubs, even the two that belonged to him, with a big gang and a batch of fancy women. Johnny had all his parties in the suite on the top floor of the Baker Hotel. All kinds of wine. Good musicians.

And, of course, Bonny was always with him. Always the same girl. Bonny Gerlacher is the right name. Bonny Powers, she called herself.

Five-foot-two on tiptoe with ocean-color eyes, dark red hair, and a build you wanted to tack on the wall over your bed.

Twenty-three or so, and looked sixteen.

Nobody messed with Bonny. And kept on living. Not with Johnny Howard around.

Well, things went along for a few years, and I guess Johnny was filling up safe-deposit boxes all over this part of the country with that green stuff. Johnny and Bonny. He was smart. Nobody could touch him. Estimates on his personal take went as high as a million and a half a year. He paid taxes on the net from the two clubs. Nothing else. The Feds smelled around for a long time, but they couldn't find anything.

The way he kept on top was by cracking down on anybody who stepped out of line so hard and so fast that it gave you the shivers.

Then Satch Connel got sick and the doc told him to retire and go to Florida if he wanted to live more than another half-hour.

Satch Connel ran a store next to the big high school. And he gave his regular payoff to Johnny Howard. Howard's boys kept Satch supplied with slot machines for the back room, reefers for the kids, dirty pictures and books. Stuff like that. I don't think Johnny Howard's end of the high school trade ran to more than three hundred a week. Peanuts to a guy like Johnny Howard.

So Satch sold out and a fellow named Walter Maybree bought it. This Maybree is from out of town and he had the cash in his pants and he buys it.

The same week he takes over, he tosses out the pinball machines and the punch boards and the other special items for the high school kids. You see, this Maybree has two kids in the high school. It gave him a different point of view from what Satch had. With Satch, nothing counted.

This Maybree paints the place inside and out and puts in a juke box and a lot of special sticky items at the soda bar and pretty soon it is like a recreation room you can maybe find run by a church.

Johnny Howard sends a few boys over to this Maybree, but Walt Maybree, being fairly husky, tosses them out onto the sidewalk. If that was all he did, maybe Johnny would have let the whole thing drop. But, no. Maybree writes a letter to the paper, and the stupid paper lets it get printed, and it says some pretty harsh things about a certain racketeer who wants him to cheat the school kids and sell them dope and filth.

Some of the wise boys around town talk to Johnny Howard and Johnny says, in that easy way of his, "Maybree'll either play along or stop breathing."

You got to understand about a statement like that. Once Johnny makes it, he has to follow through. If he doesn't, every small fry in town will figure Johnny is losing his grip and they'll try to wriggle out from under and maybe the organization will go to hell.

So, being in the line of business he's in, once Johnny Howard makes a statement like that, he has to do exactly like he says.

It would have been like pie, a shot from a car or even a ride into the country, except that a number of citizens are tired of Johnny Howard, and they get to Maybree and convince him that he is in trouble. The next thing, Maybree's wife and kids leave town with no forwarding address and the talk is that when the heat's off they'll come back and not before.

Walter Maybree moves a bunk into the back of the store, so there is no chance of catching him on the street. A whole bunch of square citizens get gun licenses before Johnny can get to the cops to stop the issuing of them, and they all do guard duty with Walt Maybree.

Business goes on as usual, and Maybree has a tight look around his mouth and eyes, and without it being in the paper all of Baker City knows what's going on and are pulling for Maybree. That's the trouble with ordinary citizens. They sit on the sidelines and cheer, but only once in a blue moon is one of them, like Maybree, out there in front with his guard up.

The bomb that was tossed out of a moving car didn't go over so good. The boys in the car were in a hurry, so the bomb bounced off the door frame instead of going through the plate-glass window. It busted the windows when it went off, but it didn't do any other damage. At the corner, the sedan took a slug in the tire and slewed into a lamppost and killed the driver. The other guy tried to fight his way clear and took a slug between the eyes.

The next day Johnny Howard was really in trouble. His organization began to fall apart right in front of his face, and everybody in the know was laughing at him because a punk running a soda shop was bluffing him to a standstill.

I can't tell you how I found out about this next part, but Johnny spends two days thinking, and then he gets hold of Madge Spain, who keeps the houses in line, and gives her some orders, and she shows up at the Baker Hotel with three of her youngest gals.

Johnny looks them over carefully, but they won't do because they look too hard and no amount of frosting on the cake is going to make any one of them look like a high school kid. Their high school days are too far behind them.

But he knows the idea is good and he is doing a lot of brooding about it and he has the dope he wants from Doc Harrington, one of his boys, who is sort of an amateur physician. He has the method all worked out, but nobody who can do it.

Bonny is worried about him, and finally she gets him talking and he tells her all about his plan, and she says that the whole thing is simple. *She'll* do it.

You've got to understand that in their own funny way they love each other. It just about makes Johnny sick to think of his Bonny killing anybody, because that is not woman's work. And maybe Bonny wouldn't normally knock anybody off, but because it is her Johnny who is in this mess, she will wiggle naked over hot coals to get him out of it.

The plan isn't bad. As soon as Maybree dies, all this trouble Johnny is having dies with him. It doesn't much matter how Maybree gets it, as long as he does.

This Doc Harrington has got hold of some curare. It is a South American poison and they use it in this country in small doses to make convulsions ease up when they give people shock therapy. It paralyzes muscles. Jam a little bit in the bloodstream and it will paralyze the heart action. *Poof!* Like that. Quick as a bullet.

The bodyguards that are protecting Walt Maybree during business hours are on the lookout for hard characters who look like they might rub Maybree out in a direct way. Johnny Howard figures they will not be on the lookout for high school gals.

For the next two days he had Bonny practicing with a soda straw and these little wooden darts he has fixed up. They just fit in a soda straw. A needle on one end and paper things on the other to make them fly right.

Walt Maybree works behind his own soda fountain.

The idea is that Bonny goes in there as a high school girl and she has the little dart with the curare on the end in her hand. She sits at the fountain and tucks the dart in the end of the soda straw, puts it up to her lips, and puffs, sticking the little dart into the back of Maybree's hand, or, better yet, his throat.

When he keels over, she goes out with the crowd.

Probably Bonny laughed and kidded a lot when she was up in the suite practicing on the cork target with the little darts. Probably Johnny Howard kidded back, but neither of them must have thought it was very funny. To Johnny Howard it was okay to rub out the competition with hot lead, but sending your gal out to kill somebody with a blowgun is something else indeed.

Anyway, the pressure on Johnny was getting worse every day, and his boys were mumbling and it was only a question of time until somebody turned hero and blasted Johnny.

On the day that was set, Bonny went in her black dress and her high heels and her dark red hair piled high on her head and unlocked the door to the room she had rented near the high school. The little dart with the sticky stuff on the needle end was wrapped in tissue paper and was in a little box in her purse. She had a suitcase with her.

The black dress fitted snugly on Bonny's curves. She took off the dress and the nylons and the high-heeled shoes and put on scuffed, flat moccasins and shortish tweed skirt and a sloppy sweater. She let that wonderful dark red hair fall around her shoulders, and she tied a scarf thing around her shining head.

She had schoolbooks with her. She took them out of the suitcase, held them in her arm, and looked in the chipped mirror over the oak bureau. Carefully she smiled. Bonny the high school lass. But with too much makeup. She swabbed all the makeup off and put back just a little. It looked better.

Her knees were shaking and her lips felt numb. Her heart was fluttering. No woman can go out to commit murder without something taking place inside her.

One little thing had to be added. She took the big purse she was leaving behind, took out the half-pint flask that Johnny Howard had given her two years before, and tilted it up to her lips. The raw liquor burned like fire, but it steadied her down. That was what she wanted.

It had all been timed just right. She left the room, carrying the books, and walked to the high school. She went in the door, and, when she got halfway down the hall, the noon whistle went off and the doors opened and the hall filled with kids.

Bonny felt funny until she saw that she wasn't being noticed. She went right through the building and out the other door and became part of the crew that stormed the gates of Walt Maybree's Drugstore.

Between the thumb and first finger of her right hand she tightly held the little messenger of death.

The liquor was warm in her stomach, and she made an effort not to breathe in anybody's face. She was a little late to get a seat at the counter, and so waited, quietly and patiently, and while she waited she thought of Johnny Howard. It was only by thinking of Johnny that she could go through with the whole thing.

When there was a vacant stool she edged in, piled her books on the counter, made her voice higher, her eyes wider, and ordered what she had heard one of the other kids order—''A special milkshake.''

She selected a straw out of the metal container near her, peeled the paper off it, and waited. Maybree was down at the other end of the counter, and a boy with a pimply face made her milkshake and put it in front of her. It was ''special.'' It contained two kinds of ice cream, a handful of malt, and an egg.

Bonny dipped her straw into it and sucked up the sweet, heavy mixture. She kept her eye on Maybree. He began to move up toward her. She pinched her straw so that it was useless, selected a fresh one, and stripped the paper off it. With a deft, practiced gesture, she slipped the little dart, point first, into the end of it.

She lifted it to her lips.

Maybree strolled down near her and stood still, his hand braced on the inside edge of the counter.

It was thus that he glanced at the very good-looking high school girl with the sea-colored eyes. He heard an odd sound, saw those sea-colored eyes glaze, and he gasped as she went over backward, her pretty head striking the asphalt tile of the floor with a heavy thud, her dark red hair spilling out of the bandanna when the knot loosened. She was dead even as she hit the floor.

That's why I get a bang out of the mayor claiming to have cleaned up this town. Hell, he couldn't have cleaned it up if Johnny Howard had been running things. When the mayor started his cleanup, Johnny Howard was gone, and weak sisters were trying to climb into the vacated saddle.

Yeah, Johnny Howard disappeared that same day that Bonny died. They didn't locate him for five days. They found him in that furnished room that still held Bonny's usual clothes. The landlady had been hearing a funny noise. They found Johnny Howard on his hands and knees, going around and around the room, butting his head into the wall now and then. He told them he was looking for Bonny. They've got him out in the state sanitarium now, giving him shock treatments, but they say it'll never work with him.

That's right. Bonny made a mistake. Just one mistake. You see, she didn't realize that by taking that huge slug of bourbon and then drinking half of that sticky milkshake she'd signed her own death warrant. They found the little dart embedded in the inside of her lower lip.

You can't mix bourbon and milkshake without getting a terrible case of hiccups.

ABOUT THE EDITORS

BILL PRONZINI is one of America's finest mystery/suspense writers, as well as one of its leading critics. He has published more than 30 novels and 280 stories. His fiction has been translated into 17 languages and he has edited or coedited some 40 anthologies, including, with Martin H. Greenberg, *Baker's Dozen: 13 Short Mystery Novels*; *A Treasury of World War II Stories*; and *A Treasury of Civil War Stories*. A longtime resident of San Francisco, he possesses one of the world's larger collections of pulp magazines.

MARTIN H. GREENBERG, who has been called "The king of the anthologists," now has some 125 of them to his credit. In addition to the books he has edited with Bill Pronzini, Greenberg has been a joint editor on *A Treasury of American Horror Stories* and *101 Science Fiction Stories*. Greenberg is Professor of Regional Analysis and Political Science at the University of Wisconsin-Green Bay, where he teaches a course in American foreign and defense policy.